By W. S. KUNICZAK

Novels:
Valedictory
The March
The Thousand Hour Day

Translations:
"The Trilogy" (Henryk Sienkiewicz)
I *With Fire and Sword*
II *The Deluge*
III *Fire in the Steppe*

History:
My Name is Million

Entertainments:
The Sempinski Affair

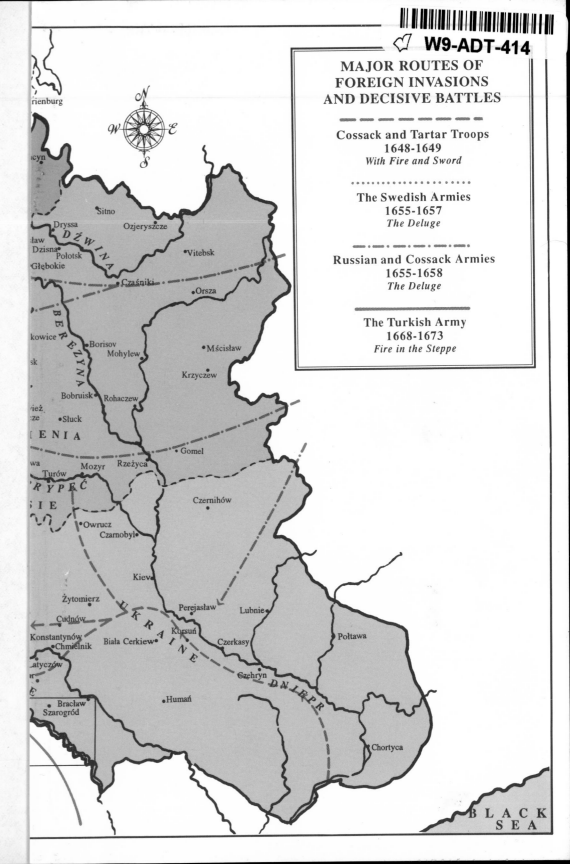

**MAJOR ROUTES OF
FOREIGN INVASIONS
AND DECISIVE BATTLES**

**Cossack and Tartar Troops
1648-1649**
With Fire and Sword

**The Swedish Armies
1655-1657**
The Deluge

**Russian and Cossack Armies
1655-1658**
The Deluge

**The Turkish Army
1668-1673**
Fire in the Steppe

Fire in the Steppe

Fire in the Steppe

Henryk Sienkiewicz

In Modern Translation by
W. S. Kuniczak

COPERNICUS SOCIETY OF AMERICA
with
HIPPOCRENE BOOKS
New York

First Edition

Copyright © 1992 by W. S. Kuniczak

All Rights Reserved

Published by the Copernicus Society of America, Edward J. Piszek, president, in its program of modern translations of Polish literary classics which begun with "The Trilogy" by Henryk Sienkiewicz, of which this book is the third in the series.

With Fire and Sword, May, 1991   ISBN 0-87052-974-9
The Deluge, October, 1991   ISBN 0-87052-004-0
Fire in the Steppe, May 1992   ISBN 0-7818-0025-0

Distributed in the U.S.A. by
Hippocrene Books, Inc.
171 Madison Avenue, New York, NY 10016
Tel. (212) 685-4371

Library of Congress Cataloging-in-Publication Data
Sienkiewicz, Henryk, 1846-1916.
Pan Wolodyjowski. English
Fire in the steppe/Henryk Sienkiewicz;
in modern translation by W.S.Kuniczak— 1st ed.
p.   cm.
Translation of: *Pan Wolodyjowski*
ISBN 0-7818-0025-0
1. Poland— History —John II Casimir, 1648-1668 —Fiction.
I.Title.

Jacket Illustration: Jozef Brandt, *Freeing the Captives* (det.), 1878, by permission of *Museum Narodowe*, Warsaw, Poland

Designed by Robert L. Pigeon

Endpaper Maps by Eugenia Gore
Printed in the United States of America

Acknowledgements

Even a labor of love such as this translation would not have been possible without the support and encouragement of many persons who believed in it. Mr. Edward J. Piszek and the men and women of the Copernicus Society of America; His Eminence, John Cardinal Krol; Mr. Edward Moskal, president of the Polish National Alliance and the Polish-American Congress, and the late Hon. Aloysius A. Mazewski; Dr. Kaja Ploss, Mrs. Debbie Majka, Mr. Joseph Zazyczny, Mr. Wallace West, Mrs. Wanda Winiarz, Ms. Mary Ellen Tyszka, Mrs. Helen Dimmett and Mrs. Anna Chrypinska of the American Council for Polish Culture; Mr. Edward G. Dykla, president of the Polish Roman Catholic Union and Mrs. Helen Wojcik, president of the Polish Women's Alliance of America; Mr. and Mrs. Artur Zygmont of the Polish-American Cultural Network of Torrance, Ca.; Drs. Jerzy R. Krzyzanowski, Thomas Napierkowski and Jerzy Maciuszko; Drs. William P. Garvey and David Palmer of Mercyhurst College; Dr. Leonard Kosinski, founder and president of the Polish Heritage Association of the Southeast and Mrs. Mary Kosinski; Mr. Joseph Gore and Dr. Albert Juszczak, present and former presidents of the Kosciuszko Foundation; Dr. Wojciech Wierzewski and Mr. Boleslaw Wierzbianski; Mrs. Wanda Cytowska, Mr. Mark Kohan and Mrs. Kathryn Rosypal; Mr. William F. Miller; Mrs. Eugenia Gore, Mrs. Eugenia Stolarczyk, and Lady Blanka Rosenstiel, founder and president of the American Institute of Polish Culture, Inc.; Mr. Robert L. Pigeon and the associates of Combined Books, Inc.; Mr. George Blagowidow and Jacek Galazka, the president and the publisher of Hippocrene Books, Inc.; Mr. Mark A. Kamienski and Ms. Susan E. Kamienski of CSA Literary Projects; Ms. Gail Rentsch and the staff of Rentsch Associates, Inc.; Dr. John G. Zawadzinski and Mr. Jan M. Lorys; Mr. Henry Morrison and the men and women of Henry Morrison, Inc; Mr. Max Gartenberg and Dr. Patricia Gartenberg; Ms. Pamela King of the Telfair Academy of Arts and

Sciences Inc., of Savannah, Ga.; Mr. Edward J. Kubinski Jr.; and Mrs. Krystyna Olszer and the officers of the Polish Institute of the Arts and Sciences in America, Inc. Each of these kind, thoughtful and hardworking persons played a role in the resurrection of the Sienkiewicz Trilogy in English. Perhaps by thanking them the publishers can thank everyone who helped.

W. S. Kuniczak

For my parents, for whom "The Trilogy" of Henryk Sienkiewicz was a source of courage; for my sister, for whom it was a source of pride; and for her children, who may enjoy it as the fine literature that it is.

—W.S.K.

Introduction

When Henryk Sienkiewicz finished writing *Fire in the Steppe* (Pan Wolodyjowski) in the spring of 1887, the final line of his epilogue read: *'Here comes the end of the books written in sweat and toil over the last few years to uplift the hearts.'* That epilogue, which is like a paean of reassurance in its projection into a distant future, and at the same time an answer to the author's contemporary critics, does not appear in this translation for reasons noted later. But it sums up a monumental effort by a selfless man who single-handedly set out to revive the national consciousness of a captive people and succeeded beyond his wildest dreams. It may be fair to say that what Sienkiewicz did for the Poles in Polish, his new American translator W. S. Kuniczak continues in brilliant modern English for a far larger audience and succeeds beyond anyone's expectations.

Writing his own foreword to this new translation, James A. Michener called the Trilogy a sacred book. In most Polish homes it stands beside the Bible. It has rallied the Polish people in their most tragic moments for more than a century, giving them faith and hope when neither appeared to be realistic, and it continues to inspire each new generation. Yet it is not merely an apotheosis of grandeur and lost glories but also a grim lesson in humanity, decency, loyalty and determination, which warns not only Poles but every other people that even the greatest civilizations fall if they lose sight of their moral and spiritual values. Written with love and that controlled, disciplined passion that makes for great writing, it has withstood every test of time, and although it has often been compared with a variety of famous English and American novels there is really nothing quite like it in any other literature beyond the works of Homer.

Like its two epic predecessors (*With Fire and Sword*, 1883-1884, and *The Deluge*, 1884-1886), *Fire in the Steppe* enthralls and captivates as a grand, love and adventure story while bringing alive a vital fragment of European history. It began appearing serially on June 2, 1887 in three Polish newspapers simultaneously—*Slowo (The Word)* in Warsaw, *Czas (Time)* in Krakow, and *Dziennik Poznanski (The Poznan Daily)* in Poznan—which, at that time, lay within the three empires of Russia, Prussia and Austria-Hungary that had partitioned Poland 92 years before, and continued running without an interruption until the middle of May, 1888. Only a part of the text was ready when the printing started and there was always the fear that Sienkiewicz, writing at great speed under difficult personal conditions and almost always traveling, might run out of material. Both the continuity of action and the cohesion of the plot had to depend upon the author's memory in those almost unimaginable days before computers, telephones, express mail delivery (or even typewriters) and it was only the prodigious mental discipline of this self-motivated literary genius that saved his novels time and time again. Even so, false tries and repetitions appeared in the printed texts of all the three books and later found their way into earlier word-for-word translations, much to the author's embarrassment and distress. It is only now that W. S. Kuniczak, working from the final definitive texts of Professor Julian Krzyzanowski's 1948-52 Collected Works edition, has been able to restore Sienkiewicz's original vision in another language. The author who turned to the 17th century to comfort his countrymen, shows us a nation rising back to greatness through courage, faith, endurance and devotion after successive devastations by rebellious Cossacks, invading Swedes and the avalanche of the Moslem world which tried to overwhelm Christianity itself in an attack on Poland. He does so honestly and fairly, showing his fictional and historical characters with all their vices as well as their virtues, and holding nothing back, no matter how painful. He speaks in the language of the century he describes which defies any orthodox systems of translation, often inventing words and phrases in a purposely antiquated Polish that only a devoted Polish-born translator could attempt to render into another language, and he creates an epos of the first magnitude which defies analysis in another culture. The fact that this translation succeeds so brilliantly in that transposition seems almost miraculous in itself.

It was the fashion for a time among the minor Polish literary critics, particularly in the years of Communist domination, and aped to this day by foreign book reviewers who cannot read Polish and must depend on second-hand opinion in their criticism, to denigrate Sienkiewicz and his work, charging him with idealizing the past, taking liberties with history, and relegating him to the role of a children's author, but even they admit that he succeeded in his self-appointed mission. His voice rang loud and clear when a desperate people needed to hear it the most. He did uplift the hearts of his grateful countrymen in his own time when there was no Poland on the maps of Europe, then through all the horrors of Nazi occupation during World War II and the dehumanizing aftermath of Soviet Communism which tried to rewrite history and subvert the character and traditions of the Polish people to suit its own purpose. He also suffered from attacks by his contemporary critics in a period ruled by social realism in literature and the arts, for whom his giant step into a more heroic age, presented in a language that could stir even ordinary people, seemed like a dangerous return to the populist romanticism of an earlier era.

Fire in the Steppe is at least in part Sienkiewicz's reply to these charges of idealizing bygone times. No other piece of 19th century literary prose possesses such graphically shocking images of human cruelty, although few match it in the simplicity of its gentleness and love, and the modern reader may well ask why Sienkiewicz does not spare us those dreadful scenes of unremitting horror. The answer goes to the very heart of this monumental work. Writing the final book of his Trilogy, Sienkiewicz took note of those critical voices among his literary peers. He was particularly aware of the admonitions of Boleslaw Prus, a literary giant in his own right, whose *The Doll* was the paramount example of socially-conscious Polish realism. Gone in *Fire in the Steppe* are some of the hyperbolic metaphors for military glory. The Homeric quality is tempered and subdued until the last moment. The obligatory final victory, essential to romantic literature, gives way to a disaster; and a single scene of horrifying cruelty, preceded by a carefully paced progressive series of accounts that document Man's inhumanity to Man, and followed by the tragedy of a young man's madness, comes as a realistic balance for Sienkiewicz's earlier glorification of the era.

Discussing *Fire in the Steppe*, a distinguished Polish literary critic, Zygmunt Szweykowski, sums up his argument in this respect as follows: "The reality of life in the Commonwealth in that time (i.e. the 17th century) shows its ugly face in all of its horror . . . The illusion of the fable is gone. However even now Sienkiewicz does not think of leaving the reader in a state of hopelessness. Over and above the illusory suggestions which served him well in the first two parts of the cycle, he wants to leave the sense of (the nation's and the era's) greatness, which in his judgment, reflects a reality that does not require irrealistic myths and can stand on its own."

This role of greatness in *Fire in the Steppe* is supplied by a historical figure rather than any character of the fiction, in the person of Jan Sobieski, Grand Hetman of Poland and later King Jan III Sobieski, who saved the Christian world from the Turks at Vienna in 1683. In his study of Henryk Sienkiewicz, published by Twayne's World Author series, Mieczyslaw Giergielewicz stresses the fact that Sobieski is shown here "not merely as a defender of his own country but also of Christendom." Sobieski's triumph over the Turks at the earlier battle of Khotim (Chocim) in 1674 appears as a detailed historical essay in the author's epilogue, set two years after the action of the book, the doomed heroic climax of the novel and the end of the story, and so it was quite properly left out of this modern translation which is designed for 20th century readers. Much as he wished to use it for its triumphant, upbeat note of a delayed victory, Kuniczak had to bow to the conventions of the modern novel which restrict material only to that which helps in character development and advances the story. Sienkiewicz's epilogue is sometimes seen as something of an afterthought, as if he were abandoning the art of the novelist for the safer province of academic history. It plucks again at those uplifting strings so dear to his Polish readers but it plays no structural role in the novel, ties no loose ends relating to the characters, and detracts some-

what from the novel's climax for the sake of an external historical effect. It is no accident, however, that in contrast to the two
preceding novels of the Trilogy, the unforgettable protagonists
of *Fire in the Steppe*—the Little Knight (Pan Volodyovski in his
transliterated spelling) and his beloved Basia—are based upon
real persons and not entirely on Sienkiewicz's art and imagination. Basia, indeed, is the apotheosis of his lost young wife.

Writing their own excellent scholarly introductions to *With
Fire and Sword* and *The Deluge*, Professors Jerzy R. Krzyzanowski
and Thomas Napierkowski more than adequately cover the
colossal impact that this epic work had on its contemporaries,
the message that it has for readers everywhere today, and its
position as a prime example of the national novel which has no
counterpart in any other literature of the world, so that no more
needs to be said on that subject here. What may be added,
however, is a brief discussion of the creative sources which
allowed Sienkiewicz to raise the epic novel so far above the
other 19th century masters of the genre. The roots of this
Homeric quality may be found in the *Iliad* and the *Odyssey*
which were Sienkiewicz's own favorite reading matter, as well
as in the period Polish writings in which he steeped himself both
in his diligent study of the times and for his private pleasure.
Principal among these were the 17th century *Memoirs* (Pamiet-
niki) of Jan Chryzostom Pasek, a fighting squire of the Polish-
Lithuanian Commonwealth who lived through many of the
events recounted in the Trilogy, knew many of the historical
figures pictured there, and was an active witness to the times and
its various peoples. Of great help to him were the *Annales*, also
known as *The Climacterics* (Klimaktery) by the Baroque chroni-
cler Wespazjan Kochowski, the *Historical Sketches* (Szkice histo-
ryczne) by Ludwik Kubala and the seminal work of another
contemporary historian, K. Szajnocha, especially his *Two Years
of Our Times* (Dwa lata dziejów naszych.) According to Samuel
Sandler, Sienkiewicz depended on both Kubala and Szajnocha
for anecdotal material and the customs of the age. It should be
noted that in preparing for the eight-year labor of his new
translation, W. S. Kuniczak went back to these and many other
sources of Sienkiewicz's fabled creativity so that he could reaf-

firm his grasp on the master's novelistic vision, and project an accurate rendering of the times for the modern reader.

More will be said later about this devoted American disciple of the Polish master. But what of the great novelist himself? How did he work? How did he manage to control, propel and maintain the massive flow of his creativity? Contemporaries have left us a picture of a man writing at a near-frantic pace, among a litter of broken pens and cascading papers, who had to be literally torn away from his writing table in order to eat. In reality, he antedated the systematic disciplined professionalism preached and displayed by every modern writer from Hemingway to Mailer, contemptuous of the Victorian amateurs of his time, and substituting hard work on a sustained basis for so-called 'inspiration.' He wrote at fixed times every day wherever he happened to be, setting himself a daily quota he never failed to meet, and seemingly oblivious of the enormous pressures required to keep control of his immense material. Considering the length, scope and breadth of his Trilogy (almost two million words in this translation), the number of characters, plots, sub-plots and story lines in the three interrelated novels, and the speed at which Sienkiewicz was obliged to work, the result can be nothing but astounding.

Sienkiewicz's method was to devise a kind of blueprint of each of his novels with as many details of time, place, action and character appearances as he was able to anticipate. Then he would put the plan on paper, fully aware that truly rendered fictional characters always took on their own lives and went their own way, and then he memorized it and let it settle in his mind. When ready to write, he would divide his material into blocks of time by weeks rather than days and let his editors decide on the daily installments they printed in their papers. Ironically enough, his systematic approach to creating his magnificent fiction earned him some scorn from his Polish literary peers who couldn't reconcile his rigidly scheduled, day-by-day production with their own 19th century notions of art by inspiration. Yet it is hard to imagine how he could have managed to produce such a vast work as the Trilogy in any other way.

It is even harder to imagine that Sienkiewicz knew what he would say in *Fire in the Steppe* before he started writing *With Fire and Sword*, and yet that conclusion is inescapable once the entire triptych is displayed for leisurely critical study and analysis. Everything that may have gone before in the Trilogy that puzzled the reader is suddenly logical and clear; everything makes sense; and even the prophetic message of triumph within disaster comes as no surprise, so that the ringing victory of the epilogue isn't really necessary after the story ends. In the long process of heroic struggle that begins with the rebellion of the Cossacks in 1648, told in such thrilling terms in *With Fire and Sword*, and then runs on through the astonishing twists and turns during the Swedish onslaught (1655-58) recounted in *The Deluge*, a single multi-level theme threads the various skeins of plot and characters together and brings them to the only logical conclusion: human beings must retain their humanity, no matter what happens to them or around them, and the salvation of mankind lies within each man.

With Fire and Sword, The Deluge and *Fire in the Steppe* are separate parts of a single, carefully designed structure and can be read as independent novels but there are marked differences between them. One of these is the harshness of reality and the cruelty of history already noted here. The other is a marvelous evolution in the role that women play in these thousands of tumultuous pages, so that what starts with the idealized figure of Helen in *With Fire and Sword*—the quintessential romantic heroine of Victorian fiction whose main role is to be the object of heroic rescue—and passes far beyond traditional limitations into the strength, courage, clear-sightedness and wisdom of *The Deluge's* Olenka, becomes at last the brave, undaunted, feminine but indomitable Basia of *Fire in the Steppe*, the most beloved heroine of Polish 19th century writing who would be quite at home almost anywhere in the 20th century. She would certainly be at home in today's America and would probably cope with it very well.

Indeed, America plays a surprising role throughout the Trilogy which may have a special meaning for Sienkiewicz's new American readership today. Critics have speculated that *Fire in the Steppe* may have been the first of the three novels that Sienkiewicz planned, because he researched the life of Jerzy Michal Wolodyjowski, a gallant little contemporary of Jan Chryzostom Pasek, several years before he started writing *With*

Fire and Sword, but his travels through America in 1876-78 suddenly changed his schedule. It was in San Francisco that he met the two prototypes of his most famous characters, the roistering Pan Zagloba and gentle Pan Longinus, and decided that one novel wouldn't be enough. In all probability Sienkiewicz's Zagloba was based upon Captain Korwin-Piotrowski, a San Francisco immigration inspector who had fought the Russians in the Polish 1830 insurrection, emigrated to America, wandered across the plains and claimed to have been both an army scout and an Indian fighter as well as a Gold Rush prospector. A prodigious drinker, good-natured braggart and teller of tall tales, he was the perfect prototype of Sienkiewicz's inimitable Zagloba, as was another Californian exile, a gentle Lithuanian of gigantic stature who turned into Pan Longinus in the young Polish writer's swift imagination.

These two providential meetings completed the main cast of the Trilogy since Sienkiewicz, barely an inch or two above five feet in height, always identified with the Little Knight, Pan Volodyovski, and the entire glorious epic of love, war, intrigue, heroism and adventure took root in the future author's mind under the western skies. Bringing the Trilogy even closer to America is the fact that the magnificent descriptions of the wild 17th century borderlands of southeastern Poland are closely patterned on the American West, as Sienkiewicz's published *Letters from America* so clearly attest. The writer had never visited those long-lost Wild Lands and Ukrainian Steppes that he recreates so brilliantly in both *With Fire and Sword* and *Fire in the Steppe*. But he saw the American plains and the western prairies, heard all the tales told around the campfires, admired the Indians, and literally fell in love with the untrammeled land and its vibrant people. Moreover, several of the early ambushes and battles in *With Fire and Sword*, as well as the raids and border skirmishes of *Fire in the Steppe*, clearly derive from American newspaper accounts of clashes with the Indians and the stories of raids and massacres popular in America during Sienkiewicz's enthusiastic visit.

American readers can be grateful to W. S. Kuniczak for an exalted reading experience. His artistry has given us a masterpiece of translation which brings continuing applause from the best American critics and resurrects Sienkiewicz in America for new generations. The superb literary skills of this Polish-born American novelist create a bridge between the Polish and Anglo-Saxon cultures and open a new chapter in the history of literary translation equal to, and at times surpassing, the original.

Jerzy J. Maciuszko, PhD.
Baldwin-Wallace College

"... to uplift the hearts."

—Sienkiewicz

Fire in the Steppe
(Pan Wolodyjowski)

Author's Prologue

NOT LONG AFTER the Hungarian War, at about the time when Pan Andrei Kmita married Panna Aleksandra Billevitchovna, everyone expected a quick wedding between Panna Anna Krasienska and Pan Jerzy Michal Volodyovski, colonel of the Laudanian Horse, whose fame and merits to the Commonwealth equaled those earned by his Lithuanian friend.

But there were serious problems that delayed that wedding. The bride-to-be was a ward of Princess Grizelda Vishnovyetzka and wouldn't even think about getting married without her permission and so Pan Michal had to leave her in the care and keeping of the Kmitas in their rebuilt Vodokty, not wanting to expose her to the dangers of travel in those violent times, while he rode alone to Zamost to get the needed blessings and permission.

His luck, however, failed him once again. The Princess had gone to the imperial court in Vienna to supervise the education of her son, and the dogged little knight followed in her tracks although it took him a long time to reach her. He did, eventually, accomplish his purpose and returned home full of hope and anticipation only to find more obstacles in the way. A fresh turmoil was sweeping through the country, discontent had split and undermined the army, Cossack rebellions kept flaring up in the Ukraine, and the conflagration raged unchecked all along the eastern borders of the Commonwealth. The border lords raised what troops they could to hold the frontiers and Pan Michal received a commission from the new *Voyevode* of Ruthenia even before he got as close to home as Warsaw.

Feeling as he did that the needs of the country must always

take precedence over private wishes, he put aside his hopes of happiness and went to the Ukraine where he served for several years among the flames and hardships of a bitter war, barely able to send a letter now and then to his beloved Anusia. After that he was an envoy to the court of the Crimean Khan; then he fought on the King's side in the terrible civil war unleashed by Crown Marshal Lubomirski, who rebelled against the great social changes with which the King wanted to strengthen the central government and rebuild the fabric of the country; and then he served in the Ukraine with Pan Jan Sobieski, the same who would become King Jan III, the nemesis of the Turks and savior of Christendom at Vienna.

All this covered him with such fame and glory that he became renowned as the 'First Soldier of the Commonwealth' but his young years went by in anxiety and longing.

Finally, in the beginning of the summer of 1668, when his commander sent him home to rest, he could at last go to his beloved, take her from Vodokty, and set out for Krakow where Princess Grizelda had come back from Vienna and waited to play the mother's role at Anusia's wedding.

The Kmitas remained in Vodokty, not expecting to hear soon from Volodyovski, and preparing for a new happiness of their own. Providence had denied them children up till then but this was now to change, much to their delight.

The year was fruitful beyond belief. The fields yielded such abundant harvests that they overflowed the barns, and the whole country became covered with open-air stacks. Fresh woodlands greened so thickly in one springtime season throughout the war-scarred countryside as would take two full years in any other time. The woods filled with game and mushrooms and the waterways were alive with fish as if this fecundity of the soil had spread to all the creatures.

Volodyovski's friends read the best possible omens for his marriage in this unusual natural abundance but fate was to prove otherwise quite soon.

Part I

Chapter One

IT WAS ON ONE of those glowing Autumn afternoons that Pan Andrei Kmita sat sipping his after-dinner mead in the cool shade of a summerhouse, gazing fondly through the crisscross bars of the leafy arbor at his wife who strolled along the clean-swept orchard avenue before him.

She was a woman of unusual beauty, with thoughtful, finely chiseled features under her fair hair, and with such a sunny look about her face that she seemed angelic. She paced back and forth slowly and with care, full of quiet dignity and joy, because God's final blessing had been granted to her marriage and she was carrying her first child.

Pan Andrei looked at her as if bemused with love, which of course he was. His eyes followed all her movements with the mute devotion of a faithful dog, but every so often his hand rose to his mustache, twisting it upward above his pensive grin, and then a broad, merry smile spread across his face. It called up images of a light-hearted, happy-go-lucky past, which wasn't all that far behind him anyway. One glance was enough to show that he was a born devil-may-care soldier who must have caused more than his share of trouble in his bachelor years.

Only the drone of insects and the spatter of ripe fruit falling to the ground broke the silence of the orchard around the summerhouse. The day glowed with all the beauty of early September. The sun no longer burned down as hotly as in the Summer months but it still shot its golden beams far and wide, ripening the crimson apples that clustered thickly in their silvery leaves, and bathing the round-crowned apple trees that crouched throughout the orchard. The heavy-laden plum trees, purple with ripe fruit, also bowed their branches to the ground, and the first gossamer threads of cobwebs spun by Autumn spiders trembled among the boughs in a gentle breeze that barely served to stir the vegetation.

It could have been just the beauty of the day that filled Pan Andrei with such pleased contentment because his face grew merrier as the afternoon went on. But then he took another sip of mead and called out to his wife: "Olenka, come here a minute! I want to tell you something."

"As long as it isn't something I'd rather not hear," she warned him.

"It won't be, by God! Come on now, give an ear!" He threw an arm around her waist, pressed his mustache close to her fair hair and whispered softly: "But if it's a boy then let's call him Michal."

She flushed a little, turned her face aside and whispered in her turn: "But you promised you'd agree to name him Heracles."

"Well, you see, I was thinking of Volodyovski..."

"Shouldn't Grandfather's memory be honored first?"

"Hmm... You're right! Where would I be without him, my dear benefactor that he was? But the second boy will have to be Michal! There's no way around that!"

Here Olenka tried to free herself from his arms and rise from the bench where she sat beside him, but he pressed her to him even more warmly than before and started kissing her lips and her eyes, saying all the while:

"God how I love you, sweetheart! You're my life, my love, my dearest everything!"

★   ★   ★

But they were interrupted just then by a servant, who appeared suddenly at the far end of the gravelled avenue which traversed the orchard, and hurried towards them, so that Pan Andrei had to release his wife.

"What do you want?" he demanded sharply.

"Pan Kharlamp has arrived, sir," said the lad. "He's waiting inside."

But Kmita had already caught sight of his longnosed, heavy-whiskered friend approaching the arbor.

"There he is!" he cried. "Dear God, look how much grey there is in that enormous mustache! Welcome, my dear comrade! Welcome my dear old friend!" And he burst out of the summerhouse running towards the newcomer with wide-open arms.

Pan Kharlamp, however, took his time in responding to this warm-hearted and sincere greeting, as if it wasn't pleasure that brought him to the Kmitas' peaceful country home. First he bowed with a stiff, formal flourish to Olenka, whom he used to see often in Keydany at the court of the late *Voyevode* of Vilna, then he pressed her hand respectfully to his dangling mustache, and only then threw himself into Pan Andrei's arms and burst into tears without any warning.

"Dear God! What's wrong, my friend?" Pan Andrei was immediately alarmed.

"God saw fit to bless one man with happiness and to withhold it from another," the visitor sighed sadly and threw a worried glance at Pan Andrei's wife. "But... I can explain my grief only to you alone."

Olenka rose at once, guessing that their guest found it difficult to unburden himself of some great personal problem while she was there to hear it.

"I'll have some mead sent out to you here, gentlemen," she said quietly.

She left, and Kmita pulled Pan Kharlamp to the arbor and seated him on the bench.

"What is it, then?" he urged. "What can I do to help you? You can count on me no matter what it is!"

"It's not about me," the old campaigner said. "Nor do I need any help as long as this old hand and saber can still do their work. But our best friend, the most deserving cavalier in the Commonwealth, is in such sore straits that I don't even know if he's alive today."

"By Christ's wounds!" Pan Andrei cried out. "Has something happened to Volodyovski?"

"Indeed something has," Pan Kharlamp replied in the tragic tone used for such occasions while fresh tears streamed down into his vast mustache. "I'm grieved to tell you that Miss Anna Krasienska is no longer with us."

"You mean she has died?" Kmita cried in shock, and seized his own head with both hands.

"Just like a bird brought down by an arrow."

Neither of them said anything for a long while after that, and only the thud of ripe fruit falling on the ground, and the shuddering sighs with which Pan Kharlamp fought to control his tears, broke the heavy silence.

Kmita was thunderstruck. He twisted his hands mutely in the air, translating Volodyovski's tragedy to himself so that he might grasp the full extent of it, and the thought made him numb with fear. "Dear God! Dear God! Dear God!" he murmured finally in horror while Pan Kharlamp nodded.

"Don't let my tears shock you," Kharlamp said at last. "Because if your heart aches just on hearing about this calamity, imagine what it's like for me who watched it happen with his own two eyes, and who saw all the agony of his grief as well."

★   ★   ★

Another servant interrupted then, coming into the arbor with a tray, a flagon of aged mead and a second goblet, and followed closely by Pan Andrei's wife. She was a thoughtful, serious-minded woman, but the natural curiosity of her gender had got the better of her, and she was eager to hear what this was all about. However, one look at her husband's deeply troubled face was enough to tell her that something terrible had happened, and her heart opened to both the men at once.

"What sort of news did you bring us, then?" she turned worriedly to Pan Kharlamp, and then urged both the men to share their trouble with her. "I may be able to cheer you up if that's what you need, or I can weep with you if that would help matters, or I might be able to offer some advice..."

Pan Andrei, however, shook his head.

"Not even your fine mind, my dear love, can come up with a solution to this problem," he said. "And I'm worried about the effect this dreadful news would have on your health just now."

But Olenka had faced up to many shocks and tragedies before. "I can take a lot," she reminded him. "It's far more upsetting to worry without knowing why."

"Anusia has died!" Kmita said.

All color drained out of Olenka's face at once. She dropped

so heavily to the bench that Kmita thought she was about to faint or fall ill. But her grief overcame the shock of the news and she began to weep helplessly, her face in her hands, while the two knights sniffed in chorus beside her and mopped their own tears.

"Olenka," Kmita said at last, trying to distract her. "Don't you think that she must be in Heaven?"

"It's not for her sake that I'm weeping," she said through her tears. "I know that her soul is at peace with God and that she'll be happy for the rest of time; I wish I were as sure of my own salvation as I am of hers. Ah, you know there was never a more decent girl, a gentler soul or a kinder heart than she. It's just that I'll miss her so much, and I'm so terribly sorry for Pan Michal in his suffering just now... Oh, my sweet Anulka! My dear, dear Anulka...!"

"I watched her last moments," Kharlamp said. "God grant the same peaceful end to everyone."

Their silence lasted long enough for their tears to ease their grief a little. Then Kmita said: "But how did it happen? Tell us, my friend. Help yourself to some mead to make the telling easier."

"Thank you," Kharlamp said, sniffed, wrung the tears out of his enormous whiskers and dipped them in the mead. "I'll take a sip or two if you'll join me, because pain is like a wolf. It bites at the throat as much as it does the heart, and when it grabs you by the windpipe it can take the breath right out of you and choke you altogether. This, then, is how it was. I was on my way home from Tchenstohova, looking forward to some peaceful years on a piece of property I'm thinking of leasing out this way in Zmudya, which is where I'm from, because it's high time I hung up my saber. I've had a bellyful of war. It was a good way for a man to live when I was a lad, and I was proud to serve, but now my thatch is all grizzled with age and it's time to rest. Of course if there's ever a need, or if can't stand the quiet in the country, I might sign up again with some regiment, but all these civil wars, army mutinies and civic disobedience have soured me on soldiering because they only serve our enemies... Swiderski was a great soldier in his time,"—he named the leader of the latest upheaval in the mutinous Crown Army—"but let God be his judge."

"Oh my dear, dear Anula!" Olenka broke in sadly. "What would have happened to us all if it you hadn't helped me? You were my shield and refuge. Oh, my dearest girl...!"

This was enough to send poor Pan Kharlamp into a fresh flood of tears, but Kmita interrupted with another question. "And where did you come across Volodyovski?"

"In Tchenstohova. They broke their journey there to dedicate themselves at the Holy Shrine. He told me all about how they got engaged, and about the Krakow wedding where Princess Grizelda was waiting to give the bride away, and how Miss Anna wouldn't marry him without the blessings of her former lady. The girl was still as right as rain and he was as happy as a bird. *'Here's my reward for all my years of service,'* he said, as pleased with himself as you could imagine. *'And isn't it a great one?'* He even poked some fun at me, God give him peace, because there was a time when we locked horns, he and I, over that girl, and we were even supposed to settle it with sabers. But where is the poor thing now?"

Here Pan Kharlamp hooted mournfully once more, but not for long because Kmita broke in again. "You say she was well? How come it came on her so quickly, then?"

"Quick was the word. She was staying with the wife of Pan Martin Zamoyski who was in Tchenstohova at that time. Volodyovski spent all his days with her, and grumbled a bit about the delay, saying it would take them a year to get to Krakow at that rate, because everybody stopped them on the way and made a fuss about them. And why shouldn't they? Everyone wants to play host to a soldier like Volodyovski, and once they've got him they hang on to him. He took me with him to visit Miss Krasienska and threatened to trim my whiskers if I turned her head. But this was just a joke, because she couldn't see the world for him, they were so much in love...

"I admit I did feel kind of sad at times," the old soldier went on. "I mean there I was, as lonely as a nail in a wall, and with old age just around the corner. But that's God's will and I'll live with it... Then one night he bursts into my quarters, eyes as big as saucers. *'For God's sake!'* he shouts. *'D'you know where I can find a medic around here?'* So I asked what's wrong. *'She's ill!'* he cries. *'She doesn't even know where she is!'* I asked when this happened. *'I just had the word from Lady Zamoyska!'* he tells me.

And all this, mind you, is happening in the middle of the night, so where were we to find some kind of a medic, especially since the monastery is the only building in one piece around Tchenstohova and the rest of the town has more ruins than people? I finally tracked down a horse doctor who put up a fuss about going anywhere so late in the night, so I had to kick him all the way to Lady Zamoyska's.

"But what they needed there was a priest more than any medic," Pan Kharlamp sighed sadly. "Indeed, one of the Pauline Fathers had already got there, and he brought her back to consciousness with prayer so that she could at least receive the last rites, and take her leave of Pan Volodyovski, and next day, by noon, it was all over with her."

"Strange are the ways of the Lord," Pan Andrei murmured.

"Indeed they are. The horse doctor said that somebody must've cast a spell on her, though that's unlikely in Tchenstohova where witchcraft has no power. But what happened with Pan Michal, what he said, is another matter. I just hope the Lord Jesus won't hold it against him because a man doesn't know what he's saying when he's torn with grief... Anyway,"—and here Pan Kharlamp let his voice drop into a whisper—"he blasphemed in his distress and despair!"

"For God's sake!" Pan Andrei murmured softly. "He blasphemed?"

"He ran from her bedside into the hall and then into the yard outside, reeling like a drunkard. There he raised both fists to the sky and started howling in a dreadful voice: *'Is this my reward for all my wounds, all my hardships, and all my sacrifices for the Motherland? I had just this one little lamb, Lord,'* he cried, *'and You took her from me. It's one thing to kill an armed man!'* he howled, *'That's God's right and duty! But who'd squeeze the life out of a harmless dove unless he's a fox, or a hawk, or a common weasel...?'"*

"For God's sake, sir!" cried Pan Andrei's wife. "Don't repeat it here or you'll bring misfortune on this house!"

Pan Kharlamp made a hasty sign of the cross. "Forgive me. That poor old soldier thought he'd finally earned his dues," he resumed. "And look at the reward he got! Ha! God knows best, though it's hard for a mortal man to grasp His reasons or understand His justice. Anyway, right after these blasphemies, he grew as stiff as a board and fell to the ground. The priest conducted an exorcism over him straight away, so that evil spirits wouldn't enter him, since they're sure to come running at a whiff of blasphemy."

"Was he unconscious long?"

"About an hour. He lay like a corpse. Then he snapped out of it, but only to lock himself up in his quarters where he refused to see anybody. I tried to talk to him during the funeral. *'Sir Michal,'* I said. *'Keep God in your heart.'* But he wouldn't talk. I sat three more days in Tchenstohova, worrying about him, but it did no good to knock on his door. He had no use for me. I could neither think nor decide what to do. Keep trying? Or give up and go on my way? How was I to leave the poor man without doing something to make him feel better? But I could see I wasn't getting anywhere so I took a chance on going to Pan Skshetuski. He's the best friend Pan Michal ever had, and Pan Zagloba is another. I thought they might find a way through to him, especially Pan Zagloba who's a clever man and knows what to say in every situation."

"And did you find Skshetuski?"

"I reached his manor in Podlasye, but as luck would have it, both he and his lady had gone visiting in the Kalish region along with Pan Zagloba. That's where his cousin Stanislav makes his home, as I'm sure you know. No one could tell me when they might be back. So I thought that since I was heading for Zmudya anyway I might as well stop here and tell you both what happened."

"I've always known you were a good friend and a decent man," Kmita told him warmly.

"It's not myself I'm concerned about," Pan Kharlamp said again. "But I'm awfully worried about Volodyovski... The way he looked, it wouldn't take much more to drive him off his head."

"God will protect him from anything like that," Olenka said firmly.

"If He does, then Pan Michal is likely to become a monk. I don't mind telling you I've never seen such grief and despera-tion, and think what a shame it would be to lose such a soldier!"

"How can it be any kind of shame if it adds to God's glory?" Olenka asked gravely, and poor Pan Kharlamp, who never had been much of a theologian, started to twitch his enormous mustache and to rub his forehead.

"Hmm. Well. As to that, my lady," he mumbled at last. "It might add or it might subtract. Just count up, if you would, how many heretics and pagans he dispatched in his time, which must've pleased our Savior and His Holy Mother more than any sermons. Let everyone serve God as best he can, I say... There're bound to be many holy men among the Jesuits who have better and wiser heads than Pan Volodyovski, but there's no other swordsman like him in the Commonwealth..."

"That's as true as there's a God in Heaven!" Pan Andrei agreed. "But where's Volodyovski now? Still in Tchenstohova?"

"He was there when I left. I can't tell what he did after that. All I know is that he's alone in his grief wherever he is, without a friend to help him and make him feel better, and to keep him from one of those desperate acts that often go hand-in-hand with misfortune."

"God keep you well, my friend!" Kmita cried out then, commending Pan Volodyovski to God's special care, and called on God's mother to intercede for him as well. "A brother couldn't have done more for me than you did!" he recalled.

*   *   *

Olenka—or rather *Pani Aleksandra*, which was her proper name and title as Pan Andrei's wife—said nothing for a time. She sat in deep thought and the silence spread from her to the two men. But then she raised her shining, fair head and turned her sky-blue eyes gravely on her husband.

"Andy, do you remember how much we owe him, you and I?" she asked.

"Remember? Good God, if I ever lose sight of it I'll get a pair of eyes from a wayside mongrel, because I won't be able to look a decent man in the face with my own."

"Andy, you can't abandon him like this," she told him.

"What do you mean?"

"Go to him. Go to him, Andy. Go!"

"What a heart this is!" Kharlamp burst out, seized Olenka's hand, and covered it with kisses. "What decency and goodness always shine from a good woman! You are truly a great lady, ma'am, a very great lady, and your feelings prove it."

But Kmita didn't like the sound of this advice.

"I'd go to the ends of the world for him, you know it yourself," he said to his wife, and started shaking his head from side to side. "I'd leave at once if you weren't likely to need me here. But now, the way things are... well, you know what's involved! God forbid something should frighten you or something violent should happen... I'd dry up with worry! A wife comes first. Even the best of friends must take second place. I'm sorry for Michal, of course I am, but... well, you see how it is!"

"I'll be in good hands with our Laudanian friends," Olenka said quietly. "Things are peaceful around here these days and I'm not likely to get frightened of just anything, you know. Nothing will happen to me unless it's God's will, and Pan Michal may be needing help."

"Oh, he does! He does!" Kharlamp interrupted.

"There, you hear it, Andy? I'm in good health. I'm fine. Nobody will harm me. I know that you don't want to leave me, but..."

"I'd rather charge a cannon with a fly whisk!" Kmita broke in fiercely.

"I know. But how can you *not* go? Won't you feel bitter each time you remember that you turned your back on a friend in need? And you might bring God's anger down on us. He could withhold his blessings. Would you want to risk that?"

"You're driving a redhot nail right through my head," Pan Andrei complained. "You say God might take his blessings from us if I stay? That I *am* afraid of!"

"Saving a friend like Michal is your sacred duty!"

"I love Michal with all my heart, you know that! And you're right, of course. What else can I do? Well, if I must go then I must and that's all there's to it! And the sooner the better since it looks as if every hour counts! But are you sure there's no other way?"

She shook her head, and he grumbled a few mild curses at Pan Yan Skshetuski and old Pan Zagloba for going off to Kalish at this of all times.

"It's you I'm worried about, my sweet love, not myself," he said to her again, "though I'd rather lose everything I own than spend one day without you! Ah, if someone ever told me I'd leave you for any reason other than service to our country, I'd shove my saber down his throat so far that he'd be chewing on the hilt!"

But she was right, and he knew it, and there was little more for him to say.

"You say this is my sacred duty? So be it then! Only a fool looks behind him when it's time to go! Ah, if it was anyone but Michal I would never do it. But if I must, I have to, and that's that!"

Then he turned to Pan Kharlamp, as brisk and decisive as he always was once a decision had been made and a path was charted. "Come with me to the stables to pick out the horses. And you, Olenka,"—he turned to his wife—"have them pack my baggage right away. Let one of the Laudanians look after the threshing...

"But you, my good friend,"—he clamped his arm around Pan Kharlamp's shoulder as they walked away—"must stay here at least through the next two Sundays. Look after my wife for me. Make sure she's alright. Maybe you'll even find something in this neighborhood you can lease so you can stay longer. What about Lubitch? Take that, if you want. Now let's go. Let's hurry to the stables. I leave in an hour."

Chapter Two

IT WAS WELL BEFORE SUNSET when Pan Andrei set out on his journey. Olenka's eyes shined with tears as he rode away and she blessed him with a crucifix in which some splinters of the True Cross were artfully set in gold. And because he was used to sudden rapid marches, these having been his specialty from his earliest years, he drove his horses and himself without pause for breath as if he were chasing Tartar raiders.

He rode to Vilna (or Vilnius, as it is known among the Lithuanians) and then through Grodno and Bialystok south into Podlasye. Passing through Lukov County, he discovered that Pan Yan Skshetuski with his wife and children and old Pan Zagloba came back from Kalish just the day before, so he decided to stop off and see them because they were the best source for advice on how to save or help Volodyovski. The stern and serious Pan Yan had been his closest friend since their old days in the service of Prince Yeremi Vishnovyetzki, in the Transdnieper country, in the Cossack Wars when Hmyelnitzki scourged Ruthenia and the Ukraine with fire and sword, and in the most recent deluge of Swedish invasion. The fat, old, one-eyed, roistering Zagloba had ridden side by side with the diminutive Volodyovski in some of the most famous of all their adventures, and exercised an enormous influence on the little soldier. Pan Andrei loved him just as much as they, owing him everything including life itself, but he knew that Zagloba and Skshetuski would always mean more to Volodyovski.

They were delighted and surprised to see him but their joy soon turned to grief and tears when he told his story. The old knight couldn't make his peace with the news all day, and wept so copiously alone by the fishpond that—as he said it later—the pond had to be saved from overflowing by opening the sluices. But having wept his fill he gave some thought to what had to be done and this is the advice he gave when they all sat down to discuss the matter.

"You can't go," he said to Pan Skshetuski, "because you've been elected magistrate, and what with all the wars we've had, and one disorder or another, there are a lot of restless spirits who must be brought to heel. And judging by what our friend Pan Kmita has just told us, it looks as if the storks will stay in Vodokty through the Winter because they've been added to the working livestock and they've a job to do.

"Small wonder then that it's a hardship for you to go traveling right now," he said to Pan Andrei. "You've shown great heart, my friend, by setting out at all, but if I'm to be quite honest about it, I'd say: go back home. What Michal needs is someone even closer to him, someone who won't take it amiss if he's snubbed, or feel hurt if he's pushed aside with a bee in his ear, and left to cool his heels. *Patientia* is the ticket, and so is a great deal of experience in dealing with human frailties and follies. And all you have to offer, my young friend, is friendship which, in this case, *non sufficit*. Don't hold it against me, but you must agree that Yan and I are older friends of his, and that we've shared many more adventures in our time. Sweet God!" the old knight wondered out loud. "How many times did I save his neck or he mine!"

"What if I resigned my post as county deputy?" Skshetuski interrupted. "I could go then!"

"Yan, that's public service!" Zagloba admonished.

"God knows," the troubled Pan Yan said, "that I love my cousin Stanislav better than a brother, but Michal means even more to me than that."

"And even more to me," said Zagloba, "since I never had close kin that I know of. But let's not waste time arguing who is closer. Think, Yan, how long it's been since this tragedy struck Michal. If it was something fresh I'd tell you myself: let your work hang and go! But count up all the time it took Pan Kharlamp to get to Zmudya from Tchenstohova, and then for

Pan Kmita to get to us from Zmudya. Now it's not just a matter
of going to Michal but staying with him too, not just shedding
tears and commiserating with him but offering reasoned arguments, not just pointing to our Savior as his best example of how
to cope with suffering and grief, but also easing his heart and
mind with a joke or two, restoring his spirits, and distracting him
with some pleasant pastimes!

"Hmm," he went on, struck by an idea. "D'you know who
should go? Me, that's who! And that's just what I'll do! If I find
him in Tchenstohova then I'll bring him here. If I don't, then
I'll go looking for him in Moldavia if that's what it takes, and I
won't stop looking until I'm too old and weak to lift a pinch of
snuff to my nose."

The two younger knights leaped up, took the old noble in
their arms and began to hug him; and he was so moved by this
demonstration of their love, respect and admiration that he
started to shed a few fresh sentimental tears, still shaken as he
was by Pan Michal's terrible misfortune and by his own anticipated sacrifice and hardships.

"Just don't you dare to thank me on Michal's behalf," he
huffed. "Because no one is closer to him than I."

"We wouldn't dream of it, sir,"Kmita said. "But we'd have to
have stone hearts, or be totally heartless, not to be stirred by
your willingness to take on such hardships for a friend's sake, and
at your age too. Anyone else of your venerable years would be
thinking only about a warm spot by the stove, but you talk about
this long and wearying journey as if you were no older than I or
Pan Skshetuski."

Pan Zagloba never made a secret of how old he was, but he
didn't like it when someone alluded to old age as a companion
to helplessness and debility; so even though his eyes were still
moist and red with tears, he threw Pan Andrei a somewhat chilly
glance.

"My dear young sir,"he growled. "When I began my seventy-
seventh year I felt a little pang at the thought of those two sevens
hanging over my neck like a pair of axes. But once I got started
on my eighties it was as if a brand new spirit leaped into my
bones. I even thought about getting married, dam'me if I didn't!
And if I had, we'd soon see which of us would've had the storks
working overtime."

"I don't deny it, sir,"Pan Andrei assured him. "And I'd be the first to trumpet your praises."

"And I'd put you in your place just as I did the late Pan Revera Pototzki, who was Grand Hetman of the Crown before Pan Sobieski, and in the King's own presence. He had the bad judgment to say something about my getting old, so I challenged him to show how many times he could roll head over heels without a break. And d'you know what happened? The lackeys had to get him to his feet after just three flips, because he couldn't do it on his own, while I did more than thirty. Ask Skshetuski if you don't believe me. He saw it all with his own two eyes."

★   ★   ★

The story, like so many of Pan Zagloba's stories, was just a figment of his imagination, and Skshetuski knew that the old knight had got into the habit of citing him as an eyewitness to all his wild claims and improbable successes, so he didn't even blink an eye and started talking about Volodyovski.

But the old knight lapsed into an unusual silence, turning something over in his mind until after they had eaten dinner, when his humor improved quite considerably.

"Let me tell you what I've been thinking for a while,"he said. "And it's not something you'd hear from just anybody, because it takes a special brain and a world of experience to come up with something this profound. In fact you wouldn't hear this from anyone but me. And what I say is that our Michal will get over this blow much easier than we thought at first."

"God grant it,"Kmita said. "But what makes you think so?"

"What makes me think so? Three things. A good head, one that I was born with, along with a knowledge of the world that you younger fellows can't possibly have acquired, and the fact that I know Michal inside out. Everybody has a different nature, and reacts differently to calamity. With one, misfortune is like a stone thrown into a river. Everything looks calm on the surface, the water runs on undisturbed as if nothing happened. But that stone is down there on the bottom, getting in the way of the natural flow, upsetting the current and tearing at the smooth order of the stream, and it'll stay there ripping things apart until all the water has flowed into the Styx. You, Yan, are one of those, and that's why your life is likely to be harder because your pain and memories stay with you for ever. Another kind of man takes his misfortunes like a fist cracking him on the back of the neck. He might get stunned at first, but he'll get back on his feet soon enough, and when the bruise is gone he'll forget about it. Those are the lucky ones, I'd say. They have it better in this world."

The younger knights listened to the fruits of Pan Zagloba's wisdom with complete attention, which made him feel much better about everything and improved his humor even more.

"I've gotten to know Michal through and through," he went on, pleased with the respectful silence with which they were listening. "God is my witness that I don't want to say anything about him that might make it seem as if I weren't devoted to him heart and soul. I am! But I think that what he misses most is the *idea* of marriage rather than the girl. Alright, so he's taken a dreadful blow just now, and he's sunk in a terrible despair, and with good reason too! This really hit him like a bolt of lightning! You can't image how eager he always was to get himself married. There isn't an ounce of greed in his entire body, he has no driving personal ambitions, and he never asked God or the Commonwealth for anything for himself. He turned his back on whatever material possessions he had, the Devil's taken everything he owned, he never grumbled about his pay or asked for promotions, and all he ever wanted was a loving wife as his reward for all those years of service. The way he looked at it was that he'd earned this tasty piece of bread, that it was his due, and it's snatched away from him just as he was about to take his first bite! And there you have it! Eat air, if you want to! So what's the big surprise about his despair? I'm not saying that he doesn't miss the girl. Of course he does! He loved her! But I'm here to tell you, as God is dear to me, that what he's really mourning is his lost chance to marry, even though he'd swear with all his heart that it's the other way around."

"God grant that this be true," Skshetuski repeated.

"Just wait a bit and you'll see," the old knight assured him. "Let these fresh wounds heal over in his soul, and let him grow some new skin over them, and we'll soon see his old spirit coming back to him.

"The true *periculum*," the old knight went on, "is in the

likelihood that he might do something hasty in his present state of anger and despair and regret it later. That's what worries me. Mind you, the worst that could've happened to him has most likely happened. Misfortune doesn't waste much time in driving people to a quick decision. If that's so then there's probably little we can do, but don't get me wrong. I'm not saying this to get out of going. In fact my lad's already airing out my shirts to pack for the journey. I said what I said to raise your spirits a little because things may not be as bad as we supposed."

"Once again, father, you'll be Michal's good medicine and cure!" Pan Skshetuski said.

"As I was yours, remember? I just hope I find him quick enough before he turns into some kind of hermit or buries himself somewhere in the Wild Lands. That's been his home since childhood, and he could run to the Steppe as if it were his mother. You, Master Kmita, made some remarks about my age a while ago. But let me tell you, that if ever an express rider made better time than I will be doing, I'll ask you to give me old socks to darn when I get back, or shell peas in the kitchen, or spin wool. Hardships won't stop me, wayside hospitality won't tempt me, and neither food nor drink will slow me down for a single moment. You've never seen the kind of speed-march that I will be making! I'm so ready for it I feel as if I was sitting on a cobbler's awl! And I've already told my lad to dip my traveling shirt in goat grease to repel the insects."

Chapter Three

AS IT HAPPENED, Pan Zagloba didn't travel as rapidly as he said he would and the closer that he got to Warsaw the slower his pace became. This was a time when King Yan Casimir, a great statesman and a truly loving monarch who had put out the worst of the many border fires, and who had brought the Commonwealth safely through a deluge of enemy invasions, sought his own peace in abdication, and renounced his throne. He had endured everything, suffered through everything, and took upon himself all the blows which came from external enemies; but, later, when he tried to bring about internal reforms, only to have opposition and revolt heaped on him by an ungrateful nation, he shed the crown which had become an intolerable burden.

The county and territorial dietines were already finished all over the country, and the Primate, Archbishop Prazmovski, had set November 5 as the date of the special convocation of parliament which was to review the candidates, seat the electoral commission, and fix the day for a new King's election.

The various candidates and parties threw themselves into early efforts to captivate electors, and though the polls themselves were to decide the issue, everyone understood the importance of this electoral convention and hurried to attend. The roads to Warsaw were jammed with territorial delegates in carriages and on horseback with their grooms and servants. The great lords of the senate came with their glittering courts, private regiments and households, and the country inns along the way were jammed to overflowing, so that finding a bed for the night was no simple matter.

Pan Zagloba's age did give him an advantage in securing quarters, but his vast fame and reputation among his brother gentry contributed a great deal to the delays throughout his long journey.

It often happened that he'd come to some crowded hostelry, occupied by some traveling personage along with his court, where the sight of his milk-white beard would prompt the residing magnate to invite him for an evening meal. Convinced that his company would delight everyone, Zagloba never refused an invitation, but once across the threshold, when his host would ask *'whom do I have the honor?'* he'd cock his fists proudly on his hips, sure of the effect, and announce in that expected mixture of Latin and Polish: "Zagloba *sum."*

These two words never failed to provoke amazement, arms flung wide in greeting, and cries of *'this must be my luckiest day!'* from the overjoyed host. Then came the calls that summoned courtiers and traveling companions who were told to feast their eyes on this *'living paragon of all the gentry's virtues,'* and at this *'gloria et decus'* or embodiment of all the qualities that made the knighthood of the Commonwealth what it was. Throngs of journeying nobles pressed together to shake his hand or to voice their admiration of him, while the younger gentry ran to kiss the skirts of his traveling coat and ask for his blessing. After which the baggage carts disgorged kegs and flagons for a celebration that might last three days.

Everyone thought that he was traveling as a regional delegate or deputy to the diet and were amazed to hear that this was not the case. But he explained that he had passed the honor to a younger man *'so that the youth of the country might acquire experience in public affairs.'* Now and again he told the real reason for his journey, but for most other audiences he'd merely say, that as an old campaigner, he wanted a last taste of war against Doroshenko's rebel Cossacks in the east.

These statements, testifying to his modesty and valor, simply added to the vast respect that everybody showed him. Nor did anyone think any the less of him because he wasn't a member of the diet, since everyone knew that the arbiters, or observers, often possessed more influence than the elected deputies themselves. Besides, each senator, no matter how powerful and distinguished, was well aware that the election was only a few

weeks away, and that the slightest comment from a man as well
known and revered as Pan Zagloba, would be worth the old
knight's weight in gold when it came to swaying the hearts and
minds of the voting gentry, so that even the greatest lords were
eager to hobnob with him and show him full honors.

The Palatine of Podlasye kept him at his table for three days
and the influential Patz family of Lithuania, whom he came
across in Kalushin, literally carried him about in their arms.
Quite a few magnates took pains to shower him privately with
expensive gifts, so that his open charabanc, with its oilskin roof
folded back for comfort, soon bulged with casks of vodka, wines,
costly ornaments, pistols and gilded sabers.

His servants had the best time of their lives with all this
adulation, but Pan Zagloba found himself traveling at such a
snail's pace that it took him three weeks just to get to Minsk in
upper Mazovia.

★   ★   ★

Minsk, however, offered him an unexpected shock. The
market square was jammed with such a brilliant retinue when his
wagon rolled into it that Pan Zagloba knew he had seen nothing
like it anywhere along the way. Whoever this splendid magnate
might have been, his courtiers strutted in dazzling livery. Only
half a regiment of foreign infantry served as the traveling potentate's ceremonial escort, since no one brought an army to an
electoral convention, but they were so magnificently uniformed
and equipped that the King of Sweden could have no finer
guards. The gilded coaches and the baggage train groaned under
cargoes of provisions, costly table settings, and oriental rugs and
tapestries used for decorating the floors and walls of hostelries
on the way, while the entire household was almost wholly
foreign so that the old knight heard few words in any language
he could understand.

But eventually Pan Zagloba spotted a courtier dressed in
Polish costume, ordered his groom to halt, and being quite sure
of an excellent rest-break in his journey, prepared to climb out.
He had already thrust one leg out of his wagon and now asked
the passing courtier: "Whose household is this?"

"Whose but our master's?" the courtier replied with a lofty
air.

"And who might that be?"

"His Highness the Prince-Equerry of Lithuania!" the courtier announced.

"Who?" asked Zagloba.

"Are you deaf or something? This is the traveling household of Prince Boguslav Radzivill, who is here as a delegate to the electoral convention, and who, God grant the day, will be our next King after the election."

The old knight jerked his leg back into the carriage as if he'd touched fire and cried to his driver: "Get going! This is no place for us!"

And then he hurried out of Minsk shaking with indignation and hardly able to believe his ears.

"Dear God!" he muttered as his carriage rattled out of town. "Your ways are a mystery, and if You don't crack this traitor in the neck with a bolt of lightning, You must have some special purpose that a mere mortal shouldn't dare to question. But looking at it from a human viewpoint, I'd say that what this son of a bitch deserves is a first class thrashing. Things can't be going well with our splendid Commonwealth if such perfidious turncoats, who are devoid of all honor and conscience, not only escape punishment but travel about as safe and powerful as ever, and even get to hold public office like good citizens...

"Where else could this happen?" he appealed to the cloudless sky. "What other country would put up with this? Are we doomed, or what? Our good Yan Casimir was a fair monarch but far too forgiving! The worst scoundrels have got used to getting away with it, though this can't be wholly Yan Casimir's fault. It looks as if the whole nation can't tell right from wrong and that it's lost all its civic conscience...!

"Tfui! Tfui!" he spat in disgust. "So he's a deputy to the diet? People entrust the safety and integrity of our Motherland to such hands as his? And aren't these the same hands that did their best to tear our Commonwealth apart and load it down with Swedish chains just a few years ago? We'll perish, there's no other answer! And they're even talking about electing him our King? How can he be a deputy anyway? For God's sake, the law is clear on that point! No one can hold public office in the Commonwealth if he also holds office in a foreign country, and he's the Governor-General of his flea-bitten uncle's Prussia, isn't he?

"Ah, but wait! Wait! I've got you!"the old knight cheered up. "What about the rules of procedure? Hmm? How about the process for seating delegates? I may be just an observer, not a deputy, but if I don't go to the meeting hall and demand some answers, may I turn into a capon with my driver here as the butcher to dress me for stuffing... There're bound to be some deputies over there who'll back me!

"Ha, you traitor!" he bellowed happily into the empty air. "I don't know if I'll manage to pull down such a great lord as you and have you thrown out of the electoral convention, but it's a sure thing that it won't help you with your own election! Poor Michal must wait for me a little longer, I'm afraid, but this is all *pro publico bono* and for the country's good."

★　★　★

Reflecting on such matters, Pan Zagloba made fervent promises to himself that he'd get busy behind the scenes, throw as much doubt as he could on Prince Boguslav's right to sit in the convention, and work among the deputies to unseat the traitor. With all this boiling in his mind, he speeded up his journey so as not to miss the opening of the convocation.

He arrived in time. In fact he came early. There were so many delegates and partisans of the various candidates already in Warsaw, that there was no room in any of the city hostelries or the inns of Praga across the Vistula or, for that matter, anywhere in the countryside around the crowded city. Nor could he very well invite himself to someone else's quarters where three or four people had to share one room.

The old knight spent his first night in the famous taproom of Fukier in the city and that passed pleasantly enough. But next day, sobering up in his wagon, he was at a loss about what to do.

"God, God!"he moaned in the worst of humor, peering along the Krakow Prospect through which he was passing. "Here's the Chapel of the Bernardines which I liberated from the Swedes. And there are the ruins of the Kazanovski Palace which I captured almost singlehanded. What an ungrateful city! I had to tear it from the enemy with my own blood and sweat and now it won't spare some quiet corner for my poor grey head."

But this was less a matter of ingratitude on the city's part than the simple fact that there was no unoccupied corner to be found anywhere in Warsaw. The old knight, however, was under the protection of his lucky star, because he barely reached the Kazanovski Palace when some voice in the street shouted at his driver: "Stop! Pull up!"

The lackey hauled back on the reins and an unknown noble approached the wagon with a beaming smile.

"Sir! Pan Zagloba!" he cried joyfully. "Don't you recognize me?"

Zagloba saw a young man, barely in his thirties, dressed in a military lynx-fur cap with a slanting feather, a scarlet surcoat and a crimson *kontush* cinched by a rich silk sash woven from gold threads. The stranger's face was unusually handsome, with a pale skin that was only partly tanned by the winds and weather, sky-blue eyes filled with some pensive sadness, and features of such delicate fragility that they seemed too beautiful for a man.

Despite his Polish costume he wore his hair full, in a long sweep falling to his shoulders, and his beard and mustache were trimmed and curled in the Western European fashion. Standing beside the carriage, he threw his arms wide-open in greeting, and even though Pan Zagloba couldn't quite place him at the moment or recall his name, he leaned out of his seat to hug him around the neck.

They squeezed and clasped each other for a while, pulling back now and then so that each could take a good look at the other, and finally Pan Zagloba said: "Forgive me, sir, but I can't quite remember where we met..."

"I'm Hassling-Ketling!" cried the laughing stranger.

"For God's sake!" the old knight exclaimed. "The face seemed familiar but your Polish clothing changed you altogether! I'm used to seeing you in a Reiter's jacket... Ha! So now you're dressing like a Polish noble?"

"That's because I am one! The Commonwealth has been a mother to me, taking me in when I was little more than an orphan lad, and giving me everything I have, so I've decided to treat her like a son. Did you know that I was given a patent of nobility after the last war?"

"That's wonderful news! You've done so well among us, then?"

"In that and more. I found a man in Courland, right across the Zmudyan border, who has the same name and origins as I, and who adopted me, admitted me to his coat-of-arms, and gave me my start. He lives in Courland but he has some lands on our side of the border and let me have some property to begin my holdings."

"Good luck to you, then! So you're landed gentry, are you now? Does that mean that you've given up soldiering altogether?"

"Just for the time being. But you can count on me to join the colors when there's a real need."

"Well done! Well spoken! That's just what I did when I was a young man, though there's some fire in the old bones yet! But what are you doing in Warsaw?"

"I'm a deputy to the congress."

"God bless you! So you're now Polish, blood and bone?"

"And with my heart and soul, which means a lot more," the young knight smiled broadly.

"And are you married now as well?"

"No," Ketling sighed. "I'm not."

"That's all that's missing, then, to make your life complete, because it's marriage that settles a man, as it did Pan Kmita. But wait a minute, could it be that your old affections for Billevitchovna are still on your mind?"

"Since you seem privy, sir, to what I thought to be my own secret, then I'll confess that no one else has come along as yet..."

"Come on now," the old knight chided the sentimental Scotsman. "You ought to have more sense, a traveled man like you. She's about to bring a little Kmita into the world, so what's the good of pining? What's the point of sighing after someone when she's so much closer to another man? It even sounds silly."

"All I said was that no one else happened to come along," Ketling said, sighed, and raised his sad eyes mournfully towards the sky.

"But they will! They will! Don't worry about that! We'll get you married yet! I know it from my own experience that too much constancy in matters of the heart is downright unhealthy. I missed a lot of chances and turned my back on some delightful little snippets in my time just because I was as faithful as a Troilus... And for what? Eh? Who needs all that fretting?"

"If only God would give everyone such a light-hearted spirit as yours, good sir!" Ketling said with fervor.

"My heart is light because I've always lived with temperate modesty," Pan Zagloba said. "Which is why my bones don't creak as they might these days. But where are you staying? Have you found an inn?"

"I've a pleasant little manor near Mokotov just across the city, which I built for myself soon after the war."

"Then you're doubly lucky because I've been searching for a room all day and I can't find anything anywhere in or around the city."

"For God's sake!" Ketling cried. "My dear friend! You must stay with me! No, you can't refuse me! There's lots of room in the manor and there are barns and a good stable for your men and horses."

"Ah, you're a gift from Heaven!" Pan Zagloba cried. "Thank God for old friendships."

★ ★ ★

Ketling climbed into the carriage and they started off. On the way Pan Zagloba told him about the misfortune that overtook Pan Volodyovski, and Ketling wrung his hands in sorrow because this was the first that he had heard of it.

"You may not know this, sir, but he and I became great friends in the recent wars," Ketling said at last. "That's what makes this blow such a frightful shock. We were together through the campaigns in Prussia and all the other sieges where the Swedes still held out in the towns and castles. We rode together in the Ukraine, and against Pan Lubomirski in his unfortunate rebellion, and back again in the Ukraine under Pan Sobieski who became Lord High Constable of the Crown after Lubomirski. One saddle served us for a pillow. We ate our rations out of the same bowl. They called us Castor and Pollux, we were that inseparable and close. The only time in recent years that we weren't together was when he went to Zmudya for Panna Krasienska. And to think that all his best hopes vanished as swiftly as an arrow in the wind!"

"Nothing is constant in this vale of tears," Pan Zagloba said.

"Except a steady friendship."

"That's true."

"We'll have to put our heads together and find out where he is. Maybe we'll hear something from Pan Sobieski who dotes on

Volodyovski as if he were the apple of his eye. And if not there
then elsewhere. Warsaw is full of delegates from every territory
and region; it's impossible that someone wouldn't have heard
the whereabouts of such a famous knight. I'll help in every way
I can, better than if my own life were at stake."

Talking like that they drove to Ketling's manor which turned
out to be a mansion rather than just a country house. The inner
rooms were richly furnished with many costly objects, some of
which Ketling bought and some that he acquired as a soldier's
booty. There was a specially fine collection of ornamental weapons hung along the walls which delighted the old knight a great
deal.

"You could put up twenty people here!" he exclaimed, peering around with pleasure. Then, switching back to the convocation, he asked suddenly: "But tell me, how do you feel about
Boguslav Radzivill?"

"I feel nothing for him or about him. I gave up his service
from the time when Pan Kmita's Tartars took me prisoner at
Warsaw and I haven't thought about it since. He's a powerful
and influential magnate but he's an evil man." And again, as Pan
Zagloba could see at a glance, he drifted into a memory of
Olenka. "I saw enough of him in Taurogen when he was laying
his foul snares against that heavenly creature..."

"Heavenly? Come on! What makes you think she's some kind
of angel?" Pan Zagloba had no patience with sentimental mus-
ings unless they were his own. "Will you get her out of your
head once and for all? She's made of the same clay as any other
woman and she can break like the rest of them. But that's not
what I want to talk about just now!"

Here Pan Zagloba turned beet-red with anger and his eyes
bulged with such passion that they threatened to pop out of his
head.

"Imagine! That scoundrel is a delegate!" he burst out. "A
member of the parliament, no less!"

"Who is?" Ketling asked, surprised, his thoughts still circling
about Olenka.

"Boguslav Radzivill, that's who! But the rules! The rules that
govern seating and verification! Listen, you're a delegate yourself, you can raise that matter from the floor and I'll support you
from the gallery, you can be sure of that! The law is with us, and

if they feel like going around the law then I'll stir up such an uproar among the observers that we'll have blood flowing in the aisles!"

"Don't do that, sir!" Ketling pleaded, because Pan Zagloba was quite capable of doing what he said. "I'll raise the matter because it should be raised. But for God's sake don't disrupt the diet!"

But Pan Zagloba was now in full gallop, letting his anger sweep him away like a runaway wild mustang. "I'll go to the Speaker, who's an old friend of mine!" he howled. "I'll set the Patz brothers baying at Boguslav! The least we'll do is remind everyone of all his past intrigues. I heard on the road that this scoundrel has the crown in mind for himself, if you can believe it!"

"The nation would have to sink to its lowest ebb and be unfit to live if his kind could be elected King," Ketling answered promptly. "But get some rest, sir. Relax a little here. And then we'll pick a day to go to Pan Sobieski to ask about our friend."

Chapter Four

THE ELECTORAL CONVENTION opened a few days later. Because this time it was the turn of Lithuania to nominate the Speaker, the post went to Pan Antoni Hrapovyetzki, the Chamberlain of Smolensk who would later become the *Voyevode* of Vitebsk, and who was known as a gentle and conciliatory man who wanted everything to happen by consensus.

Since the sole business of this diet was to set the date for the General Election and appoint the supervisory commission, and since this offered no arena for inter-party squabbles, everyone expected the convention to pass rather quietly.

But this is not what happened.

Right at the beginning, when Delegate Ketling questioned the legal standing of the Byelsk delegation, including Prince Boguslav Radzivill who owned vast possessions in that Podlasyan region, some stentorian voice boomed out among the arbiters in the gallery: "Traitor! Foreign functionary!"

Other voices took up the shout. Some deputies joined it on the floor, and suddenly the parliament split into two factions, with one demanding the ouster of the gentlemen from Byelsk and the other calling for their seating. A review commission was hastily convened to look into the matter, and eventually permitted Boguslav to remain, but the blow to Radzivill's ambitions was a serious one. The fact that his qualifications were thrown under discussion, and that all his treacheries during the Swedish war were dragged so unexpectedly into the public forum, covered him with fresh opprobrium throughout the Commonwealth and totally undermined all his ambitious plans.

Those plans had been quite logical and simple. He counted on a bitter competition among the several foreign candidates, and thought quite correctly, that when the partisans of the French Prince de Conde, the Duke of Lorraine, and the German Duke of Neuburg succeeded in discrediting each other, the compromise choice might go to a native son.

His pride and all his flatterers suggested that if that should happen then this native son could be none other than the most eye-catching of the Polish magnates, one who commanded the greatest influence and power, and whose family antecedents were the most distinguished: in other words, himself.

He kept his ambitions a close-guarded secret, biding his time until it was safe to come out into the open, but he had worked hard to put together a network of supporters throughout Lithuania and now began to set his snares in Warsaw. Right at the start, however, all his plans were ruined. The unexpected uproar about his former treason ripped such a huge hole in his calculations that, as the people said it at the time, *'all his fish escaped,'* and the crown he craved slipped out of his grasp. He boiled with rage throughout the sessions of the review commission. Ketling, as a member of parliament, was safe from his vengeance, but he let his courtiers know that he'd pay well for the name of that arbiter who had first roared *'Traitor!'* and *'Turncoat!'* in support of Ketling.

Pan Zagloba was too widely known to remain anonymous for long. Nor did he hide his part in the affair. The Prince seethed all the more when he identified the implacable old knight, who had done so much to undermine the Radzivill machinations in the last Swedish war, but he knew that a man of such enormous popularity could say pretty much whatever he pleased in the Commonwealth and get away with it.

Zagloba knew it just as well. The early rumors of Boguslav's vengeance didn't worry the shrewd old man at all. In fact he sent his own warning message to the Prince when he said at a large gathering of gentry later in the month: "I wouldn't bet much on anybody's safety if one hair falls off my head as a result of his conniving, no matter who he is. The election isn't far away, and when a hundred thousand of our brother gentry get together along with their sabers somebody could get chopped up into mincemeat without too much trouble."

★   ★   ★

The Prince got the message, bit back his own rejoinder and smiled with contempt, but privately he agreed that the old knight was right.

The next day he had apparently changed his mind about him, because when someone mentioned Zagloba during one of Boguslav's own splendid banquets, he said for all to hear: "As I have it, this gentleman is quite deadset against me. But I've always loved men of principle and valor so I'll continue to be fond of him no matter how much damage he might do to me."

A week later, when they met at a dinner given by Pan Sobieski, who was now Grand Hetman of the Crown, the Prince said the same thing to Zagloba's face.

"My dear Pan Zagloba!" he called out the length of the table. "I've heard that even though you're not a delegate, and even though I'm innocent of any wrongdoing, you did your best to have me ousted from the congress. But I forgive you, as a Christian should, and if you ever need my patronage I'll be pleased to give it."

The old knight kept his face calm and full of confidence but his heart hammered anxiously in his chest because this was, after all, a magnate of immense wealth and power, with a long reach and a well-earned reputation for crushing anybody who got in his way.

"I merely stood by the constitution," he replied steadily enough. "As for any patronage, Your Highness, I think I'd better look for it from God since I'm close to ninety."

"A fine old age," said the Prince. "If it's as full of virtue as it is of years."

"I served my country and my King, that's all, and didn't look for foreign Gods to worship."

"You served against me as well,"—the Prince allowed a shadow of displeasure to pass across his face—"I know it well enough. But let there finally be peace and amity between us. Let's forget the past, even the fact that you supported another man's private vendetta against me. I still have some old accounts to settle in that quarter but I'm willing to stretch my hand to you and offer you my friendship."

"Your hand is far too high for me to reach, Your Highness,"

Pan Zagloba answered. "I am just a smallfry in comparison with your lofty stature. I'd have to climb up to it or jump like a rabbit and I'm too old for such exercises. But if Your Highness speaks about settling accounts with my friend, Pan Kmita, I'd advise you to forget about it."

"And why?" asked the Prince.

"Because accounting is a matter of arithmetic and arithmetic has four primary functions. Pan Kmita has a lot of property, and though it's a flyspeck compared to Your Highness, he'd never go along with any division. He needs no help with his multiplication which he's handling very nicely for himself, and he won't let anyone do any subtracting. So all that's left for him is some possible addition, and I doubt if Your Highness would be pleased to see it."

Boguslav was a trained diplomat and an expert in verbal exchanges. But whether it was Pan Zagloba's smooth manipulation of the language, or his cool aplomb, he found himself so astonished by that clever broadside that he sat dumbstruck with no immediate answer. Others, however, began to shake and choke with swiftly stifled laughter, and Pan Sobieski let his own deep laugh boom right across the table.

"That's an old Zbarajh hand," he said, referring to the heroic stand at Zbarajh in the Cossack Wars and the famous role that the old knight played in it. "He knows how to swing a saber but he's a master with the tongue as well! It's best to leave a man like that alone."

Boguslav saw that he'd never be able to win Pan Zagloba's neutrality, not to mention friendship, so he gave up all attempts to draw him to his side. He turned to someone else, beginning another conversation, and merely sending a malignant glance at the implacable old knight now and then.

* * *

But the exchange with the Prince put the Grand Hetman in fine humor and he turned to Zagloba with a jovial smile.

"You're a true master, brother. A true master. Have you ever found your match in the Commonwealth?"

"Only in swordsmanship, my lord," Pan Zagloba said, pleased with this public praise. "Volodyovski managed to reach my level as a swordsman. And I've taught Pan Kmita a trick or two as well."

Here he shot a sly, sideways glance at Prince Boguslav, whom Kmita fought, wounded and took prisoner in the Swedish war, but the magnate pretended not to hear and busied himself talking to his neighbor.

"Ha!" said the Hetman. "I've watched Volodyovski at work many times and I'd swear by him if the fate of Christendom depended on his skill. It's a real shame that such a dreadful thunderbolt hit such a great soldier."

"What happened to him, then?" asked Pan Sarbyevski, the Constable of Tchehanovyetz.

"The girl he loved dropped dead in Tchenstohova," Pan Zagloba answered. "But the worst of it is that I can't find out where he might be today."

"By God!" cried Pan Varshytzki, the Castellan of Krakow. "I met him on the road to Warsaw! He was also heading this way and he confided to me privately that he's grown sick of the world and its *vanitates*, and that he was on his way to the *Mons Regius* monastery not too far from here to spend the rest of his days in prayer and contemplation."

Shocked, Pan Zagloba clutched at the remnants of his hair. "He's turned into a Cistercian!" he cried in despair. "There's no harsher order!"

The castellan's news had a profound effect on the entire gathering, and Pan Sobieski, who truly loved his soldiers and knew how desperately the country needed them in those dangerous and unsettled times, was greatly saddened by it.

"God's service and a man's free will make their own laws which we must respect," he said after a while. "But it's a real pity to hear about this, and I can't hide my distress from you gentlemen. Volodyovski was a splendid soldier, from the old Transdnieper school of Prince Yeremi Vishnovyetzki, and he'll be sorely missed. He was first rate against any kind of enemy but quite unmatched anywhere against Cossacks, Tartars and other bush rangers. There's a mere handful of light cavalry commanders of his stamp in the Ukrainian Steppe, such as Pan Pivo among the loyal Cossacks and Pan Rushtchitz in the regular contingent, but even they don't come anywhere near his skills."

"It's a good thing that the times are somewhat quieter these days,"said the constable. "And that the Tartars keep to the terms of the Podhayetz Treaty which our host's invincible sword has imposed upon them."

Here the constable bowed to Pan Sobieski who didn't hide his pleasure at the compliment, which came far more rarely in the Commonwealth than complaints and censure.

"I can only thank God's kindness and the bravery of my devoted soldiers for whatever I was able to accomplish at that time," he said. "I know the Tartar Khan is anxious to keep the treaty but he has his own troubles nowadays. There are dissensions and conspiracies against him in his own Crimea, while the Belgorodian Horde won't listen to him at all. I've just had word that there's another new storm gathering on the Moldavian border and that invasion is likely any moment. I'm having the trails and the passes watched but I am short of soldiers. Every time I move a few men to patch one gaping hole I open up another. I am especially short of experienced borderers who know the way that Tartars fight and think, which is why I'm so sad about Volodyovski."

At this Zagloba dropped his fists from his temples, where he had clutched his last few strands of hair.

"He won't become a monk!"he bellowed suddenly. "Even if I have to raid the *Mons Regius* and take him out by force! As God's my witness, I'll go see him tomorrow. Surely he'll listen to my persuasion! But if he doesn't, I'll go to the Primate! Or to the Cistercians' provincial-general! I'll go all the way to Rome if I have to but I'll get him out."

The old knight's outburst might have been comical if it weren't for his evident distress and it was clear he meant every word he said.

"I don't want to interfere with God's service," he went on. "Dam'me if I do. But what kind of a Cistercian would he make when he can't even grow any hair on his chin? My fist can sprout a better beard, and God knows that's true! He can't sing a Mass properly, and all the rats will skeedadle from the monastery if he ever tries it, because they'll think it's some tomcat yowling on a fence. Forgive me gentlemen for saying the first thing that pops into my head, but that's how I feel! I wouldn't love a son, if I had one, as much as I loved that man. God be with him! God take care of him! I only want his best. Ah, if at least he joined the Bernardines, well that would be one thing. I've known some Bernardines who can work a cannon better than German gunners. But a Cistercian? Pledged to hard labor and silence? That simply can't happen! You can believe that as surely as I'm sitting here! First thing tomorrow I'll go to the Primate and get him to give me a letter to the prior."

"He couldn't have made his vows already," the constable suggested. "It's too soon for that. But don't pressure him or he'll dig in his heels and get all the more obstinate about it. And bear in mind that his intention could be a manifestation of God's will."

But the old knight would have none of that.

"God's will?" he roared. "How could it be God's will? God's will doesn't manifest itself like a pistol shot, and the old proverbs say that haste makes waste, don't they? Things done in a hurry make the Devil happy. If there'd been any sign of a priestly calling in that man I'd have spotted it a long time ago, but he was a dragoon since I've known him, not a priest, and that's a far cry from a saintly life. If he'd made this decision calmly and at leisure with nothing on his mind, and if he'd had the time to really think about it, I wouldn't say a thing. But God's will doesn't strike a man when he's half-mad with grief. It doesn't fall on him out of nowhere like a falcon on a turtle dove. No, no, I won't pressure him. Not at all. I'll have my lines well rehearsed before I go to see him, so that he won't get his back up straight away, and I think I've good reason to hope for the best. He always trusted my wits better than his own, and it won't be any different now unless he's changed beyond recognition."

Chapter Five

NEXT DAY, having planned everything carefully with Ketling and armed himself with letters from the Primate, Pan Zagloba rang the bell at the gate to the *Mons Regius* monastery. He didn't think he'd left anything to chance. His shrewd old mind reviewed every aspect of his plot, turning it over piece by piece until it satisfied him, but his heart hammered with anxiety as he tugged the bell rope. He couldn't guess how Volodyovski would react to his visit after all that time. Maybe he was too late. Even though he rehearsed all his phrases in advance he was well aware that everything depended on how he was received.

Made somewhat ill-at-ease by these speculations, he tugged the bell rope for a second time, and when the gate creaked ajar and a monk peered out, he pushed himself rather forcefully into the narrow gap.

"I know that one needs special permits to enter this place," he told the startled little brother who served as gatekeeper. "But I've a letter here from the archbishop which I trust, *carissime frater*, you'll want to take to the prior straight away."

"It shall be as you wish, sir," the gatekeeper bowed with reverence at the sight of the Primate's seal.

He then clanged his bell twice more to summon a messenger since he himself couldn't leave the gate. Another monk appeared, took the letter and vanished as swiftly and as silently as he'd come, while Pan Zagloba dropped the bundle he had brought on a nearby bench and sat down heavily beside it, puffing and a little out of breath.

"Frater," he said at last. "How long have you been here?"

"This is my fifth year."

"Well, well, so young and already a monk for five years! Too late to leave now even if you wanted, eh? But you must've felt the itch once in a while, what? Because, the way it is, some men long for a little soldiering, another might like his good times at the table, and others have the ladies on their minds..."

"*Apage!*" the little monk cried out in pious terror and scrawled a hasty sign of the cross across his chest.

"What? Weren't you ever tempted to slip out of here?" Zagloba pressed on.

But the young monk gaped in terrified amazement. The broad-shouldered, big-bellied old knight with his one blind eye, with wispy tufts of white hair standing up around his glistening bald pate and the gleam of bone shining out of an ancient wound gouged into his forehead, and with the pushy florid face of a man familiar with the flagons, must have seemed to him like that eternal tempter whom he'd just abjured to get out of sight. It was a strange emissary from the head of the Church in the Commonwealth who talked about such forbidden things.

"Whoever hears these doors close behind him," he murmured at last. "Never comes out again."

"Is that so? Well, we'll soon see, won't we. And how's Pan Volodyovski doing here? Is he well?"

"There's no one here by that name."

"Brother Michal, then?" Zagloba tried a likely appellation. "A former dragoon colonel who came here recently?"

"We call him Brother George but he's not yet taken his vows because he can't before the proper time."

"I dare say he won't," said the merciless Zagloba. "You won't believe, dear *frater*, what a terrible womanizer that man used to be. You wouldn't find a wolf that hungry for the pleasures of the flesh in all the monasteries in the country. Ah, pardon me, I meant to say in all the regiments of the standing army."

"I m-mustn't listen to such things," the shocked monk stammered, more amazed than ever.

"You mustn't? Hmm. Well. I expect that's so... But listen *frater*, I don't know the visiting rules among you, but if our meeting is to take place right here on the spot, then I'd advise you to step aside some distance, like maybe into that little gatehouse over there, because we'll be talking about some rather worldly matters."

"I'd rather leave right now," said the shaken monk and backed away as quickly as he could.

* * *

In the meantime Volodyovski, or rather Brother George, appeared in the distance, but Pan Zagloba didn't know him at first glance because he changed almost beyond recognition.

To begin with, his long white habit made him seem taller than he was in his usual trim and tight dragoon regimentals. Secondly, his normally upthrust, perky little whiskers now dangled sadly past the corners of his mouth, and he had made an attempt to grow a monastery beard, which took the form of two meager yellow wisps that clung to about half a finger's length on his naked chin. Finally, he'd lost a lot of weight and looked drawn and wasted, his eyes lacked all of their former curiosity and sharpness, and he approached at a snail's pace with his head hung low, and with both hands folded across his chest and hidden in the sleeves of his voluminous white robe.

Taking him for the prior, Zagloba rose and launched into a Latin greeting, but he'd barely got through his *'Laudetur'* when he took another, closer look, flung his arms wide and shouted: "Michal! My dear, dear Michal!"

Brother George allowed him to seize him in his arms and something like a sob shook his narrow chest. But his dulled eyes remained sad and dry. Zagloba hugged and squeezed him a long time before he could speak because he was far more shaken by this sight than he supposed he would be.

"You didn't weep alone over your misfortune," he began at last. "I wept a bucketful as well. So did the Skshetuskis and the Kmitas and Kharlamp and everybody else. But that's God's will, Michal! Make your peace with it. Let our merciful Father ease your soul and send you consolation. You did well to come here for a time and lock yourself behind these bars and walls. Nothing is better in hard times than prayer and good thoughts. Ah, but let me hug you one more time! I can hardly see you through my tears!"

Pan Zagloba spoke the truth about his tears because the misery in Volodyovski's face touched him far more deeply than

he had expected, but not so deeply that he couldn't go on with
his mission.

"Forgive me for breaking in on your meditations," he resumed. "But I had no choice, as you'll see when you hear my
reasons. Ey, Michal! We've lived through so many good and bad
times together, haven't we? But tell me, did you find a bit of
peace behind these walls?"

"I did," Pan Michal said. "I find it in these words that I hear
here and repeat to myself each day, and that I'll keep repeating
till I die: *'Memento mori.'* Death is my consolation."

"Hmm. Death's easier to come by in the field than in a
monastery where life drags on, day by day, like knitting wool
unraveling from a spindle."

"There's no life here because there are no worldly distractions
so it's like being in the afterlife already even before the soul has
left the body."

"Hmm. Well. In that case I won't tell you that the Belgorodian Horde is getting ready to hurl itself on the Commonwealth in all its strength... Because what could that matter to
you now?"

Pan Michal's whiskers twitched suddenly and his right hand
reached instinctively for his absent saber. But when he failed to
find it at his side he hid his hands once more in his sleeves and
lowered his head.

"Memento mori!" he whispered urgently.

"Quite right! Quite right!" Zagloba said at once but his good
eye twitched with some impatience. "Pan Sobieski was saying
only yesterday: *'If only Volodyovski would serve through just this one
more cataclysm and then enter whatever monastery he pleases. God
wouldn't hold that against him. Indeed such a monk would earn even
greater merit in His eyes.'* But I'm not surprised that you put your
own peace of mind above the happiness of our entire Motherland, because *'prima charitis ab ego,'* as they say. Charity does
begin at home."

* * *

A long silence hung between them after that and only Pan
Michal's droopy little mustache gave a threatening twitch, and
started moving slowly up and down like a hedgehog's spikes
when they begin to bristle on its back.

"You've not taken your final vows yet, have you?" Zagloba asked at last.

Pan Michal shook his head.

"And you can still go outside any time you want to?"

"I'm not yet in Holy Orders," Volodyovski murmured, "because I've waited for God's grace to fill me, and for all my earthly memories to drain from my soul. But the grace is near me, my peace is returning, and I don't want to go out even though I can, because it won't be long now before I'll be ready to take my vows with a clear conscience and free of all temporal attachments."

"Of course! Of course! I'd be the last to urge you otherwise," Pan Zagloba sighed. "Indeed, I admire your determination, though I remember that when Skshetuski wanted to take the habit he waited until the Motherland was safe from the onslaught. But do as you must! I won't try to change your mind because I also felt a vocation in my time for a monastic life, though God decided I could be more useful somewhere else. Ha! It was just about fifty years ago that I began my novitiate. Call me a scoundrel if I'm lying! All I'll tell you, Michal, is that you must come out with me for a couple of days."

"Why should I go out? Leave me to my peace!" Volodyovski answered.

But now the old knight raised the tail of his coat to his eyes and began to sniffle.

"I wouldn't ask you for the sake of my own life," he stammered brokenly, "even though Prince Boguslav is breathing down my neck and sends assassins against this poor old man who has nobody to defend him and protect him... I'd hoped you might do that, for the sake of our old love and friendship... ah, but forget it. Don't give it a thought! I'll always love you, even if you turn your back on me altogether..."

"What?" Volodyovski stared, astonished, and his mouth fell open.

"Pray for me though, will you?" Pan Zagloba sobbed. "Because I'll never get away from Boguslav's vengeance... But what does it matter? What will be will be and maybe I've lived too long anyway... No, no, it's not about me but about another friend of yours, one who shared his last piece of bread with you, who is on his deathbed and desperately wants to see you because he has something to confess to you. The peace of his soul depends on it, you see..."

Pan Michal, who'd become greatly moved by the recitation of Zagloba's dangers, now leaped up, seized the old knight's shoulders, and cried out: "Skshetuski?"

"No, not Skshetuski. Ketling!"

"For God's sake! What has happened to him?"

"Some of Boguslav's cut-throats ambushed him and shot him when he tried to save me. I don't know if he'll last the day! It's for your sake, Michal, that both of us fell into these dreadful straits because we came to Warsaw just to bring you some peace and distraction..."

"For God's sake! For God's sake!" Brother George repeated.

"Come out for just a day or two," the old knight kept begging, "and help your dying friend. Then you can come back and resume the habit. I've brought a letter from the Primate, ordering the prior to let you go without interference... Only hurry, will you? Believe me, every moment counts!"

"For God's sake!" Volodyovski said again. "What is this I'm hearing? They'll let me go because so far I'm here only as a postulant. It's as if I were only making a retreat... For God's sake! A dying wish is a holy duty, isn't it? I can't turn that down!"

"It'd be the most frightful mortal sin!" Pan Zagloba said.

"You're right!" As agitated as he'd never seen him, the would-be monk made clutching motions at his missing saber, and his little whiskers bristled like an angry cat's. "It's always that traitor Boguslav, isn't it? Poor Ketling! May I never come back here if I don't avenge him! I'll find those assassins! I'll track down those murderous courtiers and carve a few heads...! Ah, ah, great God, what am I doing? Here are all those sinful thoughts again... *Memento mori*... Let me just change into my old clothes, will you? Because this habit must stay within these walls..."

"Here are some new clothes!" Zagloba cried out and seized the bundle on the bench beside him. "I brought everything you need. Boots, shirt, a short-coat, a cap with a feather, a decent little rapier..."

"Come with me to my cell," said Volodyovski.

★ ★ ★

When they reappeared at the gate shortly afterwards it was no longer a white-garbed little monk who trotted beside Pan Zagloba but a small, fierce-looking cavalry officer dressed in tall, yellow boots, a white swordbelt hanging from his shoulder, and a long steel rapier dangling at his side.

Zagloba winked his good eye and grinned under his mustache at the shocked gatekeeper who opened the portals for them both. The old knight's open carriage waited nearby, lower down the slope, with two servants ready in attendance. One sat at the reins, holding two matched pairs of horses at the traces, at which Volodyovski threw an expert and approving glance; the other stood by the wagon with a mossy flagon in one hand and two great goblets in the other.

"It's a fair distance to Mokotov," remarked Pan Zagloba. "And tears are waiting for us at poor Ketling's bedside. Have a drink, my dear Michal, to put some strength back into your bones for what's ahead. I've never seen you look so drawn and grey."

With this the old knight took the flagon from the servant's hand and filled both goblets with a buttered mead of such a venerable vintage that it had thickened to the consistency of aromatic syrup.

"A noble drink," he said with satisfaction, put down the flagon and picked up the goblets. "Let's drink to Ketling's health!"

"To his health," echoed Volodyovski. "But let's not waste time! Let's hurry!"

They drained the goblets at a gulp.

"Let's hurry!" the old knight repeated. "Pour us a another cup, my good lad! To Skshetuski's health! Quickly, quickly! Let's drink up! Let's hurry!"

"Let's get started, then!" cried Volodyovski.

"You mean you won't drink to my good health?" the old knight asked sadly.

"Alright. Just as long as we do it quickly!"

They gulped down a third goblet. Zagloba emptied his at a single draught although each cup held at least half a quart of powerful vintage liquor, then wiped his whiskers with the tail of his coat and cried out: "I'd be an utter ingrate if I didn't drink to your good health, my friend! Pour us some more, my good lad!"

"Thanks very much," said Brother George. "Very kind of you."

The bottom of the flagon was now in plain sight. Zagloba seized it by the neck and smashed it against the nearest carriage wheel because he couldn't stand the sight of an empty bottle. Then they climbed hastily into the carriage and set off. The vintage mead filled their veins with a blissful warmth and their hearts with hope. Brother George's drawn cheeks became somewhat flushed and the old brightness reappeared in his sharp, quick eyes. His hand rose to his little mustache almost as if it possessed a will of its own and twirled the sharp points upward like a pair of needles, and he began to peer around with a great deal of interest at everything around him.

Suddenly Pan Zagloba slapped himself mightily on both knees and shouted out for no apparent reason: "Ho! Ho! I believe that when Ketling catches sight of you we'll see a resurrection! Ho! Ho! Hup!"

And seizing Pan Michal by the neck he began to hug him and embrace him with all the strength in his crusty old bones. Volodyovski didn't want to seem ungrateful, or indifferent to these signs of his old friend's affection, and hugged him back for all he was worth.

Chapter Six

THEY DROVE IN SILENCE for a while but it was a blissful and contented silence and, soon enough, they started catching sight of the little houses that dotted the countryside on both sides of the road. Crowds of burghers clustered near these small summer homes, servants in livery of every hue and color bustled about on a variety of errands, and throngs of gentry, some of them dressed with more regard to opulence than function, paced in all directions.

"You can't imagine what a swarm of people has come down for the electoral convention," the old knight lectured as they rode along. "Most of them, of course, aren't members of parliament but each of them wants to see and hear everything, and to be here for the deliberations. Every inn and dwelling is packed hereabouts so that it's just about impossible to find a place to stay. And as for all the good-looking gentlewomen you'll see in the streets, you'd have an easier time counting the hairs in your beard. Ah, they're so pretty, those tempting little creatures, that a man feels like a rooster in a henhouse now and then, ready to flap his arms and crow. Look over there! See that dark-haired beauty with the long eyelashes? Hmm? The one with the lackey carrying the green cloak behind her? Not bad, eh? Hmm? What d'you think?"

Here Pan Zagloba nudged Volodyovski who threw a quick glance in the right direction, twitched his little whiskers, and showed a sudden gleam in his merry eyes. Then, as if remembering who he was and what he planned to be, he dropped his gaze, let his head droop mournfully on his chest, and said: "Memento mori!"

But Zagloba threw his arms again around his neck.

"Listen!" he burst out suddenly. *"Per amiciatam nostram!* If you really loved me or ever respected me and trusted my judgment...Get married!"

Brother George stared at his old friend in utter amazement. He thought at first that his old friend was drunk. But he remembered Pan Zagloba's immense capacity for liquor, recalled that the old knight could guzzle three times the amount of mead he had just tossed down without any visible effects, so he must have been talking out of some great upsurge of emotion. But any such suggestion, made for whatever reason, was so far removed from Pan Michal's thinking at this time that astonishment overcame his first shock and anger.

Even so, bitter resentment glittered in his eyes as he turned coldly on Zagloba. "Is that the mead talking?"

"Far from it. This comes from the heart. Get yourself a wife!"

Volodyovski's stare hardened even further.

"Memento mori!" he murmured gloomily as if to drive away the vanities of the flesh and avert temptation.

But the old knight seldom gave up without a fight once he had got started.

"Michal," he urged. "Do me this one favor, if I ever really meant anything to you, and send all your *mementos* to the Devil. I repeat, do what you wish about your Holy Orders, but I think that everyone should serve God with whatever he was created for, and you were made first and foremost for the sword. Otherwise why would God let you get so good with it? If He wanted you to be a priest He'd have given you a different set of wits and an aptitude for books and for Latin. Notice, moreover, that the warrior saints are as highly regarded in Heaven as the best of the canonized philosophers and clergy. They serve in the celestial host and go campaigning against the powers of Hell, and they draw promotions and rewards straight from God's own hands when they come back with captured battle flags. You won't deny that all this is true?"

"I won't deny it, and I know that it's a waste of time to match wits with you. But you can't deny that the best nourishment for sadness is a monastery."

"All the more reason to leave such provisioning to the monks,"Pan Zagloba said. "A man's a fool if he feeds his sadness instead of letting it starve to death like any other monster."

Pan Volodyovski failed to find a suitable response just then so he kept quiet for a little while. Then he said sadly, in a voice made plaintive with longing:

"Don't mention marriage to me, my old friend, because such thoughts only stir up my grief all over again. I don't have my old eagerness for it because I've wept it all out of me, nor am I young enough for all those illusions. My hair's turning grey already. I'm forty-two. Twenty-five years have gone by in war, hardships and campaigning. That's no joke, you know. No, that's no joke!"

"Have mercy on him, God, and don't punish him for such a blasphemy!" Pan Zagloba cried and spat in disgust. "So he's forty-two! I've more than twice that many years weighing on my shoulders, but I still have to get the leech to bleed me every Spring to thin out my blood, and have my hide flogged every now and then to beat my amorous inclinations out of me like dust from an old coat. Honor the memory of that poor dead girl!" he shouted finally into Volodyovski's face. "Don't insult her so! So you were good enough for her, were you? But you're too cheap for others? Too old?"

"Enough, old friend,"Volodyovski answered in a thin, pained voice and fresh tears started dripping into his little whiskers. "Enough, I beg you..."

"That's all I'll say," Zagloba announced. "Just give me your word of honor that you'll stay with us for at least a month no matter what Ketling's condition might turn out to be. You have to see Skshetuski too, you know. You owe him that much for all the tears he shed on your behalf. No one will get in your way if you still want to wear a habit after that."

"You've my word!" Pan Michal said, too distraught to argue.

★ ★ ★

Talk turned to other matters then. Pan Zagloba prattled about the convention, discoursed on all he'd done to undermine Boguslav, and threw in a few more vague allusions to Ketling's misadventure. From time to time he interrupted his harangue with a thoughtful silence which, however, must have been to his

liking because he slapped his knees with satisfaction every now
and then. "That's it then!" he cried out, grinning at Pan Michal.
"Ho Ha!"

But as they neared Mokotov a certain hesitation crept into his
features and, at last, he turned uneasily to Volodyovski.

"You'll stay with us at least a month, is that right?" he asked
urgently. "No matter what's happening with Ketling? You gave
your word, remember?"

"I did and I'll stay," Volodyovski answered.

"Here's Ketling's manor," Pan Zagloba cried. "He lives well,
doesn't he?" And then he shouted at his driver: "Crack your
whip, lad! Let them know we're coming! There'll be a celebration in this house today."

The whip snapped and crackled like a pistol volley, but they
had barely cleared the gateway and rode into the courtyard when
a crowd of Volodyovski's friends poured out of the manor. Some
were old comrades from the Hmyelnitzki wars, like Pan Orlik
who wore a gold plate in his skull where a Swedish shrapnel-
bomb had chipped a hole in it, and the fierce Pan Rushtchitz,
the half-wild Steppe raider whose fame almost equaled Volodyovski's own. Others, like Pan Vasilevski and Pan Novovyeyski,
were newer men, little more than youngsters who ran away from
school to serve with Pan Sobieski in the Ukraine, and who had
ridden with Pan Michal in the latest fighting. These he was fond
of more than any others.

All of them ran to the wagon shouting: "He's here! He's
here! Zagloba succeeded! Here he is!"

Then they seized the little knight, hoisted him into the air and
carried him on their shoulders to the spacious manor, shouting
and repeating: "Welcome home, back among the living! We've
got you now and we won't let you go from us again! Long life
to you! *Vivat* Volodyovski, our finest knight and pride of all the
army! Into the Steppe with you beside us, brother! Into the
Wild Lands! Let the wind burn all your sadness out of you!"

They set him down on the porch where he shook hands
warmly all around and started asking everyone about Ketling's
health.

"How is he? Is he still alive?"

"Yes, he's still breathing, still alive," they answered in chorus,
and the old soldiers' lips twitched under their whiskers in a

curious smile. "Go in and see him before he dies out of sheer impatience."

"I see that he's not as close to death as Pan Zagloba tells me," said the little knight.

★　★　★

Meanwhile they pushed into the hall and a large bedchamber beyond it. A long table, heaped with meats and spirits waited in the center of the room, while Ketling lay in one corner on a low divan covered with white horsehides.

"My dear friend!" Pan Volodyovski said, hurrying towards him.

"Michal!" Ketling cried and leaped to his feet. He seized the little soldier in his arms and swung him high into the air as if he were a cat.

"They told me to simulate illness and act like a dead man," he confessed with a helpless smile. "But seeing you proved too much for me. I'm as right as rain, as you see, and nothing happened to me at all. We just wanted to get you out of that monastery... Forgive us, Michal! We played this little trick on you out of sheer affection!"

"Come to the Wild Lands with us!" all the knights shouted out again and started slapping their sheathed sabers with their heavy fists so that a harsh, threatening rattle echoed through the room.

But Pan Michal stood as still and silent and disbelieving as if he'd been dumbstruck with shock and surprise. He let his eyes fall on each of them in turn and shook his head slowly at Zagloba.

"Oh you traitors," he said at last, more saddened than angry. "I thought Ketling was on the point of death!"

"What do you mean, Michal?" Pan Zagloba cried. "Are you upset because Ketling is alive? You'd rather see him dead than well? Has your heart turned to stone to such an extent that you'd be glad to see all of us stretched out on a slab? You want Ketling dead? And Pan Orlik, and Pan Rushtchitz and these young fellows here? And Skshetuski too, I imagine. And me! Me who loves you like a son!"

Here the old knight thrust both fists into his eyes and moaned more piteously than ever: "Ah, we might as well be dead, for all that he cares. There's nothing left for us in this life, gentlemen, because there's no more gratitude in this world! All that's left is cold-hearted indifference!"

"For God's sake!" Volodyovski broke in finally. "I wish you all nothing but the best. It's just that you had no respect for my grief."

"He wants us dead!" Zagloba kept repeating. "He hates us!"

"Give it up, will you?" the little knight protested.

"He hates us," Pan Zagloba moaned. "He says we didn't care about his grief but what about those rivers we wept over his misfortune? Weren't they real rivers? That's the truth! God is my witness that we'd have made mincemeat of your sadness if we could, because that's what good friends are for, and now you want to hate us! But since you gave your word that you'd spend a month with us then love us for at least that long!"

"I'll love you all as long as I live anyway," Volodyovski said. "You know that."

★ ★ ★

The arrival of a new guest interrupted whatever else they might have wished to say. Busy with Pan Volodyovski, the soldiers didn't hear the carriage and the escort rolling up and clattering outside and saw the man only when he appeared in the chamber doorway. He was a gigantic, heavily-built man with the proud bearing of a monarch, and the face and features of a Roman Caesar, in which however lay a truly royal kindliness and kindness. He seemed like part of an entirely different species than the gathered soldiers, as greater in comparison with them as an eagle among hawks and falcons, and he stood among them like some vast winged apparition among mere birds of prey.

"The Grand Hetman!" Ketling cried and ran to welcome him into his house.

"Pan Sobieski!" echoed all the others, and all heads bowed low with immense respect.

Each of them except Volodyovski knew that the Grand Hetman was coming, because he promised Ketling that he would, but his entrance had such a stunning impact on them all that for some time none of them dared to speak.

It was, of course, a sign of extraordinary favor for the commander-in-chief of all the Polish armies to come calling on a group of officers at a private gathering. But Pan Sobieski truly loved his soldiers, especially those with whom he crushed so many Tartar *tchambuls*. He thought of them as his family, which is why he went to such unusual lengths to welcome Volody-ovski, give him whatever consolation he was able to offer, and keep him in the service by this special show of favor and affection.

Having exchanged the normal courtesies with Ketling, he stretched his hands at once towards the little knight who ran to him, and knelt and clasped his knees, while he pressed the soldier's bowed head fondly with both hands.

"Well, faithful comrade," he said in a deep but gentle voice. "God's hand has pressed you to the ground, but it will also lift you up and soothe you. His mercy be with you. And I expect you'll want to stay with us, now that you know how we feel about you and how much you're needed, am I right in that?"

A deep sob echoed in Pan Michal's chest.

"I'll stay," he said through tears.

"I'm glad! I can't have enough men like you. And now, old comrade, cast your mind to all those times in the Steppes when we feasted under canvas after a great victory. I feel so good among you! Alright then, our dear host, let's begin the banquet!"

"Vivat Joannes dux!" all the voices shouted, the feast began, and lasted long into the night.

Next day the Hetman sent Volodyovski a costly gift of a bay thoroughbred.

Part II

Chapter Seven

THE TWO FRIENDS, Ketling and Volodyovski, promised each other that they would never be apart again, that they'd ride side by side once more as soon as the country's need called on them to do so, and that they'd share the same campfire, sleeping on the same saddle for a pillow, as they did before.

But, as it happened, the unexpected separated them only a week after their reunion. A messenger from Courland brought word that the young Scotsman's benefactor and adoptive father, the same who bestowed his name and property upon him, had fallen ill and wished to see him. The young knight mounted up and rode away without another thought.

The only thing he asked Zagloba and Volodyovski was that they should consider his house their own and stay in it as long as they wished or until it bored them.

"Perhaps the Skshetuskis will arrive,"he said. "He's sure to be here for the General Election but even if he brings his wife along with all their children there's enough room for everyone. I've no blood kin anywhere but no brother could be closer to me than the two of you even if I had one."

Zagloba was particularly pleased with this invitation because he was having a great time in the comfortable, well-provisioned house, but Michal also found it unexpectedly useful because while the Skshetuskis didn't come to Warsaw at this time, Volodyovski's sister, who was married to Pan Makovyetzki, the *Stolnik* or magistrate of Latitchev in southern Podolia, sent word that she was coming from the East. Her messenger went to the Hetman's headquarters to find out if any of Pan Sobieski's aides

could tell him where to look for the little colonel and they, of
course, sent him to Ketling's manor.

Volodyovski was delighted at this chance reunion because
Madame Makovyetzka was his only sister, and many years had
gone by since he'd been able to see her, and when he found that
she was staying in a dilapidated, shabby little hovel in the Rybaki
quarter, unable to find decent accommodations anywhere else,
he galloped straight off to bring her to the manor.

It was already getting grey outside when he burst into her
dingy little quarters but he recognized her straight away even
though two other women were sitting there as well. She—just
as diminutive as he but as plump and rounded as a ball of
yarn—also knew at once who he was, and they threw themselves
joyfully into each other's arms, too moved to say a word and
quite ignoring the two other women, who stood as still as a pair
of candlesticks and watched their tearful greeting.

Madame Makovyetzka was the first to regain the power of
speech and started crying out in a thin and somewhat squeaky
voice:

"So many years! So many years! God save you, dearest
brother! As soon as we heard about your misfortune I got ready
to go to you there and then. My husband didn't stop me either
because there's big trouble brewing in the Budjak country, and
we're down there, you know, in Lower Podolia. People are also
talking about the Belgorodian Tartars... The Steppe trails are
sure to darken again come Spring because the birds are swarming
in great flocks this year and that's what happens every time
before an invasion.

"God comfort you, my dear precious brother!" she cried and
babbled on with hardly a breath between her exclamations. "My
husband plans to be here himself for the election, so he told me
to go on ahead. *'Take the girls and go,'* he said. *'Michal,'* he said,
*'needs a bit of solace. And we'll also need to find some good refuge
before very long, because the Tartars are as sure to come as lightning
from a storm cloud, and all this country hereabouts is going to be on
fire, so you'll be killing two birds with one stone. Go,'* he said, *'to
Warsaw and find rooms for us in a good hostelry so we'll have
somewhere to stay when the storm breaks out.'* He, in the meanwhile,
is taking some local volunteers to watch the southern trails.

There aren't enough soldiers in the borderlands, and that's the whole trouble, but isn't that the way it always is with us?"

"If I could just say a word," the little knight began but she caught his hands and pulled him to the window where the light was better.

"Ay, my dearest Michal, let me look at you! Your face is thinner, you poor dear, but that's what grief does every time. It was easy for my husband to say way down in Ruthenia: *'Go find us a hostelry.'* But where am I to find it? Here we are, alone in this wretched hovel, and the best I could get were three thin bundles of straw for us to sleep on."

"If you'll allow me, sister," Pan Michal tried again but there was no way for him to get a word in edgewise. The voluble, squeaky little woman rattled on like a grinding-mill running at full speed.

"So we put up here, the three of us, because where else was there? The landlord doesn't look good to me; he has shifty eyes like a hungry wolf and it could be that he's planning something. It's true that we have four good servant lads with us, and the three of us aren't all that fearful either, because even women know how to take care of themselves in our part of the country or they wouldn't last there very long. I've a nice little musketoon I always bring on journeys, and Basia here,"—she waved an arm towards one of the two young women—"has a pair of pistols. It's only Krysia who doesn't care for weapons. But since this is like a foreign town to us, we'd rather find safer quarters in a good-sized inn..."

"Allow me, sister," Volodyovski tried to interrupt but with no better luck than he had before.

"And where are you staying, Michal?" asked Madame Makovyetzka. "You must help us find a decent hostelry since you know your way around Warsaw..."

"I have a place for you all ready and waiting!" Pan Michal finally succeeded in breaking through his sister's uninterrupted prattle. "I'm staying in the manor of Captain Ketling, a dear friend of mine, whose home is good enough for a magnate's household, and I'll take you there at once..."

"But there are three us, remember!" she rattled out again. "And two maids! And four servant lads..." And suddenly she recalled that she was yet to introduce her two traveling companions. "But wait! Let me present these young ladies here!"

With this she faced the two younger women.

"You know who he is," she said with the direct abruptness of the border gentry. "But he has no idea who you are. It's dark in here, they haven't even lit a fire for us, but make your acquaintance as best you can. This,"—and she pointed to one of the young women—"is Panna Krystyna Drohoyovska, and this,"—she waved towards the other—"is Panna Barbara Yezorkovska. My husband is their guardian and looks after their properties because they are orphans, and they live with us because it isn't right for two unmarried girls to live on their own."

While she was talking, Volodyovski bowed in the easy military manner, the two young ladies courtseyed, and Miss Yezorkovska tossed her head with the spirited impatience of a yearling colt.

"Well then, let's get ready and set out at once," Volodyovski said. "I'm sharing Ketling's manor with Pan Zagloba and I already asked him to see about our supper."

"The famous Pan Zagloba?" Panna Yezorkovska demanded at once.

"Quiet, Basia!" the Magistrate's Lady hushed her spirited young ward. "I'm just afraid we might be too much trouble, with supper and all..."

"You can be sure that when Pan Zagloba starts thinking about supper there'll be enough for twice as many as anybody needs," said the little knight. "So have the servants start carrying out your things, young ladies. I've brought a baggage cart, and Ketling's charabanc is so roomy that the four of us will fit in it quite nicely. But here's a thought,"—he turned to his sister—"if your lads aren't tipplers, too fond of the bottle, you could leave them here till tomorrow with your horses and your heavy baggage and take just what you'll need for now."

"Oh, we don't have to do that," said Madame Makovyetzka. "Our carts are still loaded. All the lads need to do is harness the horses and everything can come with us straight away. Basia, you go and make sure that they do it right!"

Miss Yezorkovska ran out into the hall and came back in less

time than it takes to say half a dozen prayers with the announcement that everything was ready.

"Then let's get started," said Volodyovski.

★ ★ ★

In a few moments they were in the charabanc on their way to
Mokotov. The Magistrate's Lady and Miss Drohoyovska took
the main seat in the rear of the carriage, while Volodyovski sat
with Miss Yezorkovska on the facing seat, their backs to the
driver. Darkness had fallen and he didn't get a good look at the
younger women.

"Are you young ladies familiar with Warsaw?" he asked,
leaning forward towards Drohoyovska and trying to make himself heard above the clattering of the carriage wheels.

"No," she replied in a low but pleasantly melodious voice.
"We're really quite provincial and we've neither seen any major
cities nor met famous men."

Here she inclined her head slightly towards Volodyovski, as if
excluding him from this generalization. *'This girl has some polish,'*
he thought, pleased with the compliment, and began to rack his
head at once for some courteous phrase to offer in return.

"Even if this town were ten times larger than it is you ladies
would be its principal ornament," he managed at last.

"How can you tell in the dark?" Miss Yezorkovska shot at him
suddenly.

'And this one's just a wild young colt,' he thought.

But he said nothing and they rode in silence for some time
until Miss Yezorkovska turned to him with another question.

"Do you know if the stables are big enough for all our
animals?" she asked. "Because we've ten draught horses and a
pair of hunters."

"There'd be room for thirty."

"My, my," she said, unimpressed.

"Basia!" Madame Makovyetzka said in a pleading voice.

"Aha! Here we go again! It's always *'Basia, Basia!'* And who
had to make sure the horses were alright all the way from home?"

★ ★ ★

That's how they talked and whiled away the time until they
drove up to Ketling's country house where every window was
brightly lit in honor of Madame Makovyetzka.

The house servants poured out of the house as soon as the charabanc drew up before the porch, led by Pan Zagloba who skipped to the side of the carriage as nimbly as his age and girth allowed. Spotting three women there, he asked at once with the flowery courtesy of the times:

"In which of you ladies do I have the honor to greet my esteemed benefactress and, at the same time, the sister of my best friend Michal?"

"It is I," squeaked the Magistrate's Lady.

At which Pan Zagloba seized her hand, smacked a number of rapid kisses on it, and exclaimed: "My most profound respects!"

Then he bustled to assist her dismount from the carriage and led her with great ostentation to the manor. "Allow me, madam, to present my compliments once more beyond the threshold," he insisted.

Meanwhile Pan Michal was helping the young women. The charabanc was quite tall, and the mounting step was hard to find in the dark, so he caught Miss Drohoyovska by the waist, whirled her lightly into the air and set her on the ground.

She offered no resistance. On the contrary, leaning against his chest with her own for a breathless moment she murmured a soft "Thank you."

He then turned towards Miss Yezorkovska but she had already jumped off on the other side so he offered his arm to Drohoyovska and led her inside. Once everyone had crowded into the reception room, the young women were introduced to the old knight, who fell into such superb high humor at the sight of them that he invited them at once to the supper table. This, as Pan Michal had foreseen, was weighed down with enough steaming dishes to satisfy twice the number of residents and guests.

They sat down to eat—Madame Makovyetzka in the place of honor, the old knight on her right and Pan Michal on the left, with Miss Drohoyovska next to Volodyovski and Miss Yezorkovska beside Pan Zagloba—and it was only then that the small knight had a chance to get a good look at both the young women.

Both were attractive but each in her own way. Drohoyovska was blue-eyed, with hair and eyebrows as dark as a raven's wing, and with such a delicately pale, olive-tinted skin that he could see the small blue veins pulsing in her temples. A soft, barely noticeable down lay on her upper lip, giving her mouth a look of sweetness that begged for a kiss.

She'd lost her father recently, so she was in mourning, and her somber dress heightened the sense of gravity and sadness suggested by her pale features and black hair. At first glance she seemed older than her spirited companion but this was deceptive. A more careful study, surreptitious though it might have been, quickly convinced the small knight that she was still in the first bloom of youth, and the more he looked at her the more he admired the gravity she projected, her distinguished bearing, the gentle curve of her poised, swanlike neck, and the slim form full of delicate girlish charm.

'*This,*' he told himself, '*is a great, high-minded lady! The other's just a tomboy.*'

It was an apt comparison.

The Yezorkovska girl was much smaller than her willowy, tall friend, and built throughout on a rather diminutive scale, although there was nothing skinny about her. She brought to mind a pink rosebud with yellow hair which, however, must have been cut short at one time because of an illness, and which she wore in a gold-mesh net.

But since this hair grew on a restless, impatient young head it had its own unruly character and poked its shortened ends out of the net through almost every opening. Bunched on her forehead in a tumbled fringe, it had the look of a Cossack forelock, which together with her restless, darting eyes and devil-may-care expression, made her seem like a mischievous little schoolboy always on the lookout for a chance to pull some harmless prank without getting caught.

She was, however, so fresh and pretty in that impish image that it was hard for anyone to tear his eyes away. She had a small, slightly tilted nose with flared little nostrils that seemed constantly on the move, and dimples in both her cheeks and chin which were a clear sign of a happy nature. She was sitting quietly enough at the moment, enjoying her supper, and shooting quick, curious glances at Pan Zagloba and Pan Volodyovski as if they were strange, legendary creatures brought unexpectedly to a child's attention.

★ ★ ★

Pan Volodyovski didn't have much to say that night. He felt
he had to make conversation with Miss Drohoyovska, as eti-
quette demanded, but he had no idea how to start. The little
knight wasn't very skillful at entertaining women anyway, and
it was all the more difficult for him at this moment because both
these fresh young girls reminded him so sharply of the beloved
Anusia he had lost.

However Pan Zagloba more than made up for his friend's sad,
introspective silence, regaling Madame Makovyetzka with tales
of her brother's extraordinary adventures as well as several
ringing exploits of his own, and wholly capturing the absorbed
attention of Miss Yezorkovska.

She stared at him as if entranced—her dimpled chin propped
in both her fists, her elbows on the table and her supper forgotten altogether—and listened to every word he said as if he were
an oracle.

"Aha! Aha! And then what?" she burst out now and then.
"And what happened then?"

But when halfway through the dinner he launched into the
tale of how he, Zjendjan and Pan Michal rescued Skshetuski's
bride, the Princess Helen Bulyhov-Kurtzevitch, from a whole
tchambul of pursuing Tartars, and then how Pan Kushel's dragoons arrived in the nick of time, jumped on the Tartars and
sabered them to ribbons across half a mile of pursuit on a
midnight highway, Miss Yezorkovska forgot the rest of her
manners, clapped her hands together as hard as she could, and
cried out:

"I wish I'd been there, blast my eyes!"

"Baska!" the round, redfaced Madame Makovyetzka called out
in her turn, and went on to admonish the flushed young woman
in her own lilting accent and distinctive Ruthenian intonation:
"You've got to break your rough border habits and act like a
lady! You're in polite society now, in Warsaw, not in the tall
grass in the Steppe somewhere! All we need now, God help us,
is to hear you shouting: *'Damn my gizzard!'*"

The girl broke into a light-hearted, silvery peal of laughter,
slapped her knees suddenly like a bluff young soldier, and cried
out: "Alright then, auntie! *'Damn my gizzard!'*"

"Dear Lord! It's enough to shrivel the ears!" the Magistrate's Lady lifted her eyes and arms helplessly to the ceiling, and appealed for understanding to everyone around her, even though she'd begun to quiver with laughter of her own. "Tell everyone you're sorry!"

Miss Basia apparently wanted to begin her penance with Madame Makovyetzka because she jumped to her feet to hurry around the table but, in the process, she knocked her knife and spoon to the floor and dived under the table to retrieve them.

The round, plump Magistrate's Lady could no longer hold her laughter at this sight and she had a most peculiar way of laughing. First, she began to quiver all over her body, as if she were dancing a jig in her chair, and then she started giggling in a shrill, gasping series of thin piping squeaks. This was enough to send everybody into open laughter and Pan Zagloba was simply enchanted.

"Will you just look at all the trouble I have with that girl!" Madame Makovyetzka gasped at everyone around, still shaking and laughing.

"A sheer delight!" Pan Zagloba chortled. "As I live and breathe, she's an utter joy!"

Meanwhile Miss Basia crawled out from under the table. She had found her knife and spoon but lost her golden net, and her hair tumbled altogether down over her eyes. She straightened up, flared her little nostrils and said: "Aha! You're laughing at me, are you? You think I am funny?"

"No one is laughing at you!" Pan Zagloba stated with complete conviction. "No one, nobody at all! We're just happy, my dear, that God sent us so much joy in your lovely person."

Chapter Eight

AFTER THE DINNER they passed into the inner or reception rooms where Panna Drohoyovska saw a lute hanging on the wall, took it down, and ran her fingers lightly across the strings. Volodyovski asked her to sing something to the chords she strummed, and she answered with a simplicity and kindness that robbed him of breath.

"Gladly, sir," she told him. "If it will help to drive the sadness from your heart."

"Thank you." The little knight felt suddenly warm and grateful.

The song she sang warned the knights that their shields and armor wouldn't protect them against the pangs of love, no matter how strong, brave or resolute they were.

> *"Your armor will fail you*
> *When Cupid assails you*
> *With his tender arrows.*
>
> *"The bravest of hearts*
> *Won't survive those darts,*
> *But perish like sparrows."*

"I've no words to thank you, ma'am," Pan Zagloba kept saying in the meantime to Madame Makovyetzka, as he sat nearby beside her and rained smacking kisses on her hands. "Both that you came yourself and that you've also brought us two such sprightly, dainty girls that all the graces of antiquity could be chimney sweeps beside them. I'm especially taken with that puckish little ragamuffin because she chases gloom away

86

better than a ferret going after a nestful of field mice. And what after all is sadness if not a mess of mice that gnaws the joy out of people's hearts? I ought to tell you, ma'am, that our former King, *Joannes Casimirus*, found such *comparationes* of mine so striking that he couldn't do without them for a single day. I had to compose special aphorisms and wise maxims for him, which he had his court chamberlain reciting to him every night before he went to bed, and on which he based all his policies so that he ruled the nation with kindness and wisdom...

"But that's neither here nor there," he went on. "I'm hopeful that Michal will forget his troubles altogether with such two *deliciae* around him. You don't know this, ma'am, but I pulled him out of a monk's habit just a week ago because he was all set to take Holy Orders! But I talked the Papal Nuncio into threatening the Cistercians with press-ganging the lot of them into the dragoons if they didn't let Michal go at once. He'd have been useless there! Thank God things turned out well! Give these two beauties a few days and either one of them will strike such sparks off his sentimental nature that his heart will burn up like a piece of tinder."

Meanwhile Drohoyovska went on with her singing, asking *'what poor, weak women could do,'* and how they could possibly save themselves, if even a strong man's weaponry offered no protection against the shafts of love.

"Women fear that king of archery just about like a dog fears a slab of bacon," Pan Zagloba whispered to the Magistrate's Lady. "But admit it, my dear benefactress! You didn't bring those two tempting morsels without something special on your mind. Fine girls, both of them! Especially that lively little scamp, as I live and breathe! I'd say Michal has a sly, cunning little sister, wouldn't you? Eh? Hmm?"

★ ★ ★

Madame Makovyetzka did her best to look sly and cunning which didn't suit her kindly and honest face at all.

"One thinks of this and that," she bridled a little, "since with us women there's seldom a lack of calculation in the things we do. My husband was coming here for the election anyway, and I took the girls ahead because we'll have Tartars rampaging in our country any day. But if something good comes out of it for

Michal I'd be glad to make a pilgrimage on foot to some holy shrine."

"It will, it will!" Zagloba assured her.

"Both the girls come from distinguished families, and each is quite wealthy, and that also means something nowadays..."

"I'd be the last to argue on that score," Zagloba said quickly. "Michal's property has gone to the Devil in all our wars, although I know he has a fair amount of money put away with some of the great lords he served at one time or another. We also took quite considerable booty in our years of service, and though we'd hand that over to the Hetman's treasury, according to custom and the regulations, a good amount came back as 'the saber's dowry,' as we soldiers call it, or as our campaign share. Michal would be sitting pretty nowadays if he'd kept it all. But a soldier lives a day at a time and doesn't give much thought to his tomorrows. He'd have thrown all of it away if I weren't there to urge him to temperance and restraint. You say then, milady, that these are well-born girls?"

"Drohoyovska comes of senatorial stock. It's true that those border castellanies of ours aren't anything like the one of Krakow, and there are some that no one in the Commonwealth has ever even heard of, but once someone sits in the great chair he passes his splendor to his heirs nonetheless. And when it comes to bloodlines, Yezorkovska reaches even higher."

"Really... do tell," Pan Zagloba leaned forward with interest. "I myself trace my lineage to certain Masagetian Kings, so I like to hear about the family trees of others."

"Yezorkovska's roots don't begin that high," said the Magistrate's Lady, "but if you'd care to hear about them, sir, I'll be pleased to list them. We can all count each other's family connections on our fingers back there in our country. Well then, she's kin to the Pototzkis, the Yazlovyetzkis and the Lashtches, and that's just a start. And this is how it all came about, you see."

Here Madame Makovyetzka settled herself comfortably in her chair, shook out the voluminous folds of her dress so that nothing would get in the way of her favorite pastime, spread out the fingers of one hand into an open fan, and poised the index finger of the other to serve as a pointer.

"Elizabeth, the daughter of Pan Yakob Pototzki by his second wife," she began, *"de domo* Yazlovyetzka, married Pan Yan Smyotanko, the Seneschal of Podolia..."

"I have it noted," Pan Zagloba said.

"This marriage produced Pan Michal Smyotanko, also a seneshal..."

"Hmm!" Pan Zagloba mused. "A most distinguished title and position!"

"His first wife was a Dorohostayska... no! She was a Rozynska... no! A Voronitchovna? How do you like that, I seem to have forgotten...!"

"God rest her soul whatever her name was," Pan Zagloba offered.

"But his second wife was certainly a Lashtchovna..."

"Aha! Now I've got him placed! And what was the *effectus* of this happy union?"

"None of his sons survived..."

"All joys are perishable in this imperfect world," Pan Zagloba sighed and nodded profoundly.

"But the youngest of his four daughters, Anna, married Yezorkovski, whose armorial bearings have the name of *Ravitch*, and who was first a border commissioner for Podolia and then, if my memory isn't failing me, the territorial marshal down there in the lower country."

"He was, I remember!" Pan Zagloba nodded as if he'd never been more certain of anything in his life.

"And it's this marriage, as you see sir, that produced our Basia."

"I also see that right now she's taking aim with Ketling's fowling piece."

Miss Drohoyovska and Pan Michal were deep in a low-voiced, private conversation of their own at the other end of the spacious chamber, and Panna Basia, left to her own devices, whiled away the time by sighting through the window with Ketling's light musket, which caused Madame Makovyetzka to quake and quiver once more in her chair.

"You can't imagine what I go through with that girl," she squeaked, shaking with the giggles. "She's a real borderland rapscallion! A real bush-ranger!"

"If all the bush-rangers were like her I'd join them in a minute!" Pan Zagloba cried.

"All she has on her mind are weapons, horses and warfare! There was this one time when she got away from the house and went duck hunting with a bird gun. She crawled into the reeds down by the river, if you can imagine a snip of a girl doing such a thing, and what do you think she saw? The head of a Tartar scout bobbing in the reeds as he was creeping up on the village further up the stream. Any other child would've died of fright, but she just let fly at him with the bird gun and the Tartar plopped into the river and went down like a stone! She knocked him over on the spot, would you believe? And with what? A handful of birdshot!"

Here Madame Makovyetzka began to squeak and quiver once again with her infectious laughter as she recalled the Tartar's misadventure, then added much more seriously:

"Though, to tell the whole truth about it, she saved all of us because there was a fair sized little *tchambul* behind that snooping Tartar. But she raised the alarm when she got back home, and we had the time to get our whole household away into the woods! You understand, of course, that this kind of thing isn't all that strange in our part of the country..."

Zagloba's face became suffused with such a look of wonder that his good eye blinked shut in sheer admiration. Then he leaped up, seized the unsuspecting girl, and planted a big smacking kiss on her forehead before she could guess what he had in mind.

"Take this from an old soldier for that Tartar in the reeds!" he said with great feeling.

The girl shook her head with fierce determination, sending her tumbled hair flying in all directions.

"Hah! I peppered his hide for him good and proper, didn't I?" she called out in her fresh, childlike voice which sounded startling in that warlike context.

"Yes you did, my sweet rapscallion!" Pan Zagloba said in a voice deepened with emotion.

"But what's a single Tartar?" Basia shrugged. "It's nothing! You gentlemen cut them up in thousands, along with Swedes, Germans, Hungarians and God only knows what... What do I amount to next to such great knights who don't have an equal in the Commonwealth? Nothing! I know it well enough!"

"Then we'll have to teach you a little sword-play, if you've so much spirit. I'm a little slowed down nowadays but Michal is also a master with a saber."

The young lady literally hopped up in delight, kissed Pan Zagloba's hand in gratitude, and courtseyed to Pan Michal.

"Thank you for the promise!" she cried out. "I already know quite a bit about it!"

But Volodyovski was totally absorbed in his conversation with Panna Drohoyovska. "Whenever you wish, milady," he said in a distracted voice.

★ ★ ★

Meanwhile Pan Zagloba sat down again next to the Magistrate's Lady, his full, florid face quite aglow with admiration and enthusiasm.

"I know how delicious are the Turkish sweetmeats and desserts, milady," he told her, "because I spent long years in Istanbul in my time. But I also know that few can resist them! How is it, then, that no one has gobbled up this tasty little morsel already?"

"Dear God, we've not lacked for suitors for both of them!" said Madame Makovyetzka. "We even joke at home that Basia is a three-time widow because she had three first-rate cavaliers knocking on her door all at the same time. There was Pan Svirski, Pan Kondratzki and Pan Tchvilihovski... all of them notable gentry in our parts, and all of them men of standing and property as well... whose antecedents I can spell out for you straight away."

The Magistrate's Lady immediately prepared the fingers of her left hand for counting and raised the index finger of the right, but Pan Zagloba hastened to distract her.

"And what happened to them?"

"All three died in the war, which is why we call Basia a widow three times over."

"Hmm! And how did she take that?"

"Well, you see sir, that's quite a normal thing down in the borderlands, and few people live to see a natural death after a certain age. We've even a saying that it isn't right for the nobility to die in their beds. But how did Basia take that? She sniffled a bit, poor thing, mostly in the stables, because if something bothers her she runs to the hayloft! I went after her one time, and I asked her: *'Which one are you mourning?'* And she said: *'All three!'* Which makes me think that she didn't favor one over another. Her head is still full of other things, you see, and she hasn't felt God's will upon her up to now, if you know what I mean... Krysia, yes. She's much more aware of her role and feelings as a woman. But I don't think Basia gives two hoots about it one way or another."

"She will!" Zagloba stated categorically. "We know that well enough, you and I my lady! Oh, she'll wake to all those feelings, there's no doubt about it. Yes, she will! She will!"

"That's the destiny of our sex," sighed the Magistrate's Lady.

"That's it exactly!" Pan Zagloba nodded with absolute conviction. "I couldn't have said it any better myself!"

★ ★ ★

Volodyovski and both the young women took this moment to approach the old knight and Madame Makovyetzka and put an end to their confidential chatter.

Pan Michal was now quite at ease with Krysia, and she—probably out of the pure goodness of her heart—showed him the gentle sympathy and kindness of a nurse towards a troubled patient, which may have been why she was more friendly than their brief acquaintance would normally permit.

But since Pan Michal was the brother of her guardian's wife, and since she herself was related to Pan Makovyetzki, no one thought twice about it.

Basia was somewhat pushed aside that evening, and largely ignored by everyone but Zagloba, but she didn't seem to mind. In the beginning she stared at both the knights with wide-eyed admiration but she seemed just as fascinated with Ketling's beautiful collection of weapons hung around the walls. Then after a while she started to yawn, her bright blue eyes blinked sleepily once or twice, and then she blurted out in that blunt, unaffected manner that endeared her so much to the old knight: "I think that when I hit that pillow I won't get up till day after tomorrow."

After that the evening came quickly to an end, particularly since the women were tired from their journey and waited only for the servants to make up their beds. But when Pan Zagloba found himself finally alone with Volodyovski he started making sly, knowing faces at him, winked at him in a manner meant to denote something significant and pointed, and bombarded him with a quick shower of jabs to the ribs.

"Michal!" he cried. "Hey, Michal, and what do you think of that? What a pair of peaches, eh? Hmm? Ripe and sweet as a couple of turnips, what? So you'd be a monk, eh? And what about that Drohoyovska, then? Isn't she a succulent little raisin? And that pink rapscallion, isn't she a picture? What do you say to that, Michal, eh?"

"What should I say? Nothing," the little knight replied.

"I'm particularly fond of that spirited little ragamuffin. I tell you, when I sat next to her at supper, she radiated warmth like a redhot brazier."

"She's still a child. The other's more mature."

"Drohoyovska is a juicy plum, I agree. And that other is a hazelnut! Blast my eyes, if I still had my teeth... But I swear, if I had such a daughter, I'd give her to you and nobody else. An almond, by God! An honest to God almond!"

Volodyovski, however, lost his cheerfulness because he suddenly remembered all the ways in which the voluble old knight once described Anusia. She rose up in his memory as if she were still alive and breathing. He saw her small, pert face, her dark braided hair. He heard her silvery laughter and the innocence of her childlike prattle. He felt the stirring and appealing warmth of her sidelong glances. These two were younger, perhaps even prettier, but surely she was a hundred times more precious than any young beauty...

The little knight hid his face in his hands and gave way to a wave of mourning which was all the more overwhelming because it was so utterly unexpected.

Zagloba stared at him, alarmed and surprised. He kept quiet for a time, watching his friend with great anxiety, and then said: "What's wrong, Michal? What's the matter? Hmm? For God's sake, say something!"

"So many of them are alive," the small knight said at last. "So many walk the earth... Only my own sweet lamb is no longer here. It's only her I'll never see again...!"

Then pain gripped him as if in a vise and he hissed out through clenched lips:

"God... God... God...!"

Chapter Nine

MISS BASIA SAW TO IT that Pan Volodyovski kept his promise to teach her the arts of fencing, and he was glad to go along with it because he became as fond of Basia as everybody else after a few days, although he much preferred the quieter and more dignified Panna Drohoyovska.

So one morning he gave her the first lesson, prompted to some extent by her bragging and her confident insistence that she already knew quite a lot about it, and that she could hold her own with almost anyone.

"I was taught by experienced soldiers," she said. "There's no lack of them in our parts, and everyone knows that they're the best swordsmen... In fact I wonder if you gentlemen wouldn't find your match among them."

"What are you saying, girl!" Pan Zagloba cried. "The whole world doesn't have our equals!"

"I'd like to show that I am also equal," she said. "I don't expect it but I'd like to see it."

"If it came to musketry," said Madame Makovyetzka and began to giggle. "I'd also try my hand in a little contest."

"For God's sake!" said Zagloba. "Are there only Amazons living in the Latichev territory?" Then he turned to Panna Drohoyovska. "And what's your favorite weapon, milady?"

"I have none," Krysia said.

"Aha! None indeed!" Basia cried, and giving a passable imitation of Krysia's winsome manner, broke into a song.

> *"Your armor will fail you*
> *When Cupid assails you*
> *With his tender arrows.*
> *"The bravest of hearts*
> *Won't survive those darts,*
> *But perish like sparrows."*

"That's her chosen weapon," she told Zagloba and Volody-ovski. "And she's a champion with it, don't worry about that!"

"Take your position, young lady," Pan Michal barked roughly, trying to hide his sudden embarrassment and confusion.

"Dear God!" cried Basia, turning quite pink with joy. "If only I could show what I'd like to show!"

She came at once to the *on guard* position, holding a light Polish saber in her right hand, the left cocked behind her back. She looked so young, pretty and alive with her head held high and her breast thrust forward, that Zagloba sighed, shook his head, and whispered in Madame Makovyetzka's ear: "Not even a flagon of hundred-year-old Malmsey could delight me more than this lovely sight."

"Take note, young lady," Volodyovski said. "All I'll do is defend myself. You do the attacking. I won't strike one offensive blow but you press me as hard as you like."

"Very well. Just tell me when you've had enough and I'll stop at once."

"That could happen anytime I want."

"And how could it happen?"

"Simple. It's no problem to disarm this kind of opponent."

"We'll see about that!"

"No we won't, because I'll spare your feelings."

"Never mind my feelings! Do it if you can! I know you're better at this than I, sir, but that's one thing I won't let anybody do!"

"You'll allow me, then?"

"Yes!"

"Have mercy, my sweet little warrior!" Pan Zagloba cautioned. "He's done that to experts!"

"We'll see!" Basia said.

"Let's begin!" said Volodyovski, somewhat irritated by the young girl's bragging.

★ ★ ★

They started. Basia struck a ferocious blow, hopping like a grasshopper as she did it, while Volodyovski stood stock still as he always did, barely moving the point of his saber and not paying much attention to her fierce assault.

"Not fair!" Basia cried, annoyed. "You're making no effort! You're just brushing me aside as if I were a fly!"

"I'm not dueling with you," the little knight reminded. "I'm giving a lesson. "That was good! Not bad for a woman... Easy with that wrist!"

"Not bad for a woman? Take this for that *woman!* And this! And this!"

But Pan Michal wasn't taking anything, in spite of the fact that Basia showered him with her most expert strokes. On the contrary, he started chatting with Zagloba to show how unconcerned he was by Basia's best efforts.

"Step away from the window," he asked the old knight. "You're blocking the young lady's light, she can't see her saber. True, a saber's a lot longer than a sewing needle, but she has more experience with sewing than sword-play."

Basia's small nostrils were now distended as far as they would go and her hair had tumbled altogether across her sharp, bright eyes.

"You take me for nothing, sir?" she demanded, short of breath and gasping.

"Not the person, no. But your swordsmanship is another matter."

"I hate you!" she cried.

"There's your payment, teacher," Volodyovski sighed and turned to Pan Zagloba. "Is it snowing outside? Hmm... I believe it is!"

"Here's your snow!" Basia cried and attacked with fury. "And here! And here! And here!"

"That's enough, Basia," urged Madame Makovyetzka. "You're gasping like a bellows."

"Hold your blade steady," warned the little knight, "or I'll strip it right out of your hand!"

"We'll see!"

"As you wish!" said Pan Volodyovski and Basia's saber whirled suddenly out of her little fist and clanged on the floor beside the tall porcelain stove in the corner.

"That was me, not you!" the young woman cried with tears in her voice. "I did that myself!"

And she ran to her fallen saber, swept it up, and attacked again.

"Try that again if you can!" she cried.

"As you wish," said Volodyovski and Basia's sword flew once more towards the stove. "That ought to be enough for today."

Madame Makovyetzka quaked and squeaked even louder than before, while Basia stood alone in the middle of the room—feeling ashamed, confused, out of breath, biting her lips and trying to hold back her tears. She knew that everyone would laugh at her all the harder if she burst out crying and she was determined that this wouldn't happen. But her angry tears welled up anyway and she ran out of the room before they could spill.

"Dear Lord!" cried Madame Makovyetzka. "She's probably run off to the stables and she's all disheveled and warm and out of breath... She's bound to catch a chill! I'd better go after her. Krysia, you stay here!"

★ ★ ★

She snatched up a warm fleece-lined short-coat in the hall and ran to the stables, and Pan Zagloba, anxious about his beloved *little warrior*, galloped at her heels.

Drohoyovska also wanted to run after them but the little knight caught her by the hand.

"You heard the order?" he asked. "I'll hold you here until they come back."

And he did, holding that velvety soft hand, and feeling as if some warm, soothing current flowed from those slim fingers deep into his bones, so he clutched it all the harder while a light flush appeared in Krysia's pale face.

"I see that I'm a prisoner," she said.

"The Turkish Sultan would give half his possessions for such a captive," Volodyovski said. "And even that wouldn't be enough."

"But you wouldn't sell me to him, would you?"

"I'd sooner sell my soul to the Devil!" he burst out. Here it flashed into Pan Michal's head that his enthusiasm was carrying him too far, so he added quickly: "Just as I wouldn't sell my sister!"

"And that's just what I can be to you," the girl answered gravely. "I love your lady sister as if she were my own and I can offer you that same sisterly affection."

"Thank you with all my heart,"Pan Michal said gratefully and kissed her hand. "I need that these days."

"I know,"she said, and a small tear rolled down from her eye and settled briefly on that soft, downy lip. "I know. I'm also an orphan."

Volodyovski watched that tear and those shaded lips and felt another soothing warmth flooding through his veins.

"You're as good and kind as an angel,"he said. "I'm already better."

"God give you peace, sir."Krysia smiled gently.

"He already has!"

It occurred to the little knight that he'd feel even better if he kissed her hands a few more times, but Madame Makovyetzka entered the room just then.

"Basia took the jacket," she said. "But she's so embarrassed that she won't come back for anything! Pan Zagloba is chasing her all over the stables."

★ ★ ★

Pan Zagloba was, indeed, in hot pursuit of the elusive Basia and he finally drove her out into the cold, hoping that this might help him to convince her to come back inside. But she darted away from him no matter how he pleaded and cajoled.

"No I won't!"she cried over and over. "I don't care if I freeze to death! I won't go back in, I won't!"

Then she caught sight of a climbing pole propped against the house with a long ladder extending above it, scooted up both of them as nimble as a squirrel, and didn't stop until she felt the edge of the roof behind her.

"Alright then!" she laughed and called down to Zagloba, already turning the pursuit into a game, and settled herself comfortably on the roof. "I'll go in if you climb up here after me!"

"What am I," the old knight bellowed. "Some kind of a tomcat to be chasing you across the tiles? Is that how you repay my affection for you?"

"I love you too, sir," she grinned down. "But only on rooftops."

"Bah!" he snorted. "A man says his thing and a woman always has her answer. Come down at once!"

"I won't!"

"It's a joke, really, to be that embarrassed over something as trivial as this! You're not the only one to whom Volodyovski did that, you pesky little ferret! He did it to Kmita, who had the reputation of a master swordsman, and he did it in a serious fight not some parlor game. For God's sake, the greatest German, Swedish and Italian duelists couldn't hold out against him longer than one Hail Mary, and here's one snippet of a gadfly taking it to heart. Shame on you for making such a fuss over nothing! Come down! Come on down! It was just a lesson!"

"Maybe so. But I can't stand Pan Michal!"

"Why, for God's sake? Because he's an expert at what you'd like to learn? You ought to love him all the more for that!"

Pan Zagloba had hit on a truth, although he didn't know it, because Basia's admiration for the little knight had soared even higher despite her embarrassment, but she remained adamant none the less.

"Let Krysia love him!" she shot back from her perch.

"Come down!"

"I won't!"

"Alright, sit there then. But I've got to tell you that you're creating quite a spectacle up there on that ladder. Ha! A lot of people would pay for the view that I have from here."

"No they wouldn't!" she cried and wrapped her skirts and coat closely about her knees.

"I'm an old man," Pan Zagloba shrugged. "My eyes have seen enough. But I'll go and call everybody else so they might learn something."

"I'm coming down!" Basia cried at once.

But Zagloba turned suddenly towards the angle of the house.

"Somebody is already on his way," he said.

★ ★ ★

Young Pan Novovyeyski appeared at that moment, coming around the corner of the house. He had ridden up on horseback, tied his mount to the rail at the side porch, and was now walking

around the manor house to reach the main entrance. Seeing him,
Basia flew to the ground in two leaps, but he had already seen
what there was to see.

He stood stock still—flushed, embarrassed and surprised—
which is exactly how Basia stood before him.

"Another predicament!" she cried out suddenly.

Highly amused, the old knight blinked his good eye for a time
from one of the young people to the other, and offered his
version of an introduction.

"This is Pan Novovyeyski," he said. "A friend and junior
officer of our dear Pan Michal. And this is Miss Ladderovska...
tfui, my error... I meant to say Yezorkovska!"

Novovyeyski gathered his wits together soon enough. And
because, young as he was, these wits were sharp and quick, he
bowed with a flourish, raised his eyes to the beautiful apparition
before him, and cried out: "For God's sake! Roses bloom in
Ketling's garden even in the snow!"

Basia dipped a courtsey. "But not for *your* nose," she said
under her breath.

Then she assumed the proper winsome smile and invited him
graciously inside. She led the way with flying skirts and feet,
burst into the reception room where Pan Michal sat with the
other women, and pointed to the crimson-coated officer behind
her.

"It must be Spring!" she cried. "A robin has come calling!"

Then she plopped down on a stool, folded her hands modestly
in her lap, and put on the innocent expression of a well-trained
young lady.

★　★　★

Pan Michal introduced his young friend to his sister and
Krysia Drohoyovska, which threw the youth into another bout
of embarrassment and confusion. One stunning girl encountered
unexpectedly was bad enough; two was too much, even if each
was absolutely different. He covered up his nervousness with a
deep bow and reached for his mustache to give himself a brave,
heroic air by twirling it upward. He had not yet, however,
grown a mustache big enough to twirl.

Having twirled his finger along his upper lip, he turned to
Volodyovski and told him what he had come about. The Grand

Hetman, it appeared, was anxious to see the little knight. As far as Novovyeyski guessed, it was a matter of military function and appointment; Pan Sobieski had just received a bundle of letters from Pan Viltchkovski, Pan Silnitzki, Colonel Pivo, and several other detachment commanders scattered throughout Podolia and the Ukraine. The latest situation in the Crimea didn't promise well. And the Budjak country—or all the Tartar-Turkish holdings on the north shore of the Black Sea—was like a roiled beehive, even though this was the wrong season for military campaigns.

"The Khan and the Sultan both want to keep the treaty we made with them at Podhayetz," he added. "But all the Budjak country is up in arms already, and the Belgorodian Horde is champing at the bit. They pay no attention to the Sultan or the Khan..."

"Pan Sobieski has already told me all about it," Zagloba broke in, "and asked my advice. But what do you hear around him about events we might expect in the Spring?"

"It looks as if all that vermin will stir again once Winter is over," said Pan Novovyeyski. "And that we'll have to crush it once again."

With this he struck such a martial pose, and twirled his finger so fiercely beside his upper lip, that the whole lower part of his cheek turned scarlet.

Basia's quick eyes noted it at once. She edged her chair slightly behind the youth to where he couldn't see her, and started twirling her own nonexistent whiskers, mimicking all his martial airs and gestures to perfection. Madame Makovyetzka sent her a sharp, warning glance, while at the same time biting back her laughter and quivering like a mound of aspic. Volodyovski gnawed the ends of his mustache, and Krysia dropped her eyes so low that her long lashes created a deep shadow on her cheeks.

"You're still a young man, sir," Pan Zagloba said. "But it's clear that you're a seasoned soldier."

"I'm twenty-two but I've served our country for seven years now," the young man replied. "Because I ran away from school and joined the colors when I was fifteen."

"And he knows the wilderness of the lower Dniester like few

others," Pan Michal threw in. "He knows how to trail Tartars in
the grass and leap on them like a fox on a flock of quail. He's a
first-rate borderer and there aren't many Tartars who can dodge
him in the Steppe."

★ ★ ★

Pan Novovyeyski flushed bright red with pleasure to be
praised by such a famous soldier in the presence of the two
young women. He looked exactly what he was—the finest
possible example of the young Steppe hawks who ranged the
wild borders in those times—but he was also an extraordinarily
handsome youth, with finely chiseled features which had been
deeply tanned by the winds and the weather. His eyes were sharp
and clear, accustomed to scanning distances near the horizon,
and his bushy eyebrows dipped to a point just above his nose and
arched back in a double curve like a Tartar horn-bow. He wore
his thick, black hair in an unruly cockscomb on top of his skull,
with the sides and back of his head shaved high above the ears
in the manner of the military gentry.

Basia liked his clean-cut looks, his confidence, and his way of
speaking, but that didn't stop her mocking imitations.

"Well, well," said Pan Zagloba. "It's good for old men like me
to see that the new generation follows in our footsteps and is a
credit to us."

"I've a long way to go before I claim such credit," answered
Novovyeyski.

"Your modesty is also impressive! It won't be long before
you're entrusted with small independent commands of your
own."

"He's already led his own troops!" cried Volodyovski. "And
fought his own campaigns!"

Pan Novovyeyski tugged at his fuzzy lip so fiercely that he
just about ripped it off his face, and Basia, who watched his
every gesture, raised both her hands to the corners of her mouth
and mimicked every twirl.

But the sharp-eyed young soldier soon noted that everybody's
glances were slipping past him, and darting behind his back to
where the beautiful young woman he had seen jumping off the
ladder was perched on her stool, and he caught on quickly that
she must be up to something he ought to know about. So he

went on talking as if he hadn't noticed anything unusual, and plucked at his skimpy mustache as before, until he picked a moment to spin around and to catch the girl with her eyes fixed on him and her hands still busy at her face.

Caught in the act, she turned an instant scarlet and rose to her feet, not knowing what to do. Nor did anyone else. There was an awkward silence.

But suddenly Basia slapped the folds of her gown with both hands. "A third embarrassment!" she cried out in her silvery voice.

"My dear young lady!" Novovyeyski said to her in a lively and good-natured tone. "I knew straight off that there was some kind of ambush being set behind me. I admit I'm anxious to have a real mustache, and if I don't get the time to grow one it'll be because I've died in our country's service. In which case, I hope I'll have earned your tears rather than your laughter."

Eyes lowered, Basia stood ashamed all the more by his youthful honesty and the sincerity that rang in his voice.

"You must forgive her, sir!" Zagloba insisted. "She's a lively thing, that's all, because she is young. But it's a heart of pure gold, believe me!"

And she, as if to confirm Pan Zagloba's words, whispered at once: "Forgive me, sir... I am very sorry."

Pan Novovyeyski seized both her hands at once and kissed them with enthusiasm.

"For God's sake, milady!" he cried. "Don't take that to heart! After all, I'm not a barbarian. It's up to me to ask forgiveness for spoiling your amusement. We soldiers love horseplay of all kinds ourselves! It's all my fault, *mea culpa*! Let me kiss those little hands again, and if I'm to kiss them until you forgive me, then—by all that's holy!—I hope you don't forgive me until nightfall."

"Now there's a courteous cavalier!" said Madame Makovyetzka. "Did you hear it, Basia?"

"I heard," Basia said.

"All's well's then!" cried Pan Novovyeyski.

He straightened up, and reached for his mustache as before, but caught himself at once and burst into open laughter. Basia also trilled her silvery laugh and then was everyone laughing as ease and merriment returned to them all. Zagloba ordered one or two special bottles brought up from Ketling's cellar and they spent a very pleasant morning.

Pan Novovyeyski was in excellent form. He clicked his spurs together, tangled his topknot even more with excited fingers, and treated Basia to an ever warmer set of fiery glances. He thought she was just splendid. He also became as eloquent as never before, and because he was an aide to the Grand Hetman and lived at the center of the most important political events of the day, he had a lot to say.

He told them all about the electoral convention and how it had ended, and how the stove collapsed in the Senate chamber under the weight of all the arbiters hanging onto it.

He didn't leave until long after the midday meal, and he rode away with Basia's lovely image filling his eyes, his heart, and his soul.

Chapter Ten

ON THAT SAME DAY the little knight reported at the Hetman's headquarters and Pan Sobieski ordered him admitted at once.

"I must send Rushtchitz to the Crimea," he said, "to watch for whatever might be in the wind, and to keep trying to induce the Khan to honor the treaty. Would you like to go back on active service and take over his command? You, Viltchkovski, Silnitzki and Pivo will keep an eye on Doroshenko and the Tartars who can never be completely trusted."

Pan Michal's face fell a little and his spirits sank. His best years had gone by in service. He hadn't given a thought to himself in more than ten years. He'd spent his life in gunsmoke, fire, and the hard riding of innumerable campaigns; he'd gone sleepless and hungry, and without a dry roof over his head more times than he could remember, and often without even a dry handful of straw to use for a pillow. God only knew what sorts of blood had drained off his saber. He'd neither married nor secured his future. Men who were a hundred times less deserving were already settled on comfortable estates, living on the fruits of their merit, and rising to high titles, honors and positions; while he had been better off when he started serving than he was right now.

But here he was again, he thought bitterly, ready for use like a worn old broom even though his soul was ripped in two with such recent suffering. And he'd no sooner found a pair of sweet and friendly hands, which had begun to heal his wounds a little, when he was ordered to leap up again and hurl himself to the distant wilderness of the Commonwealth's far-flung eastern borders, without a thought to the heartsick weariness of his mind and soul.

And, he remembered, if it weren't for just such sudden leaps and flights into the unknown, which had devoured all that precious time since the Swedish wars, he'd have had at least a few years of joy with Anusia.

A well of bitterness seemed to surge upward out of him under the weight of his disappointments. But since he thought it beneath his dignity to tout his own merits, and to remind people of the services he'd rendered, he merely said:

"I'll go."

It was the Hetman who reminded him: "You're not on active service. This isn't an order. You can decline. You know best if it isn't too soon for you to get back in harness."

"It isn't even too soon for me to die," said Volodyovski.

★ ★ ★

Pan Sobieski paced a few times up and down the chamber, then stopped before the small knight who sat on a hard chair with his head slumped resignedly on his chest, and placed a strong, steady hand on Pan Michal's shoulder.

"If your tears are still wet, the Steppe winds will dry them," he said to him quietly. "You've labored all your life, little soldier, labor a little more. And if you ever think that you've been forgotten, that you've been used without a letup or reward, that you've earned a dry crust for yourself instead of buttered pastries, that all you have to show for all those years are wounds and suffering rather than ease and a high position, just clench your teeth and say: *'It's for you, my country!'* I've no other consolation I can give you. And though I'm not a priest, and I don't speak for God, I can swear to you that you'll get farther on your worn-out saddle than others in their gilded coaches drawn by six white horses, and that you'll see gates opening before you that close for those others."

'It's for you,' Pan Volodyovski told that vision of his country he carried in his heart, wondering at the same time how the Hetman could penetrate his most secret thoughts with such unerring judgment.

Meanwhile Pan Sobieski drew up a chair and sat down across from Pan Volodyovski.

"I want to talk to you as a father to a son," he said, "rather than as your military commander. Back in those days when we lived constantly in flames and fire, at Podhayetz and earlier in the Ukraine—when we could hardly keep our heads above those oceans of enemies against us, while here, in the heart of the country, evil, heartless people sat safe behind our backs and thought only about themselves—it often struck me that this Commonwealth must perish. There's too much selfishness among us. Too many go their own way and don't give enough thought to discipline and order. Private concerns have ruled too long here over the public good, and you don't find that among any other people to such a degree. I gnawed on these dark thoughts at night in my tent, and in the field in daylight, and I thought: *'We're dying here in this constant fire. We'll perish to a man, but that's our duty and our fate as soldiers! And if we only knew that our blood was buying our country's happiness and salvation, we'd all do it gladly!'* But no! We were denied even that simple consolation!

"I lived through some hard, bitter days in those Podhayetz trenches," he resumed, "even though I showed you men only a smiling face so you wouldn't think that I'd despaired of victory. *'We lack the men!'* I thought. *'We don't have enough people who truly love their country!'* And I felt as if someone were driving a dagger through my heart...

"But one day—it was the last day at Podhayetz, the day we attacked the Horde—when I sent two thousand of you against twenty-six thousand Tartars, and you charged into certain death, galloping to that slaughter with such fire and fervor as if you were all going to your weddings, I had to ask myself: *'But what about my soldiers?'* And God at once lifted that boulder off my heart and my vision cleared.

"*They*, I told myself, are dying out there from a pure love of our mother country. You won't see *them* joining any mutinies or rebellions. It's *they* with whom I'll form that sacred brotherhood, that school of patriotism and honor for all our future generations. They'll set the example. It's they who'll bring a new life to this wretched nation, so that it can finally turn its back on anarchy and selfishness and greed, and rise as mighty as

a lion that feels its power in every limb and sinew, and amaze
the world with what it can accomplish!"

★ ★ ★

Here Pan Sobieski flushed deeply, moved by his own vision,
and lifted his arms skyward.

"Lord!" he cried. "Don't write *Mane, Tekel, Fares* on our
walls! Don't doom us! Allow me to resurrect our country!"

A long silence followed.

The little knight sat with his head bowed down on his chest
and felt his whole body quivering as if in a fever, while the
Hetman paced rapidly through the room and stopped again
before Volodyovski.

"We need examples," he said. "We need to show the country
every day what duty and sacrifice are all about. Volodyovski! I
counted you among the first in that brotherhood. Do you want
to join it...?"

The little knight got slowly to his feet and sank down to the
floor to kneel before the Hetman.

"Here it is," he said in a voice shaken with emotion. "Here's
the truth of it. I thought myself wronged when I heard that I
was to go off again. I thought I had the right to get through my
suffering in peace. But now I see I've sinned... and I curse myself
for having thought such thoughts, and I'm ashamed even to
mention it..."

The Hetman reached for him, and pulled him to his feet, and
pressed him to his chest in silence, just as a loving father would
embrace a son.

"There's just a mere handful of us," he said at last, speaking
quietly but with absolute conviction. "But others will follow
when we've blazed the trail."

"When am I to go?" asked the little knight. "I can go to the
Crimea, if you wish, sir. I've been there before."

"No," said the Hetman. "I'm sending Rushtchitz there. He
has blood-brothers among the Tartars, along with some cousins
swept up by the Horde as children. They were raised as Muslims
and climbed to some high offices over there. They'll help him
in every way they can. I need you in the field since there's no
one who can handle Tartars better than you can."

"When am I to go?" the little knight repeated.

"Within two weeks, no longer. I need to talk to the Chancellor and the Lord Treasurer, and to write the orders and instructions for Rushtchitz. Be ready, though, because I'll be in a hurry when I send for you."

"I'll be ready from tomorrow on."

"God bless you, but it won't be quite that soon. Nor will you be gone for long, because I'll need you here during the election if the peace still holds. You've heard about the candidates? What is the gentry saying?"

"I'm fresh from the monastery, sir," said Volodyovski. "They don't discuss worldly matters there. All I know is what I hear from Pan Zagloba."

"Good, I can ask him. He speaks with a big voice among our brother gentry. And who do you think you might vote for?"

"I still don't know, sir. But it seems to me that we need a Soldier-King more than any other."

"That's it! That's it exactly! I have one in mind who'd make all our enemies shake with his name alone. We need a warrior lord of the same stamp as Stefan Batory. Alright then, take care of yourself, little soldier. We need a Warrior-King, tell that to everyone... And God bless you now... God reward you for being so ready!"

Pan Michal bowed and left.

On his way home, riding back towards Ketling's manor, he drifted into a variety of thoughts. For all his readiness, he was glad that he still had a week or two, because Krysia Drohoyovska's gentle hands and friendship pleased him a great deal. He was also glad that he'd be coming home for the election so that he felt as if he didn't have a worry in the world. The Steppes also exercised a certain eager fascination on him that translated itself unknowingly into longing. He had become so accustomed to those vast, endless distances, in which a mounted soldier feels more like a bird in flight than a mere horseman, that it seemed like home.

'Well, so I'll go again to those seas of grass,' he mused on his way. *'To those frontier forts and old burial mounds, and sample the old life. I'll be leading men on long marches, keeping a hawk's eye on the border trails, bathing once more in those tall Spring grasses like fish in the ocean... So I'll go! I'll go!'*

★ ★ ★

He put his horse into a rapid gallop and let it run all out, because his thoughts reminded him of how much he missed that pounding speed and the hiss of the wind in his ears.

The day was clear and dry but the frost crackled in the air. The early snow already lay in a crisp, icy sheet across the fields, and creaked under the horse's hooves which flung it back along the road in small, frozen clods. Pan Volodyovski flew at such a headlong pace that his groom, riding a lesser horse, was soon left far behind.

The sun was about to set. The red glow of sunset burned across the sky and bathed the snowy spaces with a violet light. Stars had begun to glitter in the deepening crimson overhead, and a new moon swung upward like a silver sickle. The road was empty. The speeding knight passed nothing on his way except an occasional creaking peasant cart, and he didn't begin to rein-in his horse, and to allow his groom to catch up with him, until he saw the lights of Ketling's manor gleaming in the distance.

And suddenly he saw a tall, willowy figure coming towards him along the road and recognized Krysia Drohoyovska. Surprised, but delighted even more, he leaped off his horse, tossed the reins to the groom behind him, and ran forward to meet her.

"It's an old soldiers' superstition," he told her, "that all sorts of supernatural beings can be met at sunset, from which all kinds of omens can be read. But I can't think of a prophecy that might mean more to me than just seeing you, my lady."

"Pan Novovyeyski has come calling again," Krysia answered softly. "Basia and Madame Makovyetzka are entertaining him, and I went out to meet you, because I was worried about what the Hetman might have had to say."

Her openness, and the genuine anxiety he read in her voice, moved him close to tears.

"Are you really that concerned about me?" he asked in a voice made diffident by his hopes and longings.

"Yes," she said quietly.

Volodyovski kept his eyes on her the rest of the way because she'd never seemed that beautiful to him before. She wore a warm Winter cloak. A velvet hood trimmed in swans' down framed her pale features. Moonlight played in that small, delicately tinted face, along those thoughtful brows and on her lowered eyes, on the soft shadows thrown by her long eyelashes, and on that barely perceptible darkening above her upper lip. There was peace in that face, he thought; great peace and decency and goodness.

He saw it instantly as the face of friendship, along with a gentleness and warmth that must be close to love. A sudden wave of longing for that love and peace swept over him just then and he said, in a voice made suddenly hoarse by feeling: "Ah...! If it weren't for the groom behind us, I'd throw myself at your feet to thank you."

"Don't do that yet," she said simply, "because I've done nothing to deserve it. Just tell me that you won't be leaving us and that I'll be able to comfort you longer."

"But I am leaving!" Pan Volodyovski answered.

Krysia stopped suddenly. Her eyes were wide with shock and disappointment. "But how can that be?"

"Service," he said. "Quite normal for a soldier. I'm going to Ruthenia, out towards the Wild Lands."

"Quite normal for a soldier," Krysia said softly like a distant echo.

★ ★ ★

Suddenly silent, she started walking quickly towards the house. Pan Michal trotted beside her feeling foolish and heavy-hearted at the same time. He wanted to say something. He wanted to resume their conversation but somehow he couldn't get it going. It seemed to him that he had a thousand things to tell her and that now was the time while they were still alone with no one intruding.

'*The main thing is to start,'* he told himself and turned to her again. "When did Pan Novovyeyski come today?" he asked. "Long ago?"

"Not long," she replied.

'*That's not the way to go,'* he thought. *'If I can't do better then this, I'll never get to tell her anything important. Seems like the few wits I've had are all dried up with mourning.'*

He trotted along beside the tall, striding girl for a while longer, saying nothing but moving his little whiskers faster with each step. But when at last they reached Ketling's threshold he stopped abruptly and blurted out:

"Well, you see my lady... if I've been putting aside my own happiness for so many years, just to serve our country... how am I to do something different now?"

It seemed to Volodyovski that such a simple argument would appeal to Krysia more than fancy speeches. But it took her some moments to reply.

"The better that one gets to know you, sir," she said both gently and sadly. "The more one must honor and respect you."

* * *

They could hear Basia's loud, excited cries as soon as they stepped into the house. Pan Novovyeyski crouched blindfolded in the middle of the reception room, with his arms reaching out into empty air, while Basia darted away from him and hid in the corners, luring him on with Tartar battle cries. Pan Zagloba and Madame Makovyetzka conversed near the window.

The entrance of Krysia and Volodyovski brought it all to an immediate end. Novovyeyski tore off his blindfold and ran to greet his colonel, with the breathless Basia, Zagloba and the Magistrate's Lady close behind.

"What's the news, then?" they pressed anxiously around the little knight. "What's happening? What did the Hetman have to say?"

"If you've any letters, sister, you'd like delivered to your husband, then here's your chance!"said Volodyovski. "I'm going to Ruthenia."

"They're sending you off already? As God lives, dear brother, don't enlist so quickly!" Madame Makovyetzka did nothing to hide her distress. "Why can't they give you a moment of rest?"

"Really? You've a job to do?" Pan Zagloba was clearly unhappy to hear about the little knight's assignment at this of all times. "Madame Makovyetzka is right, you know. You need to stay here for a little longer. They're whirling you about like an old flail! Enough is a enough!"

"Rushtchitz is going to the Crimea and I'm to take his regiment," Volodyovski shrugged. "It's as Pan Novovyeyski mentioned the other day, the trails will be swarming with Tartars in the Spring and they must be watched."

"Are we the only ones to guard this Commonwealth like a pair of watchdogs?" Pan Zagloba shouted. "Others don't even know which end of a musket to point and which to hug, but there's never a break for us!"

"Enough! Enough!" Volodyovski quietened down all these pleas and protests. He was a simple and straightforward man who found his comfort in simple and straightforward answers. "Duty is duty, you know that. I gave the Hetman my word that I'd go back in harness, and it makes no difference if it's now or later. Besides,"—and here Pan Volodyovski laid a finger alongside his nose and drew on the argument he had used with Krysia—"if I've been putting service to the Commonwealth ahead of my own ease for so many years, how can I stop doing it now, just for the solace that I find with all of you?"

No one could find a convincing answer, as he knew they wouldn't. But Basia moved impulsively towards him, frowning and pouting like a disappointed child.

"We'll miss Pan Michal," she said. "Yes we will!"

Volodyovski laughed, both amused and pleased.

"God bless you, my girl!" he cried out and went on to tease her. "It was just yesterday you said you hated me worse than any Tartar!"

"I never said anything of the kind! A Tartar, indeed! The truth is that you'll be having a merry old time with the Tartars over there, and we'll just sit here missing you, alone in this house."

"Not for long, *little warrior,*"Pan Michal assured her, using Pan Zagloba's favorite name for the brave, bright, determined and beautiful young girl, and thinking that the old man's nickname for her fit her like a glove. "The Hetman made it clear that this command is not a permanent commission. I'll leave in a week or two but I must be back in Warsaw before the election. That's set for May so I'll be back by then even if Rushtchitz is still in the Crimea. That's what the Hetman wants himself so that's how it'll be."

"Oh well! That's fine, then!" Basia cried.

"I'll be going too, I expect," Pan Novovyeyski tried a saddened sigh as he peered hopefully at Basia. "If the colonel has to go I won't be far behind..."

But Basia wasn't in a mood to show him any mercy.

"Go then!" she said. "Go! Pan Michal might enjoy your company. It's a wonderful thing for a soldier to serve under such a great commander, and there'll be many like you crowding to be there."

The youth sighed sadly, ran his hand slowly through his tumbled hair, and flung his arms wide, growling like a bear. "But first I'll catch Miss Barbara!" he threatened. "As God's my witness, I'll catch her!"

"Allah! Allah!" Basia let fly with her Tartar war cry and beat a hasty retreat away from his hands.

Meanwhile Drohoyovska came closer to Pan Michal, and her face was glowing with a happier light than the one she showed on the moonlit highway.

"Pan Michal is a better friend to Basia than to me," she murmured, full of quiet joy. "He's cruel to me. Cruel."

"I'm cruel?" he cried, astonished. "I'm better to Basia?"

"You told Basia that you'll be back for the election, but if I had known that, I wouldn't have been so upset that you're going away."

"Oh, my sweet love!" cried Volodyovski, then caught himself, shocked by his own presumption, and went on in a quieter vein. "My dearest friend! I almost told you something else back there on the highway... But I just lost my head."

Chapter Eleven

IN THE NEXT FEW DAYS Pan Michal started getting ready for departure, continuing with Basia's fencing lessons because he liked her more each day, and with his solitary walks with Krysia Drohoyovska whose gentleness and goodness seemed like a balm on his troubled senses. The balm seemed to be effective because his humor improved almost daily, and he even began to take part in some of Basia's games with young Novovyeyski who called every day.

The young cavalier was now a frequent and most welcome guest in Ketling's house. He rode over either close to midday or first thing in the morning, and stayed until nightfall, and because everyone liked him and was glad to see him he was soon treated like a member of the family. He escorted the ladies to Warsaw, shopped for them at the clothmakers', pursued the uncatchable Basia with enthusiasm in the evening games of blindman's buff, and swore that he'd capture her come what may.

"Sooner or later you'll get caught," Pan Zagloba told her. "If not by him then by another."

But she always managed to elude young Pan Novovyeyski who made no secret of the fact that he wanted to catch her very much indeed. Something along those lines also must have occurred to *the little warrior*, because she became so thoughtful now and then that her unruly mop of bright, golden hair tumbled down altogether across her eyes.

★ ★ ★

But Pan Zagloba had his own ideas about who should catch

her, so one night, when everyone had gone to bed, he knocked on Volodyovski's door.

"I'm so sad that we've got to be apart again," he told him, "that I've come over to take another look at you, because God only knows when we'll get to see each other again."

"I'm sure to be back for the election," the little knight squeezed him in his arms. "And I'll tell you why. The Hetman wants as many men whom the gentry look up to and admire to work for his candidate. And because, God be praised, my name is well known to our brother gentry, he's sure to bring me here. He's counting on you too."

"Ha! He's using a pretty wide net to catch me if that's what he's doing," Pan Zagloba grumbled. "But even though I'm somewhat on the fat side I think I'll slip through. I won't vote for the Frenchman that he favors."

"Why not?"

"Because that would mean *absolutum dominium* here, that's why! We don't want some damn foreigner who believes in the Divine Right of Kings and absolute royal power. We are a republic."

"The Prince de Conde would have to sign the usual *pacta conventa*, guaranteeing all the freedoms of the gentry. And he's said to be a really great military commander, famous for his battles and campaigns all over the world."

"We don't have to look for our military leaders in France, thank God!" Pan Zagloba grunted. "Pan Sobieski himself is at least as good as de Conde. And bear in mind, Michal, that Frenchmen wear pantaloons and stockings, just like Swedes, so they probably don't keep their promises any better. *Carolus Gustavus* was ready to swear an oath every hour and break it half an hour later. They think no more of lying than of cracking walnuts. Oaths and articles of agreement are useless when there's no honesty behind them."

"But the Commonwealth must have help!" the little knight insisted. "We need a warrior on the throne! Ah, if only Prince Yeremi Vishnovyetzki was alive! We'd make him King without a single vote cast in opposition!"

"His son's alive!" Pan Zagloba noted.

"Yes, but what a difference! That lad is more like a lisping lackey than a Prince. You wouldn't think it's the same blood at all. I might vote for him just to honor the memory of his father, if the times were different. But the way things are now we have to give first thought to the public good! Skshetuski will tell you the same thing, you'll see. I'll do whatever Pan Sobieski does and says to do because I trust in his commitment to the country."

"Yes," Pan Zagloba nodded thoughtfully. "It's time for me to start pondering all these things as well. We didn't do so badly at the last election, you and I, remember? It's too bad you're leaving."

"And what will you do?"

"I'll go back to the Skshetuskis. Those pesky little kids torment me now and then, but I miss them when I don't see them for a while."

"If there's a war after the election then Skshetuski is also sure to go. Who knows, you might still decide to go yourself. Maybe we'll be campaigning together in Ruthenia like before, eh? We had some good times there didn't we? And some bad times too."

"You're so right! As I love God, you are! Our best years passed there. I wouldn't mind taking another look at all those places that witnessed our glory..."

"So come with me now, why don't you? We'll have a good, merry time together, and in five months we'll come back right here to Ketling's home. He'll be here by then, and the Skshetuskis too..."

"No, Michal, now's not the time for me," Pan Zagloba said, and launched into the subject that he had really come to see the little knight about. "But I promise to go with you to Ruthenia if you marry some girl who has property out there. I'll escort you and your bride to your new home and see you take possession."

★ ★ ★

With this, the old knight blinked rapidly at Pan Volodyovski, who lost some of his composure but recovered quickly.

"Marriage," he said, "is just about the last thing on my mind these days. And your best proof of that is that I'm going back into the service."

"And that's what worries me," Pan Zagloba told him. "There are two fine girls to choose from right here, and so I figured, *'well, if he doesn't take one, he'll take the other!'* For God's sake,

Michal, will you think about this? Ask yourself where you'll find a better opportunity than you have right now. Think of the years ahead when you'll wonder why every other man has a wife and children, while you stand alone like an old pear-tree in an open field. And grief will clutch at you! And you'll be sad with longing! I wouldn't say a thing if you'd been able to marry that poor girl you lost and if she'd left you children. At least you'd have had some focus for your affections and hope for the future. But the way things are, and the way they're going, you might find yourself alone in your old age, looking about in vain for somebody who loves you and cares about you, and you'll wonder if you're living in a foreign country, because you won't hear a kind word anywhere around you!"

Volodyovski said nothing for a while, he sat thinking deeply, so Pan Zagloba began to speak again, keeping a calculating eye on the little knight.

"My heart and head both tell me that Basia, that pink little rosebud, is for you. Why Basia? In the first place because that girl is pure gold! And, in the second place, because you and she would produce such a fighting brood that the world has never seen such soldiers..."

"She's a whirlwind," said the little knight. "Besides, Novovyeyski wants her."

"But that's just it! That's it, don't you see? Today she'd still probably pick you over him, because your great fame is so close to her heart and her imagination. But when you go and he stays—and he'll stay, the rascal, you can be sure of that, because it's not a real war that you're going to—who knows what'll happen?"

"Let it happen then! Let him take her! I wish him the best because he's a first-rate fellow!"

"Michal!" Zagloba begged, pressing his hands together as if in a prayer. "Think of the children those two scatterbrains would have!"

"I knew a couple of good men at one time whose mother was a Drohoyovska," the little knight blurted out, giving away much more than he intended. "And both of them were great soldiers, as I recall..."

"Ha!" cried Zagloba. "Now I've got you! So that's the road you're taking?"

But at this unwanted self-betrayal, Pan Volodyovski lost whatever poise he had. His whiskers twitched violently up and down as he struggled to cover up his naive admission.

"What are you saying?" he mumbled at last. "I'm not taking one road or another. It's just that when you mentioned Basia's temperament which, I grant you, is as spirited as any cavalier's, I thought at once of Krysia whose nature is far more feminine. When you hear about one of them, the other comes quite naturally to mind because they're always together."

"Alright then! Alright! God bless you with Krysia, though if I were still in the marriage market I'd fall head over heels for *the little warrior*. You don't have to leave a wife like that at home when you go to war. She can ride beside you, and sleeping in a tent will suit her just fine! And when it's time for her to give birth to a baby, even if it's in the middle of a battle, she'll do what she has to with one hand, and she'll be firing a musket with the other. And how good she is, how honest...!"

"Hey, my sweet little warrior!" the old knight cried sadly. "They don't appreciate you around here! They don't know what they're missing, I'm sorry to say! But if I were sixty years younger I'd know whom to make my Mrs. Zagloba!"

"I'm not saying anything against her!" the little knight protested.

"It's not a question of you saying anything but of doing something. But you prefer Krysia!"

"Krysia is my friend."

"A friend but not a girl-friend, is that it? That must be because she has a mustache. I'm your friend! Skshetuski is your friend! You don't need another friend, you need a good woman. Knock that into your head once and for all and stop fooling yourself. Guard yourself, Michal, from friendships with women, even those with whiskers, because either you'll betray her or she'll betray you. The Devil doesn't sleep, mark my words, and he's always glad to sit among such friends. Adam and Eve are your best example because when they got friendly poor Adam just about choked on the apple she fed him."

"Don't you say a thing against Krysia, you hear?" the little knight cried out. "I won't stand for that!"

"Who's saying anything against her? Let God take care of her and all her good intentions. She's a fine girl, though there's no one like the little warrior! All I want to say is that your face turns red when you sit beside her, and you twitch your whiskers like a bug in May, and your hair stands on end you are so excited, and you shuffle your feet and paw the ground like a stallion trotted out to pasture, and that has nothing to do with any kind of friendship! Tell those fairy stories to somebody else because I'm an old bird at this game."

"So old that you're seeing things that aren't even there..."

"I wish I didn't! I wish you'd feel like that about my little warrior. But goodnight, Michal. It's time I went. Sleep well. Take the little warrior, she's prettier! Take the little warrior, I tell you, take the little warrior...!"

And with this, Zagloba rose and left.

★ ★ ★

But Pan Michal didn't sleep well that night. He tossed about. Troubling thoughts darted through his mind. Drohoyovska's face hung before him wherever he turned, along with her eyes fringed with their long lashes, and the soft down along her upper lip. From time to time he drifted into sleep but the images didn't leave him even for a moment.

Waking, he thought of Pan Zagloba's words and remembered how seldom that man's wits had failed in the past. Sometimes Basia's pink face glimmered in the darkness, suspended for a moment between his consciousness and sleep, and this gave him rest.

But Krysia replaced her almost immediately and his sleeplessness returned. Whether he turned to the wall or to the darkness of his room he could see her eyes, full of dreamy welcome. Sometimes they closed, as if in submission. He almost heard her voice saying *'Thy will be done.'* And then the little knight would sit up on his bedding and make the sign of the cross over his chest and shoulders.

By dawn the last vestiges of sleep left him altogether. He was depressed and listless. Anusia's white, dead face rose up for a fleeting moment in his memory. He felt ashamed, and cursed himself bitterly for failing to keep that poor lost love faithfully in his heart, and for filling his eyes, mind and soul with those unnerving images of a living girl. He was sure that he had sinned against Anusia's memory, so he shook himself once or twice, jumped out of bed, and started on his morning prayers even though it was still dark in the room around him.

"I'd best leave as soon as I can," he told himself once the prayers were said. "Pan Zagloba could be right again. I've got to put a stop to that budding friendship."

After which, much calmer and in a better frame of mind, he went down to breakfast.

Chapter Twelve

THE FIRST DAY of Pan Michal's new determination passed almost entirely with Basia. He gave her another fencing lesson after breakfast and, for the first time, noticed how eye-catching the girl really was, how pretty in her breathlessness and excitement, and how captivating with her small, flared nostrils and her heaving breast.

He avoided Krysia.

She noticed it, of course, and her glances followed him about, wide with surprise and questions, but he avoided contact even with her eyes. He hated himself for doing it but did it anyway.

After the midday meal he took Basia to the storehouse where Ketling kept a whole armory of captured weapons, showed her the most unusual of them, and explained their use. Then they spent the afternoon in target practice with Astrakhan longbows. The girl was so delighted with this entertainment that she became even more rattle-brained and mercurial than before until, at last, Madame Makovyetzka had to put a stop to her frivolity.

The second day passed in much the same way. On the third day Pan Michal and Zagloba rode over to Warsaw, to the Danilovitch Palace where Pan Sobieski maintained his head-quarters, to pin down the little knight's departure date, and Pan Michal announced to the women when they returned for dinner that he'd be leaving no later than a week.

He said it lightly, in an offhand manner, and he didn't even look in Krysia's direction.

Alarmed by his coldness, she tried to ask him about this and that, and while he was polite enough in his replies he spent more time with Basia. Pan Zagloba, thinking that all this was due to his advice, rubbed his hands with glee. But because his sharp eyes never missed a thing, he noticed Krysia's sadness.

"She's upset," he muttered to himself. "She's really hurting, you can see it written all over her face. Well, that's too bad, but that's how it is with women. They take things to heart. I've got to admit that Michal changed course faster than a wind-spout and a lot sooner than I thought he would. He's a great fellow but he's always been impulsive in his love-life and he always will be!"

But because under all his posturings and bluster Pan Zagloba was really a warm, kind-hearted man, he felt sorry for the slighted girl.

"I won't say anything to her *directe,*" he told himself at once. "But I'll have to think of something to make her feel better."

What he did was take advantage of the privileges accorded to him by his venerable years, came up to her as she sat alone after supper, and began to stroke her glossy black hair with the affection he'd show a troubled child. He said nothing and she said nothing to him. But she raised her gentle eyes towards him with a look of gratitude.

Later that night, at the door of Volodyovski's room, the fat knight elbowed his small friend sharply in the side and gave him a wink.

"I was right, wasn't I?" he grinned. "There isn't anybody like the little warrior!"

"She's a pleasant snippet," said Volodyovski. "She can cause more turmoil in the house than a squad of troopers. A real fire-spitting drummer boy!"

"A drummer boy, is she? Heh heh heh! Let's hope she'll be carrying your drum pretty soon!"

"Goodnight, sir!" Volodyovski said.

"Goodnight! Women are strange creatures, don't you think? Did you notice how upset Krysia was today just because you got a little closer to Basia?"

"No! I didn't notice!"

"She looked quite stunned, poor thing. You'd think somebody beaned her with a hammer!"

"Goodnight!" Volodyovski said again and stepped into his room.

★ ★ ★

But Pan Zagloba had made a serious error. He had been counting on the little knight's well-known affinity for changing his affections, but he'd been clumsy in mentioning Krysia's anguish, and Pan Michal felt so guilty and upset about it that he started feeling like a criminal.

"What's the matter with me?" he muttered, disgusted with himself. "Is this the way to pay her for her kindness, and for the trouble she took to make me feel better?"

Puzzled by the way his plan was turning out, he started wrestling with his thoughts all over again.

"But what is it that I've actually done? I've slighted her, that's what! I've ignored a sweet, decent girl for three whole days, which is a rude and cruel thing to do in any event. And why did I do that? Because she wanted to heal my wounds for me?"

He cursed himself, angry to have shown such ingratitude, and sorry to have behaved so badly.

"If I at least knew how to keep it all in some kind of proportion," he accused himself, "and to cool down the friend- ship without making her feel abandoned and ignored! But it looks as if my wits are too dull even for that much..."

The more he thought about it the angrier he became. Pity for Krysia took precedence over all his senses. He started thinking of her as a precious, gentle and beloved being who had been badly injured through no fault of her own, and his anger with himself mounted to a rage.

"I'm a crude savage!" he hissed over and over. "A real *barbarus*! A primitive barbarian!"

And then his anger turned against poor Basia who hadn't done a thing to injure anyone.

"Let her go to whoever wants her!" he snarled. "Let her go to Novovyeyski or the Devil, for all that I care. What do I want with that restless, rattle-brained chit? That frivolous tomboy?"

Before the night was over Krysia's image quite overshadowed Basia in his mind, and it never even occurred to him that he might be hurting Basia far more with his anger than he hurt Krysia with his pretended distance and indifference.

* * *

She, in the meantime, had come to some conclusions of her own. Her instincts told her very quickly that Pan Michal was going through some important changes. She was both flustered and dismayed that he seemed to be avoiding her but, at the same time, she realized that a serious change had entered their relationship. Their former friendship would never be the same again. It would either climb to new and warmer heights or it would shrink and dwindle into nothing.

This made her anxious for some resolution, and this anxiety pierced her all the deeper because Pan Michal was leaving so soon. She'd never fallen in love with anyone before, and her feelings for the little knight were still more sisterly than passionate, but she felt closer to him than she'd ever felt to any other man. She was certainly ready to love and to be loved by someone, and he could have turned her head just a little.

Perhaps she had been a bit overwhelmed. Volodyovski was one of the most famous soldiers of his time. Every noble in the Commonwealth spoke of him with immense respect. His sister praised his decency to high heavens, he was cloaked in all the drama of misfortune, and in addition, living with him under the same hospitable roof, Krysia had got accustomed to the way he looked.

Moreover, it was her nature to like to be loved, so that her self-image suffered heavily when Pan Michal started treating her so coldly a few days before. But, being basically a good and caring person, she didn't get angry or impatient in her disappointment; on the contrary, she decided to win him over with gentleness and kindness.

This came all the easier to her because, the next day, Pan Michal wore a hangdog look, no longer avoided her company, and stared into her eyes as if to say: *'Forgive me! I shunned you yesterday but today I'm sorry.'* This and the many other messages he sent with his glances brought the blood surging into Krysia's face and her anxiety sharpened even more. She knew that something important would happen very soon.

It did that afternoon.

Madame Makovyetzka took Basia to Warsaw to call on one of Basia's kinswomen, the wife of the Chamberlain of Lvov, who

was spending some time in the capital. Krysia developed a
convenient headache to stay behind in the manor because she
was suddenly impelled to discover what she and Pan Michal
might say to each other once they were alone.

True, Pan Zagloba also stayed behind. But he'd become
accustomed to taking a nap in the afternoon, which sometimes
lasted for several hours, because—as he said it—an after-dinner
snooze protected him from lethargy and sloth and fired up his
wits for the evening pastimes.

In this respect he was even better than his word. He put on
his usual amusing performance for an hour or so, babbling about
this and that to Krysia and Volodyovski, and started getting
ready to go to his room.

Krysia's heart seemed to miss a beat. The moment was coming. But, once again, she was to be sorely disappointed because
Pan Michal leaped to his feet as soon as Zagloba stirred to leave
and followed him outside.

'*He'll come back soon,*' she thought.

She took up her embroidery frame and bent over her needle-
point. It was a new crown for a cap which she was working in
gold thread for Pan Volodyovski. Her eyes lifted every other
moment to the tall Gdansk clock that ticked gravely in the
corner of Ketling's sitting room.

But an hour passed, and another followed, and Pan Michal
showed no sign of coming back.

"He's afraid," she murmured, laid her embroidery on her
knees and folded her hands across it. "It's going to take him
some time to drum up his courage. Meanwhile the others might
come back and we won't get to say anything to each other. Or
Pan Zagloba might wake up..."

She was quite sure at this point that they were to discuss
something really urgent which Volodyovski's hesitation would
delay indefinitely.

At last, however, she heard his footsteps in the adjoining
room.

"He's pacing, "the girl told herself and bent once more over
her needlework.

★ ★ ★

The little knight was, indeed, pacing the floor and trying to calm himself enough to go in and face her. He circled the room like a captive bear but he couldn't make himself open the door between them. In the meantime the sun started to turn crimson and dipped towards the west.

"Sir Michal!" Krysia called out.

He entered and found her at her needle-point.

"Did you call me, my lady?" he asked.

"I wanted to make sure it wasn't some stranger walking about in there... I've been sitting alone here for two hours..."

Volodyovski brought a chair closer and perched on its edge. There was another long, wordless moment. He sat in silence, fidgeting a little, and trying to hide his feet under his chair while his whiskers twitched nervously up and down. Krysia put down her work and looked up at him and then they both looked down when their glances met. The last slanting beams of the sun fell across her face, edging her hair with gold, and when he raised his eyes to her again he almost gasped at how beautiful she seemed.

"You're leaving in a few days, then?" she asked so softly that he barely heard her.

"That's how it has to be."

"I thought, in the last day or two," she said after another pause, "that you were angry with me..."

"Nothing of the kind!" cried Volodyovski. "I wouldn't be able to face you if that was the case."

"What was it, then?"

"Let me be honest about it," he said, fumbling for his words. "Honesty is always better than glib, fancy phrases... But I don't know how to say how grateful I am for your kindness and for all the peace you've poured into my heart!"

"I wish it could always be like that," Krysia said and crossed her hands once more on her embroidery frame.

"Ah, if it only could!" Pan Michal nodded, resigned into sadness. "If it only could! But Pan Zagloba told me that friendship with women is a dangerous thing. Forgive me, but I'm speaking as openly as if I were confessing to a priest. Because—well, as he put it—there may be a far different feeling hidden under it, like hot coals under ashes. And I thought that he could be right. He usually is. And—again, I ask you to forgive me because I'm just a rough, simple soldier, without the smooth words to dress up what I say—I'm sick to death at the way I've shunned you in the last few days... I simply can't stand it any longer!"

Pan Michal's pointed little mustache was now twitching with the desperate fierceness of a panicked beetle. Krysia lowered her head and two small tears rolled down from under her lashes.

"If you'd rather that I weren't like a sister to you," she murmured. "If it would make things easier for you... then I'll hide my feelings."

But the sight of those two tears seemed to rip Pan Michal's heart apart altogether and he jumped up toward Krysia and seized both her hands. The round embroidery frame slipped off her knees and rolled into the middle of the room, but the small knight paid no attention to anything around him. He pressed those warm, velvet-soft hands to his lips and begged her to stop crying.

"Don't cry, milady!" he said over and over. "Don't cry! For God's sake don't cry!"

He went on covering her hands with hot, desperate kisses even when she tore them out of his grasp and laced them on top of her head, keeping them locked there in a flurry of sudden fear and dismay. Indeed he kissed them all the harder, while the warmth beating from her hair and forehead flooded all his senses as if he were drunk.

Then, not even knowing how or when it happened, his lips were on her forehead; then he was kissing her closed, tear-wet eyes, and the world seemed to be spinning madly all around him. Then his mouth brushed the soft down on her upper lip, and then their lips joined and pressed passionately together for a silent moment, and that breathless silence stretched on and on while the clock ticked quietly in the corner of the room.

★ ★ ★

But suddenly a door slammed outside, Basia's running footsteps sounded in the hall, and then they heard her voice repeating like a child: "Frost! Frost! Frost!"

Volodyovski leaped away from Krysia like a lynx driven from his prey by the horns of approaching hunters, just as Basia burst noisily into the room, still babbling her childlike "Frost! Frost! Frost!"

But suddenly she tripped over the embroidery frame in the middle of the room. She stopped then, startled and surprised, and shot a puzzled glance at the needle-point, at Krysia and at Volodyovski.

"What's going on here?" she asked. "Were you throwing that thing at each other?"

"Where's... auntie?" Drohoyovska asked, too loud and out of breath, trying to speak in a normal voice and to restore calmness to her breathing.

"Auntie is clambering out of the sleigh," Basia answered quietly, but her voice was suddenly as strange and strained as Krysia's. She threw another quick glance at Krysia and Volodyovski—who, in the meantime, picked up the framed needle-point—spun on her heels and went out of the room.

The round, plump Madame Makovyetzka waddled in just then, Pan Zagloba came downstairs as well, and they started talking about Basia's relative whom she and the Magistrate's Lady had just seen in Warsaw.

"I had no idea she was also Novovyeyski's godmother," said Madame Makovyetzka. "He must have told her something about Basia, because her ladyship teased her mercilessly about him."

"And what did Basia say to that?" Pan Zagloba asked.

"Eh, what would you expect? She can be as blunt as a mallet, and just as direct. She told her ladyship: *'He has no mustache and I'm a rattle-brain. Who knows what either of us wants?'*"

"I know she has a quick tongue in her head," Pan Zagloba answered. "But who can tell what's really on her mind? Women are cunning creatures anyway."

"With Basia what you see is what you get. Besides, I told you that she still hasn't felt God's finger upon her. She is still a child. Krysia is much more aware of her place in life."

"Auntie!" Krysia broke in quickly.

A servant came in just then to announce that supper was ready and waiting and they all trooped to the dining room. But Basia was missing.

"And where's the young lady?" Madame Makovyetzka asked the servant.

"The young lady's in the stable, ma'am. I told her that supper was on the table and she said *'Good!'* and went on to the stable anyway."

"Did something upset her?" Madame Makovyetzka turned to Pan Zagloba. "She was in such good spirits just a while earlier!"

"I'll run out and see," said Pan Volodyovski, quite aware of his guilty conscience.

★ ★ ★

He found her sitting on a bail of straw just inside the stable doors. She was so deep in thought that she didn't even hear him coming in.

"Miss Barbara!" he said, leaning down towards her.

Basia jumped slightly as if wakened from a dream, turned her pink face towards him and looked up at him, and he saw two large, swollen tears shining in her eyes.

"What's wrong, for God's sake?" he cried out. "You're crying?"

"I'm doing nothing of the kind!" she cried out in turn and jumped to her feet. "I wouldn't dream of it! It's just the cold, that's all..."

Her silvery laughter rang out at once as if to turn the whole thing into a joke, but it didn't ring true. Then, to turn Volodyovski's attention elsewhere, she pointed to a barred stall that held the bay stallion given to him by Hetman Sobieski.

"You were saying, sir, that it's too dangerous to go into that stall?" she asked brightly. "Well, now we'll see!"

And before Pan Michal could catch her or stop her she leaped into the cage. The half-tamed animal reared up, backed off, pressed his ears flat against his head, and started stamping the ground with his iron-shod hooves and flaying the air.

"For God's sake! He'll kill you!" Volodyovski shouted and jumped into the cage after her.

But he need not have worried. Basia stood at the horse's head, patting the animal's arched, glistening neck and saying: *"Let him kill me! Let him! Let him!"* while the stallion nuzzled her slumped shoulder with his steaming nostrils and whinnied with pleasure.

Chapter Thirteen

NONE OF VOLODYOVSKI'S restless nights were as bad as the one that followed his encounter with Krysia. The only way he could view his own behavior was as a betrayal of his beloved Anusia. Moreover, he'd abused Krysia's trust, exploited her friendship, made some sort of serious and far-reaching commitment, and acted like a man quite devoid of decency and conscience. Any other soldier would have shrugged the whole thing off, he knew very well; at most he'd have remembered those kisses with amused contentment. But Pan Volodyovski, like any man whose heart and soul were torn with recent loss, had scruples about such things especially since Anusia's death.

So what was he to do about it now?

There were only a few days left before his departure and that would or could put an end to everything. But would his conscience let him simply go away without saying anything to Krysia, leaving her without a word as if she were some chambermaid from whom he'd snatched a kiss? He couldn't stand the thought. It troubled all his notions of honorable behavior. But even as he tossed and turned in his bed that night, racked by all that guilt and anger with himself, the memory of Krysia filled him with a warm, blissful sense of happiness, while the remembered kisses made his heart beat faster.

He hated himself for this urge to dwell on his own sinful satisfactions, but he had no way to stop himself remembering the delights of that stolen moment, even as he took the full weight of blame upon himself.

"I led Krysia to this," he told himself, contrite and ashamed.

"I brought her to this pass. There is no way I can leave without an explanation."

So what was he to do? Ask her to marry him and leave as her fiance?

The answer that his guilty conscience thrust upon him was no answer at all. In his mind's eye he glimpsed the whiteness of Anusia's shroud, and then her lifeless face gleamed like a waxen effigy before him, and she rose up like a wraith before him with her eyes fixed on him in mute accusation.

'*Don't I deserve at least to be remembered?*' she seemed to ask from beyond the grave. '*Haven't I earned your tears? You wanted to become a monk, and to cry over me for the rest of your life, and now you're ready to take up with another woman even before my poor soul's had the time to reach the Gates of Heaven? Couldn't you wait, at least, until I've found my way to my final peace, and no longer looked down upon the Earth in sorrow and remembrance?*'

It seemed then to the little knight that he had gone back on his pledge to that pure lost soul, whose memory he should honor and revere as if it were something irreplaceable and holy. Sorrow, bitterness and self-contempt racked him mercilessly. He wished he were dead.

"Anula, my dearest," he murmured on his knees. "I'll weep for you until my dying day. Yes I will! But what am I to do right now?"

The disappointed wraith offered him no answer, the spectral apparition slipped away like mist from his imagination, and in its place he saw Krysia's dark, warmly glowing eyes. He felt again the touch of that soft, downy upper lip on his, and then a swarm of urges and temptations hissed in his ears like a flight of deadly Tartar arrows.

He'd have managed to overcome his own sensual cravings, he was sure, but he could do nothing against his own conscience. '*You'll do an evil and dishonorable deed,*' it told him bleakly, '*f you go your way and leave this young woman, whom you led astray, to her own guilt and shame.*'

★   ★   ★

His troubled mind swayed back and forth like that all night long, torn between his cravings and temptations and his sense of what was right and required of him, and bringing him nothing except further torment.

He thought at times that he should go at once to Pan Zagloba, whose sharp wits could find a way out of every trouble, confess to everything and ask his advice. Hadn't that wise old man foreseen all of this? Didn't he warn against forming those dangerous *amitiae* with women?

But it was precisely that warning, or his reaction to it, that now gave him pause. Because wasn't it the little knight himself who ordered Pan Zagloba to watch his tongue when he spoke of Krysia? And who was it who had treated the girl with real disrespect? Who was wondering right now if he shouldn't simply go away and leave her, as if she meant no more in his scheme of things than some cheap, passing fancy?

"Ah... if it weren't for that other poor, dear soul," the little knight murmured wretchedly, wrestling with himself. "I wouldn't hesitate even for a minute! I wouldn't have a care in the world! On the contrary, I'd be overjoyed at getting a sample of such rare delights which I wouldn't mind sampling a hundred times more...!"

But then he clamped his hand across his mouth. Such musing was sure to toss him back into temptation. He shook himself like a wet dog shedding drops of water, struggled out of the pleasures of his imagination, and tried to reason his way out of his dilemma.

'Alright,' he thought. 'What's happened has happened. Since I've behaved like a man who wants more than friendship, then that's the road I'll take. And I'll ask Krysia to marry me the first thing tomorrow.'

This led to another long moment of pondering, and also of some pleasant speculations, but his decision seemed to make everything permissible and clear.

"A decent, honorable proposal will take care of today's improprieties,"he assured himself. "And... it'll let me commit a few more straight away!" And then slammed himself in the mouth with an open palm.

"'*Tfui!*' he spat in disgust. "What's the matter with me? There must be a whole *tchambul* of devils scratching behind my collar!"

But once made, his decision to propose remained through the night. He reasoned calmly that if this slighted the memory of his

lost Anusia, he'd make amends to her with prayer and Masses for
her soul, which would testify to his continuing loyalty and
affection at the same time.

Besides, he thought, even if people laughed at him for trying
to become a monk just a few weeks ago, and now running to
another woman with offers of marriage, the embarrassment
would be his alone. Otherwise he's have to share the jokes, jibes
and sly malicious gossip with that dear, caring and considerate
young girl who hadn't done anything to earn them.

'*Alright then,*' he thought. '*I'll propose tomorrow and that'll be
that.*'

This brought him a considerable measure of peace. He said his
prayers, begged God to look kindly on Anusia's soul, and fell
sound asleep.

★ ★ ★

Awake at dawn, he repeated his determination. "I'll propose
today...!"

But this wasn't easy.

Pan Michal didn't want to blurt out his proposal in front of
everyone. He wanted to talk it over privately with Krysia and
then do whatever seemed best to both of them. Unfortunately
for him, Novovyeyski arrived first thing in the morning and
seemed to be everywhere at once for the rest of the day.

Meanwhile, Krysia looked as if she were ill. She was as white
as a sheet. Occasionally she broke into a scarlet flush of such
intensity that it spread like fever across her neck and shoulders.
She seemed exhausted; her eyes had a dazed, sleepy quality; and
she kept looking at the floor as if unable to meet anybody's eyes.
At times her lips trembled as if she were about to burst into tears.
At other times she seemed barely conscious as if she were
drifting in a dream.

It was hard, under all these circumstances, for the little knight
to approach her and then to stay with her for any length of time.
The crisp December day was sunny and clear, and he could have
taken her for a stroll outside as he had many times before. He'd
have done that without a second thought if their relationship
remained what it had been. But now, he thought, everyone
would guess his intentions, so he didn't dare.

Luckily for him, Novovyeyski came to his assistance. He

asked for a private talk with Madame Makovyetzka and had a lengthy conference with her in another room. But when they came to where Pan Michal and Zagloba sat with the young women, Madame Makovyetzka suggested that "the two young couples" should go on a sleigh ride.

"Why don't you?" she asked. "It's crackling fine weather. The snow's so fresh and crisp it's sparkling in the sun."

"I beg you, milady" Volodyovski whispered at once into Krysia's ear. "Ride with me. I have a lot to say."

"Very well," she nodded.

Pan Michal and Novovyeyski hurried to the stables with Basia close behind them, and a pair of light running sleighs drew up at the manor a few moments later. Krysia and Volodyovski took one of them and Novovyeyski and the little warrior climbed into the other. Since each of the men acted as his own driver, they rode away with their privacy assured.

"Pan Novovyeyski has asked for Basia's hand," Madame Makovyetzka told Zagloba as soon as the pair of sleighs had swept out of sight.

"How's that?" the old knight was immediately alarmed.

"His godmother, who is the wife of the Lord High Chamberlain of Lvov, will come here tomorrow to speak to me formally about it. In the meantime Pan Novovyeyski asked if he could sound out Basia on his own, even if it's only indirectly. He's a bright young man, and he understands that if she doesn't care for him then all these formal chats and applications would just waste everybody's time."

"Hmm. And that's why your ladyship sent them off sleigh riding?"

"That's why. My husband is a thoughtful and considerate man. He often told me: *'I'll take care of their properties while they're in my keeping. But let each of them pick the husband she likes best. All I care about is that they be good, decent men even if they can't match the girls coin for coin and acre for acre.'* Besides, they're both old enough to make their own decisions."

"And what do you intend, ma'am, to tell her ladyship tomorrow?"

"My husband is due here in May. I'll let him do all the serious talking. But I'm sure it's going to be the way Basia wants it, because that's the only way it can be with that girl."

"Novovyeyski is still a barefaced youngster!" the old knight protested.

"But Michal himself says he's a splendid soldier who's already earned his spurs several times over. He is well settled on good property, and as for his family connections, his godmother told me all about them! You see, it all began like this. His great grandmother was a daughter of Prince Syenutovski. Her son was first married to..."

"What do I care about his family trees?" Pan Zagloba burst out, too upset to care about politeness. "He's neither this nor that as far as I'm concerned, and no kin to anybody that I want to know! I don't mind saying that I've already picked the little warrior for Michal, because if there's a better and more honest girl on two feet anywhere on earth, then I'll go about on all fours like a bear from now on!"

"Michal is still far from thinking about marriage," said Madame Makovyetzka. "But even if he does, it's Krysia who seems to have caught his eye... Ha! It's all up to God, anyway, and His judgments are beyond our question."

"Maybe so. But I'll get drunk with joy like I've never been drunk before, if that barelipped whipper-snapper gets the gate as he ought to," added Pan Zagloba.

★ ★ ★

Meanwhile the fates of the two knights were being decided in the sleighs. Pan Volodyovski struggled a long time to find the right words.

"Don't think, milady," he began at last, "that I'm some shallow, irresponsible jack-in-the-box, who pops out of nowhere with a wild notion, and doesn't think about what he's doing. I'm too old for that."

Krysia kept silent, waiting.

"Forgive me for what I did yesterday," he struggled on. "That came from such powerful feelings that I didn't know how to cope with them... Milady!"—and he cleared his throat, and dropped as much of the formality as he dared—"My dearest and beloved Krysia...! Note, if you would, that I'm a simple soldier, not a courtier, and that I spent the best part of my life in the field, tracking the Tartars in the Steppe, not bowing and scraping in someone's antechambers... Yes, I know, anyone else would put on a show of manners, and try to dazzle you with all his fancy phrases, and then move to action. Well, with me it came the other way around! Remember that even a well-trained horse can take the bit and carry off its rider, so how much more likely it is for love to do the same thing? Especially since it's so much more powerful than a bolting mustang? That's what it was yesterday, you see. That's why I got swept away like that, because I care for you so much...

"Ah, my dearest Krysia!" he burst out. "You could pick among senators and castellans, nobody is too high for you. But if you won't look down in disdain at a simple soldier—who may not have two coins to rub together, but who served his country honestly and with all his heart and earned some respect—then I'd throw myself on my knees before you and ask: '*Will you have me?*' Can you even think about me without revulsion and contempt?"

"Sir Michal...!" Krysia whispered in reply, and then her hand slipped out from under the fur wraps and hid in his own.

"You'll have me then?" asked Volodyovski.

"Yes!" she replied firmly. "And I know I wouldn't find a better or more noble man anywhere in Poland!"

"God bless you, sweetheart!" he cried out and covered her hand with kisses. "God reward you! Nothing could make me happier! Just tell me that you're not angry with me for yesterday so I'll feel less miserable about it!"

Krysia half-shut her eyes. "I'm not angry," she said.

"Damn these sleighs anyway!" Volodyovski shouted. "There's never a way in them to fall at anybody's feet!"

They rode in silence for a time, saying nothing, and only the hiss of the sleigh runners in the snow and the spattering of frozen soil thrown back by the hooves broke into their stillness.

"I'm just surprised that you could care for me," Volodyovski admitted at last.

"It's even more of a surprise to me that Pan Michal could love me so quickly...!" Krysia answered softly.

"Yes, dearest,"—Volodyovski's radiant face grew somber and thoughtful—"it may seem to you that it all comes too fast... that I've fallen in love with one girl even before I've buried my grief for another. I'll also confess to you that I wasn't exactly constant

in my affections when I was a youngster. But that's another
story. No, my dearest girl, I haven't forgotten about that other
poor dear soul and I never will. I love her to this day and you'd
be moved yourself if you knew how many tears I still save for
her..."

★ ★ ★

Here the little knight's voice cracked with feeling. He turned
his face away for a moment, and perhaps that's why he failed to
notice that his words didn't seem to have much effect on Krysia.

"I'll do my best to keep consoling you," she said.

"That's why I fell in love with you so quickly," the little
knight confided. "Because you helped to soothe my pain from
the first few days. What was I to you then? Not a thing! But you
started caring for me straight away, and making my life easier,
and that's why I owe you so much I can hardly say it. People
who don't know about this might think badly of me. I mean
there I was, all set to be a monk in November and here I'm
talking marriage in December. Pan Zagloba will have a field day
for his jokes and jabs because he never misses a chance to have
his fun with people. But let him joke as much as he wants! I
don't care about that, especially since I'll be the butt of his
humor, not you..."

But at this point Krysia started staring thoughtfully at the sky.

"Must we tell everyone about our engagement?" she asked
finally.

"What do you mean?"

"Well," she said with that third-person formality she maintained throughout. "Pan Michal is leaving in a few days..."

"I've no choice about that."

"I'm also wearing mourning for my father. Why give people
a chance to raise their eyebrows at us? Let our decision stay our
secret until Pan Michal comes back from Ruthenia... Don't you
think that's a good idea?"

"But shouldn't I say something to my sister?"

"I'll tell her myself after you are gone."

"What about Pan Zagloba?"

"He'd only poke fun at us if he knew about it. It's best to keep
him in the dark for a little longer. Basia would also play little
tricks on me, and she's been in an odd mood in the last few days,

blowing hot and cold for no good reason like never before, as changeable as the weather. Ah, it's best not to tell anybody anything."

And here Krysia raised her deep blue eyes skyward once again.

"God is our witness," she said. "People don't need to know."

"I see that you've thought it out very carefully," said Volody-ovski. "Alright, I agree! Let God be our witness! Now lean against me, dearest, come a little closer. There's nothing wrong with that now that we're engaged. And don't worry! I can't repeat yesterday's behavior no matter how I'd want to because I need both hands for the horses!"

She did as he asked and he soon said to her again: "I suppose we'd better keep things formal with the others. But why don't you call me by my Christian name when we are alone?"

"I don't know," she said, smiling at him warmly. "I just don't seem to be able to do it."

"I'm doing it," he said.

"That's because Pan Michal is a soldier," she said. "Because he has courage..."

"Krysia! My dearest...!" he cried out.

"Mich..." she began but couldn't finish it and hid her face behind the upraised edge of her traveling robe.

★ ★ ★

Soon afterwards Pan Michal turned for home. They didn't say much more to each other the rest of the way. But he asked one more question as they were driving through the gates.

"About yesterday," he said. "You know... Were you terribly upset about it?"

"I felt upset," she said. "And sad. But also strange and different..."

And, at once, they dressed their faces in polite indifference so that no one at the manor would be able to spot that anything had happened between them. But they need not have gone to any trouble. No one was paying them the slightest attention. Pan Zagloba and Madame Makovyetzka ran out into the hall to greet the two returning couples, but they had eyes only for Basia and Novovyeyski.

Basia was flushed bright crimson, either with feeling or the cold, and Novovyeyski looked as if he'd swallowed a plateful of poison.

He started taking his leave of the Magistrate's Lady right there in the hallway, even though she tried her best to get him to stay. Volodyovski, who was as pleased and happy as a bridegroom, also urged him to join them for dinner, but he excused himself with duty and rode away quickly.

Madame Makovyetzka kissed Basia on the forehead without another word, and the girl flew off to her room and didn't come back until dinnertime.

It wasn't till the next day that Pan Zagloba cornered her and asked: "So what happened yesterday, my little warrior? Hmm? Young Novovyeyski looked as if he'd been struck by lightning."

"Maybe he was!" she said.

"So what did you tell him?"

"He's a straightforward lad, and quick to the point, so he didn't waste any time in asking. But I don't like to beat about the bush either, so I told him right away the answer was No!"

"God bless you!" the old knight cried out, overjoyed. "Let me hug you! That's the way to do it! But didn't he have anything else to say?"

"He asked if I could change my mind with time. I felt sorry for him but a No is a No! It just can't be any other way!"

Thoughtful, but strangely saddened at the same time, Basia shook her head with such firm conviction that her mop of hair tumbled down across her eyes, and her sharp little nostrils flared with determination.

"Could you... ah... tell me why you did that?" Pan Zagloba asked.

"That's what he wanted to know too. But there's no point in anybody asking. I didn't tell him and I won't tell anybody else!"

"Hmm..." Pan Zagloba peered sharply into her oddly sad and troubled eyes. "Could it be that there's some other affection hidden in your heart?"

"A fig for all affections!" she cried out, and flushed like a child caught redhanded in some kind of mischief.

Then she jumped to her feet as if a whirlwind had swept her from her chair and started babbling rapidly to hide her confusion: "I don't want Pan Novovyeyski! I don't want Pan Novovyeyski! I don't want anyone! Why don't you leave me alone, sir? Why won't everybody just leave me alone...?"

And she burst angrily into sudden, bitter and unexpected tears.

Pan Zagloba soothed and consoled her as best he could but she stayed sad and angry for the rest of the day.

However during dinner, the old knight said lightly to Volodyovski: "You're leaving, Michal, and Ketling will come back while you're away, and he's a handsome devil! I don't know how our young ladies will manage with him here, but I've a feeling you'll find them both head over heels in love when you've come back home."

"Excellent!" said Volodyovski. "We'll make a match for him with Panna Basia straight away!"

But Basia fixed him at once with a stare as sharp and piercing as a lynx. "Why don't you show such kind concern for Krysia?" she demanded.

The little knight flushed and lost his aplomb altogether and managed merely a weak rejoinder in return. "You don't know the power of Ketling's charm, milady," he mumbled at last. "But you'll get to feel it."

"And why won't Krysia feel it? I'm not the one who sings about poor, weak women who can't protect themselves from Cupid and his arrows!"

Then it was Krysia's turn to flush with embarrassment and to drop her eyes, but the small gadfly wasn't finished with her yet.

"I'll borrow an old shield from Pan Novovyeyski if I can't think of anything better for myself," she said to Volodyovski. "But I don't know what Krysia will use for protection, sir, once you are away."

But, in the meantime, Pan Volodyovski had pulled himself together. "Perhaps she'll find something that'll serve her better than anything you can do, young lady," he said somewhat sternly.

"And why's that?" she asked.

"Because she's less scatterbrained than you, she is more grown-up, and she has a deeper and more thoughtful mind."

Pan Zagloba and Madame Makovyetzka thought at once that the quick-tongued, combative little warrior would pick up the challenge and do instant battle, but—to their amazement—she only let her head droop sadly towards her breast, fixed her eyes on her plate like an admonished child, and said in a soft voice after a short silence:

"If I've offended you sir, I'd like to say I'm sorry. To you and to Krysia."

Part III

Chapter Fourteen

PAN MICHAL HAD leave to choose any road he wished on his journey to Lower Podolia, so he took the long way round, riding by way of Tchenstohova and Anusia's grave, where he shed the last of his tears before heading east into the vast, open spaces of Ruthenia.

His visit to Anusia's grave brought her vividly to his mind again, and shadowed his thoughts at each step of the way, so that he started thinking that his secret engagement to Krysia had been premature. He felt that there was something holy in sorrow and remembrance—something which should never be disturbed—and that grief should be borne in patience, and endured as simply as if it were the inescapable will of God, until it lifted on its own like a morning mist and dispersed invisibly in the sky.

Others, he knew, when widowed, remarried within a month or two, but that was not for him. They didn't start from a deep retreat into a monastery, nor did their tragedies strike them on the threshold of a happiness that they had longed for anxiously for years. And anyway, he reasoned, why should he follow the example of crude, unfeeling simpletons who didn't know how to honor the sanctity of mourning?

He made his long way deep into Ruthenia, and a troubled conscience rode with him through each mile of the road. He had never been much of a philosopher, but he was fair enough to take all the guilt and responsibility on himself and laid no blame on Krysia. Indeed, foremost among his many worries was the thought that she too might think badly of him because of that hurry.

"She wouldn't have done that in my place," he told himself. "And never on her own. Having a great and noble soul, she's sure to expect a great soul in others."

And then it seemed to him that he must appear to her as poor and puny in his heart and spirit, as he was small and insignificant in body.

*   *   *

As it happened, these fears were quite groundless. Pan Michal's mourning didn't affect Krysia as much as he supposed; in fact it annoyed her when he talked overmuch about it.

Krysia, as this narrative has noted, liked to be loved, and resented sharing his attentions with a ghost. Wasn't she worth at least as much as the dead Anusia? Or was she worth so little that she had to compete with a memory? If Pan Zagloba had been let into their secret he'd have assured Pan Michal that women have remarkably little mercy on each other.

Nevertheless, Krysia was quite astounded by everything that happened, and walked about in a daze after he went away, not quite able to believe that this was now forever.

On her way to Warsaw, which she had never visited before, she imagined something altogether different. The city, she was sure, would be full of brilliant courts and households belonging to the various dignitaries and bishops coming for the election and the convocation. A glittering knighthood would hurry there from every corner of the Commonwealth. There'd be no end to balls, tourneys and other entertainments, and—in all of this excitement and activity—she'd meet the kind of fascinating stranger that young girls see only in their dreams. He'd fall desperately in love with her, play the zither under her windows, stage countless cavalcades for her entertainment and wear her favor on his shining armor, and only then—after he overcame innumerable obstacles, loved her long and faithfully, and suffered through a long period of unrequited sighing—he'd fall at her feet and win her affections.

But none of that happened.

The rainbow mists of her imagination blew away and her knight turned out to be nothing like she expected. True, he was widely admired and respected. His name was on every lip. He was revered everywhere as the First Soldier of the Commonwealth and a great cavalier, but he was nothing like that anticipated stranger. Nor were there any cavalcades, tourneys, and ballads at her window. None of her ribbons were pinned to anybody's armor. There were no grand balls and no crowds of splendid knights swarming everywhere around her, nor was there anything that creates that gossamer, fairy-tale aura which captures the imagination, overwhelms the senses, sends the blood rushing hotly to the face and makes the heart beat faster.

All she'd had was a country house with Pan Michal in it. Then there came one unguarded moment, a single unexpected intimacy, and that was that! There'd be nothing more. The rest was gone, lost and extinguished like a moon swallowed by the clouds, never to return.

Ah, if at least this Pan Volodyovski had come to her after all the other things she'd dreamed and expected, she'd have been glad to have him. She had no doubt she loved him. Thinking about his fame, his sense of honor, his honesty and his courage—which made him the glory of the Commonwealth and the terror of all her enemies—she knew she loved him, or admired him, a great deal. It was just that she felt as if something precious had passed her by, or as if he had robbed her in some unknown way; she even thought herself deprived and injured by him, and by the speed with which everything had ended.

★ ★ ★

Thus the haste of their precipitous engagement oppressed both of them, although for different reasons. It was like a small, bothersome grain of sand working within a wound. And because each day put more distance between them, this little grain rubbed and gnawed at both of them and began to fester. Again, had he been consulted, Pan Zagloba might have pointed out that human feelings often were like that, and that some barely perceptible irritation that aches under the skin like a splinter unseen to the naked eye, will either heal or turn into a sore that fills even the greatest love with bitterness and pain.

Pain and embitterment were still far away from each of them. Pan Michal, in particular, relished the thought of Krysia as a source of peace, and her remembered image clung to him like a shadow.

He thought that she'd become even dearer to him the farther he rode away from her, and that he'd long for her and miss her all the more, but that didn't happen. His journey had its own excitements and distractions. Her time, however, lay more heavily upon her. No one came calling at Ketling's manorhouse since the small knight's departure, and the days dragged by in monotony and boredom, and each of them was exactly like the one before. Madame Makovyetzka talked only about her husband, counting the days until the election. Basia sunk into an owlish gloom so that the old knight poked fun at her about missing young Pan Novovyeyski. She too had lost much of her mercurial spirit, and knew that she'd have welcomed even those uninvited visits if they broke the tedium, but he kept away. *'There's nothing there for me,'* he had told himself and prepared to follow Pan Volodyovski.

Pan Zagloba did a lot of muttering about heading back to the Skshetuskis—grumbling that he missed *'the pesky little scamps,'* as he called the Skshetuski children—but he put off his departure from one day to another, feeling dull and strangely heavy-hearted, and he teased Basia that it was all her fault. He'd fallen in love with her, he said, and planned to ask for her hand in marriage.

In the meantime, he offered his company to Krysia each time that Basia and Madame Makovyetzka went calling in Warsaw. Krysia never joined them on these visits to Basia's kinswoman because her ladyship frankly couldn't stand her.

However Pan Zagloba also hurried often to the capital—where, as he put it, he was *'obliged to keep in touch with polite society'*—and he'd seldom come back until the next day, often still tipsy after his carousing, so that Krysia spent most of her time with no company at all.

She'd muse then, lonely in her solitude, about Pan Volodyovski, and wonder about all those things that had never happened, and tried to imagine what that unknown stranger might have looked like if the doors hadn't slammed forever on her dreams.

★   ★   ★

So it was that she sat one day alone by the window, plunged deep in thought and staring blindly at the chamber door which seemed to burn with the golden fires of the setting sun, when she suddenly heard the jingle of a sleigh-bell coming from the other side of the house.

It passed through her mind that Basia and Madame Makovyetzka must have returned from Warsaw but she was too absorbed in her lonely musing to give it any further thought. In fact she didn't even lift her eyes away from the glowing doorway which, in the meantime, opened quietly, and the girl's pensive stare fell upon a stranger.

Her first clear thought was that she was looking at a marvelous painting or that she'd slipped into a dream and was now gazing at a miraculous illusion.

She saw a young man dressed in black, Western European costume with a white lace collar falling to his shoulders. As a small child, Krysia had once seen Pan Artishevski, the famous, foreign-trained general of Crown Artillery who had served many years abroad, and whose customary foreign dress and striking good looks stayed for a long time in her memory.

The young man who now stood before her might have been his image except that his beauty far exceeded that of Artishevski, or for that matter, of any other man she had ever seen. His long hair, cut evenly on his forehead, fell in thick, golden locks to his shoulders, framing a face of such stunning beauty that it simply robbed the girl of breath. His dark brows lay perfectly defined on a forehead which seemed to glow as white and pure as marble. His eyes seemed filled with gentleness and a poetic sadness. His golden hair, his pale mustache, and his trim, neatly pointed beard, were as soft and feathery as freshly combed, bleached hemp; his features bore the stamp of manliness and nobility; and his whole face and bearing made him seem both chivalrous and angelic.

Krysia could hardly breathe, unable to tell if she were looking at a man or an apparition. She thought that her eyes were playing tricks on her. He also stood still and speechless for a moment, either astonished by her beauty or making a polite pretense of astonishment. Then he advanced from the door, his plumed hat in his hand, until he stopped before her with the dark ostrich feathers sweeping the floor at her feet in a courtly greeting.

Krysia rose but her legs trembled under her. She closed her eyes, flushing and growing pale by turns, and then she was listening to his voice which seemed as deep and rich and as soft as velvet.

"I'm Ketling of Elgin," he said courteously and quietly. "A friend and comrade of Pan Volodyovski. The servants told me that I've the happiness and inestimable honor to lend my roof to the sister and kinswomen of my dear brother-in-arms. But forgive my confusion, most distinguished lady, because they failed to prepare me for what my eyes are seeing, and what they see quite blinds them with your beauty..."

These were the courtly and poetic phrases with which Ketling greeted Krysia, but she didn't offer him a like compliment in reply, because she couldn't find a word she'd trust herself to say.

Her eyes remained closed.

She guessed, when he finished speaking, that he was bowing to her again because she heard the whisper of his plumes on the hardwood floor. She felt an urgent need to give some sort of answer, to find a compliment that might match his own so that he wouldn't think her foolish and provincial, but there seemed to be no air in her lungs, the pulse was hammering in her arms and temples, and her breast rose and fell as if she were suddenly exhausted.

Eyes ajar at last, she saw him standing bowed slightly before her, with admiration and respect etched in that miraculously handsome face. Her fingers flew to the edges of her gown so that she might at least offer him a courtsey but, luckily for her, a loud shout of *"Ketling! Ketling!"* boomed out in the hall and Pan Zagloba burst into the room with his arms wide open.

★   ★   ★

Ketling and Pan Zagloba threw their arms warmly around each other, and the breathless girl had time to regain her poise while throwing one or two calmer glances at the beautiful young man.

He hugged the old knight with obvious affection but also with that extraordinary courtliness and dignity which marked all his movements, and which he'd either inherited from his high-born ancestors or acquired at the courts of various Kings and magnates.

"How are you?" boomed the overjoyed Zagloba and went on babbling one thing over another as if trying to tell Ketling everything at once. "I'm as glad to see you in your house as I'd be in my own! Let me look at you! Ha! You've lost weight! Are you in love or something? By God but you look poorly! You know, of course, that Michal went back on active service? I'm so glad you're back! He's given up thinking about monasteries, God be thanked, and his sister's here along with two young girls! A couple of ripe little plums but as well-packed as turnips! Ah, for God's sake, Miss Krysia is here! Forgive my outburst, but anybody who'd deny that you two girls are as sweet as peaches had better get himself another pair of eyes, which—as far as your own looks are concerned—is something that this cavalier doesn't need to do."

Ketling inclined his head for the third time in a courtly bow.

"I left my home as barren as a guardhouse," he said with a smile. "And I find it as dazzling as Olympus since the first being I see here is a goddess."

"How are you, Ketling!" the old knight boomed again since one greeting didn't seem like enough to him, and threw his arms around the young man.

"Ah, but wait till you see *the little warrior!* One is as tasty as whipped cream but the other's like a honeycomb! Pure honey, I tell you! Well? Are you pleased with your guests? Madame Makovyetzka stopped off here for a time because an inn is just about impossible to find, but I imagine she'll move out now along with the young ladies... It's awkward for them in a bachelor house, and we don't want gossip."

"For God's sake, no!" Ketling cried at once. "I'll never allow that. I'm Volodyovski's brother as much as a friend so I can receive Madame Makovyetzka in my home as I would a sister!"

And then he turned to Krysia as if in appeal.

"I'll beg you first, my lady, to intercede for me with Madame Makovyetzka, and if I have to do it on my knees then I'll be pleased to do it!"

★   ★   ★

Down on one knee before her, the young knight seized her hand and pressed it to his lips; his eyes pleaded with her with a disconcerting blend of merriment and sadness; and she felt her face flushing once again, especially since Pan Zagloba shouted out at once:

"Look at him! Barely home and he's on his knees before her already! By God, I'll tell Madame Makovyetzka that that's how I caught you...! Sharply, Ketling, sharply...! And you take note, Krysia, on how things are done!"

"I'm not accustomed to such courtesies," the young woman whispered in confusion.

"May I count upon your intercession, then?" Ketling kept on asking.

"Please get up...!"

"But will you speak for me? I'm Pan Michal's brother! He'll feel badly hurt if this house stands suddenly empty and abandoned."

"My wishes don't matter very much," Krysia said with a measure of steadiness and calmness. "But I am deeply grateful, sir, for your kind intentions."

"Thank you!" Ketling said and pressed her hand once more to his lips.

"Ha!" bellowed Pan Zagloba. "The frost outside cuts like rawhide whip, and Cupid runs about without any clothes! But I've a feeling he'd be warm enough if he ever got inside this house!"

"Oh, do be quiet, sir," Krysia begged, embarrassed.

"I can see it already, ho ho! We're in for an early thaw this year with all the warm sighs drifting around here. Nothing but sighs everywhere I turn!"

"I'm glad to see you haven't lost your merry disposition, sir," Ketling said. "That's always a sign of good health."

"And of a clear conscience, my good friend!" Pan Zagloba answered. "And of a clear conscience! Wise maxims say: 'He who itches, scratches!' And since I don't itch anywhere, I'm as pleased as punch! Hey, how are you, Ketling? Ah, but what is this I see? The last time I set eyes on you, you wore a lynx cap with a feather, Polish boots and clothing, and carried a saber, and here you are changed into some kind of Englishman who stalks around on legs like a crane."

"That's because I was in Courland for so long, where you don't see much of Polish dress and manners, and also because I just spent two days with the English minister in Warsaw."

"Ah, so you're just back from Courland, are you?"

"Yes. My adoptive father passed away and left me another property up there."

"May he rest in peace. He was a Catholic, of course?"

"Of course."

"That, at least, must be a relief. But surely you won't turn your back on us for your new Courland possessions?"

"This is the place for me to live and die," Ketling answered simply, looking up at Krysia, and her long eyelashes fell at once to cover her eyes.

Chapter Fifteen

DEEP TWILIGHT had already fallen when Madame Makovyetzka returned from Warsaw. Ketling crossed the courtyard as far as the gate to greet her and to lead her into his house with all the ceremony due a reigning princess.

She wanted to look for lodgings in the city the very next day but her protestations were quite unavailing; the young knight begged, cajoled and pleaded on his knees, calling upon his status as Volodyovski's blood-brother, until she relented and agreed to keep on staying in his house. Her one requirement was that Pan Zagloba should also stay longer so that his age and dignity might shield the women from malicious gossip. He agreed readily enough, having grown very fond of his little warrior, and because he started pondering a certain stratagem which depended on his presence there.

The young women were both pleased to stay; indeed, Basia sided with Ketling from the start.

"We can't move tonight anyway," she told the hesitating Madame Makovyetzka. "And later on it won't make any difference to the gossips if we stay one day or twenty."

She liked Ketling's looks quite as much as Krysia but all women liked him. Besides, she'd never seen a foreign cavalier before. The few Western Europeans she came across here and there in the past were officers of foreign mercenary infantry, who were not particularly highborn and lacked Ketling's polish, so that she walked around him as if he were some sort of rarity never displayed anywhere before, staring at him with the stub-

154

born curiosity of a child, until Madame Makovyetzka had to take the edge off her intrusive snooping with a quiet rebuke.

That didn't stop her from watching him from a distance or questioning the old knight about him.

"What kind of a soldier is he?" she whispered to Zagloba. "I mean, is he any good?"

"You couldn't ask for better," the old man replied. "He's got a great deal of experience, don't you see, because he's been in harness since he was fourteen, which is when he first fought Cromwell's English rebels in defense of the Faith and his King. He's also a highborn noble which you can see from the way he acts."

"Have you ever seen him under fire?"

"A thousand times! He'll stand as still as if it were just another outing in the country. He won't even frown. He might pat his horse's neck now and then and if he says anything it's likely to be some romantic love story."

"A love story? Is it the fashion to tell love stories at such times?"

"What's fashionable is whatever shows indifference to the bullets."

"How about hand-to-hand? Is he as great in a single duel?"

"Ha! A horsefly doesn't sting more fiercely!"

"But can he hold his own against Pan Michal?"

"No. That he can't do."

"Ha!" Basia cried out, proud and pleased, and clapped her hands together. "I knew he wouldn't! I knew it right away!"

"Are you that fond of Michal, then?" Pan Zagloba queried.

Basia gave a violent shake to her tousled hair and then breathed a hushed, regretful sigh. "Fond?" she asked quietly and then shrugged. "I'm glad for him because he's one of ours, not a foreigner, that's all."

"But take note of something else, my sweet little warrior," Pan Zagloba cautioned. "Because if it's hard to find a better man than Ketling on a battlefield, it's even harder to find a smoother courtier. He's a real terror among the women who fall head over heels for his good looks! He's a real expert when it comes to loving!"

"You'd better tell that to Krysia, then," said Basia. "Because that's her field." Then she turned to Drohoyovska and beckoned

her over. "Come here for a second, Krysia!" she called out.
"We've something to tell you!"

"What is it?" Krysia asked.

"Pan Zagloba says that no girl can look at Ketling without
falling for him. I've looked him over from every angle and
nothing's happened yet. D'you feel anything?"

"Baska! Baska!" Krysia said in a pleading tone.

"He caught your eye, did he? Hmm?"

"Be sensible, Basia, will you? Stop prattling such nonsense.
Especially now that Pan Ketling is coming over this way."

★ ★ ★

Krysia hadn't yet had the time to seat herself when Ketling
drew near and asked: "May I join your company?"

"Please do!" said Yezorkovska.

"And may I know what your conversation is about?" he asked.

"Love!" Basia fired without a second thought.

"Really?"

Ketling found a chair beside Krysia. Both he and she kept
quiet and sat unnaturally still. Calm and self-controlled as she
usually was, the young woman found herself strangely shy and
diffident beside this cavalier, so it was up to him to break this
awkward silence.

"Are you really discussing such a winsome and engaging
subject, milady?" he asked her.

"Yes!" Drohoyovska answered in a low voice.

"Nothing would please me more than to hear what you think
about it."

"Forgive me, sir," she answered, looking for refuge in modesty and politeness. "But I lack both the wit and the experience
to say anything worth hearing. It seems more likely that I could
hear something new from you."

"Krysia's right!" Zagloba interrupted. "We're all ears! We're
listening!"

"Ask anything you wish, milady," Ketling said.

He raised his eyes to the ceiling, thought deeply for some
moments, and then—even though no one asked him any questions—he began to speak softly as if to himself.

"Love is a heavy burden," he said and nodded quietly. "Because it turns a free man into a slave. Just as a bird shot on the

wing by a hunter's arrow falls to the ground at its slayer's feet, so a starstruck lover loses all his power to fly away from the dear object of all his affections...

"Love steals the senses," he went on, "because it blinds the lover to the world around him. All he can see and hear and taste and feel is his own great passion...

"Love is a sadness," he murmured as if in his own unhappy resignation. "When else are more tears shed? When do we hear more sighing? He who falls in love loses all his feeling for games, pastimes, dances, dice and hunting... He's quite prepared to sit in contemplation, hugging his own knees, and given over to longing and sentimental musing as if he'd just lost his dearest relative or friend...

" It's also an illness," he sighed again. "A man grows pale when he is in love. He walks about with sunken eyes, talking to the moon; his hands tremble as if in a fever; he becomes drawn and thin and thoughts of death and dying are never far away... Or he'll stare mindlessly around him as if he'd gone mad, scratch that precious name in the sand before him, and then think it a tragedy if the wind blows it all away... And the tears always flow."

★   ★   ★

Ketling fell silent for a long thoughtful moment as if he'd plunged deep into his own reflections, and Krysia savored the echo of his words as if they were poetry and music ringing in her ears.

Her whole soul seemed to stir and lift towards him. Her soft lips parted and her eyes seemed fixed on the young knight's face, entranced with his beauty. Basia's unruly hair had tumbled down right across her eyes so there was no way to tell what she was really thinking but she sat as quietly and as subdued as Krysia.

Only Pan Zagloba seemed unimpressed with Ketling's definitions of love and of loving. He yawned noisily, blew out his breath like a snorting buffalo, stretched his legs out before him as if they'd gone asleep, and grunted:

" You can feed that kind of loving to the dogs!"

" But even so," the young knight resumed his interrupted thought. "If love is a hardship, then it's much harder not to

love at all... Because who'd be satisfied with fame, riches, jewels,
perfumes and every other pleasure or delight, if he never loved?
Who wouldn't want to say to his beloved: *'I'd rather have you
than a kingdom, a throne, my health and the long years of a fine old
age...?'* And since everyone would gladly die for love, then love
is worth more than life itself."

With this, Ketling finished.

The two young women sat quietly, huddled against each
other, entranced by the depth of feeling in his words and by
those strange poetic sentiments, quite foreign to Polish cavaliers,
which were his Western heritage from the age of troubadours
and jousting knight-errants. Pan Zagloba, who had begun to nod
sleepily towards the end, woke suddenly, blinked his eyes, stared
like an owl at all three of them in turn, and finally boomed out
in stentorian tones:

"What are you saying, then?"

"To you sir, we say *'Goodnight!'* Basia said.

"Aha! I remember! We were talking about love. So what did
the discussion amount to in the end?"

"That the lining is better than the coat," Basia told him.

"Ah, it's a dull subject anyway," Pan Zagloba grumbled sleepily. "Hmm... I dropped off a little there with all that crying,
sighing and dying! And I've a couple of other rhymes to go
along with that, like *boring* and *snoring*, which might be the best
of the lot because it's late already. So goodnight to all of you and
let me get away from all this so-called *loving*!

"Tfui!" he went on, struggling to his feet. "A cat meows until
he's gobbled up the bacon and then smacks his lips and grins
from ear to ear... Still, I was just like Ketling in my time—in fact
you'd have taken us for twins if you could've seen us—and I was
so pie-eyed and moonstruck with my loving that a ram could
bang my backside for an hour before I'd pay attention... At my
age, however, I'd rather take it easier, especially if a good host
sees me off to bed and has a nightcap with me."

"I'm at your service," Ketling said at once.

"So let's go, hmm? What do you say? Look how high the
moon has climbed already. It'll be a fine day tomorrow, the
night is as clear as daylight, and Ketling could sit here lecturing

on love until the cows come home. But you two snippets ought to bear in mind that he's had a long, weary trip and he's sure to be quite worn out."

"Not at all," Ketling said. "I've had two good days' rest already in the city. I'm just concerned that the ladies may not be used to sitting up so late."

"The night would pass quickly in listening to you, sir" Krysia said.

"There is no night, milady," he replied immediately, "where a sun is shining."

★   ★   ★

They said goodnight to each other after that and went to their rooms because it really was much later than they were used to staying up and talking.

The two young women shared a room and usually chatted a long time before they fell asleep; but this time Basia, who felt like babbling cheerily until dawn, couldn't get Krysia going no matter what she tried.

Krysia was either quiet or answered her with short, half-hearted phrases, and whenever Basia started giggling about Ketling, thinking up all sorts of sly comparisons and comments about him, poking goodnatured fun at him and imitating some of his words and gestures, she hugged her with more than usual feeling and begged her to stop.

"He's our host here," she reminded Basia. "We're living in his home... And I could see from the start that he's fond of you."

"How could you tell?" Basia asked.

"How could he help it?" Krysia threw her arms around the other girl, hugged her and kissed her fondly. "Everybody loves you. And I do too, more than I can say..."

They finally went to bed but it was a long time before Krysia could close her eyes in sleep.

She was unsettled to the point of fear.

Her heart beat so rapidly now and then that she pressed her hands to her breast to still it. At other times, especially when she tried to close her eyes, it seemed to her that some beautiful, strange face—as thrilling as a miracle and as gentle as a dream—was bowing down towards her, and that a soft voice whispered in her ear:

'I'd rather have you than a kingdom, a throne, my health and the long years of a fine old age.'

Chapter Sixteen

SEVERAL DAYS LATER Pan Zagloba wrote to Pan Skshetuski, warning him not to be surprised if he didn't get home before the election.

'*That's not because I don't care about you,*' he ended his letter, '*but mischief doesn't sleep and I'd rather end up with a bird in hand than a fistful of feathers. It won't be good if I can't tell Michal after he returns: "That other one's taken but the little warrior is ready and waiting." Everything is in God's hand, of course, but it seems to me that Michal won't need any further pushing after that, and that he'll make his move by the time you get here.*

'*Meanwhile, remembering Ulysses, I'll have to use my wits and, perhaps, even lie a little, which won't come easy for me because I've been devoted to truth all my life and, as you know, never veered from it before. But I'll take on even that distasteful burden for the sake of Michal and the little warrior because they're both pure gold.*

'*With which,*' the old knight finished, '*I embrace you both, and press you to my heart along with your scamps, committing you all to God's love and mercy.*'

Done with his letter, Pan Zagloba scattered fine sand over the page to blot and dry the ink, smacked it with his palm to brush off the sand, and read it once more while holding it as far away from his eyes as his arms could reach. Satisfied, he slipped his signet ring off his finger and licked it in preparation to fixing his seal.

That is how Ketling found him.

"Good morning to you, sir," he said, coming in.

"Good morning! Good morning!" Pan Zagloba answered cheerfully, delighted with himself. "The day looks fine, God be praised, and I'm about to send a messenger to Skshetuski."

"Send him my best, will you?"

"I already have. That's the first thing I thought of. *'I've got to send them Ketling's greetings,'* I told myself right off, so that's what I did, especially since the whole letter is about you and our two young ladies. Yan and Helen will both be happy to get some good news."

"You wrote about me and the ladies?" Ketling asked, surprised.

Zagloba placed both hands firmly on his knees, drummed on them with his fingers, cocked his head askew and shot a glance at Ketling from under lowered brows.

"My dear Ketling," he said. "It doesn't take a prophet to anticipate a fire where there's flint and tinder. You're as smooth as silk and the girls are something special too, as I'm sure you've noticed."

Ketling flushed hotly, as if the sly old knight had laid bare all his secret thoughts.

"I'd have to be either blind," he said, embarrassed, "or some kind of a primitive barbarian, not to see and admire their virtues and their beauty..."

"Quite right!" Pan Zagloba boomed, pleased with the tell-tale flush on the young knight's face. "But because you're *not* a *barbarus*, or a Turk who marries a whole harem at a time, you've got to settle on one of them and forget the other!"

"How can you... ah... suppose, sir," Ketling stammered, "that I'd... ah... have anything like that in mind?"

"Suppose? I'm not supposing anything, just thinking aloud. But you've warbled so much about love to those little snippets that Krysia's been walking about for three days as pale and drawn as if she'd taken a purge. I'm not surprised, though! I remember when I was a hot young lover, standing in the cold outside a certain window with a lute in my hands, and singing love songs to a blue-eyed, dark-haired beauty who was a spitting image of Krysia Drohoyovska."

Here Pan Zagloba struck a minstrel's pose and belted out a few lines he composed on the spot.

"There you lie, warm and snoozing,
While I'm freezing to this music.
Hop! Hop!"

"I'll let you use that song if you like," he went on. "Or, if you'd rather, I'll compose another because I've a million of them in my head. But did you notice how much Drohoyovska looks like Billevitchovna? True, she's dark-haired while the other's as fair as bleached hemp, and then there's that little smudge on her upper lip, but a lot of people take that as a mark of beauty and find it exciting. You've made a big impression on her, I see that in her eyes. I've just told Skshetuski all about it. Don't you think she looks like Billevitchovna?"

"I didn't note the likeness at first glance," said Ketling. "But it could be so... Her height and poise are similar..."

"Hmm. Well. Now mark my words because I've something important to tell you. In fact I'm trusting you with a family secret, so to speak. Make sure that you don't spoil things for Michal, because Madame Makovyetzka and I have one of those girls earmarked for him."

Here Pan Zagloba peered sharply and insistently at Ketling who lost some color in his face and asked at once: "Which one?"

"Dro-ho-yovska," the old knight stretched out the name and let it drop like stones, a syllable at a time. Then he thrust out his lower lip and started blinking rapidly with his one good eye.

But Ketling said nothing. In fact his silence dragged on for so long that the old knight had to break it on his own. "Well?" he asked. "What do you say to that?"

Ketling's voice grew thick with disappointment but when he spoke again he did it with conviction.

"You can be sure," he said, "that I won't let my heart lead me anywhere that'll do harm to Michal."

"You're quite sure of that?"

"I am sure. I've suffered a lot in my life," the young knight replied. "But I'll pledge my word: I won't let it happen!"

Zagloba threw his arms wide open to hug him and grinned from ear to ear.

"Ketling!" he cried. "Let it happen! Let it! I was just testing you! The girl we have in mind for Michal is the little warrior, not Drohoyovska at all!"

Ketling's face lit up with relief and joy, he seized the old knight in his arms and held him hard and long.

"They love each other, then?" he asked at last. "There's no doubt about it?"

"Of course they do! They must! Can you think of anyone who wouldn't love that frisky little sweetheart?" Zagloba replied.

"True! So you've already had the betrothal and all that?"

"No, not yet. Michal's hardly had the time to shake off his grief. But we'll have it! Just you let me worry about that! The girl acts like she doesn't know her mind, and she wriggles around like an eel in a lobster pot, but she's head over heels about him because she's a proper little warrior and a good saber is all that counts with her."

"I've noticed that!" Ketling cried, delighted. "As God's my witness, I noticed!"

"Ah! You noticed? Michal's still mourning that other poor woman, but if either of our two young beauties finds her way into his heart it ought to be the little warrior, don't you think? She's more like the one he lost, only she flirts less, being so much younger. Things couldn't be much better, eh? We'll have two weddings here by election time, you just mark my words."

Too moved to speak, Ketling threw his arms again around Pan Zagloba and squeezed him so hard to his chest that the old knight gasped and struggled for his breath.

"Ho!" he wheezed happily. "So Drohoyovska got under your skin so much already, has she?"

"I don't know," confessed Ketling. "I simply don't know. But it was clear to me the moment I set eyes on her angelic beauty that she's the only one my heart could adore, and I spent the whole night sighing for her and thinking about her. She's not been off my mind since then because she's taken over all my thoughts and reigns over them like a queen. If this is love or some other feeling I've no way to tell."

"Ah, but you know it's not a cocked hat, nor a yard of cloth to sew a pair of breeches, nor a set of reins, nor a tail-girth, nor a plateful of scrambled eggs and sausage, nor a vodka bottle. If you're sure of that much then you can ask Krysia about the rest. Or I'll ask for you if you like!"

"Don't do that, sir," Ketling laughed, shook his head and

smiled. "If I'm to drown, then let me think for at least a day or two that I'm still afloat."

"Hmm. I see the Scots are handy on a battlefield," Pan Zagloba said, "but they've a thing or two to learn about making love. You've got to charge straight into the smoke with women, my lad! Just as you'd leap on the enemy! *'Veni, vidi, vici,'* has always been my maxim..."

"If... what I wish for more than anything has the slightest chance," Ketling sighed and said, "I might ask you to intercede for me with Madame Makovyetzka..."

"Don't give it a thought!" Zagloba interrupted. "It's as good as done! Madame Makovyetzka is a real music-box, if you get my meaning. All I've got to do is wind her up the right way and she'll play any tune I want. I'll go see her at once. She's got to be forewarned about your intentions because your Scottish way of doing things—all those *moons* and *Junes!*—is different from our styles of courting, and she might get her back up about it if she doesn't understand what is going on. Of course I won't propose in your name, it's too soon for that, but I'll just let drop a word or two that the girl caught your eye, and that it would be a good thing to knead a tasty loaf out of that sweet flour. I'm off to her right now, as God is my witness, and you don't need to worry about what she'll think. So she'll be hearing about this second-hand, so what? I've every right to tell her whatever's on my mind."

★   ★   ★

Ketling tried to protest and stop him for a moment longer, a little startled and alarmed by the speed with which everything was happening, but Pan Zagloba paid him no attention, leaped to his feet and went off in search of Krysia's guardian.

On his way, he came across Basia who was hurrying somewhere at full tilt as she always did.

"Seems like our Krysia has Ketling standing on his ear," he told her. "His goose is cooked, and there's no doubt about it. He's sunk like a boulder."

"He's not the first," she muttered.

"And you don't care about that?"

"Ketling's a stuffed doll! I'm not saying he's not a smooth

talker and a polished cavalier but he's a prancing puppet anyway, and that's all there's to him."

"So why are you frowning?"

"Because I ran into a wagon tongue out there by the stables," she said, stooped and began to rub her knee as if it really hurt her, and peered up at the old knight watchfully at the same time.

"Be careful, for God's sake! Where are you off to now in such a hurry?"

"To Krysia."

"And what is she doing?"

"She? All she does these days is kiss me all the time and rub her face against me like a cat."

"Just don't let on that she has gobbled up poor Ketling, sighs and all!"

"Ha!" Basia cried. "As if I wouldn't be able to keep such a secret!"

Pan Zagloba knew very well that this was exactly what Basia would never be able to do, which is why he mentioned it all. He went on down the corridor, highly pleased with himself and congratulating himself on his cunning, while Basia burst into Krysia's room like an exploding bomb.

"I've banged my knee!" she cried out from the threshold and rattled off everything at once. "Ketling's head over heels in love with you! I didn't notice that wagon tongue sticking out of the carriage house and bang, that's all it took! I think I saw every star in the sky but it's over now. Pan Zagloba asked me not to tell you anything about it. Ha! Didn't I tell you that's how it would be? Well, didn't I? And you wanted to push him off on me! Don't worry, though, I know your little ways! Ouch, that knee still hurts! I didn't try to palm off Pan Novovyeyski on you because he's too wild but Ketling's something else! Oho! He's walking around the house with his head in his hands and mumbling to himself. Nice work, Krysia! Nice work! Very nicely played!"

And Basia started teasing the startled and astonished Krysia, poking her fingers into the girl's face, and chanting: "Scat Scot, scat Scot!"

"Basia!" Drohoyovska cried.

"Scat Scot! Scat Scot!"

But Krysia burst suddenly into unexpected and unhappy tears.

Puzzled, because she didn't know about her secret understanding with Pan Volodyovski, Basia started soothing and consoling the distraught Drohoyovska but that didn't help and the poor girl gave way to a flood of weeping as never before.

"Oh dear God," she sobbed. "How unlucky and miserable I am! Oh dear, dear God!"

★　★　★

No one in the entire household knew the full extent of Krysia's misery. She had been feverish for days but her face had greyed. It lost its health and color. Her eyes were dull and sunken in deep-seated circles. Her breath came in short, intermittent gasps, and something strange and frightening seemed to be happening to her all the time. She seemed drained of strength and powerless to help herself, nor did all this happen gradually; it had all come upon her violently, all at once, like a hurricane, and swept her away. It seemed to her as if her blood were suddenly on fire and her imaginary visions blazed in her like lightning. She had no way to rest or defend herself against this merciless assault. Her peace of mind had vanished along with her strength and all her willpower seemed like a bird with a broken wing.

She didn't know if she loved or hated Ketling, and a numbing fear gnawed at her at this question, but she was sure of this much: her heart was hammering so violently in her breast only because of him; it was he who sent her mind spinning in confusion. Her whole being had filled up with his words, his voice, and his glowing beauty. He—or her thoughts of him—was or were everywhere around her, in her and above her, and there was nothing she could do to protect herself against this constant presence.

It would be easier not to love him than not to think about him, she was sure, because her eyes seemed to come to life only when she saw him. Her ears could hear only what he said and his voice had become a strangely vibrant music that pierced and penetrated her entire being.

Sleep offered no relief from these persistent visions because she no sooner closed her eyes when his face bowed over her to whisper: 'I'd rather have you than a kingdom, a throne, or fame and riches...' And his imagined head came so unnervingly close to hers in such moments, and lay so near to hers on her tumbled pillow, that a blood-red flush burned in her cheeks even in the darkness.

It was all new to her, and strange and violent and unexpected, but it was not unnatural.

She was a *Rusinka*, a woman of Ruthenia, no matter how Polish she was in every other way. The hot, restless blood of the savage borderlands pounded through her veins and filled her breast with fierce though unexperienced fires that she had never even suspected in her before, and which inflamed her fear, scorched her modesty, glowed like hot coals under her helplessness, and—at the same time—soothed and cajoled her senses with a painful and luxurious lethargy that robbed her of all her powers to resist them.

Nights brought no rest.

She felt herself more exhausted every day as if she'd been struggling under a backbreaking strain.

"What's wrong with you!" she cried out at herself when she was alone. "What's the matter with you!"

But she was too far gone in her own turmoil and her inner chaos for any help or answers even though nothing real or tangible had happened. She hadn't yet exchanged two words alone and in private with Ketling, and some kind of self-protecting instinct warned her constantly to be on guard against him, and to keep out of his way whenever he came near, even though he filled her mind completely and overpowered all her thoughts in her waking moments.

She gave no thought to her understanding with Volodyovski simply because nothing had happened as yet between her and Ketling, and because she didn't think about anyone or anything but Ketling, not even herself, and that was her only source of respite, peace of mind and calmness.

She kept it all hidden in the deepest recess of her soul, looking for comfort in the thought that no one suspected what was going on inside her, and that no one had put the two of them together. But Basia's outburst showed her the frailty and futility of that falsely merciful illusion. She knew that her secret was now out in the open for everyone to see, that everyone would guess and know what she had tried so hard to bury and conceal, and that she and Ketling would be linked together in their minds from this moment on.

Worry, shame, guilt and pain came suddenly together and she burst into tears like an injured child.

But Basia's thoughtless prattle was only the beginning of those pointed comments, those meaningful glances, those winks and head shakings and ambiguous phrases that she had to bear, all of which started that afternoon at the dinner table.

Madame Makovyetzka kept shooting curious glances back and forth between her and Ketling, which she had never done before.

Pan Zagloba hurrumphed in a signifying manner.

From time to time a deep and total silence settled around the table for no apparent reason, and once, in one such moment, the rattle-brained Basia called out loud and clear:

"I know something but I won't tell!"

Krysia felt as if her face was burning, then turned as white and pale as if a sudden danger had brushed her in passing. Ketling also looked down at the floor to hide his emotions. Each of them knew immediately that this was aimed at them even though they'd taken great pains to avoid talking to each other and that she hadn't glanced in his direction even once. But it was instantly clear to them both that something definite was happening between them, that each of them shared the other's turmoil and confusion, that a powerful, unknown force had thrust itself suddenly between them even as it drew them both irresistibly together, and that they'd gone far beyond the possibility of an ordinary friendship.

Luckily for them, no one paid any attention to Basia's exclamation because Pan Zagloba was getting ready to go to the city, and planned to come back that evening with a swarm of guests, and that occupied and distracted everybody's thinking.

* * *

It happened then that Ketling's country house blazed with lights that night. Some dozen knights and officers arrived along with a band which the gracious host ordered for the ladies' entertainment. There could be no dancing because it was Lent, and because Ketling was officially in mourning for his adoptive father, but the evening passed pleasantly in talk and listening to the music. The ladies dressed as if for a court reception. The Magistrate's Lady appeared in oriental silks. The *little warrior* glowed in a variety of colors and delighted the gathered military with her round pink face and her tousled, fair mop of hair which tumbled down across her eyes every other moment. They were especially taken with her resolute, straight-from-the-shoulder speech and the way she acted: in part a blunt and carefree Cossack lad who was afraid of nothing and, in part, a charming and innocent young girl.

Krysia, whose mourning for her father was just about over, looked stunning in a white gown worked in silver thread. The admiring knights compared her both to Juno and Diana, but none of them edged up to her or made any overt amatory gestures. No one curled or twisted the ends of a mustache, or shuffled his feet, or tossed the split sleeves of his *kontush* coat behind him like a preening bird, and no one threw her any fiery glances or talked about love. Instead—and she noticed it at once—those who threw her their admiring glances would then, immediately, toss a glance at Ketling. Others came up to him and shook his hand as if congratulating him on a great achievement while he spread his hands and lifted his shoulders as if denying something.

Being both sensitive to everything around her, and as perceptive about other people as she'd always been, she knew at once that they were talking to him about her and treating her as if she were already his fiancee.

'Why?' she wondered, upset and ill at ease. 'How could they know anything? How could they suspect?'

But because she could have no idea that Pan Zagloba had already dropped a few leading comments here and there, and that he'd planted a few ideas in everybody's ears, she puzzled over this apparent universal knowledge and couldn't understand it.

'Do I have something written on my forehead?' she worried, full of alarm and shame.

Then she began to pick up words and phrases meant, apparently, for other ears than hers, but spoken so loud that she couldn't fail to hear them.

"What luck for Ketling!" one or the other of the gathered

soldiers boomed out to another. "Must've been born with a silver spoon in his mouth... or wearing a cowl. Small wonder though. He's just as handsome himself, lucky devil!"

Others who made polite conversation with her, and wanted to say something that she might like to hear, talked only about Ketling and sang paeans of praise for his courage, generosity, courtliness and the antiquity of his family and name.

She had to listen to all this whether she wanted to or not.

Her eyes seemed to have acquired a will of their own and sought out the object of all this adulation without being told. Now and then they'd meet Ketling's eyes turned helplessly towards her and then she'd feel herself swept up, transported by the magic of her own emotions into love and wonder, and lost irretrievably in his poise and beauty.

He was, she thought, as different from those bluff and rough-hewn warriors as day is to night.

'*A Prince among his retainers*,' Krysia thought bemused, her eyes fixed on that lofty, aristocratic head, on those angelic eyes full of poetry and sadness, and on that high, noble forehead framed in fair hair.

Her heart beat up rapidly at such moments and she felt as weak and helpless as if this beautiful, sculpted head belonged to a God whose will had to be her own.

He saw this. He tried to keep away from her so as to spare her any more embarrassment. But once in a while, when someone else sat near her, he also came over and then her panicked heart beat harder than before.

He couldn't have treated her with greater courtliness and respect, she thought, if she were a queen.

Whenever he spoke to her, his head dipped in admiration and his legs assumed the stance of a man who was about to kneel. His measured words fell with a natural, inborn dignity, never presuming to witty, joking phrases, although he shot some light-hearted comments in Basia's direction.

He treated her in all his words and gestures with the highest possible consideration and regard, and with that strange, melancholy dignity and reserve which suggested the utmost devotion mixed with quiet sadness, as if she were both unforgettable and unattainable to a mere mortal. Thanks to this restrained, respectful admiration no one else allowed himself any jocularity, or said

anything too pointed and direct, as if all were convinced beyond
any doubt that she stood far above them, both in birth and
station, and that they couldn't be too courteous or polite.

★   ★   ★

It was a troubling evening for Krysia but it was also pleasing
and exciting and she was full of gratitude for Ketling's considerate attention.

Near midnight the orchestra put away its music, the ladies
took their leave, and the assembled soldiers turned to a more
noisy celebration over cups and goblets, with Pan Zagloba
taking the place of honor.

Basia flew upstairs as happy as a bird because she'd had a most
enjoyable time among those dashing cavaliers and warriors, and
she joked, prattled and darted about like swallow, mimicking
various guests before she knelt for prayers.

"It's super to have your Ketling here!" she said to Krysia,
clapping her hands together. "At least we won't run short of real
soldiers! Oho! Just let's get done with Lent and I'll dance myself
into the ground! What a time we'll have! And what a time I'll
have at your betrothal and then at your wedding! Ha! May the
Tartars get me if I don't turn the whole house upside down, but
wouldn't it be something if they did? I like your Ketling! It's
you for whom he imports those musicians but I'm having a great
time right along beside you. And he'll do more, much more for
you before he does this!"

And Basia threw herself down on her knees before Drohoyovska, clutched her with both arms, and started imitating
Ketling's firm, low voice.

"Milady!" she mimicked. "I can't breathe for the love of you...
I love you on foot and on horseback, and after dinner and on an
empty belly, and in the Scottish fashion and forever... Will you
be mine?"

"Enough, Basia!" Krysia cried. "Enough! Or I'll get angry
with you!"

But instead of getting angry she threw her own arms around
the laughing girl and started hugging her and kissing her eyes
while pretending that she was merely trying to lift her to her
feet.

Chapter Seventeen

PAN ZAGLOBA KNEW perfectly well that the little knight felt more drawn to Krysia than to Basia, which is exactly why he pushed so hard to put her out of reach and clear the way for the little warrior. Knowing Volodyovski as well as he did, he was convinced that Pan Michal would turn to Basia just as soon as he saw no other choice, while the old knight himself was so totally entranced by the lively Basia that he was quite unable to imagine that anyone might pick some other girl over her.

He reasoned that he couldn't do more for Volodyovski than to get him married to Basia Yezorkovska and simply melted at the thought of the amazing children that would spring from this providential union. Annoyed at Volodyovski, he was also quite put out with Krysia, and even though he'd have much rather seen Pan Michal married to her than not at all, he was determined to do everything to hook him up with Basia. The quicker that Krysia and Ketling became linked officially together, the better, he was sure.

His conviction suffered a small shock when Skshetuski wrote a few weeks later, urging him to mind his own business and not to interfere. *'Otherwise,'* Pan Yan wrote, *'you might create a serious discord among two good friends.'* Since that was the last thing Zagloba would have wished, he suffered a few qualms. But he soon argued himself out of them.

"It'd be one thing," he reasoned, "if Michal and Krysia had reached some serious understanding and if I then tried to drive Ketling between them like a wedge. Solomon said: *'Don't stick your snoot in another's boot,'* and he got that absolutely right. But there's no harm in wishing the best for everyone. Besides, looking at it realistically, what harm did I do? Can anyone accuse me of hurting anybody?"

Having absolved himself of any wrongdoing, Pan Zagloba cocked his fists aggressively on his hips and stared around the walls of his room as if daring them to launch an accusation. But since the walls didn't say a word one way or the other he took their silence for assent.

"I told Ketling that I've earmarked the little warrior for Michal," he went on aloud, glowering at his walls. "And what's wrong with that? Isn't that my right as a friend? Well? Isn't it? Besides, it's nothing but the truth! May the agues bite me and may I get the shakes if I ever wished anyone else for Michal!"

The walls said nothing to deny it and the old knight decided that his conscience was absolutely clear.

"I told the little warrior that Ketling's been bowled over by Drohoyovska," he went on. "Anything false about that? Hmm? Didn't he say as much himself, sighing like a bellows into the fireplace so that the ashes flew back all over the room? I only told others what I saw myself. Skshetuski is a realist, I agree, but my own wits aren't exactly a handful of pebbles that you'd throw at a pack of mongrels to drive them away. I know what can be talked about and what's best left unsaid... Hmm! He writes that it's better not to meddle. Maybe so. I won't push myself where I am not wanted. So if I ever find myself alone with Ketling and Krysia I'll go off and leave them to manage on their own, and I dare say they'll manage very well. Push them? I don't need to push them! They're pulling towards each other so hard their eyes are popping right out of their heads. Moreover Spring is coming. It's not just the sun that burns hotter at this time of year but other things as well... Very well! I'll give up all this *interfering*, as Skshetuski calls it, and we'll see what happens."

★   ★   ★

The results of all that weren't long in coming. Ketling and all his guests moved to Warsaw for the duration of Holy Week, and put up at the hostelry on Dluga or Long Street to be closer to the major churches, go to all the services, and to enjoy the holiday bustle of the town.

Here too, as in his own house, Ketling took the role of host because he knew the capital inside-out even though he came from a foreign country; he had friends and contacts everywhere, and he could arrange everything anyone might have wanted.

He went to such extraordinary lengths to amuse and entertain the ladies—and especially Krysia—that it seemed as if he knew how to guess and anticipate their wishes. All three of them became very fond of him. Madame Makovyetzka, whom the old knight had alerted to the young man's feelings, began to look at him and Krysia with a sympathetic eye, and the only reason she didn't say anything to the girl about it was that he hadn't yet declared his intentions.

It seemed, however, quite natural and proper to the kindly *auntie* that the young cavalier should pay court to Krysia, especially since he was a truly splendid knight, one who was treated with respect and friendship everywhere he went, and not merely by people of lesser importance but also by powerful and distinguished men high above his station. His physical beauty had its effect on her just as it did on every other woman, and she was quick to appreciate all those qualities that made him so admired. Gentle, obliging, courteous and generous in peacetime—and brave in war—he seemed like something from a fairy tale.

'*What will be, will be,*' the warmhearted Magistrate's Lady told herself in private. '*God and my husband will decide what's best. But I'm not going to get in their way.*'

Thanks to this decision, Ketling was spending more and more time with Krysia, even more than he had at home. The whole company went everywhere together anyway. Zagloba usually offered his arm to Madame Makovyetzka, Ketling walked with Krysia, while Basia—being the youngest and quite on her own—darted about alone, either ranging far ahead or dropping behind them in the bazaars to gape at the overseas goods displayed in the open-air stalls which she'd never seen anywhere before.

All this gave Krysia time to get used to Ketling so that when she walked beside him nowadays, resting her hand on his arm and listening to his comments, her heart no longer hammered in her breast with its former anxiety and violence. She could look into that noble face without all her strength draining from her body, and a feeling of great peace and calmness replaced her earlier fears and confusion.

They were together almost all the time, kneeling beside each other in the churches—and their voices blended into one in the hymns and prayers—but the word *love* hadn't yet been spoken between them.

Ketling, of course, had no doubts about it; he knew his own feelings beyond any question but the laws of chivalry forced him to be silent for a little longer.

Krysia kept saying to herself that she wasn't sure, either because she lacked the daring to say exactly what she felt, or because she wanted to convince herself that her feelings hadn't carried her beyond the point of safety. The phrase '*I love you*' seemed to hang everywhere in the air around them but she hadn't said it. This love, however, was now a foregone conclusion, made all the deeper by their genuine fondness for each other and by the fact that they liked each other as the best of friends. But since that love was still an unacknowledged presence, their time together passed almost like a dream, and the sun seemed to shine upon them wherever they turned.

Soon, all too soon, this warm illumination would be clouded over by Krysia's sense of guilt in respect to Pan Volodyovski but at this happy time these clouds were still crouched beyond the horizon. All of Krysia's anxiety and alarm had been put to rest in just that new closeness. The friendship which bloomed between them along with their love had put an end to all her doubts and fears; her feelings were no longer ripped apart by the violence of her imagination; and the instincts which seemed to set her blood on fire were lulled into stillness. It was enough for her to know that they were together, that this made them happy, and she gave herself heart and soul to that blissful sense of untroubled rightness. She didn't want to think that it might ever end or that a single phrase could blow this dream apart as if it had never existed at all; yet all that Ketling had to say to her was '*I love you*' and the illusion would burst and disappear.

★ ★ ★

That phrase was soon spoken. Basia and Madame Makovyetzka went one day to visit her ladyship of Lvov who had fallen ill and Ketling talked Krysia and Zagloba into touring the public rooms of the Royal Castle which Krysia hadn't seen before and which were famous throughout the whole country.

So they went together with Pan Zagloba puffing along as their corpulent duenna.

Ketling's largess opened every door, and all the various porters and custodians bowed so low before Krysia that she felt as if she were a queen entering her own palace. Knowing his way around the castle very well, Ketling led her through a long series of magnificent corridors and chambers.

They saw the Royal Theatre and the King's Baths where hot and cold water ran out of the wall through gilded copper pipes.

They admired the huge canvasses that depicted the great battles and military victories of Kings Sigismond and Vladyslav over the eastern hordes.

They stood on the tiered terraces outside from which they could see far into the countryside beyond. Krysia couldn't get over her amazement at all this, and Ketling showed her everything, explaining the history, origins and function of every precious object, and his eyes told her clearly whenever he fell silent that none of these accumulated treasures meant anything in comparison with her.

Then he stopped at a hidden doorway in one of the King's private rooms where he conducted Krysia with Pan Zagloba plodding stoically behind them.

"This is the way to the cathedral," he said. "There's a long corridor behind this door which leads to a small gallery beside the main altar. Their Majesties usually heard the Mass from there."

"I know that passage well," Pan Zagloba said. "King Yan Casimir relied on my judgment and consulted me in everything important, and Queen Marie-Louise loved me with a passion, so they often invited me to join them for Mass. This was in part to enjoy a bit more of my company but also so that they might seek inspiration in my piety."

"Would you like to visit there, milady?" Ketling asked and signaled to the porter to open the door.

"Yes I would," she said.

"Go on without me," Pan Zagloba told them. "You're young and your legs are in good shape but I've trotted about enough for today. Go, go. I'll stay here with the porter. Oh, and take

your good time about it, will you? I won't mind how many
prayers you say over there and I'll get a chance to rest at the same
time."

They passed through the door.

He took her hand and led her through the long corridor
which, in point of fact, was a hollow bridge that spanned the
open space between the palace and St. John's Cathedral. But he
didn't hold that hand too warmly, nor press it to his heart. He
walked in thoughtful silence. Small transept windows cast intermittent beams of light, which brushed them with sunshine, and
then they walked again in a mysterious twilight. Her heart beat
a little faster because this was the first time that they were alone
but his quiet silence put her mind at rest. And then at last they
stepped into the little gallery fixed to the western wall of the
cathedral just beyond the high-backed stalls reserved for dignitaries.

They knelt to pray. The church was hushed and empty. Two
tall candles burned before the main altar but the nave lay
shrouded in a somber but uplifting twilight. Only the rainbow
shafts of multicolored light streamed down from the stained-
glass windows along the nave, and bathed those two miraculously beautiful young faces plunged in their own reflections,
and as at peace with each other and themselves as the angelic
figures they resembled.

Ketling was finished first. He rose and whispered, as his
respect for the church required: "Look, milady, at these velvet
armrests. You can see where their Majesties rested their heads in
prayer. The Queen sat over there, nearer to the altar... Why
don't you sit and rest there for a moment in her place?"

"Is it true that she was unhappy all her life?" Krysia asked,
taking her place in the Queen's private chair.

"I know her history from tales heard in childhood because it
was told in all baronial halls throughout the West. She may have
been unhappy because she couldn't marry the man she loved the
most."

Krysia pressed her head back into the high-backed chair, in
the exact spot where Queen Marie-Louise had rested her head,
and let her fringed eyelids drop across her eyes. She felt a strange
coldness welling up and rising from the empty nave and chilling
that peaceful warmth which had filled her entire being all this

time. Ketling said nothing. He stared at her in silence which seemed suddenly both sacred and profound.

Then he knelt slowly at Krysia's knees and began to speak in a quiet voice which, however, was alive with feeling.

"It's no sin," he said, "that I kneel before you in a sacred place, because where else if not in a church, should a pure and honorable love come to ask for blessings? I love you more than life, I love you above all the treasures of the world, I love you with all my soul and with all my heart, and I confess that love here, in the sight of God and His holy altars!"

All blood drained at once out of Krysia's face.

White as a sheet of canvass, she leaned her head against the velvet armrest of the prie-dieu before her, and kept as still as someone who'd been suddenly overwhelmed by a forgotten and disregarded danger.

"So here I am at your feet," he went on, "and pleading for your verdict. Am I to leave here feeling as if the Gates of Heaven stood open before me, or so sick with sorrow that the pain will surely stay with me all my life..?"

He waited for her answer but, when it didn't come, he bowed his head so low that it came close to touching Krysia's shoes. His voice began to tremble with a rush of feeling, breaking as if he couldn't fill his chest with sufficient air.

"My life and happiness are in your hands," he said. "Have mercy, because I can't bear it all much longer..."

"Let's pray for God's mercy!" Krysia cried out suddenly and fell to her knees.

Ketling didn't understand what happened but he wouldn't think of countering such intentions, so he knelt down beside her, full of anxiety and anticipation, and they started praying together again. Their voices called out strangely mournful echoes from the dim-lit shadows of the nave.

"God have mercy on us!" Krysia prayed.

"God have mercy on us!" Ketling responded.

"Take mercy upon us!"

"Take mercy upon us!"

After that she prayed silently to herself but Ketling saw that her entire body was shaken by sobbing. It took a long time for her tears to ebb, and even longer for her to rise from her knees.

"... Let's leave," she said.

They came once more into the long, narrow passage. Ketling thought that she would give her answer sometime along the way, so he walked beside her, looking down into her eyes, but to no avail. She walked so swiftly, as if in a hurry to reach the chamber where Pan Zagloba waited, that he had little choice. They were within a few dozen paces of the little doorway when Ketling caught the trailing edge of her ribboned gown.

"*Panno Krystyno!*" he said in purest Polish. "By all that is Holy...!"

Then Krysia spun around, seized his hand so swiftly that he couldn't stop her, and pressed it to her lips.

"I love you with all my soul!" she said. "But I can't be yours!" And before the astonished Ketling had time to speak a word, she added: "Forget everything that happened!"

And then they were both in the chamber beyond the door. The porter was snoring in one chair and Pan Zagloba in another but their entry made them both open their eyes. The old knight blinked once or twice as he struggled back to reality but it took him a moment to remember who was who and where they all were.

"Ha! It's you two!" he said clambering to his feet, as he hauled his sash down across his belly. "I dreamed that we had a new candidate-elect but it was old King Piast, with whom our first Polish dynasty began. Were you in the gallery?"

"Yes."

"And did you happen to see Marie-Louise's poor unhappy ghost?"

"Yes," Krysia said in a hollow voice.

Chapter Eighteen

KETLING, WHO NEEDED TIME to get over his shock and disappointment, and to come to terms with the way that Krysia had acted, said his goodbyes hastily to her and Pan Zagloba as soon as they reached the palace gates again, and the old knight took the girl back to the hostelry. Basia and Madame Makovyetzka were already back from their visit, and the older woman greeted Zagloba with a flood of news.

"I've heard from my husband!" she cried out and then rattled on with a breathless stream of gossip and reports, none of which had much to do with each other and the rest.

"He's at the army post with Michal!" She used the old Polish military term *stannitza* for the border fort. "They're both well and hope to be here soon! There's a letter for you, sir, from Michal, with only a *post scriptum* for me from my husband who writes that he's settled some trouble we had with the Zuber family over one of Basia's holdings... Our local legislatures will meet any day, to pick our candidate for the throne, and my husband says that everyone's going to vote for Pan Sobieski's choice. The Grand Hetman means a lot to the people in our part of the country. Everybody who is anybody is going to be here for the election and it looks as if Pan Sobieski's candidate will carry the day... The weather's fine back home though it rains a lot... Our farm in Verhutka burned down because one of the workmen didn't watch the fire, and since the wind blew up suddenly it got out of hand..."

"Where's Michal's letter to me?" the old knight interrupted, breaking into the plump, excited lady's babble of news and trivia.

"Here!"she said and handed him a letter. "As I was saying, the wind blew up suddenly, and..."

"How did these letters get here to us in Warsaw?"Pan Zagloba asked.

"They came to Pan Ketling's manor and a groom brought them over here today. There was this wind, then, as I was saying..."

"Would you like to hear, ma'am, what Michal has to say?"

"Gladly, if you'd be kind enough..."

Pan Zagloba cracked the seal that closed Volodyovski's letter, glanced through it quickly while muttering in his whiskers, and then read it out for everyone to hear.

'*This must be the first and last letter I'll send you from here,*' Pan Michal had written. '*Primo because the mails are unreliable and, secundo, because I'll be with you soon in any event. It's good to be out here in the field but my heart is with all of you, and there's no end to the reflections and the recollections, so that I'd rather be alone, in solitudo so to speak, than with a lot of people. The work I expected doesn't amount to much because the main Tartar hordes keep as quiet as field mice. All we get are loose bands rampaging in the Steppe, and we've had a couple of good outings against them, coming up on them unexpectedly and hitting them so hard that not one of them got away to report what happened.*'

"I bet Pan Michal made it hot for them!" Basia cried out, delighted. "There's nothing like a soldier!"

'*Doroshenko's Cossacks,*' the old knight read on, '*would love to dance with us a little but they can't do much without Tartar help. Prisoners tell us that none of the bigger tchambuls are going to stir just now, and I think so too, because we've had new grass in the Steppe for more than a week, and if they were going to do something this Spring they'd have already done it. There's still some snow in the ravines here and there but the High Steppe is green with fresh growth and there's a warm wind blowing. The horses are also getting their new coats and there's no surer sign of good raiding weather...*'

'*I've already asked the Hetman to let me come home,*' the letter continued. '*Pan Novovyeyski can take over the watch on the border trails which call for so little work just now that Makovyetzki and I have been chasing foxes all day long just to keep ourselves from dying out of boredom. Their Spring pelts are useless, by the way, but it keeps us busy. There's a lot of birdlife too, and my groom shot a pelican the other day... Kiss my sister's hands for me,'* Volodyovski ended, *'and also Miss Krysia's, to whose kind thoughts I commend myself, praying to God that I might find her of the same mind and feeling as before. Give my regards also to Miss Basia. Novovyeyski is still angry about his rejection but he's working it out on the marauders around here so it's all to the good.'*

Then he signed off, commending Pan Zagloba warmly to God's keeping.

"Is that all?" Basia asked.

"There's a *post scriptum,*" Pan Zagloba said and read it out aloud. *'I bought a bale of fine ermine tails for Miss Krysia from some Armenian traders which I'll bring myself. And there'll be some Turkish sweetmeats for our little warrior.'*

"Let Pan Michal gobble them up himself!" Basia cried, annoyed and flushed with quick anger. "I am not a child!"

"Won't you be pleased to see him, then?" Pan Zagloba asked. "Are you upset with him?"

She muttered something brief and biting under her breath, deeply hurt and angered that Pan Michal treated her with so little seriousness and feeling. But her anger didn't last longer than a moment and her thoughts flew to the wild birdlife he'd described and especially to that pelican he'd mentioned.

★ ★ ★

Krysia, however, sat through the reading in torment and despair. She turned her head away from the light and kept her eyes shut tight, taking it as a real stroke of luck that the others couldn't see her face, or they'd have guessed at once about that hurricane of feeling that was sweeping through her.

What happened in the cathedral, followed so quickly by Pan Volodyovski's letter, was like a double blow with a battle hammer. The precious dream in which she'd been living was gone at a stroke, the wretched girl stood face to face with things as they really were, and that reality was as merciless as it was hard to bear.

Her first thoughts were chaotic, little more than a whirlwind of jumbled emotions. Volodyovski's blunt, straightforward letter seemed so crude and clumsy after Ketling's ornate courtesies that she was immediately repelled. His bale of ermines, along with his offhand homecoming announcement, made him seem so shallow and unpolished that her first feeling was one of revulsion. Ketling had never seemed more dear to her than now. Just thinking about him filled her with a sense of wellbeing and wonder. She loved every feature of his beautiful, fairy-tale face, adored each word he'd said, and even his disappointed sorrow seemed precious and rare.

And now she'd have to walk away from that impassioned love and all that adoration. She'd have to turn her back on this splendid man to whom her heart soared like a homing dove and whom her arms wanted to embrace with all of her strength. She had to leave him in despair, to an endless sorrow, abandon him to his desolation and give her soul and body to another man who seemed suddenly as small and trivial as a cruel joke, and whom she hated just because he wasn't the one she wanted.

'*I won't be able to stand it!*' she wailed bitterly in her thoughts. '*I simply can't do it!*'

She saw herself as helpless and bereft as a Tartar captive, her hands bound with rawhide, and yet she knew that she had tied those cruel knots herself because she could have told Volodyovski that she'd never be able to be more than a sister to him.

Here her mind flashed on that kiss which she'd accepted and returned, and she was sick with shame and self-contempt. She asked herself if she had been in love with Volodyovski and knew that she hadn't. Far from it! She'd felt compassion, yes, but also just a plain curiosity and a desire to sample something new, all covered up with an artificial sisterly affection.

'*A kiss from the heart*,' she thought, '*is as different from that kind of kissing as angels are from devils!*'

Anger leaped up in her along with self-disgust and she turned them both against Volodyovski.

He too was to blame!

Why should all the guilt, bitterness and penance fall on her alone? Why shouldn't he taste that harsh, embittering cup of gall that made her sick with loathing? Why shouldn't he share in her disappointment?

Couldn't she say to him, as soon as she saw him: "I was wrong! It was a mistake! I took my pity for you for deeper affection. You too were mistaken. Now leave me and forget about me as I leave and forget about you!"

... But what would happen then?

Fear of the rage with which that dangerous man would avenge himself suddenly lifted the hair on her head. She felt no fear on her own behalf—that didn't matter to her just then, not much anyway—but for that dear, loved man who'd have to pay the price of her mindless folly.

In her mind's eye she could see Ketling, sword in hand, facing that unsurpassed duelist and swordsman, and falling like a flower scythed down in a meadow.

She watched his spilling blood.

She saw his bleached, lifeless face, and his eyes closed in death for ever, and her tortured thoughts cracked through all her barriers of restraint. She leaped to her feet and hurried to her room so as to get out of everybody's sight and so that she wouldn't have to hear them talking about Volodyovski and his coming home.

In her heart, which was so full of Ketling, she felt a storm of rage gathering against the little knight.

* * *

But thoughts of Ketling tracked her to her room. They stayed with her throughout her jumbled prayers. They crouched at her bedside when she threw herself down on her pillows, exhausted by her turmoil, and spoke to her as clearly as if they were real apparitions and not just the reflections of her tortured mind.

Pity asked: *'Where is he now? He didn't come back to the inn. He's wandering about somewhere in the night, cracking his knuckles with pain and disappointment. You'd give him Paradise itself if that was in your power. You'd die for him, you say. Instead you've fed him poison and drove a knife straight into his chest...'*

Regret said: *'It's your own foolishness that did it! It's that urge you have to captivate everyone around you and tempt each man you meet! It could have been all different for you but what do you have instead? Emptiness! Desolation! Nothing but pain and tears!'*

'It's all your fault,' Bitterness accused. *'You're the one to blame!'*

'Why didn't you have any mercy on him,' Pity asked again, *'when he was kneeling in that church before you? Why wasn't your heart breaking when he looked into your eyes and told you he loved you? It*

was right for you to pity a stranger, but what about him who means so much to you? God help him now! God show mercy to him.'

'*If it weren't for that trivial, empty mind of yours, you could have been his wife,*' said Bitterness.

'*For ever,*' said Regret.

'*It's all your fault!*' Bitterness said again.

'*Weep now,*' Pity whispered.

'*That won't do any good,*' Bitterness said at once. '*That won't make amends.*'

'*It's not too late,*' Pity said, '*to offer him some hope... some consolation...*'

'*Yes it is!*' Fear, Bitterness, Anxiety and Regret said immediately. '*Because Volodyovski is going to kill him!*'

An icy sweat flooded over Krysia.

She sat up in bed. Bright moonlight spilled into the room and filled it with strange and terrifying shadows.

"What is this?" Krysia murmured to herself. "There's Basia sleeping in her bed. I see her. The moon is shining straight into her face. But when did she come in? When did she get undressed and get into bed? I never closed my eyes... I never slept, not even for a moment... but I didn't see her, never noticed her...! What is happening with me? What's wrong with my poor head?"

Exhausted, she fell back among her pillows, but Bitterness and Regret perched again on the edge of her bed like two river spirits who floated in and out of that silvery moonlight whenever they wished.

"I won't sleep at all tonight!" Krysia told herself and her mind turned to thoughts of Ketling with even greater sorrow than before.

But suddenly Basia's plaintive voice rose from that night-time silence.

"Krysia!"

"Aren't you sleeping?"

"I had a bad dream. I dreamt that some Turk shot Pan Michal with a bow and arrow. Sweet Jesus! What a nightmare! I'm shaking like a leaf! Let's say a litany so that God might avert the danger!"

'*I wish someone would kill him!*' flashed like lightning across Krysia's mind. But the full horrifying force of her own malevolence sent her trembling into self-disgust and terror, and although it took a superhuman effort on her part to pray for Volodyovski's safe return at this of all times, she answered:

"Very well!"

Both the young women left their beds, knelt on their bare knees in that pool of moonlight, and began the recitation of a litany. Their voices played against each other, rising and falling in a measured rhythm, so that it seemed as if their bedroom had suddenly changed into a convent cell in which two young, white-garbed nuns said their midnight prayers.

Chapter Nineteen

NEXT MORNING Krysia was much calmer because she found a way out of her dilemna. The road she chose among the many tangled paths and blind alleys was an immensely difficult one but, at least, it was sure and safe. If nothing else it pointed to a definite direction she might take. But first she wanted to see Ketling and to talk to him, for what would be the last time, so that she might help to protect him from any misadventure. This wasn't an easy thing to do because Ketling kept away for the next few days and didn't come back to the inn at night. Krysia began to get up at first light, and go to a nearby Dominican church, in hopes that she might run into Ketling on some morning and talk to him in private.

This happened just as she had hoped. She met him a few days later at the hostel gates. Seeing her, he bared his head, bowed to her in silence, and stood waiting as mute and still as a marble statue. Lack of sleep had stamped his face with lines of weariness and pain. His eyes had fallen back into tired circles. His pale skin had acquired a waxy sheen as if he were ill, so that, at first glance, he seemed like a beautiful flower that had begun to wilt. Krysia felt as if her heart would rip itself in two when she looked at him, and though any firm, decisive step cost her a great deal, since she was naturally diffident and timid, she stretched her hand towards him and broke the heavy silence.

"May God bring you peace," she said, "and help you to forget."

Ketling took her hand, pressed it first to his feverish forehead and then to his lips where he held it a long time and with all his strength.

"There's no such thing for me," he said with resignation as if he were exhausted to the point of death.

There was a moment when Krysia needed all her strength not to throw her arms around his neck and cry out: *'I love you more than anything! I want to be yours!'*

She felt that if she were to give way to the tears that welled up inside her this was exactly what she would cry and do, so she stood before him in silence for several long minutes, struggling with her anguish. But she won her battle, crushed her grief, and started speaking in a steady voice, although her words spilled out in a breathless hurry.

"Perhaps it might make it easier for you if you know that I won't marry anyone," she said. "I'm entering a convent. Don't think badly of me because I'm heartsick and miserable enough! Promise me... give me your word of honor... that you won't tell anyone about your love for me. That you won't confess it to anybody, not even your dearest relative or friend, and that you'll never mention what happened between us. That's the last thing I'll ever ask you. You'll know in time why I have to do it but try to be understanding even then. I can't tell you more than this today because I'm too heartbroken about it as it is. Promise me that much, so I can breathe a little easier, will you? Otherwise I think I wouldn't want to live."

"I promise," Ketling said. "You have my word of honor."

"May God repay your kindness and I thank you with all my heart! Try to hide your feelings when others are present and show them nothing that might help them guess."

Then she took back her hand and broke away from him. Her voice remained firm and low and steady but she couldn't control its breathless, interrupted quality.

"It's time for me to go. I don't know how to thank you for your goodness. We won't see each other alone from now on. We'll always be with other people near. Tell me again that you don't feel any anger with me. Suffering is one thing, neither one of us can help the pain we feel, but hostility is something else again. Remember that it's God to whom you're giving me, not anyone else."

Ketling felt a desperate need to speak. He wanted to say

something too—this, after all, was their last time together—but
he was too broken-hearted to utter a word. He merely touched
her temple lightly with his fingers and held them there in silence
as if to show that he felt no ill-will against her and that she had
his blessings and support.

Then each of them went their own way: she to the church,
and he back into the street so as not to come across anyone he
knew in the hostelry.

★   ★   ★

Krysia didn't come back until noon and, when she did, she
found an eminent caller at the inn. This was the Reverend
Monsignor Olshovski, Undersecretary of State for the Polish
Kingdom, who paid a wholly unexpected visit to Pan Zagloba
to—as he put it—"meet such a distinguished cavalier, whose
victories in war are an example to the entire knighthood, and
whose great mind is a guide to all the gentry of the Commonwealth."

Pan Zagloba was totally amazed but just as much delighted by
this astounding honor which came to him in front of the ladies.
He huffed and puffed and strutted about, as proud as a peacock;
his face glowed like a crimson lantern and he sweated buckets in
nervous excitement; and, in the meanwhile, he tried to show
Madame Makovyetzka that he was quite accustomed to visits
from all kinds of dignitaries, even the most lofty, and that this
was a perfectly ordinary event in his life.

Krysia, introduced to the distinguished prelate, kissed his
hands with every sign of piety and respect, and sat down next to
Basia, glad that her face betrayed no signs of her recent emo-
tional upheaval.

Meanwhile, the politician-priest poured such a flood of compliments over Pan Zagloba that it seemed as if he drew them by
the bucketful out of his violet, lace-edged sleeves.

"Don't think, dear sir," he said, "that I'm here only in response to my curiosity, and an anxiety to meet the flower of our
knighthood. While it is true that admiration is the due of heroes,
people also make their pilgrimages to those rare places where a
clear mind and a wealth of experience in public affairs live side
by side with valor."

"Age alone gave me my experience," Pan Zagloba tried a

modest tone. "Especially in military matters. And perhaps that's why the late, great Pan Konyetzpolski, the father of the present Seneschal of the Crown, came to me sometimes for advice on the battlefield. After that there was Grand Hetman Pototzki, Prince Yeremi Vishnovyetzki, Pan Sapyeha and even Pan Tcharnyetzki, but I've always protested against the name of *Ulysses* by which I am known."

"And yet that name is so closely linked with yours in peoples' minds," the prelate replied, "that they sometimes say *our Ulysses* when talking about you, without the need to use your proper name, and everyone knows at once to whom they're referring. So I told myself, in these difficult and contrary times when many people don't know what to do, where to turn, and whose lead to follow: *'I'll go to see him! I'll hear his opinions, put my doubts to rest, and seek the light of his sage advice.'* You've guessed of course, dear sir, that I'm speaking about our nearing elections, in which every analysis of the candidates may lead to something useful, but what could be more illuminating than your views? I've heard our knighthood say with great enthusiasm that you're inclined to take a dim view of all those foreigners who are trying to crowd onto our splendid throne. The Vasa dynasty—as you are supposed to have said—had Yagellonian blood running in its veins so, as people quote you, it couldn't be regarded as foreign! But these current foreigners, as you're reported to have said, know nothing of our ancient Polish customs, nor can they respect our privileges and freedoms, and so *absolutum dominium* might easily result. These are profound thoughts, sir, as I readily agree, but forgive if I ask whether you actually spoke those words, or if it's just the normal run of things by which *opinia publica* ascribes every wise sentiment to you?"

"These ladies can attest to it," Pan Zagloba answered rather grandly. "And though it's not a subject suited to their interests, let them confirm that I've often said it, since Providence, acting in its own unfathomable manner, saw fit to give them voices."

His Reverence the Undersecretary threw a quick glance at Madame Makovyetzka and at the two young women who sat close together side by side. None of them, however, said a word.

And then Basia's silvery voice rang out in the silence. "I never heard you say it!"

After which Basia flushed all the way to her ears, and glanced at her hidden shoes, terribly embarrassed, especially since Pan Zagloba said at once:

"Disregard this outburst, Excellency! She's a young thing so she's still a bit on the wild side! But *quod atinet* the candidates, or as concerns their fitness, I often said that Polish freedoms will weep over all these foreigners."

"I fear that too," Monsignor Olshovski inclined his head profoundly. "But even if we wanted to elect another *Piast*, a man of our own blood and bred to the bone among us, where do you think our hearts ought to turn? Your thought to pick a Polish candidate, distinguished sir, is of course quite brilliant and it spreads like wildfire throughout the whole country since, as I hear it, every legislature in the territories which is yet unbribed and uncorrupted cries in one voice for a King born and bred in Poland!"

"And quite right too!" broke in Pan Zagloba.

"However," the Undersecretary went on smoothly. "It's easier to call for a much needed Piast than to find one who would fit the need. Don't be surprised then, most eminent sir, if I ask whom you had in mind?"

"Whom did I have in mind?"

Pan Zagloba sounded at a loss for a ready answer, as indeed he was. He frowned with fearsome concentration and pushed out his lower lip in a deep and sagacious manner but nothing, or rather no one, came to mind. This was due largely to the fact that he had never given serious thought to any candidate, any more than he voiced such views and sentiments as the shrewd Undersecretary just planted in his head. He knew it, as he knew perfectly well that the cunning prelate was trying to pull him over to somebody's side, and he was pleased to let him do it by the hour if that's what it took, because it flattered him immensely to have such attention.

"I spoke in general terms," he said at last. "Stating *in principio* that we need one of our own people on the throne. But I haven't named anyone as yet."

"I've heard about some ambitious plans that Prince Boguslav Radzivill has for the election!" the Monsignor muttered as if merely reflecting on a rumor.

"Never!" roared Zagloba. "Nothing will come of them as long

as there's still some breath in my lungs and one drop of blood boiling in my heart! I wouldn't live in a nation that would choose its own worst Judas for its King as a reward for all his villainy!"

"I hear the voice of reason... and civic virtue too!" the Undersecretary murmured once again, and Pan Zagloba took a thoughtful measure of the man before him.

'Hmm,' he thought. *'You want to pull me somewhere, do you? Let me give you a little tug as well.'*

But the Monsignor heaved a sigh and addressed himself to a higher audience.

"Where oh where," he cried as if to the Heavens, "will our racked and battered ship of state find a safe harbor in these troubled times? What new storms and shoals wait for you, my unhappy country? Ah, verily I say, it will be an evil day when a foreigner takes your helm, but that seems to be what'll have to happen since there isn't a better man among your own sons!"

His fingers shined with rings as he spread his white hands in a helpless gesture.

"So... it must be de Conde?" he mused. "Or the Prince of Neuburg? Or the Lotharingian?"

"It cannot be!" said Zagloba. "It must be one of ours!"

"But who?"

Again there was a moment of heavy, wondering silence and then the Undersecretary continued his musing.

"Is there one we'd all agree upon?" he asked. "One who'd catch the gentry's hearts so firmly that no one would dare to raise a voice against him? Ah,"—and he smiled sadly—"There was one once, oh yes, the greatest and the most deserving—and a dear friend of yours too by the way," he prompted, "my very dear sir—who walked in his own glory as if it were both the sunlight and the sun..."

"Prince Yeremi Vishnovyetzki!" the old knight interrupted.

"That's the one! But he is in his grave..."

"But his son's alive!" Pan Zagloba answered.

★　★　★

The Undersecretary, who was of course seeking support for the young Michael Vishnovyetzki's party, closed his eyes as if unable to believe the perceptiveness and wisdom that he had just witnessed, and sat, apparently bemused, through a moment's silence. Then he looked up at Pan Zagloba and started speaking in slow, reverent tones.

"I thank the Lord that He inspired me with the thought to meet you, sir," he said. "That's it exactly! The son of the great Yeremi is alive among us, a young Prince who can trust in a hopeful future, and who is heir to a debt that's long overdue in the Commonwealth. But there is nothing left of the Vishnovyetzki fortune. His sole inheritance is glory. So where, in these corrupted times when all eyes turn only to where gold beckons to them, will we find the man who will nominate him? Who'll first submit his name as a candidate? You sir? Yes! But where to look for others such as you? It's no surprise that one who spent close to a century of his life in heroic service on every battlefield has the courage to speak for Right and Justice in the election field as well. But will others follow...?"

Here the prelate-politician sat quiet for a moment, as if plunged in thought. "God has the greatest power," he mused out loud. "Who can plumb His judgment? Who can tell? When I think how our entire knighthood trusts you, sir, and believes everything you say, I'm amazed to notice some hope in my heart. Tell me though, sir. Honestly. Has the impossible ever existed for you?"

"Never!" said Pan Zagloba with absolute conviction.

"It wouldn't do, though, to push this candidate too sharply on our brother gentry. Not at first. Let that name start ringing in people's ears, let everyone get used to the idea, but don't let it seem threatening to the opposition. It'd be better if they laughed and jeered than put up a struggle. Perhaps God will grant that his name rises to the surface once the other parties have destroyed each other. Perhaps that could happen. So blaze his trail for him, sir. Clear the way slowly, step by step, and never cease your labors, because he is *your* candidate, worthy of *your* wisdom and experience. And may God bless your efforts."

"Am I right in thinking," Zagloba asked quietly, "that Your Excellency also had Prince Michael in mind?"

The prelate drew a small book out of his sleeve and handed it to Pan Zagloba. *"Censura Candidatorum, or Critique of the Present Candidates,"* he read off the cover. "Read it, sir! Let the book speak for me."

* * *

The Reverend Undersecretary—who was also Deputy Chancellor and member of the Privy Council, and whose chancery title was Keeper of the Lesser Seal—started getting ready to make his departure, but Pan Zagloba stopped him for a moment.

"Permit me, Excellency, to say something in reply," he said and smiled slightly. "But first let me thank God that our Lesser Seal lies in such skillful hands that they turn people into sealing wax to mold as they like."

"What do you mean, sir?" asked the astonished prelate.

"Let me tell Your Excellency from the start that Prince Michael's candidacy is close to my heart because I knew and loved his father, Prince Yeremi, and fought under him along with all my friends, and that we'll all be delighted to show the son the love we had for his father. I'm therefore seizing his nomination with both hands and I'll get to work today. I'll have a talk with his lordship, Pan Kritzki, who is a territorial chamberlain of great influence and power, and a good friend of mine. He has a vast following among the gentry because he's generous, and sets a fine table, and because it's awfully hard not to love that man. We'll both start doing what we can and if that's the way God wants it then that's what'll happen."

"May the angels guide you," said the priest. "If that is settled then it's all that matters."

"With your permission, Excellency, but there is also something that matters to *me*. I'd be obliged if Your Excellency didn't leave here thinking: *'I've shoveled my own wishes into his mouth like slops to a hog, convinced him that Prince Michal was his own idea,'* and in short, that you molded yet another dimwit according to your fancy like a lump of wax."

"Good God, sir!" the politician-prelate stammered out. "Whatever do you mean?"

"Here it is then, sir." Pan Zagloba smiled. "I'll work for Prince Michael because I feel something for him. That's my only reason. Since, as I see, this goes hand in hand with Your Excellency's wishes, I say all the better! I'll push his cause for his mother's sake, for my friends,"—and here the old knight acknowledged the councillor with a courtly bow—"and with respect for the trust I place in the distinguished mind from which this great idea sprung like Minerva, the Goddess of Wisdom, who leaped full-grown out of the head of Jove. That's why I'll do it, sir, not because someone talked me into thinking it was my idea as if I were a child, or because I'm stupid. There's one thing about old Zagloba, sir, that you ought to know. Namely, when a wise man tells him something wise, old Zagloba says: *I agree!"*

Finished, the old noble bowed again and stood waiting quietly.

Monsignor Olshovski kept his own embarrassed silence for a lengthy moment, caught in his own snares and not quite knowing what he ought to say. But since the old knight spoke in such a bantering, pleasant tone, and since the politics were going in the right direction anyway, he burst into hearty laughter and clutched his own head in genuine amazement.

"Ulysses!" he cried over and over. "As I live and breathe, a real Ulysses! Ah, my dear brother, if someone wants to bring about something good he has to take a roundabout path with all sorts of people. But with you sir, I see, it must go straight from the shoulder to the heart of things. I've really gotten awfully fond of you!"

"As I have of Prince Michael!"

"May God keep you healthy! Ha! I'm outfoxed but I'm very glad! You must've been fed on nightingales' tongues when you were in your crib, you've a brain like crystal... Anyway,"—and the Monsignor started tugging at one of his rings—"do take this little signet ring in memory of our chat."

"Hmm. Let that little signet ring stay just where it is," Pan Zagloba said.

"But do me the favor..."

"Impossible! Quite out of the question!" Pan Zagloba said. "Perhaps another time... like after the election..."

The astute prelate understood, gave up insisting, and left smiling broadly.

★ ★ ★

Pan Zagloba escorted him all the way beyond the hostel gates and, on his way back, muttered with contentment.

"Ha! I taught him a lesson! That's what you get when you try to throw a saddle on a fox! But the honor of the thing remains, there's no doubt about it! We'll have all sorts of dignitaries pushing through these gates before very long... Hmm! I wonder what the ladies thought about it all?"

The ladies were most definitely impressed and Pan Zagloba soared in their estimations as high as the ceiling, especially in the eyes of Madame Makovyetzka. "You sir," she cried with enthusiasm, "exceed Solomon himself!"

"Who? Solomon? Just wait a bit, dear lady, and you'll see this place so full of Hetmans, senators, castellans and bishops that we'll have to chase them off like flies or hide behind a curtain!"

Ketling walked into the room just then and put an end to the conversation if not to Pan Zagloba's sudden glimpse of influence and power.

"Ketling!" the old knight shouted, carried away by the vision of his own importance. "How would you like a step up in rank?"

"Thank you, no," the young knight said sadly. "There is another long journey waiting for me just now."

Pan Zagloba gave him a closer look. "Why do you look so down-in-the-dumps?" he asked.

"Because I am leaving."

"Where to?"

"I've had word from some of my father's former friends in Scotland, and from my own as well. Some important matters need my attention there, perhaps for very long. I'm sorry to be losing your company, sir, and that of the ladies, but I have to go."

Pan Zagloba walked out into the middle of the floor, and stared as if dumbstruck at Madame Makovyetzka and each of the girls in turn. "Did you hear?" he asked in a bewildered voice. "In the name of the Father, the Son and the Holy Ghost, why now of all times?"

Chapter Twenty

NO MATTER HOW ASTONISHED Pan Zagloba was by Ketling's announcement it didn't occur to him to suspect his reasons. In fact no suspicions of any kind popped into his head. It was easy to suppose that King Charles II of England and Scotland, who'd been restored to the throne of the United Kingdom after the Puritan dictatorship of Cromwell, would have remembered the loyal services rendered to the Stuarts by the Ketling family and wanted to show his gratitude to the last of that line. Indeed, the opposite would have been more of a surprise. Moreover Ketling showed Zagloba some letters from abroad, written in a language the old knight didn't know, and convinced him totally.

In its way, however, this precipitous departure threatened the old knight's best-laid plans, so that he looked into the near future with some trepidation. Volodyovski, to judge by his letter, was due back any day. The Steppe winds would have swept the last of his mourning from his head. *'He'll come back,'* Pan Zagloba thought, *'more decisive, more determined, and more resolute than ever,'* and since he'd been drawn more to Krysia than to Basia he might propose marriage on the spot. *'And then what?'* Pan Zagloba worried. Then Krysia would accept, because how could she refuse such a cavalier who was, moreover, Madame Makovyetzka's brother? And then the poor little warrior would be left high and dry.

Meanwhile, driven by that willful, persistent and unreasonable stubbornness common to old age, Pan Zagloba was deadset on getting the little knight hooked up with Basia at all costs.

Neither Skshetuski's persuasions, nor the arguments which

198

the old knight occasionally chewed over on his own, did the slightest good. Once in a while he'd swear to stay out of it all, and stop trying to pull everybody's strings, but then he'd jump back into his machinations with even greater fervor and persistence. He'd ponder all day long how to get Basia and Pan Michal walking up the church aisle side by side. He weaved his plans, tore them apart, rewove them and created innumerable stratagems, and he was so engrossed in this occupation, and so utterly determined to tie the knot he had fixed upon, that when he did flash on some workable idea he'd shout: "God give you long life and happiness together," as if the wedding had already taken place.

What he saw now, however, was nothing less than the ruin of everything he wanted. All he had left, he thought, was giving up, the end of all his efforts, with God taking over the course of events in His own unfathomable manner, because that dim thread of hope that Ketling would make some decisive move towards Krysia before his departure, couldn't keep dangling much longer in the old knight's head. So it was more out of deep and resigned sorrow rather than curiosity that he decided to question the young knight, and to get out of him what he planned to do before his departure, as well as the actual date that he picked to leave.

★ ★ ★

"Too bad!" he said when Ketling came to see him in response to an invitation for a talk. "It can't be helped. Each man knows best what he ought to do, so I won't try to talk you into staying. But I'd at least like to know when you're coming back…"

"Can I foresee what's waiting for me where I'm going?" Ketling asked. "Anything might happen. If I can come back sometime I will. If I can't, I'll stay."

"You'll miss us," Pan Zagloba assured the young Scotsman. "You'll see. Your heart will nag at you night and day to come back to us."

"May I be buried in this hospitable soil which gave me everything it could," the young man said sadly.

"Ah, you see? A foreigner is always just a stepson in any other country, but our good Motherland will stretch her arms to him and hug him to her breast from the start."

"That's true. That's very true. Ey, if it was only up to me, if only I could... The fact is that anything might come my way in my former country... except happiness."

"Ha!" Pan Zagloba snorted. "And didn't I tell you? Didn't I say you ought to get married? But you wouldn't listen! You'd have to come back, being a married man, unless you wanted to transport your wife across all that dangerous, wild water, which I don't think you would. I told you and I told you but you wouldn't listen!"

Here Pan Zagloba started peering carefully into Ketling's face, wanting some clear explanations out of him, but the young man said nothing. He merely hanged his head and stared at the floor.

"And what do you say to that, then?" the old knight demanded.

"There's been no likelihood of anything like that,"the young knight said slowly.

Zagloba started pacing up and down the room, then stopped in front of Ketling's chair, stared down at him like a judge, and clasped his hands behind his back.

"And I'm telling you there was!"he said. "If there wasn't, may I never get this belt around my belly from this moment on! You've a friend in Krysia!"

"I hope she'll always be one, even though there'll be seas between us."

"Why should there be seas between you if you stay together? But why don't you make a move, for God's sake? Why don't you tell her something?"

"There's nothing more to say!"

"What? Did you pop the question to her, then? No? So why didn't you?"

"Let me be, sir, will you? I feel bad enough about leaving as it is."

"Ketling! There's still time! Talk to her! I know that you love her! D'you want me to find out exactly how she feels about that?"

Ketling thought that since Krysia was so anxious to conceal the fact that they loved each other, she might be glad of a chance to deny it outright in the open.

"I assure you, sir, that it's all been for nothing," he told Pan

Zagloba. "And I'm so certain of this that I've done everything I know to knock those feelings out of my heart and head. But if you expect miracles, then ask her!"

"Ha!" Pan Zagloba grunted with some bitterness. "If you've really knocked her out of your head then there's really nothing to be done. Let me tell you, though, that I gave you credit for a lot more sense."

★ ★ ★

Ketling leaped to his feet, jerked both his hands feverishly up into the air, and answered with a degree of violence than Pan Zagloba never saw in him before.

"What good is it for me to crave one of those stars up there? I can't soar up to her and she won't come down to where I am standing! Those who sigh for the moon are cursed!"

But Pan Zagloba had also come to the end of his tether and he began to huff and hiss as if he'd been insulted. Indeed, he found himself in such a sudden fury that he was lost for words, and it was only after a long period of snorting and puffing that he managed to bring his rage to heel.

"My... dear fellow," he growled among pauses, half stifled with anger. "Don't treat me like a dimwit. If you have a reasonable argument to offer, then give it quick, like you'd do for any man who gets his nourishment out of bread and meat not cobwebs and stardust! Because if I lost all my wits right now, and told myself that my cap is really a lunar apparition which I'll never reach, I'd walk about town with my bald pate shining in the moonlight while the frost is gnawing on my ears! That's not my way of thinking, but I know this much: that this girl is sitting on her backside three rooms away from here, that she eats when she's hungry and drinks when she's thirsty, and that her legs have to cross each other when she walks. I know that her nose gets red with the cold in Winter and peels in the Summer, that she itches when a mosquito bites her, and that her only similarity to the moon is that both of them are beardless. But the way you see things you might as well say that a turnip is an astrologer. As far as it concerns Krysia, if you've tried and failed that's your private business; but if you've got the girl all stirred up to love you and then you go off talking about moonshine, then both your mind and your honesty are easily satisfied!"

"I can't feed my hopes on ashes," Ketling said, distraught. "I'm going because I must, that's all I can say. I won't plead because there is nothing I can hope to get. But you see me wrong sir! God knows you see me wrong!"

"Ketling!" Zagloba cried, as upset by all this as the bitter Scotsman. "I know that you're a decent man, it's just that I can't make head or tail of these convoluted foreign manners of yours! In my time, a man went to a girl, looked her straight in the eye, and put it to her more or less like this: *'If you don't want to try, I don't want to buy.'* And everybody knew which end was up and where matters stood. If someone had straw for brains, and didn't know how to go about it, he'd send somebody with a tongue in his head to do his asking for him. I said I'd speak for you and I'll say it again. I'll go, I'll speak, I'll bring your her answer, and then you can decide to go or to stay..."

"I'm going! That's how it has to be because there isn't any other way!"

"But you'll come back...?"

"No! Do me the favor, sir, and don't ask me any more about it. If you want to satisfy your curiosity elsewhere, then do so. But not in my name..."

"For God's sake!" Pan Zagloba cried. "Did you ask already?"

"Let's not talk any more about it! Do me that favor, sir!"

"Fine, then let's talk about the weather! May lightning strike you along with your fancy manners. You have to go and I've got to swear!"

"Goodbye, sir."

"Wait! Wait! This will blow over in a moment. I get upset too easily, that's always been my trouble. My dear Ketling! I wanted to talk to you about something... Ah, when are you leaving...?"

"As soon as I've settled everything here. I'd like to wait until my quarter rents come in from Courland, and I'd be glad to sell that little house where we all stayed together, if I came across a ready buyer."

"Let Makovyetzki buy it. Or Michal! For God's sake, man, surely you won't go without saying goodbye to our dear friend Michal?"

"I would give everything to be able to do it!"

"He'll be here any day! Any moment! Maybe *he'll* help you out with Krysia..."

* ★ *

Here Pan Zagloba became suddenly uneasy and broke off what he'd begun to say.

"I've tried to do Michal a good turn in good faith," he growled under his breath. "But it's been damned little according to his fancy. If the end result is to be *discordia* between him and Ketling, then maybe it's best if Ketling goes his way."

Here the old knight started scratching his bald head and pondered for a moment.

"I say this and that," he muttered, backing off a little. "But it's only because I really think the world of you, you know... See, I've got so fond of you that I'd like to keep you with us by fair means or foul, so I dangled Krysia before you like a slice of bacon..."

Then, suddenly worried that he had really stumbled into something where he had no business intruding, he backed off even farther.

"But it's all out of wishing you the best. None of it is any of this old man's business anyway. It's just because I'm so fond of you, you see, nothing more. I mean, I don't make a living as a marriage broker, because if I wanted to play the arranger I'd arrange a wedding for myself, first and foremost. Here, Ketling! Let me give you a good hug... and don't be angry with me."

Ketling at once threw his arms around the old knight who immediately let the sentimental side of his nature get the better of him, sniffed once or twice, and called for a flagon of Ketling's best Malmsey.

"We'll empty one to your voyage every day before you leave," he said.

They drank it dry together and then Ketling said goodnight and left.

The wine did for the old knight what he always said it did: it sharpened his wits and lifted his spirits. He plunged into some profound reflections on Basia, Krysia, Ketling and Volodyovski, brought them together like marionettes and paired them off together, murmured his blessings, and then decided that he missed the two girls wherever they were and wanted to see them. "I'll go and see what those young goats are up to," he muttered.

The young women sat sewing in a room across the hall. Pan Zagloba grunted some kind of a greeting, nodded to them, and started walking up and down the room, dragging his legs a bit because they no longer served him as well as they used to, especially after wine.

Walking, he peered down at the girls who sat so close together that Basia's bright, fair head was almost touching Krysia's midnight hair. Basia's eyes trailed after him and Krysia sewed with such rapid concentration that he could hardly catch the darting of her needle.

"Hrumph!" Zagloba said.

"Hrumph!" Basia mimicked.

"Don't make fun of me because I'm still angry!"

"Ah!" Basia cried with pretended fright. "Maybe he'll cut my throat!"

"Rattle on, rattle-brain! Your tongue ought to be cut out, that's what!" With this, Zagloba marched right up to the girls, cocked his fists on his hips, and fired without warning or preamble: "D'you want to marry Ketling?"

"And five more like him!" Basia said at once.

"Quiet, you pesky fly, I'm not talking to you! I'm speaking to you, Krysia. D'you want to marry Ketling?"

Krysia lost some color in her face even though she thought at first that Pan Zagloba was asking Basia, not herself; then she lifted her beautiful dark-blue eyes to the old man's face.

"No!" she said quietly.

"Well, well! *No!* At least it's short and to the point. Well, well! And why doesn't your ladyship want him, if I may be so bold?"

"Because I don't want anyone."

"Krysia! Tell that to somebody else!" Basia broke in quickly.

"And what has made the institution of marriage so repulsive all of a sudden?" the old knight demanded.

"It's not repulsive," Krysia said. "It's just that I have a vocation for the convent."

There was such quiet dignity in her voice, along with so much sadness and acceptance, that neither Basia nor Zagloba thought that she was teasing, jesting or being facetious even for a moment. But they were both so utterly astonished that they stared at her and at each other as if they couldn't believe their ears.

"Wha-a-at?" Zagloba was the first to recover.

"I've a vocation for the convent," Krysia said once more, as gently and as softly as if it were a dream.

Basia glanced at her once or twice, her small mouth gaping in amazement, then suddenly threw her arms around Krysia's neck, pressed her pink lips to her cheek, and started to speak with such a rush of feeling that her words ran into one another in one chaotic, incoherent jumble.

"Krysia, I'll bawl! Tell me at once that you're just joking with us or I'll bawl. I'll bawl, by all that's holy!"

Chapter Twenty-one

AFTER HIS TALK WITH ZAGLOBA, Ketling paid a call on Madame Makovyetzka whom he informed that he must stay in the city for some days, and that he might have to go to Courland for a few weeks before his sea voyage, so that he wouldn't be able to act as her host in person in his country house. He begged her, however, to keep treating his manor as her own private residence, and to stay in it along with Michal and her husband throughout the election which was drawing near. Madame Makovyetzka agreed readily enough, because otherwise the pleasant little manor would have stood empty and useless to anyone, which would have been a waste.

After this conversation Ketling disappeared and no one saw him again at the inn or in the manor house when Madame Makovyetzka and the two young women returned to the country. Only Krysia, however, felt his absence. Pan Zagloba was busy with the election, while Basia and Madame Makovyetzka were so shaken by Krysia's decision that they could think about nothing else.

Madame Makovyetzka did nothing to try to get Krysia to change her mind, and doubted whether her husband would make any effort, because in those days opposition to that kind of calling was looked upon as an insult and injury to God.

Only Pan Zagloba would have dared to put up a fuss if it served his purpose but, since it didn't, he kept quiet about it. In fact he was quite pleased that events had taken such a course that Krysia was removing herself on her own from between the little knight and the little warrior. He was now quite convinced that his fondest wishes would come true and he was free to throw himself headlong into his political agitation. He spent his days either in hobnobbing with the gentry who swarmed through the capital, or talking with Monsignor Olshovski whom he came to like a great deal in the end, and whose willing partner and confidant he became.

Each such talk sent him home burning with ever greater zeal for a new Piast on the Polish-Lithuanian throne, and even more inflamed against the foreigners. Acting in line with the Reverend Undersecretary's prompting, he still kept his full fervor to himself, but hardly a day passed without him capturing some voter for Prince Michael's cause. What happened then is what normally happens with such accidental commitments: he turned into such a fierce and unmitigated zealot, and he was swept away by such a fiery enthusiasm, that the election of Michael Vishnovyetzki became his second most important goal, next only to hooking up Basia with Volodyovski.

★　★　★

Meanwhile the election drew closer every day. Spring had already freed the waters from their bonds of ice; strong, warm winds began to breathe new life into the budding trees; and the chains, which according to the beliefs of the simple folk, hold the swallows locked under the ground, flew open and spilled their darting little prisoners out of the icy depths into a sunlit world. Strings of returning wildfowl weaved through the skies along with the swallows, and all sorts of foreign visitors started arriving for the great assembly.

First came the merchants who looked for rich harvests in those electoral meadows where more than half a million of the voting gentry would throng together with all the great magnates, their suites and servants and followers and escorts and their private armies. They came from England, Holland, Germany and Russia. There were Tartar traders, Turks, Armenians and even merchant caravans from Persia, carrying fine cloth, bolts of woven woolens, canvass for the tents and pavilions under which all of the Polish-Lithuanian knighthood would live and debate, cloth-of-gold and damask, furs, jewels, perfumes, honeyed dates and oriental sweetmeats. Open-air stalls sprung up in the streets and beyond the city, packed to the rafters with every kind of foreign goods and products. Many of these bazaars spread even among the neighboring country hamlets, since everyone knew that not even one tenth of the electorate would find quarters within the city walls, and that the vast majority would pitch its camps in the countryside, which is what happened at every election.

Then the highways darkened under the arriving gentry who thronged to the capital in such overwhelming numbers that no enemy would set foot within the Commonwealth if they ever came as readily to defend her borders.

Most people thought that the election would be a stormy one because the whole nation seemed split between the three main candidates: de Conde of France, the Prince of Neuburg, and the Prince of Lorraine known as the Lotharingian. There were insistent rumors that each candidate's supporters were ready to impose their choice by force of arms if everything else failed.

Alarm gripped many hearts and everyone seethed with a ferocious zeal that far exceeded mere determination. Some people spoke darkly about a civil war, pointing to the huge military contingents surrounding the magnates. These too came early so as to have enough time for intrigue and negotiations.

It was a strange time, with many strange and sobering revelations about the Commonwealth, its great lords and its turbulent mass of lesser nobles, landowners and gentry. Neither the King nor the Hetmans could field more than a handful of devoted soldiers when the Commonwealth was threatened, and when the enemy pressed his dagger to her throat. Now just the Radzivills alone came with an army of some twelve to twenty thousand men, either defying or disdainful of the law and the rules of the electoral convention. The Patz family led an almost equal force; and neither the powerful Pototzkis, nor any of the other Polish, Lithuanian and Ruthenian 'kinglets' were very far behind.

"When and how can we sail this battered ship of state into a safe harbor?" Father Olshovski asked more and more often, but even he had some private interests to support. As for the rest of the ruling classes, which with rare exceptions thought only about themselves and the power of their own families and Houses, they was so egotistic, and so riddled with self-interest and corruption, that any of their members could throw the country into civil war at a moment's notice.

The crowds of lesser gentry swelled to such proportions every day that few people doubted who'd have the last word once the General Diet finished its deliberations and the vast swarms of voters spilled out into the election field. Not even all the power and resources of the mighty magnates could challenge those overwhelming numbers. But even those huge, swirling and unruly crowds were both unable and unfit to steer the Commonwealth into peaceful waters, because their own heads were dim with ignorance, and dulled by preoccupation with their own best interest, and their hearts and spirits were, for the most part, corrupted and rotten.

★　★　★

With all these threats and fears in the wind, the election began to assume an almost monstrous quality even before the fact, and no one guessed that it would turn out merely pathetic. No one except Pan Zagloba could look forward to a satisfactory outcome, even among those who worked for a Polish-born candidate as hard as the intrigues of the magnates and their own provincial mindlessness permitted, and no one dreamed that they'd be able to elect Prince Michael. But Pan Zagloba swam in those roiled waters as happily as a fish. He found quarters for himself in the city just as soon as the diet started its deliberations, and showed up in Ketling's manor only when he thought he missed his little warrior. But since Basia also lost much of her cheerfulness, directness and joy since Krysia's decision, he took her often back to Warsaw with him so that she might find some pleasure and distraction among the merchants' stalls.

They usually left early in the morning and Pan Zagloba brought her back past nightfall and sometimes quite late into the night.

As he supposed, these expeditions did her a lot of good. Her spirits lifted among the surging throngs of citizens and gentry, the glittering private regiments and courtiers of the magnates, the visitors from across the seas whose dress, looks and manners were quite new to her, and the assembled goods and treasures of the foreign merchants. Her eyes would glow and sparkle as brightly as two little coals, her head twisted about as if it were mounted on a revolving screw, and she buried Pan Zagloba under an avalanche of questions which he was pleased to answer because it displayed his scholarship and knowledge.

It often happened that a large troop of young officers clustered around the pony cart in which they did their traveling, and much of the young knighthood admired Basia's beauty, the quickness of her mind, her self-reliance and directness in everything she said. Pan Zagloba never failed to tell them the story of the Tartar shot with a load of birdshot to stun them into even greater admiration.

★   ★   ★

One evening they were returning very late because it took them the whole day to review the household troops of Pan Feliks Pototzki. The night was warm and clear. White cloudlets hovered above the meadows. Pan Zagloba always urged caution with such large swarms of lackeys, grooms, servants and soldiers everywhere, fearing that roguery wouldn't be far behind them, but this time he slumped into a heavy sleep. The driver also nodded at his reins, and only Basia was still wide awake because a thousand pictures galloped across her mind.

But suddenly she became aware of hoofbeats behind them. She pulled Pan Zagloba's sleeve, shook him more or less awake, and said urgently: "Riders are coming up at a bound behind us!"

"What? How? Who?" gasped Pan Zagloba, struggling out of sleep.

"Riders are coming at a bound!"

At this Pan Zagloba came all the way awake.

"Oh! *At a bound!* Right away they're *at a bound!* All I hear are hoofbeats, maybe it's some other travelers taking the same road..."

"I'm sure it's bandits!"

Basia was so determined that it should be bandits because she wished with all her heart for some adventure that included bandits; she wanted to test her courage with a stand against them and to show the old knight just how steady she was in danger, and how good with pistols. With this in mind, she started nagging Pan Zagloba to give her one of the pair of pistols that he always carried under his carriage seat on the off-chance that something unforeseen might happen.

"Don't worry, I won't miss!" she insisted. "I'll hit the first one that comes near. Aunt Makovyetzka is a real dead-eye with a musketoon, but she's blind at night. I'll swear that it's bandits! Ai, God, don't let them miss us! Hurry up with that pistol, sir!"

"Alright," said Zagloba. "But you've got to promise that you'll shoot only on command and never before me. The command is *'Fire!'* A scatterbrain like you, armed with some firepower, might blast the first poor gentleman who happens along, without even a *'Who goes there'* to warn him, and then there'll be trouble!"

"So I'm first to ask *who goes there?*"

"Ha! And what if it's a bunch of drunks who'll tell you something rude when they hear your voice and know it's a woman?"

"Then I'll blast them, right?"

"Here's my penance for taking such an all-fired, hotheaded jack-in-the-box to the city!" Pan Zagloba groaned. "I'm telling you, missy, that you mustn't shoot without a command!"

"I'll ask *'who goes there'* in such a gruff voice that they won't know the difference."

"Alright, let's that do. Ha! I can hear them near now. You can be sure that these are solid people because bandits would have jumped at us out of the ditch without any warning."

But because there were all kinds of troublemakers on the roads these days, Pan Zagloba ordered the groom to pull up in the middle of the moonlit highway rather than turning into a grove of trees that loomed beyond the bend.

★ ★ ★

Meanwhile four riders drew to within some dozen steps in the darkness, and Basia managed a deep growling challenge worthy, she thought, of a dragoon.

"Who goes there?"

"And why are you standing in the middle of the road?" asked one of the riders who must have thought that either their carriage had broken down in some way or their harness traces had become entangled.

But Basia, when she heard that voice, at once lowered her pistol and said quickly to Zagloba: "That sounds like Uncle! Oh my lord!"

"What uncle?"

"Makovyetzki."

"Hey there!" Zagloba shouted. "Could that be Pan Makovyetzki with Pan Volodyovski?"

"Pan Zagloba?" the little knight asked clearly from the darkness.

"Michal!"

Here Pan Zagloba scrambled in great hurry to get his legs over
the rim of the pony cart, but he'd barely got one of them
flapping in the air when Volodyovski leaped out of his saddle
and stood beside the cart. Recognizing Basia in the moonlight,
he caught her hands and cried out: "It does my heart good to see
you again! And where's Panna Krysia? And my sister? Is everyone well?"

"Yes, thanks to God! Ah, that you've finally come back, sir!"
Basia answered, with a quickened heartbeat. "Is Uncle here too?
Uncle!"

She seized Pan Makovyetzki around the neck just as he
walked up to the pony cart while Pan Zagloba opened his arms
in welcome to Volodyovski. After a long moment of greetings
on all sides, the Magistrate was presented to Pan Zagloba, and
both the newly come gentlemen threw the reins of their horses
to their grooms and climbed into the wagon. Makovyetzki and
Zagloba took the main seat in the back of the cart while Basia
and the little knight perched on the forward bench.

★   ★   ★

Swift questions brought quick answers, as is the usual thing
between people who haven't seen each other for some time. Pan
Makovyetzki asked about his wife. Volodyovski asked again
about Krysia's health. He was astonished by Ketling's imminent
departure but he had no time to think much about it because he
was pressed to tell everything he'd been doing in that borderland
stannitza, how he raided, trapped and ambushed the Tartar
marauders, how he missed everyone, and how good he felt in
this brief return to his old Steppe life.

"I thought at times," he said, "that I was back in Lubnie, back
in the old lost Transdnieper country with Prince Yeremi, riding
with Skshetuski, Kushel, Vyershul and the rest of us... It wasn't
until they brought me a pail of water to wash with in the
morning, and I'd catch sight of that grey hair on my temples,

that I'd remember I'm no longer the man I was. Though, on the other hand, it seemed that a man doesn't change a lot as long as the spirit is the same."

"That's it! You've hit that dead-center!" Pan Zagloba said. "I see that you've had a chance to hone your wits in that tall grass as well, because they weren't quite so sharp before. Spirit is the thing! Nor is there any better purge for melancholy."

"What's true is true," added Makovyetzki. "There're a lot of wells in Michal's *stannitza* because there's no open water anywhere near. Well, I tell you sir, when the soldiers start working those well-beams in the morning, you wake so full of energy and fire that you feel like thanking God that you're alive."

"Ha! If I could spend just one day out there!" Basia cried.

"One way to do it," Pan Zagloba said, "is to marry a border captain."

"Pan Novovyeyski will get his captaincy sooner or later," Volodyovski added.

"There you go already!" Basia cried, eyes snapping with anger. "I didn't ask you for Pan Novovyeyski!"

"That's why I brought you some Turkish *bakalia*," he teased her, "to sweeten your tongue while that poor devil chews on bitter seeds."

"Then you should've given the sweetmeats to him! Let him gnaw on them until his whiskers grow!"

"Imagine, sir," Zagloba turned to Pan Makovyetzki. "They're always like that with each other. It's a lucky thing, as the *proverbium* has it, that sharp words strike warm sparks."

Basia said nothing in reply. Volodyovski shot a merry glance at her small, brightly moonlit face, as if expecting some sharp new rejoinder, and he thought her so pert and pretty that he told himself, quite against his will: *'That little sprite looks good enough to strike a man blind.'*

But something else must have leaped up in his mind because he turned to the driver at his back and ordered: "Tickle those ponies with a whip, will you? Let's look more alive."

The little pony cart rolled far more snappily after that, so much so that they sat in silence for a while, and it wasn't until they slowed on the sandy side-road that Volodyovski spoke again.

"I can't get over this sudden trip of Ketling's," he said. "It's

odd it should happen just when I've come home. And on the
eve of the election, too..."

"The English care about our elections about as much as they
do about your homecoming," Pan Zagloba answered. "Ketling
himself walks around like a half-drowned corpse, he's so upset
at the need to leave us."

'*And especially Krysia,*' Basia almost said.

But something stopped her just in time. Instinct or intuition
told her not to mention what she knew of Ketling and Krysia
and Krysia's decision; both, she guessed, would touch and hurt
Pan Michal from the start, which somehow brushed against her
own most fragile feelings, so she bit back the comment despite
her usual impulsiveness and directness.

'*He'll hear about Krysia's wishes soon enough,*' she thought. '*But
it's probably best not to mention them just now, especially since Pan
Zagloba hasn't breathed a word.*'

★ ★ ★

Meanwhile Volodyovski turned again to the coachman's box.
"Drive with a bit of life, will you?" he ordered.

"We left our people, carts and horses in the Praga suburb,"
Pan Makovyetzki was telling Zagloba. "And we set out on
horseback as you see, with just the two grooms behind us even
though night was falling, because both I and Michal were
anxious to get home."

"I can believe it, sir," Pan Zagloba said. "Did you see what a
swarm of people has crowded into Warsaw? There are so many
camps and trading booths at the city limits that it's almost
impossible to get through. Some men are saying the strangest
things about this election, which I'll be glad to pass on at home
at a better time..."

Politics occupied them for a while after that, with Pan
Zagloba trying to sound out Pan Makovyetzki's leanings and
opinions, and then he turned to Volodyovski.

"And whom are you going to vote for?" he asked without
preamble.

But Volodyovski had been thinking about something else and
jumped a little at Zagloba's question, as if pulled without warning out of a musing dream.

"I wonder, will the ladies be asleep?" he asked. "And will we get to see them before tomorrow morning?"

"They're probably sleeping," Basia answered softly, as if she were dreaming on her own. "But they'll get up to greet you, sir, I am sure of that... They'd hardly want to miss seeing you come home."

"You think so, m'lady?" the little knight asked joyfully and looked again more carefully at Basia. *'My God, she's pretty,'* he told himself once more. *'Especially in this moonlight...'*

★   ★   ★

Krysia and Madame Makovyetzka had gone to bed already, and only the cooks, grooms and table servants were still up and about because they waited with supper for Basia and Zagloba. But Pan Zagloba ordered more people routed out of bed, so that the new arrivals could get a hot dinner, and the whole household was soon on its feet.

Pan Makovyetzki wanted to go up to his wife at once but she'd already heard the commotion in the house, guessed who must have come, and ran downstairs in a hastily-donned gown, out of breath, with joyful tears in her eyes and her lips full of happy smiles. There was then a flurry of hugs, kisses, greetings and a babble of excited questions, interrupted now and then by loud cries of pleasure.

Pan Volodyovski kept glancing at the door which closed behind Basia and where he expected to see a radiant Krysia appear at any moment, aglow with quiet joy and with her hair hastily set in order. But time passed, the upright Gdansk clock kept ticking in the corner, dinner came and went, and Pan Michal's loved and longed-for girl didn't show herself.

Basia came in at last but she was alone and oddly grave and subdued both at the same time. She neared the table, shielding her candle with her tiny hand.

"Uncle," she said to Makovyetzki. "Krysia's a bit unwell and won't be coming down. But she asks that you go up, at least as far as her door, so she can tell you how happy she is you've joined us."

Pan Makovyetzki rose and went out at once with Basia behind him. Disappointment put an edge on Pan Michal's voice. "That

I did not expect,"he said. "I mean that I wouldn't get to see Miss Krysia here tonight. Is she really ill?"

"No, she's alright," said Madame Makovyetzka. "She just doesn't have much use for people nowadays."

"And why's that?"

"Didn't Pan Zagloba tell you anything about her vocation?"

"What vocation's that, by Christ's wounds?"

"She's entering a convent..."

Pan Michal started blinking rapidly like a man who didn't quite catch or understand what he had just heard. His face sagged. He rose and then sat down heavily again. Sweat burst out on his forehead and he rubbed it with both hands as if not quite aware of what he was doing. The room was as quiet as a tomb around him.

"Michal..." his sister murmured.

But he stared at her with unseeing eyes and then, at last, said to her and Zagloba in a terrifying voice: "Am I cursed?"

"For God's sake, Michal!" Pan Zagloba cried. "Keep God in your heart! Have mercy on yourself!"

Chapter Twenty-two

VOLODYOVSKI'S CRY revealed the secret of his heart to the old knight and Madame Makovyetzka, and when he leaped up suddenly, and rushed from the room, they stared at each other as if stunned and alarmed at the same time.

"For God's sake, sir!" she urged at last. "Go after him, explain, or calm him down. Or I'll go, if you won't!"

"Don't do that, my lady." Zagloba shook his head. "He doesn't need either one of us. He needs to see Krysia. But if that can't be, it's best to leave him on his own, because comfort offered at the wrong time is like a condolence. God knows where that might take him!"

"Now it's as plain as the nose on my face that he wanted Krysia! Think about it, sir! I knew that he liked her and went out of his way to spend time with her, but it never even glimmered in my head that he'd go to such lengths over her!"

"I wish *something* glimmered somewhere... He must've come here with a declaration ready on his tongue, thinking he'd finally found his happiness, and it's as if a thunderbolt hit him on the threshold!"

"So why didn't he say anything to anyone about it? Neither to me, nor you sir, not even to Krysia... Maybe the girl wouldn't have made that vow..."

"It's a strange thing," the old knight wagged his head. "After all, he confides in me, and trusts in my wits better than his own. However, he not only kept absolutely quiet about this attachment, but he even told me once that all he wanted from Krysia was friendship."

"Ah, he's always been secretive about everything!"

"What? You must not know him very well, my lady, even if you're his sister. He wears his heart right out in the open, the way a carp swims around with its eyes popping straight out of its head. I've never met a less devious or more honest fellow. But I admit that this time he did something different. And are you quite sure, ma'am, that he didn't say anything to Krysia?"

"Dear God, he couldn't have! Krysia is the mistress of her will, because my husband made it absolutely clear, speaking as her guardian: *'As long as it's a decent man with good blood in his veins,'* he told her, *'you don't have to think about his means.'* If Michal talked to her before he left she'd have said yes or no, and no bones about it, and he'd know what to expect when he came back."

"Hmm. It did seem to strike them both like lightning," Pan Zagloba mused. "Your female reasoning hits the nail right on the head, my lady."

"Forget the nails and the reasoning, dear sir! Let's decide on something!"

"Let him take Basia, then!"

"How, when he likes the other better? Ha! If it had only glimmered in my head...!"

"I wish it had glimmered."

"How was it to glimmer for me if it didn't for a Solomon like you, sir?"

"And how do you know it didn't, ma'am?"

"Because you pushed for Ketling."

"I? As God's my witness, I didn't push a soul! I said he liked her and thought a lot about her, which was true. I said that Ketling was a worthy cavalier, which was also true. But I leave the role of go-between to women who are better at it. My dear lady! Don't you know that half the problems of the Commonwealth are weighing on my head? Do I have time to think about something other than public affairs? I'm so rushed sometimes I don't have time to eat!"

"So think now, for God's sake! Everyone says that no one else has a head like yours."

"People gab about my head as if it was an object of public veneration. I wish they'd give it up. But as for a solution, there are two: either Michal takes Basia, or Krysia goes back on her announced intention. Solemn vows are one thing, but an expressed intention is something quite different. It's not as if she'd taken Holy Orders, after all."

* * *

Pan Makovyetzki rejoined them just then and his wife quickly told him everything. The stout, easy-going gentleman looked troubled and upset because he really cared for Pan Michal and valued him highly but, at the moment, he couldn't think of anything to offer.

"If Krysia gets her hackles up about it," he said and rubbed his forehead, "there's not even a way to discuss it with her..."

"She'll get her hackles up!" Madame Makovyetzka said. "She's always been like that!"

"But what was Michal thinking of, not to make sure of her before he went away?" asked the puzzled noble. "A worse thing might've happened... He could've come back to find that the girl gave her heart to another man... Do you suppose she did?"

"Then she wouldn't be entering a convent," his wife pointed out. "Don't forget, she's free to decide everything for herself."

"True!" said Makovyetzki.

* * *

But a spark of light, weak though it was at first, blinked to life in Pan Zagloba's head. Everything would have been clear as day if he had known Krysia's secret with Volodyovski, without which it was really hard to put two and two together and come to grips with what was going on. His shrewd brain, however, started to pierce the fog, and to grasp the reasons for Krysia's decision and the little knight's despair, and—in another moment—he was sure that Ketling stood at the heart of the matter in some way.

But suppositions weren't proof, so he decided to seek out Pan Michal and to probe a little deeper into the situation.

On his way he became uneasy.

"There's a lot of my own meddling in all this," he grumbled. "I wanted to sweeten the mead for Basia's wedding with Michal but it seems I might've brewed some sour ale instead. Ah, what'll happen if Michal takes his cue from Krysia, goes back to his old idea, and puts on a habit of his own...?"

An icy chill shook him at this thought and he put on a burst of speed to send some heat running through his veins and get away from his guilty conscience.

Soon after, he was in Pan Michal's room. The little knight circled the walls like a small, caged bear. His brow was fiercely furrowed. His eyes were fixed in a glassy stare, seeing next to nothing, and quite unable to understand anything around him. It was painfully clear that he was in torment. Catching sight of Zagloba, he stopped his frantic pacing, stood stock-still before him, and hugged his own chest as if he were freezing.

"Tell me," he demanded, dull with shock. "What does it all mean?"

"Michal," soothed Zagloba. "Think of how many girls enter convents in any one year. It's a normal thing. There are even some who do it against their parents' will, trusting that Lord Jesus will be on their side, so what's the big surprise about a girl who's free to make her choices for herself...?"

"There's no secret to keep anymore!" Pan Michal broke in sharply. "And she's *not* free to choose because she promised me her love and her hand before I went away!"

"Ha!" said Zagloba. "That I didn't know."

"It's true!" Pan Michal said.

"Then maybe she'll listen to some persuading?"

"She doesn't care about me anymore!" the little knight burst out, overwhelmed by sadness and self-pity. "She didn't want to see me! I rode day and night to get here and she doesn't even want me back! What did I do, in Christ's name? What sins weigh down on me so terribly that God's anger hounds me everywhere and whirls me around like a dried-out leaf? One died, the other's entering a convent, God himself took both away from me... I must be cursed! Everyone else can hope for grace and mercy, why can't I...?"

Pan Zagloba shuddered, worried to the bottom of his soul that the little knight would get carried away by this latest blow and start to blaspheme as he did at the time of Anusia's death.

"Michal," he said to turn his thoughts elsewhere. "Don't lose faith. God's mercy is with you as it is with every decent man. It's a sin to doubt Him and how do you know what's waiting for you just around the corner? Maybe Krysia will recall how you were orphaned and left alone that other time, change her decision, and keep her promise to you? And in the second place—listen to me carefully—isn't it better that it's God who plucks these doves out of your hand rather than some man? Tell me yourself, would that make it better?"

But the little knight's reaction was quite the opposite to what the old knight wanted. His whiskers twitched savagely. He ground his teeth together, and then he shouted out in a cracked, stifled voice: "If it was a man? Ha...! I wish there was one! I'd rather... At least I'd have vengeance..."

"Instead you have prayer," Pan Zagloba said. "Listen to me, old friend, because you won't hear better advice from anybody else... Maybe God will change things... I myself, as you know, wished something else for you. But I'm the first to share your pain, seeing how this hurts you, and I'll beg God on my knees, right here beside you, to comfort you and bend that useless girl towards you again."

The honest tears that Pan Zagloba started mopping then in both his red-rimmed eyes were wrung out of him by pity and devoted friendship. Too late, the old knight knew that he'd undo everything he'd done to get Krysia out of Volodyovski's reach, and that he'd be the first to throw her into his arms if that were in his power.

"Listen!" he said after another moment. "Have one more talk with Krysia. Let her see your grief. Explain your suffering and then let God and nature take care of the rest. She'd have to have a stone heart not to be moved by the ache in yours. But I think she will be. A nun's habit is all very well but not when it's stitched out of another's misery. Tell her that, hmm? And then you'll see a difference."

Hope flickered in Pan Michal's eyes and the old knight heaved and hid a vast sigh of relief.

"Hey, Michal!" he cried as if convinced. "Here we're shedding tears, you and I, and tomorrow we could be getting drunk at your betrothal! I'm sure that's how it'll be! Look, the girl got lonely, that's all, and that's how the convent popped into her head. Sure, she'll take Holy Vows, why not, but they'll be the kind where you get to ring the christening bell... And maybe she is really feeling a bit ill and told us all that stuff about nuns and habits to throw sand in our eyes... Why not? Did you hear all this out of her own mouth? No you didn't and you won't, God grant it! Ha! So you made a secret pact together, and she didn't want to give the game away, so she dreamed up this idea to throw everybody off the scent! That's what it is! That's what it has to be! It's just another shrewd piece of female cunning, as I live and breathe!"

★   ★   ★

Zagloba's words acted like a tonic on the heavy-hearted little knight. Hope burst to life within him anew. His eyes filled with tears of relief and a long time passed before he could trust himself to speak. It wasn't until he got a grip on his restored confidence and new anticipation that he threw himself into Pan Zagloba's arms.

"No man deserves a friend as good as you," he said. "If only it would happen as you say it will."

"There's nothing I wouldn't do for you, you know that!" the old knight huffed and sniffled, quite as relieved and moved as Volodyovski. "It'll happen! Of course it'll happen! Have you ever known me to be wrong in my prognostications? Do you no longer trust my wits and experience?"

"You can't imagine how I love that girl," the little knight rushed into a confession. "It's not that I've forgotten all about the other; not at all, I pray for her faithfully every day! But this one too caught my heart like a bird in a snare. Ah, how I love her! I thought about her all the time out there in those grass-lands; morning, noon and night! I even got to talking to myself, not having anyone with whom to share such thoughts. I swear, my head was full of her even when I was going at full speed after some damned Tartar!"

"I can believe it!" The old knight nodded in complete under-standing. "I did so much weeping after a certain girl when I was a youngster that one of my eyes floated right out of my head! Or if it didn't, it turned blind, in any event."

"So don't let it surprise you," Pan Michal went on. "I mean, I barely get here, I've hardly caught my breath, and the first word I hear is *convent!* But I must believe in persuasion and trust the power of reason, and I can't lose faith in her promises and the goodness of her heart as well. How was it you phrased it? '*A habit is a good thing...*' but what?"

"But not when it's stitched out of another's misery."

"Wonderfully said! Why couldn't I ever put an epigram together? They'd have passed the time on guard-duty and spared me a lot of dull, witless moments. Ah, I'm still on tenterhooks, my friend, but you've stirred all my hopes again... Yes, of course, we agreed to keep it all a secret, she and I, so it makes sense for her to talk about Holy Orders to divert suspicions... There's one more top-notch *argumentum* you cited a while back but I can't quite recall it... Ah, I feel much better."

"So come up to my room, why don't you? Or I can have a demijohn brought here from the cellars. Come on, you'll think of all my maxims on the way."

They went to Pan Zagloba's quarters with no more discussion or delay and sat there over a demijohn of mead until very late.

Chapter Twenty-three

NEXT MORNING PAN VOLODYOVSKI dressed himself with a great deal of care, assumed an air of gravity, armed himself with all the arguments he could think of as well as those proposed by Pan Zagloba, and feeling himself remarkably well equipped, went down to the dining room where everyone usually met for breakfast. Only Krysia was still absent but even she didn't keep him waiting long. The little knight had barely sipped two spoonfuls of broth when he heard the rustle of her gown in the doorway and watched the girl come in.

She appeared so swiftly and moved in such a feverish hurry that it was more like bursting in rather than an entrance. Her cheeks were flushed deeply. Her eyelids were lowered. Some fear and a sense of being rushed and pressured were evident in her face and her every movement.

She went straight to Volodyovski and gave him both her hands, as one did in welcome within one's family and among close friends. But she didn't look up at him even once, and when he started kissing those hands with a warmth that went beyond any kind of friendship, she blanched and couldn't find a word to say to him in greeting.

His heart and mind, however, were immediately filled with love, anxiety and wonder at the sight of that delicate face which seemed to change color and shimmer before him like a holy icon. Despite all his newfound gravity, he found himself quite swept away by that tall, slim figure which he loved so much, and which still carried the warmth of interrupted sleep. He was even touched by the fearfulness and constraint flitting across her face.

'*Ah, my dearest flower*,' he said deep inside him. '*Why are you afraid? Don't you know I'd give my life for you?*'

But he didn't say this out loud for everyone to hear. He just pressed his pointed little whiskers to her soft hands with such strength and feeling that he left a red imprint on them both.

Looking at all that, Basia ran both hands through her unruly hair and pulled it down across her eyes so that no one would be able to read her own thoughts and feelings, but she needn't have worried about that because no one paid any attention to her just then. Everyone stared at Krysia and Pan Michal and the silence became difficult and heavy.

Volodyovski was the first to break it.

"I spent the night in anxiety and sadness," he said quietly and looked at Krysia with love and understanding. "Why? Because I saw everyone yesterday except you, my lady. And I was told such things that I felt more like shedding tears than sleeping."

Krysia grew even more pale at this straightforward openness and frankness, so much so that Volodyovski thought she was about to faint. She didn't, but he went on hurriedly anyway: "We must talk about that. But not yet, not now. You need a little time to get over the shock and the upset and get your thoughts together. I'm not a savage, after all, nor some kind of wolf, and God himself knows best how much I care for your wellbeing."

"Thank you!" Krysia murmured.

Pan Zagloba and the Makovyetzkis started shooting questioning glances at each other, as if trying to encourage one another to begin a normal conversation, but somehow none of them could manage it for a very long time.

"We ought to go up to the city, gentlemen" the old knight said at last to Michal and Pan Makovyetzki. "You won't believe the excitement there nowadays because everyone's out and pushing his own candidate for all he is worth. And on the way I'll tell you who, in my opinion, ought to get our votes."

No one said a word and Pan Zagloba stared owlishly up and down the table and then turned to Basia.

"And you, my little Junebug. Will you go with us, then?"

"I'll go to Ruthenia, if you like," she shot back abruptly.

Another heavy silence followed after that and the rest of the breakfast passed in much the same way, with a few more vain

attempts to piece together an easy conversation that simply
wouldn't or couldn't get going that morning.

★ ★ ★

But at last the difficult meal was over and everybody rose
while Volodyovski went at once to Krysia.

"I have to talk to you alone,"he said, gave her his arm and led
her to the adjoining room which, as it happened, was the one
where they'd exchanged that kiss.

He seated her gently on the sofa, sat down beside her and
began to stroke her hair as if he were consoling an unhappy
child.

"Krysia,"he murmured. His voice was quiet and soothing and
full of care and feeling. "Are you now calm enough to talk to
me without anxiety and fear?"

"I am,"she said softly.

"Is it true that you've made a commitment for the convent?"

"Don't hate me for it,"she said, or rather pleaded, and pressed
her hands together as if in a prayer. "Don't curse me. But I
have."

"Krysia," he said again. "Is it right for you to trample on
someone's happiness the way you're trampling over mine? What
happened to your word and to our agreement? I can't go to war
with God over you, but I'll tell you what Pan Zagloba said to
me last night, that a nun's robe oughtn't to be sewed out of hurt
inflicted on others. Mistreating me isn't going to add to God's
glory because He is the King of everything anyway. His are all
the nations, all the lands and seas and rivers and birds in the air,
and the animals in the woods, and the stars and suns. He has all
that, along with anything you can think of and a lot more
besides, and all I have is you to love and to hold. You're my
entire happiness and all that I can count on. Do you suppose that
God, who has such vast riches, needs to tear this one precious
treasure out of the hands of a poor soldier who has nothing else?
That He, in all His goodness, will agree to this? That He'll be
pleased rather than insulted...?

"Look at your gift to Him," he went on gently but with a
wealth of feeling carefully controlled. "You're giving Him yourself. But you are mine, because you pledged yourself to me, so
you are giving Him something that isn't yours to offer anymore.

You're giving him my tears, my pain, and perhaps my death as well. Think, do you have the right to do that? Ask both your heart and your conscience too... It'd be one thing if I offended you, or perjured my love, or forgotten you, or let myself commit some kind of a crime... Ha! That'd be one thing, I don't deny it. That'd be a reason. But I went to watch the Steppe trails for the Tartars, track the marauders in the border wilderness, and serve our country with all my strength and health and whatever blood I still have left unshed, and loved you all the while, and thought about you day and night, and longed for you like a thirsty deer longs for a clear stream, needing you like a bird needs air, and crying for you like a child taken from its mother or like a parent who misses a child... And, after all that, is this the welcome and the *solatium* you've prepared for me? Is this what I've earned?"

He paused, caught up for a moment in his own emotions, but then went on as gently and as firmly as before.

"Krysia, my dearest love... my most precious friend... be frank with me. Tell me why you've changed. Show me your reasons as honestly and as openly as I've shown you all my rights and expectations. Keep faith with me, don't leave me to my own devices with nothing but confusion and misfortune. You gave me the right to hope and to believe... don't banish me from happiness. Don't make me an outlaw!"

★　★　★

The wretched little knight went on, more eloquent than he'd ever been before, but unaware of the oldest and most compelling truth of all.

He felt that he had all the right to speak as he did but he'd forgotten the first law of nature which is more powerful and binding than any man-made statute, and which rules that love breeds love and begets love and reaches out to love despite all argument and reason, but that it can't be stirred to life once it has died away, any more than a guttered candle can be lit again after it has melted.

He'd never thought about it so he didn't know it, and he pressed his head to her knees and pleaded and begged, and she answered him with a stream of tears because her heart could no longer speak to him at all.

"Krysia," the little knight said at last, getting to his feet. "I didn't ask you to drown my happiness in tears. I need you to save it!"

Sobbing bitterly, the girl tried to answer as best she could.

"Don't ask me to explain!"Her broken voice quavered among tears. "Don't ask why! That's how it has to be, that's all, there is no other way. I'm not worth a man like you and I never were... I know how much I'm hurting you. Believe me, that pains me more than I can say, and I just can't cope with that! I know it's wrong, I know...! Dear God, I can't stand it! Forgive me, will you? Please? Don't leave me in anger...forgive me, don't curse me...!"

And suddenly Krysia threw herself on her knees before Volodyovski.

"I know that I've wronged you!" Pale as death, her face was a mask of tragedy. "But I beg your forgiveness and your understanding. I beg you for mercy!"

Krysia's dark head bowed almost to the ground and Volodyovski reached down at once, swept her to her feet, and forced her to sit on the couch again. Then he began to pace desperately through the room like a caged animal unable to find a way out of the trap. Now and then he'd pause, stand still and press both fists to his head, and then he'd lurch forward in another series of mindless steps to nowhere.

At last he halted before Krysia.

"Give yourself some time before you decide and leave me with at least a shred of hope," he urged. "Think... I'm not made of stone anymore than you are...! Why are you torturing me like this? Can't you find any mercy in yourself? It's as if you were scorching my skin with a branding iron! Look, I'm a patient man, but there's a point at which even the greatest patience must snap and give way when a man's hide starts to hiss and crackle under a hot iron...! I don't even know how to tell you how much I am hurting. God help me but I don't! I'm a simple fellow, you see, not good with fancy phrases. War's been my nursery and my only schoolroom..."

Shaken and shamed more than he'd ever been before, Volodyovski fought against a quick upsurge of anger.

"For God's sake!"he cried. "Sweet Jesus! This is the room in which we loved each other! *Krychna!"*—the diminutive of her name rang in his ears like a drowning man's last shout of despair—*"Krychna*! I thought you'd be mine the rest of my life, and now there's nothing! Nothing! What happened to you? Who changed your heart? I haven't altered! I'm the same man I was before! And this is worse for me than for some other fellow because I've already lost one love..."

Angered by his own inability to get through to her, the little knight turned bitterly towards the bright morning sky visible through the windows.

"Jesus!" he cried. "What am I to say to break into that heart? All I'm doing is just torturing myself... Ah!"—and this had to be his last appeal—"Leave me some hope, at least! Don't rob me of everything at once!"

But she said nothing. She felt as if she had been scorched and ripped apart by her own streaming tears and that chaotic sobbing, while Volodyovski struggled with his grief and disappointment and that rush of anger that threatened to unhinge his mind and hurl him into violence.

"Leave me some hope, at least!" he cried. "Do you hear me?"

"I can't!" She could say nothing else. "I just can't!"

Pan Volodyovski threw up his hands, went over to the window, rested his forehead against the chilly glass, and stood there a long time looking out at nothing. Then he turned and took a few steps back towards Krysia.

"Be well, my lady," he said quietly, resigned and without reproach. "There's nothing here for me, that's clear even to a fool. I wish you as much good as I've had evil and that ought to be enough for anyone. You ask me for forgiveness and for understanding... Well, they're yours, as much as my poor, stumbling words can make them so. God grant that my heart can do as much eventually. Next time around, though, have a little feeling for the suffering of others and don't be quite so quick with your promises... Ah, but why go on with this? What's there left to say? I'm not going to find any happiness in this house, that's certain. So be well!"

★ ★ ★

His pointed little whiskers twitched up and down with more than their usual mobility and violence, and then he bowed politely and stepped from the room. Pan Zagloba and both the Makovyetzkis leaped to their feet in the adjoining chamber when he came in among them, and stared at him in anxious expectation, but he merely snapped his hand coldly in the air as if to dismiss their questions before they could ask them.

"It's no use," he said. "It's all been for nothing. Just don't bother me with it any more."

A narrow little corridor led from the dining chamber to his own, and it was there, at the foot of the stairway that rose towards the young women's room on the upper floor, that Basia appeared before him like a shadow.

"May God comfort you, sir," she said in a voice that trembled with her own tears and pity. "And may Krysia change her heart and mind..."

He walked passed her without a glance and without a word. But suddenly rage seized him by the hair, bitterness burst through all those restraints he'd struggled to impose on himself with Krysia and flooded into him like a tide of lava, and he spun around, faced the poor girl who had never done him any harm, and hissed at her in a voice full of contempt and loathing.

"Why don't you promise yourself to Ketling?" he snarled through his teeth. "Go on, make him love you, and then trample him, rip his heart in two and run to a convent!"

"Sir Michal!" Basia cried, astonished.

"Go on, amuse yourself!" he lashed out. "Get a taste of kisses and then turn yourself into a nun! Ah, to the Devil with all of you!"

But this was more than Basia was willing to take. God alone could tell what it cost her to express the wish that Krysia might change her heart, and how much of her own best hopes for herself she sacrificed to say it, and all she got for it were insults, jeers and an unjust accusation right at the point when she was ready to do almost anything to console this ingrate.

Her quick, proud soul flamed with sudden anger; her cheeks flushed with fire; her small pink nostrils flared in disdain and she gave a violent shake to her tumbled mop of fair, unruly hair.

"It's not I who am going to a nunnery for the sake of Ketling!" she snapped out, just as unthinking and blinded by hurt pride as he was himself.

And then she darted up the stairs and disappeared from Pan Michal's view.

Left alone with this shocking revelation, the little knight stood as still as if he'd been turned to stone, and then he started blinking foolishly at whatever his eyes happened to rest upon, and to rub his face like a man waking from a nightmare.

Then a rush of blood surged into his face, he clutched savagely at the saber dangling by his side, and shouted out in a voice thick with murderous fury: "Death to the traitor!"

Fifteen minutes later he was on horseback and galloping to Warsaw with such reckless speed that the wind was howling in his ears, and his horse's hooves flung a hail of cold gravel and frozen earth behind him.

Chapter Twenty-four

BOTH THE MAKOVYETZKIS saw him galloping away, and so did Pan Zagloba, and a profound anxiety gripped all three of them. *'What has happened?'* they read the same worried question in each others' eyes. *'And where's he going now?'*

"Great God!" cried Madame Makovyetzka. "He's likely to hide somewhere in the Wild Lands and I'll never set eyes on him again!"

"Or,"—Pan Zagloba ranted in utmost consternation, sounding as if he were about to give way to despair—"he'll take a page out of that blasted girl's prayer book and lock himself in a monastery like she's going to do!"

"We need to think and talk about this!" the Magistrate suggested.

But just then the doors flew wide open and Basia burst into the room, or rather whirled into it like a windstorm, all overwrought and white-faced with distress, jammed both small fists into her eyes like a frightened child, began to stamp her feet impatiently in the middle of the room, and burst into a series of alarming squeals.

"*Rety!* Help! Pan Michal went to kill Ketling! Go after him someone! Stop him! *Rety! Rety!*"

"What's wrong with you, girl?" Pan Zagloba shouted and seized her by both hands.

"*Rety!* Pan Michal will kill Ketling! There'll be blood spilled because of me, and Krysia will die, and it's all my fault!"

"Explain!" roared Zagloba and shook her with both arms. "How do you know? And why because of you?"

"Because I got angry and blabbed out to Pan Michal that they love each other and it's because of Ketling that Krysia wants to become a nun! Ride after him everyone, if you believe in God! Stop him! Go at once, sir! Let's all go!"

Pan Zagloba was quite unaccustomed to wasting time in an emergency; he was out of the door in one jump, in the yard in another, and bellowing at the top of his lungs for the charabanc and horses.

The Magistrate's Lady wanted to question Basia a bit more, since this was the first she'd heard about anything serious happening between the young Scotsman and Krysia, but Basia catapulted into the courtyard right after Pan Zagloba. She helped to take the horses from their stalls, backed them into their traces, jumped up on the high driving seat, seized the reins, and pulled up before the main porch where the men were already waiting.

"Get down from there!" Pan Zagloba told her.

"No I won't!"

"Get down, I say!"

"I won't get down! You can get in if you want to but I'm staying here, and if you don't then I'll go alone!"

She gathered up the reins, as if to snap them down on the horses' rumps, and the two men gave up any thought of arguing with the stubborn girl. She was determined to stay where she was and it would just waste time to try to talk her off the driver's box. Meanwhile a groom came running with a coach whip, and Madame Makovyetzka managed to run out with a warm short-coat and fur cap for Basia because a sharp morning chill still hung in the air.

Then they started out.

Basia remained perched on the high box of the open carriage. Pan Zagloba wanted to talk to her some more, and kept appealing to her to jump down into the well of the coach where the two men were seated, but she was in no mood to obey. Perhaps she was afraid she'd be chided for her outburst before Volodyovski. Whatever her reason, he was forced to interrogate her at a distance, talking to her back, and she replied without looking at him or turning around.

"How do you know those things you said to Michal about that other pair?" he demanded.

"I know everything!"

"Did Krysia tell you something?"

"Krysia told me nothing."

"Then was it the Scotsman?"

"No, but I know that's why he's going to England. He fooled everybody except me."

"Amazing!" said Zagloba.

"It's all your doing, sir," Basia said. "You shouldn't have pushed them at each other as hard as you did."

"You just keep quiet up there, you pesky scamp, and don't stick your nose where it doesn't belong!" answered the old knight who was especially galled to have this accusation, true and accurate as it was, thrown into his teeth when the Magistrate could hear it. Pan Makovyetzki's title and position, both as a Justice of the Peace and a regional administrator, placed him among the foremost of the middle gentry; he was, therefore a man of stature and importance.

"I pushed them?" he added gruffly after a short pause. "Ha! I like that! As if I'd push anybody into anything."

"Ha!" the girl fired back at once. "And I suppose you didn't?"

And they drove the rest of the way in silence.

★   ★   ★

Upset as he was to have his interference pointed out before Pan Makovyetzki, Pan Zagloba couldn't quite shake off the realization that the girl was right, and that he *was* responsible for much that had happened. This ugly thought gnawed at him relentlessly as the charabanc rattled on, and because the conveyance bucked and bounced like a mustang each time it hit a pot-hole in the pitted highway, the old knight fell into the worst possible humor and didn't spare himself his own accusations.

'It'd be right and proper,' he grumbled wordlessly, careful to keep his own recriminations to himself, 'for Ketling and Volodyovski to get together and slice off my ears. Marrying off a man against his will is about as smart as putting him on horseback with his face to the horse's tail. She's right, that little gadfly! If those two actually get to fight each other then Ketling's blood will be on my head. That's what comes of flexing mental muscles at my age! Tfui! What the Devil did

I think I was doing anyway? And, as if that weren't bad enough, those two made a proper jackass out of me, because I didn't even guess why Ketling was in such an all-fired hurry to get overseas, while that other empty-headed magpie headed for the nunnery. But wouldn't you know it, the little warrior got it all figured out a long time ago...'

Here Pan Zagloba slumped into some thinking.

"She's a sharp little rascal," he growled under his breath after a moment. "Michal must've borrowed his eyes from a bat, or maybe from a crayfish, to pass her up for that vapid puppet."

★　★　★

Meanwhile they reached the city but that was only the beginning of their difficulties. None of them knew where Ketling was staying nowadays, nor where Volodyovski might have gone to find him, and searching for either one of them in those enormous crowds made as much sense as looking for two grains of sand in a peck of birdseed.

Their first stop was at the headquarters of Hetman Sobieski in the Danillovski Palace, where they were told that Ketling planned to leave that very morning and was probably already on his way north out of the city. Yes, Volodyovski had been there as well, asking about Ketling, but no one knew where he went after that. Some of the Hetman's officers suggested that the little knight might have gone visiting in the regiments bivouacked outside the city.

Pan Zagloba had the charabanc turned around and driven to the camp but nobody there could tell then anything. They looked for Volodyovski in all the inns and taverns along Dluga Street, and drove through the rowdy suburb of Praga as well, but it was all for nothing.

Night fell in the meantime, and since there was no hope of finding rooms in any of the hostelries where they could stay till morning, they turned back for home. It was a downcast trip for all of them. Basia sniffed and sniffled now and then, the pious Magistrate gave himself to prayer, and Pan Zagloba fretted worse than ever although he tried to lift everybody's spirits as well as his own.

"Ha!" he suggested. "Here we are, worrying ourselves sick, and Michal is probably home by now. What do you think of that?"

"Or he is dead!" Basia said and sniffed and started to weave and twist about on the coachman's box. "Cut out my tongue, somebody!" she wailed. "It's all my fault! It's all my fault! Sweet Jesus, I think I'll go mad!"

"Quieten down, my girl," Zagloba said at once. "Come on now, listen to me, and set your mind at rest. It's not your fault at all. Sooner or later the truth was sure to pop out anyway. And I might as well tell you that if anybody's been killed in a duel it wouldn't be Michal!"

"Yes, but I'm sorry for the other man as well. Dear God, we really paid him handsomely for his hospitality and kindness, didn't we?"

"That's the sad truth of it," added Makovyetzki.

"Ah to the Devil with all this!" Pan Zagloba was becoming as exasperated as he was uneasy and upset. "Why assume the worst? Ketling is probably a lot closer to Prussia than he is to Warsaw. You heard them say he'd left. I also trust in God's mercy and I hope that they'll remember their old friendship and all the dangers and campaigns they've shared. For God's sake, they rode stirrup to stirrup for years, used the same set of saddle-bags for a pillow, went on raids together, and dipped their arms in the same blood! Their friendship was so famous in the army that the regimental wits called Ketling '*Volodyovski's wife,*' out of regard to their closeness and his pretty looks. It's just impossible for them not to think of this when they face each other!"

"It happens, though," offered the cautious Magistrate, "that it's the greatest friendships that turn into the most unforgiving hatreds. Down in my country, Pan Deyma killed Pan Ubish with whom he lived in perfect amity for more than twenty years. I can give you a complete account of this sad affair if you'd like to hear it."

"Ah, if only my mind was less cluttered than it is right now," Zagloba assured him. "Just as I'm always glad to take advice from your kind Lady Wife, who also likes to give detailed accounts, down to the genealogies involved. But I'm struck by what you just suggested, sir, about love and hatred. God forbid that anything like that should happen this time! God forbid!"

"One was named Deyma and Ubish was the other!" Pan Makovyetzki was either still following his own line of thought or he was reinforcing his own argument. "Both were worthy fellows and old comrades in arms as well..."

"Oy! Oy! Oy!" Zagloba said darkly. "Let's trust in God that it won't be like that this time, but if it is then Ketling is a goner!"

"A tragedy," the Magistrate said after a while. "Yes, yes! Deyma and Ubish were the names! I remember it like it was yesterday! And the quarrel was also about some woman."

"It's always the women!" the old knight muttered. "Take any of those noisy, pushy magpies and you'll choke on the stew that she'll cook for you."

"Don't you attack Krysia, sir!" Basia cried out suddenly.

"I wish Michal had the good sense to fall for you!" the old knight shouted out in exasperation. "We'd have avoided all this trouble we've had..."

★   ★   ★

Talking and fretting and snapping in this manner at each other, they finally reached the little country house in Mokotov they had left that morning. Their throats tightened and their hearts beat a little faster at the sight of lights blazing in all the windows because they thought that Volodyovski might have come back before them.

But they were received only by Madame Makovyetzka. She was very worried and upset. She gave way to a flood of bitter tears when she was told that all their searching had been quite for nothing and started to lament that she'd never see her brother again. Basia sniffed and sniffled in chorus and Pan Zagloba also couldn't shake off his anxiety.

"I'll go again tomorrow," he said. "This time I'll go alone. Maybe I'll pick up some word about them somewhere."

"We'd do better to look for them together," the Magistrate suggested.

"No! You sir had best stay here with the ladies. I'll send word if Ketling's still alive."

"For God's sake!" exclaimed Pan Makovyetzki, horrified by the impropriety they were all committing if Ketling were dead in a duel with Volodyovski. "We're still staying in that man's house! We simply must find some hostelry tomorrow. It'd be better to pitch tents in the open field than to keep abusing his hospitality like this!"

"And I say that you'd best wait for word from me," Pan Zagloba urged them. "Otherwise we'll all get lost and won't know where to look for each other. If Ketling's been killed..."

"Quieter, sir, by all that's holy! Don't say such things so loud!" urged the Magistrate's Lady. "Or the servants will hear it and blab it out to Krysia and she's half dead with worry as it is."

"I'll go and sit with her!" Basia said.

★ ★ ★

She ran upstairs. The rest of them stayed where they were, anxious and fearing the worst. The thought that Ketling could be dead already filled their hearts with dread. On top of that, the night turned suddenly breathless with anticipation of a storm, clouds covered up the sky, thunder rolled heavily across the firmament and white sheets of lightning began to shred the darkness every other moment. By midnight the first of that year's Spring squalls was raging overhead so that even the manor servants woke and got out of bed.

Krysia and Basia came down to the dining room where the entire company started on their prayers, and then sat around the table, saying nothing, and merely repeating the customary phrase, *'And the Word became Flesh,'* each time a thunderbolt hit the ground outside.

The wind hissed and howled among the trees, and rattled along the shutters, and carried some strange drumming sound that, occasionally, echoed like the hoofbeats of galloping horses, and then a sick, sudden fear and a horrible premonition stirred the hair on the heads of Basia, the two men and the Magistrate's Lady, because they expected the doors to come flying open any moment and Volodyovski stepping in, splashed from head to foot with Ketling's blood. The decent, easy-going and reliable Pan Michal had become a weight on human hearts for the first time in his life, crushing their happiness like a rock, and every thought of him filled his sister, Basia and the two anxious gentlemen with terror. None of them knew what Krysia could be thinking.

But the night passed without any news about the little soldier. At daybreak, when the wind and thunder quietened down somewhat, Pan Zagloba set out for Warsaw once again.

That whole day turned into an even heavier burden of uncertainty and waiting. Basia sat perched on the windowsill until nightfall, or ran out every now and then to the gates outside, peering anxiously up the road that Pan Zagloba would take coming home, while the servants were busy packing up the visitors' belongings, as Madame Makovyetzka ordered. Krysia took on the job of supervising these preparations for departure because it gave her the chance to stay apart from the Makovyetzkis. Pan Michal's kindly sister took care not to mention his name where the girl could hear it; but just that simple fact, and that worried, uncommunicative silence, convinced the wretched Krysia that Pan Michal's love for her, as well as both their past agreement and her fresh refusal, were now common knowledge. It was hard for her to imagine how all these anxious people, who were closer than anyone to Volodyovski, could think of her without feeling bitter and resentful. Poor Krysia knew that this was the way they should have been feeling, that there was nothing she could do about it, and that these warm, loving and supportive hearts had now turned away from her, so she preferred to suffer where they could not see her.

By evening the baggage was all packed and stowed away in the wagons so that the Makovyetzkis and the two young women could leave that very day if that's what they wanted, but the Magistrate still waited for news from Zagloba. Dinner was served at last but no one wanted to eat anything, and the night began to drag past, thick with gloom and an intolerable silence, as if everyone were counting the seconds and the minutes ticked off by the clock.

"Let's move to the parlor," the Magistrate said at last, unable to stand this depressing waiting. "It's impossible to sit here any longer."

They passed into the adjoining chamber but no one had the time to say a single word before the dogs broke out in a wild chorus of barking beyond the windows.

"Someone's coming!" Basia said.

"The dogs are making such a fuss it sounds like a welcome," said Madame Makovyetzka. "As if it were somebody familiar..."

"Quiet, now!" urged the Magistrate. "You can hear some carriage wheels rattling on the road...!"

"Quiet!" repeated Basia. "Yes, they're coming closer. It must be Pan Zagloba."

Basia and Pan Makovyetzki leaped to their feet and hurried outside. Madame Makovyetzka's heart started hammering in her breast but she stayed with Krysia, so as not to give away that Pan Zagloba was bringing urgent and important news.

The rumble of the carriage wheels was now echoing right outside the windows and then there was silence. Then there were some raised voices in the hall, and suddenly Basia was back in the sitting room, as wild-eyed and breathless as if she'd seen a ghost.

"Basia!" Madame Makovyetzka's voice shook with utmost urgency and terror. "Who is it? What's it all about?"

But before Basia could catch her breath to answer, the doors flew open at her back, and Pan Makovyetzki stalked into the room with Volodyovski and Ketling walking close behind.

"And the Word became Flesh!" cried the thunderstruck Madame Makovyetzka.

Chapter Twenty-five

KETLING WAS SO sheepish and abashed that he barely managed a deep bow for the ladies; then he stood as still as a marble statue, with his eyes half-closed, clutching his hat against his chest, and looking more like a beautiful and lovingly constructed work of art than a living man. Volodyovski gave his sister a quick reassuring hug and walked up to Krysia.

The girl's face was as white and stiff as sailcloth. The soft, downy smudge above her upper lip seemed darker by contrast with her deathly pallor, her breast rose and fell, violent in its breathing, and Volodyovski took her hand and pressed it gently to his lips. He stood quietly before her for some time, as if gathering his thoughts, and his little whiskers moved up and down swiftly with the effort. There was great sadness in his voice when he began to speak but also a deep sense of quietness and composure.

"My dear young lady," he began somewhat formally and then gave it up. "Or my dearest *Krychna!* Listen to me calmly and don't be frightened by what I have to say. I'm not a Scythian of some kind, nor a Turk, nor am I a wild boar. I'm your friend. And even though I've not been all that lucky in that friendship I want to see you happy. It's all out in the open now about you and Ketling. I know you love each other. Panna Basia hurled it all into my eyes in her anger, and she was quite right to be angry with me. Nor do I deny that I burst out of here in a rage and went flying after Ketling to exact my vengeance. When a man has lost everything he dreams of, it's easy for him to crave retribution... and I, as God's my witness, loved you so terribly and in so many ways that revenge seemed like the only thing I had left. I wouldn't have been more shaken if you and I were married and if God had taken our only child from me..."

Here Pan Michal's voice shook a little and he paused for breath, but he soon got hold of himself again, twitched his little whiskers, and went on.

"Anyway, regrets are one thing, reality is another. It's no surprise that Ketling fell in love with you. I mean, who wouldn't? Nor is there much to scratch one's head about that you love him too. Maybe that's my fate and who am I beside Ketling anyway? I might compare well on a battlefield, he'll tell you himself, but that's neither here nor there...

"God blessed some men with beauty," he resumed after another pause, "denied it to another, and then rewarded him with a bit of understanding. So it was with me once the first rage was over and the wind blew the thoughts of revenge out of my head. I asked myself: *'What's there to punish them for? Why are you going to spill a friend's blood?'* So they fell in love. So that's the way God must've wanted it. The greatest sages say that even a Hetman's order can't command affection. It's God's will, that's all, that you should love each other, but you didn't do it behind my back, nor was there any breach of trust or betrayal of friendship, and that's to your credit... It'd be one thing if Ketling knew that you were promised to me. Then I might have called him to account. But he didn't know anything about it! So what's he to pay for? And what are you to pay for? Not a thing! He wanted to exile himself, you offered yourself to God, what else could you do? It's my fate that's to blame, nothing more, because it's clear that I'm to stay alone for the rest of my life... Well, anyway, I got over it. The anger is over..."

Pan Michal stopped again, breathing rapidly and deeply like a diver who breaks the surface of a lake after a long plunge into murky waters, and took Krysia's hand.

"It's easy to love in such a way that you get everything you want," he said. "Anyone can do that. But there are three of us whose hearts are torn apart, I told myself, so let just one squirm a little more and bring a little ease to the other two. God make you happy with Ketling, dearest Krysia! God bless you both! Amen! It hurts a bit, I admit, but it's not the first time... It's nothing... God bless you both, I say... I'm over the pain."

He said that he was over the pain and anger and that his hurt was nothing, but he spoke through clenched teeth as if a deep wound were on fire within him, and Basia's wail of pity and compassion broke out in the opposite corner of the room.

"Ketling!" Volodyovski cried. "Come here, brother!"

Ketling drew near, knelt on the floor, opened his arms in silence and embraced Krysia's knees with the greatest reverence and devotion.

"Take his face into your hands," Volodyovski said in a cracking, interrupted voice. "The poor man also suffered. God bless the two of you. You won't be going into a convent now... As for me, I'd rather have you think well of me than curse me. It hurts, yes, I admit, but that's the way God wants it..."

Basia, who could no longer stand his suffering and pain, burst out of the room, and Volodyovski turned quietly to his sister and Pan Makovyetzki.

"Why don't you go into the next room?" he suggested. "Let's leave these two alone. I'll also step aside somewhere and bend a knee in a little prayer..."

★   ★   ★

He left.

Halfway down the narrow little corridor, near the stairway where Basia told him angrily about Krysia's secret, he came across the girl again. But this time she stood with her forehead pressed against the wall, shaking with sobs and overcome by tears.

This was enough for the sentimental little knight to feel a pang of pity and regret over his own fate. He'd kept a tight grip on his feelings up to now, but all his disappointments broke free at this point, the dam of his sorrows cracked and fell apart, and his own tears trickled into his whiskers.

"Why're you crying, my lady?" he sniffed mournfully.

Basia lifted her teary face like a broken-hearted child, thrust one small fist after the other into each eye in turn, and answered him still racked by sobs and gasping for air through half-parted lips.

"I'm so sorry for you... Oh dear God! Sweet Jesus! You're such a good, decent man... Oh dear God...!"

"God bless you!" he cried out in gratitude and affection and

seized both her hands and began to kiss them. "God reward you
for your heart! Enough now... stop your crying."

But this made Basia weep all the harder and sob all the more.
Every nerve and fiber in her body seemed to shake with grief,
her lips seemed unable to catch enough air to breathe, and finally
she started to stamp her feet, quite carried away, and to cry out
so loudly that the whole corridor seemed filled with her voice.

"Krysia is stupid! So stupid! I'd take one Pan Michal over ten
Ketlings any day! I love him with all my strength! More than my
auntie... more than Uncle... more than Krysia...!"

"For God's sake! Basia!" cried the little knight.

He wanted to soothe her and help her calm herself so he
threw both his arms around her, but she clung to him with all
her strength, her head on his shoulder and her heart beating
against his chest like a tired bird, and he tightened his arms
around her and so they stood together.

A long silence followed.

"Basia," the small knight said at last. "Would you really want
me?"

"Yes! Yes! Yes!" she answered.

And now it was his turn to be swept away. He pressed his lips
to her soft, childlike mouth and that's how they remained.

★　★　★

Meanwhile the rattle of an open *britchka* came from the
outside, Pan Zagloba shot into the hallway, and then burst like
a bomb into the dining room where the Makovyetzkis were still
sitting quietly together.

"There's no sign of Michal anywhere!" he shouted. "I've
looked everywhere! Pan Kritzki told me he'd seen him with
Ketling... they must've fought already!"

"Michal is here," Madame Makovyetzka told him. "He
brought Ketling with him and gave him to Krysia!"

Pan Zagloba was dumbstruck with awe and amazement. His
face couldn't have mirrored a greater astonishment and surprise
than those with which Lot's Wife contemplated her transformation into a pillar of salt. The silence seemed as if it would go on
for ever. Then the old noble rubbed his eyes, shook his head and
blurted out an unbelieving: *"Wha-a-at...?"*

"Krysia and Ketling are sitting next door,"said the Magistrate. "And Michal went to pray."

Pan Zagloba spun on his heel and marched into the next room without another word, and even though he now knew every-thing, he was hardly able to believe the sight of Krysia and Ketling sitting close together, their fingers clasped in each other's hands, and their foreheads resting against each other. They leaped up and apart at the sight of him, thrown into a sudden turmoil of embarrassment, especially since the Mak-ovyetzkis walked in right behind him.

"A lifetime won't be enough to repay Michal for his generos-ity and his understanding,"Ketling said at last. "We owe all our happiness to him!"

"God give joy to the two of you," said Pan Makovyetzki. "We'll do nothing to counter Michal's wishes."

Krysia ran to Madame Makovyetzka and both of them wept with happiness, their arms around each other. Pan Zagloba went on standing, mouth agape, as if stunned and deafened. Ketling went down on one knee and clasped the Magistrate's legs like a son asking for a father's blessing, and he—either out of an excess of feelings and impressions, or out of sheer confusion in which everything had become quite jumbled together—scratched his head and said: "Imagine! And Deyma made mincemeat out of Ubish! You should thank Michal, not me! What was that woman's name anyway?" he asked his wife.

But Madame Makovyetzka had no time to answer because Basia ran into the room just then—pinker and more out of breath than ever, and with her tousled hair bunched more chaotically than usual across her eyes. She hopped up to Ketling and Krysia, and poking her finger from one to the other, started to cry out happily in one breathless outburst:

"Aha! Very well! So that's what you're up to! Go on then, keep sighing at each other! Get married! D'you think that Pan Michal will be left all alone in the world? Well, he won't be, because I'll take him, and that's because I love him and I told him so myself! Yes I did, and he asked if I wanted him and I said I did, better than ten others because I love him, and I'll be the best wife, and we'll go campaigning together! I've loved him from way back, right from the beginning, though I didn't say anything because he's the best and the dearest and the most decent man alive... And now go and get yourselves married off because I'm ready to marry Pan Michal tomorrow... and because... because..."

But at this point Basia did, finally, run out of breath.

Everyone stared at her with mouths hanging open, not sure whether she'd lost her mind or if she was, indeed, telling them the truth. Then they started gaping numbly at each other, and then Volodyovski appeared in the doorway, coming in Basia's wake.

"Michal!" Pan Makovyetzki asked once his own amazement subsided and his voice returned. "Is it true what we're hearing here?"

"God has given us a miracle," the little knight said gravely and nodded with a rare sense of wonder and importance. "And here,"—he raised his arms to the breathless girl—"is all my comfort, all my love, and my greatest treasure."

Basia ran to him like a doe.

Meanwhile the mask of shock and stunned astonishment slipped off Pan Zagloba's crimson face; his white beard started quivering with emotion and he flung his arms open as if to embrace the world.

"As God's my witness," he confessed. "I'm going to bawl! Come here, Michal! Come here, little warrior! Let me hug you both!"

Part IV

Chapter Twenty-six

HE LOVED HER with a passion, she adored him dearly, they had a good life together, and their sole complaint after four years of marriage was that they had no children. But they lacked nothing else and worked hard and well to build for the future.

Volodyovski bought several villages near Kamyenetz, using Basia's money as well as his own, and getting the properties for much less than their actual value since many landowners in Lower Podolia were anxious to sell-out and leave in fear of invasion by the Turks. He restored peace, stability and order and an almost military sense of discipline to these new estates, rebuilt the burned homesteads, and founded a number of *fortalitzye* or defensive manors throughout his possessions, which he garrisoned with trained troops until safer times. In short: he tilled his soil with just as much energy, devotion and courage as he had used to defend the rest of the country, keeping his saber handy all the time.

His name, however, was the best defense for his lands and the people on them. He *'poured water over the sabers'* with several Turkish frontier governors or *murjahs*, as the custom was among the frontier knighthood of those days, pledging friendship and becoming their blood-brother. Others he crushed. Freebooting Cossack bands, troops of independent roving Tartar raiders, Steppe bandits and marauding cut-throats from nearby Bessarabia, shook at their memories of *The Little Falcon*, so that his horseherds, flocks of sheep and water buffalo and camels, grazed undisturbed in the open Steppe, and even his neighbors were left unmolested.

His wealth increased with the help of a brave and dedicated woman. He was loved and honored by everyone around him. His country gave him rank and high position in his territory, his Hetman cared for him as if he were his son, the Turkish Pasha in the border fortress of Khotim smacked his lips in admiration of him, and his name was spoken with respect in far-off Crimea and in the Sultan's capital as well.

Work, war and love were the three cornerstones of his new-found life with Basia.

*   *   *

The hot and fruitful Summer of 1671 found Sir Michal and Lady Volodyovski in Basia's inherited village of Sokol which was the jewel of all their possessions, and it was there that they gave a rich and joyous welcome to Pan Zagloba, who had ignored the hardships of the journey and his own extraordinary age to pay them a visit, as he had sworn to do on their wedding day.

Their joy, however, and the noisy celebrations they staged for their guest, were soon interrupted by the Hetman's order for Volodyovski to take command of the *stannitza* of Hreptyov, keep an eye on the Moldavian border, listen for sounds of trouble in the vast, open wilderness that stretched south and east of this sparsely settled territory, and turn away whatever loose, freebooting Tartar *tchambuls* and bands of borderland marauders might erupt out there.

The little knight, who was first and foremost a soldier always ready to serve the Commonwealth, wasted little time. Word went out at once to all his serving people to drive his herds in from the Steppe, pack and load the camels, and to hold themselves armed and ready to ride.

But he could hardly stand the thought of separation from his wife. His love for her, he knew, was as full and passionate as a man might want, but it included something of a father's worry about his only child. He didn't think at times that he could breathe without her. But he didn't want to take her into the wilderness below Ushitza and expose her to all the dangers there.

She, however, was determined to go with him.

"Just think," she told him. "Will I be safer here than with you, surrounded by your soldiers? Your field-tent is all the home I want. I married you to share everything with you, and that means hardships and dangers as well. Here I'd be biting my nails with worry about you, but there, beside such a soldier as yourself, I'll feel safer than a Queen in Warsaw. If it comes to riding out with you I'll do that too. I won't be able to sleep or eat without you here, and in the end I won't be able to hold back anyway, and I'll run after you to Hreptyov, and if you won't let me in then I'll camp outside your gates, and plead and weep until you relent."

Volodyovski couldn't resist for long. He caught her in his arms and covered her face with kisses which she gave to him right back and in good measure.

"I wouldn't think twice about it," he said, "if it was just a matter of guard-duty and a few raids on marauding Tartars. There'll be enough good men as well, because I'll have the Tartar Light Horse of the Captain-General of Podolia, and another troop from the territorial chamberlain, along with Motovidlo's Cossack Borderers and Linkhauz's dragoons. We'll have at least six hundred first-rate soldiers and the armed grooms and herdsmen will make it closer to a thousand. The thing I'm concerned about is what all of us border people know beyond all doubt, and which all those arguing Warsaw politicians don't seem to be able to believe, namely that it won't be long before we're at war with the whole might of the Turks. Pan Myslishevski, the envoy to the Sultan, has confirmed that view, and the Pasha of Khotim repeats it every day. The Hetman is also certain that the Sultan won't leave Doroshenko without help much longer, and that he'll declare a great war on the Commonwealth, and what will I do with you then, my sweet precious flower?"

"Whatever happens to you will happen to me as well," she said. "I wouldn't want it any other way."

Here Pan Zagloba broke his silence which had lasted far too long for his liking anyway.

"If the Turks take you two," he told Basia. "Your fate will be far different from Michal's anyway. Ha! Think of it, though!" he rumbled on. "We've barely got done with Hmyelnitzki's Cossacks, the Swedes, the Muscovites and that pack of Prussians, and here comes the Turk! I told Father Olshovski: *'Don't drive Doroshenko to despair, give him what he wants, or you'll force him to turn for help to the Turks, which he'd do only if he didn't have any other choice!'* But did they listen to me up there in Warsaw? No, they didn't! They stuck their noses in the Cossacks' business, backed Hanenko against Doroshenko in the Ukraine, and now old 'Dorosh' has no place to run except crawl down the Turks' gullet. And, in the end, he'll bring them down on us whether he wants to or not. D'you remember, Michal? You were there when I warned Monsignor Olshovski."

"You must've done your warning when I wasn't there," said the little knight. "I don't remember being there to hear it. But what you're saying about Doroshenko is God's own truth, no less. The Hetman believes the same thing. People say he even has letters in which Doroshenko makes no bones about it. But whatever the rights or wrongs or politics of the matter, it's too late now for talking with the Cossacks..."

Then the small knight turned to matters closer to his heart.

"Tell me, though, should I take Basia to Hreptyov or leave her at home? I trust in your judgment. I'll just add that the settlement never amounted to much, and there've been so many Tartar *tchambuls* and Cossack *vatahas* running over it in the last twenty years that I doubt if I'll find two logs nailed together in one spot. Moreover, the territory is full of overgrown canyons, deep caves, hideouts and ravines buried in the forests where bandits roost by the hundreds, not counting those who come in from Valachia."

"The bandits are nothing with a command like yours," Pan Zagloba shrugged. "The *tchambuls* are also nothing. If they come in force you'll hear about them in good time, and if they come in small bands you'll crush them."

"What did I say?" Basia cried. "Bandits, Tartars, whatever, all of them are nothing! Michal will protect me from all the Hordes of the Crimea with a force as powerful as his."

"Don't interrupt my deliberations or I'll rule against you!" Pan Zagloba threatened.

Basia immediately clapped both hands across her mouth, and hid her small, fair head between her slim, hunched shoulders, pretending to be terribly afraid of Pan Zagloba. This pleased and flattered the old man even though he knew that she was only putting on a show for her own amusement.

"There, there, don't worry," he said at once and put his

gnarled old hand fondly on her shining hair. "I'll make you happy in a moment, you'll see."

* * *

Basia jumped up immediately and kissed the old man's hand because a great deal depended on his counsel which had always been so timely and so to the point that no one ever went wrong on his advice. He, in turn, thrust both fists into his belt, pushed-out his lower lip in an inquisitorial manner, and flipping his sound eye from one of them to the other asked without any warning: "But the progeny is a little late in coming? Hmm?"

"It's God's will, nothing else," Volodyovski sighed and raised his eyes.

"It's God's will, nothing else," Basia echoed and lowered her own.

"And would you like to have some?"

"I'll tell you honestly," the little knight replied. "I don't know what I wouldn't give to have some children, but I sometimes think I'd be asking for too much. Our good Lord Jesus sent me so much joy by giving me this kitten—or *little warrior*, as you choose to call her—and He's bestowed such honors and material blessings on me as well, that I just wouldn't dare to knock on His door with any other wishes. The way I look at it now and then, you see, is that if everyone was supposed to get what he wanted there'd be no difference between this earthly Commonwealth and the one in Heaven, which alone can give complete happiness. It seems to me that if I don't live to see a lad or two of my own down here on Earth, I'll see them over there, and they'll make war in the same old way on the powers of Hell, and win fame and glory under Heaven's Hetman, the Archangel Michael, against all that crawling nastiness spewed out by the Devil, and earn their own distinctions and good names."

The sentimental little knight found himself quite moved by his own devout rhetoric, and lifted his eyes again towards the ceiling, but Pan Zagloba heard him out with rather scant attention and blinked at him as coldly as before.

"Take care you don't blaspheme," he said. "All this self-flattery in which you're indulging, presuming that you can guess what Providence has in store, sounds like a sin for which you'll have to simmer in Purgatory like a broiled turnip. The good

Lord has wider sleeves than the Bishop of Krakow but he doesn't like people peering up them to see what he's got cooked up for everyone. He'll do what He wants, and you take care of what you have to do. But one thing is certain if you want some children: stick close together and avoid splitting up for whatever reason."

★ ★ ★

Hearing this, Basia hopped out into the middle of the room and started dancing about like a strolling player at a country fair.

"Isn't this just what I was saying?" she cried out, clapping her hands with pleasure. "Let's stick close together! I guessed at once, sir, that you'd take my side! Yes I did! Let's go to Hreptyov, Michal!" she pleaded and cajoled. "Take me on a raid against the Tartars at least once, my sweetheart! At least one little time, my dearest, my precious!"

"You hear her," the little knight sighed and spread his hands in a helpless gesture. "Now she wants to go campaigning too!"

"That's just because I wouldn't be afraid of the entire Horde if I were beside you!"

"*Silentium!*" Pan Zagloba ordered, following Basia's leaps and prances with his loving eyes, or rather with the one solitary eye he had. "I trust that Hreptyov, which isn't all that far from here anyway, won't be the last border fort before the frontier."

"No it won't. There'll be commands stationed in Mohilev and Yampol, and the last outpost will be near Rashkov," the little knight answered.

"Rashkov?" The old knight smiled fondly at his memories. "We know Rashkov well! It's out of there that we rode with Helen, Yan Skshetuski's wife, the time we rescued her from that canyon near the Valadynka, d'you remember, Michal? And d'you recall how I chopped up that *monstrum* Tcheremiss, or whatever kind of Devil he was, who was guarding her? But if the last *praesidium* will be out in Rashkov they'll be the first to hear if the Tartars stir in the Crimea, or if the whole Turkish might starts marching upon us. They'll send early word to Hreptyov so there's not much danger of surprise, which means that there isn't much danger at all!"

Nodding wisely, and smiling happily at this adoring and devoted couple, whom he loved more than anything on earth, the old knight finally gave his considered approval to Basia's fondest wishes.

"The more I think about it, Michal," he remarked, "the less I see why Basia shouldn't stay with you out there. I say this quite frankly, and you know I'd rather put my old head under the axe than risk anything happening to her. So take her with you! It'll be good for both of you! Basia must promise, though, that in the event of a major war she'll let herself be sent as far as Warsaw, if that's necessary, and not put up any fuss about it! Because when that happens there'll be some hard campaigning, and some heavy riding, and a lot of desperate battles and terrible sieges, and maybe even hunger and starvation such as we had in Zbarajh. And in such *extremis* even old campaigners find it heavy going, not to mention women."

"I'd be glad to fall at Michal's side," Basia told the old man both firmly and gravely. "But I do have a brain in my head and I know that if one can't, one can't. It's up to Michal anyway. He'll make the decision. He went campaigning with Pan Sobieski once already this year, but did I insist on going along? No, I didn't. Very well! If I can go with Michal to Hreptyov this time, then you gentlemen can send me off wherever you want in case of a great war."

"Yes, when that happens, Pan Zagloba can take you all the way to Podlasye, to the Skshetuskis," said the little knight. "Surely the Turks won't get that deep into the country!"

"Pan Zagloba! Pan Zagloba!" the old knight mimicked with some irritation. "What am I, some kind of baggage-master? Don't be so quick to entrust your wives to Zagloba, you young whipper-snappers! And don't rely on his age to save yourselves from a surprise or two. D'you think I'll hide behind some Podlasyan stove and keep an eye on the bakery when the Turks invade? I'm still not a cripple and there's a thing or two I can do to make myself useful. I admit I have to use a stool to climb up on a horse these days. But once I'm firmly in the saddle I can charge the enemy as well as any beardless whelp! There's neither sand nor sawdust leaking out of me as yet, God be thanked! I won't go out chasing after Tartars anymore, nor will I sniff the wind in the Wild Lands since I'm not a bloodhound, but you just keep close to me in a general engagement and you'll see great things!"

"Would you still like to go into the field, then?" asked
Volodyovski.

"Huh!"the old knight snorted. "D'you think that I don't want
to seal a valiant life with a valiant death after so many years in
harness? Hmm? What better end could I want? You knew Pan
Devyonkevitch, didn't you? It's true he didn't look more than
a hundred and forty years old but he was a hundred and forty-
two and he was still in service."

"Oh, he wasn't that old."

"Yes he was! May I sprout roots into this chair if he wasn't!
I'll go to a major war and that's that! And now I'll ride with you
and Basia to Hreptyov because I'm head-over-heels in love with
your wife!"

Basia leaped towards him, her face radiant with delight, and
began to hug him, and he only raised his head to the ceiling now
and then and gasped: "Harder! Harder!"

However Pan Volodyovski gave it all some more careful and
well-considered thought.

"We can't all go together right away," he decided. "That's
quite impossible because there's nothing out there, it's a sheer
wilderness anywhere you look, and there's not even a scrap of
shelter left among the ruins. I'll go first, find and survey the spot
for the encampment, put up a decent fort and barracks for the
soldiers, and build good stables for the better horses which
would get wasted under those primitive conditions. I'll also have
to dig the wells, thin-out the trails that you will be following,
and clean out the worst of the bandits out of all those dark caves
in the ravines and the hidden canyons. Then I'll send you a
handsome escort and you can come and join me. So you'll have
to wait here for at least three weeks."

Basia wanted to protest but Pan Zagloba recognized the
wisdom of Volodyovski's words and made his own decision.

"What's right is right,"he said. "You and me, Basia, will stay
here at home and it won't be so bad for us, you'll see. We'll also
have to gather a few special provisions and supplies that we'll
need out there on a chilly evening. You may not know it, you
two, by the way, but there's nothing like a dark, dry cave for
storing mead and wines."

Chapter Twenty-seven

VOLODYOVSKI WAS AS GOOD as his word. Three weeks later he'd finished with the buildings and sent a splendid escort: one hundred native Tartar Horse from the regiment of Pan Lantzkoronski, and one hundred of Linkhauz's dragoons led by Pan Snitko, a gentleman whose signet ring bore the crest of the Hidden Moon. Leading the Tartars was a *setnik*, or Leader of a Hundred, named Azia Mellehovitch, a very young man for such a command since he was only in his early twenties. He brought a letter for Basia from her husband.

'*My heart's beloved Basia!*' Pan Michal had written. '*Come at once because life without you is like a dry crust of bread, and if I don't turn into one myself out of longing for you, I'll devour your pink cheeks with kisses once you're here. I'm sending a substantial escort under experienced officers, of whom Pan Snitko is the foremost as both a wellborn noble and a man of substance, and whom you should treat with all the courtesies due to our own rank. Mellehovitch is a fine soldier but God only knows about his antecedents, and I doubt that he'd get to be an officer in any regiment other than the Native Horse, because it would be too easy for wellborn serving gentry to offer him an insult...*'

And then, again, he assured her of his love, expressed his longing to embrace her, and promised to cover her hands and feet with kisses when they met again.

'*As for the place,*' he went on, '*I've built a fine fortalitzya out of seasoned timbers and with good stone chimneys. We have a few rooms in a separate house. Everything smells of pine sap, and a whole mess of grasshoppers has crawled in everywhere, and when they start to chatter in the evening they make such a noise that they wake the dogs. A few*

*corn husks and the like would soon take care of them if you'd have the
bottoms of your wagons lined with a load of rushes. Glass is nowhere
to be found around here and we screen our windows with sacking and
tarpaulins. Pan Byaloglovski, however, has a glazier among his dragoons, so stop in Kamyenetz on your way and buy some window-glass
from the Armenians there. Only for God's sake make sure you wrap it
well because there's no way to replace it here if it should get smashed...*

'*I've had the walls of your room lined with rugs and carpets and it
looks quite good,*' he wrote, and added that he'd already caught
and hanged nineteen cut-throats he'd trapped in the gorges and
ravines, and that he expected to have a '*full gross*' of them
dangling by the time she arrived.

'*Pan Snitko will tell you how we live out here,*' he wrote at the
end. '*Meanwhile, heart of my heart, I commend you to the keeping of
the Holy Mother.*'

★   ★   ★

Having read the letter, she passed it to Pan Zagloba, who
perused it swiftly and immediately started treating Pan Snitko
with greater ceremony; not so great, however, that the officer
could fail to see that he was conversing with a more distinguished warrior and a much more highly placed personage than
himself—one, in short, who permitted intimacies only out of
kindness. Pan Snitko, however, took it in good grace and let it
all pass without a challenge. He was a good-hearted, easy-going
soldier with a fine sense of humor, and he'd learned to take
things as they came after a lifetime in the ranks. He had a great
deal of respect for Volodyovski and felt himself truly unimpor-
tant in the presence of a man as famous as Pan Zagloba.

Mellehovitch wasn't there when Basia read Volodyovski's
letter. He'd left the room after handing her the message, under
the pretext of seeing to his men, but actually to avoid getting
sent to the servants' quarters, which—in that place and
time—could be expected with a man whose background and
antecedents were open to question.

But Pan Zagloba had time to look him over and said to Pan
Snitko in a rather lofty and condescending manner but bearing
Volodyovski's words fresh in mind:

"You're most welcome here, sir. Most welcome. Well, well...
Pan Snitko... I've heard of you, of course! Yes, I have! Hmm...

The Hidden Moon... Yes, yes, a most distinguished crest... But what do they call that Tartar over there?"

"Mellehovitch."

"Can't say I like his looks all that much. There's something wild about him, like a hungry wolf. Michal writes that he's a man of doubtful antecedents which sounds strange to me because all our Polish and Lithuanian Tartars are gentry, even though they're Muslims. I saw whole settlements of them up in Lithuania. They're called *Lipki* over there though around here they're known as *Tcheremisses*. They've served the Commonwealth faithfully for an age and more, but many of them went over to Hmyelnitzki at the time of the peasant insurrection, and now, I hear, some of them are sniffing around the Horde... That Mellehovitch has a wolfish look about him. Has Colonel Volodyovski known him long?"

"Since Pan Sobieski's last campaign, when we rode across the Ukraine against Doroshenko and his Tartar allies."

"Ah, the last campaign! I couldn't take part in it because Pan Sobieski entrusted me with something else, though he missed me sorely later on... Hmm. Well, well. So your family crest, sir, is the Hidden Moon? I'm impressed...! So where's he from, this Mellehovitch?"

"He calls himself a Lithuanian Tartar, but it's a strange thing that none of them know him from before, even though he's serving in their regiment. Which is why there's some speculation about his antecedents despite his rather haughty bearing. He's a splendid soldier though he's close-mouthed about himself. He rendered fine service at Bratzlav, and at the fight in Kalnik, which is why the Hetman promoted him to Leader of a Hundred, even though he's the youngest man in his regiment. The *Lipki* think the world of him but nobody pays much attention to him among our serving gentry. Why? Because he's a gloomy fellow. And because, as your distinguished excellency has observed, there's something wolflike about him."

"But if he's a brave soldier, and shed his blood in service, we should receive him here as one of ourselves," Basia said at once. "Which is something my husband doesn't forbid in his letter. You'll permit me, sir?" she turned to Pan Snitko.

"Of course, ma'am! I'm always at the service of my Colonel's Lady!" Pan Snitko cried out.

Basia vanished behind the door and Pan Zagloba sighed with satisfaction. "And what, sir, do you think of your Colonel's Lady?" he grinned at Pan Snitko.

But the old soldier merely stuffed his fists into his eyes, leaned back in his chair, and cried out: "Ai, ai, ai!" After which he slapped his hands across his mouth and sat without a word, as if embarrassed by his admiration.

"Pure marzipan, what?" Pan Zagloba smiled.

★   ★   ★

Meanwhile *the marzipan* reappeared in the doorway, leading Mellehovitch who looked more than ever like a fierce, suspicious bird of prey.

"We've heard about your great deeds, sir," Basia was saying to him. "Both from Pan Snitko and in my husband's letter. So we'd like to meet you and know you a bit better. Dinner will be served soon. Please join us at the table."

"You're welcome, young fellow," Pan Zagloba added kindly, though keeping his distance. "Come in, if you please. That's it. Yes. Come closer."

The young Tartar's darkly handsome face didn't lose much of its glowering scowl but it was clear that he was grateful to be treated well and that he hadn't been ordered to stay among the lackeys. Basia went out of her way to show him every courtesy, having guessed by instinct, and by the gentle goodness of a woman's heart, that his suspicious pride was a defense against those painful and embittering humiliations that he must have suffered many times because of his unknown origins. She spoke to him in exactly the same tone and manner as she addressed Pan Snitko, the only difference being the deference due to the older man because of his age, and she displayed great interest in the heroic actions that brought him his promotion.

Pan Zagloba caught on quickly to Basia's intentions and also addressed himself frequently to the menacing young Tartar. He, in turn, spoke well and to the point—although it took him a long time to shed his scowling image—and his sharp answers and proud, haughty manner not only failed to betray a crude or vulgar background but actually astonished the old knight with their courtliness.

'That's not a peasant,' Pan Zagloba thought, surprised and intrigued. 'That's a noble's spirit.'

Then he addressed the young man aloud. "And where's your father living, my young sir?"

"In Lithuania,"Mellehovitch said and flushed as if challenged.

"Lithuania's a big country. It's as if you said: in the Commonwealth."

"Our land's no longer in the Commonwealth. My father had some property near Smolensk but all those territories have now fallen to the Russians."

"I also had some large holdings near Smolensk,"observed Pan Zagloba, "having come to them through a childless kinsman. But I preferred to give them up and stick with the Commonwealth and with my own kind."

"That's what I'm doing too,"Mellehovitch said.

"Which is an honorable thing for anyone to do,"Basia added warmly.

But Pan Snitko shrugged slightly as if to say: 'God only knows who you are and where you've come from, fellow,' and Pan Zagloba took note of it and said to Mellehovitch:

"And do you believe in Christ, young man? Or, putting it bluntly though with no offense intended, are you still blundering about in error and superstition?"

"I became a Christian and abandoned Islam which is why I had to leave my father's home,"Mellehovitch said.

"If that's the reason why you turned your back on your natural father then God will never turn His back on you! And the best example of his mercy is that you're now free to drink wine, which you wouldn't be able to do if you'd stayed a Muslim."

Snitko burst into laughter but Mellehovitch clearly didn't care to be questioned about his life and lineage and glared more savagely than ever.

However Pan Zagloba didn't pay a great deal of attention to the scowling Tartar. He had developed a distinct aversion for the morose young man, especially since his fierce, slitted eyes and his restless gestures reminded him of Bohun, a famous Cossack leader of another era that the old knight didn't like to think about too often.

★   ★   ★

Meanwhile dinner was served. The rest of the afternoon and evening passed in last minute preparations for the trip, and they set out next morning, even before first light, so as to get to Hreptyov in a single day.

More than a dozen wagons rolled along behind them because Basia decided to stock the Hreptyov larders in a sumptuous manner; a long string of heavily-laden camels followed behind the wagons, along with a herd of pack-horses that groaned under the weight of smoked meats and grain sacks; with a small herd of Steppe cattle and a sizable flock of sheep driven at the tail-end of the caravan. Mellehovitch and his Tartar soldiers rode at the head of the column while the dragoons surrounded the covered charabanc in which Basia drove with Pan Zagloba. She badly wanted to ride one of the remount horses but the old knight begged her to restrain herself, at least at the beginning of the journey.

"I wouldn't mind so much if you'd behave yourself and keep in one place," he told her. "But you'll start running out into the bush, and showing off your horsemanship, and galloping in and out of the column, and that won't be right."

"And why won't it be right?"

"Because it'll go against the dignity expected from the wife of a Commandant, that's why."

Basia did not protest. She was as happy and light-hearted as a bird. She wished for only two things since her marriage. One was to give Michal a son. The other was to live with him, for at least a year, in some *stannitza* at the edge of the fabled Wild Lands, to get her fill of a frontier soldier's life, to sample war and to taste adventure in the wilderness, to see the great Steppe with her own eyes, and to experience those thrills and dangers that she'd heard about from her earliest childhood. She had dreamed about all that even as a girl and here, at last, those dreams were coming true. What's more, she'd experience them at the side of the man she loved, the most famous Steppe soldier in the Commonwealth, of whom people said that he could find an enemy even underground.

She felt—this young Colonel's Lady—as if wings were sprouting from her shoulders, and the joy that swept through her was so intense that she wanted to cry out and shout and jump up and down, but the need to keep up a dignified appearance kept her still and quiet because she'd promised herself to behave like a stable and mature woman, and to win the love and admiration of her husband's soldiers.

★   ★   ★

She confided some of these thoughts to Pan Zagloba as they rode along, and he smiled at her with fond amusement as if he were humoring a beloved child.

"You'll be the apple of everybody's eye," he told her. "You can count on that. And everybody out there's going to walk around you as if you were the first of your kind they'd seen. A woman in a frontier outpost is a rarity."

"And when it comes to action I'll set a good example."

"Of what?"

"Of courage!" She used the word for courage which also means manhood and Pan Zagloba was even more amused. "I'm just afraid that there'll be other troops stationed beyond Hreptyov, like in Mohilev and Rashkov, so we won't get to see a real Tartar even if we need one."

"And I, my dear,"—Pan Zagloba grew considerably more serious—"am afraid that we'll see a lot more of them than we'd want. It's not for my sake that I'm worried about them, that goes without saying, but it's your safety that I'm thinking of. What is this, d'you think the *tchambuls* are under some kind of obligation to come out of the south and head only for Mohilev and Rashkov? They can come straight out of the east, out of the Steppe and Belgorod beyond it, or they can follow the course of the Dniester on the Moldavian side and erupt into the Commonwealth wherever they want, even above Hreptyov. What's to stop them from doing that? Eh? Unless, of course, they hear that I am now in residence in Hreptyov, in which case they'll go around, because they know me all too well."

"And I suppose they don't know Michal? I suppose they won't try to go around him?"

"They'll try to dodge him too, unless they come in great strength which can also happen. Besides, he'll be looking for them on his own."

"I thought as much! Tell me, though, is it a real wilderness around Hreptyov? It seems so close to civilization!"

"It couldn't be more real. There was a time, when I was still a lad, when this was a busy, populated country. You'd ride from one homestead to another and one small town or village to the next. I knew it well, I was here often! I remember when Ushitza was a big, bustling town! The late Pan Konyetzpolski proposed me for the post of *Starosta* there. But then there was the peasant insurrection, and the Hmyelnitzki troubles, and it all went to rack and ruin. It was already a barren wilderness when we came this way to rescue Helen, Yan Skshetuski's wife, a couple of dozen years ago, and the *tchambuls* must've gone through here twenty times since then... Pan Sobieski tore these lands out of the clutch of the Cossacks and the Tartars once again, like you'd tear a bone out of a dog's gullet, but there still aren't many people settled over here... All there's plenty of are cut-throats in their hideouts..."

Here Pan Zagloba started peering eagerly around, nodding his head and recalling former times.

"Dear God!" he mused. "It seemed to me, the time we rode through here to free Skshetuski's Helen, that old age was just around the corner, and now I think that I was a young man because it was all close to twenty-four years ago! Michal was still a young buck with less hair on his lip than I've on my fist. But it's all as clear in my mind as if it happened yesterday. The only thing that seems different to me are the forests and the wild growth everywhere around that's gotten thicker and bigger since the farming folk took themselves off to safer places."

Chapter Twenty-eight

IT HAPPENED THEN, just beyond the old Mongol trading post of Cathay-gorod, that they plunged into those deep forests which covered a large part of that country in those days. Now and then, especially in the region of the Studyennitza, they came across open land and caught a glimpse of the high, desolate banks of the Dniester River, and of the plains on the Moldavian side which spread to the highlands across the horizon.

Deep gorges and ravines, the lairs of wild beasts and much fiercer humans, cut across their path. Sometimes these chasms were precipitous and narrow. Others were broader, with mild slopes covered by tangled underbrush and a silent forest. Mellehovitch led his horsemen into those murky depths with tense, sharp-eyed caution, like all cavalrymen who enter hostile country, and when the tail end of the convoy was still perched on the high edge of the road above, its head sunk to what seemed like the underworld. Sometimes Basia and Pan Zagloba had to climb out of their wagon and walk down on foot; Pan Michal had done his best to cut a clean trail, but it was still too dangerous in places for wagons and horses.

Freshwater springs bubbled from the soil at the bottom of the canyons, or swift streams rustled there across broken stone, swelling in Spring with the snows melted off the Steppes. The sun burned hotly through the forests and the open grassland; but here, in the dark, stone gullets of the chasms, a damp chill crouched in eternal ambush and seized the passerby. The bleak, grim forest gripped those rocky slopes and clenched across the edges overhead as if to shield those murky depths from the golden sunlight. At times, however, they rode through whole stretches of mature timberland that had been toppled, smashed and splintered, with tree trunks piled across each other, the branches tangled and crushed together into an impenetrable thicket, and all of them were either dry and dead or covered with rusty leaves and pine fronds.

"What happened to these woods?" Basia asked Pan Zagloba the first time they caught sight of this devastation.

"Here and there it could be old defensive barriers, thrown up by past inhabitants against the Horde, or by the rebel peasants against our own forces. In other places, it's the Moldavian winds that batter these woods like that. Old folks say that unearthly creatures, or even the Devil, have their frolics when that wind is blowing."

"And you, sir, did you ever see such a Devils' Frolic?"

"See one? No, I can't say I saw one. But I heard devils shouting *'U-ha! U-ha!'* and having a good time. Ask Michal. He heard them too."

Basia was a brave young woman, but she was just a bit uneasy about ghosts, and feared evil spirits, so she began to make quick signs of the cross.

"What a dreadful landscape," she said.

And, indeed, some of the deeper gorges seemed ghostly and malignant because they were not only dark with a murky twilight but soundless and airless as well. No winds blew within them. Branches didn't rustle in that breathless silence. The only sounds came from the clicking hooves and snorting of the horses, the creak of the cartwheels, and the loud shouts of the wagon drivers in the most dangerous and forbidding places.

Sometimes the Tartars or dragoons chanted a Steppe ballad, but the dense forest wall made no reply, either in human voices or the cry of animals.

★　★　★

But if the gloomy gorges made a dark impression on the travelers, the upper country spread into cheerful vistas, even where the forests ran into one another. It was quiet Autumn weather. The sun rode through its own sky-blue Steppe, untroubled by the smallest cloud, and bathed the woods, cliffs and meadows in a golden glow. Seen in that light, the pines were gold or crimson; and the spiders' webs that clung to the trees, and to the undergrowth and single blades of grass, glittered as brightly as if they too had been spun from sunbeams. October had come to its golden midpoint, and many birds, especially those which felt the night chill more acutely, began their long aerial trek out of the Commonwealth towards the Black Sea. In that bright, cloudless space, long strings of cranes weaved southward, screaming their shrill cries in their intricate formations, with flocks of wild geese and other waterfowl beside them.

Here and there but high above the migrants, hung danger in the form of eagles drifting on outspread wings; grim hawks circled slowly elsewhere in hungry search of prey. Nor were the open fields deprived of winged inhabitants who'd rather look for safety among the tall grasses. Flocks of rust-colored partridges and quail burst into the air from under the hooves of the Tartar horses every other moment; Basia could also see long-billed herons standing like far-off sentries or stalking through the marshlands, and her cheeks reddened at the sight and her eyes shined brightly.

"We'll hunt them with greyhounds, Michal and I!" she cried and clapped her hands with pleasure.

"If your husband was a peaceful stay-at-home he'd soon have a grey beard with a wife like you," Pan Zagloba told her. "But I knew whom to give you to. Another woman might show a bit of gratitude, don't you think?"

Basia planted a quick warm kiss on each of his cheeks and the old man melted altogether.

"Loving hearts are as good in old age as a warm spot by the fireside," he said, then added after a thoughtful pause: "It's an odd thing. I've always liked the female gender, but I'll be damned if could tell you why. They're a devilish untrustworthy lot and as fluttery as quail. But they're all soft and helpless when they want to be, like a flock of children, and the heart squeaks in a man with pity whenever anything bad happens to one of them. Give me another hug, what d'you say?"

Basia would have been glad to hug the whole world just then so she obliged the old knight and they drove on in excellent high spirits. They traveled slowly because the heavily-laden wagons wouldn't be able to keep up with them at a faster pace, and it was too dangerous to let them lag behind with only a troop or two around them in those woods.

But as they neared Ushitza, the landscape narrowed and became more broken. The ravines were deeper and the forests darker. Time and again the wagons broke down, or the horses started backing up and refused to go ahead, and there were long delays. The ancient highway which ran to Mohilev at one time, was so thickly overgrown in the past twenty years that barely a trace of it remained here and there, and they had to follow difficult, rocky trails cut by passing armies, both those of long ago and more recent times, which often led nowhere.

Nor did they escape accidents. Mellehovitch's mount stumbled on the edge of a ravine and rolled down the slope to the bottom along with its rider, who sustained such a deep cut on the crown of his head that he lost consciousness for a while. Basia and Pan Zagloba immediately mounted a pair of spare horses, and the Commandant's Lady ordered that the Tartar be placed gently in the wagon and driven with great care. From that moment on, she halted the convoy at every freshwater spring and bound his head with cloths wrung in clear, cold water, working with her own hands to patch his wound and make his journey easier.

Most of the time he lay still and pale and kept his eyes closed. But one time, as she leaned over him to change the cold dressings, and asked him how he felt, he opened his eyes, caught her hand in his and raised it to his grey, bloodless lips in place of an answer.

It was only after a while that he seemed to regain consciousness and awareness and said in the dialect of the Little Russians: *"Oy, dobre, yako davno ne buvalo... It's a long time since I've felt this good."*

★ ★ ★

The whole day passed in that kind of journeying. At last the sun flushed an angry scarlet and rolled like a gigantic millstone to the Moldavian side. The Dniester glowed, shining in the dusk like a fiery ribbon, and a lowering darkness welled up in the east and flowed out of the Wild Lands.

Hreptyov was quite near then, or at least it wasn't far away, but the horses were desperate for a rest so they pulled up for a longer break.

It was the time for evening prayer. Here and there some dragoon began the Evensong, and the *Lipki* Tartars dismounted, spread sheepskins on the ground, and started praying with their faces turned towards the east.

Their voices rose and fell like a murmuring sea so that at times the cry of *'Allah! Allah!'* rang through whole swaying ranks; at other times, they rose to their feet, held their open palms close to their faces, and lost themselves in silent supplication as their dreamy, barely whispering voices, chanted a soft *'lahitch-men, ah lahitch-men'* like a distant sigh.

Basia watched the praying Tartars with great curiosity, sad that so many good men and fine soldiers would face hellfire after a lifetime of danger and hardships, especially since they were in daily contact with people who professed the true faith, and yet stayed blind to truth of their own free will.

Pan Zagloba, who stood closer to reality in such contemplations, merely shrugged whenever Basia made that kind of comment.

"God wouldn't let those goat-sons into Heaven either way," he observed. "For fear they'd bring their ugly insects with them."

After that, getting a bit of help from a servant lad, he put on a quilted, furlined short-coat which was the perfect wear against the evening chill, and ordered the convoy forward once again. But the wagons had barely lurched ahead when five riders appeared suddenly on the high ground before them.

The *Lipki* parted ranks at once.

"Michal!" Basia cried, spotting the rider who galloped before the rest.

★ ★ ★

This was indeed Pan Volodyovski who'd ridden out with just a few horsemen to meet and greet his wife. They spurred towards each other, shouting their joyful greetings, and then started to tell each, both at the same time, everything that happened to them while they were alone.

Basia plunged into an excited tale of their journey, telling how Mellehovitch *'banged his head on a stone,'* while the little knight reported on all his work in Hreptyov where, as he assured her, everything was ready and waiting to receive her *'because five hundred axes have been hacking at those buildings for three weeks.'*

Head-over-heels in love, the little colonel kept turning to his wife and throwing his arms around her, which seemed to go according to her mind as well because she rode so close to him that their horses' flanks brushed against each other.

The end of the journey was now clear in sight, but night had fallen in the meantime and a great golden moon brightened the bluish twilight. The darkness deepened and the moon grew whiter as it climbed higher in the sky, until at last its waning and uncertain light gave way to a reddening glow which rose before the convoy.

"What is that?" Basia asked.

"You'll see," Volodyovski and his little whiskers twitched in a mysterious manner. "Just as soon as we're through that last belt of woods that lies between us and Hreptyov."

"It's Hreptyov then? Already?"

"You'd see it plain as day if those trees weren't in the way."

They plunged into the woods. But they had barely crossed to the midpoint of the darkened thickets when Basia saw a swarm of glittering small lights, twinkling like fireflies or like a moving skyful of bright blinking stars that crowded up ahead, and then watched them rushing up towards her at great speed, and then the whole stretch of woodland thundered with cries of welcome.

"Vivat to our new lady!"* roared hundreds of voices. *"Vivat* to our exalted and illustrious *'Pani komendantova!' Vivat! Vivat! Vivat!"*

These were Pan Michal's soldiers who ran on foot to greet and welcome Basia, and hundreds of them pushed their way through the escorting *Lipki*. Each held a long, split stave with a burning brand set into the notch, or a sputtering lantern which dripped flaming pitch like fiery tears.

A mass of fierce, mustached faces—some of them frightening in their ferocity but all alight with the brightest joy—closed around Basia. Most of them had never set eyes on her before, and they expected a somewhat stately matron as their Colonel's Lady, so they went wild with pleasure at the sight of this bright young woman, so little more than a mere child, who bowed gratefully towards them on her small white palfrey, with her beautiful, rosy face overjoyed to see them, but also hesitant with embarrassment at their unexpected welcome.

"Thank you, gentlemen," she murmured to right and left. "Thank you... I know it's not just for me..."

But her silvery voice vanished in the roars of *'Vivat!'* and the whole woodland shook with the thundering voices.

Gentlemen-troopers from the regiments of Pan Konyetzpolski, the Captain-General of Podolia, and of the Lord Chamberlain of Premysl, crowded together with Motovidlo's veteran Cossack Horse and the Tartar Levies. Everyone wanted to see their young Colonel's Lady and get closer to her, and the more fiery among them grasped and kissed the edges of her coat or the boots in her stirrups. She was a sight so much beyond the expectations of those half-savage borderers who spent their lives in raids, manhunts, massacres and bloodshed, that their hardened hearts stirred and opened to feelings they had long forgotten. They had come out to greet her out of their affection for Volodyovski, and perhaps to flatter him as well, and found themselves suddenly moved in their own right. That soft, smiling face, so innocent and childlike with its small, flared nostrils and bright, shining eyes, became precious to them in a single moment.

*"Detino ti nasha!"*shouted the old Cossacks who were the true Steppe wolves of all her childhood legends. "Ey, you sweet little child of ours! *Cheruvim kajhe, pa'ne regimentar!"*they cried out to Volodyovski. "A true angel, colonel!"

"A morning star, as I live and breathe!" howled the serving gentry. "A precious little flower! We'll die for her gladly!"

The *Lipki* troopers smacked their swollen lips with every sign of oriental admiration and respect, placed their open palms reverently on their powerful chests and murmured *'Allah! Allah!'* while Volodyovski sat back, moved but also pleased, and took his pride in Basia.

The shouts went on. The convoy rolled at last out of the woods and the travelers caught sight of massive wooden structures clustered in a broad, palisaded circle on a spreading hilltop. This was the stronghold or *stannitza* of Hreptyov, as clear to see as if it were daylight, because huge bonfires burned all around the steep defensive slope, with entire tree trunks piled in the flames. The whole parade ground inside was ablaze with similar although smaller watch-fires, carefully guarded in case the flying sparks carried the fire to the fresh log buildings.

The throng of soldiers now put out their torches and each of them unslung a musket or a fowling piece and blasted out a welcoming salute in honor of their lady who, as the custom of the times demanded and required, would be as much the mistress of their fate from this moment on as if she were a sovereign princess among her retainers.

The regimental singers and musicians marched out to greet her at the foot of the fortification with the long, curved, war-horns of the serving gentry, the Cossacks' pipes, cymbals, drums and other instruments, and finally with the shrill flutes and whistles which were the heart of all Tartar music. Dogs barked and bayed everywhere in excitement, and fearful cattle bellowed hollowly to add to the uproar.

The convoy was now far behind and Basia rode at the head of the advancing column, flanked by her husband and Pan Zagloba.

Above the gates, prettily dressed in pine fronds, gleamed an inscription written on greased, transparent bladders with candles set and glowing inside them:

> *'Of happy moments may Cupid not deny...*
> *'Crescite,' dear guests!*
> *Flower and multiply!'*

"V*ivant! Floreant!"* howled the border soldiers when Basia and the little knight stopped to read the sign.

"By God," said Pan Zagloba. "I too am a guest but if those wishes for multiplication apply to me as well then I've no idea what to do about them."

But the old knight found a special, illuminated sign meant for him alone and read it out with quite considerable satisfaction and enjoyment.

> *'Long life to Pan Zagloba, a man without peer,*
> *Honored by all good soldiers to whom he is dear.'*

Pan Michal was close to bursting with his own excitement and invited all the officers and the serving nobles to supper in his quarters while one or two barrels of homebrewed vodka were rolled out into the parade ground for the celebrating soldiers. A few head of cattle also fell victim to the celebration and were soon roasting over the open fires. The border fortress boomed with shouts and volleys long past the midnight hour, so that the bands of cut-throats cowering in their forest hideouts were stricken with fear.

Chapter Twenty-nine

PAN VOLODYOVSKI HAD NO TIME to waste in his border outpost where his men worked as if their lives hung upon their labors. Fewer than a hundred soldiers were on duty at any time in Hreptyov; the rest were always out on various expeditions. Troop-sized detachments combed the caves and gorges all the way to Ushitza and beyond, living in constant war, because the bands of cut-throats fought hard for their lives and often came in superior numbers, so that it sometimes took a formal battle to beat them and crush them.

Such missions, sometimes in regimental strength, would take a week or more, while smaller columns rode as far as Bratzlav beyond the Ukraine, scouting for Doroshenko and Crimean Tartars. The task of these smaller scouting parties was the capturing of prisoners to question, so their nights and days passed in unending manhunts in the Steppe. Other patrols went down the Dniester to Mohilev and Yampol to keep contact with commandants stationed in those places. Yet others crouched in listening posts on the Valachian border, while work details and parties bridged the streams and rivers and repaired the old, abandoned highway.

A region in which there is so much activity soon becomes peaceful and secure. Such of the quieter people as still lived in the territory, and weren't committed to a life of banditry and pillage, started drifting homeward to their abandoned dwellings. At first they slunk home as carefully as wolves, but then moved boldly and in thicker numbers as the joys of banditry dimmed in the shadow of Volodyovski's gallows.

Hreptyov itself received a welcome smattering of Jewish artisans. Once in a while there'd be a visit from an Armenian trader, while lesser booth-keepers were in and out of the stronghold almost all the time. Pan Volodyovski could hope that if God and the Hetman left him in this command long enough to make an impression, the savage wilderness around him would, in time, turn into something different.

What he had done, he knew, was a mere beginning. A world of work and danger remained to be conquered. The roads were still too hazardous for travel. The glowering homesteaders, spoiled by easy pillage, were more likely to make friends with bandits than the military, and scurried back into their ravines at the first opportunity. The Dniester fords admitted large *vatahas* of freebooting Cossacks, Tartars, Magyars and Valachians—with God alone knew what else for company—and these swept across the countryside like Dobrudjan Tartars, attacking hamlets, homesteads and little market towns deep within the country, and looting whatever they could carry off. There wasn't one moment in a day when a border captain could put aside his saber or sling his musket on a hook, but a beginning had been made and the future looked promising enough.

The most sensitive listening posts, however, had to be planted in the east. Doroshenko's restless Cossack masses and their allied Belgorodian Tartars broke out of bounds almost all the time, spewed out their raiding parties which were often several thousand strong, harassed the scattered Polish military outposts, and burned and devastated whatever came their way. But because these were supposedly break-away bands which acted on their own, without the knowledge of either their ataman or their Khan, the little commandant could fall on them and crush them without bringing down a storm of retaliation on the entire country. He even hunted for them in the Steppe and left them with such memories of disaster that the most hardset and violent among them lost their taste for raiding.

★　★　★

In the meantime Basia was making herself at home in Hreptyov. She was entranced by that military life which she'd never observed at such close range before. All the activity, the expeditions, the soldiers' homecoming after a campaign—and even the

sight of prisoners—pleased her beyond measure. She told Volodyovski that she must take part in at least one mission but, for
the time being, she had to be content with sight-seeing around
Hreptyov, riding a swift Tartar pony beside Pan Zagloba and the
little knight, and running with the hounds after a fox or two. It
happened that the chase turned out a fierce wild boar now and
then, and he'd scuttle away into the tall grasses, and they'd ride
him down in the chaparral with Basia galloping right behind the
hounds so that she'd be the first to reach the beast when he
turned, tusks flashing, and fire her pistol straight between the
furious scarlet eyes.

Pan Zagloba liked falconry the best and he'd take out some of
the excellent hunting birds that a few of the officers had on
hand. She'd go out with him, relishing the sense of danger that
the chase provided in that savage country, but Pan Michal would
send a couple of dozen men to watch out for her in secret,
because although the Hreptyov garrison always knew what was
happening for twenty miles around them the little knight took
no chances when it came to Basia.

His soldiers loved her more each day because she watched
over the quality of their food and drink, looked after the sick
and saw to it that the wounded got the best of care. Even the
dour, scowling Mellehovitch, whose head injury still gave him
violent headaches, and whose heart was more hardened and
embittered than all the rest together, would brighten up at the
sight of her. Old soldiers praised her to high heaven, pointing to
her cavalier dash and her extensive knowledge of military affairs.

"Come the day we lose the Little Falcon," they'd nod to each
other, "she could take command, and it'd be no hardship to die
for such a brigadier."

It also happened that when Volodyovski was away and there'd
be some breach of discipline, or some other failure in carrying
out his orders, Basia growled at the offending troopers, and the
hardbitten borderers would take her admonishment to heart
even more than the stern disciplinary measures which her husband dispensed with an iron hand.

Trained in the school of Prince Yeremi Vishnovyetzki, the
little brigadier knew how to keep a tight rein on his fierce
command, and his ruthless Steppe borderers toed the line with

the obedience and docility of children, but Basia's presence had a powerful mollifying influence none the less on the worst of their rough-and-ready habits.

In the Light Horse Regiment of Pan Mikolai Pototzki there were many highborn nobles serving in the ranks, all of them men of breeding and civilization, who had lost most of their polish in the savagery of a lifelong war and in the rigors of frontier service, but who were still able to offer a certain leavening of chivalry and manners. These veterans of a hundred battles and campaigns would come often to their colonel's quarters, along with the officers of the other regiments, spinning their tales of past wars and adventures in which they'd taken part, and turning the long Autumn evenings into times of wonder.

Pan Zagloba was, of course, the foremost of such storytellers. He was by far the oldest man in Hreptyov. He'd seen the most and, by his own account, he had done the most, and he hardly let anybody else get a word in edgewise. But when a few quart-sized cups of mead got him nodding sleepily, and to slump for a snooze in the comfortable armchair that the others were always quick to offer him, then the floor was open to everybody else.

And they had much to tell.

There were men among them who'd traveled to Moscow and Sweden, both in war and peace. There were old Steppe warriors who had spent their youth in the Zaporohjan *Sietch* way back before the times of Hmyelnitzki and the Cossack holocaust, when the Poles and the Cossacks fought side-by-side like brothers against the Turks and Tartars. There were escaped or ransomed captives of the Tartars who had spent years as slaves and herdsmen in the Crimea, who dug the Sultan's wells in the pleasure palaces of Baktchi-saray, who had seen Asia Minor, who sailed through the Aegean archipelago as Turkish galley slaves, who prayed at Christ's sepulcher in Jerusalem, and who'd experienced every kind of hardship and adventure but, none the less, came back to the colors to spend their final years in this border service, and to expend their last breath and drop of blood in the defense of that ravaged and bloodstained frontier.

★ ★ ★

When the days became shorter in November, and the evenings lengthened, and the Steppe quietened down because the
tall grasses had begun to die, such gatherings in the colonel's
house became nightly fare.

Pan Motovidlo, the Ruthenian leader of the Cossack troopers, came often to sip the mulled wine, to talk and to listen. He
was a tall, thin man, as dry and weathered as a lanceshaft, who
had spent more than twenty years in constant border service.
Pan Deyma, whose brother had that famous fatal meeting with
Pan Ubish which Basia's former guardian liked to talk about,
was another caller, as was Pan Mushalski who'd been a man of
great wealth and possessions but who was taken captive by the
Tartars in his younger years, rowed as a galley-slave in the
Turkish war fleet, clawed his way to freedom, and turned his
back on all his properties to seek a lifelong vengeance on the
Turks and Tartars. He was a mounted archer without peer who'd
shoot a heron out of the sky anytime anybody wanted.

Others who came were Pan Vilga and Pan Nenashinyetz, both
of them great soldiers, along with Pan Hromyka and Pan Bavdi-
novitch and others of their kind, and all of the eastern world
came to its thrilling and awe-inspiring life when they started on
their evening tales.

Listening entranced, Basia saw living pictures of Baktchi-
saray, Istanbul, the minarets and mosques of the Muslim
prophet, the sky-blue waters of the Bosphorus, the sparkling
fountains and the teeming throngs of the Sultan's harem, the
swarms of people in the huge stone city, the various tribal and
imperial armies, the dreaded janissaries and the whirling dervishes, and that entire vast mass of threatening, restless and
merciless humanity that hurled itself time and time again against
these frontier territories of eastern Ruthenia, and against all the
churches and crosses throughout western Europe, and which the
Commonwealth held back year after year with her bloodstained
breast.

The old soldiers settled down in her rough-hewn parlor like
a flock of storks tired by their journeys, hunched around her
table in just the way that those far-ranging birds perched on old
burial mounds, resting in the Steppe, and filled the evenings
with their clacking voices.

Pine logs burned and crackled in the hearth, throwing harsh

beams of light into the shadows. Moldavian wine steamed on the glowing coals, set there by Basia's order, and serving lads dipped long-handled copper beakers into the fragrant liquor and kept the knights' goblets filled whenever they emptied. The cries of the sentries on the walls, calling out their *'All's well'* on the hour, came distantly from beyond the chamber. The locusts, about which Volodyovski had complained, chirped their skittery songs under the fresh, pine floorboards; and the November wind that blew out of the north, and which grew colder each night with the promise of approaching Winter, hissed harshly now and then through the cracks in the log-house walls which had been caulked with moss.

It was on such chilly evenings that she loved to sit in the quiet, brightly lit parlor of her timbered house, listening to the breathtaking tales of adventure.

Chapter Thirty

IT WAS ON JUST such an evening that Pan Mushalski told his own extraordinary story.

"May the Supreme Being safeguard the Commonwealth," he began. "Along with all of us and, in particular, her ladyship here present, who is a worthy spouse of our commandant, and whose splendors are surely too great for eyes like ours. I don't want to compete with Pan Zagloba, whose adventures would throw Dido and all her maids-in-waiting into dumbstruck wonder, but since all of you in this distinguished company demand the *casus cognoscere meos*, or an accounting of my past, I won't slight your worships by holding it back.

"In my youth I inherited some substantial properties near Tarashtcha in the Ukraine. I also had two fine villages, left me by my mother in the quiet country around Yaslo, but I preferred to make my home on my father's lands, since they lay closer to the Tartars and so promised greater challenges and adventures. A young man's fancy for adventure drew me to the *Sietch* but there was no room for our kind there any more, not after all those years of bloodshed with Hmyelnitzki. I did, however, go often to the Wild Lands with other restless spirits, and I tasted some exhilarating times out in the tall grasses. I had a good life back home on my estates and the only thing that stuck in my craw was a lousy neighbor. He was a common peasant from near Byelotzerkyev who was a Zaporohjan Cossack in his youth, served in the *Sietch*, became a regimental ataman, and spent some time as a Cossack representative in Warsaw where he was ennobled.

"His name was Didyuk," Pan Mushalski said. "I should add at this point that my family is a very old one, descended from a certain chieftain of the ancient Samnites named Musca, which means *housefly* in Polish. This Musca suffered some hard reverses in fighting the Romans, made his way to the court of Zyemovit, the son of Piast, our first Polish King, who changed his name to Muscalski for greater convenience, and which our later generations altered to Mushalski.

"Being aware, then, of such ancient and distinguished lineage, I looked with special abhorrence and contempt at this jumped-up Didyuk. I would've let him be if he'd at least show some respect for the high honor that met him when he was ennobled, and if he professed the greatness and superiority of the gentry over the lesser orders of the Kingdom like the rest of us. But he, while holding lands as a knighted member of the gentry, made light of his dignity and his sense of place, and never missed a chance to spit out some slighting jibe about it.

"Is my shadow longer nowadays?" he'd sneer. *"I was born a Cossack and I'll die a Cossack, and you can take your coats-of-arms and crests and privileges and all your noble blood and stuff it, along with the rest of your damned Polish ways and, for that matter, everything else about you snotty Poles.*

"The presence of her ladyship prevents me from showing the foul gestures he'd make at that point," the grim old archer said, "but I began to hate him with a passion. I gave him a hard time but he stood his ground. He was a hardbitten, fearless man and he gave me even better than he got. He'd have come at me with a saber but I wouldn't fight him, keeping in mind his vulgar origins. I loathed him like the plague and he paid me back with ferocious hatred. One time in Tarashtcha, he fired a pistol at me in the market square, and came within an inch of killing me, and I split his head wide open with a battlehammer. I raided him on two occasions with my manor people and he attacked me twice with mob of hoodlums. I wanted to set the law on him. But what law is there in the Ukraine where most towns are still a heap of smoking ruins? Anyone who could call out a band of cut-throats on the public highways didn't need to worry about any lawsuit in the Commonwealth! And that's what he did, without a thought for our mother country which lifted him up to a knight's estate, gave him his freedoms and his privileges which, in turn, vested him with the rights and powers of landowning gentry, and with all those liberties, excessive though they are, which are unheard of in any other nation.

"If we'd been able to meet and talk like neighbors," the gnarled borderer went on, "I might've convinced him and got him to change his ways. But the only time we ever saw each other was with a flintlock grasped in one fist and a swordhilt in the other. My loathing for him gnawed at me to such a point that my skin turned yellow, as if I were being eaten alive with fever. All I thought about was how to get my hands on him. Hatred, I knew, was a mortal sin, so all I planned to do was flay his back with a bullwhip for all those insults leveled at the gentry, and then, forgiving him like a Christian for all his personal violence against me, simply have him shot.

"But God ruled otherwise," Pan Mushalski said. "I had a fine piece of pastureland some way beyond the village and I went there one day to have a look at it. I was there just long enough for nine Hail Marys when I heard some kind of *clamor* ringing in my ears. I looked around and there was smoke hanging above the village like a storm cloud. Then people came running. *'Tartars!'* they yelled. *'The Horde!'* And right behind them came a veritable swarm of that slant-eyed vermin, thick as locusts! The arrows rained like a cloudburst all around, and everywhere I looked there were sheepskin coats and those devil faces. I jumped for my horse! But I'd hardly got one foot in the stirrup when there were five or six lariats 'round my body. I tore at them with all my strength, and I had a lot of muscle in those days... But *nec Hercules,* as the saying goes, one man's strength is futile against the many... and three months later I was in a village beyond Baktchi-saray with all the other captives.

"My master's name was Selim-bey. He was a rich Tartar but a cruel man and without any feeling for his slaves. We dug wells all day under the whip and worked in his fields. I thought I'd buy my freedom, I had the means at home, and I sent letters by an Armenian trader to my estates near Yaslo. I don't know if they ever got there, or if the ransom was intercepted somewhere along the way, but no moneys came, and in a short while they took me to Istanbul and sold me to the galleys.

"I could talk for a week or more about that city," the grim old borderer went on after a while. "I doubt if there's another like it anywhere on earth. So many great stone buildings, such ornaments and riches, and with as many people everywhere around as there are grass-blades in the Steppe or stones in the Dniester. Huge walls, so thick that a highway could run along their top, and janissaries march there forty men abreast. One great tower right next to another, and the town itself is full of wandering dogs which the Turks don't harm because, most likely, they feel kinship for them, being such dogs themselves... There're only slaves and masters in their hierarchy, and there's no slavery harder than among the heathen. God knows if this is true, but I heard in the galleys that the waters of the Bosphorus and the Golden Horn sprung from the tears of the slaves. A lot of mine flowed there as well...

"There's no match anywhere on earth for the power of the Turks," Pan Mushalski resumed after another pause. "No other potentate has as many kings and rulers for vassals as the Turkish Sultan, and the Turks themselves say that if it weren't for the mad dogs of *Lehistan*—which is their name for us and our Motherland—they'd have been masters of the world a long time ago.

"All the rest of mankind lives as infidels and blasphemes the Prophet behind the Pole's back," they say. *"Because,"*—as they put it—*"he crouches snarling at the foot of the cross like a rabid dog and bites at our hands...*

"And they're right to say it," the Steppe knight went on, "because isn't that just what we do here in Hreptyov, and in the outer posts in Mohilev and Yampol? There is a lot of evil in our Commonwealth and maybe we've a share of that right here as well, but the way I see it, God will take our service into account some day, and so might the people..."

★ ★ ★

"But let me get back to my own story," he resumed. "Those slaves who live on land, in the towns and villages, live a life of pain but they suffer fewer torments than those who must row the galleys. Because once they're chained to their bench and their oar that's where they remain for the rest of their lives. Those manacles are never opened, neither at night or in day-time, nor is there ever a Holy Day when a man might rest, and if the ship goes down *in pugna navalis,* as they say, the galley slave goes with it. They sit naked on the oar deck, exposed to the weather. They're chilled by the bitter cold of the wind at sea, scorched by the midday sun, and sluiced by every rain. Hunger torments them, and there's no relief from the tears and back-breaking labor, because the oars are so long and heavy that each needs two men to move it...

"They brought me there at night, chained me to the oar across from some other poor son of misfortune, and I got no look at him at all at night and in the shadows. Ah, when I heard the thud of that mallet and the clang and clatter of that chain... dear God! I thought that they were driving the nails into my coffin, though I'd have preferred that. I prayed. But all hope was gone. It was as if an icy wind had blown it clean out of my heart. The *Cawa-dji*, or overseer, beat me into silence with his plaited whip, and I sat through the night without a word. But then the light broke and I glanced up at the other oarsman, wanting a look at the man with whom I'd be suffering and laboring until my last moment, and—Great God alive!—can anybody guess whom I saw seated in chains right in front of me? Didyuk! It was Didyuk! I knew him at once even though he was as naked as I and so thin that every bone was showing, and he had a beard down to his waist because he'd already been in the galleys a long time...

"I started watching him and he stared at me, and neither of us said one word to the other... because, to tell the truth, what was there to say? There we were, that's where life would end for both of us, that's where everything had led us... But that hatred was still so powerful between us that we couldn't even greet each other like two Christian men. On the contrary, all those remembered injuries burst into such a flame in each of us, that we both felt a wild joy at the thought that our enemy's torments were at least no lesser than our own...

"That day the ship set sail, though it is always the galley slaves that move it. It was very strange to work the same oar with your most hated enemy, to eat such filth out of the same bowl that our dogs wouldn't touch it back at home, to bend our backs to the same whip, gulp the same breath of sea air, suffer together and weep at the same time... We went through the Hellespont and then rowed into the Aegean, past island after island, and all of it was Turkish. So were the shores all around that sea. The whole world seemed Turkish while life at those oars became a never-ending torture...

"The upper oarsmen," he went on in a measured beat, as if still breathing across his galley oar, "sit in facing pairs on an open half-deck, running along the length of the galley, and that back-breaking work under that burning sun must be like life in Hell. The sun is so hot that the water seems to catch on fire, and when that glare begins to leap and dance on the wavetops you'd think a fiery rain was coming down upon you. Sweat poured off us until there was no more. Our tongues dried up, glued to the roofs of our mouths. At night the cold gnawed on us like a dog... And nowhere was there a word of comfort, a consoling thought... Nowhere! All that we had was pain, grief for the happiness that each of us had lost, more pain and bone-wracking labor...

"Ah,"—and he gave a hopeless shrug—"words can't come near the truth of it. We sailed all over the Archipelago and then around the Pelloponnesus. Day followed day. One week replaced another. Not a word passed between me and Didyuk but God's hand began to crush us both. Work and the weather were stripping the flesh off our bones, and those wounds lashed into our backs with rhinoceros hide festered in the sun. At night we prayed for death. I'd no sooner start drifting into sleep when I'd hear Didyuk: '*Chryste pomyluy! Sviatchasta Prechistaya, pomyluy!* Have mercy, Christ! Have mercy, Holiest Virgin. Let me die. *Daiy umerty...*' And he'd hear and see me begging the Holy Mother and the Infant Jesus to end my own torments..."

Moved, Pan Mushalski shook his head slowly from side to side and stared into the fire as if it were the light of a revelation.

"It was as if the sea winds were blowing all that hatred out of both our hearts," he went on gravely. "There was less of it each day. At last, when I wept for my own suffering, I was weeping over his as well, and we were both looking at each other with new eyes. More than that, we started looking out for each other. When I shook with fever and couldn't pull the oar he did all the rowing. When he got sick I did the same for him. When they brought us food each of us saw to it that the other got his fair share. In short we began to love each other. Ah, but wouldn't you know it? Human nature being what it is, neither of us

wanted to be the first to say it. Ah, what a stubborn devil he was!
A real Ukrainian soul...!

"Then came a day when we'd both just about reached the end
of our rope, and the word on deck was that we'd be fighting the
Venetian fleet next day. Food was running out. The whipping
was the only thing that wasn't in short supply. Night came. We
were both moaning, both praying hard, each in his own tongue.
I looked up, saw him in the moonlight, and there were tears
streaming all the way down into his beard. My heart swelled
with pity, so I said: *'Didyuk! We're both from the same corner of the
world. We are landsmen, brother! Can't we try to forgive each other?'*

"When he heard this—dear God!—what a bellow! What a
flood of tears! He leaped up! All those chains were rattling. We
threw ourselves into each other's arms right across that oar,
weeping and kissing each other. I can't say how long we held
each other because all memory left us then and time just disappeared. We just stood there, hugging and shaking with tears..."

★ ★ ★

Pan Mushalski paused for a moment at this point and his
fingers groped blindly around his moist eyes. There was a long
silence which no one dared to break. Only the cold north wind
hissed between the logs, and the fire crackled in the hearth, and
the cicadas chattered in the floorboards. Then the old archer
sighed and took a heavy breath.

"The Lord God gave us His blessings and showed us His
mercy, as will become apparent in a moment,"he went on. "But
in the meantime we paid a bitter price for our love and friendship. Holding each other like we did, we tangled all our chains
and couldn't break apart again. The overseers came and tore us
loose but the bullwhip whistled over us for more than an hour.
They lashed us without caring what they hit. Blood ran out of
me like water, it flowed out of Didyuk, and dripped out of the
scuppers into the sea in a single stream. Ah, well! Old times,
dead and gone for ever, God be praised... But from that time on
it never once occurred to me that I was descended from a
Samnite chieftain while he was a jumped-up Byelotzerkvian
peasant. I couldn't love a brother more than I loved that man,
and I'd have loved him even if he weren't ennobled, though I
was glad he was. And he was just as stubborn as he'd ever been,

giving me better than he got, only now he paid with love for love instead of hate for hate. That's the way he was, you see... That's his Cossack nature.

"Well, next day there was a naval battle. The Venetians scattered our fleet to the four winds. Our galley, badly holed with cannon, hid in some empty little bay and had to be repaired. But all the soldiers had been killed and there was no one else to do the work, so they had to break our chains and give us tools and axes. We barely got to shore and I looked at Didyuk. He looked at me. We both had the same thought in our heads. 'Now?' he asked. 'Now!' I said, and I smashed the head overseer right between the eyes while Didyuk got the captain. The other slaves took our lead and threw themselves on the rest of the Turks, and it was all over in an hour. Then we patched up that galley as best we could, went back to our oars but as free men this time, and God saw to it in His grace and mercy that the winds carried us to Venice.

"We got back to the Commonwealth by begging on the roads," the old soldier said. "Once home, I shared my Yaslo properties with Didyuk and we both enlisted with the colors straight away to pay the heathen dogs for all our blood and tears. Didyuk went to the *Sietch* during the Podhayetz campaign, joined up with Sirko's Zaporohjans, and raided the Crimea. What they did there, and what a diversion they provided for us, all you gentlemen know well enough so I don't have to tell it because it's all now a matter of history. On his way home, Didyuk took an arrow in some ambush and died of his wound, having settled his scores with interest, like he always did, and I am still here. And each time I draw my bow these days against a Turk or a Tartar I do it for Didyuk. And if that's given rest or pleasure to his soul, then all you gentlemen here will admit that he must be happy."

Here Pan Mushalski paused once more and, once again, there was only the hiss of the wind and the crackling of the fire to break the heavy silence. The old warrior fixed his eyes on the flaming logs, thought deeply for another long and moving moment, and finished his tale with these words:

"There was Nalevayko and Loboda," he named dead leaders of past Cossack risings. "We had Hmyelnitzki and his insurrection, and now we have Dorosh. Our soil stays wet with blood, we keep quarreling and fighting each other, and yet God has planted some kind of seed of love deep in all our hearts. It's just that this seed lies buried in rocky soil, as it were, and it takes oppression, whips and blood and tears to get it to flower, and it gives fruit only when in chains."

But Pan Zagloba snapped awake just then, having heard nothing of the tale beyond its beginning, and throwing in his comment where he thought it fit.

"Once a peasant, always a peasant!" he said.

Chapter Thirty-one

MELLEHOVITCH, who was still licking himself back to health after his fall and injury in the canyon, took no part in the long-range sweeps and raiding expeditions, and no one gave him much thought while he sat shut away in his quarters, until something happened that suddenly turned everyone's attention upon him.

Pan Motovidlo's Cossacks caught a suspicious-looking Tartar who had been sniffing around the outskirts of the stronghold, brought him in for questioning, and discovered that he had serious business in Hreptyov itself. He turned out to be one of those Lithuanian Tartars who abandoned their homes in the Commonwealth, abjured their oaths of service, and placed themselves under the rule of the Sultan. He'd come from the south bank of the Dniester, and carried letters to Mellehovitch from a former *Lipki* colonel named Krytchinski who now served the Turks. This immediately alerted Pan Volodyovski who summoned all his senior officers to council.

"Gentlemen," he told them. "You all know how many of our *Lipki* have gone over to the Horde, even from among those who've been living here in Ruthenia and in Lithuania for centuries. The Commonwealth took them in, allowed them to settle within our borders, gave them lands and accorded them the privileges of the minor gentry, and they repaid this generosity with betrayal. It's right, then, not to trust all of them unduly and to keep a sharp eye on what they are doing.

"We have a troop of them here as well," he said while the others nodded. "One hundred and fifty men and horses, led by Mellehovitch. I've not known this Mellehovitch long, and all I know about him is that the Hetman promoted him to Leader of a Hundred for outstanding service, and that he sent him to me along with his men. I must say I wondered why none of you ever came across him before he joined the service, or even heard of him. Our *Lipki* think the sun sets and rises by him, and follow him as blindly as a pack of dogs, and I explained that to myself by his demonstrated bravery and the acclaim he'd won in some hard-fought actions. But it seems that they themselves aren't sure who he is or where he had come from...

"I had no suspicions about him until now," the little knight went on, "nor did I ask him to tell me anything about himself, assuming that the Hetman knew everything he needed to know about him and that he wouldn't have promoted him if he couldn't be trusted. There never seemed much of a doubt, however, that Mellehovitch was a man with some sort of secret. Still, even that didn't bother me too much. People do odd things they don't like to talk about later in their lives, and I don't think that's any of my business as long their work gets done. What happened, though, is that Pan Motovidlo's men caught a Tartar with letters to Mellehovitch from Krytchinski. Is there anyone among you who doesn't know Krytchinski?"

"I knew him personally," said Pan Nenashinyetz. "And now everybody knows him as a turncoat."

"We went to school togeth..." Pan Zagloba started but cut himself short, realizing that this would make Krytchinski more than ninety years old, at which age few men get involved in conspiracies.

"To put it simply," said the little knight, "Krytchinski is a Polish Tartar. He was a colonel in one of our *Lipki* regiments, broke his allegiance and went over to the Dobrudjan Horde where, as I hear it, he has a high position because they expect him to pull all our other *Lipki* to their side. That's the kind of man this Mellehovitch has been dealing with, as this letter proves, and this is what it says."

Here the little colonel spread out a roll of paper, slapped it flat with the back of his hand, and began to read.

'*Dearly beloved brother,*' Krytchinski had written. '*Your courier reached us safely and delivered your letter...*'

"He writes in Polish?" Zagloba interrupted.

"Krytchinski, like all our Tartars, spoke only Polish and

Ruthenian," said Volodyovski. "And I doubt if Mellehovitch knows more than a word or two in the Tartar language. But listen carefully, gentlemen, and don't interrupt me. Where was I? Ah, here it is... *'delivered your letter, and God will grant that all will be well and that you'll achieve that which you so dearly want...*

"I meet here often with Moravski, Aleksandrovitch, Tarasovski and Groholski, and we write to our other Brothers for advice on how to bring about that which lies so close to your own heart as swiftly as we may. And since, as word has reached us, you are in ill-health, I am sending a man to you, my dear brother, so that he can see you with his own eyes and lift the worry from our hearts.

"Just make sure that everything stays secret because God forbid that it should all be known before its time. May God give you descendants as numerous as the stars." Pan Volodyovski read the Islamic formula of greeting and conclusion, and added: "Then he signs it. The name is *Krytchinski.*"

Finished, the little knight peered sharply at the others, looking from one face to the next and waiting for comment, but when they remained silent, he explained: "Tarasovski, Moravski, Groholski and Aleksandrovitch are all former captains of our Tartar Horse and now each of them's a traitor."

"As are Poturtchinski, Tvorovski and Adurovitch," Pan Snitko tossed in.

"What do you think of this letter, then, gentlemen?"

"Clear treason," Pan Mushalski shrugged. "There's no need to say another word about it. They're sniffing around our *Lipki* to pull them over to the Horde, and Mellehovitch goes along with it."

"My God! What a *periculum* for the whole command!" called several voices. "Those *Lipki* would give their souls for that Mellehovitch, and they'll strike at us at night whenever he orders!"

"The blackest treason under the sun!" Pan Deyma cried out.

"And to think it was the Hetman himself who made him Leader of a Hundred," Pan Mushalski said.

"Ha!" Pan Zagloba stirred with indignation and turned on Pan Snitko. "What did I say when I saw Mellehovitch? Didn't I tell you that he had the eyes of a renegade and traitor? Ha! One look was enough! He could fool everyone but not me! Tell everybody what I said about him, Master Snitko! Don't change a word! Didn't I say that he was a traitor?"

But Pan Snitko merely buried his legs deeper underneath his chair and lowered his eyes.

"Your ah... perspicacity, sir, is worthy of the highest admiration," he murmured at last. "But to tell the truth I don't recall you calling him a traitor. What you said was that his eyes reminded you of wolves."

"Ha!" the old knight roared. "So you think that a dog's a traitor, but a wolf is not, and that a wolf won't bite the hand that strokes him and feeds him? So only dogs are traitors? And now maybe you'll defend this wolf Mellehovitch and turn the rest of us into traitors? Hmm?"

Thrown off track, and both astounded by the undeserved violence of the attack and embarrassed by it, Pan Snitko opened his eyes and mouth as far as he could, and sat unable to utter a word. Luckily, Pan Zagloba soon fell asleep again, lulled by the warmth of the fireside and flagon of mead beside him.

⋆ ⋆ ⋆

Meanwhile Pan Mushalski, who liked things done quickly, said that there were only two things that needed to be done.

"The first is to thank God that such a dangerous and vicious plot has come to light in time," he offered. "And the next is to detail six dragoons to put him up against a wall."

"And then appoint a new Leader of a Hundred," added Pan Nenashinyetz. "The treason is so clear there can't be a mistake about it."

"No," said Volodyovski. "First we must question Mellehovitch, get to the bottom of the plot, and send a full report to Hetman Sobieski. I know he's most concerned about the loyalty of our Tartars. I had a talk about that recently with Pan Bogush who's close to the Hetman."

"Why bother, sir? Your Excellency can have Mellehovitch shot out of hand under the Articles of War, like any other lowborn enlisted man," said Pan Motovidlo. "He's not a regular member of the serving gentry and so he doesn't need a trial before a court-martial."

"I know my rights where he's concerned," Volodyovski

snapped. "And you, sir, don't have to remind me about the regulations."

But now some of the others had begun to shout: "Get him over here, the damned dog! Let's have a look at that turncoat and traitor!"

Pan Zagloba had been snoozing quietly in his chair, which had begun to happen to him both regularly and often, but the loud shouts jerked him awake again and he wasted no time getting back into the conversation.

"No, no, Master Snitko," he picked up his last remembered comment. "The moon might be hiding in your coat-of-arms, but your wits are even better hidden. In fact you wouldn't find them with a candle. Imagine saying that a dog, *canis fidelis* as he is, and known as man's most faithful friend among the *animalia*, is a traitor and that a wolf is not!"

★　★　★

Poor Pan Snitko raised his eyes to Heaven, as if to appeal for justice in this persecution, but he didn't want to upset the old gentleman with an argument. Luckily for him, Volodyovski ordered him just then to fetch Mellehovitch, and he hurried out of the room as quickly as he could, glad to get out of range of Pan Zagloba's unjust accusations. He was back just as quickly, leading the young Tartar who had apparently not heard about the captured courier, because he marched in calmly and quite without a qualm. His dark, handsome face had lost a lot of color while he was laid up, but now his strength was back and he no longer wore bandages on his head. Instead, he kept it covered with a Crimean skullcap made of crimson velvet.

All eyes in the room fixed themselves immediately upon him as he bowed with deep respect to Volodyovski and then nodded somewhat haughtily to all of the others.

"Mellehovitch!" Volodyovski said without preamble, and fixed him with his own sharp, penetrating stare. "Do you know Colonel Krytchinski?"

A sudden, tense shadow passed across the young Tartar's face and his narrow eyes became dark and threatening. "I do!" he said sharply.

"Then read this!" the little knight snapped out and passed him the intercepted letter.

Mellehovitch read the letter quickly and his features calmed and relaxed by the time he'd finished.

"I await your orders, sir," he said as he returned the letter.

"How long have you been plotting treason? And who are your accomplices in Hreptyov?" the little knight demanded.

"Am I charged with treason?"

"You're here to answer questions, not ask them!" the little knight said sternly.

"Then here's my reply," Mellehovitch said to Volodyovski and turned his eyes coldly on the rest of the assembled officers. "I've plotted no treason, I have no accomplices in Hreptyov, and those I may or may not have elsewhere are beyond your reach."

This haughty answer brought instant growls of anger from the officers, all of whom were gentry, and a number of them burst out at once: "Humbly, you Tartar dog! Humbly! Watch your manners, fellow! You're standing before your betters!"

The look that Mellehovitch threw at them would have frozen Summer.

"I know my duty to my commandant," he said and bowed again to Pan Volodyovski. "I also know that I'm of little worth to the rest of you gentlemen, which is why I don't expect to find friends among you. Your Worship asks about my accomplices in the work I'm doing here in Hreptyov? Very well. I've two. One is Pan Bogush, the *Podstoli* of Novgorod. The other is the Grand Hetman of the Crown."

This reply dumbfounded everyone and, for a time, no one could think of anything to say. Then Volodyovski twitched his little whiskers and asked: "How can that be?"

"This is how, Your Honor. Krytchinski, Moravski, Tvorovski and the rest of them went over to the Horde, and already did a lot of damage to the Motherland, but they've found neither luck nor fortune in their new allegiance, nor are they happy there. Maybe their consciences bother them, I don't know, but the Sultan's service isn't what they hoped for and they're fed up with being known everywhere as traitors. The Grand Hetman is well aware of this and he instructed Pan Bogush and Pan Myslishevski to get them back under the banners of the Commonwealth, and Pan Bogush used me in this work, ordering me to make contact with Krytchinski. I can show letters from Pan

Bogush that Your Worship can believe better than anything I say."

"Let's see those letters.

"They are in my quarters."

"Go with Pan Snitko and bring them here at once," said Volodyovski.

* * *

Gentlemen!" the little knight turned quickly to the others when the door had closed behind Mellehovitch. "We may have done this soldier a great injury with our quick suspicions and our rush to judgment. Because if he does have those letters and if he speaks the truth—which, I'm beginning to believe, he is—then he's not only a fine cavalier who's won renown in war, but he's a man who is sensitive to the country's good, and he deserves reward rather than suspicion. I hope to God we can repair the damage!"

No one said anything. All of them felt uneasy and ashamed, and each kept his eyes fixed on the toes of his boots, and Pan Zagloba thought it both wise and expedient to close his eyes, nod his tired old head, and pretend to have slumped into another accidental snooze.

In the meantime Mellehovitch had come back, and handed Volodyovski the letter from Pan Bogush, which the little knight read out for all to hear.

'I hear tell everywhere,' the Novgorod administrator had written. 'that you're the best man for this work we'll find anywhere, and that's because of that strange devotion that all of our Tartars seem to have for you. The Hetman is ready to forgive those renegade captains who have gone over to the Horde and he vouches for the Commonwealth's forgiveness as well. Keep in close touch with Krytchinski through men you can trust and promise him any reward you care to. Don't for God's sake, however, breathe a word of this to anyone, because if a hint of it should reach their new masters it would doom them all. You can tell the secret to Pan Volodyovski because he's your commanding officer and he'll be able to do a lot to help you. Don't spare any efforts, keeping in mind that 'finis corona opus,' or 'the end crowns the work,' as we say in Latin, and you can be sure that our grateful country will return your affection with a mother's love.'

"I've had a strange sort of gratitude here today," Mellehovitch snapped.

"For God's sake!" Volodyovski cried at him. "Why didn't you ever say a word to me about this?"

"I meant to tell Your Excellency but there's not been time since that head-wound knocked me off my feet and kept me on my back for the past few weeks. As for you, gentlemen,"—and here Mellehovitch turned coldly to the others—"you had no need to know what doesn't concern you! I trust that Your Excellency will now order silence in this matter so as not to place those other men at risk."

"Very well," Volodyovski said. "You're clear of suspicion. In fact any suspicions would be as unjustified as they'd be unjust, the evidence is clear. Carry on your mission with Krytchinski. No one will interfere with you and everyone will do their best to help you, on which I'll shake your hand as a good officer and an honorable man. Come and take supper at my home tonight."

Mellehovitch shook the hand that Pan Volodyovski held out to him, and bowed once again, while several other officers began to move towards him.

"We didn't know you," they started to assure him. "But no good man should refuse to shake your hand."

But the young Tartar only stiffened and jerked back his shoulders, and his tilted head acquired the sharp, threatening stance of a bird of prey.

"I'm standing before my betters," he said, cold as ice, and walked out of the room.

★   ★   ★

Tension left with him and the officers gathered around the refreshment table to reassure each other that not much damage had been done.

"It's not surprising he's angry," they said. "His head is still on fire with the accusation, but that'll pass. We have to treat him far differently from now on. He's got the dash and fire of a real cavalier! Yes, yes, the Grand Hetman knew what he was doing! Strange things are happening, though, hmm? Strange things, I must say."

Pan Snitko enjoyed a moment of quiet triumph, but at last he could no longer hold himself in check, and he sidled up to Pan Zagloba.

"Allow me sir," he grinned as he bowed. "But it looks like that wolf's not a traitor either...?"

"Not a traitor?" the old knight shot back. "Of course he is, but he's an *honorable* traitor, because he's plotting treason against the Horde, not us... Don't worry, Master Snitko, I'll pray every day that your dim wits might find some illumination. Maybe the Holy Ghost will take mercy on you!"

Basia was also very pleased when Pan Zagloba told her about the whole affair because, being a gentle and warmhearted woman beside all her other traits and characteristics, she felt a great deal of sympathy and kindness towards the young Tartar.

"Both Michal and I should go with him on his next dangerous expedition," she suggested quickly. "There's just no better way to show him we trust him."

But the little knight laughed, shook his head and began to stroke her small, pink face.

"Oh, you persistent fly!" he teased. "I know what you're up to! You're not concerned about trust or Mellehovitch, you want to break out into the Steppe and get a taste of battle! But it won't work, my dear... It won't work!"

And he planted one kiss after another on her lips and laughed between the kisses.

"*Mulier insidiosa est!*" Pan Zagloba pronounced with dignity and conviction and then, for no reason that anyone could see, repeated in Polish: "Women are tricky people."

★   ★   ★

Meanwhile Mellehovitch sat in his quarters with the Tartar courier, talking in low voices. They sat so close to each other that their foreheads almost touched each other's. A short tallow candle made of mutton fat flickered on the table, throwing a yellow light on Mellehovitch's open and unguarded face which bore a vivid imprint of an ancient hatred, anticipated cruelty and a fierce new joy.

"Listen to me, Halim" he whispered to the other.

"I hear you, *Effendi.*"

"Tell Krytchinski that he's smart because he wrote nothing that could hurt me here. Tell him he's smart, you hear? He's never to write any other way... They'll trust me now more than ever, all of them! The Hetman, Bogush, Myslishevski, this command, the lot! Are you listening? May the plague strangle every one of them!"

"I hear you, *Effendi.*"

"I'll go to Rashkov like it's planned to meet in secret with Krytchinski and the others, but then I must come back here for a while."

"*Effendi*, young Novovyeyski is in Rashkov now. Won't he recognize you there?"

"No. Why should he? He saw me at both the battles where we served together, at Bratzlav and Kalnik, and he didn't know me. He stares at me, he wrinkles up his brow, but he can't tell anything for sure. He was fifteen when he ran away from home and the Steppe has seen eight Winters since that day. I've changed a lot. Old Novovyeyski might know who I am but never the young one... Anyway, I'll signal you from Rashkov. Let Krytchinski be ready to move without notice and hold all his men close to the border. You must have full control of the river crossings and there's another regiment of ours in Yampol that I've got to visit before we are ready. I'll get Bogush to get me orders seconding me to Yampol, on the pretext that this will help me put pressure on Krytchinski, but I must come back here for a while afterwards."

"Back here, *Effendi?*"

"Yes! I must! I don't know how things will go for me, or even what'll happen with Bogush and the Hetman... But she's more important. I can't sleep nights, it's like I'm in a constant fever, and there's no cure for it... Ah, I'd have died if it hadn't been for her..."

"Blessed are her hands, *Effendi.*"

Mellehovitch's bluish Tartar lips had begun to tremble. He bowed even closer to the older Tartar and started whispering as urgently as if fever had set his brain on fire:

"Halim! Blessed are her hands, blessed is her head, blessed is the ground she walks on, d'you hear me, Halim! Tell them I'm well—thanks to her!"

Chapter Thirty-two

THE REVEREND KAMINSKI, once a fine Steppe soldier and a cavalier of great dash and daring, was living out his final years in Ushitza where he had set himself the task of rebuilding the parish. But because the church was a heap of rubble, and he had no live parishioners to speak of, this pastor without a flock came often to Hreptyov, where he stayed for weeks at a time and did his best to uplift the knights with his moral lessons.

It happened then, that having listened with great attention to Pan Mushalski's story, he turned to the gathering a few evenings later with a tale of his own.

"I've always liked sad stories with a happy ending," he said, "because they show that God's hand can lift a man from the cruelest trap and bring him safely home even from the Crimea. Which is why all you gentlemen ought to remind yourselves that nothing is impossible for God in His mercy, and that you should place your trust in Him at even the worst of times. That, you see, is what it's all about.

"It's to Pan Mushalski's credit that he came to love a lowborn man like a brother," he went on. "The Savior gave us the best example of that kind of love. He loved the common people even though He came of royal blood, and He made some of them into His apostles and helped them to rise in the world, and now they sit in the celestial Senate.

"But private love between individuals is one thing, and the love of one People for another is something quite different, and that's something else that our Heavenly Master told us to pursue. But look around and tell me, where is this love between differ-

ent nations? All a man sees in the world around him are such
hardened hearts, and so much unforgiving hatred, that it seems
as if people followed the teachings of the Devil rather than those
of God."

"My dear sir," Pan Zagloba was moved to interject. "You'll
have a hard time convincing us that we should love the Turk,
the Tartar or some other heathen *barbarus* who must give God a
queasy stomach anyway."

"That I don't attempt. I merely hold that children *eiusdem
matris* as it's said, or of the same mother like we and the
Cossacks, ought to love each other. Instead of which all these
lands of ours have been dripping blood since Hmyelnitzki's days,
and that was already thirty years ago."

"And who's to blame for that?"

"He who is first to admit his guilt will be the first whom God
will forgive."

"Your Reverence is wearing clerical skirts today," Pan
Zagloba noted. "But you did your share of pounding on the
rebels when you were a young man. And you did a nice job of
it too, as we hear it told..."

"I pounded on them because that was my duty as a soldier,
and that's not my sin. Where I went wrong was hating them like
the plague. I had my reasons, which I won't mention here
because it was all a long time ago and those wounds have healed,
but my fault lies in doing much more than I had to.

"I had a hundred men under my command in those days," the
old priest went on. "Hard men from Pan Nyevodovski's Dragoon Regiment, and we were often detailed on our own to track
down the rebels, and kill and burn whatever came to hand. You
gentlemen know what those times were like. The Tartars called
in by Hmyelnitzki burned and slaughtered everything that came
their way. So did we. The Cossacks also left nothing but
scorched earth and water behind them, doing even worse things
than we or the Tartars. There's no conflict on earth more
terrible than a civil war and there's no word to describe the
horror of those times. Let it suffice to say that both we and they
were more like mad dogs than people, and leave it at that. But
one day my brigade got word that the rebel hoodlums were
besieging old Pan Rusetzki in his manor and I was detached to
go to the rescue. I got there too late. The *fortalitzya* was burned

to the ground. But I caught the peasants, most of them too drunk to put up a fight, and I slaughtered all of them but a few who hid in the wheat field, and those I ordered taken alive to hang as a warning to others of their kind. But where and how? There wasn't a building or a tree left standing in the village. Even the wild pears had been chopped down on the boundary line. I had no time to build a gallows, nor were there any woods around, that being pure Steppe country. So what was I to do?

"I took my prisoners and went on," the old priest continued, "thinking I'd find some wild oak somewhere. I went a mile, then two, but there was nothing but the Steppe around me, as flat and treeless as a bowling green. At last, near evening, we came across the traces of some burned-out village. And again there was nothing I could use for a hanging tree. Here and there I'd see a heap of charcoal or some other scorched and blackened rubble. Everything else was just old, grey ashes blowing in the wind. But there was a wayside cross on a little mound: a tall, broad-armed crucifix nailed together out of good oak timbers, and fairly recent to judge by the pale, unweathered wood that glowed in the sunset as if it was on fire. There was a flat, cut-out image of Christ hanging from that cross, painted on tin and so true to life that it looked quite real unless you saw it from the side. But seen head-on, it looked like a real man, with a face drawn and pale with suffering and pain, with the crown of thorns pressed into the brow, and with upraised eyes that were full of terrible grief and sorrow.

"My first thought when I saw it was: '*Here's some upright timber so I'll use that, there's nothing else around,*' but then I got scared. In the name of the Father, the Son and the Holy Ghost! How could I hang anybody on a cross? But the way I saw it, I understood that I'd please Christ if I cut the heads off those murderers who spilled so much innocent blood, and if I did it right before His eyes.

"*Dear Lord,*" I said. "*Let it seem to you that these are the ancients who nailed you to your cross because these evil creatures are no better than those that killed you.*

"So," the old priest said, "I had them seized and dragged and beheaded one by one on top of that hillock, laying them out like a wreath at the foot of the cross, old gray-haired peasants and young lads alike.

" '*By the Lord's suffering,*' the first of them begged me. '*By that Christ up there, have mercy on us, master.*' But I just said '*take off his head,*' and the dragoon swung his saber and sliced his neck in two. They dragged up the second and he said the same thing to me: '*By that merciful Christ, good master, show mercy!*' And I said again: '*Take off his head!*' It was the same with the third, and fourth, the fifth and the rest of them. There were fourteen of them all told and each of them begged me to have mercy in Christ's name... The sun had set by the time we'd finished. I ordered them laid out in a circle around the cross. Fool that I was, I thought I'd please the Son of God with the sight of those jerking arms and legs and those twitching bodies, but they were soon quiet and still.

"Night had come by then," the old white-haired priest went on, "and I decided to bivouac right there on the spot although there was nothing we could use to get a campfire going. Still, God gave us a warm night, so my men stretched out on their saddle blankets, glad enough to get a bit of shut-eye, and I went up to the cross to say my evening prayers at Christ's feet and to ask His blessing like I always did. I thought my prayers would be all the more welcome to the Savior because of the day's hard work, and because of all those things I'd done which I thought would please Him."

★ ★ ★

"It often happens to a tired soldier that he'll fall asleep during his evening prayers," said the former raider. "And it happened to me. My dragoons, seeing me kneeling with my head against the cross, thought I'd become immersed in pious contemplation, so none of them wanted to disturb me. Meanwhile my eyes had closed and a strange dream came to me from that cross and the figure on it. I won't say that I had a vision, because I was as unworthy of one then as I am now, but fast asleep as I was I saw the whole torment of the crucifixion as if it was happening right there and then.

"Tears flowed from my eyes and an immeasurable sorrow gripped me at the suffering the Lamb was enduring. '*Lord,*' I said. '*I've a troop of good lads on hand and ready to work. If you'd like to see what Polish cavalry can do, just nod your head, and I'll have those sons of bitches, those executioners of yours, sliced into mincemeat and trampled into dust faster than it takes to say a Hail Mary!'*

"I'd no sooner said this when the whole scene vanished and all there was before me was this wayside cross, with Christ weeping bloody tears on it, and I threw my arms around the foot of it and burst into tears as well.

"I don't know how long all that lasted but eventually I got myself together and I said again: *'Lord, Lord! Why did you spread your Holy Word among those ancient Hebrews who were too far gone in their hard-hearted ways to hear you and receive it? Why didn't you come here to the Commonwealth? You can be sure we wouldn't have nailed you to a cross! We'd have been more likely to greet you with a banquet, give you lands, privileges and every kind of benefice in plenty, and find you a place among the gentry for the greater glory of your name... So why didn't you do that, Lord?'*

"I said that and I looked up—and this was all in a dream, gentlemen, remember—and what did I see? Our Lord was looking down at me like an angry judge. His eyes were bitter and his brows were furrowed. *'Your knighthoods are too cheap for me,'* he said in a great voice. *'Any rich furrow-jumper could buy one in the time of the Swedish wars, but that's another matter... You're well-matched, you and these blood-mad peasants, and I wouldn't give the lot of you for one of those old, mistaken Jews, because they cried for my crucifixion only once, while you nail me to a cross each and every day! Didn't I order you to love your enemies and to forgive all trespasses against you? And don't you all claw and tear at each other like wild beasts, drunk on each other's blood? And you—yes, you!—who wanted to ride to my rescue and then invited me here to your Commonwealth, are you any better? What have you just done? Corpses are littering the foot of my cross. Blood has splashed my feet. And yet there were innocent men among these victims, either too young or too ignorant to know what they were doing and merely following the lead of another like a flock of sheep...*

"'Did you have mercy on them? Did you judge them before you had them slaughtered? No! You didn't! And you thought you'd please me? Verily I say unto you it's a different thing to punish and admonish the way a father or an older brother corrects a younger brother or a son, than it is to spill blood in vengeance, without trial or judgment, and to know no limits in your cruelty. Things have gone so far in these lands of yours

that wolves are more merciful than people, that your grass sweats blood
instead of dew, that winds howl with horror when they fly above you,
rivers flow with tears, and all mankind merely begs for death, calling it
Salvation...!'

"Lord!" I cried. "Aren't they worse than we are? Who's been
the most implacable and cruel? Who brought in the Tartars?"

"*'Love them even as you judge and punish them,'* said the Lord,
'and then their blindness will fall from their eyes, their hearts will grow
gentle, and my mercy shall lie upon you all. Heed my Word, or an
implacable enemy will engulf you all, lock yokes around your necks, and
you'll groan and weep under his oppression—both you and these
others—until the day you've learned how to love each other. And if you
continue in your blind savagery and your stone-hearted hatred, there'll
be no mercy for anyone among you and heathen rule will grip these lands
for ever!'

"I was struck dumb with terror," said the priest. "It took a
long time before I could speak. But, at last, I threw myself down
on my face before the Lord and asked: *'Lord? What must I do to*
be forgiven?'

"*'Go and spread my Word!'* He said to me. *'Preach love!'*"

★   ★   ★

"With these words my dream disappeared," Father Kaminski
said. "Summer nights are short so dawn came soon after and I
woke wet with dew. I looked, and there were all those heads in
a ring around the cross, livid now and graying. It was a strange
thing, I'd been so pleased with myself the day before, now I was
horrified. There was this one head in particular, a seventeen-
year-old... I had the troopers give them a decent burial and,
from that moment on, I was a different man.

"In the beginning, in the early days, I'd think: *'ah, it was just*
a dream, a nightmare that's all.' But it stayed with me and it started
to intrude more and more on my everyday reality. I didn't dare
to suppose that the Lord had been talking to me because, as I
said, I didn't feel worthy. But it could've been the voice of my
conscience which had crouched out of sight in wartime, like a
Tartar hiding in the grass, and which now woke so suddenly to
reveal God's will.

"I went to confession and the priest who heard me confirmed

this supposition. *'It's clear,'* he said, *'that you've had a warning. Follow God's will or you'll finish badly.'*

"From then on I started preaching love. But my fellow officers and the rest of the fighting gentry laughed into my face. *'What are you,'* they'd ask. *'Some kind of a preacher? Who are you to lecture anybody? Haven't those sons of bitches done enough to disgust God himself? How many more churches do they have to burn? How many more altars and crosses d'you want them to desecrate? And are we to fall in love with them because of all that?'* In short, nobody would listen.

"So right after the Battle of Berestetchko, when we crushed the rebels and finished the war, I put on these skirts and became a priest, all the better to preach the Word of the Lord. I've been doing it day-in, day-out for more than twenty years. My hair's turned white but people still don't listen. I don't expect that God will hold it against me that I'm like a man crying out in a wilderness, but I wish that just once somebody would hear me.

"Gentlemen," said the old priest. "Love your enemies, punish them like a father corrects an erring son, admonish them like an older brother admonishes the younger, otherwise woe to you and to them and to the Commonwealth as well.

"Ask yourselves, what has this endless fighting and all this fratricidal hatred been about? And where have they brought us? There's an empty wilderness where once there were cities. I have tombstones for parishioners in Ushitza. Churches, towns and villages lie in ashes, and the might of the pagans swells above us like a tidal wave that threatens to engulf us all."

★ ★ ★

Pan Nenashinyetz listened to Father Kaminski's story with such intense feeling and attention that sweat burst out all over his forehead.

"I don't deny there are some fine men among the Cossacks," he said in the silence that followed the priest's tale. "Pan Motovidlo, whom we all love and honor, is the best example. But when it comes to universal love, which Father Kaminski preached to us with such eloquence, there—I admit—I've lived in deep sin up to now, because I had none in me, nor did I try to find it. Father Kaminski opened my eyes somewhat. But it'll take God's special grace to wake that love within me, and that's because of a particularly cruel blow which I can't forget, and which I'll relate to you in a moment."

"Why don't we have something warm to drink?" Zagloba interrupted.

"And throw another log on the fire," Basia ordered.

The servant lads jumped to obey, the spacious room glowed with fresh light in a moment, and each knight soon had a quart mug of mulled hot ale before him. They dipped their whiskers eagerly in the steaming liquor, took a good swallow once or twice, and Pan Nenashinyetz took the floor again, rattling on in a harsh, cracked monotone like a runaway wagon.

"Before my mother died," he said, "she placed my sister in my care. Halshka was her name. I wasn't married and I had no children so I loved that girl like the apple of my eye. She was twenty years younger than me and I carried her about in my arms as if she were my own only daughter. Then I went campaigning and the Horde swept through my lands and took her. I thought I'd go mad after I got back home. The property had gone up in smoke during the rebellion but I sold my last saddle, got what money I could, and went to the Crimea with some Armenian traders, to buy back her freedom. I found her in Baktchi-saray. She was only twelve so she wasn't in the harem yet, but that's where they kept her. I'll never forget how she threw her arms around my neck, or how she kissed my eyes when I tracked her down! But what could I do? The money I'd brought wasn't enough for ransom. The girl was just too beautiful. Yehu-aga, the *murjah* who'd seized her, wanted three times as much. I offered myself in her place but it did no good. I watched her sold in the slave market to the great Tuhay-bey himself, that terrible and implacable enemy of ours, who wanted to keep her with his women for two or three years and then turn her into one of his many wives.

"I made my way home tearing the hair out of my head," the fierce old soldier said. "Somewhere along the road I heard that one of Tuhay-bey's wives was living in a settlement near the Black Sea coast with his favorite child, a little boy called Azia. Tuhay-bey, you see, kept his wives scattered through many towns and villages so that he could always sleep under his own roof wherever he went. Anyway, I heard about this favorite son of his, and right away I knew that God had given me a last chance to save my little Halshka. If I could get my hands on the boy, I knew, I'd be able to trade him for my girl. But there was no way for me to do it all alone. I had to get a band of raiders together in the Wild Lands or the Ukraine, the kind who'd do anything for good pay and pillage, and that wasn't easy in those days for what I had in mind. Tuhay-bey was feared throughout Ruthenia, his name was enough to scare off the bravest, and besides, he was the Cossacks' best ally against us in those years.

"Still, the Steppe is always full of freebooting Cossacks who'll risk anything for loot no matter where it comes from, and I gathered a sizable bunch together. I won't waste time telling everything we went through before we could get our boats out to sea, because we had to do everything in secret, hiding from the Cossack leadership all the way. But God blessed the venture. I seized the boy along with a good amount of loot. We got away from the pursuit and reached the Wild Lands again, on our side of the sea, and I hurried towards Kamyenetz to start the negotiations through the traders there.

"I gave all the loot to my Cossack rovers," the Steppe knight went on, "keeping only Tuhay-bey's whelp for myself. I thought that since I'd been so generous with those men, and since I'd risked my neck for them time and again in all those adventures we had shared together, they'd follow me to Hell if necessary and that I'd won their hearts for all time. But I was soon to pay bitterly for that illusion. I'd forgotten that these wild dogs tear their own atamans to pieces just to get their claws on their leaders' loot. I'd forgotten that there's no such thing as loyalty, decency, gratitude or conscience among them. So, near Kamyenetz, they got a hankering for the rich ransom they'd get from Tuhay-bey for his little Azia. They came at me like wolves in the night, choked me with a rope and knifed me all over, and then left me for the jackals in the wilderness and got away with the child.

"God sent me help in time. I survived. I patched myself together. But my dear Halshka was lost to me for ever. Maybe she's still alive somewhere over there. Maybe some other savage took her for a wife after Tuhay-bey was killed at Berestetchko. Maybe she embraced Islam, like so many do, and maybe her son will one day spill my blood... And there you have my story."

★ ★ ★

Finished, Pan Nenashinyetz sat in heavy silence, staring gloomily at the floor, and Pan Mushalski sighed, shook his head and said: "Ah, think of it! How much of our blood and how many of our tears have flowed for this country..."

"Thou shalt love thine enemies!" said Father Kaminski.

"Didn't you look for that Tartar puppy once you'd got your health back again?" Pan Zagloba asked.

"As I heard it later," said Pan Nenashinyetz, "my band of marauders got itself attacked in turn by another bunch who robbed them and slaughtered them all. They must've carried off the child along with the loot. I looked for him everywhere for years afterwards but he'd vanished like a stone cast into the sea."

"Perhaps, sir, you came across him later on somewhere," Basia suggested quietly, "but you couldn't recognize him after all those years...?"

"Perhaps, my lady. He was hardly more than a baby, three years old at most, when I captured him. He hardly even knew that his name was Azia. But I'd have recognized him well enough if I ever got my hands on him because he had a blue fish tattooed over each breast."

Mellehovitch had been sitting quietly in a corner but now he broke in suddenly in a strange, tense voice. "The fish tattoos wouldn't be enough," he said. "Many Tartars wear them. Especially those who live near the sea."

"That's not true!" said the venerable Pan Hromyka. "We all had a good look at Tuhay-bey's carcass after Berestetchko, because it had been left abandoned on the battlefield, and I know for a fact that he had blue fishes tattooed on his chest while all their other corpses carried different markings."

"And I tell you, sir, that many Tartars wear the fish tattoos."

"Yes, but only if they've Tuhay-bey's foul blood in their veins."

★ ★ ★

Whatever else they might have had to say was interrupted just then by Pan Leltchitz whom Volodyovski had sent out that morning on patrol and who had returned to Hreptyov a few minutes earlier.

"Commandant!" he said right on the threshold, coming in.

"There's a big *vataha* gathered at the Orphans' Crossing, on the Moldavian side, and it looks like they mean to come across the Dniester."

"Who are they?" asked Pan Michal.

"Marauders, for the most part. There are a few Valachians, a few Hungarians, and a lot of Tartars. About two hundred men all told."

"That must be the same bunch I'd heard about plundering downriver on the Valachian side," said Volodyovski. "The Turkish governor must've squeezed them hard so they're trying to sneak over to our side. But if that's who they are then it's a bigger party than you've figured, Leltchitz. They've at least two hundred renegade Tartars among them, not counting all those others. They'll come across under the cover of darkness and we'll slip in behind them, cut them off from the river, and hit them at first light."

The quiet evening was over, there would be no more stories told that night by the crackling fireside, and the little colonel was all business as he issued orders.

"I want Mellehovitch and Pan Motovidlo ready to ride at midnight," he commanded. "Drive a small herd of cattle towards them to bait the trap, and now back to your quarters, gentlemen! Let's get some rest for what's left of the night."

The officers started taking their leave, bowing in turn to their commander and his lady, but they were not all gone from the room when Basia ran up to her husband, threw her arms around his neck, and started whispering something urgently in his ear. He smiled and kept shaking his head but she apparently insisted all the harder.

"Oh, let her go this one time, Michal," Pan Zagloba said, guessing what this urgent whispering was about. "Take her along, why don't you? Do it this once, and even I'll climb up on some sorry nag and keep you company, old as I am for this kind of thing."

Chapter Thirty-three

THE ROBBER BANDS which infested both sides of the Dniester contained men of all the nationalities that inhabited the adjoining regions. Deserters from the Dobrudjan and Belgorodian Hordes, much braver and fiercer than their Crimean brothers, were always the majority in these swarms of cut-throats, but there was no dearth of Valachians, Cossacks, Magyars and runaway Polish lackeys, grooms and drovers who deserted from one or another of the border forts that lay along the river. They terrorized both the Polish and the Valachian territories that adjoined the Dniester, crossing to one country or the other as they were squeezed by Polish border captains or Turkish commandants.

The forests, caves and canyons of the wilderness gave them safe hideouts wherever they appeared.

Their main objectives were the horse and cattle herds which belonged to the border outposts and never left the Steppe, wandering across the plains even in the Winter, and foraging for their feed under the banks of snow. But they attacked anyone and anything: small towns and villages, frontier settlements, Polish traders and Turkish merchant caravans, and negotiators who carried ransom to the Crimea. All these bands had their own rules and their special leaders but they seldom joined one another; in fact it often happened that the larger gangs attacked and massacred the smaller. They had proliferated in vast numbers throughout the territories of eastern and southern Ruthenia, especially since the Cossack-Polish wars when all protection vanished from these lands. The Dniester bands, swollen by deserters from the Hordes, were particularly dangerous. Some of them numbered upwards of five hundred men whose chieftains gave themselves the Turkish military title of *Bey*. When they attacked, they devastated the countryside with the coldblooded thoroughness of Tartars, falling upon their victims so suddenly and fiercely, that the border captains sometimes couldn't tell if they were dealing with bandits and marauders or with the lead *tchambuls* of an invading Horde.

None of these bands could stand up to regular army regiments, especially to the cavalry of the Commonwealth, but they fought like demons whenever they were cornered, knowing that capture meant a hangman's noose. Their weapons varied. They were usually short of firearms and horn-bows which were of little use in night raids anyway. Most of them carried Turkish scimitars, the long, curved daggers known as *yataghans*, pole-axes, Tartar sabers, and the lower jawbone of a horse let into the split end of a green oak stave and fastened with rawhide. These primitive Steppe versions of the battle axe were particularly deadly in a mounted, hand-to-hand encounter because they could smash through almost any saber if their wielder put muscle behind the blow. Some of them carried long-poled pitchforks, heavily banded and reinforced with iron, and with especially sharp and elongated tines; yet others fought with broad-bladed spears with which they'd hedge themselves against cavalry.

★ ★ ★

The *vataha* which halted at the Orphans' Crossing must have been particularly powerful, or it had found itself in especially dire straits on the Moldavian bank, since it dared to come so close to the Hreptyov garrison despite the terror that Volodyovski's name inspired in all the cut-throats on both sides of the river. Indeed, a second group of scouts soon confirmed that the marauders numbered more than four hundred fighting men, led by a famous bandit named Azbah-bey, who had been terrorizing the borderlands for years.

Pan Volodyovski was pleased to hear who he'd be dealing with and immediately issued the necessary orders. The Lantzkoronski and Pototzki regiments went out as well as Mellehovitch and Motovidlo, slipping out while it was still dark, and riding off in what seemed like several unrelated directions. But this was a ruse. They spread far and wide, like fishermen who wade into a river on a broad front driving their catch before them, only to come together in one predetermined spot. Volodyovski's horsemen rode out in just such a broad, encircling maneuver, casting a long net which they'd tighten at first light at the Orphans' Crossing.

Basia's heart beat quickly with excitement as her twinkling eyes darted about the departing columns.

This was to be her first major expedition.

She felt the pride of a real commander as the trained and experienced Steppe wolves vanished beyond the gates. Not one bridle jingled to betray their presence, no iron stirrup clicked against another, no sabers rattled and no horse was allowed to neigh. The night sky was cloudless and bright under a full moon which cast a sparkling light over the *stannitza* hilltop and the sloping Steppe around and beyond it. And yet no sooner had the regiments emerged through the palisade, no sooner did the moonlight break and flicker on their naked sabers, when they sunk from view like a flock of partridges in the tall Steppe grass. There was something mysterious and unearthly in this silent progress.

It seemed to her that she was watching hunters going out to some exhilarating chase that was to start at dawn, and creeping up quietly on their quarry so as not to startle the animals too soon, and she was full of confidence and anxious to take part in the pursuit.

Pan Volodyovski voiced no objections to her participation. He agreed with Zagloba that this was probably as good a time as any to let Basia have her way, especially since the bandits were unlikely to be armed with firearms and horn-bows. They didn't leave, however, until three hours after the borderers' departure since that was what Pan Michal's plan required. They rode out with Pan Zagloba, Pan Mushalski and two hundred of Linkhauz's Mazurian dragoons—picked men as tough and unbending as a stand of oaks—whose heavy sabers guaranteed that Basia would be just as safe among them as she'd have been in her husband's chamber.

Riding a man's saddle, Basia was suitably attired in voluminous, pearl-grey, velvet trousers, so wide that they seemed almost like a skirt tucked into saffron-yellow boots, and a grey

military short-coat lined with soft, white lambswool and decorated with gold-stitched embroidery along the cuffs and seams.
Slanting across her breast was a beautifully tooled cartridge-box
of silvered metal; a light Turkish saber dangled at her hip from
a silken swordstrap; and a pair of pistols protruded from the
holsters at her saddlebow. On her head she wore a wide *kolpak*
cap with a slanting top of Venetian velvet, decorated with a
heron feather, and with lynx-fur trim along the lower edge. Her
small, pink face—almost childlike with excitement and curiosity—peeked out eagerly from under this martial headgear, and
her two bright eyes glowed in the moonlight like a pair of coals.

Thus uniformed and armed, and sitting astride a dappled grey
Tartar runner which was as swift and gentle as a doe, she seemed
like a Hetman's son riding out on his first campaign under the
watchful eye of experienced warriors. They too were delighted
with her looks and spirit. Pan Zagloba and Pan Mushalski
nudged each other with their elbows as they rode behind her,
and kissed their upraised fists now and then in sheer admiration,
and they joined Volodyovski in assuring her that she'd be missing nothing just because they started out so late after the others.

"You don't know enough about military tactics," the little
knight was saying. "And that's why you suspect us of bringing
you out after everything is over. Some of our troops are going
straight for the kill. Others must circle around, to cut the fords
and crossings, and only then will they all come secretly together
and spring the trap on the enemy. We'll get there in good time.
Nothing will start without us. Every hour has been calculated
and every movement has been planned in detail in advance."

"But what if the enemy should catch on and slip through the
net?"

"They're quick and cunning but we also know a bit about this
sort of fighting."

"You can trust Michal," Pan Zagloba cried out with absolute
assurance. "There's no one like him for this kind of warfare.
Those scurvy cut-throats may not know it yet but they've run
plumb out of luck."

"I was just a young whipper-snapper in Lubnie," Pan Michal
observed, "but even then I ran this kind of operation like it was
second nature. And this time, wanting to give you a real show,

we buttoned-up everything with even greater care. The enemy won't see hide nor hair of our regiments until they're all charging him at once like a single whip-crack."

"And... and...!"—Basia squealed, delighted, and stood up in her stirrups to throw her arms around the little knight—"will I be allowed to charge as well? Will I, Michal? Will I?"

"I won't let you get into a general free-for-all melee because it's too easy to get hurt in that kind of tight-packed milling crowd, or your horse might get bowled over and fall. But I gave orders that a bunch of them should be driven up to us after they're smashed and scattering, and then we'll charge and you can cut down two or three of them as they bolt and run. Just remember always to come up on them from the left. That way the man you're chasing has a problem reaching you across his own horse and body from the right while you have him right under your saber."

"Ho! Ho!" Basia said at once. "I'm not a bit worried! You said yourself that I'm now better with a saber than Uncle Makovyetzki. None of them will get away from me!"

"Be sure to have a tight grip on your reins," Pan Zagloba added. "They've got their own tricks. It could happen that you're after one and he'll suddenly set his horse in place and you'll sweep past him at a gallop but he'll be able to reach out and get you. An experienced rider never lets his horse run wild beyond control but works him fast and slow as the situation calls for."

"And never lift your saber too high above your head so you can switch quickly to a thrust if you have to," threw in Pan Mushalski.

"I'll keep close to her just in case," the little knight assured the other two, then turned with a last bit of instruction to Basia. "You see, my love, the hardest thing in a cavalry fight like this is to remember everything at once. You've got to watch your horse, the enemy, your reins, your saber, your downstrokes and your thrusts all at the same time! It all comes naturally once you've had a few skirmishes behind you, but even the best sword-fighter can get into trouble on his first time out. All it takes is an experienced horseman, no matter how inferior with a sword, and the best beginner can go down before him. That's why I'll keep close beside you at all times."

"Just don't try to do all my work for me, will you?" Basia was insistent. "And order the others not to rush to help me unless it's really needed."

"We'll see how you feel about that in the thick of things," the little knight smiled.

"Or if you won't grab one of us by his coat-tails!" Pan Zagloba added.

"We'll see!" Basia cried, incensed and indignant.

★   ★   ★

Talking back and forth like this, they rode into a flat, open region dotted with chaparral and dwarf shrubs crouched here and there in the dark. Dawn wasn't far away but, in the meantime, the moon had set and the night grew thicker. A light mist had also started to rise from the soil, screening distant objects. Those wisps of mist, and that deepening half-light, made the black undergrowth seem alive and threatening in Basia's stirred imagination, and time and again she thought that she could see moving men and horses.

"Michal," she whispered, and thrust a questioning finger at a looming blackness. "What is that?"

"Nothing," he said. "A tangle of bushes."

"I thought it was horsemen... How soon will we be there?"

"Another hour and a half. It'll all start then."

"Ha!"

"Are you scared?"

"No, I'm just eager to get on with it, that's all... That's why my heart is hammering like this... Me, afraid? Not a bit of it! Look at the frost around here... You can see it even in the dark."

They had ridden into a stretch of the Steppe where long-stemmed thistles bowed under a covering of pale grey frost. Pan Volodyovski threw a glance at them and said:

"Motovidlo passed this way. He's gone to ground no farther off than a mile ahead. Look, the dawn is breaking!"

The first light of day had edged the horizon as he spoke and the darkness started to recede. The sky and the earth grew grey together, the air around them turned a pale blue, and the tops of trees and bushes gleamed under the silvery sheet of advancing daylight. Farther away, clumps of trees and bushes began to appear as if someone were lifting a series of succeeding curtains.

But suddenly a horseman rode out of the nearest thicket and came towards them at a silent run.

"From Pan Motovidlo?" Volodyovski asked when the Cossack trooper reined-in right beside him.

"Yes, Your Honor!"

"What's new?"

"They crossed the ford. Then they headed for Kalusik where they heard the cattle. Now they've picked up the herd and they're standing in the Yurkov meadows."

"And where's Pan Motovidlo?"

"He's covering the ridge out there to the front. Pan Mellehovitch is circling up from Kalusik way. I don't know about the other regiments, Your Honor."

"Very well," said Pan Volodyovski. "I know where they are. Now off you go to Pan Motovidlo and pass the word to close up on them. And have him string out a connecting line of men towards Pan Mellehovitch."

The Cossack trooper flattened himself across his horse's neck, sped off like an arrow shot into the night and vanished in the shadows, and they rode on even more quietly and cautiously than before.

Chapter Thirty-four

MEANWHILE THE DAWN had risen everywhere around them. The mist which had drifted upward from the ground at the break of day sunk into the grasses, and a long band of rosy light appeared at the edge of the eastern sky, tinting the air, the intermittent high ground, and the jagged edges of ravines and hilltops.

Suddenly the riders heard a loud, jumbled cawing from the direction of the Dniester, and a great flock of ravens appeared high above them and in front of them, flying into the sunrise. Lone birds broke away from this dark mass now and then, dropped lower, and circled above the Steppe like hawks seeking prey.

Pan Zagloba raised his saber and pointed to the carrion birds with its crooked end.

"It's amazing how smart these creatures are," he said to Basia. "They can always tell when a battle is about to be fought and they'll come flying in from all sides as if they've been spilled out of a sack. There's next to no sign of them when it's just one army on the march, or if it's to be a meeting of friendly forces, that's how well they guess what people have in mind even though nobody sends them an announcement. Mere instincts of the species or *sagacitas narium* doesn't account for that altogether, so it's really something for you to see."

Meanwhile the birds had come closer, cawing all the louder, and Pan Mushalski tapped his bow and turned for permission to the little knight.

"My Lord Commandant," he said. "Will you permit one shot in honor of her ladyship? It won't make any noise, after all."

"Bring down a couple, if you want," said Volodyovski, knowing how much the old soldier liked to display his skill.

The matchless archer reached into the quiver hanging on his back, drew out a feathered arrow, notched it to his bowstring, and then raised the bow, cocked his head, stared at the sky and waited.

The ravens flew closer. Everyone reined-in and halted, looking at the sky. Then the bowstring twanged, the arrow soared like a homing swallow and disappeared in the flock ahead. At first sight it might have seemed that Pan Mushalski missed, when suddenly one bird flipped over, started tumbling head-over-tail towards the ground, and finally planed straight down with outspread wings just like a falling leaf.

A moment later the carcass bounced on the ground a few feet ahead of Basia's horse, an arrow right through it.

"For a lucky omen," Pan Mushalski said and bowed to Basia. "I'll also keep an eye from a distance on your ladyship, and if there's a need I'll let loose another little arrow. Even if it buzzes real close, my lady, it won't scratch, of that I assure you."

"I wouldn't want to be the Tartar at whom you aim your arrow, sir!" Basia answered.

Volodyovski ended further conversation, pointing at a fairly lofty height-of-land a few furlongs distant.

"We'll take our stand there," he said.

★ ★ ★

After this they moved forward at a trot. Halfway up the slope the little knight ordered them into a walk and halted them just short of the summit.

"We won't ride all the way up," he said. "They'd catch sight of us from quite far away on such a bright morning. But if we dismount right here we can walk to the top and look across the skyline."

He jumped to the ground, followed by Basia, Pan Mushalski and several others. The dragoons held their horses in the rear and stayed well below the skyline while they moved up to a grass-screened spot where the ridge plunged straight down to the Steppe below them.

Dense undergrowth, tall enough to hide a mounted man, hugged the foot of the escarpment which made an almost sheer wall of eroded limestone several dozen feet behind and above it, with the low flat grassland rolling out before them as far as they could see. A slow brown stream cut across this greening plain towards the Kalusik which, in turn, was a minor tributary of the Dniester, winding among thick, widespread clumps of thorn and thistle of the same kind as the man-high, tangled growth below the observers. Thin streams of wood smoke climbed towards the sky out of the largest of these natural hideouts.

"There," Pan Volodyovski said to Basia. "That's where they've gone to ground."

"I see the smoke," Basia said, while her heart beat swiftly in her breast. "But I see neither men nor horses."

"The bush conceals them though an experienced eye can spot them. Look over there, see? Two, three, four... there's a whole bunch of horses. See the piebald one? And the white one? It looks blue from here."

"How soon will we ride down towards them?"

"Our men will drive them to us but there's still some time. It's a good half a mile to them."

"And where are our men?"

"See that belt of trees way ahead? The edge of the forest? Pan Pototzki's regiment ought to be getting in position in those trees just about now. Mellehovitch will come out from the other side. Our other Light Horse regiment will hit them from that large rockfall over there. When they've caught sight of our men they'll break out towards us on their own because they can get back to the river through the broad, light chaparral below us while on the other side there's a steep, impassable ravine that would bar their way."

"They're in a trap, then?"

"As you see."

"Oh dear God!" Basia squeaked, excited. "I can hardly keep still, I'm that impatient for it to begin!" But, after a moment, she turned to Pan Michal with another question. "And what would they do if they were smart?"

"They'd charge straight into the smoke, hit the Pototzki Horse with everything they've got and carve their way through them to the woods behind. Then they'd be free to run and probably get away. But they won't do that."

"And why won't they do that?"

"First, they never like to go head-to-head with regulars. And, in the second place, they'll be afraid that there are other troops waiting in the forest. So they'll come towards us."

"Bah!" Basia snorted. "But how will we hold them? We've only two hundred men."

"What about Motovidlo?"

"That's right! Pan Motovidlo!" Basia cried. "Where is he?"

Instead of answering, Pan Volodyovski uttered a sharp, shrill scream, exactly of the kind that a hawk would give at the sight of prey, and—at once!—similar cries replied from the foot of the cliff below them. These, Basia realized at once, were Motovidlo's troopers, who were so well hidden in the nearest thicket that she hadn't spotted them at all even though she stood a scant fifty feet above them.

So for a while she peered down, astonished, then shot an especially measuring glance at her little husband, and suddenly her cheeks flushed with admiration and she threw her arms once again around Pan Michal's neck.

"Michalku!" she cried, using the family diminutive of his name. "You must be the greatest commander in the world!"

"I've just a bit of experience." Volodyovski smiled, feeling an overwhelming wave of love and affection for this extraordinary young woman. "But don't you go fluttering about here with excitement, hear? Remember that a good soldier is a calm one."

★   ★   ★

But the rebuke did little good. Basia felt as if she was in the grip of fever. She wanted to jump back on her horse at once and ride down into the thicket where Motovidlo's Cossack companies were hiding. But Volodyovski kept her still for a little longer because he wanted her to get a good look at the start of the action.

Meanwhile the morning sun had climbed over the horizon and its cold, brassy light bathed the entire plain like a reflection cast by a gilded mirror. The nearby thickets leaped brightly into prominence and acquired texture; the more distant copses became more distinct; frost glittered whitely here and there at the bottom of a gulch; the air became translucent like water under ice, and the eye flew as far as it could reach, seemingly beyond limits.

"Pan Pototzki's regiment is coming out of the woods,"Volodyovski said suddenly. "I see the men and horses."

And indeed a long line of horsemen emerged from the darkened wall of the trees behind them, looking starkly black against the silvery sheen of the woodland meadow. The white, frosted space between them and the forest began to widen slowly. They were apparently in no hurry, waiting for the other regiments to appear.

Volodyovski turned towards his left. "And here's Mellehovitch," he said. And a moment later, with quiet satisfaction: "The Chamberlain's Horse is here too. Everyone came together right on time."

Then his sharp, pointed little whiskers twitched and started moving swiftly up and down as he shot a sharp, satisfied glance towards the bandits' hideout.

"Not one of them should get out of this alive!"he said. "And now, mount up!"

They turned quickly towards the dragoons, leaped back into their saddles, and rode down and around the side of the ridge into the tall coppice below the escarpment where they joined up with Motovidlo's Cossacks. After which, all of them moved carefully forward at a walk until they halted at the edge of the thicket, staring straight ahead.

Their quarry must have caught sight of the approaching troop that was now coming at a fast trot from their left because the widespread copse in mid-plain suddenly erupted with groups of hurrying horsemen who darted into the tall grass before them like a herd of deer. More and more of them spilled out of the undergrowth every moment, turning at first into a long chain of animals and riders, and trotting lightly at the edge of their concealing hedges. The riders lay flat against their horses' necks, becoming practically invisible, so that a careless glance thrown at them from a distance might dismiss them as only a string of mustangs trailing through the thicket. They must not have been sure if the Pototzki Horse were coming straight at them, or if it was only a detachment patrolling the countryside. If the worst should happen, they could expect that the thick veldt bush would hide them for a little longer.

From where Volodyovski stood at the head of Motovidlo's Cossacks, the enemy's quandary was evident and clear. Their

movements showed the nervous, darting quality of animals that
had sniffed out a danger but weren't sure exactly what it was.
Their pace increased to a ragged canter as they broke out into
the open plain and then the front ranks reined-in suddenly and
the rest of the *vataha* came to a halt behind them.

They had caught sight of Mellehovitch's Tartar Horse coming
at them from the opposite side.

They spurred ahead at once, wheeled sharply away from the
thicket, and their eyes fell on the Chamberlain's regiment now
coming at them at a trot in full battle order.

Now they could have no doubt. Each of them would know
in a flash that all these troops knew exactly where they were, and
that they weren't here on any routine sweeping operation but
that they'd come to kill them. Wild shouts of rage and panic
burst out of the milling ranks that piled upon each other in
disorder. The regiments thundered with an answering cheer,
broke into a canter, and the entire plain filled at once with the
quick drumming of their horses' hooves. At once, as if spurred
by a dangerous beasts's instinct for survival, the whole bandit
mass broke into full gallop and ran as fast as their breathless
horses could take them straight towards the ridge under which
Volodyovski and Motovidlo's men were waiting.

The intervening distance narrowed with terrifying speed.

Basia grew somewhat pale. It wasn't fear as much as sheer
excitement, and her heart hammered in her breast even more
swiftly than before. But she was aware that other eyes could see
her, and saw no alarm in any other face, so she brought herself
quickly under firm control. Her whole attention focused on the
rushing mass before her. She tightened her reins, and her fingers
gripped the hilt of her little saber, and a new rush of blood
mounted to her face.

"You're doing well," came the calm voice of the little knight
beside her.

She threw him a swift wide-eyed glance, her little nostrils
flared, and she whispered quickly: "Are we charging soon?"

"There's still some time," Pan Michal replied.

Out in the open country that spread out before them, the
greyish mass of galloping marauders was now in full flight,
running like a fieldful of panicked wild hares which hear the
baying of the hounds behind them. No more than half a furlong

now lay between them and the long, crimson-coated line of silent Cossack troopers who waited for them in their concealing thicket. She could see the outstretched necks and the bobbing heads of their panting horses, the wildly flared nostrils, the glaring eyes, and the flat, slanting masks of the Tartar faces crouched just above the manes...

And now they were closer. She felt, more than saw, Pan Michal's arm going up in the air beside her. She saw the bared teeth and heard the whistling breath of the animals that hurtled towards her at a pace that robbed them of breath. But in that instant Volodyovski dropped his upraised arm and a hedge of muskets dipped as one towards them all along the line of Motovidlo's men.

"Fire!" the colonel shouted.

A thunderous blast swept out of the thicket. Smoke billowed like a storm cloud. A windstorm seemed to slash through the charging mass and hurl it out of sight like a mound of husks on a threshing floor.

In one brightlit moment, the whole *vataha* burst apart and fled in all directions, howling and screaming in wild rage and terror.

★　★　★

The little knight spurred into the open, the ranks of Cossacks and dragoons broke through the underbrush behind him and, in that instant, his three other regiments closed the circle around the milling mass, swept the scattering marauders back into the center, and squeezed them into another tightly-crowded mob. Wild-eyed Tartars galloped in all directions, trying to slip out in small groups or alone but to no avail. In vain they darted to the left, then to the right. They tried to turn back and then whirled around to the front again, but the ring of galloping cavalry was now closed around them and the howling swarm compressed even tighter, and then the charging regiments were upon them with a dreadful roar.

The marauders knew at once that the only man who would live beyond this day was the one who could break out of this iron vise, and so even though they were crushed together in wildest disorder, they started fighting with fierce desperation. Right from the start, when the charge had hit them, they littered the field with their dead and dying, and the terrible harvest went on unabated.

The soldiers who forced their horses forward despite the tight-pressed throng before them, cut them down and stabbed them with that merciless efficiency that only veteran professionals can acquire. The thick hammering of their blows welled out of this human whirlpool much like the rapid thud and clatter of flails swung in a circle around a threshing floor. The Cossacks, the *Lipki*, and the fighting gentry who served as rank-and-file troopers in the two Light Horse regiments, slashed at Tartar heads, cut through bowed necks and slanting backs and shoulders, and through the desperate hands with which the stricken bandits tried to shield their faces, and they fought back whichever way they could. Beaten without rest, without time for breath, with no thought of mercy, and lacking any hope for life if they should surrender, the bandits struck back with knives, sabers, spears and their horse-jaw axes. Their horses, giving way before the crushing pressure of the cavalry around them, fell back on their haunches or tumbled on their backs on the ground behind them. Others bit each other savagely, squealing in their terror, or reared up on their hind hooves and flailed the air above them, creating an indescribable confusion.

After a short, bitter stand fought in savage silence, a long howl burst out of all the Tartar breasts; they were crushed by greater numbers, better weapons, and a degree of skill that went far beyond their own. They understood at last that there was no salvation for anyone among them; and that none of them would get away with his loot or even escape alive.

In the meantime, the soldiers warmed up to their work and hacked and thrust at them all the harder. Some of the battered bandits jumped out of their saddles in an attempt to slip through to safety between the horses' hooves; they died moments later, either trampled by that stamping mass of raging, terror-stricken horses, or nailed to the ground by the sword-thrust of a passing soldier. Some played dead among the carcasses of their horses and the corpses of their fallen comrades in a vain hope that this crushing vise would pass over them as the Polish ranks pressed on towards the center, and that they'd be able to hide and crawl away.

Meanwhile the hard-pressed core of their doomed resistance

was shrinking by the moment as men and horses toppled to the ground. Seeing that no other hope remained, Azbah-bey forced what men he could into a wedge formation and hurled himself, and them, against Motovidlo's troopers, wanting to break out of the killing-circle at all cost. But the Ruthenian soldiers did not break, and the remorseless killing match turned into a massacre as Mellehovitch, raging like a flame, charged into the bandits from the rear.

In moments, the swarm was split in two.

One half was immediately surrounded by Volodyovski's two other Light Horse regiments, while Mellehovitch and his *Lipki* horsemen joined Motovidlo's Cossacks in slaughtering the rest.

A handful of the bandits saw their chance as the tight ring around them all parted for a moment, and they burst through and scattered across the plain like a fistful of dry leaves flung into the wind. But the soldiers in the rear ranks, who had been crowded out of the fight in the compressing circle, broke away and chased after them at once. The rest were simply put to the sword, and—despite a desperate defense—fell where they stood in much the way that corn topples to the ground when determined reapers attack it from all sides.

Chapter Thirty-five

BASIA RODE INTO the battle with Motovidlo's troopers, trilling in a high, thin voice to whip up her fervor, because in the first few moments she got rather dizzy both from the speed and violence of the charge and the heavy onrush of emotions. Having reached the enemy, all she could see in the beginning was a dark, swirling mass and she was gripped by an overwhelming wish to close her eyes. She overcame that longing practically at once but, even so, she flailed about with her saber in a somewhat blind and haphazard fashion.

This slight bewilderment, however, passed almost straight away. Her courage nullified and reversed the shock and confusion, her daring took over, and she saw things clearly. First she saw heads of horses. Then her attention focused on red, savage faces. One of these flashed near. Basia whirled her saber down on it with gusto and the face vanished as if it were only a bad dream.

Then she heard her husband's calm voice close beside her ear. "That was good! Well done!"

This quiet praise did wonders for her confidence and calmed her down completely. She uttered an even higher squeak, her bright, wide eyes shined with even greater curiosity and enthusiasm, and she began to inflict damage on the enemy with complete awareness of where she was and what she was doing.

Here, then, loomed another dreadful face with bared teeth, a flat nose and protruding cheekbones... she swung at it and it disappeared! There a fist flew up, clutching a broad-bladed spear; Basia slashed at it and it vanished too. A thick back and

326

shoulders hunched over in a raw sheepskin coat leaped up before her eyes... one thrust and they were gone! Then she cut left and right and straight ahead, and at each stroke a man toppled to the ground, dragging his horse down as he fell and vanished under-hoof, and Basia wondered why it was all so easy, when it ought to be so difficult and dangerous.

It was easy because the little knight rode next to her stirrup on one side and Pan Motovidlo on the other. The former kept a close eye on his heart's delight and snuffed bandit lives right and left as if they were candles, slicing off an armed fist with a shallow stroke when it came too near, or slipping his saber blade like a shield between his wife and some other enemy, and husking bandit weapons high into the air as if they were birds scampering in panic.

Pan Motovidlo—a phlegmatic, unperturbable old soldier—guarded the other flank of his valiant lady. He moved so quietly and calmly beside her that he brought to mind a gardener walking through an orchard, clipping a dry branch in passing here and there without thinking any more about it, so that there seemed to be no connection between him and the men who tumbled to the bloodstained soil before him. Both soldiers knew perfectly well when to allow Basia her own independent action and when to intervene.

She had another distant and invisible guardian in the matchless archer who took his place where he could see everything around her, and notched an arrow to his bowstring time and time again, and sent his shafts hissing into the thick of the mob with unerring aim.

But the crowd became so dense, and the maddened Tartar horses were so dangerous—biting, rearing up, and slashing the air with their hooves everywhere around her—that Volodyovski ordered Basia to pull out of this frenzied and chaotic uproar and wait at the side with a few men to guard her.

She obeyed at once, both because she'd given him her word that she'd do exactly as he told her, and because her woman's consciousness had started to revolt. Her courage and enthusiasm kept on urging her to stay in the fight but all the gentle facets of her nature rebelled at the carnage. The reek of spilled blood and the stench of sweat choked her small, flared nostrils. The howls

of rage and fear, the groans of the wounded, and the dreadful
rattling of men's dying breaths, began to sicken her, and she
backed her horse slowly out of the melee.

Released from their guard-duty, the little knight and Pan
Motovidlo, could now indulge in the bloody business of their
trade, while Basia sat her horse safely outside the killing ground
and tried to catch her breath.

★   ★   ★

Meanwhile Pan Mushalski, who had been standing nearby
with his bow, rode up to her and bowed.

"Your ladyship rode like a real cavalier," he told her with the
flowery but sincere courtesy of the times. "Someone who didn't
know you might believe that the Archangel Michael had come
down from Heaven to hurl some thunderbolts at those heathen
dogs. Ah, what an honor it is for them to die at such lovely
hands... which, perhaps, I may be permitted to kiss in honor of
the occasion."

With this the old Steppe ranger seized her hand and buried it
for a moment under his thick whiskers.

"You saw me, sir?" Basia gasped, gulping the air with her
parted lips, and still too overcome by her own excitement. "Did
I really do well?"

"A cat wouldn't do better in a ratpack, ma'am. It really was a
joy to see you! I really felt uplifted, as God is my witness! But
you did right, my lady, to withdraw just now because things
always get most chancy right before the end of a fight like this
one."

"My husband ordered me to pull back and I promised him
before we set out that I'd obey him like any other soldier."

"And quite right too! Hmm. Should I leave my bow with
you, my lady? No? I won't have much use for it from now on
because I'd like to jump in there with my saber before it's all
over... Ah, I see three men coming up; the Colonel must've
ordered them out to protect your ladyship, otherwise I'd have
sent some. But now I'll take my leave with your kind permission, because things are coming to an end over there and I have
to hurry."

Three dragoons did gallop up just then, detailed to guard their
Colonel's Lady, and Pan Mushalski spurred his horse and

charged into the battle. Basia wondered for a moment whether she should stay where she was, or ride around the flank of the escarpment and climb to the top of the ridge where she had watched the field before the battle. But she felt rather tired and thought she would stay.

Her natural, womanly revulsion in the presence of such wholesale slaughter rang even more urgently within her. The last surviving remnants of the massacred marauders were being sabered down a scant two hundred paces from where she was standing, and the black mass of animals and men that boiled across the battlefield whirled more frantically than ever.

Screams of despair tore at the air around her, and she—who only moments earlier had been so full of fire and enthusiasm—started to feel both dizzy and sick to her stomach. She was terrified that she might faint, and it was only her fear of displaying weakness before the three dragoons that kept her in the saddle. She did, however, turn her face away from her three grim watchdogs so that they wouldn't see how pale she'd become. The fresher, cleaner air outside the killing ground helped to restore her strength and fortify her spirits; but not, however, to such a point that she wished to leap back into the battle. The only reason she thought she'd do it now would be to plead for mercy for the slaughtered Tartars. But since she knew that this would do no good, she simply waited for the end and prayed that it might come soon.

★　★　★

Meanwhile, out in the field, the sabering and the battering went on. The shouting and the sound of blows didn't abate even for a moment. A half hour had gone by, perhaps a little more, and the remorseless vise of Volodyovski's horsemen squeezed tighter than ever, when suddenly a small group of bandits hacked its way out into the open and flew like the wind towards the escarpment. Running along the edge, they could indeed reach the spot where the ridge sloped gently to the grassland floor, and look for safety in the open Steppe. But Basia and the three dragoons were standing in the way. The sight of this danger pumped instant courage into her heart and spurred her to immediate awareness and attention. She understood at once that to stay where she was would mean death; because the tightly

packed crowd of fugitives would bowl her over along with her
horse just by sheer speed and the weight of numbers, not to
mention that twenty sabers would make short work of her and
her dragoons.

The dragoon sergeant came apparently to the same conclusion, because he seized the bridle of Basia's horse, pulled it
around to face open country, and shouted in a desperate voice:
"Run for it, m'lady...!"

Basia shot like an arrow into the Steppe but she flew alone.
The three faithful soldiers turned like a living wall to face the
onrush and halt it long enough to give their beloved lady time
to get away. Other soldiers broke away at once to go after the
fugitives; but this, in turn, cracked the killing circle which up
till then clenched tightly around the marauders; and they began
to slip away one at a time, then in small groups, and then in
thicker numbers. The main body of the massacred *vataha* lay
littering the field, but several dozen including Azbah-bey managed to break free. All these bands and units were now galloping
towards the ridge with all the speed they could get from their
tired horses.

The three dragoons couldn't hope to turn this tide.

The onrush slowed and milled around them only for a minute; they fell dead from their saddles after a short fight only
moments later; and the whole swarm galloped after Basia around
the escarpment and broke at last into open country. The Polish
regiments, with the Tartar Light Horse flying in the lead, poured
into the Steppe a few dozen horses' lengths behind them and
formed a sort of serpent that twisted through that broken,
ravine-dotted country with Basia as the head, the bandits as an
ever-lengthening neck, and the thick mass of the pursuing
cavalry as the broadening body. Mellehovitch galloped like a
madman with his *Lipki* troopers crowding at his heels, while
Volodyovski rode with terror in his heart and his spurs buried in
his horse's flanks, with the dragoons behind him.

At the moment when the first handful of marauders broke out
of the circle, he had been busy on the other side and that was
why Mellehovitch beat him to the rescue. But now the hair
stood erect on top of his head at the thought that Basia might be
swept up by the fugitives, or that she might become disoriented
and ride towards the Dniester, or that some bandit might saber

her or knife her as he galloped past. His heart constricted with anxiety about her. Pale as death and with a hurricane of terrifying thoughts howling through his head, he bowed so low in his saddle that he was practically lying on his horse's neck, roweled its flanks bloody with his spurs, lashed it on with the flat of his saber, and flew at full tilt just above the ground like a heron before it lifts itself into the air.

'God grant that Mellehovitch reaches her in time!' he cried silently to himself, shaken with despair. *'He's riding a good horse...'*

★ ★ ★

But his fears proved to be for nothing and Basia's danger wasn't quite as pressing as the enamored little knight was certain. The fleeing Tartars were far too concerned about their own skins. They heard the *Lipki* horsemen too close behind their backs to waste time on a single rider, even if she were the most desirable *houri* in the Prophet's Paradise and wore a cloak studded all over with emeralds and rubies. All Basia had to do was swerve towards Hreptyov to shed her pursuers, because they'd surely not follow her into the lion's den with the river-crossing straight ahead of them, and with all their hideouts and ravines waiting just beyond it. Moreover, Basia rode an incomparably swifter animal than the sturdy, shaggy-haired Tartar ponies, which may have been known for their great endurance but which could never catch a running thoroughbred. As for the rest of Pan Volodyovski's worries, she not only kept her head and had no thought of panic, but her natural daring awoke in her again, leaped up in full force, and fired her senses.

Her horse bounded ahead like a deer, the running wind was whistling in her ears, but rather than feeling any kind of fear, she felt exhilaration.

"They can chase me a year for the good it'll do them," she said to herself. "I'll go on a bit, then swing around and face them, and then I'll either let them go on by, or—if they keep on coming after me—I'll draw them after me to our people's sabers."

Sabers, in turn, brought to mind the thought that if the fleeing ruffians had scattered in the Steppe behind her, she might come face to face with one when she made her turn, and actually cross sabers in a sword-to-sword, hand-to-hand encounter.

'*And what's wrong with that?*' she asked her valiant spirit. '*Michal taught me so much that I can try my hand without worrying about it. If I don't, they'll all think that I'm running because I'm afraid, and they won't take me with them on the next campaign, and Pan Zagloba will make jokes about me.*'

A quick glance back across her shoulders showed that the cut-throats were still running in a tight-knit cluster. A saber duel was out of the question but Basia was suddenly determined to show all the soldiers that she wasn't just running blindly for her life.

She remembered that her saddle-holsters held a pair of hand-picked pistols that Michal himself had carefully primed and loaded before they left Hreptyov, and she began to rein and slow her horse, turning as she slowed towards that distant refuge.

To her surprise, the whole band of fugitive marauders veered slightly to the left, changing the direction of their flight towards the slope which brought the ridge gently in line with the grassy uplands. Basia let them come to within a few dozen paces, fired both her pistols into the thick of the huddled horses, then wheeled around and spurred towards Hreptyov.

But her horse took barely a dozen paces when a wide Steppe gully yawned darkly right before his hooves. She lifted him into a leap without a moment's thought and the brave animal rose to the occasion. Only his front hooves, however, found purchase on the opposite edge of the crevasse. His back legs stamped and scrambled madly for a moment, struggling to dig into the sharply slanted wall of earth under him, and then the loose, thawed soil crumbled under him and he plunged into the chasm taking Basia with him.

Luck and her own quick wits saved her from being crushed. She kicked her feet out of the stirrups, threw herself out of the saddle even before the horse cartwheeled to the bottom, and landed on a thick pad of moss which spread like a furry carpet on the gully floor. But the force of the fall jarred the breath out of her and knocked her unconscious.

Volodyovski didn't see her fall because the galloping *Lipki* blocked it from his sight, but Mellehovitch screamed in a fright-ful voice, waved to his men to keep going after the fleeing bandits, reached the crevasse in one mindless bound and hurled himself headlong into the gorge.

He was out of his saddle in a flash and caught her in his arms. His sharp, hawklike eyes scanned her instantly from head to foot, saw no blood, fixed on the bank of moss and understood why she and her horse were still alive, and a muffled cry of joy burst out of the young Tartar.

Basia lay heavily in his arms and he pressed her to his chest with all his strength; then started kissing her eyes and cheeks with his bloodless lips; then fixed them to her mouth as avidly as if he wished to suck the soul out of her; and then the world spun crazily around him, and all the lust and longing that lay hidden in his chest like a crouching monster, leaped into the open and seized him like a storm.

Just then, however, the rapid drumming of many horses' hooves rang in the Steppe above and nearing voices started to cry out: "Here! In this gorge! Here!"

Mellehovitch placed Basia carefully back upon the moss and shouted up to the arriving horsemen:

"Here! Come here! She's here!"

A minute later Volodyovski sprung into the gorge with Pan Zagloba, Pan Mushalski, Pan Nenashinyetz and several other officers behind him.

"She's alright!" cried the Tartar. "The moss broke her fall!"

Volodyovski caught his unconscious wife in his arms, the others ran for water, and Zagloba seized Basia's temples in both hands, bellowing with worry:

"Basia! Dearest Basia!"

"She's alright!" Mellehovitch said again, pale as a corpse.

★ ★ ★

In the meantime Pan Zagloba slapped his hip, found a full canteen, splashed some coarse, home-brewed vodka into this hands, and started rubbing the alcohol into Basia's temples. Then he tipped the flask to her lips which seemed to help at once because she opened her eyes even before the others found and brought a cupful of water. She gasped for air, coughing a little as the harsh liquor burned her tongue and throat, but a few minutes later she was completely conscious.

Volodyovski kept kissing her and squeezing her in his arms, oblivious of the officers and soldiers who clustered around them, and murmuring in relief:

"Ai, my sweet love! I thought I'd die! Are you alright, though? Does anything hurt?"

"I'm fine!" Basia said and focused her eyes on all the anxious faces. "Aha...! I see now that I must've been knocked out for a moment because my horse fell with me... Is the battle over?"

"All done. Azbah-bey is dead. Let's get home quickly now because I'm afraid you might get sick with all this excitement and fatigue."

"I'm not a bit tired!" Basia said at once.

Then she threw a quick, careful glance around the circle of relieved officers and soldiers and her little nostrils flared in instant challenge.

"Just don't start thinking, gentlemen, that I was running out of fear!" she said. "Oho! I wouldn't even dream of that! I was just sort of galloping along, out of sheer pleasure, and then I fired both my pistols at them!"

"You brought down one of their horses, my lady," Mellehovitch said. "And we took the bandit alive."

"There, you see? Anybody can take a tumble in a jump, can't he? No amount of skill or experience can keep a horse from stumbling, am I right? Ha! But it's a good thing that you gentlemen saw me right away, or I might have been stuck here for quite a while."

"Pan Mellehovitch was the first to see you and first to get to you," said Volodyovski. "We'd gone after the others."

"Thank you, sir, for your thoughtfulness," Basia said and offered her hand to the pale young Tartar.

He said nothing in reply, merely pressed his lips to her hand with utmost respect, and then bowed as low before her as if he were a peasant, embraced her feet in homage, and touched the tips of her boots with his forehead.

*   *   *

Meanwhile more and more of the returning companies gathered around the gully. The battle was over. Pan Volodyovski dispatched Mellehovitch on a rapid manhunt after the few bandits who managed to hide in the tall grass and avoid pursuit, and the whole column turned towards Hreptyov.

Basia caught one last sight of the battlefield. Dead men and horses lay all across the plain, singly and in heaps, and the calm blue sky discharged ever greater swarms of cawing carrion birds which settled around the edges of the field, waiting until the last few troopers mounted and rode away.

"Look at those croaking creatures," Pan Zagloba said, pointing at the birds with the curved end of his saber. "They're not called a soldier's grave diggers for nothing. The wolves will come next, just as soon as we are out of sight, and ring out a fine funeral dirge with their teeth for these miserable scoundrels. This is a major victory, even though the enemy were all worthless scum, because this Azbah fellow raised Hell for years all along the border. The local commandants hunted him all over, and always for nothing, until his luck ran out and he met with Michal. And that was his inevitable end."

"Azbah-bey is dead, then?" Basia asked.

"Mellehovitch was the first to reach him and, I tell you, when he cracked him in the ear, the saber didn't stop until it reached his jaws."

"Pan Mellehovitch is a good soldier," Basia said, then turned to Pan Zagloba. "And you, sir! Did you do well today?"

"Well," the old knight flipped a sly, merry glance at her and grinned from ear to ear. "I didn't squeak like a mouse, or jump up and down like a flea because I leave such pleasures to the insects, nor did they have to search for me in the moss as if I were a mushroom, nor did anyone have to pinch my nose or blow air into my mouth like some people I know..."

"I don't like you at all, sir!" Basia said, annoyed, and reached for the tip of her pink nose before she stopped herself.

But he continued to look at her, and smile, and tease, and mutter with amusement.

"You fought like a hero," he said. "You ran like a hero. You flipped a most heroic cartwheel and now you'll wear a hot buckwheat poultice, also like a hero, to get the aches and pains out of your heroic bones. We, in the meantime, will have to keep the birds away from you or they'll gobble up the poultice along with your heroics, seeing that they're awfully fond of hot buckwheat groats."

"And you, sir, are already trying to make sure that Michal doesn't take me on another expedition. I know that very well!"

"On the contrary! On the contrary, my dear! I'll keep on begging him to bring you along whenever he goes nut-picking, because you're light and nimble and the branch won't break under you. Dear God, is this gratitude? And who convinced Michal to let you come with us? Hmm? I did! And now I'm sorry that I did, especially since you pay me back in such miserable coin. Wait, though, wait! We'll whittle you a wooden sword and you can cut the heads off all the thistles around Hreptyov! That's what comes of taking snippets on a military mission! Another woman might give an old man a hug for getting her invited, but not this pesky gadfly! First she scares the living daylights out of me and then she attacks me!"

Basia immediately twisted in her saddle and threw her arms around the old knight's neck, which delighted him, and he went on in a much more proud and thoughtful tone.

"Hmm. Ahem! Well, well. I must say, though, that you had quite a part in today's victory because all the soldiers fought like wild furies trying to show their best."

"As God's our witness!" shouted Pan Mushalski. "A man doesn't mind dying before such an audience!"

"*Vivat* to our lady!" Pan Nenashinyetz shouted.

"*Vivat!*" roared a hundred other voices. "God give her health and happiness!"

"After she's had her baby," Pan Zagloba murmured in her ear.

They rode on in high spirits after that, calling out and shouting, and sure of a splendid victory celebration before the night was over. The day glowed with all the beauty of the Steppe around them. The regimental trumpeters blew their horns, the drummers pounded on their kettledrums, and they rode into Hreptyov with a great commotion.

Part V

Chapter Thirty-six

IN HREPTYOV, much to everyone's surprise, the Volodyovskis found unexpected guests. These were Pan Bogush, who picked Pan Michal's outpost as a place to stay for a month or two while he and Mellehovitch were negotiating with the Tartar captains who had gone over to the Sultan's service; old Pan Novovyeyski with his daughter Ewa; and Lady Boska, wife of one of the Hetman's most cherished old soldiers, with her young and extremely pretty daughter Zosia.

The sight of women in the harsh, wilderness surroundings of Hreptyov delighted the soldiers, but their astonishment exceeded even their delight. They, in turn—these female visitors who amazed them so—couldn't believe their eyes when they saw the commandant and his lady. In Pan Michal's case, judging by the widespread awe attached to his name, they imagined some kind of a giant who terrified people with a single glance; his wife, they thought, had to be a glowering giantess with the booming voice of a sergeant-major. Instead they saw a pint-sized little soldier with a cheerful face and a friendly smile; and an equally elfin woman, pink as a rosebud and as trim as a china doll, who was more like an extraordinarily slim and pretty youth with her saber and her riding pants than a grownup person. None the less, their host and hostess greeted them with open arms. Basia exchanged warm kisses with all three women even before the formal introductions, and then, when they told her who they were and where they had come from, she said:

"I'd gladly give you ladies whatever your hearts desire! I'm awfully glad you've come! And I'm really happy that no harm came to you in this wilderness of ours, but it's just today that we crushed the worst of the bandits."

Then, seeing that Lady Boska was staring at her with rising stupefaction, she slapped the little saber dangling at her side, and added with a definite swagger in her voice:

"I also fought in the battle! Ha, as if I wouldn't! That's how things are with us around here! Ah, but let me go and change into something more suitable to our sex, and to wash some of this blood off my hands, because we've just come back from a most frightful battle. Oho! If Azbah-bey weren't smashed and killed, perhaps you wouldn't have reached Hreptyov so happily, my lady. I'll be back in a flash, meanwhile Michal will serve your ladyship."

★ ★ ★

With this she vanished behind the door, and the little knight who had already greeted Pan Bogush and Pan Novovyeyski, approached Lady Boska.

"God gave me a woman," he said, "who is not only a sweet home companion but knows how to be a brave comrade in the field as well. And now, by her order, I am at your ladyship's service."

"May God bless everything about her, as He's already blessed her in her beauty," Lady Boska said, and then proceeded to introduce herself and the reason for her being there. "I am the wife of Antoni Boski, and I didn't come here to extract services from you, sir, but rather to beg you, on my knees, for your help and rescue in my terrible misfortune. Zoska!"—she signaled to her beautiful young daughter—"Get down on your knees as well before this knight, because if he can't help us then nobody can!"

Then the stately matron did, indeed, throw herself down on her knees before the little soldier, her daughter followed suit, and both burst into tears.

"Save us, sir knight!" they cried. "Have mercy for the orphaned!"

A crowd of officers gathered curiously around, drawn by the sight of the kneeling women and especially by the lovely Zosia, and the little knight, thrown suddenly into discomfiture and mystification, struggled to get Lady Boska back on her feet again and then to seat her on a bench.

"For God's sake!" he hurried to help her to compose herself. "What are you doing, ma'am? It's I who should show my respect by kneeling. Tell me, dear lady, what I can do to help you, and as God's in his Heaven I won't fail to do it!"

"He'll do it!" Moved by the women's tears, Pan Zagloba broke in with conviction. "And I'll do my part as well! Zagloba *sum!*" he added the fearsome power of his name. "Your ladyship doesn't need to hear any more than that!"

Lady Boska nodded at her daughter who quickly found a letter tucked into her bodice and handed it to Pan Volodyovski.

"From the Hetman!" he murmured as he glanced at it.

'My very dear and most valued Volodyovski!' the Hetman had written. *'Accept my warmest wishes through Pan Bogush who'll also give you new instructions from me. But there's another matter which needs your attention. May God forget me if I ever fail any of my soldiers and here's a case in point. Pan Boski, a cavalier of great merit and a fond companion, was carried off by the Horde near Kamyenetz a few years ago. His wife and daughter found shelter with me in Yavorov but their hearts are torn with grief for husband and father. I've written through Ambassador Piotrovitch to Pan Zlotnitzki, our resident in the Crimea, to search everywhere for Boski, and I hear they've found him. But the Tartars promptly hid him from us, so we couldn't get him back with the others in the prisoner exchange, and he's probably rowing a galley somewhere to this day. His wife and daughter have now lost all hope, and they no longer even turn to me to save him, but their grief rings just as loud in silence and I can't miss any opportunity to help them.*

'You're closer to it all out there,' the Hetman went on, *'and you've poured water over the swords with several of the murjahs. I'm sending the ladies to you, and you do all you can. Piotrovitch will be going soon to the Crimea again and he'll stop in to see you. Give him letters to all those blood-brothers of yours. I can't write either to the Khan or to the Grand Vizier because they're not well-disposed towards me; what's more, they might take Boski for some well-connected and influential person and raise the ransom to impossible proportions. Call in all your favors, urge Piotrovitch to do his best and tell him not to come back without Boski, and don't forget your own influence among*

the border murjahs. They may be pagans but they always keep the friendship oaths they swear, and their respect for you must be truly great.

'*Do what you wish and can, I give you a free hand in this matter,*' Pan Sobieski wrote. '*You can even offer their negotiators three of the most distinguished prisoners we have, as long as Boski comes back if he's alive. No one knows better than you how to go about such things since, as I hear, you've ransomed some of your own kin in the past. God will bless you for whatever you do and I'll add my own thanks as well because you'll be lifting a great weight off my heart.*

'*Word of your good work in Hreptyov has already reached us,*' the Hetman concluded, '*but that is only what I expected of you. Be sure to keep an eye peeled for the bandit Azbah. Pan Bogush will tell you all the public matters that concern us here, but for God's sake keep an ear cocked sharply at Valachia because it seems that we won't be able to avoid a great cataclysm from there...*'

Then Pan Sobieski urged the little knight again to have Lady Boska's interests close to heart, and signed off with every sign of devoted friendship.

★   ★   ★

Lady Boska sobbed throughout the reading of the Hetman's letter, and Zosia sniffed tearfully beside her and lifted her cornflower eyes towards the sky.

In the meantime Basia had run in, now properly attired in a gown and ribbons, and started to question everyone anxiously about what had happened. She listened closely when Pan Michal read her the Grand Hetman's letter and gave it her immediate, whole-hearted endorsement.

"The Hetman has a heart of gold," she said, embracing her husband. "But we won't show a worse one, *Michalku!* Lady Boska will make her home with us until her husband has returned, and you can have him back from the Crimea in three months! Three or two, isn't that correct?"

"Or tomorrow," Volodyovski teased. "Or within the hour. As you see, my lady,"—he turned to Lady Boska—"my wife is a woman of quick determination."

"May God bless her for it!" the sobbing woman said again. "Zosia! Run and kiss the hands of the Commandant's Lady!"

However the Commandant's Lady wasn't about to have her hands kissed by the sad young girl, with whom she felt an instant bond of sympathy and friendship, so the two young women merely hugged and kissed each other again, and then Basia turned once more to her husband, Pan Zagloba and the officers.

"Let's have some thoughts about this, gentlemen!" she cried. "But quickly! Quickly!"

"Hurry, because her head's on fire!" grunted Pan Zagloba.

But Basia only shook her tawny hair. "It's not my head that's burning but those ladies' hearts!"

"No one argues with your good intentions," said Volodyovski. "But we must hear her ladyship's detailed account before we know exactly what to do."

"Zosia!" urged the sobbing matron. "Tell everything that happened because my tears won't let me."

★ ★ ★

At first, however, poor Zosia was no more able to speak than her mother. She didn't know where to begin. She was overcome with shyness. So many people were staring at her and crowding around her that she became tongue-tied; she flushed as crimson as a ripened cherry, scrunched down her eyes and fixed them on the floor.

Luckily Basia helped. "Zoska," she asked. "When was your father taken prisoner?"

"In 'sixty-seven," she answered in a thin silvery little voice, keeping her long lashes lowered across her eyes. "Five years ago."

But the ice was broken and she plunged in breathlessly as if to tell the story all at the same time before she had to stop to come up for air.

"There were no raids along the borders then," she sniffed. "The Tartars were quiet, and Daddy's regiment was in camp near Panovtze, and Daddy and Pan Bulayovski were keeping an eye on the grooms in the cattle pastures, and then the Horde came from the Valachian Trail and swept up Daddy and Pan Bulayovski, but Pan Bulayovski came back two years ago and Daddy is still gone."

Two small, crystal tears coursed down her cheeks and Pan Zagloba was moved to immediate pity.

"Poor little rabbit," he sniffed in his turn. "Don't worry, child, don't worry. Your daddy will come back and dance at your wedding."

"And that's when the Hetman wrote to Pan Zlotnitzki?" Volodyovski asked.

"Yes sir,"Zosia hurried on as if reciting a well-learned history lesson. "The Hetman wrote about Daddy to the Constable of Poznan, and then Pan Piotrovitch and the Constable went to the Crimea and found Daddy with the Tartar Agha called Mussa-bey."

"Good God, I know that Mussa-bey!" cried Volodyovski. "His brother and I had an oath of friendship. And didn't he want to let Pan Boski go?"

"There was an order from the Khan to set Daddy free, but Mussa-bey is harsh and cruel and he hid Daddy somewhere, and then he told Pan Piotrovitch that he sold Daddy a long time ago to somebody in Asia. But other captives told Pan Piotrovitch that this wasn't true, and that Mussa-bey was just saying that so he could keep Daddy longer, and torment him, because he's the worst of all the Tartars when it comes to prisoners. It could have been that Daddy wasn't in the Crimea at that time because Mussa-bey has his own galleys and always needs slaves to row them but everyone said that he hadn't been sold. Mussa-bey would rather kill a slave than sell him, everybody said..."

"That's absolutely true," broke in Pan Mushalski. "That Mussa-bey is known all over the Crimea. He's as rich as Croesus but he is strangely twisted with hatred for our nation because he lost four brothers in campaigns against us."

"Would he have a blood-brother somewhere among us?" asked Volodyovski.

"That's most unlikely!" everyone said at once. "Seeing how he hates us!"

"Will someone tell me what this blood-brother business is all about?" Basia interrupted. "And all that stuff about pouring water across swords?"

* * *

This gave Pan Zagloba the chance to monopolize the floor which he did with alacrity and a great deal of profound clearing of the throat.

"The way it is," he said, "when talks begin right after a war, the soldiers visit each others' camps and get to know each other. It might happen then that a gentleman-trooper will get to like some *bey* or *murjah*, and the *murjah* likes his looks as well, so they'll vow lifelong friendship to each other and that's known as the friendship oath and makes them blood brothers. The more famous the Polish cavalier, like our Michal here, or like Pan Rushtchitz who is the commandant in Rashkov, the more he's wanted for a blood brother by the more powerful and important *murjahs*. There's no need to say that such distinguished soldiers wouldn't swear their friendship with any pipsqueak Tartar that happened along, but also look for their blood brothers among the best and most famous of the Horde. The custom is to pour water over their sabers and pledge their friendship to each other, is that all quite clear?"

"And what if there's another war?"

"They can fight each other in an all-out war but if they should come across each other in the field, or meet as skirmishers before the battle, then they just greet each other and each goes his own way. If one gets taken prisoner the other is bound to do his best to sweeten his captivity and, if all else fails, make his ransom for him. Ha! I've even heard of some who shared their possessions! When it comes to finding somebody in each other's country, or to helping some other acquaintance or friend, one blood brother will turn to the other, and pure justice requires me to say that no nation sticks to such an oath better than the Tartars. Their word is their bond! And you can bet your life on a friend like that."

"And does Michal have a lot of them?"

"I have three powerful and wealthy *murjahs,*" said Volodyovski. "One, named Agha-bey, goes back with me all the way to the years in Lubnie. I begged his life one time from Prince Yeremi and he'd give his head for me any day. The other two are just as sure to help."

"Ha!" Basia said. "I'd like to take a blood-oath with the Khan himself and free all the captives!"

"I'm sure he'd like that," Pan Zagloba grinned. "I'm just wondering what kind of tasty little *praemium* he'd want in return?"

"Let's give some serious thought to this, ladies and gentlemen," said Volodyovski. "I've heard from Kamyenetz that

Piotrovitch will be here in two weeks or less with a large negotiating party. He's going to the Crimea to arrange the ransom for some Armenian traders who were robbed and thrown in prison when the new Khan took over from the old one. They're all rich men, and they're ready to spend a lot of money, so Piotrovitch will be well supplied. He should have no trouble on the way. It's not long till Winter and the *tchambuls* stay quiet when the grass turns yellow. Besides, he's traveling with a delegate of the Armenian Patriarch and two high-ranking Anardrates from Kufa who have passes from the young new Khan. I'll give Piotrovitch letters for the Commonwealth resident with the Khan and all my blood-brothers. Besides, as all of you know, Pan Rushtchitz, the commandant in Rashkov, has blood-kin in the Horde who were seized as children, grew up as true Tartars, and rose to some high positions over there. They'll move heaven and earth for him, try negotiating, and if Mussabey gets too stubborn about it they might even twist his neck for him in some quiet corner. So I think we can hope that if—God grant it!—Pan Boski is still alive somewhere, I'll be able to get him back in a few months just as the Hetman orders, and as my nearer *Hetman,*"—and here Pan Michal bowed smiling to his wife—"wants to see it done."

The nearer Hetman jumped up at once and ran to throw her arms once more around the little soldier, while Lady Boska and her lovely daughter merely pressed their hands together as if in grateful prayers.

Chapter Thirty-seven

EVERYONE, INCLUDING THE TWO grieving women, cheered up considerably after that, and the talk slipped into general speculations.

"Everything would go smoother if the old Khan was still alive," said Pan Nenashinyetz. "He ended up being truly well-disposed towards us, which can't be said about the man who replaced him. Those Armenian merchants that Pan Zaharias Piotrovitch is going to try to ransom were jailed in Baktchisaray and the young Khan is said to have ordered it himself."

"Give the young whelp time and he'll change his tune just like the old one did," Pan Zagloba shrugged. "I knew the old goat well. I sat through seven years in his captivity, and there wasn't a worse enemy for the Commonwealth until he learned that we could be as decent as we are. May the sight of me give you hope, dear lady,"—the old knight nodded gravely to Lady Boska and edged his chair beside her. "Seven years is no joke! But I got back alright, and I sent so many of those Tartar dogs to Hell afterwards that there're at least two of them squirming on the coals for each day of my captivity, with maybe three or four for the Holy Days and Sundays."

"Seven years!" Lady Boska sighed.

"May I drop dead right here if I exaggerate by a single day!" Pan Zagloba swore, and then blinked rapidly with his one good eye as if about to confide an important secret. "Seven years in the Khan's own palace! And people say the new Khan looks like my mirror image..."

Here the old knight began whispering something into Lady
Boska's ear, burst into a loud *"Ha! Ha! Ha!"* and started pounding his knees in sheer enthusiasm. Then, as if absentmindedly,
he patted Lady Boska's knee as well.

"Those were good times, eh?" he chortled. "When one is
young there's a fine fight in every field and each day brings its
own happy little pastimes! Ha!"

★　★　★

The staid and proper matron flushed hotly with embarrassment at Pan Zagloba's secret and moved her chair slightly away
from the chortling noble; the young women also guessed at once
that the merry old knight's confession wouldn't sit well with
their natural modesty and quickly dropped their eyes, especially
since all the soldiers burst into a great roar of approving laughter.

"We must be sure to send word quickly to Pan Rushtchitz,"
Basia added swiftly. "So that Pan Piotrovitch will find the letters
ready when he gets to Rashkov."

"By all means hurry," urged Pan Bogush. "Hurry while the
Winter's here because the *tchambuls* don't come out till Springtime. And God only knows what will be happening here this
coming Spring."

"Did the Hetman hear something from Istanbul?" asked Volodyovski.

"He did, and we'll have a talk about that later. What's certain,
however, is that we've got to finish with those Tartar captains as
soon as we can. Much depends on Mellehovitch in this matter.
When is he due back?"

"Any minute now. All he had to do was track down the rest
of the bandits and bury the fallen. He should be back no later
than tomorrow morning. I told him to bury just our own dead,
Azbah's corpses can stay where they are. Winter is just around
the corner so there's not much fear of disease. Besides, the
wolves will clean them up."

"The Hetman asks that Mellehovitch should have a free hand
in his work," Pan Bogush insisted. "And that he should go to
Rashkov anytime he wants. The Hetman also asks that he be
absolutely trusted in all things since he's sure of his love and
loyalty to the Commonwealth. He's a great young soldier and
we expect some great things from him."

"Let him go to Rashkov or anywhere else he needs to," the little knight assented. "I don't even need him all that much now that Azbah's finished. We won't see any other big gang of cut-throats around here until the new grass."

"So Azbah-bey is so completely shattered?" asked Pan Novovyeyski.

"He's been so thoroughly destroyed that I doubt if two dozen of his people got away, and they'll be fished out of the grass soon enough if Mellehovitch hasn't caught them and strung them up already."

"I'm delighted to hear it!" old Pan Novovyeyski said. "Because that means the road to Rashkov will be safe and clear." Then he turned to Basia. "We can take with us those letters to Pan Rushtchitz that your ladyship just mentioned, since we'll be going on to Rashkov as soon as we can."

"Thank you," Basia said. "But there's no need. We send regular couriers all the time."

"All the commands must keep in close contact at all times," Pan Michal explained, and nodded towards Ewa Novovyeyska. "But does this mean that your worship plans to go all the way to Rashkov with that beautiful young lady?"

"She's just a Plain Jane, kind sir, not any sort of beauty," the old noble said with the gruff, false modesty of his kind which took great pride in any praise of their families or children. "And we're going to Rashkov because that's where my worthless rascal of a son is serving in Pan Rushtchitz's command. It's been ten years since he ran away from home and all I've had from him were a dozen letters."

"Ah!"—and the little knight slapped his hands with pleasure—"I thought straight off that you must be young Adam Novovyeyski's father. I was about to ask only we became so taken with Lady Boska's troubles. Yes, the family likeness is quite clear! Well, well! So Adam is your son!"

"So his late mother was good enough to tell me. And since she was a truthful and virtuous woman I've no need to doubt it."

"That makes you doubly welcome, sir! Only don't call him a worthless rascal! He's a splendid soldier and a worthy cavalier who adds the greatest possible glory to your name. He's the finest borderer in his regiment, next only to Pan Rushtchitz, and

the apple of the Hetman's eye! Young as he is, he's been
entrusted with whole brigade commands and he's always come
through with the most resounding success possible."

Crimson with pleasure, Pan Novovyeyski made a quick, self-
effacing gesture.

"You know how it is, Colonel," he murmured. "A father
often says something slighting about his child only to hear
somebody else deny it. I can't think of anything that warms a
parent's heart better than to have this kind of contradiction
thrown into his teeth. I've heard a bit about Adam's honorable
doings, but it's only now, when I hear his record confirmed by
such famed lips as yours, that I'm truly happy. I'm told he's not
only a brave soldier but a thoughtful and serious-minded man as
well, which amazes me because he always was as wild as the
wind. He was all fired up to go to war from his youngest years,
the fidgety young rascal, and the best proof of that is that he ran
away from home when he barely knew how to walk on his own
hind legs. I admit that if I'd have caught him then, I'd have
given him something *pro memoriam* that he wouldn't have forgotten in a hurry. But now I see I'll have to let it go or he'll hide
somewhere else for another ten years and I miss him in my
twilight years."

"And he never came home once in all that time?" Pan Volodyovski wondered.

"He couldn't. I forbad it. But it's time to forget about all that
and here I am, making the first move, since he's under orders
and can't stir without one. I wanted to ask you and your lady,
my dear and honored host, to keep my girl here while I went to
Rashkov, but since you say that the trail is clear and everything
is safe I'll take her along. She's a curious magpie and wants to
see a bit of the world, so let her."

"And let the world get a good look at her!" Pan Zagloba
added.

"It wouldn't see much!" threw in the young woman whose
deep, dark eyes and full, pouting lips promised something altogether different.

"A Plain Jane, that's all, as I said," Pan Novovyeyski muttered,
pleased with this praise for his daughter's beauty as he'd been
pleased with praise for his son's gallantry and courage. "A Plain
Jane, that's all! But when she sees some handsome officer you'd

think she'd sat down on a needle, the way she'll start squirming. That's why I took her with me in the first place, especially since it isn't safe to leave a girl alone in a country house. But if it does happen that I must go to Rashkov without her, I'll ask your ladyship to have a string tied around her collar or she'll kick over the traces and gallop off somewhere!"

"I wasn't any better," Basia said, "before I got married."

"They used to give her hemp to spin," Pan Zagloba said with a grin at Basia. "And she'd dance with the spindle if there was nothing else to dance with. But you're a merry soul yourself, my dear Novovyeyski! I'd like to clink a glass or two with you because I'm also fond of jokes now and then..."

*　★　★　★*

Meanwhile, before the supper was set on the table, the doors swung open and Mellehovitch came into the room. Pan Novovyeyski didn't notice him at first, because he was huddled with Pan Zagloba in a private chat, but Ewa caught sight of him at once, flushed as suddenly as if her face had burst into flames, and then became as pale as a sheet.

"Commandant," the young Tartar reported to Volodyovski. "All those other bandits have been caught as ordered."

"Very well! Where are they?"

"I had them hanged already, as by standing orders."

"Very well! Are all your men back with you?"

"I left some behind as a burial detail but the rest are here."

"Good God!" Pan Novovyeyski looked up at that moment, rose to his feet, and the most intense amazement flooded his face with color. "What is this I see?"

Moving as if he could hardly believe what he was doing, he marched straight up to Mellehovitch.

"Azia!" he shouted. "What are you doing here, you scoundrel?"

He reached up and clutched at the young Tartar's collar but the Light Horseman flared as if someone had thrown a handful of gunpowder on a bed of coals, became deathly pale, crushed the old man's hand in an iron grip and snarled: "I don't know you, mister! Who the devil are you?"

Then he shoved Novovyeyski away with such force that the old man staggered back into the middle of the room. He stood

there for a moment, so choked with rage that he couldn't
stammer out a word, then he caught his breath and started
shouting like a man gone mad.

"Commandant! That's my man! My servant! And a runaway
at that! He lived in my house since he was a puppy and now he
denies it! Scoundrel! That's my fellow! Ewa, who is this? Speak
up!"

"Azia!" said Panna Ewa, trembling all over as if she were ill.

Mellehovitch didn't even spare her a passing glance. His eyes
were buried like twin daggers in Pan Novovyeyski, his nostrils
flared back with a choking rage, his fist clutched the handle of
the knife sheathed inside his sash, and he glared at the bellowing
old noble with a depth of hatred that defied description. His
quivering nostrils set his mustache jumping and bared sharp,
wolflike teeth that brought to mind the snarl of an infuriated
beast.

The officers surged forward in a circle and Basia bounded into
the center between Mellehovitch and Pan Novovyeyski.

"What is the meaning of this?" she demanded.

★ ★ ★

Her angry frown brought the two antagonists back under
control, but not enough to make any difference.

"The meaning? Commandant, it means what I said!" cried Pan
Novovyeyski. "This is my houseman, a fellow named Azia, and
a runaway. I picked him up as an abandoned infant in the Steppe
when I was a young soldier in the Ukraine. He was half-dead
when I came across him and I took him home. He's a Tartar
foundling. He lived twenty years in my house and shared my
son's tutors. When my son ran off he gave me a hand with
running my estates until he got a hankering to try his luck with
Ewa. I had him well whipped for it and he ran away soon after.
What does he call himself here?"

"Mellehovitch!"

"Then he's living under a false name! He's called Azia, nothing more! He says he doesn't know me, but I know *him*, and so
does my Ewa!"

"How can that be?" Basia said. "Your son saw him with us
many times. Why wouldn't he know him?"

"My son may not be able to recognize him because they were

both only fifteen-years-old when Adam ran away from home, and this one stayed another six years with me, when he changed a lot, grew up, and sprouted a mustache. But Ewa knew him right away. Ladies and gentlemen, surely you'll take the word of a noble and a citizen of the Commonwealth over the word of some Crimean vagabond?"

"Pan Mellehovitch is a Hetman's officer," Basia said. "We have no right to touch him or insult him!"

"At least you'll allow me, sir, to ask him a few questions," the little knight moved forward to stand beside Basia. *"Audiatur et altera pars!* A look-alike is a possible explanation."

But Pan Novovyeyski fell into a rage and was in no mood to listen to anyone.

"Pan Mellehovitch!" he spluttered with contempt. "He's no *Sir* or *Squire!* He's not landed gentry! He's my runaway groom masquerading under a false name. I'll have this *Squire* clip my dogs tomorrow! I'll have this *Squire's* hide flogged the day after, and not even the Hetman will get in my way because I'm a noble and I know my rights!"

At this Pan Michal's mustache twitched and his voice tightened dangerously.

"And I'm not only a noble but a commanding officer and I know my rights as well. You, sir, can go after your man in the courts and make your application at the Hetman's chancery, but I'm the man who gives orders here and nobody else!"

* * *

Pan Novovyeyski backtracked immediately, remembering that he was speaking to a military commander, as well as to his own son's superior officer and the most famous knight in the Commonwealth.

"Colonel," he said in a far softer tone. "I won't try to take him against your will, I'm merely trying to elucidate my rights and I ask that they be taken seriously and heard as the truth."

"What do you say to all this, Mellehovitch?" asked Pan Volodyovski, then added, when the Tartar stared fixedly at the floor and didn't say a word: "We all know that your first name is Azia!"

"Why look for further proof?" asked Pan Novovyeyski. "If

he's my man then he has a pair of blue fishes tattooed on his chest!"

But hearing this, Pan Nenashinyetz gasped, opened his mouth and eyes as far as they would go, and finally clutched his head with both trembling hands.

"Azia Tuhaybeyovitch!" he shouted suddenly in a frightful voice.

All eyes swung to him at once and he stood shaking as if all his ancient wounds had burst open anew, and he stammered over and over in a voice full of suffering and sorrow: "That's my captive...! That's the son of Tuhay-bey...! For God's sake, that's he...!"

The young *Lipki* Tartar lifted his head proudly, swung his lynxlike stare over the gathering, and suddenly tore his clothes open across his wide chest.

"There are the blue fish!" he said. "I am Tuhay-bey's last surviving son!"

Chapter Thirty-eight

THE SHOCK OF HEARING the name of the awesome warrior silenced everyone.

It had been Tuhay-bey, after all, who'd shaken the Commonwealth to her foundations along with the terrible Hmyelnitzki, who spilled a sea of Polish blood, who ground the territories of the Ukraine, Volhynia, Podolia and Halitch into dust under his horses' hooves, who turned cities into smoking ruins, burned the villages, stormed and gutted citadels and castles, and carried off a hundred thousand captives into slavery. Now that man's son was standing before this gathering and spitting fire right into their faces.

'I have the blue fishes tattooed on my breast!' he told them with his burning eyes, as fierce and savage as a hawk and as proud and haughty as the Devil. *'I am Azia, blood and bone of Tuhay-bey, your exterminator!'*

But such was the respect which the people of those times had for great military leaders and distinguished lineage, that Mellehovitch soared in their eyes to the gigantic stature of his terrifying father despite the dread which seized every soldier at the sound of that near-legendary name.

They stared at him as if transfixed, especially the women for whom a mystery is the source of the most gripping fascinations. He, in turn, stood before them in such haughty splendor as if his admission had invested him with his father's greatness.

"This noble," he said at last, and nodded towards Novovyeyski, "says that I'm his man. And I say to him that my father mounted his horse off the bowed backs of greater men

than he. It's true that I lived with him. It's true that my back
bled under his whip, which I won't forget, so help me God! I
called myself Mellehovitch to escape his clutches. But now,
though I could have run to the Crimea, I spill my blood and risk
my life in service to this country, so I belong to the Hetman and
nobody else. My father was kin to Khans. A life of wealth and
pleasure waited for me in the Crimea. But I stayed here, despised
and humiliated, because I love this Motherland, the Hetman and
those who never showed me their contempt."

With this he bowed respectfully to Volodyovski, bent so low
before Basia that his head almost brushed her knees, ignored all
the others as if they didn't exist, tucked his saber under his arm
and walked out of the room.

The silence continued for a while longer until Pan Zagloba
shook off his own stunned stupor and remarked: "Ha! And
where's Pan Snitko? I told him that this Azia had eyes like a
wolf, and he's a wolf's son."

"A lion's son, more likely," said Volodyovski. "And who
knows if he didn't inherit the greatness of his father."

"Good God," said Pan Mushalski. "Did you all notice how his
teeth gleamed and flashed? Just like Tuhay-bey when he was
enraged! I'd know him by that if nothing else, because I used to
see old Tuhay-bey often enough..."

"But not as often as I!" threw in Pan Zagloba.

"Now I understand why he has such a following among the
Lipki and the *Tcheremisy*," Pan Bogush exclaimed. "Tuhay-bey's
name is holy among them. As God's alive, he could take every
one of them into the Sultan's service any time he wished,
heaping an irreparable misfortune on the Commonwealth!"

"That he won't do," said Pan Volodyovski firmly. "What he
said to us about loving this country and the Hetman is quite true.
Otherwise he could've gone to the Crimea a long time ago and
lived like a prince. He certainly hasn't found much joy in staying
among us!"

"That's right, he won't!" Pan Bogush echoed Volodyovski
with conviction. "He'd have done any time he wished if that's
what he wanted. Nothing could have stopped him."

"On the contrary," added Nenashinyetz. "I can now believe
that he'll succeed in bringing all those traitor captains back into
the service of the Commonwealth."

"Master Novovyeyski," Zagloba said suddenly. "If you'd known that this was the son of Tuhay-bey, would you have still... I mean, would you... what?"

"I'd have ordered three thousand lashes for him instead of three hundred!"shouted the old noble. "May lightning strike me if I wouldn't have! Gentlemen! I find it very strange that he didn't run off to the Crimea, being the whelp of Tuhay-bey. Unless it's something that he's just discovered because he didn't know a thing about it when he was with me! It's strange, I agree, but I find it threatening! For God's sake don't trust him! I've known him a lot longer than you and I'm telling you that the Devil isn't as changeable as he, a mad dog isn't as dangerous, and a wolf isn't as cunning, cruel and vicious as this man! Mark my words, he'll cause us all a lot of trouble before he's done with us!"

"What are you saying, sir!" Mushalski shrugged, dismissing the warning. "We've seen him at work at Kalnik, Uman, Bratzlav and a hundred other fights and battles!"

"He won't let go of what belongs to him," appealed Pan Novovyeyski. "Mark my words! Remember what I told you! He'll have his revenge!"

"You should have seen him carving Azbah's cut-throats and bandits this morning, sir! What are you trying to tell us anyway?"

★ ★ ★

Basia, meanwhile, was burning with excitement, quite fascinated with the Mellehovitch story. But her own eager, warm-hearted and idealistic nature wanted the end of this story to be as thrilling and romantic as its beginning, so she shook Ewa Novovyeyska by the shoulders and whispered in her ear:

"Evka! You loved him, didn't you? Admit it, don't deny it! You loved him? Ha? And you still love him, yes? I am sure you do! Be honest with me. Whom can you trust if not another woman? Ah, you see? Think of it, that's almost royal blood! The Hetman will get him ten patents of nobility, not just one, and your father won't be able to object. I'm as sure as anything that Azia must still be in love with you as well! I know it, I know all about it. Trust me, don't be afraid! He respects me and he won't hide anything from me. Ha! I'll put him under an interrogation straight away and I know just how to go about it. He'll tell me everything without a bucketful of hot coals to loosen his tongue, believe me. Were you terribly in love with him? Do you love him still?"

But Ewa sat as if she were stunned.

She was a child when Azia first showed his interest in her but then he disappeared, she didn't see him for years, and she stopped thinking about him altogether.

All she remembered of him through those years was a fiery image of an impetuous young lad, in part a playmate and companion of her brother and, in part, a servant. But now, when she suddenly saw him again after that supposedly endless separation, he was someone quite unknown, unimaginable and new: a fierce young man, as beautiful and dangerous as a falcon, an officer and a famous borderer, and the son of princes even though a foreigner.

So now even the earlier Azia looked entirely different, and what she saw confused her, dazzled her, and—at the same time—stirred her and aroused her. The half-forgotten memories came to life within her. Basia's whispered questioning filled her with unanswered questions of her own and resurrected all her buried excitements and feelings, as if she'd suddenly plunged into a fairy tale. She couldn't fall in love with this fabulous young man in one impassioned moment, but she felt willing and ready to do so with a little time.

★   ★   ★

Unable to get anything out of her in the crowded parlor, with all the others jostling and arguing with each other everywhere around them, Basia took Ewa and Zosia to an adjoining study and started pressing her with questions even more urgently than before.

"Evka! Speak up, and be quick about it! Do you love him still?"

"I don't know," Panna Novovyeyska said after another moment of uncertainty.

"But you don't deny it? Oho! Then I know! Just don't be afraid! I was the first to tell Michal straight out that I loved him, and that was that! You understand? You must've loved each other terribly in the past! Ha! Now everything is clear! So it was out of love for you that he walked about here as gloomy as a wolf... The poor soldier just about dried up with longing! What happened between you?"

"Nothing..."

"Nothing?"

"He caught me in the wash-house," whispered Novovyeyska. "He told me he loved me..."

"In the wash-house! Well, isn't that something? And what happened then?"

"He got hold of me and started to kiss me," Panna Novovyeyska whispered even more softly than before.

"Well, he's really something, that Mellehovitch! And what did you do?"

"I was afraid to call out..."

"Afraid to call out? Zosia, do you hear this? And when did all this loving come out into the open?"

"Father came along, caught us, knocked him down with a mace, whipped me, and had him whipped so badly that he couldn't get to his feet for two weeks!"

Here Panna Novovyeyska burst into tears in part out of shame and sorrow and in part out of sheer confusion. This was enough to fill Zosia Boska's sky-blue eyes with tears but Basia started to soothe and comfort Ewa.

"Everything will end well, don't worry, I'll see to it all. I'll harness Michal and Pan Zagloba to this work as well. I'll put the bug in their ears, you can be sure of that! Nothing and nobody can hold out when Pan Zagloba starts working on something. You don't know him yet! Now stop crying, Evka, because it's time to go in for supper."

⋆ ⋆ ⋆

Mellehovitch didn't come to supper. He sat in his quarters, warming a mixture of mead and vodka on his hearth, and then pouring it into a small metal cup from which he sipped the aromatic liquor while he chewed on a piece of hardtack.

It wasn't until late at night that Pan Bogush came to see him to find out the latest about his dealings with the Tartar captains. The young Tartar seated him courteously on a stool padded with a sheepskin, placed a tin cup of hot liquor before him, and asked:

"Does Pan Novovyeyski still talk about turning me into his peasant?"

"No one is even thinking about it any more," said the *Podstoli* of Novgorod. "Pan Nenashinyetz might have some claims on you but even he doesn't need you any more, because his sister is either dead already or wouldn't want to change her situation. Pan Novovyeyski didn't know who you were when he had you whipped for getting too close to his daughter. But even he is walking around just now as if he'd been hit on the head with a battle mace because, even though your father did terrible harm to our country in his time, he was a great warrior nonetheless, and blood isn't water. God is my witness that no one here will crook a finger at you as long as you stay loyal to the Commonwealth, especially since you have friends in high places everywhere."

"Why shouldn't I be loyal?" Azia answered. "My father pounded you but he was a heathen while I follow Christ."

"That's it! That's what it's all about! You can't go back to the Crimea now without a change of Faith, and since that would mean the loss of your salvation, there are no earthly goods that might make it up to you. Come to think of it, you owe a debt to both Pan Nenashinyetz and Pan Novovyeyski, because the first one got you away from pagans and the second raised you in God's Faith."

"I know what I owe them," Azia said, while his cold eyes glinted. "And I'll do my best to pay them both in full. You're right to say, sir, that I have many benefactors among you!"

"Ah, Azia, you say it as if it burned your mouth. But count them up for yourself. You've many well-wishers."

"His Lordship the Hetman and yourself, first and foremost," Azia nodded slowly. "I'll say that to my dying day. But I don't know who else..."

"And the Commandant out here? Do you think that he'd let anyone get his hands on you even if you weren't the son of Tuhay-bey? And what about her? What about Lady Volodyovska? I heard how highly she spoke of you at the supper table... Bah! And even before, when Novovyeyski recognized you, she took your side at once! Pan Volodyovski would move heaven and earth for her, because he's blind to the world where she is concerned, and a sister can't care for her brother as much as she cares for you. You were all she could talk about at supper..."

★ ★ ★

The young Tartar bowed suddenly over the half-quart cup he
clutched in both hands, blowing into the steam, and his distended, bluish lips made him look suddenly so fierce, so savage
and so much like a wild Dobrudjan, that Pan Bogush shuddered
and shook his head.

"It's amazing how much you resemble old Tuhay-bey right
now," he said. "I knew him well and I saw him often, both in
the field and in the Khan's court as well. And I must have been
at least twenty times in his Summer tents."

"May God bless the righteous," Azia muttered darkly. "And
may the plague choke those who injure others. Long life to the
Hetman!"

"Long life and good health," Pan Bogush echoed and tossed
down his cupful. "He has only a handful of men like us around
him but we are real soldiers. With God's help, we'll stand up to
all those fat-bellied country politicians who can't do anything
except snipe and bicker at their petty diets and accuse the
Hetman of bad faith to the King! Ah, the scum! The scoundrels!
Here we stand in the Steppe, face to face with the enemy night
and day, and they stuff themselves with tubs of cabbage stew and
bang-out their drumrolls with a fork and spoon! That's their
commitment! Here the Hetman sends one courier after another
begging for some armaments for Kamyenetz while there's still
time to strengthen the defenses; here he is, crying out his
warnings like Cassandra before the Siege of Troy, prophesying
the fall of Ilium and the death of Priam, and all they think about
is who did what to undermine the King!"

"What's this you're saying, sir?"

"Eh, nothing. It was just a thought. I made a *comparationis*
between our Kamyenetz and Troy but you probably never even
heard about the Trojan War. Let things quieten down a bit and
the Hetman will get you properly ennobled, I'll bet my neck on
that! Such times are coming that you won't lack an opportunity
to cover yourself in glory."

"I'll either walk in glory on this earth," Azia said and
shrugged, "or lie dead under it. You'll hear about me as surely
as there's a God in Heaven!"

"And what about those others? What's Krytchinski thinking? Will they come back or not? And what are they up to?"

"They've gone to Winter quarters. Some are camped in the southern Steppes, others farther off. It's hard for them to keep in contact now because of the distance. They've orders to go to Adrianople in the Spring and take as much food and fodder with them as they can."

"By God, that's important news! Because if there's to be a great military *congressus* in Adrianople then war with us is a certainty. The Hetman must be told about it right away. He also thinks that a war is certain but that would be the last sign he needs."

"Halim told me there's talk among the Tartar captains that the Sultan himself will come to Adrianople with all of his armies."

"Dear God almighty! And here we've barely a handful of soldiers. Kamyenetz is our only hope. Does Krytchinski have any new conditions?"

"They're more concerned with their old complaints than any new conditions. What they want is what they've always wanted: a general amnesty, readmission to the rights and privileges of the gentry which they had before, and restoration of their rank as captains. But since the Sultan has already given them a lot more than that, they are hesitating."

"What are you saying? How can the Sultan give them more than the Commonwealth? The Turks live under an absolute monarchy where all laws are subject to a Sultan's whim. Even if the one who rules them now should keep all his pledges, what's to stop his successor from breaking every promise and trampling on them all as much as he pleases? But with us a privilege, once granted, is a holy thing, and the King himself can't take anything away from a man who becomes a noble."

Azia shrugged.

"They say they were gentry but they were treated no better than dragoons, and that the county sheriffs had them doing things that not even the Ruthenian petty boyars are obliged to do, not to mention nobles."

"But since the Hetman has given them his word..."

"None of them doubt the magnanimity of the Hetman, and all of them love him secretly in their hearts, but this is what they say: the Hetman himself is accused of treason by the politicking gentry, he's hated and distrusted at the King's court, and now the military confederations threaten him with trial. So what can he do?"

Pan Bogush started to rub his head in perplexity. "So what will they do?"

"They don't know themselves. They can't make up their minds."

"Will they stay with the Sultan?"

"No."

"Bah!"—and the troubled noble made a disbelieving gesture—"And who'll make them return to the service of the Commonwealth?"

"I will."

"You? How can you?"

"I'm the son of Tuhay-bey," said Azia Mellehovitch.

Chapter Thirty-nine

ANOTHER SILENCE FOLLOWED the young Tartar's abrupt exclamation and Pan Bogush stared at him for a moment with surprise and doubt etched into his face. Then he shrugged. He sighed.

"My dear Azia," he said and shook his head. "I don't deny that they might take great pride in Tuhay-bey and honor your lineage, even though they're our own Polish Tartars and Tuhay-bey was our bitterest enemy. I understand such things because there are some among our gentry who like to say that Hmyelnitzki was a Polish noble, and that his roots lay within our nation, in Mazuria, and not among the Cossacks, and they take pride in that... Amazing, what? You wouldn't find a worse demon anywhere in Hell, and he slaughtered more of our people and of the Jews as well than any murderer in history, but he was a first-rate soldier, that no one can deny, and so they're glad to claim him as their own. That's human nature! That's just how people are. But I don't see how descent from Tuhay-bey gives you the right to force obedience on any and all Tartars."

Azia sat thinking for a time, then rested his palms on his thighs, leaned slightly towards Pan Bogush, and spoke in a quiet but firm and thoughtful voice, nodding all the while.

"Then let me tell you, sir, why Krytchinski listens to me and why the others listen. Because, beside the fact that they're just common *Tatarchuki* and I am a prince, there is something else. I've a power in me. I've a way. It's something none of you people can see, neither you nor the Hetman... But all of *them* can see it."

"What power? What way?"

364

"*Ya toho skazaty ne umiyo,*"Mellehovitch answered in Ruthenian. "I can't explain it to you. But why is it I can do things that the others can't? Why can I think of things nobody else can think of?"

"What are you talking about, boy? What did you think up?"

"What I've thought up,"Azia said, "is that if the Hetman gave me the right and the power I wouldn't just bring back those two dozen Tartar colonels and captains. No! I'd put half the Horde at the Hetman's orders. How much free soil is there in the Wild Lands and in the Ukraine? How much unpeopled space is there in the Steppes? Let the Hetman just send out the word that every Tartar who comes to the Commonwealth will become a noble, that he'll be free in his religion, serve in his own Tartar regiments, and follow his own Hetman just like the Cossacks do, and I'll see to it that they'll fill the Ukraine from one end to the other. You'll get back your *Lipki* and your *Tcheremisy*, every last one of them. You'll get Tartars from Dobrudja and from Belgorod. They'll come from the Crimea in their tens of thousands. They'll bring their herds and cattle and their wives and children. Don't shake your head, sir. They'll come! Just like those others who came before, and settled among you, and served the Commonwealth faithfully for centuries! In the Crimea and everywhere else where you find the Tartars, the Khan and the *murjahs* squeeze them and oppress them, and here they'll be gentry, and they'll wear a saber and go to war under their own Hetman. I swear they'd come because the soil is rich here and the pastures run from one horizon to the other, and out where they are right now they starve to death in a hungry season. And when the word spreads among the *yurts* that I am calling them in the Hetman's name, *and that it's the son of Tuhay-bey who is calling*, then thousands will come."

Pan Bogush grasped his head.

"For God's sake, Azia!" he cried in amazement. "Where do you get such ideas? How? Can you imagine what would happen then?"

"What would happen,"the young Tartar said, "is that there'd be a Tartar Nation living in the Ukraine, as there's a Cossack one! You gave the Cossacks their privileges and their Hetman, why can't you give the same to us? You ask, sir, what would happen? There'd never be another Hmyelnitzki, that is what would happen, because we'd put our heel on the Cossack's throat right from the beginning. There'd be no peasant outbreaks, no massacres, no ruin and no devastations. There'd be no Doroshenko because I'd throw him on a leash at the Hetman's feet the first time he stirred! If the Turkish armies wanted to move against you, we'd fight against the Sultan! If the Khan wanted to send his *tchambuls* raiding through this country, we'd make war on the Khan! Isn't that what your Polish and Lithuanian Tartars used to do for years even though they stayed faithful to their Mohammedan religion? Why should we do something different, we Tartars of the Commonwealth! We nobles! We gentry? Now, sir, count your profits: the Ukraine quiet and at peace, the Cossacks muzzled, a shield against the Turks, and tens upon tens of thousands of new soldiers more...

"You ask what I've been thinking?" the young Tartar asked and stared into the fire. "That's what I've been thinking! That's the idea that's been growing in my head. That's why they listen to me over there, all of them—Krytchinski, Adurovitch, Moravski, Tvorovski and the rest—and that's why half of the Crimea will come running to these Steppes when they hear my call!"

Pan Bogush was so astounded by these words, and felt himself so narrowed and diminished by the vastness of the Tartar's vision, that he'd have been no less shaken if the walls of the room in which they were sitting suddenly burst apart and he found himself confronting a new world.

Minutes passed before he could say a word; he sat numbed, watching the young Tartar who started pacing the room in great strides.

"Such a thing couldn't happen without me," Azia said firmly and nodded quietly to himself with absolute conviction. "Because I'm the son of Tuhay-bey, and there's no name that rings louder among the Tartars from Belgorod to the Black Sea and from the Danube to the Dnieper."

And, after a while, he added:

"What do I care about Krytchinski and the rest of them! This isn't a question of a few thousand Polish and Lithuanian Tartars but of the Commonwealth herself! People say there'll be a great war in Spring against all the power of the Turks, but give me the nod and I'll boil up such a ferment among all the Hordes that the Sultan will scald his hands in it."

"For God's sake, Azia!" Pan Bogush cried out, dazzled by this vision. "Who are you?"

The young man raised his head and his voice rang out: "The future Hetman of the Tartars!"

★ ★ ★

The firelight fell on Azia in that moment, illuminating his proud and cruel features, and there was such a wealth of power and magnificence beaming from that face that Pan Bogush gasped, thinking for an instant that some strange, legendary figure had sprung up before him. The old statesman knew instinctively that what Azia told him was the truth. If such a call came from the Hetman of the Crown, all of the Polish and Lithuanian Tartars would come back at once, of that he was certain, and many of the other Tartars would follow in their wake. Pan Bogush knew the Crimea very well. He had been twice a slave there, and an ambassador after the Hetman ransomed him; he knew the ins and outs of the Khan's court at Baktchi-saray. He knew the Hordes that spread along the Black Sea from Dobrudja to the River Don. He knew that hunger stalked among the black, horsehide tents in Winter, that the European *murjahs* snarled and fretted under the grasping despotism of the Khan's *baskaks* or roving governors and other tax-collectors, and that bloody riots often broke out in the Crimea itself. It was as clear as day that a promise of rich grants of land and the vast privileges of the Polish-Lithuanian gentry would lure all those who found themselves stifled, threatened or abused in their old allegiance.

It was even more certain if the call came from the son of Tuhay-bey. He alone could do it, no other name had such a powerful natural influence among the *yurts*, not even that of the Khan himself! His father's fame was immortal among the Hordes. A call from the son would ring like a summons from the father among the tent cities of the plains, arm one half of the Crimea against the other, draw the savage legions of the Belgorodian Horde, and shake not only all of Tartary but the vast power of the Sultan as well.

If the Hetman wished to avail himself of this opportunity, the

old statesman thought, he could view this son of Tuhay-bey as
a gift from Providence.

So now Pan Bogush looked at Azia with new eyes and started
wondering how such far-reaching thoughts could have sprung
from that youthful head. Sweat burst out along the old man's
forehead at the enormous implications of what he had just heard.

But there were still some doubts locked in his heart and mind
and so he asked after a long moment: "And do you know that
there'd have to be a war with the Turks over a thing like this?"

"There'll be a war anyway!" Azia snapped, impatient. "Otherwise why would they order the Hordes to go to Adrianople?
The only way a war can be avoided now is utter chaos among
the Turks. And if they move against us anyway, half the Hordes
will ride with us, not with them."

'*He has an answer to everything,*' Pan Bogush thought, dazzled
and impressed.

"This is enough to make a man dizzy," he said after a long,
silent moment. "It's not an easy thing, you see... I mean, you're
talking about settling a new nation in the Ukraine! What would
the King say to that? What about the Chancellor? And what
about the Estates General, the parliament, the diets? Most of the
gentry is ranked against the Hetman nowadays..."

"All I need is the Hetman's permission in writing to send out
the call!" Azia said coldly and spat into the fire. "Let them try to
get us out of here once we've come and settled! And who's
going to drive us out anyway? And with what? You'd like to get
rid of the Zaporohjans in the *Sietch* but you've no way to do it."

"The Hetman might not be able to take on such responsibility..."

"There'll be fifty thousand Tartar sabers ranked behind the
Hetman, not counting the troops he already has."

"And the Cossacks? You forget the Cossacks! They'll rise up
at once!"

"That's why you need us here in the first place, to have a
sword hanging over the Cossacks' necks. What keeps Doroshenko going? Tartars! He'd be lost without them. Let me grasp
all the Tartars in my hands and Dorosh must go down on his
knees before the Hetman! He'll have no other choice."

★   ★   ★

Here Azia stretched out his hands before him, and spread his fingers as if they were the talons of an eagle, and then he clutched the hilt of his saber.

"This is the law we'll show to the Cossacks!" he snarled savagely. "They'll go back to the furrows, like the peasants they are, and we'll be the masters of the Ukraine! Listen to me, Master Bogush, and listen well. You thought me just a little man, all of you, but I'm not as small as it seems to your Novovyeyski, and the Commandant out here, and the officers, and you too as well! I've thought about this day and night for a long, long time. I didn't eat, I didn't sleep, I got as thin as a rail thinking about all this until my face turned dark and the flesh fell away from my bones, as if I was eaten up with an inner fever. But what I've thought up I thought up well, and that's why I told you that I've the power and the way. These are great matters for great men, as you can see yourself, so go now to the Hetman and be quick about it! Tell him what I've said. Tell him that all I need is a letter from him and I won't care about your parliaments and diets. The Hetman has a great soul. He can see far beyond an ordinary eye. He'll know that this is the power and the way! Tell him that I'm the son of Tuhay-bey and that I'm the only one who can do this for him. Tell him. Make him agree. But hurry, man, hurry! There is no time to waste. All this must happen now, in Winter, while the Steppe is buried under snow, because Spring means war! Go quickly and come back just as fast so I'll know what I will have to do."

Pan Bogush was so shaken by what he had heard that he didn't even notice that Azia spoke to him in a commanding tone, ignoring all the normal courtesies of rank, as if he were already a Hetman giving orders to a lesser officer.

"I'll rest tomorrow," he said after a while, "and leave the day after. God grant that I'll find the Hetman at home in Yavorov! He makes decisions quickly so you'll have your answer very soon."

"And what do you think he'll say? Will he agree?"

"It's possible he'll order you to come to see him so don't go to Rashkov just now to meet with Krytchinski. You'll get to Yavorov faster from here than there. I don't know if he'll agree or not but he'll certainly think seriously about it because your reasoning is most persuasive. By God, Azia, I didn't expect something like this from you, but now I see that you're not an ordinary man, and that God has destined you for greatness..."

Bemused, he shook his head in wonder.

"Well, well," he said. "Azia... who'd have thought it. Just a lieutenant in a *Lipki* regiment, nothing more, but he has such things stirring in his head that they can scare the daylight out of people... I wouldn't be surprised to see a heron's feather in your cap and a horsetail standard waving over you... no, not after this! Yes, I can well believe that this has gnawed at you through the nights for years... Yes, I'll set out the day after tomorrow, one day's rest will do, but now I've got to go to bed because all this is roaring through my head like water in a millrace... Stay with God, Azia, son of Tuhay-bey!"

Pan Bogush squeezed the Tartar's bony hand and turned towards the door. But he stopped once more on the threshold, deep in thought, as if recalling the young Tartar's vision.

"Could it be?" he murmured. "New armies for the Commonwealth, the Cossacks cowed and muzzled, Dorosh brought down at last, the Crimea shaken, the Turks weakened... the end of Tartar raiding in Ruthenia... Dear God! Dear God! Could it really be?"

Then he left, and Azia stared darkly after him for a moment longer.

"And for me," he whispered, "a Hetman's *bulava* and a horsetail standard... and *her*, whether she wants or not! Otherwise... death to all of you!"

Then he drained the last of the liquor from his cup and threw himself down on the cot that crouched in the corner of the room under a pile of sheepskins. The fire dwindled in the hearth but the window glowed with the pale light of a golden moon which had climbed high into the cold winter sky.

Azia lay quietly for some time but, apparently, he couldn't sleep that night. At last he rose, came over to the window, and stared in silence at the crescent moon which sailed like a lone ship, bound for unknown places, across the unfathomable darkness.

The young, silent Tartar stared at it a long time. Then he clenched his fists close against his chest, raised both his index fingers straight into the air, and the mouth which uttered Christ's name only an hour earlier now spilled the soft, lilting chant of a Moslem prayer.

"*Llachai, illachai, Llacha illacha... Mohammed Rossulah...!*"

Chapter Forty

BASIA WASTED NO TIME the next day in mobilizing her husband and Pan Zagloba to help the young lovers. They laughed and teased her, amused by her enthusiasm, but in the end they let her have her way as they always did, and promised to do everything they could.

"The best thing," said Zagloba, "would be to convince old Novovyeyski to leave the girl behind when he goes to Rashkov, what with the Winter winds starting to blow and the roads not being all that safe. While he's away your lovers can get themselves enamored good and proper."

"That is a first-rate thought!" Basia cried.

"Maybe it is and maybe it isn't," answered Pan Zagloba. "You just make sure you keep an eye on them. You're a woman and you'll glue them both together in the end because women always get what they're after one way or another. But the Devil also does his work so watch for monkey-business. You'd be ashamed later that you had a hand in it."

Basia spat at him like a kitten while he winked and nodded and then she said: "You, sir, boast that you were a real Turk when you were young and you think that everybody is a Turk! Azia's not like that!"

"That's right. He's a Tartar, not a Turk. A mighty fine distinction! Listen to her guaranteeing a Tartar's honorable intentions!"

"Both of them think more about weeping than... than... What I mean is they're too love-sick to... to... well you know what I mean! And anyway, Ewa's a decent girl!"

"Right. She just has a face that looks as if she had *'come and get it'* written on her forehead. Hooo! What a jaybird! I noted last night at supper that when she looks at a good-looking man she starts to pant so hard her plate flies away and she's got to pull it back to her again."

"Shame on you, sir!" Basia threatened. "D'you want me to leave the room?"

"You won't leave when you've got the chance to play the matchmaker," Pan Zagloba said. "You'll stay put, ho ho! We know all your tricks, though it's a bit early for you to be a marriage broker because that's a matron's occupation. Lady Boska told me that when she first caught sight of you strutting around in breeches yesterday she thought you were Lady Volodyovska's whipper-snapper son who'd been jumping fences on a pony. You don't much care for a mature image but maturity doesn't love you either, which is clear to all who see you hopping about like a schoolboy. What a jack-in-the-box you are! Dear God, how the women have changed! There was a time that if a wench sat down on a footstool it would screech like a dog whose tail got trampled underfoot, but you my girl could ride bareback on a cat without putting the beast under any strain... People say, by the way, that women who start to play the go-between don't ever have children."

"Is that true?" the little knight asked, alarmed. "Is that what they say?"

But Pan Zagloba only started laughing and Basia pressed her pink face to her husband's cheek.

"Eh *Michalku,*" she murmured. "We'll make a pilgrimage to Tchenstohova when we have a chance and perhaps the Holy Mother will bring about a change."

"There's no surer way," Pan Zagloba said, although it was clear from his tone that he could think of several.

The couple gave each other a quick hug and Basia said: "Let's get back to Azia and Ewa. What can we do to help them? We're so happy together, let them be happy too."

"They'll be a lot happier when Novovyeyski leaves," said the little knight. "There's no way for them to meet while he's here, especially since Azia hates the sight of him. If the old man would just let him have Evka they might forget their past differences and start to love each other like in-laws sometimes do. The way

I see it, it's not a question of getting the young couple together, since they're already in love with each other, but of winning over the old man."

"He's an old sour-puss!" Basia said.

"Baska!" the old knight huffed. "Imagine that you have a daughter and that you've got to marry her off to some slant-eyed Tartar! What would you say then?"

"Azia is a prince!"

"I don't deny that Tuhay-bey was a blueblood, at least by their reckoning. But Ketling also comes from noble stock and yet Krysia Drohoyovska wouldn't have married him if he hadn't been ennobled in Poland as well."

"Then get Azia ennobled!"

"Just like that, eh?" The old knight threw up his arms and wagged his head as if he'd never heard anything so foolish. "D'you think it's that easy? Even if someone did admit him to his coat-of-arms, he'd have to get it confirmed by the diet, and that needs strong backing and a lot of time."

"That's the part I don't like," Basia said. "I mean that it takes time. The backing could be found. I'm sure the Hetman wouldn't refuse to use his influence because he loves soldiers. Michal! Write to the Hetman! D'you need ink? Pens? Some paper? Write at once. I'll bring you everything you need. Candles? Sealing-wax? I'll get them right now!"

Volodyovski started laughing.

"Dear God," he sighed. "I prayed for a calm, cool-headed wife and you sent me a whirlwind!"

"Keep saying that and I'll die and leave you!"

"Not on your life!" the little knight cried out at once. "Not on your life! Don't even say such things! Tfui! Tfui! Turn the curse away! Throw it on a dog!" Then he turned anxiously to Pan Zagloba. "D'you know some good incantation to turn away curses?"

"I do," the old knight said. "And I've already said it!"

"Write!" Basia cried. "Or I'll leap out of my skin with impatience!"

"I'd write twenty letters to please you," said Volodyovski. "But I don't know what good it'll do because this is something not even the Hetman can move before its time and he can't exert his influence until the process starts. My dear, sweet Basia, Panna

Novovyeyska let you in on her secret, and that's fine and good. But you haven't heard a word from Azia and you don't even know if he feels the same way."

"Of course he feels the same way! How is he to feel if he kissed her in the wash-house? There!"

"Ah, what a Heart of Gold!" Zagloba rocked with laughter. "She's like a newborn babe except that her tongue wags faster! My sweet child, if Michal and I wanted to marry every snippet we kissed now and then we'd have to turn Moslem! I'd have to be at least the Padishah and he'd be the Khan! Isn't that right, Michal?"

"Hmm. I once had some suspicions about Michal, back then before we married," Basia said, wagged a finger right under his nose and began to tease him. "Come on now, twitch your whiskers, go ahead! You won't keep it from me. I know and you know too... in Ketling's house, remember?"

The little knight was indeed moving his whiskers fiercely up and down, both to give himself a more determined air and cover his confusion. He didn't like to think about his foolishness with Krysia Drohoyovska.

"But you still don't know if Azia's in love with Novo-vyeyska," he said to change the subject.

"Just wait a bit! I'll get him face to face and I'll get the answers. But of course he's in love! He has to be in love! Otherwise I don't want to know him!"

"Dear God," Zagloba sighed. "She's ready to talk him into it."

"And I will, even if I've got to lock myself up with him every day!"

"Question him first," the little knight suggested. "He may not admit it straight away because he's a wild one. But never mind. You'll win his trust, get to know him better, understand how his mind works, and then you'll know what to do about him."

Satisfied with his own advice, the little knight turned to Pan Zagloba. "She gives the impression of a rattle-brain," he said, "but she is a sharp one!"

"Some snippets are," Pan Zagloba nodded.

★ ★ ★

The rest of the discussion had to be deferred because Pan Bogush burst into the room like a cannonball, barely took the

time to kiss Basia's hands, and started shouting as if he'd had a
stroke of revelation.

"God love that Azia! I couldn't close an eye all night, may he
suffer for it!"

"What did poor Azia do to you, sir?" Basia asked at once.

"Can you all guess what we did last night, he and I?" The
excited noble stared from one of them to the other with eyes as
big as saucers. "D'you have any idea?"

"No! What?"

"We were making history, as I live and breathe!"

"What history?"

"The Commonwealth's history! That is, to put it simply, a
great man. Even Pan Sobieski will be amazed when I tell him
about Azia's ideas. A great man, I say again, and I'm only sorry
that I can't tell you any more about it because I'm sure you'd be
as amazed as I was. All I can say is that if things go the way he
intends then there's no limit to how high he'll go!"

"For example?" Zagloba voiced his doubts. "Will he become
a Hetman?"

"That's it!" Pan Bogush cocked his fists on his hips and rolled
his eyes triumphantly at the others. "He'll be a Hetman! I wish
I could say more... But, yes! He'll become a Hetman and that's
that!"

"Whose?" the old knight remained unconvinced. "The dogs'?
Or is he going to command a goat-herd? The rabble also have
their so-called hetmans. Tfui, sir! What are you babbling about?
So he's the son of Tuhay-bey, so what? Huh! If his kind gets to
be a Hetman, what will I become? Or Michal? Or yourself? His
hetmancy is about as likely as for the three of us to become the
Three Kings of the East after Christmas, always supposing that
Casper, Melchior and Balthazar will abdicate in our favor. The
gentry at least made me a Generalissimo at one time, which I
resigned in favor of Pan Sapyeha out of sheer friendship, but I
can make no sense whatsoever out of you prophecies!"

"And I tell you that Azia's a great man!"

"And didn't I say so from the start?" Basia said and turned
towards the door through which her other guests were entering
the room.

★   ★   ★

First to come in was Lady Boska with the blue-eyed Zosia, and then Pan Novovyeyski and Ewa who hadn't slept very well that night but who, none the less, looked even fresher and more tempting than before.

She didn't get much sleep because she'd been disturbed by strange dreams. She had dreamt of Azia but it was a far more handsome and aggressive Azia than she'd ever known, one who did a lot more than just try to kiss her. Ewa's face blazed with color when she recalled that dream because she was certain that everyone could read it in her eyes.

But no one paid her much attention. Everyone was busy saying their *good mornings* to the Commandant's Lady, and then Pan Bogush launched into his praise of Azia and his prognostications about his future greatness, and Basia was delighted that Ewa and Pan Novovyeyski were obliged to listen to it all, especially since it came from such a source.

She was quick to note that the old noble seemed to have gotten over his outrage over the young Tartar and that he was much more relaxed and calmer than the day before. He said nothing more about him as *his fellow*, nor staked any claims, and the truth of it was that he was most impressed by the discovery that Azia was a Tartar prince, born to the purple as it were, and a son of Tuhay-bey as well.

He listened with great interest to accounts of the young man's bravery and daring, and to the revelation that the Hetman himself thought so highly of him that he'd entrusted him with the important mission of bringing all the renegade Polish and Lithuanian Tartars back into the service of the Commonwealth. At times, in fact, Pan Novovyeyski thought that all this praise must deal with someone altogether different, because this new, great and influential Azia didn't seem like anyone he had known before.

Meanwhile Pan Bogush kept repeating with a most mysterious air that all this was nothing in comparison with what was to come. "I'm not free to say a word about it," he assured them all. "But what he is or what he was is but a shadow of what he's going to be!"

And then, because some of the others shook their heads in doubt, he shouted out, still dazzled by the visions of what he'd

heard from Azia: "There are two truly great men in the Commonwealth: Pan Sobieski and this Tuhaybeyovitch!"

"For God's sake!" Pan Zagloba burst out at last, driven out of
patience. "No matter what kind of a Tartar prince he is, what
could he ever be in the Commonwealth, not being a noble? He
still doesn't have a patent of nobility, does he?"

"The Hetman will get him ten patents!" Basia cried. "You'll
see!"

Ewa Novovyeyska listened to all these prophecies and praises
with half-closed eyes and a heart that fluttered in her chest like
a startled bird. No one could say—indeed, she didn't even know
it for herself—if she'd have been that moved and that entranced
if Azia was a poor, unknown stranger, or even the captive Tartar
houseboy she barely remembered. But she felt strangely weak
and helpless at the thought of this new, soaring Azia whose
stature as a valiant knight grew with every telling, and whose
future seemed to be so great.

These conquered doubt. Her recent dream inflamed her, as
did the sudden recollection of those remembered kisses, and she
felt herself shuddering with mysterious tremors throughout her
whole body.

'Such a great man,' she thought, remembering her dream. 'So
powerful and strong. No wonder he's as quick as fire to take what he
wants.'

Chapter Forty-one

BASIA QUESTIONED THE TARTAR the very same day, but having been warned about his primitive lack of polish and his feral fierceness, she took her husband's advice and decided not to press him directly from the start.

Even so, he had no sooner appeared before her when she fired point-blank: "Pan Bogush says that you're a most unusual man. But I think that even an extraordinary man doesn't shun affairs of the heart."

Azia half-shut his eyes and bowed his assent.

"Your ladyship is quite right," he said.

"Because the heart follows its own rules, you see. One look and it's all over!"

Having fired her opening shot, Basia tossed her tawny head and started blinking in a manner meant to suggest that she too knew all about such things and that both of them must know what she was driving at. Azia, in turn, raised his gloomy eyes and embraced her whole winsome being with a single glance. She had never seemed more dazzling and enticing to him than now, with her bright eyes alight with curiosity and excitement, and with her pink childlike face lifted towards him full of encouragement and smiles.

But the more innocence she projected, the more he was stirred to lust and possession; he wanted to carry her off and drink her as if she were wine, giving up every desire except one: to take her from her husband, keep her for himself, fix his mouth on hers and feel her arms winding around his neck, and to keep loving her no matter what happened in the world around him, even if this meant his death along with her own.

He was caught in the vortex of his own emotions, the earth seemed to spin around him like a whirling sandstorm, and all his hidden cravings crept out of his soul like serpents from dark crevices underneath a rock. But this was also a man who had lived for years under an iron self-control and possessing a truly terrifying will and so he told himself: *'Not yet!'* and held himself hobbled like a maddened mustang.

He stood before her outwardly unmoved, although flames seemed to scorch his mouth in anticipation, and to leap from those dark, hooded eyes that told her everything his lips would not utter.

Basia knew nothing of this. Her heart and mind were simply too honest and straightforward, the currents of her soul were as crystally clean as a freshwater spring, and her thoughts were elsewhere; she was preoccupied just then with wondering what else to say to the Tartar. At last she lifted one small finger and said:

"Many people hide their warmest feelings, not daring to share them even with a friend, but they might hear something good if they'd only speak up honestly."

Azia's face darkened. A wild hope flashed through him like a thunderbolt, but he stifled it and asked: "What does your ladyship wish to talk about?"

"Some women would press you into an admission," Basia said. "Some of us lack thoughtfulness and patience. But I'm not that kind. I'd be glad to help you—very glad!—but I don't demand confessions as a precondition. I'll say just this for now: don't hide your feelings, come to see me as often as you like, every day if that is what you need, because I've already talked this over with my husband; you'll get used in time to trusting me, you'll see how well-disposed I am towards you, and you'll know that I'm not questioning you out of sheer curiosity but only through compassion. If I'm to help you then I must be sure about your feelings. It's really up to you in any event to be the first to show them and if you'll do that then I'll be able to tell you something too."

The Tartar understood at last how fleeting and unreal that wild flash of hope had been.

He grasped at once that all this had to do with Ewa Novovyeyska and all the hatred that he nurtured for that entire family in his vengeful soul flooded his mouth with curses. A murderous fury burst into flame within him, all the more violent for his disappointment, but he controlled even this terrifying rage. He was not only a complete master of his own emotions but he possessed that calculating shrewdness common to Eastern peoples. He knew in an instant that if he spat out his venom at the Novovyeyskis he'd lose Basia's friendly interest in him and his chance to see her every day. On the other hand, he didn't think he'd manage to control himself, at least not just then, if he were to lie to this woman whom he craved so badly, and to pretend that he loved another.

So it was out of a real inner turmoil and from a genuine torment of the soul that he threw himself on his knees before her, kissed her feet in the manner of the times, and found himself speaking a truth that would not offend her.

"My life and soul are in your hands, my lady. All I want to do is what you say I should; your will is my own! Do what you want with me! I live in pain, my days are a torment! Have mercy on me, ladyship! Because I'd sooner die than go on like this!"

The deep groan he uttered was also genuine and real because the pain of his repressed desires scorched him like a fire. Basia, however, took his outburst for an expression of his long and painfully concealed love for Ewa, she was gripped by pity, and two small tears appeared in her eyes.

"Get up, Azia," she said to the kneeling Tartar. "I always liked you and I want to do whatever I can to help. You come of noble stock and your great merits are sure to get you a patent of nobility. Pan Novovyeyski will let himself be convinced because he's already looking at you with quite different eyes, and Evka..."

And here Basia rose off her bench, stood on tiptoe, lifted her pink, smiling face towards Azia's ear and whispered:

"Evka loves you!"

His face, however, twisted as if wrenched by a spasm of hatred, he seized his topknot with both hands, and losing sight

of the shock that such a cry would be sure to cause, groaned out
in a harsh, snarling voice:

"Allah! Allah! Allah!"

And then he hurled himself out of the room.

★ ★ ★

Basia stared after him for a moment. His shout hadn't startled
her particularly—even Polish soldiers used the name of Allah
now and then as an exclamation—and she totally misread his
explosive violence.

'What a whirlwind,' she told herself about him. 'He's quite mad
about her!'

Then she rushed, as if carried off by a whirlwind of her own,
to report all this to her husband, the old knight and Ewa
Novovyeyska. She found Volodyovski at his headquarters, going
over his regimental rosters, and practically leaped on him where
he sat and wrote.

"I spoke to him!" she cried. "He threw himself down on his
knees before me! He's off his head about her!"

The little knight put down his quill and looked at his wife.
She was so full of life just then, and so adorable in her young
excitement, that his own eyes filled with laughter, alight with
pleasure at the sight of her, and he stretched out his arms towards
her.

"Azia is mad over Evka!" she cried out again.

"As I am over you!" he said and pulled her closer.

Not long afterwards Pan Zagloba and Eva Novovyeyska knew
every detail of her talk with Azia.

The old knight didn't really care about it one way or another—his interest in the Tartar's lovelife was confined to pleasing his beloved little warrior—but Eva was swept away by an
onrush of thoughts and feelings she'd never experienced to this
extent before. She gave herself totally to anticipation of that first
fond meeting, and even more to wondering what would happen
when the two of them were finally alone together and able to
exchange that magical phrase with which love began. In her
mind's eye she already saw Azia's dark face bending over her
knees, felt the touch of his mouth as it covered her hands with
kisses, and drifted into that sweet languor with which a young

woman's head bows towards her beloved's shoulder while her lips whisper: *'And I love you too.'*

Meanwhile she showered Basia's hands with her grateful kisses, glancing every moment towards the door, and wondering when the darkly beautiful young Tartar might appear there.

★   ★   ★

Azia, however, didn't show himself anywhere in the garrison because he spent the day secluded with Halim, who had been one of his father's most trusted retainers and who was now an important *murjah* among the Dobrudjans.

This time Halim had come quite openly because the Hreptyov officers knew that he was an intermediary in Azia's negotiations with the turncoat captains. The two of them locked themselves in Azia's quarters where Halim prostrated himself on the pineboard floor, rendered the salaams due to a son of Tuhay-bey, then placed his arms across his chest and shoulders, bowed his head, and waited for his master's questions.

"Have you brought me anything in writing?" Azia asked.

"No, *Effendi*. The message is verbal."

"Speak then!"

"The war is now certain. All of us are to go to Adrianople in Spring. The Bulgarians are stocking the oats and hay over there already."

"And where will the Khan be?"

"The Khan will go straight across the Wild Lands into the Ukraine to join up with Dorosh."

"What do you hear in the Winter camps?"

"Everyone's pleased about the war and longing for Spring because times are hard under the tents these days even though it's just the start of the Winter."

"Are they really having such a hard time, then?"

"They lost a lot of horses. The grass was scarce in the fall because the sun burned it out in the Steppe through Summer. And yes, the hunger's great. Many warriors sell themselves into slavery in Belgorod just to last out till Spring."

"And have they heard about the son of Tuhay-bey?"

"I spread the word as far as you allowed it, *Effendi*. The *Lipki* and the *Tcheremisy* passed it on through the Hordes but no one knows anything for sure. They're also saying that the Common-

wealth wants to give them land and freedom and to call them to
service under the heir of your father's greatness. Just a hint about
this was enough to throw the outlying encampments into ferment. They want it, *Effendi*! Oh yes, how they want it! But
others tell them that it isn't true, that the Commonwealth would
send armies against them if they came, and that there is no son
of Tuhay-bey. We've had traders come from the Crimea who
said: '*Yes! Tuhay-bey's son is alive and real!*' But others say: '*No!
It's all a lie!*' and hold back the rest. But if it became known
through all the Hordes that Your Enlightened Worship summons them to freedom, land and service, they'd pour out of all
the camps like a sea of ants... Just give me your permission,
Effendi, to speak freely..."

Azia's face flushed with pleasure and he began to stride up and
down the room, deep in his own thoughts. Then he turned to
Halim.

"Be welcome under my roof, Halim," he made a kindly
gesture, "because you bring good news. Sit down and eat!"

"I am your dog, *Effendi,*"murmured the old Tartar. "I am your
humble slave."

Tuhay-bey's heir clapped his hands and one of his own
Lithuanian Tartar orderlies appeared at once to hear what he
wished. Azia ordered a meal for Halim and the orderly returned
with a flask of harsh, homebrewed Cossack vodka, a bowl of
smoked mutton, a loaf of dark bread, a few sweetmeats, and a
handful of dried watermelon seeds which all Tartars loved almost
as much as they liked sunflowers.

"You're my friend, not a mere servant," Azia said to Halim
after the orderly was gone. "Be welcome, I said, because you
bring good news. Now sit down and eat!"

★   ★   ★

Halim bent over his food at once and they said nothing to
each other until he was done. But he finished quickly and then
sat mute and still, following Azia about the room with a fixed,
doglike stare and waiting for him to speak.

"They already know who I am over here," Azia said at last.

"They do, *Effendi*? And what do they say?"

"Nothing. They look at me with more respect than ever. I'd
have to tell them anyway when the time was ripe. I delayed the

telling because I wanted to hear your news about the Hordes and to let the Hetman know before the others. But Novovyeyski got here and he recognized me."

"The young one?" Halim asked quickly with a touch of fear.

"No. The old one. Allah sent the whole pack of them because the girl is here as well, may the *Djins* possess them! Let me become a Hetman and I'll make them dance! They want to marry me off to the wench but who cares what they're hoping for? A harem can always use another slave!"

"Who wants to marry you off, *Effendi*? The old man?"

"No! *She* does! She! She thinks that I love that other one, not her!"

"Effendi," Halim murmured, bowing to the ground. "I am a humble servant of your House and I've no right to draw breath or speak without your permission. But I was the first to recognize you among the Lithuanian Tartars. I told you way back at Bratzlav who you were and I've served you faithfully ever since. I told all the others to look upon you as their master and to serve you with all their hearts and souls. But even though they love you and would die for you none of them love you as much as I... May I speak freely?"

"Speak."

"Watch out for the little knight, *Effendi*. Take care with the Falcon. He is a deadly warrior, famous in the Crimea and throughout Dobrudja."

"And you, Halim," Azia asked him coldly. "Did you ever hear about Hmyelnitzki?"

"I have, *Effendi*. I served with your father when he warred on the Poles along with Hmyelnitzki, and burned their castles and took loot among them..."

"And do you know that Hmyelnitzki took Tchaplinska from her husband and lived with her and had children by her? And what happened then? There was a war and all the armies of the King and of the Hetmans and of the Commonwealth couldn't tear her away from him. He beat the Hetmans and the King and the Commonwealth herself because my father helped him and because he made himself the Hetman of the Cossacks. And what will I be? The Hetman of the Tartars. They'll have to give me a lot of land and some big city for my capital, and on that good rich soil around that capital will stand the tent cities of good

Tartar warriors, many warriors with many bows and sabers! And if I then seize that bright-eyed beauty and take her to my capital, and make her into a Hetmans' wife, who will take her from me? Who'll have the power that decides what will be and what will not be? I shall! Who'll challenge it? The little knight alone... if he's alive to do so! But even if he is alive and howls like a wolf, and complains to the King himself about his injury, d'you think they'd start a war with me over a woman? They already had a war like that and half the Commonwealth went up in fire and smoke. Who'll be able to hold out against me? His lordship the Hetman? Then I'll unite with the Cossacks, make Dorosh my blood-brother, and give my lands and people to the Sultan. I'd be a second Hmyelnitzki but better than Hmyelnitzki, because I've the heart and blood of a lion in me!

"Look you, Halim," he went on, dark and cold as Winter and glowering like a storm, "this is how it will be. If they let me have her I'll be their hammer of the Cossacks, and I'll fight the Khan and the Sultan for them. But if they don't, I'll trample all of *Lehistan* under my horses' hooves, and drag all their Hetmans on a rope's end to the auction block, and crush all their armies, and burn down their cities, and put half their nation to the sword! I will because I can. I can because I'm the son of Tuhay-bey, the Lion of the Tartars!"

★   ★   ★

A crimson light flared suddenly in Azia's eyes and his teeth gleamed whitely just like Tuhay-bey's used to do when his will was challenged. He raised his clenched fist high above his head and shook it savagely towards the heart of the Commonwealth in the North and West, and he was so great and terrifying in his fury, and so dark and dazzling in his ferocity and determination, that Halim threw himself facedown on the floor before him and started whispering humbly:

"*Allah kerim! Allah kerim!* May your great will be done."

The silence lasted a long time while Azia Tuhaybeyovitch slowly brought himself back under control.

"Bogush was here," he said. "I showed him my power and revealed my thoughts that there should be a Tartar Nation in the Ukraine as there are now the Cossacks, and that there be a Tartar Hetman where there's a Cossack one."

"And he agreed, *Effendi?*"

"He grasped his head, he was so astonished, and then he just about salaamed before me and ran to the Hetman the next day with the happy news."

"Effendi!"Halim dared to ask. "And if the Great Lion refuses?"

"Sobieski?"

"Yes, *Effendi.*"

The dark red lights glinted again in Azia's narrowed eyes but only for as long as it took him to blink them away. His face calmed at once. He sat back down on the bench, leaned across the table with his forehead resting on his fists, and gave himself to thought.

"I've weighed in my mind," he said at last, "what the great Hetman could say when Bogush brings him this welcome information. The Hetman is wise. He will not refuse. The Hetman knows that in the Spring there'll be a general war against the Sultan, for which the Commonwealth has neither the money nor the men, and when Doroshenko and the Cossacks line up beside the Sultan, he may well witness his country's last hour. All this, mark you, is especially true since neither the King nor the ruling classes believe there'll be a war and do nothing to prepare for it. I take note of everything from here, Bogush doesn't hide a thing from me, and I know all that's said and done at the Hetman's court. Pan Sobieski is a great man and he will consent. He knows that if my Tartars come here to new land and freedom, there will be rebellion and a civil war in the Crimea and in the Dobrudjan Steppe, the Hordes will be torn apart and lose all their strength, and the Sultan himself will first have to think about putting out that fire, and that will take time! Meanwhile the Hetman will gain breathing space to prepare himself, and Doroshenko's Cossacks will start shaking in their loyalty to the Turks and start looking to the safety of their own necks. This is the only way for the Commonwealth to save itself, Halim! For all its vastness, this country is so weak and powerless that it has to worry about the return of a few thousand Polish and Lithuanian Tartars. The Hetman knows all this. He is a wise man. The Hetman will give me what I need."

"I am awed by the depth and greatness of your wisdom, *Effendi,*"said the old Dobrudjan. "I am blinded by the power of your mighty vision. But what will happen, Lord, if Allah de-

prives the Great Lion of enlightenment or if Sheitan fills him
with such pride that he will cast your plans aside?"

Azia pressed his savage face close to Halim's ear and whispered with a terrible intensity:

"You stay here now, till we hear from the Hetman. And I
won't go to Rashkov either till the answer comes. If that man
over there rejects what I've envisioned then I'll send you to
Krytchinski and the others. You'll give them my order to come
as close to Hreptyov as they can on their side of the river and
hold themselves ready, and I and my *Lipki* will storm the barracks and take this command on the first dark night, and"—and
he made a slashing gesture across his throat—"that's what I will
give them!"

And, after a contorted moment, he choked out in a stifled
growl: *"Kesim! Kesim! Kesim!* Kill!"

Halim pressed his head down into his shoulders, like a vulture
squatting to its kill, and an evil smile glowed in his bestial face.

"Allah!" he said. "And the Little Falcon too... you agree
Effendi?"

"Him first!"

"And then we go to the Sultan?"

"Yes! With *her!"*

Chapter Forty-two

AN ICY WINTER sheathed the forests with a thick carapace of snow and piled it in such deep banks throughout the wilderness that the billowing whiteness filled the gorges to the brim. It was a time of such overwhelming snow squalls that whole herds of cattle vanished in the flurries, travelers lost their way and died on the buried trails, and whole merchant caravans simply disappeared. Nevertheless Pan Bogush hurried to Yavorov to share Azia's great vision with the Hetman as quickly as he could.

Born and bred as he was in the farthest reaches of the Commonwealth's Ruthenia—which, by the way, had nothing to do with Russia and the Russians, and whose great lords, now wholly Polish in culture and tradition, derived from the Kievan and Novgorod empires of a much earlier century than the upstart Moscow—the old noble could hardly contain his eagerness and excitement.

Raised in the so-called *Kresy* borderlands where the air itself trembled with the threat of Cossack and Tartar incursions, he was preoccupied throughout his whole life with Tartar raids, rebellions and Turkish encroachments, and saw the ultimate salvation of his Motherland in young Azia's vast and stirring vision. He was convinced that Grand Hetman Sobieski, whom he loved like all the other people of the *Kresy* with passionate devotion, wouldn't hesitate even for a moment when it came to multiplying the might of the Commonwealth, so he was filled with joy as he traveled west along those lost, blind trails.

At last, on a Sunday morning, he stumbled into Yavorov

along with a snowstorm, and finding the Hetman at home on the
family estate had himself announced immediately. He was
warned at once that the Hetman was so busy night and day with
couriers and dispatches that he hardly ever found time for a meal
but, unexpectedly, the Commonwealth's principal military
commander had him called after only a short wait, and the old
border soldier bowed gratefully to his beloved leader.

He found Pan Sobieski greatly changed, his face harrowed
with anxiety, because these were the heaviest years of his life.
His name was still to echo like a clarion through all the nations
of the Christian world, but he was already known in the Commonwealth as a great commander and a fierce conqueror of the
Turks and Tartars.

Thanks to this hard-earned fame, he had been entrusted some
years earlier with the gold *bulava* of the Grand Hetman of the
Crown, along with the duty of saving and protecting all the
lands along the eastern borders, but he'd been given neither men
nor money to carry out that task. Victory marched in his footsteps none the less, following him as faithfully as a shadow trails
the striding man who casts it. With hardly more than a handful
of devoted troops, he fought the long and arduous Podhayetz
campaign and forced a peace treaty on the Turks and Tartars. He
swept like lightning through the length and breadth of the
Ukraine, crushed the raiding Hordes which often numbered tens
of thousands of ferocious warriors, scattered their *tchambuls* like
chaff before a windstorm, stormed rebel fortresses and recap-
tured cities, and hammered those eternally flaming eastern territories into a smoldering but quiescent order and obedience.
But now, in the midst of that unusual and desperately needed
peace, the luckless Commonwealth faced a war against the most
terrifying power of the times: the vast immensity of the Muslim
world ruled by the Turkish Sultan, with all its myriad peoples,
nations, treasures and resources.

It was no longer a secret for Sobieski, that when the implacable rebel Doroshenko offered the Cossacks and the Ukraine as a
fief to the Turkish Sultan, this mightiest of all living monarchs
promised to call out all the swarms of Turkey, Asia Minor, Syria,
Arabia, Egypt and both the north and central lands of Africa
from Morocco down to the Sudan, declare a Holy *Jihad*, or War

for the Faith, and come in person to demand his new *pashalik*, or province, from the Commonwealth.

Total destruction hung like a bird of prey over Ruthenia while, in the meantime, the Commonwealth bordered upon chaos; the gentry churned and squabbled in defense of its inept and pliable young King, the charming but ineffectual son of the great Prince Yeremi Vishnovyetzki; the great lords intrigued against each other in endless political disputes; and if any of them had some kind of war in mind it would be another civil war. The Commonwealth's seemingly inexhaustible resources were drained to the bottom. The whole country was morally and economically exhausted by fifty years of almost endless war, invasions, mutinies and rebellions; it had become a land ripped apart by envies and suspicions which drained both honesty and honor out of all the classes of society and poisoned one heart against another. No one was willing to believe in a Turkish War. The great commander was universally denounced as an alarmist who created war-scares to divert attention from his own domestic political ambitions. He was even more cruelly accused of actually calling in the Turks himself so as to give the upper hand to his party's backers; he was, in short, slandered throughout the country as a traitor, and he'd have been dragged and hounded through the courts already if it weren't for the loyalty and devotion of his soldiers.

He knew that he was facing war against uncounted thousands, which were about to flood out of the East, with such a mere handful of hard-pressed regulars that just the Sultan's household dwarfed them with its numbers. He had no money, no means of repairing the ruined or dilapidated fortresses. There was no hope of saving anything, far less some dream of victory. He couldn't even find sustenance in the conviction that his own death might waken the conscience of the country, summon an avenger, and bring about the kind of moral restoration that followed the death of the great Hetman Zolkievski in a Turkish War of an earlier century. Anxiety crouched along his forehead in a permanent, deep frown; and his magnificent face, which brought to mind the stern and noble features of triumphant Caesars, carried the traces of sleepless nights and a hidden sorrow.

★　★　★

Careworn and troubled though he was, he found a genuine smile for the devoted Bogush, and stooped to raise him from his knees where he had fallen to greet his commander.

"Welcome, old soldier, welcome!" he said with affection. "I didn't expect to see you quite this soon but that just makes me all the happier that you're here. Where are you coming from? Kamyenetz?"

"No, Illustrious Hetman. I didn't even stop there on the way. I come straight from Hreptyov."

"And how's my little soldier doing there? Is he well? And has he managed to clean out the Ushitza wilderness at least by a little?"

"The wildlands are so quiet over there now that a child could walk through them in safety. The cut-throats have been either hanged or killed in battle, and in recent weeks Azbah-bey has been totally destroyed along with his *vataha*. Not one of them got away alive. I arrived in Hreptyov on the day he was crushed and beaten."

"That's Volodyovski," the Hetman smiled and said. "Only Rushtchitz in Rashkov can compare with him. But what did you hear from the Steppes? Is there some new information from Belgorod? Are the Tartars stirring?"

"It's bad news I'm afraid. There is to be a great *congressus* of all the Sultan's forces in Adrianople in the last days of Winter."

"That I already know. There is no news except bad news nowadays. Bad from the country, bad from the Crimea and bad from Istanbul."

"Not altogether, however, most illustrious Hetman. Because I myself bring you word of such happy prospects that if I were a Tartar or a Turk I could ask for a province in return."

"Then you're a gift from heaven!" Pan Sobieski cried. "Quickly, then, quickly! Speak up and blow away some of these troubles for me."

"Yes sir... It's just that I'm so chilled by the journey that my brain seems to have frozen in my head."

★ ★ ★

The Hetman clapped his hands and ordered a page to bring some mead. A few moments later his servants brought a mossy flagon and several candelabra filled with glowing candles because, although it was still early in the day, the snowclouds cast such a gloomy pall across the landscape that twilight seemed to grip the countryside and darkened all the chambers.

The Hetman poured the cups and toasted his guest who bowed at the honor, drained his own goblet, and began making his report.

"The first news is that this Azia, whom we were using to bring the renegade Polish and Lithuanian Tartar captains back into the service of the Commonwealth, is not named Mellehovitch but that he is the son of Tuhay-bey!"

"Tuhay-bey?" said the astonished Hetman.

"Yes, Your Illustrious Worship. It's now come to light that he was seized while still an infant by Pan Nenashinyetz and carried off from the Crimea as an act of vengeance, but that Nenashinyetz lost him on the way and he was raised in the household of Pan Novovyeyski, quite unaware of who he was and from whom he was descended."

"I wondered," said the Hetman, "why he had such a following among all our Tartars, as young as he was. But now I understand it. All one needs to remember are the Cossacks, even those who remained faithful to their Motherland, for whom Hmyelnitzki has become some kind of holy image in which they take such an amazing pride."

"That's it, that's just it, sir!" Pan Bogush assured him. "That's just what I told Azia!"

"God truly moves in mysterious ways," Pan Sobieski mused. "Old Tuhay-bey drained rivers of blood out of our country and the young one serves it. Or at least he served it in the past, because I don't know if he'll now want a taste of Crimean greatness."

"Now, Excellency? Now he's more faithful and devoted than ever! And this is the beginning of my second news in which—God willing!—we can find the power and the means to save our troubled and unhappy Commonwealth in the hour of her greatest danger. God is my witness that I spared neither hardships nor avoided risks to bring this good news to Your Excellency and help to ease the burdens in your heart."

"I'm all attention," Pan Sobieski said.

★　★　★

Pan Bogush began to expound the young Tartar's ideas and he presented them with such enthusiasm that he soared into real eloquence.

From time to time he refilled his cup with mead—his hand unsteady and trembling with emotion and splashing the noble liquor over the goblet's edge—and his voice soared on, and vivid pictures of a glowing future seemed to flow past the Hetman's startled eyes. He could see Tartar warriors in their tens of thousands trekking with their herds and their wives and children; the Steppelands filling with this new fighting gentry of the Commonwealth; the Cossacks, stunned with terror, beating their foreheads on the ground before the King, the country and the Hetman. He looked into an age free of bloody risings and rebellions in the Ukraine. He saw a century when the *tchambuls* no longer spilled out of the ancient trails to turn Ruthenia into a sea of flames, and in their place—riding along the borders beside the Polish and Cossack armies with a blare of trumpets and the thunderous music of the kettledrums—swarmed legions of the new Ukrainian gentry of the Tartars.

And year after year thereafter, as he looked and saw, the long parade of high-wheeled Tartar *arbas* rolled on and on into the Ukraine, carrying fresh populations to be rooted in the rich, black soil. It was an ingress that would never stop, in spite of all the orders of the Khan and Sultan, as long as all those vast restless masses of primitive humanity could choose between tyranny and freedom and bread over hunger.

The Hetman saw into an era when the age-long nemesis of the Commonwealth had become her servant. The Crimea emptied, becoming a state without a population, and a land devoid of half its swarming people. His sharp, clear mind could project itself into the helplessness and fear of both the Sultan and the Khan as they watched their former power slipping from their fingers, and as they looked with trembling premonition towards the Steppes, the Wild Lands and the Ukraine, where staring fiercely back into their worried eyes, stood the new Hetman of the newly crested Polish Tartar gentry, the faithful guardian and defender of the Commonwealth, the famous son of a terrifying father: the Young Tuhay-bey.

A high flush erupted on the face of the old borderland

diplomat and soldier. His own words seemed to carry him into the heights of intoxication; and, at last, he lifted both his arms into the air and cried out:

"This is what I bring you! This is what that strange spawn of a dragon hatched in the Hreptyov wilderness. And all he needs now is Your Excellency's permission, in writing, to send the word ringing from the Crimea to Belgorod and beyond! Ah, Your Illustrious Worship! If this young man does nothing more than throw the Crimea into chaos, create a ferment among all those Hordes from the Don to the Moldavian Steppe and from the Danube to the Adriatic, awake the many-headed monster of a civil war and arm one Tartar clan against another, then—on the brink of the most terrible war in our country's history... yes sir, I'll repeat it... on the threshold of a storm beyond anything we've ever experienced—he'd have rendered the Common-wealth a service beyond price."

★   ★   ★

But Pan Sobieski merely paced with great strides through the chamber and kept a stubborn silence. His classic features were dark with a heavy frown, almost threatening in its grim intensity. His outward silence was so deep that it suggested an internal dialogue; but Bogush couldn't tell if he was speaking to himself or listening to God.

At last, however, the Hetman found and turned some criti-cally vital page within him, halted and faced the expectant speaker.

"Bogush," he said. "Even if I had the right to give such permission, I wouldn't give it if my own life depended upon it."

His words fell with the weight of lead, as dark as cast-iron, and they crushed Bogush so utterly that he lost his voice, bowed his head and shoulders low towards the floor, and stammered out painfully only after a protracted silence:

"W-hy, Your Excellency...? W-why...?"

"First I will answer you as a man of some political and military experience. The name of Tuhay-bey's son could bring a *certum quantum* of Tartars, if they were also promised lands, freedom and the privileges of the gentry. But they wouldn't come in the numbers that both of you imagine. What's more, calling the Tartars into the Ukraine would be an act of madness. We can't cope with the Cossacks there, for God's sake, and you want to settle yet another nation? You say there'd be immediate conflicts between our new Tartars and the Cossacks, and that we'd have a ready sword suspended over the Cossacks' necks. But who'll guarantee that this sword will never run as red with the blood of our own people here...?

"I didn't know this Azia until now," Sobieski nodded grimly. "But now I see that he carries the dragon of ambition and pride in his breast, so I'll ask you again: who can assure you that a second Hmyelnitzki isn't sitting in that heart as well? Oh, he'll hammer the Cossacks, if that's to his liking. But if the Commonwealth fails to satisfy him in some way, or if it calls him to account for some act of violence or abuse of power, he'll join with the Cossacks, call in fresh swarms out of the East in just the way that Hmyelnitzki called in Tuhay-bey, submit to the Sultan just as Doroshenko has submitted, and then instead of adding to our power we'd drown in a new sea of blood and feel the weight of a new disaster."

"Your Excellency! Having become gentry, the Tartars will stand loyally by the Commonwealth...!"

"And didn't we have our *Lipki* and our *Tcheremisy*? And weren't they gentry from the start among us, and isn't that why they went over to the Sultan?"

"Their privileges weren't honored..."

"And what'll happen if the gentry fights the extension of their privileges, as is sure to happen? And by what process of reasoning, and through what act of a misguided conscience, do you propose to give the right and the power to decide the destiny of the Commonwealth to a swarm of savage looters and marauders who have been ravaging our country for centuries? Is that how they earned the right to elect our King, sit in the parliament, and send their deputies to our diets? What madness set fire to that young Tartar's head that he came up with this insane idea? And you, old campaigner, what demon possessed you to let yourself be fooled and led astray, and to believe in such dishonest and impossible solutions?"

★　★　★

Pan Bogush shuddered, stared at the floor, and said in an unsteady voice:

"I knew it from the start, Your Illustrious Worship. I mean about the gentry and their opposition. But Azia said no one would ever manage to drive out the Tartars once they'd come and settled with Your Excellency's permission."

"For God's sake, man! So he's already making threats, he's already shaking his sword at the Commonwealth, and you failed to see it?"

"Your Excellency!" Desperation trembled in Bogush's voice. "Not all the Tartars need to be ennobled. Perhaps just their leaders? And the rest could be declared as freedmen, subject to the law, free to till their own land after military service and free to settle off the properties of a master... They'd come anyway if the son of Tuhay-bey called them with your permission."

"Then why not declare all Cossacks as freedmen instead, rather than trying to force serfdom upon them all? That's been the source of all their discontent! Cross yourself, old soldier, because I'm telling you that you've been blinded by an evil spirit."

"Your Excellency..."

"And I'll add this much," Pan Sobieski said, while another deep and threatening frown settled on his brow and his eyes flashed fire. "Even if all things were as you say they would be, if we gained new strength through it and if the Turks were weakened, and even if all the gentry called for it in one voice, I'd still fight to stop it just as long as my fist could lift a saber and my hand could make the sign of the cross. So help me God! I'll never allow it!"

"Why not, Excellency?" Bogush said again, twisting his hands in anguish.

"Because I'm not only a Polish Hetman but a Christian one as well! Because I guard the Cross! And even if the Cossacks clawed at the guts of the country far more cruelly than they already do I wouldn't punish them with the swords of pagans! They may be wrong, misled and misguided, but they're a Christian people, and to send a Muslim horde against them would disgrace everything we have tried to do. It would be like spitting on the graves of all our ancestors, and at all the blood, ashes and tears spilled by them, and by my own progenitors, for the old Commonwealth they founded...

"As God's alive!" Sobieski cried out suddenly. "If we're to be

destroyed, if our name is to become the name of a vanished
people, then let there be at least a heritage of glory left among
our ashes. Let the world remember that we did the duty to
which God assigned us. And let future generations say, looking
at the crosses on the mass graves above us: '*Here lie those who
defended Christ's Cross against the Muslim hordes to their last breath
and their last drop of blood, dying for all the other nations in the
Christian world...*'

"This is our task and duty, Bogush," he went on more calmly,
but still as stern and forbidding as a judge. "We are the fortress
in whose walls Christ has affixed the symbol of his suffering, and
you are telling me that I—God's soldier, and commander of
God's soldiers—should be the first to break down the gates, let
in the savages like wolves into a sheepfold, and throw Christ's
children to slaughter by the pagans? I'd rather that we went on
suffering the *tchambuls* for ever, bear the burdens of endless new
rebellions, go to that terrible Turkish War and die along with
the entire Commonwealth, then shame our name, dishonor our
guardianship, forswear our holy service, and betray the duty laid
on us by God!"

With this, Pan Sobieski stretched to his full height, and his
eyes blazed with the light of mystical devotion. "God wills it!"

Pan Bogush suddenly saw himself as worthless and as insignificant as a speck of dust beside these soaring phrases, and Azia was
even less than dust beside the Grand Hetman, and all the young
Tartar's fiery ideas seemed to turn suddenly as black as soiled
ashes.

What could he say after the Hetman's statement that it was
better to die in God's service than abandon it? What other
arguments could he find and offer? The racked old noble could
no longer tell if he should throw himself on his knees, keep
pleading for Azia's vision or beg the Hetman's forgiveness, or
beat his own chest, saying: "*Mea culpa, mea maxima culpa...* the
sin is mine, O Lord!"

But suddenly the sound of churchbells rang out of the nearby
Dominican *collegium*.

Pan Sobieski heard them.

"They're ringing for vespers, Bogush," he said. "Let us go and
commend ourselves to God."

Chapter Forty-three

JUST AS PAN BOGUSH HURRIED from Hreptyov to the Hetman, so now he showed no hurry whatsoever in going back to Hreptyov. He stopped for at least a week, sometimes even two, in every larger town. He spent the Christmas holidays in Lvov, and he was still there in the New Year.

It was true that he was carrying instructions from the Hetman, directing Azia to bring his dealings with the *Lipki* renegades to a quick conclusion, and containing a rather dry and admonitory order for him to abandon all his grand designs, but since the young Tartar could do nothing anyway without the Hetman's guarantees in writing, the old frontier noble didn't see the need for rushing with a quick delivery of Pan Sobieski's letter. So he dragged himself along, taking quite literally one slow stage at a time, and stopping off in many churches all along the way to do his penance for having fallen in with Azia's mad ideas.

Hreptyov, meanwhile, became filled with guests right after the New Year. These were some leading members of the great and rich community of Armenian Christians settled in the Polish bastion of Kamyenetz, the strongest fortress and the oldest city in Lower Podolya, who were on their way to the Crimea with ransom and petitions. Leading them was Master Naviragh, a representative of the Armenian Patriarch, and two skilled theologians from the faculty of Kufa, whose numerous followers and servants became objects of curiosity in their outlandish clothing. The soldiers gaped, appreciative though amused, at their violet and crimson skullcaps, their extraordinarily stretched satin and velvet collars whose points dragged behind them as they walked,

399

and—with far more respect—at the intelligence of their olive-
tinted faces and the grave dignity with which they paced like
herons through the fort's enclosure.

Acting as their guide was Pan Zaharias Piotrovitch, famous for
his constant journeys to the Crimea and even among the Turks,
and for the painstaking care he took in searching for hidden
hostages and slaves and buying their freedom. Pan Volodyovski
immediately counted out to him the sum needed to ransom Pan
Boski. But since Lady Boska didn't have enough money of her
own, he made up the difference out of his own pocket, while
Basia secretly sold her pearl earings to help the mourning gen-
tlewoman and the charming Zosia. The other guests included
Pan Seferovitch, a rich Armenian merchant and a City *Praetor* of
Kamyenetz whose brother was a captive, and two Armenian
ladies, both still young enough to retain their looks although
they were somewhat on the dark-skinned side. They wanted the
return of their hostage husbands.

These were, for the most part, troubled visitors. But there was
no shortage of merry ones as well since Father Kaminski sent his
niece, Panna Kaminska, to stay in Basia's keeping for the holidays. On top of that, young Pan Novovyeyski who heard about
his father's arrival, took a short leave from his troop in Rashkov
and hurried to meet his gruff progenitor halfway.

★　★　★

For those who'd known him earlier, young Pan Novovyeyski
had changed almost beyond recognition in the past few years. To
begin with, his upper lip now sported a short but thick and curly
mustache, which didn't hide his laughing mouth and gleaming
white teeth, but which he could twist nicely with one finger.
He'd never lacked for size but now, at twenty-five and after ten
years of frontier service, he'd grown into a giant. It seemed that
only a head as huge as his could carry such a heavy tangle of
trimmed but tumbled hair, and that it took just such a massive
set of shoulders to support that head. His face, burned by the sun
and scorched by the Steppe winds, was now as dark as any of the
Eastern races. His eyes, black as coals, were full of life and
daring. His hamlike fists could hide a fair-sized apple so completely that he could play guessing games with it, and when he

spilled a handful of hazelnuts on his muscular thigh, and pressed down on them with his open palm, he ground them to powder.

All his flesh seemed to have gone into strength and sinew. He showed no fat anywhere, his belly had sunk out of sight, and only his huge, muscled chest hung suspended over his hard, lean waist like a wayside chapel perched on its narrow stand. He was so strong that he snapped horseshoes with very little effort and amused himself by twisting iron bars around his soldiers' necks, and he seemed even bigger than he was. Floorboards groaned under him when he took a step, and he chipped the corners off a bench when he bumped against it.

In short, he was the kind of man described in those times as *setny*, or one-in-a-hundred, in whom life, health, strength and dare-devil courage leaped and boiled like water in a kettle, as if even his enormous body couldn't contain all the rough-and-ready turbulence within it. In this respect he looked like what he was: a young Steppe rover, a borderer and a frontier soldier who seemed so full of fire that people glanced instinctively at his head to see if smoke or steam were coming out of it, which often did in any event because he liked his liquor as much as any man of his time and station.

In battle, he fought like a demon, laughing all the while like a neighing horse, and the blows he struck were so Herculean that soldiers gathered afterwards in the battlefield to admire his work. But, accustomed as he was from boyhood to life in the Steppe, and to the raids and ambushes along the frontier, he was as watchful and as careful as he was impulsive. There was nothing about fighting Tartars that he didn't know, and he was widely thought to be the best frontier soldier after Pan Rushtchitz and Pan Volodyovski.

★　★　★

Old Novovyeyski had been full of threats and grumbling about his son but, when it came down to receiving him, he bit back on most of his complaints. He was afraid that if he harangued him as harshly as he used to do, the fiery young man might take himself off for another ten or eleven years and that would be the last he'd ever see of him.

Besides, the old country noble was as self-centered, egotistic and parsimonious as most of his kind, and he liked this devil-may-care, independent son who never asked for money from home, took excellent care of himself in the world, won the respect of his comrades and superiors, and acquired an officer's sash and the Hetman's favor which no amount of string-pulling could get for very many others. The shrewd old man also figured out that this wild Steppe warrior might not take kindly to discipline by a ranting father and he thought he'd better not put it to the test.

The son went down on his knees before him, which simple filial duty demanded in those times, but he stared boldly into the old man's eyes and fired bluntly and point-blank at the first paternal admonition.

"You've got a mouthful of complaints, father," he grinned, "but in your heart you're pleased with me, as you ought to be, because I've brought no shame to you or our name. And the fact that I ran off to the regiment... well, that's why I'm a noble, isn't it?"

"And maybe a heathen too, by now," the old man had to grumble. "So why didn't your show your face at home for eleven years?"

"I was afraid you'd try to whip me, sir, which would insult my rank and go against my dignity and position, so I wouldn't have been able to let it happen, if you know what I mean. I waited for some word that you've forgiven me. Since I neither got nor saw a letter from you, *you* didn't see *me.*"

"And now you've lost all your fear of me, have you?"

The young man showed his white teeth in a broad, slow smile. "We're under military authority here, which takes precedence even over a father's wishes. But hey, d'you know something, sir? I think you'd better give me a good hug because I can see you're dying to do it anyway."

★   ★   ★

With this he threw his arms wide and old Novovyeyski found himself unsure what to do about it. He couldn't quite get used to this laughing giant who'd run away from home as a mere youngster and who was now returning as a grown man and a seasoned warrior. All this and more flattered the gruff old noble's vast parental pride, and he'd have been glad enough to press this wayward son to his chest once more, but his consciousness of his own age, dignity, appearances and position was getting in the way. But the young man solved the problem by himself. He leaped up, seized his father and squeezed the amazed old man so hard that his bones creaked in that bear-hug, and this display of strength, love and determination melted down whatever reserve Pan Novovyeyski had.

"What can I do?" he gasped, struggling for breath and dignity. "The rascal knows he's in the saddle here and that's all he cares about! Look at him, if you please! If we'd been home, back in my own parlor, I wouldn't let myself be swayed like this. But what can I do here? Come and give me another hug, then, if that's the way it's going!"

They squeezed each other again and then the young man started asking urgently about his sister.

"I told her to stay outside until I called her in," the father said. "She's in the next room and just about ready to jump out of her skin."

"Let's get her here, by God!" the young giant shouted, ran to the door and roared "Evka! Evka!" in such a thundering voice that a booming echo rattled off all the walls.

The girl was in the room in a moment, laughing with joy to see him, but she'd no sooner managed to cry out "Adam!" when those powerful arms locked about her and twirled her practically as high as the ceiling.

Her brother, as she knew very well, loved her terribly, always did his best to shield her from their father's tyranny, and often took the whipping for her childhood misdeeds. Old Pan Novovyeyski ruled his family with an iron hand, and often a cruel one at that, so that the girl got used to looking at her brother for refuge and protection. He, in turn, kissed her hair, her eyes and her hands, then pushed her away from him long enough to see how she'd grown, and shouted out:

"A fine-looking wench, as I live and breathe! Look at the size of her! She's as solid as a brick stove and grown like a pinetree!"

★ ★ ★

Laughing and smiling into each other's eyes, they started babbling excitedly about all the years since they'd seen each other while old Novovyeyski stamped back and forth around them, muttering like a bear.

His son impressed him a great deal, he had to admit, but he
also felt a pang of worry about his own future as the undisputed
ruler of his hearth and home. These were already times of great
parental authority which, in the years to come, would harden
into just that kind of autocratic *absolute dominion* that the gentry
fought so bitterly in their Kings and diets. But this strange,
rediscovered son wasn't likely to bend to anybody's will. He
was, after all, a fierce Steppe borderer, a soldier from the outposts of the wilderness, who—as Pan Novovyeyski grasped at
once— *'rode in his own saddle and went his own way.'* The old noble
was just as jealous of his rights as any other member of the landed
gentry, and this huge, laughing, powerful young man seemed to
threaten all his prerogatives as a father, on which he based his
sense of propriety and order.

On the one hand, the old man was sure, his son would always
honor him and give him his parental due. But could that broad
back still bow before the whip? Could he be shaped and molded
to his father's will like a ball of wax? Would he put up with
everything he'd endured while he was at home?

'Bah,' thought the old noble. *'Would I even dare to treat him like
a whipper-snapper? The son of a gun's a lieutenant now... he's a
seasoned soldier... and I must say he's an impressive devil!'*

And to make matters worse, Pan Novovyeyski felt his fatherly
affection swelling by the minute and knew that he'd have a real
weakness for this gigantic son.

★ ★ ★

Meanwhile Evka went on twittering like a bird and bombarded Adam with a barrage of questions. When would he come
home? When would he settle down? Did he give any thought to
getting married soon? She—as she hurried to make clear—didn't
know about such things for certain, but she'd heard, yes she'd
heard somewhere as she could swear by her love for Papa, that
soldiers were quick to fall in love... Yes, yes, she even thought
she could remember that Lady Volodyovska had told her the
same thing.

"Ah, what a beautiful and kindhearted lady she is, this Pani
Volodyovska...!" she bubbled on excitedly. "You'd be unable to
find a prettier or a better woman throughout all of Poland!"

Only Zosia Boska could compare with her, she added as if in afterthought.

"What Zosia Boska is that?" Adam started asking.

"The one who's here in Hreptyov with her mother because the Horde carried off her father. You'll see her for yourself and I'm sure you'll like her!"

"Let's have Zosia Boska here and now!" the young officer shouted out at once, and Ewa and their father burst out laughing at his ready fervor.

"Yes, yes," he went on, eager and content. "Love and death come to everyone. I was still walking about with a bare lip, and Pani Volodyovska was just a young girl, when I fell in love with her like you wouldn't believe! Ey, dear God, how I loved that Baska! But what could I do? I told it to her once, and it was just like getting a fistful of knuckles in my teeth! Scat from the cream, kitty-cat! It turned out later that she was in love with Pan Volodyovski even then. And by God, she couldn't have made a better choice!"

"And why is that?" asked old Pan Novovyeyski.

"Why is that?" The young man's hero-worship glowed in all his features. "Well, to begin with, there isn't another man alive who'd last more than five minutes against me with a saber, if you'll permit a boast, but he would put me away in two Hail Marys! And besides, he's the perfect borderer, a Steppe commander unmatched in the Army, before whom even Pan Rushtchitz gladly bares his head. But forget Pan Rushtchitz! Even the Tartars turn him into legends. He is the greatest soldier in the Commonwealth!"

"And oh, how he and his wife love each other!" Ewa threw in quickly. "Ay, ay, it hurts the eyes to see it!"

"Do I hear envy?" Adam asked, laughing at his sister. "Yes, by God, you're envious! And why not? It's getting close to your time as well!"

He loomed over her, his fists cocked on his hips, laughing and grinning from ear to ear and tossing his head like a young mustang in a Springtime pasture, and she dropped her eyes modestly and said: "I haven't even thought about it."

"Why not? There's no dearth of officers and fine gentlemen-at-arms in this command, is there?"

"Ah!" Ewa appeared to want to change the subject. "But did Papa tell you that Azia is here?"

"Azia Mellehovitch? The Tartar? I know him, he's a damn good soldier."

"What you don't know, though," old Novovyeyski said, "is that he's not any Mellehovitch but our own Azia, the same one I raised right along beside you."

"For God's sake!" Nothing could have amazed the young soldier more. "What is this I hear? Imagine that... Come to think of it, I did have some such thoughts now and then but people said his name was Mellehovitch so I thought it couldn't be the same one, especially as Azia's a common name among them. It's been so long since I've set eyes on him that it's small wonder I couldn't be sure! Besides, our Azia was a rather ugly little fellow, set close to the ground as I remember, and this man could be called a beauty if he were a woman!"

"No, no, he's ours alright!" said old Novovyeyski. "Or rather not ours at all, as it appears. D'you know whose son he turned out to be?"

"How should I know?"

"The great Tuhay-bey himself!"

The young man slapped his knees with such force that it sounded like a clap of thunder.

"I can't believe my ears! The great Tuhay-bey? Then he's a *Knazh*, or a Tartar prince, and blood-kin to the Khans! There's no lineage any higher in all of the Crimea than that of Tuhay-bey!"

"Say rather that he's kin to dogs," old Novovyeyski muttered. "That blood is pure poison."

"His father's blood may have been pure poison, but the son serves with us! I've seen him in combat myself at least twenty times. Ha! Now I understand where he gets that Satanic courage. Pan Sobieski praised him in front of the whole army and gave him a battlefield commission on the spot! I'll be really happy to see him again, he's a first-rate soldier. I'll greet him with all my heart!"

"Just don't get too familiar with him," the old noble grumbled.

"And why not? Is he my servant or some groom of ours? I'm a soldier and he's a soldier. I am an officer and so is he. Bah, if this was some yokel from the infantry who dresses his ranks with a reed cane, I might put him in his place. But if he's the son of Tuhay-bey then his blood is as good as any. He's a prince, and that's that, and as for his Polish coat-of-arms, the Hetman will see to it himself. How am I to keep my nose in the air around him when I'm blood-brother to the Baktchi Agha and the *Murjah* Kulak and to Sukyman-Ulan, and each of them would be proud to herd sheep for Tuhay-bey?"

Ewa felt a sudden overpowering urge to kiss her brother all over again, then sat down close beside him and started stroking his wild mop of tumbled and unruly hair with her beautiful white hand.

★   ★   ★

Pan Volodyovski's entrance put a sudden end to this family interlude. Young Novovyeyski leaped to attention to greet his superior, and started making his apologies for not reporting to the commandant the first thing on arrival. But this wasn't a service matter, after all, he'd come on a private family affair, and the little knight was too fond of him to be a stickler for formalities.

Instead he hugged the young soldier with genuine affection. "Who could blame you, my good comrade-in-arms, for hurrying to your father's knees after so many years of separation? It'd be different if you were under orders. But I don't suppose you have anything for me from Rushtchitz?"

"Only his best salutations, colonel. Pan Rushtchitz is also gone from Rashkov at the moment, off with a column to the Yahorlik and beyond, because he'd heard that there were many horse-tracks in the snow out in that direction. He got Your Honor's letter and sent word straight away to his kin and blood-brothers in the Horde, but he says he won't write you a reply because his hand is too heavy for the quill and he has no experience in the art of writing."

"He's not fond of it, I know," Pan Michal said and smiled. "The saber is his thing." And then he added with a sly, teasing smile: "But you Rashkov soldiers fished for Azbah-bey for two months and came up empty-handed."

"And Your Honor gulped him down like a pike takes a goldfish!" Novovyeyski cried out with enthusiasm. "God

must've scrambled Azbah's wits altogether so that he slipped out
of Pan Rushtchitz's grasp only to come near yours, sir. What
foresight, eh? Well, it serves him right!"

★   ★   ★

Pan Michal wasn't averse to a little flattery, which always
pleased the haughty and quick-tempered gentry of his day, and
he repaid one piece of praise with another.

"God hasn't given me a son as yet," he turned to old Pan
Novovyeyski. "But if He ever deigns to do so I'd be glad to have
one just like this cavalier."

"Oh, he's not much! He's not much at all!" the old man shot
back promptly. "There's nothing special about this young rascal."

But he was so pleased that he turned quite crimson and
wheezed with contentment.

Meanwhile Pan Volodyovski started stroking Evka's face as he
would a child's. "I'm no Spring chicken, as you can see, young
lady," he said. "But my sweet Baska is close to you in age and I
do my best, whenever I can, to see that she has some good
entertainment suited to her years. It's true that everybody here
loves her, but I expect you'll agree she's worth it?"

"Dear God!" Evka cried out. "There isn't another like her in
the entire world! I've just finished saying it!"

"Did you now!" The little knight was so pleased and delighted
with praise for his beloved Basia that his whole face lit up. "You
said it, eh?"

"She said it!" father and son answered him in chorus. "As I live
and breathe!"

"Then I'll advise you, young lady, to put on your pretties,"
the little knight confided, "because I've ordered a surprise for
Basia. I've had an orchestra sent secretly from Kamyenetz and it
got here today. I had them hide their instruments in the straw
and told Basia that they were wandering Gypsies come to shoe
the horses. I'm giving a ball tonight, with music and dancing.
She loves that even though she likes to play the matron."

With this Pan Michal started to rub his hands, pleased with
himself and everything around him.

Chapter Forty-four

SNOW FELL SO THICKLY that night that it filled the deep defensive ditch dug outside the earthworks and turned the tall, wooden palisade into a wall. But if the night outside played host to a howling January blizzard, the main hall of the *fortalitzya* was ablaze with light and alive with music.

There were two fiddlers and a man who sawed on a large bull-fiddle, two flute-playing pipers and a man who blew on a thick, curved horn something like a tuba. The fiddlers pulled their bows from straight beside the ear, and with such verve that they almost twirled around in the process, while the pipers and the tuba-player blew so hard into their reeds that their cheeks ballooned and their eyes bulged out. The oldest among the officers and the serving gentry sat shoulder-to-shoulder all around the walls, at ease and content on their wooden benches like rows of aging, silver-headed pigeons perched along a rooftop, and sipped their mead while they looked at the dancers winding across the floor.

Basia danced in the first pair with Pan Mushalski, who was as light of foot as he was unerring as an archer. Dressed in a silver gown of embroidered silk, she looked like a fresh rose thrust into new snow. Everyone, no matter what their age, wondered at her beauty, and shouts of awe, *"Rety!"* and "God have mercy!" tore out of many chests. Zosia Boska and Evka Novovyeyska were a little younger, and quite extraordinary in their eager beauty, but she was clearly the most beautiful of them all. Joy burned along with gaiety in her bright blue eyes. Passing the little knight, she thanked him with a smile for the pleasure he'd created for her,

409

and her shiny white teeth gleamed merrily in her parted lips. Gleaming all over in her silver gown, she seemed at times like a beam of moonlight or a turning star, and she dazzled eyes and hearts alike with the beauty of a woman, a child, and a flower all at the same time. The long split sleeves of her silver *kontush* fluttered behind her like the wings of a giant butterfly, and when she lifted the edges of her overskirt to courtsey to her partner, it was as if she were a radiant apparition returning to the soil, or one of those dancing lights that glow on bright Summer nights around the rims of the canyons in the wilderness.

Outside in the snow, the private men-at-arms who were not members of the serving gentry, pressed their fierce, mustached faces to the window panes, and flattened their noses on the frosted glass as they peered into the bright-lit room. All of them were Basia's vehement supporters and took it as a point of pride that their adored *Pani Komendantova* should put the other dancers to shame. They heaped slighting comments on poor Zosia Boska and Ewa Novovyeyska, and let fly with a ringing cheer each time that Basia danced across their window.

Inside, Volodyovski swelled with pride as if he'd been fed a bucketful of yeast, and bobbed his head in time to Basia's movements. Pan Zagloba, who stood beside him with a huge stone mug of ale in his hand, kept time with his boots, and they turned and peered mutely at each other every now and then, and sighed in sheer pleasure.

And Basia gleamed and flickered all across the hall, ever merrier, brighter, more spectacular and winning. This was her idea of a frontier outpost in the wilderness! A battle one day, a hunt the next, and then happy times and dances; musicians, soldiers everywhere, and her husband the greatest and the foremost among them, a man she loved with all her heart as he loved her with all his heart and soul. She felt that all was going right with her. Nothing could be better. Everyone liked her. She was admired and valued. This made her husband happy. Her husband was happier with her every day and her own happiness soared accordingly, until she felt as light as the birds that surge into a May sky to cry their joy at the advancing Spring.

★   ★   ★

Novovyeyska, wearing a flared crimson short-coat over her

gown, danced in the second pair with Azia Mellehovitch. The young Tartar didn't say a word to her, drunk as he was on that silvery vision that glittered before him, but she thought it was the depth of his feeling for her that rendered him voiceless, and tried to encourage him with a soft and then more insistent pressure of her fingers in his hand.

His own hand tightened on hers now and then with such savage force that she barely managed to stifle a cry of pain, but he never noticed either her gasp or that sudden clenching of his fist. His hand clenched on its own, it didn't represent any kind of signal; Basia was all he could think about, all he saw, and deep inside he repeated his terrible promise to himself: that he'd possess her if he had to burn down half of Ruthenia to get her.

Now and then, when his madness ebbed long enough to show him some glimpse of the reality around him, he felt like seizing Ewa by the throat. He wanted to crush it, feasting on her terror, just because she broke into his dream with those pressing fingers and because she stood between him and Basia. Then his fierce falcon eyes clawed at her with hatred and she thought that his ferocity came from love and passion.

Just behind them, dancing in the third pair, came the huge Adam Novovyeyski and the tiny Zosia. She, reminding watchers of a forget-me-not, trotted beside him with cast-down eyes and delicate little steps, both bemused and frightened; he, looking next to her like a prancing stallion, took wild mustang leaps in his cleated boots, ripping white splinters from the shuddering floor. His hair shook and quivered like a wind-swept mane, his face flushed with fire, his nostrils flared with the ferocity of a Turkish charger, and he whirled Zosia off the floor as lightly as if she were a leaf carried by a whirlwind. There seemed to be neither end nor limit to the joy he felt; and because he spent his years at the far edges of the Wild Lands, where he'd see no woman for months at a time, he was so immediately taken with Zosia Boska that he was instantly head-over-heels in love.

From time to time he glanced down at her lowered eyes, her flushed cheeks and her rounded bodice, and a roar of happy laughter burst out of him at this gentle sight; and then his iron-shod heels struck even thicker sparks and splinters from the floor; and he pressed Zosia to his massive chest even tighter on the twists and turns, and leaped and bounced and hissed with joy like a boiling kettle, and loved her all the harder.

Too much? Zosia may have thought so, but if she felt a touch of helplessness in the grip of this laughing whirlwind it was the kind of fearful helplessness that makes its own joy. She liked that sense of breathless, airy lightness with which she flew and soared, secure in his hands. *'A dragon,'* she thought. *'Nothing else but a fire-breathing dragon!'* She'd seen some dashing cavaliers in Yavorov, in the Hetman's mansion, but never one as fiery as this one. None other danced like this. None swept her this close. Really, a dragon...! Smoke, fire, sparks and all! What could she do in the grip of such a hurricane? How does one resist a wild force of nature?

★   ★   ★

Panna Kaminska danced in the fourth pair with a well-born trooper, and the two Armenian ladies pranced in the fifth and sixth; they were invited to the gentry's frolic even though they were only the wives of merchants, not the landed gentry, but they were rich enough so that it made very little difference and they displayed the courtly mannerisms and graces of the higher classes.

The grave Naviragh and his theologians stared with amazement at the dash and fire of these Polish dances. A high, crackling murmur came from the older men gathered around the flagons, bringing to mind the chatter of grasshoppers in the dry corn-husks of a harvest field. But the music overwhelmed all other sounds and voices and the joy and gaiety soared ever higher in the middle of the room.

But suddenly Basia abandoned her partner, ran to her husband all flushed and out of breath, and clasped her fists before him as if in a prayer.

"Michalku!" she cried. "It's such a cold night! The soldiers are so cold out there beyond the window... Couldn't they have a barrel?"

"I'd slit my veins for them if that made you happy!" he shouted, seized her small fists and covered them with kisses.

Feeling so full of happiness that he could hardly stand it, he hopped outside in person to tell the soldiers just whose thoughtfulness was sending them a liquor barrel, because he wanted them to be grateful to her and love her all the more.

And when they raised such a thundering cheer in reply that an avalanche of snow cracked off the roof and tumbled down among them, he shouted: "Fire off a musket volley there, will you? To salute the Lady!"

Back inside, he found Basia dancing with Mellehovitch, as he still thought of the *Lipki* Tartar.

The world was gone for Azia, whirling among strange stars, when he felt his arms close around that light, lambent figure, felt her warmth near him and her breath brushed across his face. His eyes turned up and vanished as if seeking refuge deep under his skull, and he renounced all the joys promised by the Prophet, all his eternity of bliss, and all the *houris* of the Moslem paradise, if he could just have this one.

But Basia caught sight of Evka's crimson jacket whirling on the arm of another dancer and became curious whether Azia had told the girl he loved her.

"Have you said anything?" she asked.

"No!"

"Why not?"

"It's not the time for it yet," the Tartar murmured with a strange expression.

"And do you really love her?"

"More than life!" the son of Tuhay-bey cried out in a low, throaty voice whose trembling gutturals sounded like the caw of a raven.

★ ★ ★

They danced on then, right behind Zosia and Novovyeyski who had moved up to become the first or leading couple. Everyone else had changed partners twice already but Pan Adam he wouldn't let Zosia move into anybody else's arms. He'd seat her on a bench now and then, to rest and catch her breath, and then he swept her up again and whirled her away.

At last he stamped to a halt before the musicians, threw one arm around Zosia and cocked the fist of the other on his hip.

"Play a *Krakoviak,* lads! Jump to it!"

True to his order, the fiddlers and the pipers and the tuba player swung into a lively, whirling dance from the Krakow

province, while Pan Novovyeyski stamped his heels to the
tripping four-two beat, and started singing in a voice that shook
the caulking from between the timbers:

> *"Flow the waters brightly*
> *And the Dniester takes them*
> *So my heart is flowing*
> *Into you, my dearest!*
> *U-ha!"*

He yelled that *'U-ha!'* so much like a Zaporohjan Cossack that
poor little Zosia wanted to sit down out of sheer fright, as did
the grave Naviragh who stood nearby, and as did the two
wide-eyed Armenian theologians.

But Pan Novovyeyski led the dancers far across the hall, and
then brought them twice around the walls and back to the center
of the room, where he stopped before the musicians just like he
did before and sang another quatrain that dealt with the heart:

> *"Flowing but not dying,*
> *Just to spite the water,*
> *And finding at the bottom*
> *A ring for me to offer!*
> *U-ha!"*

"Very handsome sentiments!" called out Pan Zagloba. "I can
judge that better than anyone because I've composed quite a few
pretty songs myself! Keep fishing, cavalier, keep fishing! And
when you've fished out that wedding ring then I'll sing you this
one:

> *"Every boy's a flintstone*
> *Every girl is tinder,*
> *Get the sparks aflying*
> *If you want some 'kinder!'*
> *U-ha!"*

"'*Vivat! Vivat* Pan Zagloba!'" thundered all the officers and
gentry, so that the grave Naviragh became alarmed again, and so
did his two Armenian theologians, and they started looking at
each other with astonished glances.

★   ★   ★

Pan Novovyeyski circled the walls twice more and then seated the breathless Zosia on one of the benches. She liked him very much; he was so dashing and so daring, and as honest and straightforward as a leaping fire. But he was also bold beyond belief, and she had never met anyone like him before, and this both frightened her a little and threw her into great confusion, so she kept her sky-blue eyes fixed even closer to the floor and sat as quiet as a field mouse in a furrow.

"Why're you so quiet, m'lady?" Novovyeyski asked, concerned. "Why so sad?"

"Cause Daddy's a captive," she replied in a tiny voice.

"That's why it's good to dance!" said the merry giant. "Take a look through this hall, m'lady. There's three or four dozen of us here and not one will die of old age in his bed. There's either a galley-oar or a pagan arrow waiting for each of us. His turn today, mine tomorrow, that's the way we see it! Everyone in here in the *Kresy* borderlands has lost someone dear and that's why we're having a good time, so that God won't think we're complaining about the service. That's what it's all about, m'lady! It's right to be dancing! So give me a smile, will you? And show me your eyes, or I'll start thinking you don't want to look at me at all!"

Zosia didn't lift her eyes as he urged, but the corners of her mouth began to move upward and two dimples showed in her apple cheeks.

"D'you like me at least a little, m'lady?" asked the cavalier.

"A... little," Zosia answered in an even smaller voice.

At this Pan Novovyeyski leaped up on the bench as if someone had stabbed a cobbler's awl into his vast haunches, seized her little hands in his own huge paws, rained kisses upon them, and threw all his cautions to the winds.

"I'm lost and that's all there's to it!" he shouted. "I'm stuffed, cooked, roasted and head-over-heels about you, may I drop dead right here if I'm lying! I don't want anybody else, just you! Ay, my sweet pretty! *Rety!* How I love you, m'lady! I'll go on my knees to your mother tomorrow... Tomorrow? The Devil take tomorrow, I'll do it today, just as long as I know you care for me a little!"

Just then a wall-shaking blast of musketry rattled the windows from the other side as the celebrating soldiers fired their salute to Basia. It quite drowned Zosia's answer. The grave Naviragh worried for the third time, and so did the frightened theologians, and Pan Zagloba started to comfort them in Latin.

"*Apud Polonos,*" he told them. "*Nunquam sine clamore et strepitu gaudia fiunt,* as the saying goes. The more noise you hear from and among the Poles, the less there is to be afraid of no matter what the dangers. The time to worry, my dear sir, is when they're sitting quiet."

And it seemed as if everyone had waited only for that blast of salutatory thunder to let loose the reins on their exuberant wild spirits.

The usual courtliness of the gentry gave way altogether to the devil-may-care here today, gone tomorrow fierceness of the Steppes.

The music crashed out again, the dancers swept into an even madder whirl, eyes flamed and steamy exhalations curled upward out of all those crimson faces and the sweated hair. Even the most staid and stable officers hurled themselves into the dance, wild cheers shook the rafters every other moment, liquor flowed by the barrel, and the good times went on.

They drank toasts out of Basia's slipper, fired pistols at the cork high-heels of Evka's discarded dancing shoes, and all of Hreptyov boomed and shook and thundered all night into the morning, so that even the beasts of prey that crouched in the wilderness around it sought shelter in the deepest thickets they could find.

And because all this was taking place on the eve of a desperate war with all the vast multitudes of the Muslim world, and the grim shadows of death and devastation lay over all those people, the grave Naviragh looked with sheer amazement at these Polish soldiers, and so did his two staring theologians.

Chapter Forty-five

EVERYONE SLEPT LATE the next day, except for the sentries huddled on the walls, and Pan Volodyovski who was up as usual because he never let anything interfere with his service duties.

Young Pan Novovyeyski also leaped out of bed early in the morning because catching another sight of Zosia Boska was more important to him than getting some rest. He dressed himself from the start in his finest clothing, went to the scene of last night's celebration, and pressed his ear to the walls in hopes of hearing some sign of stirring in the women's quarters on the other side. There were, indeed, sounds of movement in the room assigned to Lady Boska, but the young man was so impatient to catch a glimpse of Zosia that he pulled out the long, curved, ornamental Turkish dagger he wore in his sash and started chipping with it at the moss and clay which caulked the narrow crevices in the thick log walls.

He was caught redhanded in this work by Pan Zagloba who came by in just that moment with a sandalwood rosary clutched piously in his hand, realized at a single glance what was going on, crept up on the absorbed young giant on the toes of his boots, and started lashing his broad back with his string of beads.

The young man fled, twisting this way and that and very much ashamed although he tried to cover it up with laughter, and the old man chased him up and down the room, whacked him with his rosary, and cried over and over:

"Oh you Turk! You Tartar! Take this! And take that! *Exorciso te*, let me drive the Devil out of you! Where's your respect? So you're peeking at the women, are you? Take this, you scoundrel! And take that!"

"Kind sir!" boomed Novovyeyski. "It's not right to turn holy beads into a horsewhip! Let me go because I didn't have any bad intentions!"

"What do you mean it's wrong to whip somebody with a rosary?" bellowed Pan Zagloba. "Palm fronds are also holy on Palm Sunday but people get whacked with them anyway! Ha! These used to be heathen worry-beads and they belonged to Supankhazi-agha till I got them away from him at Zbarajh and then the Pope's Nuncio blessed them. Look, see? It's real sandalwood!"

"If it's real sandalwood then it should smell like perfume."

"If I have a nose for holy beads, you have one for girls!" the old noble grunted. "I've got to give you a good beating with it because there's nothing like a rosary to drive the Devil out of a sinful hide."

"I didn't have any kind of sin in mind!" the young man protested. "May I drop dead right here if I'm lying!"

"And you were just digging out a peephole out of piety, is that it?"

"Not out of piety but out of such huge love that it'll blast me apart like a bomb if I don't get to do something about it soon! Ah, but why beat about the bush? The truth is the truth and that's all there's to it! Horseflies don't pester an animal in Summer worse than I itch with all this loving right now!"

"Just make sure it's not a sinful itch!" threatened Pan Zagloba. "Because when I caught you, you were hopping from one heel to another like a firewalker."

"I didn't see a thing, as God is my witness, because I'd just started digging out a peep hole!"

"Well that's youth for you," the old knight observed. "Hot blood is not cold water! Even I have to restrain myself now and then because the old lion still roars here and there inside me... But if you've good intentions you must be thinking about getting married?"

"Am I thinking about getting married? Dear God! What else would I be thinking? I'm not just thinking about it, I am feeling it, because it's like getting jabbed with a branding iron! I don't suppose you know, sir, that I've already made my proposals before Lady Boska and that I have my father's consent as well?"

"Already?" Pan Zagloba smiled. "You don't waste much time, may the Devil take you! Sheer sparks and gunpowder, that's what you are made of... Ah, but if that's the case then everything's alright and aboveboard and there's not much of a Devil in you, the way that I see it... So come on now, tell me, how did it all go?"

★ ★ ★

Spared further lashes with the old knight's rosary, the young man breathed a vast sigh of relief and told him how he followed Lady Boska to her room last night when she went to get a shawl for Zosia.

"She turned around and there I was," he said. "*Who's there?'* she asks. And bang I go on my knees before her. *'Let me have Zoska, mother,'* I tell her. *'Because I can't live another day without her! Beat me if you want to, but I've got to have her!'* Well, it took her a while to get over the shock, but then she says: *'Everybody says good things about you and you've got the looks of a fine cavalier. My husband is in captivity and Zoska has no protection in this world. Still, I won't give you my reply today, nor even tomorrow, and you first need to get your father's consent anyway.'* That's what she said and went her way, thinking most likely that I'd had a snootful, which of course I did..."

"So did everybody else," Pan Zagloba shrugged. "Did you notice how Naviragh and his theologians ended up with their pointy skullcaps dangling from their ears?"

"No I didn't because I was trying to figure out how best to get that consent out of my father."

"And was it hard going?"

"We went to his quarters right around sunrise, and since the best time to hammer out a horseshoe is when the iron's hot, I thought I'd at least find out how the old man might feel about all this. So I told him: *'Listen, father, I want Zoska worse than anything and I need your consent right away, but if I don't get it then I'll go and enlist with the Venetians or someone and that's the last you'll ever see of me.'* God sir, you should've heard him! *'Oh you misbegotten whelp!'* he yells at me, mad as the Devil and ready to burst with fury. *'You know all about getting a father's consent, don't you, before you run away from home! You know how to do without it well enough! Take the girl and go to the Venetians for all that I care, but there's one thing I'll tell you: I won't give you a tin penny from my money chest, or your mother's either, because it's all mine, you hear me?'"*

"Oy, that's bad," Pan Zagloba muttered.

"Wait sir, it gets better. As soon as I heard this I said: *'Who's asking for your money? Who needs it? I want your blessing, that's all, because all the heathen goods that fell to me as my campaign shares are enough for a good lease or freehold, or even to buy a fair-sized village. Let mother's dowry go towards Evka's, and I'll even throw in a handful or two of jewels, and some brocades and velvets, and if a bad harvest thins out your incomes, father, in some unlucky year, I'll help out with cash!'"*

"That got his interest, I imagine," Pan Zagloba said.

"It did. Right away he asks me: *'You're that rich, then? Where'd you get it? Loot? Because when you left home you were as naked as a Turkish saint!'"*

"And what did you tell him?"

"*'God love you, father!'* I said right away. "*'It's not like I've been flailing about with my saber for the fun of it for eleven years, and I don't do it badly either, as some people say! I helped storm rebel cities where the cut-throat scoundrels and their Tartar allies piled up a stock of treasure. I did my share of slicing up various Tartar murjahs and rich bandit chiefs, and the goods kept coming.'* I took only what the Hetman granted, taking nothing that I didn't earn, but it grew and grew, and if it wasn't for the fact that I like to have a good time and enjoy myself I'd have twice as much as all of father's properties bring in every year."

"And what did your old man say to that?" the old knight asked, amused.

"He was dumbstruck, because that was the last thing he expected, and he started on me right away for being a spend-thrift. *'There'd have been something to build on,'* he says. *'But such a whirlwind-rider, such a tadpole from a village pond who puffs himself up like a toad and likes to play the magnate, he'll throw it all away,'*—he says—*'he won't keep anything.'* Then his curiosity got the better of him and he starts to question me, in detail, about what I have. I saw at once that I'd ride that wagon to where I want to go, so I not only didn't hide a thing but I lied up a storm of stuff besides. I don't usually like to stretch the truth, because truth—the way I see it—is oats, and lies are chopped straw."

"I couldn't have said that any better myself,"Pan Zagloba said. "And your father heard all this?"

"Father couldn't get over it. He kept clutching at his head and making all kinds of plans for me. *'This or that,'* he says, *'we can buy. This or that lawsuit'*—he goes on—*'we can win. We'd live across a furrow from each other and I could keep an eye on it all when you're away.'* And here that good old man burst out crying. *'Adam!'* he says. *'I really like that girl for you, especially since she's the Hetman's ward which also might be useful. Adam!'*—he tells me—*'Only you take good care of this second daughter of mine, and don't you hurt her any, or I'll curse you in the hour of my death.'"*

"Very nicely put," Pan Zagloba grunted. "And was he still weeping as he said all this?"

"He was and I was. Because just the thought of something hurting Zosia made me bellow like a water-buffalo! So we fell into each other's arms, Pa and me, and we wept until the first cockcrow."

'That old country skinflint!' Pan Zagloba thought and shook his head in wonder, because it was quite clear that the sly, tyrannical, penny-pinching father was as true to type as the brave young son. But, in full voice, he said: "Ha! So we might have a wedding in Hreptyov soon, and another jolly time like last night!"

"It'd be tomorrow if it was up to me!" Novovyeyski shouted. "But here's the thing, my leave is almost up, and duty is duty, and I must go back to Rashkov. Pan Rushtchitz will give me another leave, that isn't a problem, but I don't know if the women won't hold things up, like they always do. I went to the mother again. She said: *'My husband's in captivity.'* I went to the daughter, she said: *'Daddy is a captive.'* Ay! What's that to do with me? Have I got this Daddy locked up somewhere and groaning on a chain? I'm awfully worried about all these obstacles, otherwise I'd grab Father Kaminski by his skirt-tails and hold him till he tied the knot for me and Zoska. But once a woman pounds an idea into her head, you wouldn't get it out with a pair of pliers. I'd spend my last penny to get Daddy out

of whatever galley he is sweating in, I'd go for him myself, but
there's no way to do that! Nobody even knows where he is. He
might be dead, and there's a task for you! If those two women
make me wait for him I'll dry up like a thistle!"

"Piotrovitch, Naviragh and those theologians are leaving tomorrow. You'll have some news soon."

"Sweet Jesus help me! So I'm to wait for news? That won't
come till Spring and I'll dry up by then, as God is my witness!
My good, kind sir,"—the desperate young man turned to Pan
Zagloba—"everyone has faith in your wisdom and experience.
Knock this thing about waiting out of the women's heads!
Spring, sir, means war! God only knows what'll happen then! It's
Zoska I want to marry, not her daddy, so why should I be sighing
for his return?"

"Convince the women that they should go to Rashkov and
settle there for a time," Pan Zagloba said. "The news will come
there first and so will Pan Boski himself if Piotrovitch finds him.
Moreover, I'll do what I can, but you ask Lady Basia to intercede
as well."

"I will! I will! Otherwise the Devil..."

                                    ★   ★   ★

But whatever the young man thought the Devil might do was
left unsaid just then because the doors creaked and opened and
Lady Boska came into the room. Pan Zagloba hardly had the
time to turn towards her when Novovyeyski hurled himself to
the floor before her, landing so hard that the pineboards shuddered under him and taking up a vast amount of space with his
enormous body, and started shouting till the rafters rattled:

"Give me Zoska, mother! Give me Zoska, mother! Give me
Zoska, mother!"

"Give him Zoska, mother!" Pan Zagloba added his hoarse bass
in chorus, and all this uproar brought everybody else running
from their rooms.

Basia entered. Pan Michal showed in the door of the orderly
room. Zosia herself appeared a moment later. The girl wasn't
supposed to know what was going on; conventions required that
she should be oblivious of Novovyeyski's interest. But a deep
red flush bloomed on her cheeks at once, she assumed all the
expressions of modesty and compliance expected of a gentle-

woman, folded her little hands, and stood against the wall with her eyes fixed on the floor before her. Basia immediately added her entreaties to those of Novovyeyski, and Pan Michal took off at a run to bring the young man's father. He, once he got there, showed himself quite shocked that his son had neither left the matter to parental discretion, nor made his plea in a sufficiently eloquent and high-minded manner, but he too begged Lady Boska to relent.

Lady Boska, who really had no one else in the world who might offer her some care and protection, let her tears flow at last, and agreed both to Adam's pleas and to the idea of going to Rashkov with the Piotrovitch party, and waiting for news of her husband there.

Then, at last, she turned her tearful face towards her daughter.

"Zoska," she said. "And are you of like mind about Pan Novovyeyski's feelings and ideas?"

All eyes turned at once on Zosia who still stood quietly against the wall, scarlet as a poppy and with her eyes riveted to the floorboards.

"I want to go to Rashkov...!" she breathed out at last in such a tiny voice that they barely heard her.

"My precious!" bellowed the enormous Adam and seized the girl in his huge embrace. And then he started shouting with such force and power that dust and splinters billowed from the timbers: "Zoska is mine now! Mine! Mine! Mine!"

Part VI

Part VI

Chapter Forty-six

YOUNG PAN NOVOVYEYSKI left for Rashkov right after his engagement to find and prepare a place where Lady Boska and Zosia could stay in that outpost, and two weeks later all the other temporary Hreptyov guests set out in his tracks. The caravan consisted of Naviragh and his theologians, the two Armenian ladies, Seferovitch, Zosia and Lady Boska, old Pan Novovyeyski and the two Piotrovitch brothers, as well as several other Armenian traders from Kamyenetz, and a crowd of armed grooms and drovers to guard the sleighs and wagons, the remount herd and the baggage animals. The two Piotrovitches and the representatives of the Armenian Patriarch were to rest only a few days in Rashkov, find out the condition of the road ahead, and then go on to the Crimea. Everyone else decided to settle in Rashkov for a time and to wait there, until at least the first Spring thaws, for the return of the captives.

The trail was a hard one since it ran through deep forests and precipitous gorges. Fortunately for the travelers, the thick carapace of snow created a perfect sleighing surface, while the presence of military outposts in Mohilev, Yampol and Rashkov itself assured a safe journey, especially since Azbah-bey's *vataha* had been crushed, the other local bandits were either hanged or scattered, and the Tartars didn't send their raids across the border in the snowbound season when there was no grass on which to feed their horses.

The journey was a brisk and cheerful one. They felt all the safer since Adam Novovyeyski promised to bring out a troop of cavalry to meet them halfway just as soon as his commandant,

Pan Rushtchitz, gave him permission to do it. Zosia would have gone gladly to the ends of the world just as long as Pan Adam would be there as well, while Lady Boska and the two Armenian merchants' wives were looking forward to getting their husbands back again. True, Rashkov lay in the midst of a forbidding wilderness at the outer limits of the Christian world, but it wasn't as if they meant to spend the rest of their lives among those gloomy forests, or as if their stay would stretch beyond Spring; the end of the Winter would bring war, this was common knowledge in the borderlands, so they would have to head back to civilization with the first warm breezes, or just as soon as they recovered their loved ones, to save their own lives from the coming storm.

Ewa stayed in Hreptyov, kept back by Basia Volodyovska. Her father didn't put up much of an objection knowing that she'd be well looked after among such good people. He was a decent enough man by the gentry's standards of his time, but he was far more fascinated by Adam than by Ewa—boys being more important than girls in the family hierarchy of the landed gentry—and he wanted to enjoy his rediscovered son without a ripe young female to worry about in a military outpost, and more or less underfoot in a largely male society, so he gave an eager ear to Basia's arguments.

"I'll make sure she'll join you safely when it's time to send her," she assured the noble. "Or I'll bring her over to Rashkov myself because I'd really like to see, once and for all, that terrible frontier wilderness I heard so much about when I was a child. My husband won't allow me go in the Spring, when the *tchambuls* spill out across the trails, but taking Evka to Rashkov will give me a good excuse to see it all now. I'll start to hint about it in a week or two and in three weeks I'll probably win him over."

"Nor will your husband let you go without a good escort, I expect," the old noble said.

"He'll come himself, if he can. If he can't, then I'm sure he'll be glad to entrust me to Azia who has been seconded to Rashkov. And that means two hundred men or more to look after us."

★ ★ ★

That was the end of that conversation and Evka stayed behind.

Basia, of course, had other reasons for wanting her in Hreptyov. She was concerned about the girl's love affair with Azia who was beginning to worry her a bit. The young Tartar met all her questions, whenever they were alone, with assurances of his love for Evka, but whenever he was alone with the girl he had nothing to say.

Meanwhile the girl had tumbled head-over-heels in love. She hardly knew what she was doing any more. His savage but appealing beauty, the hardships of a childhood spent under the heavy hand of Pan Novovyeyski, his highborn lineage as Tuhaybey's son and heir, the thrilling mystery that went with the long secret he'd carried within him, and finally his dazzling fame as a heroic soldier, entranced her altogether. It was quite clear to Basia that the girl was only waiting for the moment to fling open that glowing heart and tell him: *'Azia! I've loved you since I was a child!'* And then to throw herself headlong into his arms and swear to love him as long as she lived.

He, in the meantime, clenched his teeth and didn't say a word.

Evka thought at first that he held back because her father and her brother were there. Then she became alarmed. Because even if there was opposition from her father and Adam—and there'd surely be some until Azia could become ennobled—he could, at least, open his heart to her, and he should have done so. The more difficulties there might lie ahead, she thought, the more they should trust each other and confide in each other.

But he said nothing.

Doubt crept into the girl's troubled heart at last and she voiced her worries and complaints to Basia who did her best to calm her and console her.

"I can't deny that he's a strange and secretive kind of man," she said. "But I'm sure he loves you. In the first place, that's what he told me himself at least a dozen times, and in the second place, he looks at you in a different way than he does at others."

"But is that a look of love?" Evka shook her head, sad and unconvinced. "I sometimes think he hates me."

"My dear Evka, don't babble such nonsense, why should Azia hate you?"

"And why should he love me?"

But here Basia began to stroke the girl's face with her gentle hand. "And why does Michal love me? And why did your brother start loving Zosia the moment he saw her?"

"Adam was always quick off the mark..."

"Azia, meanwhile, is proud and fears a rebuff from your father, even though your brother might be more understanding when it comes to the torments of affection, having just fallen into love himself. That's the problem here! Don't be stupid, Evka, and don't be afraid. I'll give Azia a good talking-to and you'll see what a gallant he'll turn out to be."

Basia made sure that she cornered Azia that same day and ran in to see Ewa after a short meeting.

"It's all as good as done!" she announced right out of the doorway.

"What is!" Evka cried, flaming like a poppy.

"This is what I told him: 'What do you think you're doing, cavalier? Are you trying to insult my generosity? I went out of my way to keep Evka here so that you might have an opportunity, but if you don't take advantage of it in two weeks then know this: in two weeks, or three at the latest, I'm sending her to Rashkov, and I might go with her myself, and you'll be left swinging on the gate.'

"His whole face," Basia went on, "changed at once. He got so upset he got down on his knees and almost beat the floor with his forehead before me. 'What do you mean to do, then?' I asked. 'On the road,' he answered. 'On the road I'll declare everything that is in my heart. On the road,' he insisted, 'will be the best chance, it's on the road that everything will happen that is supposed to happen, all that is ordained... That's when I'll drop all pretense and reveal everything about me, because I can't live with this secret torment any longer!'

"His lips began to shake, he was so moved," Basia said, "especially since he had some bad news from Kamyenetz this morning. He told me that he must go to Rashkov anyway, that my husband holds the Hetman's order to that effect, and that the only reason why it hasn't been carried out till now was that the time wasn't ripe for those negotiations that Azia is conducting with those *Lipki* captains.

"'But now,' he said, 'the time has almost come that I must go to Rashkov and even beyond to get closer to them, so I'll be glad to escort your ladyship and Panna Evka all the way.'

"I told him I wasn't sure that I could come as well, because that must depend on Michal's permission, and he was almost scared to death when he heard this. Ha! You're stupid, Evka! You say he doesn't love you, and he loves you so much he threw himself on his knees before me, and he begged me so hard that I should come as well, that—I tell you—he made me think of a crying puppy, or an injured child, and my heart went out to him with pity. And d'you now why he did that?"

"No! Why?"

"He told me at once: 'I will show everything that is in my heart, but it won't work with the Novovyeyskis, the father and the son, without your ladyship's intercession, and all I'll do is stir up their anger and hatred along with my own. My life is in your hands, your ladyship,' he went on. 'You alone hold my fate, my suffering and my salvation, because if your ladyship won't be coming with us then I'd rather that the earth swallowed me up or that a living fire devoured me.'

"That's how he loves you, Evka," Basia finished. "It's almost frightening how intense he is about it. And it'd scare you too if you'd seen what he looked like then."

"No! I'm not afraid of him!" Evka assured Basia as much as herself, and started to kiss Basia's hands in gratitude and pleading. "Come with us! Come with us!"

Quite swept away with feeling, she sounded as distraught as a needy child.

"Come with us! You're the only one who can help us, save us... only you are brave enough to tell Father that we love each other, no one but you would get anywhere with him! Come with us! I'll beg Pan Volodyovski on my knees to let you go. Without you, Father and Azia will leap on each other with knives in their hands! Come with us! Come with us!"

"With God's help, I'll do it!" Basia said. "I'll explain everything to Michal and I won't stop pestering him until I have my answer. It's almost safe for a woman to travel alone in these parts these days, so how much safer will she have to be with such a heavy escort? And maybe Michal will come too!"

Basia, for all her open, honest and devoted love, obviously knew her husband very well.

"But even if he can't come with us," she remarked, "he'll let me go without him. He has a heart. He's sure to agree. His first word will be 'No,' but let me just start looking a little sad, and he'll start walking in circles around me, and peering into my eyes, and then he'll say 'Yes.'

"I'd rather he came with us," she went on, "because I'll miss him terribly, but if he can't, he can't, and there is nothing to be done about it! I'll go anyway to help you two a little... My goodness, this isn't just a whim of mine anymore, it's a matter of life or death for Azia and you! Michal likes you and Azia very much. He'll go along with this."

★   ★   ★

Azia, meanwhile, ran to his quarters from that meeting with Basia so filled with hope and expectations as if he'd just come back to health after a long illness.

A murderous despair clutched him by the throat only moments earlier. He had received a short, dry letter from Pan Bogush only hours before, in which all his dreams shattered and crumbled into dust.

'*My dear Azia,*' the old border noble addressed him abruptly. '*I've halted at Kamyenetz and I'm not coming on to Hreptyov at this time, in part because the journey has finally worn me down and, in part, because there's no need. The Hetman not only denies your request, and won't be made a part of your lunatic ideas, but he orders you, under the threat of losing his patronage and favor, to give them up at once. I also came to the conclusion that everything you've told me is out of the question; first because it'd be a sin for a civilized Christian nation to enter into such plots with pagan barbarians; and, in the second place, because it would shame us in the eyes of the entire world if we were to give the privileges and rights of ennobled gentry to thieves, robbers, pillagers and murderers who have spilled so much innocent blood through so many centuries.*

'*Come to your senses as well in this matter,*' urged Azia's former patron, '*and give up your grandiose visions of yourself even if you are the son of Tuhay-bey. You are not a Hetman, nor will you ever be one, and if you want to come back quickly into Pan Sobieski's favor then be satisfied with the rank you're given, and bring your work with Krytchinski, Tvorovski, Adurovitch and the others to a quick conclusion, since that's your best road to merit and advancement.*

'I'm sending the Hetman's note about your duties to Pan Volodyovski, along with an order that you and your men be free to come and go as you please. I expect that you'll soon set out to your meeting with those turncoat captains. Hurry with that and let me know everything you hear on the other side.'

Then he commended Azia to God's keeping.

★   ★   ★

The young Tartar fell into such raging fury when he read this letter that the faithful Halim feared for his life. He ripped and shredded the offending letter and stamped it into dust; he stabbed and gouged the tabletop with his Turkish *kindjhal* and threatened to turn the deadly weapon on himself; and at last he turned on the kneeling Halim who begged him to do nothing until he recovered from rage and despair.

The letter was, beyond all doubt, a devastating blow. The castles that his pride and ambition had created for him were gone in an instant, as shattered as if they'd been blown up by a charge of powder, and all his plans had tumbled into ruin. He'd seen himself as the third ranking Hetman of the Commonwealth, taking precedence even over the Hetman of the Cossacks, and holding much of the country's destiny in his hands, and here he was to remain an ordinary officer whose highest realizable ambition could be only membership in the serving gentry.

His inflamed imagination had shown him vast throngs salaaming before him, and now he was to go on his knees to others, and—all at once—everything was for nothing! It didn't matter that he was a son of Tuhay-bey, and that his veins carried the blood of princes; it made no difference that he could see beyond the horizons, and create visions that others failed to grasp. Nothing! All of this meant nothing! He'd live unrecognized and die in some Godforsaken outpost, forgotten and unknown. One word had crushed his wings and sent him tumbling to earth out of the skies. A single 'No!' forced him to forget about the dreams of eagles and to stay crawling on the ground like the meanest insect.

But even that was nothing beside the joy he'd lost. *She*, for whose possession he would shed seas of blood and give up all his hopes of eternity and salvation, for whom he burned like fire and whom he craved with every pulse and sinew of his body, would never be his. That letter took her from him just as surely as it robbed him of a Hetman's baton. Hmyelnitzki could steal another man's wife and then fight all the might of the Commonwealth to keep her, and Azia could've done the same if he were a powerful warlord leading his own nation. But how could he do that if he was just a *Lipki* lieutenant who led a hundred men and served under her husband?

The world darkened for him. It became desolate and empty. He knew it would be better just to kill himself than live without a reason for living, without happiness or hope or the woman that he needed like he needed air.

The shock was all the more brutal because it was so wholly unexpected; he'd convinced himself that the Hetman would not be able to refuse him, bearing in mind the condition of the Commonwealth, the dearth of troops, and the certainty of the coming war. Each day confirmed him in his suppositions. If he'd have done it if he were the Hetman, why wouldn't Pan Sobieski?

And now all his dreams were gone at one cruel stroke, blown away like mist by a cold morning breeze, and what did he have left? How could he turn his back on fame, glory, power, happiness and greatness?

He couldn't do it.

A mindless rage seized him at this thought. Despair clawed at him along with his anger. He felt as if the marrow in his bones had turned into fire, and he howled aloud and hissed and ground his teeth, and his chaotic thoughts were no less murderous than his disappointment. He wanted vengeance on the Commonwealth, the Hetman, Volodyovski and even on Basia. He was primed and ready to send his *Lipki* on a bloody rampage, slaughter the entire garrison, murder all the officers, burn Hreptyov, kill Volodyovski, seize Basia and carry her off to the Moldavian bank, then run with her into Dobrudja or even to Istanbul itself if that's what it took to keep her in his grasp, or hide her in the vastness of continental Asia.

But the faithful Halim kept an eye on him and soothed him

and calmed him, and he too finally managed to get through his fury and despair and to recognize the impossibility of what he had in mind.

Azia had one more quality in common with Hmyelnitzki: he carried within him both a serpent and a lion, he was both brave and cunning.

So he'd strike at Hreptyov with his loyal *Lipki*, he began to reason finally. And then what?

Would Volodyovski, a skilled Steppe borderer and a man as watchful as a stalking crane, let himself be caught by surprise? And if he was, could he be defeated? He had more men and better soldiers close to hand, and what about his fearsome reputation?

And finally, even if Azia did bring him down by some inexplicable stroke of luck and break out of Hreptyov, what could he do beyond that? Follow the Dniester to the Yahorlik and the Tartar treaty lands beyond it? But what about the army regiments in Mohilev, Yampol and Rashkov right on the Tartar border? Could he surprise and exterminate them all? And if he didn't go downriver but merely crossed right here to the Moldavian side, how could he cope with the Turkish border governors and commanders, all of them friends of Volodyovski, and that included his blood-brother, the all-powerful Pasha of Khotim who'd hang him out of hand as a common bandit?

That left the Steppe itself and Doroshenko's rebels out towards Bratzlav and beyond, but what about the Polish troops stationed along the way and filling the wilderness with their patrols and columns even in the Winter?

Faced with all this, the Tartar felt his own impotence and weakness. His dark, glowering spirit plunged into icy gloom like a wounded beast that seeks shelter in the depths of a forbidding cave, and there it crouched, convulsed with rage and hatred, but silent and still.

But just as even the worse and most gnawing pain eventually devours itself and dissipates in the dullness of exhausted senses, so his own fury ebbed and left him weak and spent and stunned and with all thought gone.

It was at this moment that an orderly reported that the Commandant's Lady wished to talk to him, and he went off to

that brief meeting with Basia which she already related to Ewa
Novovyeyska.

*   *   *

When he came back from that meeting he seemed like a man
reborn. Halim himself almost didn't recognize him, the change
was so total. All the stiff, moribund deadness had fallen from his
features. His eyes gleamed with the savage eagerness of a lynx
which perceives the quiet and unsuspecting approach of his prey.
His face was full of fire and alight with hope. His long white
canines flashed under his mustache, and he was so like his
terrible father at that moment, that the old Tartar fell to his
knees in homage.

"Lord," he murmured. "By what means did God bring peace
to your troubled soul?"

"Halim!" Azia answered. "God creates daylight after the darkness of the night and commands the sun to rise out of the sea.
Halim!"—and here he seized and shook the Dobrudjan by the
shoulders—"In just one more month she'll be mine for ever!"

His dark face glowed with such a radiance then, and he was
so magnificent in his reawakened power, that Halim began to
pound the floor with his forehead at his master's feet.

"You are great, son of Tuhay-bey," he murmured and then
cried: "You have the might and the power, and the malice of the
unbelievers will fail against you!"

"Listen!" Azia ordered.

"I hear you, *Effendi!*"

"This is what I've decided. We will go to the purple sea where
the Winter snows lie only on the mountains, and if we ever
come back to these parts it will be with *tchambuls* as numerous
as the desert sands, and as thick as the leaves in these immeasurable forests, bringing death and fire. You, Halim, will get on
your way today. You'll find Krytchinski and tell him to creep up
on Rashkov on the other side of the river with all his men and
horses. And Adurovitch, Moravski, Groholski, Tvorovski and
every other man alive among the *Lipki* and the *Tcheremisy* must
go there too and wait for my coming. Send word to the Dobrudjans who are in Winter quarters beside Doroshenko to give me
a diversion and make a sudden raid out towards Uman, so that
all the Polish garrisons come out of Mohilev, Yampol and

Rashkov and head into the Steppe. Let the road I'll take be clear of all troops, so that when I leave Rashkov there'll be nothing but ashes behind me."

"Allah protect you, Lord!" Halim said, making his salaams, and Azia leaned over him and hissed urgently:

"Send out the word! Send messengers everywhere! There's only one month left!"

★ ★ ★

Left alone, Azia began to pray because he was filled with happiness and gratitude to God.

As he prayed he glanced now and then through the window at his *Lipki* troopers who'd just begun to lead their horses out of the sheds and stables and water them at the troughs set beside the wells. The whole parade ground darkened under them. The men were chanting their monotonous Tartar songs, pulling down on the creaking well-beams and splashing water into the open troughs. Twin columns of condensing steam rose from the nostrils of each horse and gave the picture the hazy quality of a dream.

Pan Volodyovski emerged just then from the main building of the *fortalitzya*, dressed in a long sheepskin coat and tall, untanned leather boots, and started saying something to the *Lipki* soldiers who stiffened to attention before him and bared their heads in the oriental manner.

Azia gave up his prayers as he watched.

"Yes, you're a Falcon," he murmured to himself, his eyes fixed coldly on Volodyovski. "But you'll fly neither as far nor as high as I will, and I'll take all your happiness away, and you'll stay here in Hreptyov, alone with your pain."

Pan Volodyovski finished talking to the soldiers and turned back to the headquarters building, and the broad open space within the fort's enclosure filled again with the droning chant, the creak of the well-beams and the snorting of the watered horses.

Chapter Forty-seven

THE LITTLE KNIGHT did just what Basia expected him to do, and his first reaction when he heard about her intentions was to cry out that he'd never let her go on such a trip without him; and since it was impossible for him to go at this time, the whole venture was out of the question. He was then bombarded from all sides by such a barrage of pleadings and entreaties that he was soon shaken in his decision.

Basia pressed him about it far less than anyone expected, because she badly wanted him to come along, and the expedition lost much of its charm without him. But Evka went on her knees before him, kissed his hands as if he were her father, and begged him by his love for Basia to agree.

"No one else would dare to tell my father about this," she argued every time she caught him. "Neither I nor Azia nor even my brother! Only Lady Basia could make him listen because there's nothing he wouldn't do for her."

"It's not Basia's business to play the marriage broker!" he said. "And besides, all of you will be coming back this way from Rashkov. Let her do it then."

Evka replied with tears. God only knew what would happen before they came back, she wailed, and she was quite sure she'd die in the meantime out of sheer sorrow, but perhaps that would be the best thing for her anyway since, apparently, there was no mercy for her in this world.

The little knight was known to have a soft-spot for tender-hearted moments, and his response to such piteous laments was to set his little whiskers twitching violently and to start trotting around the room. One day's separation from his Baska was more than he wanted to think about, and here he was being asked to send her off for weeks!

But Evka's pleading moved him none the less; he could not ignore them; and a few days after this assault, his firm decision showed the beginning of a breach.

"I wouldn't say anything if I could come with you," he told Ewa one evening. "But I can't go. I have duties here."

His dedication to his duty was one of the things about him that Basia honored and admired the most but she ran to him at once, pressed her pink lips to his cheek and started repeating in a childlike tone: "Please come with us *Michalku*! Please! Please!"

"Absolutely not!" he said with determination.

Another day or two passed in this three-way struggle, in which the little knight tried to find some way to please his Baska without coming into conflict with his military duties, and at last he went for advice to Pan Zagloba. He, however, for the first time in all the years that Pan Michal knew him, refused to advise him one way or the other.

"If," he said, "it's only your feelings for Basia that stand in the way of letting her go to Rashkov, and if there's no other obstacle you know of, then what's left to say? Make up your own mind. Sure this place will be empty without the little warrior. I'd go myself if I weren't too old to rattle around in the wilderness and if the road was better, because the days without her won't be fit for living."

"There you are!" said Volodyovski. "That is just the problem. There really are no other obstacles. It's a bit cold, true, but not unusually so for this time of the year. The country is quiet and there are army posts all along the way. But time hangs so heavy without her and nothing means much when she's gone."

"That's why I said: make your own decision!"

★　★　★

After this unsatisfactory conversation Pan Michal was more unsettled and unsure than ever. Once shaken, his decision wavered, and he began to try to see both sides of the question. He was sorry for Evka. He wondered if it was right to send the girl alone with Azia on such a long journey and, even more, if he weren't doing a serious wrong by refusing to help two decent young people, especially since there were such good means at hand to do them a service.

'What is this really all about?' he asked himself. Two or three weeks without Basia was all the sacrifice he was asked to make. And even if there was no more at stake here than to give her what she wanted, a chance to see Mohilev and Yampol and Rashkov, then why not give it to her? Azia had to take his men to Rashkov anyway and his two hundred *Lipki* were more than enough for any kind of escort, especially since the bandits had been crushed and the Hordes were quiet for the Winter.

This sapped the walls of his resistance even further which the besieging women caught sight of at once and they redoubled their bombardment: one pointing to a good deed, to his obligation as a decent man, and to his duty as the girl's host and temporary guardian, the other threatening to drown him with her tears.

Finally Azia Mellehovitch came to bow before his commandant and to add his assurances about Basia's safety. He said he knew he hadn't earned the favor of such an assignment, but that he'd shown so much loyalty and devotion to the colonel and the Colonel's Lady, and he was so anxious to demonstrate it further, that he now dared to ask for the task.

"I'll never forget the way her ladyship dressed my wounds," he said. "She was more than my commander's wife in that respect, your honor. She was like a mother."

He'd already given proofs of his gratitude in the battle against Azbah-bey, he said, and in the future, should the need arise, although God forbid that she should be in any kind of danger, he'd gladly die in her defense.

Then he told about his boyhood love for Evka which he could not forget through all its evil and unlucky turns. Ah, he cried out: he found it difficult just to live without her! He'd loved her through all the years of their separation, although there'd been no hope of any kind, and he'll never stop. The gap, however, that yawned between him and Pan Novovyeyski, was the unbridgeable chasm that lies between a master and a former servant, and so was the hatred.

"Only her ladyship can smooth the ground between us," the young Tartar had become eloquent in his desperation. And, he went on, even if she failed to move the old noble, she'd at least help to shield that poor, dear girl from the old man's tyranny, from being locked away, and from his whip.

Volodyovski would've liked it better if Basia hadn't got herself involved in that affair but, as he reasoned, how could she help trying to help others? He was also fond of doing what he could for people so why should it surprise him that she'd take that matter to her loving heart? It would be out of character for her not to do so.

That night, however, he didn't give Azia any kind of answer, and spent more and more time in the next few days alone behind closed doors, pondering in his office.

★ ★ ★

And then one evening he came out to dinner without a cloud of worry in his face and, when the meal was over, he turned unexpectedly to the dour young Tartar.

"Azia," he said. "When will you be ready?"

"In a week, Your Honor!" The Tartar sounded worried and uncertain. "Halim must've finished his arrangements with Krytchinski."

"Then have the large sleigh well padded," Volodyovski told him. "You'll be taking two women with you."

Basia clapped her hands when she heard this and ran to her husband. Evka followed. Azia jumped up and bowed all the way down to his colonel's knees, a look of wild joy burning in his face, and the little knight found himself suddenly showered with gratitude from all sides.

"Leave me alone, for God's sake!" He flapped his arms in goodnatured protest as if driving off a swarm of pestering flies. "What is this now! It's hard not to help people when there's a chance to do it and I'm not a tyrant after all. You, sweetheart,"—he turned fondly to Basia—"come back as quickly as you can. And you, Azia, look after her well. That's the only thanks I need from either of you. Now come on, stop all this nonsense and leave me alone."

Hard as he tried to sound stern, his little whiskers went into a powerful fit of twitching as if to hide his own stirred sadness, resignation and regret, and the quick pang of sympathy he felt for all that youthful enthusiasm and exuberance around him.

"There's nothing as bad as those female tears," he grumbled

to Zagloba, largely to bolster his own resolve. "All I need is to catch sight of some and I'm as good as finished! And you, Azia, thank my wife as well as me, and don't forget this young lady here who trailed me like a shadow with her tears and pleading. You must pay her well for all that love and caring, you hear?"

"I'll pay her! She'll see how I'll pay her!" the Tartar answered in a strange, thick voice, seized Evka's hands in his own and kissed them with such violent fury that it seemed as if he were tearing at them like a dog.

"Michal!" Pan Zagloba groaned suddenly and tossed a slow, sad nod towards the happy and excited Basia. "How are you and I going to get by here without that dear kitten?"

"It won't be easy," sighed the little knight.

Then he murmured privately into the old knight's ear. "But maybe God will bless us later for this good deed... do you get my meaning?"

Pan Zagloba did, of course. But before he could come up with a smart rejoinder Basia thrust her bright, inquisitive head between them.

"What are you two muttering about?" she asked.

"Eh... Nothing," the old knight shrugged. "We're just saying that the storks will probably come in Spring."

Basia did something then that made her seem even more like a kitten: she started rubbing her pink cheek against her husband's.

"Michalku!" she murmured in a lowered voice. "I won't stay there long."

★　★　★

More discussions occupied everyone after that conversation but they dealt with preparations for the journey.

Pan Michal took charge of everything himself. He had the large sleigh put in perfect shape and padded with fox furs, dozens of which had been hunted down on horseback with the hounds in Autumn. Pan Zagloba brought down his own quilts so that the two young women would have something in which to wrap their legs on the long journey in the open sleigh. The convoy was to include some carts with warm bedding for the night-halts, and Basia's horse as well, so that she could mount up in those places where the ravines made sleighing dangerous. Pan

Michal was especially worried about the descent into Mohilev which lay at the bottom of a really precipitous ravine where the trail plunged as suddenly as a waterfall.

Although there wasn't the slightest probability of some attack or ambush, the little knight ordered Azia to exercise every caution common to the border, always to send out a strong advance and point-guard, and to stop for the night only in localities which held army posts. The convoy was to set out each day at dawn, halt for the night while it was still daylight, and waste no time along the trail but press on as swiftly as it could. Pan Michal was so totally absorbed in making sure that nothing was forgotten to ensure Basia's safety, that he loaded and primed the pistols for Basia's saddle-holsters with his own hands.

$\star$ $\star$ $\star$

At last there came the moment of departure. It was still dark outside when two hundred troopers of the Tartar Light Horse formed ranks in the courtyard. The main chamber of the Commandant's house was also full of people. Pine logs were blazing in the hearth and crackling and spluttering with sap. All the officers gathered to say goodbye, along with all the enlisted gentry from the senior Polish regiments. Baska and Evka, still pink and warm from sleep, were sipping hot wine toddies for the road.

Volodyovski sat next to his wife, holding her close with his arm around her waist. Zagloba poured the steaming liquor with his own two hands, filling the women's cups as soon as they emptied, and urging them to drink up because of the biting frost outside. Basia and Ewa both dressed in men's clothing for the journey because that was the way that women traveled in the borderlands. Basia wore her saber, a lynxfur jacket edged with otter along the cuffs and collar, a warm ermine cap with earflaps, a pair of such wide breeches that they looked no different than a skirt, and soft leather kneeboots with a lambswool lining.

Warm hooded cloaks and fur wraps were to go over all that clothing, protecting her face from the bitter cold, but now this face was still open and uncovered, and the gathered soldiers stared at her with their usual fondness and respect. Others shot greedy glances at Ewa, whose lips were moist and parted as if for a kiss. Yet others didn't know which of them to look at. Both

were so beautiful, each in her own way, and the grim old
borderers were so taken with them, that their departure
prompted the men's own regrets, loneliness and longing.

"Ay... It's hard for a man to live in this wilderness," they
sighed and whispered to each other in the dark, cold corners of
the room. "The Commandant's so lucky... And Azia's lucky
too...! Ah, I tell you...!"

The fire in the hearth was now crackling cheerfully, and
roosters started crowing in the pens, calling out the sunrise. The
day dawned slowly. The air was crisp and bright with shimmer-
ing particles of ice, and the thick mounds of snow piled on the
roofs of stables, sheds and barracks, gleamed with a pale pink
glow.

All the air in the flat white space of the parade ground seemed
to fill with the brisk sound of snorting Tartar horses, and the
creak of snow under the boots of the gathering gentry and
dragoons, who were assembling from their sheds and taprooms
to wish a safe journey and Godspeed to Basia and her escort.

At last Volodyovski said:

"It's time!"

Basia jumped up at once and threw herself into her husband's
arms. He pressed his lips to hers and then held her with all his
strength against his chest, and kissed her eyes and forehead and
mouth all over again. They held each other a long time in
silence, too moved to say a word, and missing each other even
before they parted. The moment lasted and lasted, protracted to
infinity in their imaginations, because they loved each with all
their hearts.

Pan Zagloba took his turn in hugging and kissing Basia when
Volodyovski finally let her go, and then the other officers and
enlisted gentry came up one by one to bow over her hand, and
she repeated in her silvery, childlike voice:

"Stay well, gentlemen! Keep well."

Then both she and Evka left for a moment to put on their
lined traveling cloaks, which were slit at the sides in the place of
sleeves, and with the thick, hooded furs laid on top of them in
such profusion that both the women seemed to disappear in a
heap of clothing. The doors were flung wide so that they could
edge out into the freezing air and then the whole gathering
spilled into the courtyard.

The daylight sharpened all around them and the air brightened with the cold white glare of a Winter sun reflecting on the snow. A glittering frost had settled on the thick Winter pelts of the *Lipki* horses, and on the sheepskin jackets of the mounted troopers, so that it seemed as if they were all uniformed in silver and sat on silver horses.

Basia and Ewa slid into the softly padded sleigh while the dragoons and men-at-arms clustered all around and sent out a ringing cheer for good luck on the journey.

This shout sent a cloud of crows and blackbirds hurtling into the sky out of the eaves and crannies of the buildings where they'd taken shelter from the savage Winter and set them wheeling in the pink, dawn-tinted air overhead with their shrill screams and angry, raucous cawing.

The little knight leaned once more into the sleigh and plunged his face into the deep fur hood that hid and shielded his wife's face and features.

It was another long, protracted moment.

Then the Commandant pulled away, stepped back, and made the sign of the cross above Basia and the sleigh.

"Go with God!" he cried.

"In God's name! In good health!" roared the assembled soldiers, and Azia rose suddenly in his stirrups, his face alight with joy and the dawn's red glare.

He signaled sharply with his ridged, short-handled iron battle mace, making his movements so abrupt and violent that his cloak ballooned and spread out in the air behind him like the wings of a dangerous bird of prey, and then he uttered a shrill, ear-splitting, scream: "By the right wheel, forward at a wa-a-alk...! Column, ha-a-arch!"

Snow scrunched and creaked under the horses' hooves. Steam billowed thickly from the snorting nostrils. The leading ranks moved forward at a walk, followed by the next bobbing, shuffling ranks of the point detachment; then the sleigh surged ahead, then came another troop of escorting horsemen, and then the rest of the men and wagons of the convoy wound down the slope towards the open gates within the palisade.

The little knight watched them riding out of the fortifications and scrawled his quick, anxious crosses in the air behind them. And then as the sleigh glimmered for a moment in the arch of the gateway he put his palms beside his mouth and shouted: "Be well, Baska!"

But his only answer came from the shrill pipes and flutes of the departing Tartars and from the vast, skyborne cawing of black birds.

Chapter Forty-eight

A DETACHMENT OF SOME DOZEN horsemen went about a mile ahead of the convoy to clear the trail, warn the local commandants about the arrival of Lady Volodyovska, and make sure that she had good quarters for every halt. The main force of the Tartar Light Horse rode watchfully behind this advance guard, followed in turn by the large sleigh that carried the two young women and a smaller sleigh that contained their maids, with another *Lipki* troop surrounding the baggage wagon and closing off the escort.

Thick banks of snow piled up by the winds made progress difficult. The pine woods, which retained their bushy fronds in Winter, kept the worst of the snow off the trail beneath them, but the leaf-bearing forests that stretched along the Dniester, and consisting for the most part of oak, chestnut and birches, admitted so much snow through their naked branches that the drifts rose halfway up their trunks, packed the narrow gorges, and loomed so high above the travelers that they seemed like tidal waves frozen at convulsion's peak but ready to crash down at any moment and meld with the surrounding whiteness.

The Tartar troopers held the sleighs on ropes during those dangerous descents into the ravines and guided them to safety along the icy slopes, and it was only on the high plateau where the winds smoothed out the polished carapace of snow, that the convoy could make better time, following in the tracks left by Naviragh's earlier caravan.

Hard though the going might have been at times, it wasn't anywhere as bad as it often proved in this broken, thickly wooded country which was full of ravines, sudden streams and

rivers and deep cataracts and canyons, so the travelers were
pleased to think that it would still be daylight when they reached
that cavernous, sheer-cliffed gorge in which Mohilev nested not
too far ahead.

Moreover, it looked as if the good weather would hold
through the day. After a bright, pink dawn, the sun burst redly
into a pale blue sky, and the cliffs and canyons and thickly
padded forests flashed with their own reflected fires. Branches
seemed studded with glittering pinpoint lights. Sparks gleamed
and flickered off the snow so brightly that they hurt the eye.
From the high wooded places that lifted like a tabletop almost
to the tree crowns, the gaze flew across unexpected clearings far
towards Moldavia, carried as freely through those sudden spaces
as if it were cast through an open window, and lost itself in the
sunbathed, bluish-white horizon.

The air was dry and crisp. It was the kind of day when animals
and people share a sense of confidence and wellbeing. The
horses fired off sharp, healthy snorts among the ranks, and the
Tartars sang light-hearted Lithuanian or Ruthenian ballads even
though the frost snapped at their legs so fiercely that they tucked
them constantly under their sheepskin caftans.

★ ★ ★

The sun climbed at last to the top of its celestial arc and the
air warmed slightly. Basia and Evka found themselves too warm
in the sleigh under their robes and furs so they loosened the
wraps around their heads, threw back their hoods, showed their
pink faces and started to peer around. Basia looked eagerly at the
countryside through which they were traveling. Evka looked for
Azia. He was nowhere in sight, riding ahead with the advance
guard which scouted the trail and swept the snow out of the way
whenever necessary. This even troubled Evka and a sullen cloud
settled on her face, but Lady Volodyovska told her not to worry.

"They're all like that," she said to comfort her companion.
"That's what it's like to be married to a soldier. Service first! My
Michal's the same. He won't even look at me when it's time to
take care of military matters. And so it should be, because if
you're going to love a soldier you'd best love a good one."

"But he'll be with us on the halts, won't he?"

"You might see more of him than you want. Did you note

how happy he was when we were setting out? You'd think he was on fire, the way he was glowing."

"I saw that! He was very happy!"

"So just imagine what he'll be like once he has your father's blessings and permission!"

"Dear God!"Evka groaned. "I don't even want to think about what's still ahead! But let God's will be done, even though I'm half dead with fright about my father. What if he starts shouting? What if he gets his back up and refuses? I'll really feel like a fool then, after we've gone back home."

"Hmm," Basia mused. "D'you know what I think?"

"What?"

"There's no playing games with Azia, you know! Your brother could put up a fight against him, he has troops. But your father can't! So what I'm thinking is that if your father gets stubborn about this, Azia will take you anyway."

"What do you mean?"

"He'll just carry you off, that's all! Azia doesn't joke around, you know. He goes after what he wants and gets it no matter what, just like Tuhay-bey... He'll simply seize you, carry you off, and get the first priest he finds to tie the knot. Anywhere else you'd need to post banns, get consent, permissions, and sign a marriage contract, but in this wild country almost everything gets done a bit in the Tartar fashion..."

Evka's face brightened.

"Oh! Oh! That's what I'm worried about!" she cried. "Azia will do anything that pops into his mind. Yes, that's what I'm scared of!"

Basia turned her head, gave the girl a long, careful look, and suddenly burst into a silvery peal of her childlike laughter.

"You're about as scared of that as a mouse is of a slab of bacon," she said. "And don't you try to tell me any different!"

Flushed from the cold, Evka turned an even deeper crimson.

"I'd be afraid of my father's curse,"she said. "And Azia's likely to pay no attention to anything."

"Hope for the best," Basia told her then. "You'll have me to help you as well as your brother. Real love always gets its way. That's something Pan Zagloba told me long before Michal even thought about me."

* * *

Having got going on the subject of their men, the two young
women rattled on at full speed, with Basia talking about her
Michal and Evka about Azia. A few hours passed this way until
the convoy stopped in Yaryshov for their first brief halt. The
little town had never amounted to much, and all that was left of
it after the peasant rising of the 1640's was a single tavern which
had sprung up when the frequent passage of the frontier patrolling detachments promised a sure profit. The two young women
found it occupied by an Armenian trader who was carrying a
load of saffron to Kamyenetz from his home in Mohilev. Azia
wanted to have him tossed out into the weather, along with his
Tartar and Valachian escort, but the women let him stay and
only his people had to move outside.

Finding out that his unexpected company included the wife
of Pan Volodyovski, the trader showered her with effusive
greetings, praising the Hreptyov commandant to the skies, to
which she listened with delight and a great deal of pride. Then
he went to his baggage and returned with a horn-shaped basket
of honeyed dates and sweetmeats along with a box of Turkish
aromatic herbs which were a sure-fire cure for a variety of
illnesses.

"Take this as a token of my gratitude, my lady," he said. "Ah,
it had got to the point around here that none of us could stick
our heads out of the town, what with Azbah-bey and all those
other bandits. But now the trail is safe and we are back in
business. We can travel again! May God increase the days of the
Commandant of Hreptyov, and make each day so long that it
lasts through a journey from Mohilev to Kamyenetz, and may
every hour seem as long as one of those days. Our Mohilev
commandant would rather sit in Warsaw, but your ladyship's
husband watched over all of us so well, and cleaned out the
bandits so completely, that they'd rather die nowadays than
come across the Dniester."

"Does that mean that Pan Revuski isn't at his post in Mohilev?" Basia questioned him.

"He just brought the garrison but I don't know if he spent
three days in the town. Not all our local commandants are like
Pan Volodyovski! Ah, but will your ladyship try this small dark

fruit here? It's what they call a raisin, which is a dried wine grape. And this is a special fruit that comes from far off in Asia and grows on a palm-tree. Even the Turks don't have anything like it in their gardens. No ma'am, Pan Revuski is away in Warsaw and now all the cavalry is gone as well. They rode out suddenly yesterday out towards Bratzlav. And these are dates, may your ladyships enjoy them in good health. All we've left in Mohilev is Pan Gojhenski with the infantry but the cavalry's all gone."

"Why would they leave so suddenly?" Basia turned to Azia. "Isn't that unusual?"

"They probably left to exercise their horses," the young Tartar said. "These are quiet times."

"People in the town are saying that Dorosh is on a sudden rampage," the Armenian said.

Azia laughed.

"And what's he going to use for fodder this time of the year?" he asked and smiled at Basia. "Snow?"

"Pan Gojhenski will inform Your Excellencies much better than I," the merchant agreed.

"I also think that this isn't anything to worry about," Basia said after a moment's thought. "Because my husband would be the first to know if something was wrong."

"There's no doubt about that!" Azia assured her quickly. "Your ladyship doesn't have a thing to fear."

"I?" she said, lifting her proud, bright face towards the Tartar and letting her little nostrils flare with disdain. "Afraid? That's really a good one! Did you hear that, Evka? As if I would be afraid of anything!"

Evka couldn't answer straight away. She was by nature a bit of a glutton, and she had stuffed her mouth full of honeyed dates, and it was only after she gulped them down that she could reply while staring at Azia with the same greedy eyes which she directed at the sweetmeats basket.

"I wouldn't be afraid either," she said, "with such an officer to guard me."

Then she shot him a fond glance, full of hidden promises and meanings, but since all he had for her was a seething anger and a suppressed loathing, made all the deeper since she became an obstacle to his plans, he kept his eyes averted.

"We'll see in Rashkov if I've earned such trust," he said in a
harsh, low voice which sounded almost threatening. But since
both the women knew by this time that this strange, moody son
of Tuhay-bey never did or said things quite like anybody else
they paid no attention. Besides, he started pressing them at once
to get back on the road again because there were steep, rough
hills this side of Mohilev which ought to be crossed in daylight.

★   ★   ★

They set out soon after, riding rapidly as far as those sharp,
forbidding hills clustered around Mohilev, which Basia wanted
to traverse on horseback, but Azia convinced her to keep Evka
company in the sleigh.

The mounted Tartars held the sleigh firmly on their lariats and
lowered it with extreme care down the icy slopes while Azia
walked beside it on foot all the way to the bottom of the steep
escarpment. He said almost nothing to either of the women,
wholly engrossed in their safety and his mission, but the sun set
before they managed to get across the mountains, and the Tartars
of the lead detachment lit blazing bonfires beside the trail that
they cleared ahead.

A Tartar trooper was left beside each of these bonfires to feed
them constantly with brushwood, so that the convoy moved as
if through a crimson corridor of fire with a fierce sheepskinned
warrior crouched beside each blaze. Harsh cliffs and threatening
chasms loomed in the twilight behind these savage figures,
thrown into sharp relief by the light of the fires, giving the
journey a quality of mystery and tension.

All of this added up to novelty and excitement, suggesting
some kind of dangerous and secret expedition, and Basia thought
herself in seventh heaven. She felt immensely grateful to her
husband for allowing her this new experience in a strange and
thrilling country she'd never seen before, and also to Azia for
the skill with which he led the convoy.

It was then that she finally grasped the full, true meaning of
an army column on the march along the frontier, seeing with her
own eyes all those obstacles and dangers she'd heard so much
about from experienced soldiers, and getting a real taste of life
on the trail.

A wild joy seized her as she traveled along those dizzying

heights and precipitous gorges. She'd have insisted on mounting her thoroughbred racer, to be sure, if it weren't for the fact that siting next to Evka in the sleigh she could whisper frightening stories into the girl's ear, so that when the lead detachments disappeared from view and started calling out to each other in the ghostly darkness, Basia would turn to Evka and seize her hands in pretended fear.

"Oho!"she said then. "Did you hear that? It's vampires crying out in the wilderness. Or maybe the Horde!"

But Evka only had to think of Azia, the son of Tuhay-bey, to calm down at once.

"Even the vampires wouldn't trouble him," she'd answer. "Even the Horde would be afraid to touch him."

And then, leaning closer to Basia's ear, she whispered in a voice that trembled with feeling: "I'd go all the way to Belgorod... or to the Crimea... as long as he was there."

Chapter Forty-nine

THE MOON HAD SAILED high into the sky by the time they rode out of the hills, and into the thickly wooded plain, and then they saw a scattering of lights that glittered far below them as if a handful of spangles had been flung into the dark depths of an endless chasm that opened ahead.

"That's Mohilev," a voice said behind the two young women.

They turned around. They hadn't heard Azia's quiet approach but now he stood right behind the sleigh.

"The town lies at the bottom of a canyon, then?" Basia asked.

"It does." Azia leaned forward across the back of the sleigh and thrust his head between theirs. "The hills shelter it completely from the winds. You'll note, my lady, that even the air is different here. It's warmer and quieter. Spring also comes here ten days earlier than on the other side of the hills and the trees bud quicker. Those low grey shrubs you see there on the slopes ahead, they're grapevines, only they're still buried under snow."

Snow lay glittering in the moonlight everywhere they looked but the air was warmer, just as Azia said, and it was quiet and still. More and more lights clustered ahead of them as they made their way to the canyon floor.

"It looks like a fairly decent town," Evka said. "And sizable too."

"That's because the Horde didn't burn it down at the time of the Hmyelnitzki rebellion. Cossack troops wintered in this valley and there had almost never been any Poles living hereabouts."

"Who lives here, then?"

"Mostly Tartars, who have their own small wooden mosque and minaret because anyone can practice any faith he likes in the Commonwealth. And there's a fair bunch of Valachians and Armenians. Also Greeks."

"I saw some Greeks in Kamyenetz," Basia said. "They come from very far away but they always find their way anywhere there's trade."

"The town is also laid out differently than others you might've seen, my lady," Azia said. "Lots of different peoples come here to do business. All kinds of nationalities from many distant places. That settlement we passed a while back on the trail is called Serby and it was built by Serbs."

"And here we are," Basia said, peering eagerly around. "Entering the town."

★ ★ ★

And so they were. A strange acidulous smell of untanned hides and fermentation filled their nostrils right at the outskirts of the town; it was the aroma off manufactured saffron, the main occupation in Mohilev of almost everyone who lived there, especially the Armenians. The town was just as Azia said it would be, different from every other that Basia ever saw anywhere before. The houses seemed to have come straight out of Azia Minor, with arched windows screened by narrow wooden trellises and gratings, or showing no windows at all on the outside walls, while open fires blazed within the enclosed inner courtyards. None of the streets were paved although there was no shortage of stone in the surrounding country. Odd structures, with translucent, latticed walls that seemed to have been made out of a webwork of lace, stood almost everywhere. These, as Azia pointed out, were drying sheds for grapes, used in the manufacture of raisins. The rich smell of saffron hovered over the entire town.

Pan Gojhenski, the commander of the infantry detachment, had been warned by Azia's point-guard that the Hreptyov commandant's lady was on her way, and he rode out to meet her at the entrance to the town. He proved to be a middle-aged, stammering man who lisped when he spoke because he had once been shot through both cheeks by a Turkish janissary, so that when he launched into his slurred and stuttering speech of welcome, going on and on about *'the star which rose so brightly above the skies of Mohilev,'* Basia almost choked on her stifled laughter.

But he received her with all the hospitality he could provide at such short notice. A supper waited for her in the fort, along with a superbly comfortable bed, soft goosedown pillows and fresh, clean quilts requisitioned from the richest Armenians in the town. Moreover, while Pan Gojhenski may have had trouble with his diction, what he had to say over the supper table was so interesting that he was worth hearing.

A strange, restless wind had blown up suddenly and unexpectedly out of the Steppe, according to his story, and the powerful *tchambul* of the Crimean Horde which supported Doroshenko's Cossacks had stirred without warning and moved swiftly into Commonwealth territory near Haysin in the Uman region, with several thousand of the Cossackry riding along beside it. There were other unseasonable and alarming stirrings reported in other quarters but Pan Gojhenski didn't attach a great deal of importance to them.

"And that's because it's Winter," he explained, "and Tartars have never moved in the wintertime since God created the earth and put people on it. They don't use wagon trains, you see, and carry only what they can tie behind their saddles, so they can't bring fodder for their horses which they feed off the land. We all know that only the ice and snow hold the full might of the Turks at bay right now, and that we'll have visitors here just as soon as the Spring thaw brings us the new grasses, but I don't believe that anything can happen until then."

All this took a very long time to say, with Pan Gojhenski stumbling on every consonant, and Basia waited patiently until he was done.

"What do you see then, sir, in that sudden stirring of the Horde towards Haysin?" she asked.

"I'd say that their horses must've dug up all the grass from under the snow in their present area, so they want to pitch their camp in some other place. It could also be that camped as near as they are to Doroshenko's people they're at odds with them. It's always been like that when Tartars serve with Cossacks. I mean they're supposed to be allies and all that but there's never any love lost between them. Let them just pitch their camps near each other and they start fighting in the pastures straight away."

"That's what it has to be this time as well," said Azia.

"What's more," went on Pan Gojhenski, "all these reports didn't come from our own patrols, but from passing drovers and the local Tartars hereabouts who started babbling about it straight out of the blue. It's only three days ago that Pan Yakubovitch brought in some prisoners to question and our cavalry moved out right away."

"So all you have here, sir, is your infantry?" Azia asked.

"And a pitiful little bunch they are too!" Pan Gojhenski said. "Forty men! Barely enough for a proper guard-mount. I'd have trouble defending the fort if just our local Tartars here in Mohilev got it into their heads to start some sort of trouble."

"But they won't, will they?" Basia asked.

"They've no reason to. Most of them have been living in the Commonwealth a long time, with their wives and children, and those that came in from outside are here for trade not war. They're good, decent people"

"I'll leave you a troop of fifty of my *Lipki,*" Azia offered.

"God bless you, sir!" The stuttering old commander seemed vastly relieved. "That'll help a lot. I'll have horsemen to send for news to our cavalry. But can you spare a troop?"

"Surely. There'll be new men coming into Rashkov anyway, all the companies of those Tartar captains who'd gone over to the Sultan and now want to come back to the service of the Commonwealth. Krytchinski will come at once with at least three hundred, and maybe Adurovitch with two hundred more, while the rest come later. I'm to take command of them all by the Hetman's orders, and we'll have a whole division gathered there by Spring."

★ ★ ★

Hearing this, Pan Gojhenski bowed to Azia with formal respect. He'd known him a long time but didn't pay much attention to him since the young Tartar's unknown origins and doubtful antecedents made him an inferior to the serving gentry. But now he knew him to be the son of Tuhay-bey, having heard about that from Naviragh's caravan which passed through Mohilev a week or two earlier, so he felt duty-bound to honor his

distinguished lineage even though it was the blood of a bitter
enemy. Moreover, he was pleased to honor a fellow-officer to
whom the Hetman had entrusted such an important mission and
command.

Azia went outside to issue orders to his troop commanders,
summoned the *Setnik* David Aleksandrovitch, and gave him his
instructions.

"David, son of Iskander," he said. "You'll stay here with fifty
men, and you'll watch and listen for everything around you."

"I hear and obey, Great Lord."

"If the Little Falcon sends any messages after me from Hreptyov, you'll intercept the courier, take the writings from him,
and send them on to me by one of our own people. You'll stay
here with your troop until you hear from me. Then, if my man
tells you that it's *nighttime*, you'll ride out quietly and join me
wherever I am. But if he tells you that *'the dawn is coming'* you'll
storm the fort, set fire to the town, cross over to Moldavia and
then go wherever you are told to go by whoever tells you. Is
that clear, then?"

"You have spoken, Lord!" David said. "I will watch with my
eyes and listen with my ears. I will stop all couriers from the
Little Falcon, take their writings from them, and send them on
to you by one of my own men. I'll stay here until I get your
orders. Then, if your messenger tells me it is night I will ride out
quietly. If he says that the dawn is coming I will raze the town,
cross over to the Moldavian side, and go where they tell me."

★   ★   ★

Next morning the convoy set out again, smaller by fifty men
of the *Lipki* escort. Pan Gojhenski accompanied Basia all the way
to the far end of the Mohilev valley. There he stammered out
his farewell oration, and turned back to the town, while the rest
of them hurried towards Yampol. Azia was so unusually merry
and drove his men and horses with such urgency that even Basia
was surprised about it.

"Why are you in such a hurry?" she asked him.

"Everyone hurries to his happiness," he answered. "And mine
begins in Rashkov."

Evka took this as applying to herself, smiled at him fondly,
and murmured: "Only my father might stand in the way..."

"Pan Novovyeyski won't get in anybody's way," the Tartar shot back, and a dark, cruel spasm flashed across his face.

They found almost no troops of any kind in Yampol which was little more than a huddle of huts and recently rebuilt dwellings thrown around the old scorched ruins of the little castle. There'd never been any infantry stationed here, and the cavalry had all gone out as in Mohilev, so there was only a handful of men left on guard in the tumbled fort.

The beds had been prepared for the traveling women but Basia slept badly. She was uneasy about the threatening news that came from the Steppe. She was particularly troubled that the little knight would worry about her if it turned out that Doroshenko's auxiliary contingent of Tartars was really on the move. Her one consoling thought was that this might prove just another rumor.

She wondered if she shouldn't take an escort from Azia's small command and return to Hreptyov but there were two reasons why she couldn't do that. First, Azia was under orders to reinforce the Rashkov garrison so he'd be unable to spare more than a few dozen men, especially since he'd already detached a troop in Mohilev; in the event of any real danger such a small escort would be worse than useless. Finally, they were already two thirds of the way to Rashkov which always housed a powerful garrison, along with an officer she knew very well, and which would be further reinforced by Azia's contingent and the companies of the returning captains. Considering all that she decided to go on with her journey.

But sleep eluded her.

She was uneasy for the first time since they'd set out from Hreptyov, as if some unknown danger were hovering above her. Yampol itself might have contributed to her sleeplessness because it was a place of blood and horror which she knew about from the tales told by her husband and by Pan Zagloba. It was here that the main force of the Podolian rebels, led by the fearsome Burlay, had made their war camp in the years of Hmyelnitzki's terrible insurrection. It was here that prisoners were brought for sale to the eastern slavers or to be murdered after gruesome tortures. And, finally, it was here that Pan Stanislav Lantzkoronski, the *Voyevode* of Bratzlav, launched a frightful slaughter in the spring of 1651, falling upon the town in the midst of a crowded market day, burned the whole place, and perpetrated a horrifying massacre that lived-on in the memories of the Dniester region. It seemed to her that the smell of blood still hovered over the entire settlement. The black, scorched scars of the devastation still lingered among the ruins; and the pale, ghostly faces of slaughtered Poles and Cossacks still seemed to peer off the walls of the ruined castle.

Basia was brave but her courageous heart quailed at the thought of ghosts, and the old stories told that bitter moans and weeping echoed at midnight in the dank, dark gorges of the nearby Dniester, in Yampol itself, and at the confluence of the Dniester and the Shumilovka rivers where the waters ran red in the moonlight as if stained with blood.

Such thoughts filled Basia with distress and dread. She lay awake for most of the night, listening despite herself for the ghostly weeping and the groans of the unburied dead in all the rustling night-sounds that came from the river, but all she heard was the drawn-out *'All's well'* of the watching sentries. This brought to mind the peaceful and secure walls of Hreptyov, her husband, Pan Zagloba, and the friendly faces of Mushalski, Motovidlo, Nenashinyetz, Snitko and the others. But rather than soothing or consoling her, they merely reminded her that she was very far away from them, alone in strange country, and she was seized by such an overwhelming longing to be back in Hreptyov that hot tears welled in her sleepless eyes.

It was already near dawn when she finally closed her eyes and slept but even then her dreams haunted her with strange and troubling visions. Burlay, the murderous rebels, Tartars and the bloody images of slaughter flowed across her eyes, along with Azia Tuhaybeyovitch whose dark face loomed time and again out of these nightmare flashes of massacre and bloodshed. But it was a strange sort of Azia she'd never seen before: as if he were in part a wild, fierce Cossack, in part a savage Tartar, and in part the terrible Tuhay-bey himself.

⋆ ⋆ ⋆

She rose early, glad that the night and its frightful visions were over.

She decided to ride the rest of the way on horseback so that she might get some exercise and also to give privacy to Evka and

her Tartar. Rashkov was drawing near, she thought, and so was
the threatening image of old Pan Novovyeyski, and the two
young lovers needed to decide how to confront him with their
news and get his consent.

Azia held her stirrup for her with his own hands but didn't
get into the sleigh with Evka. At first he rode out again to his
former place at the head of the column and then dropped back
to keep close to Basia.

She also noticed straight away that they were riding with a
smaller troop than they'd brought to Yampol and asked him
about that.

"I see, sir, that you left another detachment in Yampol," she
said.

"Fifty men," he answered. "As in Mohilev."

"And why's that?"

His smile was a strange one. His lips curled upward in a
sudden spasm like a snarling dog's, baring his sharp white teeth,
and it was only after a moment that he said: "Because I want
those posts held by my own men and assure your ladyship's safe
return."

"The posts will be strong enough once the cavalry comes back
from the Steppe."

"The cavalry won't come back all that soon."

"And how do you know that?"

"Because they must find out what Doroshenko's up to and
that'll take them a good four weeks or more."

"Hmm. If that's so, sir, then you did well to leave some men
behind."

They rode in silence for a while after that. Azia kept glancing
at Basia's pink face, half-hidden though it was by her raised
cloak collar and her sable cap, and each time he looked at her he
half closed his own narrowed eyes as if wanting to fix her
fetching image in his memory for ever.

At last she said:

"You ought to have a talk with Evka, sir. In fact it's very
strange how little you do talk to her and she is getting quite
upset about it. It won't be long before the two of you stand
before Pan Novovyeyski. I'm uneasy about that myself. You
really should decide how the two of you are going to broach the
subject, don't you think?"

"I'd rather first talk to your ladyship," Azia answered in an odd, strained voice.

"Then why don't you do it?"

"Because I'm expecting a courier from Rashkov. I thought I'd find him waiting for me in Yampol but he wasn't there. I'm looking for him any minute now."

"What does a courier have to do with a conversation between you and me?"

"I think that's him up ahead!" the young Tartar said avoiding an answer, and spurred forward to the head of the column, but he was back alone a few moments later. "No! That wasn't him!" he said.

There was such a feverish air of anxiety in his voice, his glances, his words and his whole posture, that it began to infect Basia as well. But she did not suspect him even for a minute. His excitement found an easy explanation in the nearness of Rashkov and Evka's fierce father, and yet Basia began to feel as chilled and uneasy as if her own life and fate were unaccountably in danger.

★ ★ ★

She drew closer to the sleigh and rode for a few hours next to Ewa, talking with her about Rashkov, both the Novovyeyskis, Zosia Boska and, at last, about the countryside around them which became an even grimmer and more savage wilderness as they rode deeper into it. The wilderness began in its full and proper sense right after Hreptyov, but there at least would be a column or two of smoke lifting into the air above the horizon, showing the presence of some distant settlement or dwelling. Here there were no traces of human habitation, and if Basia didn't know that she was on her way to Rashkov, which was inhabited by several hundred people and where a strong Polish garrison stood guard, she would have thought herself carried off into unknown deserts, and into foreign countries at the edge of the world.

Peering around her, she reined-in her horse without being quite aware of what she was doing, so that she was soon riding at some distance behind the sleigh, the convoy and the escort. Azia dropped back to join her after a little while, and since he knew this southern edge of the Steppes quite well, he pointed out and named various landmark features.

But this didn't last long because the countryside began to vanish under a thick white mist. Winter didn't grip the land as fiercely in these southern reaches as it did in the thickly wooded country around Hreptyov. There were thin sheets of snow spread in the ravines, in the cracked, dried-out river beds, on the north slopes of hillocks and escarpments and along the edges of the scattered rockfall, but most of the earth hereabouts was free of its Winter covering, and showed dark clumps of vegetation everywhere around, and gleamed yellowly with splashes of wet, wilted grass.

These patches of moist grassland now exuded a light, steamy mist that hovered close to the hidden soil, making it seem as if some broad waters spilled to the horizons, filling the invisible gullies and ravines, and covering all of the open landscape. These mists rose and lifted higher by the minute, drifting skyward and blotting out the sunlight, so that the crisp, bright day became grey and gloomy.

"There'll be rain tomorrow," Azia said.

"Just as long as it stays dry today. How far is it from here to Rashkov?"

The son of Tuhay-bey peered into the lunar landscape through which they were passing, almost invisible in the clouds of mist.

"It's closer to Rashkov now," he said, "then back towards Yampol."

And he sighed deeply with relief and with satisfaction as if a great weight had fallen from his chest.

★ ★ ★

In that instant they both heard the muffled drumming of a horse's hooves, and the dim figure of a hurrying horseman showed like a ghostly apparition in the mists ahead, coming towards them from the south and the direction of the hidden convoy which moved invisibly before them.

"That's Halim! I recognize him!" Azia cried.

It was, indeed, the old Dobrudjan *murjah* who galloped up to Basia and Tuhaybeyovitch, leaped out of his saddle, and started

to beat his forehead in oriental homage against the young Tartar's stirrup.

"You come from Rashkov?" his master demanded.

"From Rashkov, my lord!" said Halim.

"What's the word from there?"

The old man raised his ugly, worn face towards Basia, as if to
ask if he could speak openly before her, but Tuhaybeyovitch said
at once: "Speak freely! Has the garrison ridden out?"

"It has, Great Lord. There's just a handful left."

"Who took out the column?"

"Young Pan Novovyeyski."

"The Piotrovitch party's gone to the Crimea?"

"Long ago, Great Lord. Only the two women stayed behind
and old Pan Novovyeyski with them."

"Where's Krytchinski?"

"Across the river, lord. He's ready and waiting."

"Who's with him?"

"Adurovitch, lord, with his whole command. They both kiss
your stirrups, son of Tuhay-bey, and place themselves in your
hands along with all their people. They and all the other captains
who haven't yet had the time to get there."

"Very well!" Azia said, with fire in his eyes. "Fly like a bird to
Krytchinski and tell him and the rest to occupy Rashkov."

"Your will is theirs, Great Lord!"

In the next instant Halim leaped back into his saddle and
vanished in the mists just as he had come, gone in a moment like
an apparition.

A terrible light seemed to shine from Azia's darkened face.
The moment he had waited for had come, the time of decision
that would determine his happiness and his life hereafter, but
some moments passed before he could speak. His heart was
hammering so rapidly in his chest that he could hardly breathe.
He rode in silence beside Basia for a while longer until he was
sure that his voice wouldn't fail him, and then he turned his
gleaming eyes on her in an unfathomable stare.

"Now is my time to talk frankly with your ladyship," he said.

"Speak," Basia said. "I'm listening."

And she peered sharply into his altered features as if to read
the secrets they contained.

Chapter Fifty

AZIA EDGED HIS HORSE so close to Basia's that their stirrups almost touched each other and went on riding in silence for a few more paces. He used that time to get a tight grip on his sense of triumph, wondering why it took him such an effort to calm down, since Basia was in his grasp and there was no human power left on earth that could take her from him.

It wouldn't occur to him that this desired woman might want him as he wanted her. That lay against all likelihood and probability. But some dim spark of hope glimmered in his soul, remote though it was, and his need for her was so overwhelming that it shook him like a spasm of fever. He had no illusions that she'd open her arms to him, or throw herself into his own. He'd never hear her say '*Azia, I'm yours,*' nor would she ever cling to his hungry lips, as he had dreamed so often. But how will she take his words? What will she say in turn? Will she lose all feeling like a dove in the talons of a bird of prey, and lie limp and fainting in his hands just like a helpless pigeon in the grasp of a hawk? Will she beg him tearfully for mercy or fill the wilderness with her screams of terror? Will all this add to his sense of triumph and possession or will it rob him of some of his victory?

Such questions created a whirlwind of doubt and hesitation in the Tartar's mind. The time had finally come to stop his pretending, to shed all his simulated respect and loyalties, and to show her his terrible, true face. Hence the sudden fear! Hence the gnawing worry! A moment more and everything he wanted would begin to happen!

At last, however, these tremors of the soul began to change into another feeling. Rage seized him, in just the way that a wild beast's fear turns into murderous fury, and he found himself even more excited and feeding on his frenzy.

'She's mine whatever happens!' he thought. *'Mine in body to do with what I want. And I'll have her today, and more of her tomorrow, and then there'll be no going back to her husband for her. She'll go where I take her. She'll have no other choice.'*

A wild joy gripped him at this thought and his own voice sounded to him as new as a stranger's when he finally turned to her and spoke.

"Your ladyship didn't know me up till now," he said.

"Your voice sounds so different in these mists," Basia said uneasily, "that you really seem like someone I don't know."

"There are no Polish troops in Mohilev," he grated out, biting his lips and quivering with passion. "None in Yampol... None in Rashkov! I'm the master here! Krytchinski, Adurovitch and the rest of them are mine body and soul... They're my slaves to do with as I want because I'm the son of a prince. I'm their only ruler! I'm their Vizier, their highest *murjah*, their supreme commander, like Tuhay-bey was a ruler and commander. I'm their Khan! I alone have the strength and the will. Mine is the power here...!"

"Why are you saying this?" Basia asked, surprised.

"I'm saying your ladyship didn't know me until now. Well, Rashkov is near and you'll know me there. I wanted to be the Hetman of all the Polish Tartars and to serve the Commonwealth, but Pan Sobieski wouldn't let me do it. Well, I'm not going to be just a *Lipki* rider anymore, I won't serve under others or take orders from anybody else! I'll be my own commander, leading great *tchambuls* against Doroshenko or the Commonwealth, it's all one to me. I'll go against one or the other, whichever you want, whichever you order...!"

"Whichever I order?" Basia cried, shaken and astonished. "Azia, what's happened to you?"

"What's happened is that everybody serves me here and I serve you! Who cares about the Hetman? What's the difference if he agrees or not? Give me the word, my lady, and I'll throw the Crimea at your feet! I'll give you Ackerman... Dobrudja... And all the Hordes that live below the Dniester, and those camped in the Wild Lands, and those in Winter quarters everywhere around here will be your servants like I am your servant! Order me, and I'll turn on the Khan and I'll fight the Sultan! I'll help the Commonwealth and create a new Horde in these territories, and I'll be its Khan, and you'll be the only supreme ruler over me! Say the word and you'll be a queen, and I'll bow down before you alone, begging your grace and mercy!"

And suddenly he leaned and reached out of his saddle and seized the terrified and stunned young woman by the waist and shoulders.

"Couldn't you see that you're the only one I love?" he hissed out in a thick, grating voice. "Ay, how I suffered! And I'll have you anyway, one way or the other! You're mine now, and you'll stay mine no matter what happens! No one will tear you out of my grasp! No one! You are mine!"

"Jezus Maria!" Basia cried.

★ ★ ★

Her terror lasted only a fraction of a moment. He crushed her in his arms as if he wished to strangle her. His ragged breath beat against her face. His eyes were glassy and his stare unfocused. At last he dragged her off her horse and pulled her to the pommel of his saddle before him, crushing her breasts against his chest and seeking her lips with his thick, bluish mouth.

She made no sound after her first, shocked cry, but she started struggling against him with unexpected strength. They fought in grim silence, interrupted only by their rasping breath. The violence of their movements and the nearness of his face to hers galvanized her repugnance and resistance.

She experienced a moment akin to clairvoyance, sharpening all her senses and perceptions in the same way that a drowning person grasps every facet of his or her existence, and suddenly everything was clear. The ground had split apart under her feet, a vast well had burst open beneath her, and he was dragging her down into it at all cost. She saw his passion in all its dreadful forms; she understood all his duplicity and treason and, at the same time, all of her own helplessness and the full horror of her fate. She was afraid, yes; she knew that no one would be able to save her, and she was almost overwhelmed at first by hopelessness and pity for herself. But, in that same instant, she felt the

hot, bitter rush of a measureless indignation and immense resentment, and her determination turned into furious anger.

There was so much courage in this child of a long line of
warriors, and in this chosen wife of the Commonwealth's bravest knight, that her first thought was: *'he'll pay dearly for this!'*
And only then did she think: *'It's all up to me! I must save myself!'*

All of her mind focused upon this task just like an iron bow
bends to propel its arrow, and her clarity of vision became almost
a miracle of lucidity. In all their struggling and clawing at each
other, her hands searched him for weapons she might use, and
finally found the thick bone handle of an oriental pistol in his
sash. But at the same time she was aware enough to realize that
even if the pistol was primed and fully loaded, and even if she
had the time to cock it, twist her hand and press the barrel up
against his head, he'd be sure to catch her wrist and tear this last
means of salvation from her fist, so she decided on a different
stroke.

All of this took no longer than a blink of an eye. He guessed
at once what she intended to use to defend herself, and reached
out for her wrist with the speed of lightning. But he failed to
calculate her unexpected stroke, and their hands passed each
other in the air as Basia struck him right between the eyes with
the hard, bone handle of the pistol, putting all of her desperate,
young strength behind the blow.

The blow was so frightful that Azia couldn't even cry out as
he toppled backwards off his horse, pulling her to the ground
behind him.

Basia jumped to her feet at once, leaped back on her horse,
and shot off like an arrow carried by the wind away from the
Dniester and towards the Steppe.

The mists closed behind her. Basia's thoroughbred flattened
his ears back along his head and hurled himself into a pell-mell
run among the rocks, cliffs, boulders, crevices and ravines. One
false leap could send the animal hurtling at any moment into
some crevasse. Each pounding step could smash it and its rider
against some razor-sharp projection of limestone and granite.

But Basia paid no attention to these hazards; her peril lay in
Azia and his *Lipki* Tartars. And, strange to say, now that she'd
freed herself from his savage hands, now that he lay most likely
dead back there among the rocks, fear overwhelmed all her

other feelings. Azia terrified her much more now, as she leaned forward across her horse's neck with her face hidden in the flying mane, and fled like a doe pursued by a pack of wolves, than he did when she was struggling in his grasp. It was only now that she gave way to panic, tasted the full measure of her helplessness, and felt the lonely terror of a lost and abandoned child. Some strange, tearful voices came to life within her and started their plaintive cries for help amid the sobs and whimpers of a child's complaint.

"Help me, Michal! Save me...!"

Throughout all this, her brave horse galloped on and on, carried by some miraculous instinct across the sudden clefts that yawned under his hooves, swerving around the sharp rocky overhangs and protrusions and leaping over gorges, until the stone and shale ceased their ringing clatter underhoof. She sensed then that he must have broken out into one of those long stretches of soft pasture land that ran among the canyons and arroyos in the Steppe.

Sweat sheeted him. His breath began to rasp. But he ran on and on.

'Where should we run to?' Basia asked herself and supplied her own immediate answer: *'To Hreptyov!'*

But a new terror squeezed her heart at the thought of the vast distances that stretched across that terrifying wilderness between her and her goal. Memory rang with warning. Azia had left *Lipki* companies in Mohilev and Yampol. All were loyal to him and sure to be a part of his conspiracy. They'd seize her at once and carry her to Rashkov. She had to plunge deep into the Steppe and turn north for Hreptyov only after all the Dniester settlements were left far behind.

It was all the more important to risk that desperate gambit because if there was any pursuit sent after her it would be almost sure to run along the Dniester, while out in the Steppe, in those endless spaces, she might run into one of the returning Polish frontier forces.

The headlong rush continued but the horse's hoofbeats were starting to falter. Basia was an experienced rider and she knew at once that the animal would fall unless he got some rest, while her own instincts told her that if she were left alone and on foot in the wilderness she'd never come out of it alive.

She eased the straining animal into a trot and brought it gradually to a gentle walk. The mists were dwindling but a hot, steaming cloud rose from the horse's shuddering flanks.

Basia began to pray.

And suddenly the brief, sharp neighing of another horse rang out in the receding mists behind her. Her short, tumbled hair rose on her head in terror.

'*Mine will fall,*' she thought desperately. '*But so will theirs.*'

And she spurred her horse into another gallop.

★　★　★

The horse ran for a time with the desperate speed of a pigeon fleeing from a falcon, running long and hard almost to the last of its strength, but that distant neighing went on sounding at its back. There was something both threatening and plaintive in that animal call across the mists. But it occurred to Basia after that first onrush of instinctive fear, that if there was a rider on that horse behind her, he'd keep it from neighing so as to keep her unaware of pursuit.

'*It must be Azia's animal running after mine,*' she thought at last. '*It can't be anything else.*'

Just to be on the safe side, she pulled both her pistols out of the saddle holsters but the precaution proved unnecessary. A moment later some dark, moving shape loomed among the wisps of shredded mist that billowed to the sky behind her, and Azia's animal came bounding towards her, showing his own flared nostrils and a windblown mane.

"Here boy, here!" she called out.

The Tartar warhorse caught sight of her gelding, came on in a skipping sideways prance, and uttered a shrill neigh of greeting to which Basia's animal replied at once. Trained to the touch of a human hand he let Basia catch his bridle and she raised her eyes gratefully to heaven.

"God's mercy!" she said.

The capture of Azia's horse was truly providential.

First of all, the two best horses in the *Lipki* company were now in her possession. She'd acquired a remount. She also knew that no one would come riding after her for some time. If Azia's horse had gone running after the rest of the detachment, the *Lipki* would have turned back at once to look for their leader.

This way, it wouldn't even occur to them that something could be wrong, and if they launched a search or pursuit it would be long after she had vanished in the Steppe.

Here she recalled once more that Azia's troops were now encamped in Mohilev and Yampol.

"I have to circle far into the Steppe," she told herself grimly, "and not come near the river until I'm close to Hreptyov. That terrible man set his traps with real cunning but God will save me from them!"

That thought helped to raise her spirits and she began to make her preparations for the rest of her journey. Slung beside Azia's saddle she found a musket, a powder horn and a bag of shot, along with a satchel full of hemp seeds which the Tartar chewed almost all the time. As she shortened the stirrup straps to suit herself, Basia thought that she'd feed herself like a bird through her long flight home, and moved the seed-bag to her own saddle horn.

She decided to bypass homesteads or people she might come across because any men found in this wilderness were likely to be evil and a decent human being was a rarity. Her heart quaked at the thought that she might run out of fodder for the horses. They'd dig out their own grass from under the snow, and snip at the moss in the rocky crevices along the way, but what if they should fall out of poor nourishment and sheer exhaustion. And, after all, there was no way she could rest them for any length of time and still keep on running.

Her other fear was that she might lose her way in the wilderness. The trail was easy to follow along the course of the Dniester, but that was the one road she had to avoid. What would happen when she rode into the vast, trackless spaces and dense gloomy forests in the north? How could she plot her course if she were unable to see the sun on a gloomy day or the stars at night? She was less concerned about the wild animals that swarmed through the timberlands further along the way. She was armed and brave. True, wolf packs could be dangerous. But she was more concerned about the two-legged beasts she might encounter in the hostile wilderness.

"Ha!" she told herself aloud, resolute and determined. "God will guide my way and allow me to come back to Michal."

She made a sign of the cross, dried the chilling dew off her face with the sleeve of her coat, let her sharp, bright eyes sweep once more through the grim landscape that spread all around her, and set her horses at a gallop to the north.

Chapter Fifty-one

NO ONE THOUGHT to look for Azia, so he lay unconscious in the wilderness until he regained his senses on his own. He sat up, trying to understand what had happened to him, and started peering about in bewilderment. But it seemed to him at first that he was looking out through a reddish twilight, and seeing with only one eye. The other was either knocked out altogether or so caked with blood that he saw nothing through it.

He raised his hands to his face. His fingers brushed against bloody icicles that clung to his mustache. His mouth was full of blood. Choking and gagging, he spat it out and felt a shard of agonizing pain lancing through his head each time that he did it. He groped upward beyond his mustache, probing gingerly along the bones of both cheeks, and jerked his hands away with a moan of pain.

Basia's blow had crushed the bridge of his nose and fractured his cheekbone.

He sat through another while, as still as a stone. Then he began to search the countryside with the one eye that managed to admit some light, and he found some snow crushed in a rocky crevice. He crawled over to it, clutched it with both hands, and pressed it against his ruined face.

This brought him some relief. He pressed fresh handfuls of snow against his upper face as it melted and ran in pink streams down into his mustache, and clutched at more of it, and then began to eat it greedily. This eased his pain even more. After a while that leaden weight that seemed to crush his head in an iron vise eased off enough for him to remember everything that happened. But at first he felt neither rage, nor fury, nor despair. A purely physical agony deadened all his senses and left him with only one wish: to be quickly rescued.

He gulped down a few more handfuls of snow and started looking for his horse, but the animal was gone. He realized then that if he didn't want to wait for his men to come looking for him in this wilderness, he'd have to go after them on foot. He tried to lever himself to his feet, using both hands in the attempt, but all he managed to achieve was another bout of excruciating pain that tore an animal howl out of him.

Rocked back to ground, he sat still for perhaps another hour and then tried again. This time he managed to stagger up, long enough to put his back against a slab of rock, and stayed on his feet. But when he thought that he'd have to step away from the supporting stone, and then to start walking, he fell into such helplessness and panic that he almost allowed himself to slide down to the ground again.

However, he mastered his fear and despair. Each movement was sheer agony but he managed to draw his saber and, using it for a crutch, took his first step forward. It worked. After a few more steps he realized that his legs and body were as strong as ever, and that he could use them perfectly; it was only his head that seemed to belong to somebody else, swaying with each step loosely on his neck like an enormous weight, wagging to left and right and then back and forward. He felt as if he had to carry this wobbly, unfamiliar object with extraordinary care or it would fall and smash itself against the rocky shale underfoot. At times, this weighted head turned him completely around as if it meant to have him walking in a circle. At other times consciousness ebbed, and darkness filled his one remaining eye, and then he waited, propped on his saber with both hands.

But the vertigo began to pass gradually, the world settled down and steadied around him while the pain increased, boring into his forehead, into his eyes, and into his whole face as if he were being tortured with a red-hot drill, so that a series of thin, plaintive whimpers bubbled out of Azia.

These moans and whimpers echoed among the cliffs, and so he staggered on through that savage wilderness, more like a bloody and disfigured apparition from beyond the grave than a human being.

Twilight had come before he heard the clatter of hoofbeats before him and recognized one of his *Lipki* squad leaders riding back for orders. He had just enough strength left that night to order a pursuit, but right after that he toppled onto a pile of hides, and lay there for three days, dead to the world and seeing no one other than a Greek barber surgeon and the faithful Halim who nursed him and never left his side.

★ ★ ★

It took him four days before he could speak again and to become aware of everything around him.

He remembered everything that happened up to the moment of Basia's escape and, at once, his fevered thoughts darted after her. He saw her galloping across the cliffs and the wilderness, like a bird that was flying away from him for ever. He saw her reaching Hreptyov, safe in her husband's arms, and this sight racked him with a far more violent pain than any physical injury he'd suffered, and along with the pain came a terrible regret and an overwhelming shame at having been thwarted and defeated.

"She got away! She got away!" he mouthed constantly, and such a dreadful rage choked him at this memory that he'd almost lose his consciousness again.

"Death to them all!" he snarled at Halim who tried to calm him down and to assure him that Basia couldn't get away from the pursuing *Lipki*, and he kicked and clawed at the furs and hides with which the old Tartar tried to cover him, and he lashed out at Halim and the Greek with his knife, and howled like a wild animal, and tried to leap up and go running after her so that he might catch her, seize her and then strangle her with his own hands out of savage passion and overwhelming fury.

Sometimes he babbled in his fever, ordering Halim to bring him the head of the little knight at once, and to lock his bound wife in the adjoining room. Sometimes he talked to her, begged her and threatened her in turn, and stretched out his arms to her, and at last he fell asleep and slept through a night and a day. But after he awoke, his fever was quite gone and he could talk with Krytchinski and Adurovitch who had been waiting anxiously to see him because they didn't know what to do.

They were in Rashkov, allowed to enter the frontier town under the ruse of their return to the service of the Common-

wealth, as Azia had arranged. Pan Rushtchitz was gone, tracking
down a reported band of Tartars or marauders out towards
Bratzlav in the Steppe. The regiments that had gone out under
young Adam Novovyeyski weren't expected back for two more
weeks but some unforeseen event might bring them back
quicker and the two Tartar captains had to know how to react
to them. Neither of them was serious about coming back to the
Commonwealth but it was Azia who directed this whole operation. Only he could tell them exactly what to do and which side
promised better profits. They wanted to be told if they were to
go back at once to the Sultan's country or to keep on pretending
that they had come back to their old allegiance. And if so, how
much longer were they to pretend?

Both of them knew that Azia planned to switch sides in any
event, but they assumed he'd order them to conceal their treach-
ery until the outbreak of the war, so that their betrayal would be
all the more effective. What he told them might come as a
suggestion because he was far younger than any of the renegades
but it would be as good as a binding order because he'd thrust
himself upon them as their leader and they accepted him will-
ingly as such. He was, after all, the head of the entire enterprise.
He had planned it all. He was the most astute and cunning man
among them who had the most far-reaching and influential
connections on both sides. Moreover, he was the son of Tuhay-
bey, whose name would live for ever among all the Hordes.

They hurried eagerly to his bedside as soon as he could see
them and made their obeisance, waiting to hear what he might
have to say.

★ ★ ★

He received him with his head swathed in bandages, still too
weak to rise and with one eye gone, but wholly recovered
otherwise and in complete command.

"I'm ill," he told them right from the beginning, since they
were sure to know the whole story anyway. "The woman that I
wanted to seize and keep for myself got away from me, wound-
ing me with a pistol in the struggle, as you see. She was the wife
of Commandant Volodyovski... may the plague consume him
and all his kind!"

"Let it be as you said!" the two captains chorused.

"May God give you both the luck of the faithful," he replied. "And to you, Great Lord!"

After which they settled down to business, talking about what they ought to do.

"There's no time to waste," Azia told them. "Nor can we put off the Sultan's service until the start of the war. After what's happened with that woman they won't trust us here and they'll charge us, sword in hand, as soon as they hear about it. But we'll strike first, take the town and burn it, so that the fires may please the eyes of God and add to His glory! That handful of soldiers they've got here just now will be our first captives, as will all those inhabitants who are subjects of the Commonwealth, and whatever belongs to the Valachians, the Greeks and the Armenians will become our loot. And then we'll cross the Dniester into the Sultan's country."

Greed glittered in the eyes of the renegades. Krytchinski and Adurovitch had been a long time among the Dobrudjans, raiding and pillaging with the fiercest of all the Tartar Hordes, and they had become as savage and bloodthirsty as the worst of them.

"Thanks to you, lord," Krytchinski said, "they let us into this town, and now God puts it in our hands!"

"Novovyeyski didn't oppose your coming?" Azia questioned.

"Novovyeyski knew that we were coming over to the Commonwealth, and that you were coming to join up with us, so he took us for a friendly force, just as he takes you."

"We were camped on the Moldavian side," Adurovitch added, "but we'd come visiting with him here, both me and Krytchinski, and he received us like any other gentry. *'What you're doing now,'* he said, *'erases your past sin. And if the Hetman forgives you on Azia's guarantee then who am I to cock an eyebrow at you?'* He even wanted us to come over and move into the town but we said we wouldn't until you brought us the Hetman's permission. Even so, when he was riding out he gave us a banquet and asked us to watch over the town."

"At this banquet," Krytchinski threw in, "we saw his father, the old woman who's waiting for her husband, and that girl that Novovyeyski has a mind to marry."

"Ah!" Azia sat up suddenly. "I didn't even think that they're all here together... And I brought the Novovyeyskis' girl myself!"

He clapped his hands at once to summon Halim.

"Tell my men," he told him, "to watch for fire in the town, and then throw themselves on the soldiers here in the fort and slit their throats for them. The old noble and the women are to be bound and guarded till I give the word what's to be done with them."

Then he turned to Krytchinski and Adurovitch. "I can't do much myself because I'm still too weak. But I'll at least mount a horse and watch you at your work. So start it now, good comrades. Start it now!"

★   ★   ★

Krytchinski and Adurovitch leaped for the door and he came out after them, called for his horse and rode to the gate in the palisade beyond the earthworks, from which he could look down into the town and watch what was about to happen there.

Many of his *Lipki* also broke through the palisades and climbed up on the earthen wall to feast their eyes on the massacre. Those of Novovyeyski's soldiers who hadn't ridden out into the Steppe, and who now saw the gathering Tartar troopers, assumed that there was something interesting to see in the town below and joined them on the ramparts without a shadow of fear or suspicion. There were fewer than two dozen of them anyway, the rest being scattered in the taverns in the town.

Meanwhile the cohorts of Adurovitch and Krytchinski scattered throughout the little town in less time than it takes to blink an eye. Most of their men were former Polish or Lithuanian Tartars, at one time inhabitants of the Commonwealth and for the most part gentry, but since it had been a long time since they left their country they had become almost indistinguishable from the savage Tartars of the Steppes and Wild Lands. Their old Polish *zhupan* coats had long lost their usefulness in their years of wandering, and most of them now wore crude sheepskin jerkins, worn with the wool outside, and thrown over gaunt, naked bodies that were dark with the smoke of innumerable camp fires and the harsh Steppe winds. Their weapons, however, were far better than the arms of the ordinary Tartars. Each of them had a saber. All of them carried laminated horn bows and quite a few had firearms. But their faces expressed the same cruelty and bloodlust as those of their Crimean, Belgorodian and Dobrudjan brethren.

Now, having spread throughout the little town, they started running through the streets in every direction, galloping back and forth through the yards and alleys and across the squat enclosure of the market square, howling like wolves and uttering shrill and terrifying cries as if to encourage each other to murder, bestiality and pillage. But even though many of them had already clamped their knives between their teeth in the Tartar fashion the local people were not yet alarmed. Just as in Mohilev and in Yampol, the population of Rashkov consisted largely of Valachians, Armenians, Greeks and Tartar traders who watched the galloping swarms without the slightest fear or suspicion. All the shops were open. The merchants sat cross-legged before their stores in the oriental manner, calmly fingering their glass and sandalwood beads. The howls of the horsemen did nothing more than arouse their curiosity in expectation of some unusual game or spectacle.

But suddenly pillars of smoke shot upward at all four corners of the market square, and the howl that burst out of all the Tartar throats was so terrifying that the hair rose in terror on the heads of all the Valachians, Armenians and Greeks along with all their women and children.

Sabers flashed whitely everywhere at once. A rain of arrows fell on the peaceful people. And then their cries became one with the hurried slamming of doors and shutters, the clatter of the horses' hooves, and the baying of the murderers and looters.

The town square filled with smoke. Cries of "Fire! Fire!" echoed in the smoke cloud. Doors and shutters gave way to a ferocious battering and pounding and terrified women were dragged out by the hair, while other pillagers hurled dishes, household objects, trade goods and bedding out into the street.

Clouds of down and feathers spilled into the air out of the slit featherbeds and pillows, along with the cries and groans of murdered men, the laments and weeping, the howling of fear-crazed dogs and the bellowing of cattle trapped in the flames of their burning byres. Scarlet tongues of flame shot high into the clear light of day, as vivid against the billowing black smoke as if it were midnight.

★ ★ ★

Meanwhile in the fort Azia's horsemen threw themselves on the handful of Novovyeyski's foot soldiers, few of whom carried any sort of weapon, the moment that the massacre began in the town. There was hardly any fight to speak of. A dozen knives plunged at once into each Polish soldier's back and chest and then their heads were hacked off and piled under the hooves of Azia's horse.

Azia allowed most of his *Lipki* to run down into the town and join in the bloody handiwork of the earlier renegades while he remained where he was and watched but there wasn't a great deal to see.

Black coils of smoke obscured most of the work of Krytchinski and Adurovitch at this point. The stench of the conflagration lay thickly on the air. The town burned like a vast bonfire under its sooty smog. Once in a while a musket shot echoed in that cloud like a clap of thunder, or some desperate fugitive burst out of it pursued by troops of *Lipki*.

Azia watched with joy burning in his heart. A dreadful smile stretched his lips and his white teeth glinted cruelly under it. The smile was all the more terrible because it was laced with the pain of his clotted wound. Pride filled his chest. At last, after so many years, he'd thrown off the burden of pretending, let loose the demons of his secret hatred, and felt himself the true son of Tuhay-bey.

Yet at the same time he felt a wild regret that Basia wasn't there to watch this fire, this slaughter, and to see him practicing his new profession. He loved her but at the same time he craved a savage vengeance over her.

'*She'd stand here at my stirrup!*' he thought. '*She'd cling to my feet! And I'd be holding her by the hair, and then I'd lift her up and suck the honey out of those sweet lips, and she'd be mine! Mine! My slave!*'

Only the hope that she'd be caught by the pursuit he'd launched, or by the troops he left along the way, kept him from giving way to utter desperation. He clung to this grim hope as fiercely as a drowning man clutches at a plank, and this gave him strength. He couldn't think only about his loss because his mind was too full of the moment when he'd get her back, take her at last, and finally possess her.

★ ★ ★

He stood and waited by the gate until the sounds of slaughter began to dwindle and gave way to silence. This came quite quickly because the cohorts of Adurovitch and Krytchinski numbered at least as many men as there were people in the little town, so that only the roar of the fire lasted until evening. Azia climbed off his horse, turned into the fort, and walked slowly into a spacious room where his men piled sheepskins in the middle of the floor for him to sit on, and there he waited for the two renegade commanders.

They came not long after, along with their troop leaders. Each face glowed with savage joy and pleasure because the loot exceeded all their expectations. The small town had been prospering since the end of the peasant insurrection and had become quite wealthy. They'd also taken about a hundred young women and a flock of children from ten-years-old and up who could be profitably sold in the eastern markets. All men, older women, and the children who were too small to survive the long trail to captivity went under the knife. The hands of the killers were still red with blood that steamed in the chilly air, and their sheepskin jerkins reeked of smoke when they pushed their way into the room.

All of them found places to squat on around Azia and Krytchinski said: "There'll be only a pile of ashes here after we have gone. We could hit Yampol before the garrisons return. There's at least as much loot to be taken there."

"No!" Azia said. "Leave Yampol to the men I left there. It's time to go into the lands of the Sultan and the Khan."

"We hear and obey!" the captains and lieutenants chorused. "We'll go back with loot and glory!"

"But there's something else to do here in the meanwhile," Azia said. "There are some women here in the fort, along with that old noble who kept me in childhood. I need to pay him for it."

He clapped his hands for the guard and ordered the prisoners brought in. They came moments later. Lady Boska was sobbing and quivering with terror. Zosia was bathed in tears. Evka was as pale as a winding sheet and old Pan Novovyeyski was roped hand and foot. All of them were terrified but clearly bewildered and unable to understand as yet what had happened here.

Only Evka thought she had some idea what this was all about. She couldn't think of what might have happened to Lady Volodyovska, nor why Azia didn't show himself, nor why the town was put to the torch and its people slaughtered. She couldn't imagine why she and the others were seized and roped like captives, but she assumed it was something to do with her. What it must be, she thought, was that Azia had gone mad with his passion for her, that he was too proud to beg her father for her hand, and that he'd simply seized her to carry her off by force. It was all terrible and frightening but at least she didn't fear for her life.

★ ★ ★

The captives didn't recognize the seated Azia, whose face was almost wholly swathed in bloody rags, but the sight of him terrified the women all the more. Pushed roughly into the room, they immediately assumed that real Tartars must have somehow surprised and overwhelmed the *Lipki* companies and seized control of Rashkov. It was only the sight of Krytchinski and Adurovitch that showed them who their captors really were.

They and the Tartars stared at each other in silence for a while. Uncertainty showed in old Pan Novovyeyski's words when he broke this silence but his voice was steady.

"In whose hands are we?" he demanded.

In reply, Azia unwrapped his head. His fierce, handsome features were ruined for ever. His nose was crushed and shapeless. A blue-black stain marked the place where one eye had been. His icy smile resembled the spasmodic rigor of a corpse as he savored his anticipated vengeance.

He said nothing for another still, protracted moment, then fixed his one good eye on the old noble as if it were a white-hot branding iron.

"In mine," he said. "The son of Tuhay-bey."

But the old noble recognized him even before he named himself. Evka also knew him, although her heart tightened with fear and revulsion at the sight of that monstrously disfigured face and head. She hid her eyes behind her trembling hands while the old nobleman blinked in amazement once or twice and his mouth fell agape.

"Azia?" he asked. "Azia?"

"Yes, Azia. Whom you raised from childhood. To whom you were such a caring and devoted father. And whose back flowed with blood under your loving hand."

But the old noble's face was now red with fury and blood surged into his own raging head, drowning all thoughts of caution. "Traitor!" he said. "You'll answer for all your crimes at the bar of justice! I've still a son, you viper...!"

"And you've a daughter," Azia said, "for whose sake you ordered me whipped to death. But now I'll give that daughter to the least of my Tartars so that he might enjoy her and find some use in her."

"Give her to me, commander!" Adurovitch said suddenly.

"Azia! Azia!" Evka screamed and threw herself headlong at his feet. "I always loved you...!"

But he only kicked her in the face and Adurovitch seized her by the hair and dragged her over to where he was sitting. Pan Novovyeyski went from red to purple. His bonds creaked on his arms as he strained to break them and his mouth babbled out incomprehensible sounds of rage.

But now Azia rose and advanced upon him, at first walking slowly and then rushing forward like an animal eager to hurl itself on its prey. One bony fist seized the old man by his dangling mustache and the other started to smash his face and head, beating him senseless without pause or mercy. Hoarse, grating sounds welled out of the young Tartar's throat and when the old noble finally toppled to the floor he knelt on his chest and a long knife glittered in his hand.

"Mercy! Help!" Evka howled and sobbed.

But Adurovitch slammed a fist on top of her head and then clamped his broad hand across her mouth. Meanwhile Azia was butchering Pan Novovyeyski.

The sight was so dreadful that even the *Lipki* sergeants felt the cold clutch of fear, because Azia was relishing every moment of it and taking his time. His knife slid across the old man's throat with careful, premeditated cruelty, each stroke slow and measured, while the blood spurted ever higher out of the victim's slit arteries onto the butcher's hands, and streamed across the floor, and the air hissed and gurgled out of his severed windpipe. At last the snarling gasps and groans dwindled into a hissing silence, and only the dying man's legs still jerked and kicked convulsively on the floor.

Azia rose. His one, inflamed eye now settled on the pale, sweet face of the stricken Zosia who hung unconscious in the arms of a *Lipki* guard.

"I'll keep that one for myself," he said, "until I tire of her and either sell her or give her away."

Then he turned to his Tartars. "And now, as soon as the pursuit is back, we'll go to the Sultan."

The pursuit party came back two days later but with empty hands.

Sick with his own rage and disappointment, Azia Tuhaybeyovitch crossed into the Sultan's country, leaving only a blue-grey heap of ashes behind him.

Part VII

Chapter Fifty-two

TEN TO TWELVE Ukrainian miles separated those towns through which Basia passed on her way from Hreptyov to Rashkov, which meant that the entire Dniester trail took about thirty. It was still dark when her convoy started out at daybreak after a night's halt, and the day's ride didn't end till nightfall, but the entire journey had taken three days, including all those difficult hill and river crossings and all the stops for rest. The troops and travelers of those times seldom moved that swiftly but it was possible for those who wished to do it. Bearing this in mind, Basia concluded that the road back to Hreptyov should take her even less time than that, especially since she was covering it on horseback rather than in a cumbersome transport sleigh, and since it was a flight for her life whose success depended upon speed.

But the first day of her escape showed her that she was wrong about that, because she couldn't use the direct, comparatively simple trail but had to inscribe a wide circle far into the Steppe, which added immeasurably to the time and length of her journey. In addition, it was likely she could lose her way. She could come across thawing rivers, forests that had no one had cut through before, swamps and morasses that didn't freeze even in the Winter, and all the dangers that could come upon her from wild animals and even wilder people. So even though she intended to gallop night and day, she realized that no matter how dearly she wished it, God alone could tell how long it would take her to get back to Hreptyov.

Yes, she'd succeeded in tearing herself out of Azia's grasp. But what would happen next? Nothing could be worse than the clutch of those loathsome hands, but the thought of what else might be waiting for her turned her blood to ice.

It occurred to her almost at once that if she tried to save the wear and tear on her horses the pursuing *Lipki* would be sure to catch up with her. They knew these Steppes inside out. It was practically impossible to hide from them there. These, after all, were the men who tracked Tartars night and day through this wilderness even in Spring and Summer when there were no hoof tracks to follow in the snow or in the mud of Autumn; they could read all the signs as clearly as a book; their eyes pierced the vast, shrouded distances like eagles and they followed the scent of a fugitive like bloodhounds. Their entire lives were spent in such pursuits. In vain did the Tartars turn streams and rivers into roads, so as to leave no tracks; the Cossacks, the *Lipki* and the *Tcheremisses*—and the Polish borderers as well—knew how to find them, how to match their cunning with their own, and how to fall upon them as unexpectedly as lightning out of a clear sky. How then was she to escape getting caught by such men, unless she left them so far behind at the very start that distance itself would make pursuit impossible? But if she did that she would lose her horses.

'*They'll fall, there's no doubt about it,*' Basia thought in fear, as she looked at the sweat running down their sides and the sheets of foam that splashed off their bridles. '*I'll lose them if they run like they've been doing up till now.*'

So from time to time she'd rein them in and strained her ears to listen, but then she'd hear the sounds of pursuit in each breath of wind, in the rustling whisper of the dry leaves on the canyon floors, in the soft snap of dried-out thistle stalks tapping against each other, in the flapping wings of a passing bird, and even in the deep silence of the wilderness which rang in her ears. Then, thrown into sudden panic, she spurred ahead and fled at a wild gallop until the rasping breath of her exhausted horses told her that they couldn't run like that much longer.

The weight of her loneliness and helplessness threatened to crush her will and undermine her senses. Ah! How abandoned she felt at such times! How much unfair and undeserved bitterness she felt towards everyone, even those for whom she cared the most, for not being there when she needed them so desperately around her. And, finally, how she blamed herself!

She thought that this could be God's punishment for her insatiable craving for adventure, for her insistence on being part of every hunt, chase and entertainment, for going against her husband's reasonable objections to her forays among the military and her participation in the raids and battles, for her flightiness, her scatterbrained dismissal of good sense in favor of impetuous whims and fancies, and for her lack of stability, maturity and judgment.

She burst into open and sincere tears at this thought, feeling less sorry for herself than for the little knight, and she raised her small, troubled face towards the sky, and begged among her sobs:

"Punish me but don't abandon me! Don't punish Michal. Michal's not to blame!"

★ ★ ★

Meanwhile night was nearing. And along with twilight there came a chilly gloom, anxiety and uncertainty about the road ahead where it was so easy to go astray in the darkness. Familiar objects started to lose their shapes and to become mysterious, dim, and at the same time strangely alive and threatening. The jagged rims of the high, sheer cliffs that loomed everywhere around her looked as if they were dotted with heads dressed in spiked helmets or round hats and turbans, the heads of watchers who peered silently but with malevolent hostility out of some gigantic battlements at whoever happened to pass below. Tree branches, stirred by the breeze, acquired almost human gestures. Some beckoned to her, as if to confide some terrifying secret, Others seemed to tell her to keep away and be on her guard. The gnarled, tangled roots of uprooted trees were like the reaching tentacles of some monstrous creatures, crouched and ready to leap out upon her.

Basia was brave, indeed she was almost fearless, but she was just as superstitious as everyone of her time, and the hair lifted on her head in terror at the thought of all the evil spirits that were sure to inhabit that deepening darkness. She was especially terrified of vampires. Everyone in the Dniester country believed in their existence, close as it lay to Moldavia on the southern bank, and the area around Yampol and Rashkov had a particu-

larly evil reputation in that regard. So many people left the
world by violence in these lands, without a chance to confess
their sins or get a Christian burial, that doomed souls seemed to
whimper out of every breeze. Basia recalled all the tales told by
the knights at her fireside in Hreptyov about those bottomless
chasms in which plaintive cries of *'Jezu! Jezu!'* rose suddenly on
the wind, about misleading lights in which something growled,
about rocks that laughed, and pale, keening children with green
eyes and monstrously misshapen heads who begged to be picked
up by a passing horseman, and once picked up, clamped themselves to the horseman's neck and sucked out his blood. She
remembered everything she heard about truncated heads that
hopped on long spider legs and about the worst apparitions of
them all, the full-grown vampires, known in the Valachian
tongue as *bruholaki*, which threw themselves on people with no
ruse at all.

Riding through the first of that gathering darkness, Basia
started to make frantic signs of the cross and didn't stop until her
hand grew numb. But even then she didn't stop praying because
that was the only means to keep evil at bay. Her horses also gave
her much encouragement, since they showed no sign of fear and
snorted in good health. At time she leaned forward and patted
her animal's neck as if to reassure herself about the reality around
her.

* * *

Dark at first, the night lightened gradually and at last starlight
glimmered through the wispy mists. This served Basia well. Her
fears lessened and she could follow the Big Dipper northward
towards Hreptyov. Peering about through the wilderness she
calculated that she'd put some distance between herself and the
Dniester because there were fewer cliffs and rocks around her
now, more round wooded hillocks, and even an occasional
broad open space that ran for some miles. Time and again,
however, she had to slide down into one or another of those
sudden canyons where an impenetrable darkness contained an
icy chill. Some of these chasm were so steep that she had to find
a way around them which meant a loss of time and many miles
added to her journey.

It was even more difficult to get across the innumerable

streams and small, winding rivers which flowed in a thick irregular web south towards the Dniester. The ice had already cracked on all of them and her horses made harsh, grunting sounds of fear when she forced them into these chilly waters which were often deeper than they seemed. Basia forded them only in places where broad, flat banks on either side of a wide-spilled stream suggested a shallow bottom, but even so sometimes the horses sunk well beyond their bellies, and she'd kneel on her saddle in Steppe-soldier fashion, clutching her saddlebow with both hands in an attempt to keep her feet and legs out of the icy water. But this didn't always work for her and she was soon wet and numb with cold from her knees down to her sodden feet.

"Come dawn," she murmured to herself, "it'll go easier, God grant it."

* * *

At last she rode into an open plain dotted with sparse trees and scraggly thickets of woodland and gorse. Her horses could hardly drag themselves along so she stopped to rest them. They bent their necks at once to nibble greedily at clumps of greyish moss and dead, yellow grass. The woods were silent and unusually still. The only sounds that came to her then were the wheezing breath of her tired horses and the crunch of dry grass in their powerful jaws. Both animals showed every sign of wanting to roll themselves in this thin, anemic vegetation but Basia couldn't let them have their way. She didn't even dare to loosen their girths and climb off the saddle because she had to be ready for instant flight.

She did, however, change mounts, switching to Azia's light Tartar runner, because her own highbred racer was far more delicate and had already carried her since before Azia's sudden attack the day before. She'd quenched her thirst by scooping up handfuls of river water each time she crossed a stream but now she felt a sharp pang of hunger, so she began to eat the sunflower seeds she found in the little satchel tied to Azia's saddle. They were slightly bitter but tasty anyhow and she thanked God fervently for this providential meal.

She rationed herself carefully, however, eating a little more than a bird might peck so that this meager nourishment might last as far as Hreptyov. Then her eyelids blinked sleepily. She could hardly keep them open, struggle though she did to stay awake and aware at all times, but a piercing chill had begun to shake her as soon as the motion of the ride had stopped, and with it came a wave of sudden weakness. Her legs were numb with cold. Her whole body cried out with pain and exhaustion, especially in her back and shoulders which had expended so much effort in her struggle with Azia. The weakness settled on her like a boulder and her eyes fell shut.

But, after a mere moment, she forced them open again. "No!" she told herself. "I'll sleep in daylight, while riding. Because if I sleep now I'll freeze to death."

Nevertheless her thoughts drifted more and more, or flowed into each other, presenting a kaleidoscope of disordered images in which the wilderness, her escape, the pursuit, Azia, the little knight, Evka and everything else that had happened to her blended into one indistinguishable landscape of memory and imagination.

All of that seemed to flow together like a wave driven by the wind, and she flowed right along with it, carried forward into the unknown without fear or joy or any other feeling as if it were all arranged and preordained. Azia was supposedly chasing after her but, at the same time, he was right there beside her, talking to her and worrying about the horses; Pan Zagloba was annoyed that the dinner would be cold before she got back; Michal was pointing out the way and Evka followed in the sleigh eating honeyed dates.

Then all these figures dimmed and slipped away as if some strange misty twilight had fallen upon them, and there was only a strange, impenetrable darkness everywhere around her, all the more mysterious because it went on for ever into immeasurable distances beyond the reach of eyesight. Darkness pervaded everything. It enveloped Basia and filled her head as well, and it extinguished every thought and image in her mind just like a wind that snuffs out flaming torches carried in the night.

★   ★   ★

Basia fell asleep.

But luckily for her an unusual clamor jerked her awake before her blood cool chill. The horses leaped worriedly. Something quite out of the ordinary was happening in the thickets all around her.

Fully awake and aware at once, Basia grasped Azia's musket, leaned forward in her saddle and cocked her ears to listen while her eyes narrowed dangerously and her nostrils flared. She was one of those indomitable people in whom every danger woke an immediate watchfulness, courage and readiness to fight.

But this time her experienced ears told her that there was little to be concerned about. The sounds that had wakened her were only the commotion of wild pigs. Whether the yearling swine were trying to get at some fresh litter, or mature boars were fighting over a dam, it was enough to fill the woods with a sudden uproar. This hubbub was clearly taking place quite far away, but it reverberated so powerfully in the silence of the night that it seemed to brake out underfoot, and Basia heard not only the squeals and the grunts but also the wheezing hiss of violent breath expended in excitement. And suddenly there was the dry, snap and crackling of trampled undergrowth and the whole herd stampeded somewhere near and vanished in the darker and thicker depths of the forest.

In spite of all the terrors of her situation, the love of the chase woke at once in the incorrigible Basia and she heaved a small sigh of regret that she hadn't had a chance to see the game herd at close quarters.

"There'd be something to see,"she murmured to herself. "But no matter! Going through the woods like this I expect I'll get another chance..."

And it was only after this silent observation that she remembered it would be much better to see nothing new just now, but to get away as fast as she could, and she set out once more.

★　★　★

It was all the more important to get going again because the chill of the night gripped her more powerfully than ever, and the motion of the horses warmed her quite considerably without adding to her weariness and fatigue. The horses, however, which managed to snatch just a few mouthfuls of dry grass and moss, moved at a staggering, dispirited pace with their heads hanging to the ground. Frost had sheathed their flanks during their short rest and it seemed that they were barely dragging themselves

along. They had been going, after all, practically without a
breathing spell all the way from the Dniester.

She crossed a broad clearing with her eyes fixed on the Big
Dipper overhead, and plunged into a thicker woodland. It
wasn't dense enough to bar her way but it was rather hilly and
raked throughout by a whole series of narrow ravines. It was also
much darker there, not just because of the tree crowns which
kept out the starlight but because a grey mist coiled upward from
the soil among the trees and obscured the sky. She rode on then
as if she were blindfolded, trusting to luck and instinct. Only the
ravines gave Basia any kind of sense of her direction since she
knew that, like the streams and rivers, all of them ran out of the
east south towards the Dniester, and so by crossing them she was
heading northwest towards Hreptyov. She realized however that
even with these directional markers she was always in danger of
either moving too far away from the great border river or
circling too close. Either way was dangerous because in the first
instance it would add immeasurably to the distances that she had
to cover and, in the second instance, she might find herself
coming into Yampol where she'd fall into the hands of Azia's
detachment.

As to whether Yampol was still ahead of her, or if it lay
directly to her south, or whether she'd already left it far behind,
Basia had no idea.

"I'll be better able to tell where I am once I've passed
Mohilev," Basia told herself, "because that lies in a great canyon
that goes on for miles and perhaps I'll recognize it when I see
it."

Then she glanced hopefully at the sky, more in search of inner
reassurance than the hidden stars.

'God grant that I get at least past Mohilev,' she thought. 'Michal's
territory begins close beyond and nothing will harm me there.'

★   ★   ★

Meanwhile the night became even darker. Luckily for Basia,
there was still snow on the woodland floor whose pale backdrop
threw into relief the black tree trunks, the treacherous stumps
and the reaching branches so that she could avoid them. On the
other hand, the darkness meant that she had to be much more
careful than while galloping in the open, and slowed her horses

to a walk, so that all her fears of the supernatural gripped her again with an icy fist.

"If I see a pair of gleaming eyes close to the ground," she assured herself, "that won't mean much! It'll be just a wolf. But what if they glow at the height of a man's head...?"

And in that very moment that's just what she saw.

"In the name of the Father and the Son!" she screamed out loud.

Whether this was merely an illusion, or if a wildcat sat crouching in the branches of a nearby tree, a pair of greenish eyes was glittering right before her at the height of a man's head.

Her sudden terror blinded her for a moment. Her eyes slid out of focus and she reeled as if about to topple from her saddle, but when she blinked away that wild bout of panic there was no longer anything to see. Only the rustling of some body moving among the branches sounded in her ears while her heart hammered in her breast as if it wished to break free.

She rode on in that apparently endless darkness, praying for dawn and daylight. The dreadful night seemed to go on for ever. Soon afterwards another river barred her way. Basia was already quite far beyond Yampol, on the banks of the Rosava River, but she had no idea where she was, and she could only guess that she was still moving towards the north since yet another stream cut across her path.

She also guessed that the night was about to end. The air became much colder, painful in her nostrils, and more difficult to breathe. The mists started ebbing. Frost clenched about her throat. The stars appeared overhead again, only they seemed weaker and much more pale than before, flickering with an uncertain light.

★ ★ ★

At last the darkness all about her began to recede. Tree trunks, broad branches and even smaller twigs gradually acquired form and definition. The silence in the forest became absolute as if all the hidden life around her held its breath in anticipation. Daylight was seeping into the blue-grey darkness. After a time Basia could tell the chestnut shading in her horses' hides and then, at last, a ribbon of gold and scarlet shined brightly through the

branches behind her right shoulder. The day had come and
promised dry, good weather.

It was then that she felt immeasurably tired. Her mouth kept
opening in protracted yawns, her eyelids felt as heavy as lead,
and at last she fell asleep only to be brought sharply awake again
when a low branch struck her in the head. Fortunately, her worn
horses were barely dragging themselves along, snipping at
patches of moss along the way, so that the blow was a light one
and did her no harm. The sun, she saw at once, was already up
and its brilliant light broke through the leafless branches. Hope
filled her heart again at this sight. Miles of Steppe lay behind her
now, and so many hills, canyons and forests stretched between
her and the pursuing Tartars that she could feel encouraged and
optimistic.

"If I just don't get caught by that lot from Yampol and
Mohilev," she told herself, "those others won't get me."

But doubt wasn't laid to rest as easily as that. *'The Lipki can
follow a trail even across stone and water,'* she thought at once, *'and
they never give up a chase as long as their horses last.'*

That last assumption seemed the most likely to her. It was
enough for her to look at her own horses. Both the racer and the
Tartar runner walked with hanging heads, caved-in flanks, and
on unsteady legs. Their muzzles dipped towards every patch of
moss they passed and they snatched at whatever dried leaves they
could find on low hanging-branches. Moreover, they must have
been dehydrated by a feverish thirst because they drank greedily
at every river crossing.

Even so, breaking out of the woods at last into a wide strip of
treeless Steppe, Basia spurred both her exhausted animals into a
full gallop and drove them at a run as far as the next belt of
woods that darkened the plain ahead. Beyond that woodland lay
another clearing, even broader than the one before and dotted
with rolling mounds and hillocks. But a scant quarter of a mile
behind these piled mounds she saw a thin, blue-grey column of
woodsmoke lifting into the sky as straight and narrow as a
sapling pine.

This was the first human habitation that Basia encountered
because all of that vast, untrammeled country, other than the
land that lay along the banks of the Dniester, had long become
a savage wilderness, swept clean of people not merely by the

Tartar incursions but by the endless, bloody Polish-Cossack wars as well. After the last punitive expedition of Stefan Tcharnyetzki which destroyed the territory of Busha twenty years before, such towns as still remained scattered here and there turned into miserable little settlements, and rural hamlets returned to the forest. And how many other expeditions, battles and massacres had there been in this unhappy country since Tcharnyetzki's time? How much death had fallen on its dwindling people until the recent years when the great Sobieski wrested these lands from the enemy? Life was beginning to drift into them again but it did so fearfully and slowly, and the territory through which Basia was blazing her trail was especially barren. Only marauders made their lairs there, and most of them had been stamped out already by the garrisons in Rashkov, Yampol, Mohilev and Hreptyov.

Basia's first thought when she caught sight of that smoke was to ride towards it, find the hut, shack or cabin out of which it rose, warm herself by its fire and beg a little food. But it soon occurred to her that it was safer in these parts to trust a pack of wolves than people who were far more vicious than any animal alive. Indeed, reason dictated that she should bypass this human lair as widely as she could and ride away as fast as she was able because only death could be waiting there.

Right at the edge of the forest ahead stood a little haystack so she took the risk and stopped there to feed her two horses. They ate voraciously, plunging their heads into the stack all the way to the ears, and pulling out and crunching thick bunches of still-fresh hay. Their bridles hampered them but Basia wouldn't take them off.

'That smoke and this stack,' she reasoned correctly, *'mean that those people live there and that they have horses of their own. If they have horses they can come riding after me. So I must be ready to ride for my life at a moment's notice.'*

She did, however, spend a good hour at that little haystack, so that her mounts could get a bellyful of feed, and she herself made a meal of some of her seeds. But she'd no sooner set out again, riding a few furlongs, when she came across two men carrying bundles of firewood on their backs. One was a middle aged, savage-looking man, with slanted eyes and a cruelly pock-marked face, who seemed more like a beast of prey than a human being, while the other was a mentally retarded youth with a fixed, glazed stare and an empty smile.

Both of them threw down their burdens at the sight of an approaching rider. Both were clearly startled and afraid. But she had come up on them too suddenly for them to try to run.

"Slava Bohu," Basia said in Ruthenian. "God be praised."

"Na viki vikov. For ever and ever."

"What's the name of your homestead, then?"

"Why should it have a name? It's a hut, that's all."

"Is it far to Mohilev from here?"

"Who knows?"

The older man shrugged and started peering sharply into Basia's face. She wore men's clothes, so he'd take her for a young, beardless boy, and his own face immediately acquired a calculating ruthlessness and cruelty.

"Ey, and how come you're such a babyface, little master?" he growled in contempt.

"And what's that to you?" Basia snapped back at once.

"And are you riding out alone in the Steppe like this?" the peasant queried and took a step towards her.

"There are troops behind me," Basia said.

But the peasant stood still and peered across the wide open space behind her. "That's a lie," he said. "There's nobody there."

With this he advanced boldly forward. His slanted eyes flashed with a gloomy light, his lips pursed and he shrilled out a birdcall, as if signaling to some other person or people to come at a run.

All this was more than enough to awaken Basia to her sense of danger so she whipped a pistol from one of her holsters and aimed it at his chest without hesitation.

"Keep quiet or die!" she warned.

The peasant clamped his mouth shut at once and hurled himself facedown on the ground. The mindless youth did the same, baying like a wolfhound. It could have been that his mind was unhinged in the past by some terrible event because he now began to howl in utter terror.

Basia spun her horse around and flew into the Steppe like an arrow shot into the sky.

Chapter Fifty-three

AS LUCK WOULD HAVE IT, this stretch of woods was free of undergrowth and with quite a lot of open space between the trees. A few moments later Basia ran into another clearing, a narrow one that stretched a long way ahead. The horses, which had fed well at the haystack and acquired fresh strength, now flew like the wind.

'They'll run home, mount up and come after me,' Basia was quite certain.

But she was reassured and encouraged by the thought that it was quite far to the homestead from the spot where she met the two men and that her own horses were running well.

'I'll be two miles away or more before they get to their horses, get them saddled and start after me, if my own mounts can keep up this pace.'

And that's just what happened. But when several hours passed without pursuit of any kind behind her, and Basia slowed the pace, she gave way to a great wave of fear and despair while hot tears forced themselves into her eyes.

That woodland meeting taught her what she could expect from people she met in this wilderness, and what such people were. It really wasn't much of a surprise. She knew from the tales told by her fireside in Hreptyov and by her own experience, that all the quiet and stable former settlers and inhabitants of this savage country had either moved away, or they'd been devoured by the wars, and that those who stayed had been irreversibly changed by the very nature of life and survival. Living in the constant shadow of death and devastation, inured to all the horrors of Tartar raids and domestic slaughters and upheavals under conditions where one man was only another's prey, deprived of faith and churches and any other exemplars of humanity, held in check by no authority other than murder and the torch of arson, and knowing no law other than the fist, they were now stripped of all human feelings and became as implacable and vicious as the beasts of prey that infested their forests.

Basia knew all this without a need for any illustrations. But a lost wanderer in the wilderness, who is tormented by the cold and hunger, looks by sheer instinct for help from his own species, and she had done the same. That column of woodsmoke signaled some sort of human habitation and her weary heart had surged towards it at first sight no matter what her mind was able to tell her. She wanted to run there, greet the people with the name of God and seek a moment's rest under their hospitable roof. In the meantime, a cruel reality barred its teeth at her like a savage dog, her heart filled with bitterness, and tears of disappointment streamed out of her eyes.

'There's no help here from anyone except God,' she thought. 'Let Him preserve me from meeting any other people.'

Then she recalled the birdcalls with which the slant-eyed peasant seemed to be signaling others who may have been hidden somewhere nearby. It occurred to her that she might be in marauder country, where gangs of cut-throats would have gone to ground, close to the refuge of the open Steppe, after they'd been rooted out and driven from their lairs in the gorges and ravines of the Dniester forests in the south.

"So what'll happen," Basia asked herself, "if I meet a whole bunch of them? Like maybe a dozen? The musket will take care of one. The two pistols will settle with two more. The saber might take another one, maybe even two. But if there are any more than that I'll die a frightful death."

So just as earlier among the terrors of the night she'd prayed for daylight to come as quickly as it could and relieve her fears of supernatural evil, so now she longed for darkness which could hide her from the eyes of evil men.

★   ★   ★

Twice more during her determined flight she caught sight of people. Once she spotted a huddled cluster of cabins at the edge of a high plateau. She couldn't be sure who lived there. It need not have been a bandit lair but she took no chances and gave it a wide berth because even homesteaders in that countryside weren't much better than common marauders. At yet another time she heard the distant thud of axes in a pine grove.

At last the longed-for night settled about the earth. Basia was so exhausted by this time that as soon as she'd broken out into a gaunt, bare plain, free of woods and forests, she decided to risk sleeping as she rode.

'Here at least,' she thought, *'I won't smash myself against some low-hanging branch, even if I freeze while I'm dozing off.'*

It seemed to her just as she was about to close her eyes that there was a scattering of small black dots darting back and forth against the white backdrop of the snow far at the edge of vision in the distance and she made one last attempt to stay awake.

"It's probably wolves," she murmured to herself.

But those scurrying dots vanished before she'd ridden more than a few dozen paces so she plunged into such a deep and consuming sleep that she woke only when Azia's Steppe runner neighed shrilly under her.

She glanced quickly around. She was now at the edge of yet another forest and she'd wakened just in time or she might have ridden asleep into a tree. But suddenly she noticed that her other horse was gone.

"What happened?" she asked herself aloud, immediately alarmed.

The explanation wasn't long in occurring to her. She had tied the thoroughbred's reins to the saddle horn of her Tartar runner but her cold, numb fingers hadn't served her well and the knot wasn't drawn tight enough. It must have slipped during the night, pulled loose by the motion of the horses, and the tired animal had fallen behind, either to search for fodder or to lie down somewhere. Luckily not much else was lost. Basia was keeping her pistols in her sash rather than the saddle holsters. The powder horn and the seed satchel were also at her side. The loss of the animal wasn't as catastrophic as it might have seemed because Azia's runner was even better suited to the cold and hardships of her journey, although it may not have been quite as fleet of foot as the thoroughbred. But she had loved the lost racer, she worried about him, and her first thought was to turn back and to look for him.

What surprised her now, however, was that she couldn't see him anywhere in the Steppe behind her even though the bright moonlit night was not much darker than a cloudy day.

"There's no doubt he's back there," she told herself. "I'm sure he wouldn't have galloped off ahead. So he must have rolled into some declivity and that's why I can't see him."

The Tartar horse neighed nervously once again, gave a strange frightened shiver and flattened his ears, but no reply came from the silent Steppe.

"I'll go back!" Basia said. "I'll find him!"

But a sudden inexplicable fear seized her as she turned her animal around and she could almost swear a voice crying out in warning: '*Basia! Don't go back there!*'

And at once, almost as if answering a command, the still night air filled with protracted howls, growls, groans and moaning as if they were welling up from under the earth, and finally a short, frightful scream that ended on a half-note. It was all the more terrifying because there was absolutely nothing to see in the moonlit Steppe and Basia was immediately wet from head to foot with an icy sweat.

"What is it?" she screamed out loud through numb trembling lips. "What is it?"

She guessed at once that it was a wolf pack gutting her lost horse, but she couldn't understand why she couldn't see it, since—judging by the nearness of the sounds—this had to be happening no farther off than five hundred paces.

It was too late to rush back to save the animal. By this time it would have been torn apart or so badly wounded that nothing would heal it, so Basia fired a pistol into the air to drive off the wolfpack and set about her own salvation. She set her spurs into the Tartar runner and shot off at speed.

She tried to picture in her mind how this could have happened, and how her favorite racer might have strayed, and suddenly thought that it may not have been wolves that had seized the luckless animal and were now dragging it down invisibly into the bowels of the earth. She felt as if a swarm of ants had suddenly stirred to life all along her spine, but giving it all more thought she remembered some half-dreamed slope that she'd ridden down while dozing in her saddle, and then a sharper slope she had climbed back into the Steppe.

'*That's what it must've been,*' she thought. '*I must have crossed some ravine while asleep, and that's where my poor horse stayed, and that's where the wolves got him.*'

★ ★ ★

The rest of the night passed without any new adventures. The horse had fed itself at the haystack the morning before and now ran so steadily that Basia was filled with admiration for the animal's endurance. This was a Tartar *bahmat* of great strength and beauty, one of those indefatigable Steppe runners that could chase a wolfpack from sunrise to sunset, and whose resilience had practically no limits. At the short rest breaks that Basia allowed herself within woodland thickets he gnawed whatever feed presented itself—moss, dry leaves and even bark ripped off the wayside trees—and he pushed on and on. In the clearings, when Basia dropped her reins and spurred him into an all-out gallop, he'd grunt a little, and his breath became more resonant, but he never failed to respond. When she brought him back into a steadier trot he gasped, shuddered and let his head hang a little lower but he didn't fall.

Her thoroughbred, she knew, would never have lasted through such powerful exertions even if he hadn't fallen prey to the wolves that killed him.

With dawn, as soon as she had said her prayers, Basia made a quick accounting of her time.

"I got away from Azia close to noon on Thursday," she reasoned. "I galloped until nightfall. Then I rode through the night, then through another day, and then there was this night that is just ending. Now the third day is starting. Even if Azia's men had gone after me late Thursday afternoon they must have turned back by now, and Hreptyov can't be much farther ahead because I didn't spare the horses."

Then, after a while, she added worriedly:

"It's high time to get there! Oh it's time to get there! God have mercy on me!"

At times she felt an urge to turn south and start her circle back towards the Dniester, where she'd be able to judge with closer

certainty exactly where she was, but she was putting that off as
long as she could knowing that Azia left a troop of fifty *Lipki*
with Pan Gorjhenski in Mohilev.

Riding as far as she did into the high Steppe, she thought that
she may not have yet passed above Mohilev, that it was still
below her like a waiting threat. All the way, as long as sleep and
weariness didn't close her eyes, she kept looking for a major
canyon that might remind her of the one in which Mohilev
crouched just above the Dniester, but so far she hadn't come
across anything like it. Besides, that gorge might look entirely
different beyond the town. It might twist and turn and narrow
and dwindle into nothing. It might even end a few furlongs
beyond the settlement. In other words she had absolutely no
idea where she was right now.

She merely begged God constantly that her terrible journey
should come to a quick end because she felt that she wouldn't
be able to go on much longer, and that she could keep up her
remorseless struggle against the cold, the hardships, the exhaustion and the gnawing hunger. She'd eaten nothing for three days
except the few handfuls of seed and, careful though she'd been
to ration herself, she'd eaten the last of the seeds just that
morning.

Now she could feed and warm herself only with the hope that
Hreptyov was near. She was hot with fever. She knew that she
was about to fall into a serious illness, because even though the
whole world seemed colder every day, her arms and legs felt as
if they had begun to burn, and she was tormented by a constant
thirst.

"Just as long as I don't lose consciousness," she told herself
over and over. "Just as long as I last long enough to reach
Hreptyov, see Michal once more... Then, let God's will take
care of the rest."

There came again a whole series of streams and rivers to ford
but they caused few problems because they were either wide-
spilled and shallow or still gripped by ice under a thin coverlet
of water. But she was growing steadily more afraid of them
largely because her horse seemed to fear them. Entering the
water, or stepping on the ice, he'd make harsh, grating sounds
in his throat, flatten his ears, sniff the air as if anticipating danger,
and slide his hooves cautiously ahead as if testing a surface that

was sure to buckle under him. Moreover, she had to force him to step off the banks each time they made a crossing.

* * *

It was well after noon when Basia, riding through a densely growing forest, halted at some large river that was much wider than any of the others. She thought that this might be the Ladava or the Kalusik and her heart leaped with joy within her at this sight. Hreptyov couldn't be far away, and even if she missed it at first try, she could already think of herself as saved because it meant she'd entered a quieter and better settled country where the people could be feared less.

The river banks were tall and steep as far as she could see, except for one flat gap gouged into both sides where the frozen water spread out in a glazed sheet as if it were piled on a shallow plate. The ice looked thick and strong near to the banks, and a broad grey ribbon of water ran swiftly in midstream, suggesting a firm footing below it just as it had been in all the other rivers she had crossed.

The horse showed signs of balking, as he did before, and went in unwillingly, with his head hanging low and sniffing at the snow and scree in front of him. When he came up to the running water, Basia pulled up her legs and knelt in the saddle, holding onto the saddlebow with both hands as she always did.

The water gurgled under her. The underlying ice was indeed firm and solid. It rang as hard as a stone pavement under the horse's hooves.

But either the soaked ice was especially slippery right there, or the hackles on the horseshoes had worn off and blunted on the rock and shale over which Basia had been galloping for three days, because the frightened animal soon began to slide and slip. His stiff, trembling legs went out from under him time and again, going in every direction simultaneously, and suddenly he slipped, spun wildly and plunged down to his knees with his soft muzzle dipping in the icy stream. Terrified, he leaped up and tumbled back on his haunches, scrambled up again, and then began to flay about with his hooves in the utmost panic. Basia jerked the reins to lift him up and to hold him steady, but suddenly she heard a sharp crack and the desperate animal's rear legs vanished in the water.

"Jesus! Jesus!" she cried.

The horse made a desperate effort to scramble out onto the hard ice with his forelegs which still had a solid surface under them, but apparently the splintering ice on which his rear hooves were trying to find purchase began to slide from under him, because he only backed deeper into the cold, black stream and started uttering a thick, rasping groan.

Basia had just enough awareness and time to seize the horse's mane and hurl herself across his head onto the firm ice ahead. There she fell, immediately soaked through, but quite safe from drowning. She even tried to save the horse. She jumped up, seized the bridle and hauled with all her strength as she backed towards the far bank of the river.

But the horse could no longer even get his front hooves out on the edge of the solid ice and slid back ever deeper into the murky flood. The reins in Basia's hands stretched as tight as bowstrings and soon only the animal's neck and head protruded from the water. The horse bared all his teeth in a frightful effort. His groans were sounding almost human, and his eyes were staring up at her with an indescribable sadness and regret as if to say: "There's no help for me... Let me go or I'll pull you in as well..."

And since there really was no way to help him now, Basia dropped the reins.

The animal vanished under the ice at once. Numb with grief and fear, she crossed on foot to the next bank, sat down under a skeletal, leafless bush, and burst into tears like a child.

All her strength and energy were now gone. All the bitterness and disappointment she'd experienced when she first made contact with the people of the wilderness now came flooding back into her even more powerfully than before. Everything seemed stacked against her—the unknown distances before her, the false trails, the terrors of the darkness, the elements, the animals and the people—and only God's gentle hand extended any kind of help throughout all her hardships. She'd placed all her trust in that kind, fatherly care and even that was now taken from her, leaving her only a cruel disappointment. Basia would never voice that kind of thought which is why it struck her all the harder and she felt abandoned all the more.

What was left to her? What else could she do other than let her tears flow and sink into despair? Hadn't she shown as much courage and endurance as such a small and powerless being had in her to show? And now her horse drowned, her last hope of escape was gone, and she was left alone. She not only knew that she'd never manage to conquer the unknown distances and forests and ravines without this faithful animal companion, and cross the Steppe on foot, helpless against pursuit and whatever animals threatened her on the way, but she never felt more lonely and abandoned.

She wept until she had no more tears to shed. Then came exhaustion, weariness, and such a powerful feeling of futility that they brought her a resigned, regretful kind of peace and acceptance of what had to follow.

"I can't go against God's will," she murmured. "This is where I'll die..."

And she closed her eyes, which used to be so bright and merry and clear, and which were now so dull and sunken and rimmed with black shadows.

But even though her body grew heavier and weaker by the minute, her mind and her heart were fluttering within her like a pair of small, frightened birds. Ah, it wouldn't be so bad to drift off into that permanent, uninterrupted sleep if she were truly abandoned, unloved and alone. But she remembered how many people loved her, and how much they loved her, and leaving them was just too sharp a pain even in her terrible situation.

She tried to imagine what would happen once Azia's treason and her own escape became known in Hreptyov, how they'd search for her and then how they'd find her—blue with cold, frozen and sleeping her eternal sleep—here under this leafless bush on the banks of the river.

"Ai, but won't poor old Michal be sick about it," she told herself aloud, and then went on as if to apologize for all the trouble she was causing him, flinging her arms around his neck in her imagination.

"I tried the best I could, my dearest. I really did! But what could I do beyond that? God willed it otherwise..."

And suddenly she was gripped by such an overwhelming love

for that dear, good man, along with such a fervent wish to see him at least once more before she died, that she struggled back up to her feet and set out again.

It was, at first, almost impossibly hard going. Three days on horseback robbed her of the ability to walk and now she felt as if she were stumbling forward on legs borrowed from some other person. But at least she wasn't cold. Indeed, her fever sent her body temperature climbing to such heights that she was actually quite warm despite the freezing air.

She plunged into the woods and pressed on, taking care to keep the sun always on her left. It had moved well into the west by now, crossing the Dniester to the Moldavian side, and the time may have been four in the afternoon. Basia was less concerned now about coming too close to the river because she was sure that she must have passed Mohilev by now.

"... If only I knew for sure," she repeated, lifting her cold, blue-tinged face towards the sky, and at the same time feeling hot under the skin and burning with the fever that didn't leave her even for a moment. "If only I knew... Ah, if only some animal or some tree could speak out and tell me *'it's just a mile or two to Hreptyov, it's just a little further,'* perhaps I might make it..."

But the trees said nothing. On the contrary, rather then help they seemed to be conspiring against her, barring her way with gnarled roots half hidden in the snow, and with thick, knotted stumps over which she tripped constantly. After a while the going got even harder, she felt as if she were carrying a huge weight on her back, and she threw off the thick, warm cloak in which she was wrapped, and kept only her shortcoat around her shoulders to keep out the bone-chilling frost.

Feeling a little lighter, she went on, tripping and falling into the deeper snowdrifts at every other step, but hurrying as best she could. Her thin, unsoled suede boots may have been fine for sleigh riding and galloping on horseback, but they did nothing to protect her feet from the stones and frozen lumps of earth that she stumbled against in passing. Moreover, soaked through as they had been in all the river crossings, and kept damp and sweaty by the heat of the fever that set her legs on fire along with her body, they weren't likely to last long on the forest trails.

'*I'll get to Hreptyov barefoot,*' Basia thought. '*If I don't die that way.*'

A sad smile lit up her small face for a moment, because she was pleased that she could still keep going, and that Michal wouldn't be able to blame her for lack of trying, once he had found her dead, frozen body and seen how far she'd come.

And because she was now delirious with her fever, and talking almost constantly to her absent husband, she told him: "Ey, *Michalku*, not too many women would have got as far as I have... Evka, for example..."

She'd thought of Evka often during her ride to freedom, and she prayed for her many times as she stumbled on foot through the darkening forest, because she knew that if Azia didn't love the girl, then her fate, and that of the other captives he had seized in Rashkov, would be a frightful one.

"They have it worse than I do," she kept telling herself and this kept her going.

But now, after hours of that desperate journey, each of her steps was weaker than the one before. The sun rolled slowly across the Dniester, bathed the sky in a final scarlet glow, and then sunk and vanished deep within Moldavia. The snow acquired a deep violet hue. The gold and purple canopy overhead began to dim and narrow. What had been like a scarlet sea spilled across half the sky, now shrunk into a lake which became a river. The river dwindled into a stream that turned into a last glowing thread of light on the horizon, and then a vast darkness ascended from the west.

* * *

Night came again.

Another hour went by. The forest turned into a black, mysterious entity, hushed in the breathless stillness of the night, as if it crouched in thought everywhere around her, pondering what to do with that poor, lost creature. But there was nothing good that Basia could expect from that deathly silence; on the contrary, it betrayed only cruelty and indifference.

Basia hurried on, gasping the still, cold air with parched lips, and tripping in the darkness all the more frequently, and falling more often.

Her small, cold face was tilted towards the sky but she was no longer searching for the Dipper because she'd completely lost her sense of direction, or even the awareness that there were stars overhead to guide her. She moved just to be moving. She pressed on because she knew that death was near her now, and she began to see, hear and experience those warm, brilliant visions that come to the dying before their final moments.

The dark forest walls compressed about her and became suddenly the main hall of her home in Hreptyov. She was there. She could see every detail of that hospitable chamber. She saw the bright glow of the fire leaping in the hearth. She watched the officers ranked on their evening benches all along the walls. Pan Zagloba was poking fun and teasing Pan Snitko. Pan Motovidlo stared silently at the fire. The fire hissed and crackled like a condemned soul, and each time it did so, the old Cossack leader asked in his drawn-out, sing-song voice: *'What can I do for you, poor spirit, to ease your time in Purgatory?'*

She saw her Michal, throwing dice with Pan Mushalski and old Pan Hromyka, and she went up to him and said: "Let me sit close to you on this bench for a bit, my dear. I don't feel too well."

And there were Michal's arms thrown around her at once, and his voice whispering in her ear. "What is it, kitten? Is it maybe... are you maybe...?"

"I just don't feel well," she answered, knowing what would concern him yet please him the most.

Ah, how bright it was then in that warm, pleasant room where the evening tales would start at any moment! How she loved her Michal! Only there was this strange, unexpected illness that was settling on her; that feeling of emptiness and loss and a sudden fear...

She felt so chilled just then that her fever left her for a while. She was too weak to take another step. All her strength drained away in what had to be her last mortal moment. Cold clarity returned. Her visions disappeared. Memory was restored.

"I'm escaping from Azia," Basia told herself. "I am in a forest, at night. I can't get to Hreptyov. I am dying."

After the feverish heat that had gripped her body all this while, the sudden chill was like a shard of ice that pierced right through her deep into her bones. Her legs quivered and collapsed under her. She found herself kneeling in the snow, before a dark tree.

Not even the slightest shade of doubt or illusion clouded the crystal clarity of her mind just then. She loved her life. She didn't want to lose it. But she knew perfectly well that she was about to die, and turned to God in prayer so that He might accept her soul into His keeping.

"In the name of the Father and the Son," she began.

Ah! But what were those shrill, piercing sounds that suddenly screeched and rattled in her ears?

Basia's mouth fell open.

The question *'what is that?'* died unspoken on her parted lips. Her trembling fingers moved towards her face as if they had a will and mind of their own and wanted to pull her out of a deep, troubling sleep into a wonderful awareness.

She struggled to regain both memory and consciousness as if she were dreaming, and trying to awake so that she could believe her own startled ears, and suddenly a terrible cry burst out of her throat: "Jesus! Oh dear Jesus! Those are well beams screeching! That's Hreptyov! Oh Jesus!"

And then this poor, spent creature which was dying helplessly only a moment earlier, leaped to her feet and ran madly through the forest, choking on her own rasping breath, falling and leaping up again, and crying out to herself as if it were an incantation that would give her strength:

"They're watering the horses! That's Hreptyov! Those are our well beams! Let me just get as far as the gate! Just to the gate! O dear Jesus! That's Hreptyov... Hreptyov...!"

The woods thinned out and opened up before her into a snowy plain topped by a gentle mound from which several pairs of glowing eyes regarded her brightly.

Ah, but these weren't the eyes of wolves! Not this time! These were the gleaming windows of the *fortalitzya*, up there on the mound, whose bright, beckoning lights offered her salvation.

There was still a long way to go but Basia didn't even know when she crossed the plain. The soldiers who stood around the gate on the village side didn't recognize her in the darkness, but they assumed that this was some lad sent out by the commandant earlier on some errand so they let her pass. She ran into the fort, stumbled across the parade ground past the string of horses, just back from patrol, that the dragoons were watering at the wells, and managed to reach the door of the main house with what was literally her last ounce of strength.

★ ★ ★

It just so happened that Pan Zagloba and the little knight were both sitting astride a bench in front of the fire, sipping hot *krupnik* and talking about Basia. Both of them were gloomy and out of sorts, missing her and wondering how she was doing so far away in Rashkov, and wishing that she had never left.

"So when will she be back?" Pan Zagloba grumbled. "God save us from any sudden thaws, rains or floods or it'll be weeks before we see her here again."

"The Winter is still holding fast," the little knight offered. "Let's give her another eight to ten days before we start worrying. Though I don't mind telling you I look out towards Mohilev every day just in case she's coming home early."

"I wish she'd never left!" the old knight burst out. "I'm lost here without her!"

"So why did you advise me to let her go?"

"I advised you? I never said anything of the kind! It was all your doing!"

"Let her just get back safe and sound," sighed the little knight. "And the sooner the better."

But just then the doors creaked open. They glanced up and saw some small, bedraggled creature, covered with snow and wrapped in shreds of torn, ragged clothing.

"Michal! Michal!" the frail apparition squealed pitifully from the threshold.

The little knight leaped to his feet but in that first, startled moment he seemed to turn to stone. Amazement stunned him. He was unable to move. He only threw out both his arms in thunderstruck astonishment and stood waiting dumbly, blinking his eyes rapidly as if to focus them on something he didn't understand.

But Basia stumbled nearer.

"Michal!" she gasped, and then went on in a cracked, broken voice, that was little more than a muffled groan. "Azia betrayed us... tried to take me with him... but I got away. Help me!"

With this she pitched forward to the floor and spilled there like a corpse. He came alive with terror. He reached her in one bound, swept her up in his arms as if she were a feather, and screamed out: "Merciful Christ!"

But her worn, bloodless face lay as if lifeless on his arm, her head dangled loosely when he clutched her closer, and he began to howl in a terrible, stricken voice:

"Baska is dead! She's dead! God help me!"

Chapter Fifty-four

THE NEWS OF BASIA'S RETURN struck all of Hreptyov like a
thunderbolt, but no one saw her that night nor through the next
few days other than her husband, Pan Zagloba and the serving
women.

She had recovered consciousness just long enough to stammer
out a few bits and pieces of her story, telling what happened on
the road to Rashkov. But then she fainted once more, and even
though everyone made a desperate effort to keep her warm, to
feed her herbs and wine and even some hot food, and to keep
her from slipping into shock, an hour later she wasn't even able
to recognize her husband, and everybody knew that she was in
for a grave and protracted illness.

All of Hreptyov, however, leaped awake and stirred like a
roiled beehive. The soldiers swarmed into the parade ground as
soon as the word burst in every barrack that their Lady had come
back only half alive. The officers assembled in the commandant's
main hall, whispering worried speculations to each other, and
peering anxiously towards the sleeping quarters where Basia had
been put to bed, but it was a long time before anybody heard
anything for sure.

True, the serving women ran like deer through the gathered
nobles—some on their way to the kitchen for pails of hot water,
and others running to the apothecary's store for healing herbs
and poultices and ointments—but they wouldn't stop long
enough to exchange two words.

Uncertainty weighed like lead on everyone.

A dense crowd gathered in the *maydan*, including many people who came up from the settlement beyond the walls. Questions flew from mouth to mouth. Azia's treason was soon common knowledge, along with the news that the Lady saved herself in a desperate flight, and that she'd been on the run for a whole week without food and rest. A terrifying rage seized the assembled soldiers when they heard about this, all the more frightening because it was silent and controlled so that no loud outbursts would disturb the victim.

At last, after what seemed like an interminable wait, Pan Zagloba came out of the sickroom, his eyes red with weeping, his bald pate wet with sweat, and his scanty hair erect with despair. The officers ran to him at once and surrounded him with their fevered questions.

"Is she alive? Is she breathing yet?"

"She's still alive," the old man answered. "But God only knows if she'll last an hour..."

Here his low, quavering voice tightened in his throat, his lower lip began to tremble, he grasped his head with both his hands and sat down heavily on a bench.

Then he began to quiver with thick, muffled sobs.

At this sight Pan Mushalski threw his arms around Pan Nenashinyetz, whom he didn't particularly like, and hooted mournfully while Pan Nenashinyetz added his own low wail. Pan Motovidlo's eyes bulged out of his head, as if he'd choked on something that he couldn't swallow; Pan Snitko started unbuttoning his coat with trembling hands and for no good reason; and Pan Hromyka raised his arms to heaven and paced like that up and down the room.

The soldiers massed outside the windows took all these signs of desperation to mean that their beloved Basia had given up the ghost, and raised a fierce lament and ruckus of their own, which enraged Pan Zagloba to such an extent that he hurled himself into the *maydan* like a stone out of a catapult.

"Quiet, you dogs!" he hissed in a stifled voice. "May the lightning smash your bones to pieces!"

The soldiers understood at once that their howls of grief had been premature, and that their beloved Lady was still struggling against Death's dark shadow, but they stayed where they were, waiting in grim silence.

Meanwhile Pan Zagloba made his way back into the main hall, a little calmer than he was before, and sat down on the bench again. A woman servant appeared hurriedly in the door of Basia's room just then and the old knight leaped up and trotted towards her.

"What's happening in there?" he demanded.

"Nothing. She's asleep."

"Asleep? Then God be praised!"

"Maybe God will take mercy," the woman began but the old knight wouldn't let her finish.

"What's the commandant doing?"

"He's at the bedside, master."

"That's good!" the old man snapped. "Now off you go about your business!" Then he turned to the officers around him. "She's sleeping," he announced in a careful whisper and repeated the servant woman's prayer. "Maybe God will take mercy on her. Ah, I feel a touch of hope in me again... Phew, I've quite lost my breath..."

The others also drew a deep breath of relief. Then they crowded around the old knight with hushed, anxious questions.

"But how did all of this come about, by God? What actually happened? How could she get away on foot?"

"She was on horseback at the start," the old man murmured back, hardly able to make his voice stronger than a whisper. "In fact she had two horses, because she knocked down that damned Tartar dog, may the plague squeeze the air out of him, and took his *bahmat* for a spare!"

"A man would hardly dare to believe this!"

"She smashed him right between the eyes with the grip of his own pistol, and because they'd dropped back behind the convoy nobody else saw her do it, and she could get away. The wolves butchered one of her horses, the other drowned under ice. Oh, sweet loving Christ! Imagine that poor little thing alone in the forests, in the ice and snow... going night and day on foot without food or drink..."

Here Pan Zagloba couldn't control himself and let out another tearful bellow that broke into his story, and the officers clutched at their own heads in wonder, admiration, and pity for this brave young woman whom they all loved so much.

"When she finally came within sight of Hreptyov," Pan

Zagloba resumed his account after a long moment, "the poor thing was so spent she could no longer recognize the place and got ready to die. It's then she heard the well beams screeching in the *maydan*, figured out that she was almost home, and dragged herself here literally on her last breath."

"If God looked after her in such a terrible adventure," Pan Motovidlo murmured, wiping his wet whiskers, "then He'll protect her through this hard time as well."

"You've got that right!" all the others chorused eagerly. "That's just how it'll be!"

★ ★ ★

Meanwhile another growl of raised angry voices came from the men massed in the parade ground, and Pan Zagloba leaped up in another rage and dashed through the doors. Rows of fierce faces ranked tightly before him, but the soldiers drew back respectfully and formed a half circle when he and two other officers appeared.

"Keep quiet, you damned dogs!" he roared. "You hear me? Or I'll...!"

But before the old knight could finish his threat, a far more dangerous man stepped out of the ranks and took two steps forward. This was Zydor Lusnia, the dragoons' regimental sergeant-major, a dour Mazurian who was Volodyovski's favorite soldier, and who was known for saying exactly what he meant and never to mince his words.

"What it is, sir, by Your Honor's leave," he barked out in a voice that brooked no discussion. "That since that scurvy mongrel tried to harm our Lady, we want to march on him straight away to have our revenge. I'm the one that says it, but everybody wants it. And if the colonel can't leave the post to go after that son of a bitch himself, then we'll ride under another officer's command, all the way to the Crimea if that's what it takes, so's to get our own back on that murdering dog and pay him for our Lady!"

An ice-cold, unforgiving peasant hatred rang in the sergeant-major's voice. The dragoons and the common men-at-arms from the nobles' regiments started to snarl and mutter and grind their teeth and rattle their sabers, and the deep booming growl that swept across the *maydan* sounded as deadly as the fury of a wakened bear.

The sergeant-major stood rigidly at attention, awaiting the reply, and the grim, determined ranks stood as rigidly behind him, and each fierce, threatening face mirrored such an implacable conviction that even their iron discipline couldn't hold against it.

The silence stretched until some other voice boomed out from the rear ranks.

"That man's blood is the best medicine there is, for what troubles the Lady!"

★   ★   ★

Pan Zagloba's anger was quite gone by then. He was profoundly moved by the troopers' love for his adored little warrior. Besides, the mention of medicine lit another bright idea in his fertile mind. He decided to have a top-notch physician brought at once for Basia. Living as deep in the wilderness as all of them did, no one had thought of it at first, but there were several well-known medics living in Kamyenetz. Among them was a certain Greek—a rich, famous man who owned a lot of property in that city—and who was so skilled in his craft and practice that he was generally regarded as almost a magician. But would he come?

It seemed to Pan Zagloba that since the Greek was both so rich and famous that even magnates addressed him as *Master*, he might refuse this housecall no matter what the price, if it meant a long, hurried trip to the far boundaries of civilization. He pondered the problem for a while, then said:

"Justice and retribution won't miss that prince of mongrels. I swear it to you. And I assure you that this arch-hound would much rather have His Majesty the King vow vengeance against him than to have Zagloba doing it. But I can't swear that he's still alive because our Lady banged him in the head with a pistol-butt when she got away. But now's not the time to talk about that. Now we must save the Lady!"

"We'd gladly trade our lives for hers!" Lusnia shot back at once.

"I know. So would I. A medic would serve her better though, just now." Pan Zagloba turned a serious face on the grim sergeant-major. "Listen, Lusnia. In Kamyenetz there's a famous pill-pusher, name of Rodopoulos. You'll ride to him and you'll tell him that his lordship, the Ordinary-General of Podolia, twisted his foot right outside Kamyenetz and needs his attention. You've got that?"

"Sir!" Lusnia barked.

"And as soon as you've got him on the other side of the city walls, grab him by the neck, jam him on a horse or throw a hop sack over him, and bring him here to Hreptyov at the gallop! I'll have fresh horses posted for you in stages all along the way so you'll fly like the wind. Only make sure you get him here alive because he's useless to us as a corpse."

A growl of approval swept across the ranks, and Lusnia twitched his ferocious mustache. "He's as good as here," he said. "There's no worry about that."

"Go, then!"

"There's one more thing, Your Honor."

"What more do you need?"

"What if he croaks afterwards?"

"Let him croak, as long as he's alive while he's here! Now take six men and go!"

Lusnia vanished. A crowd of others ran to saddle horses, glad they could do something to help their sick Lady, and in about the time it takes to say six Hail Marys, six men rode out with Lusnia at a gallop, while others trotted out behind them with a herd of remounts.

★　★　★

Pleased with himself, Pan Zagloba went back to the main hall of the house, and a moment later Volodyovski came out of the sickroom.

The little knight was changed almost beyond recognition; he seemed only half aware of what was going on everywhere around him, and quite deaf to all the sympathy and commiseration that was offered to him.

All he said to Pan Zagloba was that Basia was still asleep, still breathing. And then he slumped listlessly on a bench and stared with blank, empty eyes at the door behind which she lay. It seemed to all the gathered officers that he was straining to hear something in that other room so they clamped their fists over their mouths and tried to hold their breaths. Not even a whisper broke their total silence.

At last Pan Zagloba stirred, sighed, shook himself like an wakening old hound, and approached the little knight on tiptoe. "Michal?" he said.

"Hmm?"

"I sent to Kamyenetz for a medic. But... should we maybe send for somebody else...?

Volodyovski's blank stare shifted for a moment as he tried to understand what the old knight was saying, but apparently he failed.

"For a priest?" Pan Zagloba offered. "Father Kaminski could be here by morning..."

The little knight closed his eyes at that, his face became as white as a winding sheet, and he turned away to stare into the fire.

"Oh Jesus! Jesus! Jesus!" he started to repeat in a strangled whisper.

Pan Zagloba sighed, asked him nothing more, and went out to give the necessary orders and make the arrangements.

★   ★   ★

When he returned Volodyovski was no longer there but the other officers told him that the little knight had run to his wife who had began to call for him. No one could guess, however, if Basia had called out in full consciousness of what she was doing or if it was just a cry born of her fever and hallucinations.

The old gentleman soon discovered that it was the fever.

Basia's cheeks were radiant with a scarlet flush. She seemed aglow with health. Her eyes were shining with a feverish brightness but they seemed as blank and as void of reason as if the whites had spilled across the iris and rendered her sightless. Her thin hands searched for something desperately along the quilt. Volodyovski lay with his head at her feet, looking half dead himself.

From time to time the sick woman muttered some disjointed phrases, or spoke a word or two aloud and quite clearly, and "Hreptyov" was one that came the most often. Wherever she thought she was, it must have been somewhere on her journey. Pan Zagloba was particularly worried by those restless hands because their mindless grasping at the empty air suggested the proximity of death. He was a widely experienced man who'd seen many people die before his eyes but no death had such an effect on him as the approach of this one. He thought his heart would split with grief at the sight of this small, fragile flower wilting before her time. He understood at once that there was nothing that a man could do to keep that dimming life from flickering out altogether. Only God could help. So he knelt at the foot of Basia's bed and plunged into fervent prayer.

Meanwhile Basia's quick, chaotic breathing seemed to come harder by the minute. A grim, rasping rattle sounded among the panting, shallow gasps, and Volodyovski jumped to his feet in terror. Pan Zagloba also got off his knees and the two of them stared at each other with the utmost horror and despair. They were convinced that Basia was dying. But this terrifying moment lasted for only a short while. Basia's breath soon settled down again and returned to normal.

From that moment on the two men seemed to live suspended between hope and fear. The night dragged by. Each minute seemed like at least an hour of anxiety and waiting.

The other officers also waited, whispering in the main hall. None of them went to bed that night. All sat slumped wearily on their benches and watched the closed doors of the sickroom, or wandered about the bright, spacious chamber, with their eyes fixed gloomily on the floor, or nodded sleepily where they were, lulled by the warmth of the fireside and the silence of their vigil, and snatching odd moments of sleep when it stole upon them. A servant lad entered now and then to throw another log into the crackling fire, and each time the door creaked open to let him in, the officers leaped to their feet thinking that this was Volodyovski or Zagloba, and that they were about to hear the dreaded words: "She's dead!"

★ ★ ★

Meanwhile the night had ebbed, the roosters started crowing, and the sick young woman went on struggling with her fevered illness. A howling wind rose up not long before the sunrise; it lashed the roof and the windows with dark streams of rain; it boomed and roared among the chinked logs, and within the thatch, and rattled in the rafters; it hissed down the chimney and sent thick clouds of smoke and sparks billowing into the room. Pan Motovidlo tiptoed out at first light because he had to take out a patrol that morning but all the others stayed. The new day was as pale as if it were also ill and dying and anxious to cover itself with the grey shroud of clouds. Its weak, trembling light crept in through the windows and fell on drawn and exhausted faces.

Out in the *maydan*, the routines of the outpost garrison went on with their disciplined sameness, no different than those of any other day. Hoof beats rattled on the stable ramps through the hiss and booming of the wind. The long wooden beams creaked and groaned at the wells and at the watering troughs. There was the normal sound of soldiers' voices as the men went about their assigned morning tasks. But soon another sound intruded: the thin tinkling of a bell announced that Father Kaminski had come with the holy sacrament.

When he entered the main hall, dressed in a white surplice over his black cassock, all the officers went down on their knees as if there was a special ceremonial content to the moment, after which death was sure to come. The sick woman who hardly seemed to breathe remained unconscious, locked within her fever so that she couldn't be confessed and given absolution, but the priest gave her the last rites with the holy oils, and then set about comforting the small knight, urging him to surrender to the will of God. But this had no effect on Volodyovski because no words he heard were able to pierce through the wall of pain around him.

Death hovered over Basia all that day.

It seemed to all who were there that it crouched darkly overhead like a watchful spider in some murky corner of the ceiling, and that it crept out into the light now and then and dropped down on its silvery thread towards Basia's pillow, and that its shadow brushed against her hot, pale forehead while her bright young soul spread out its wings to fly away from Hreptyov, to cross those unimaginable distances of eternity and go beyond the bounds of life to another shore.

But then death retreated. It hid again like a waiting spider in the darkened ceiling and hope gleamed once more in the hearts and minds of the gathered men.

It was, however, only a passing temporary hope. No one there dared to expect that Basia could live through such a serious illness, not after all the hardships and ordeals of her desperate journey. Volodyovski had no hope at all so that Pan Zagloba began to fear for his small friend's life, and even though he was quite heartsick and bereft himself beside Basia's sickbed, he took the time to urge the other officers to look after their over-wrought commander.

"For God's sake!" he urged one of them after another. "Keep an eye on him, will you? This is the most terrible thing that's ever happened to him. He might just turn a knife on himself!"

The thought of suicide didn't occur to Pan Volodyovski, but he asked himself constantly through that grief and pain that were threatening to tear him apart: *'How am I to stay here when she's leaving us? How can I part from that sweet, loving soul? What will she say when she looks for me on that other shore and doesn't see me walking at her side?'*

With such thoughts for company, he wanted to die right along with her. He craved that final moment of togetherness with all of his heart, because just as he couldn't imagine any kind of life for himself without her, so he believed that she too would miss him in that other world, that he was important to her happiness, and that she'd want him near her.

★　★　★

Late in the afternoon the evil spider slipped away once more into its dark shadows, Basia's flush receded, and her temperature fell enough to allow her some moments of consciousness and awareness.

She kept her eyes closed for a while, then opened them and peered carefully into the face of the little knight. *"Mihalku,"* she asked. "Am I in Hreptyov?"

"Yes, my love!" he answered, clamping his teeth shut in anguish and pity.

"And you're really here?"

"Yes! How do you feel?"

"Oh, so well..."

It was clear that she didn't know herself if she was conscious and seeing what she saw, or if she was still talking to her fevered dreams. But she regained full consciousness steadily from then on.

At nightfall, Sergeant-major Lusnia clattered into the compound along with his men, and spilled the Kamyenetz physician
out of a sack at the main house door, along with all his herbs and
medications.

The Greek looked half dead. In fact he wasn't far from dying
out of terror, and he kept fainting and collapsing for a little
while. He had assumed that he was seized by bandits and dragged
off into the wilderness for ransom, but it didn't take him long to
get the sense of his surroundings. Once reassured that he was
making only another housecall, even though it was by an unusual sort of invitation, he set about his work with energy and
skill.

He was all the more devoted to his patient's care after Pan
Zagloba showed him a satchel full of minted silver and a loaded
pistol. "That's your reward for her life,"he told him. "And that's
for her death." And late that same night, sometime towards
morning, the evil spider hid himself for good.

"She'll be ill a long time but she will get well!" the medic
announced, and this good news flew like lightning into the
maydan and beyond the walls and echoed throughout the fort
and countryside of Hreptyov.

When he first heard it, Volodyovski finally allowed himself to
break; he fell to his knees and burst into such a cleansing and
healing flood of tears that it seemed as if the sobbing would blow
his chest apart.

Pan Zagloba grew weak with relief and joy. His florid face was
quite awash with sweat. He barely staggered to a bench, crying
out "Get me a drink, somebody!" in his passing, when his legs
gave way.

All the other officers hugged and embraced each other.

Out in the *maydan*, all the dragoons, the men-at-arms and Pan
Motovidlo's Cossacks gathered as before. Only the most powerful entreaties kept them from disturbing Basia with a roaring
cheer. But they were determined to show their joy, and their
gratitude to God for her recovery, and they started pleading for
a gift of a few captured marauders from the Hreptyov cellars, so
that they might hang them as a votive offering.

But the little knight refused them.

Chapter Fifty-five

BASIA REMAINED so gravely ill for another week, that if it weren't for the assurances given by the medic, both Pan Zagloba and the little knight would have supposed that her life might flicker out at any moment.

It took the full seven days for her to improve, so that she felt much better. She was now fully conscious and aware. The medic warned that she might have to stay in bed for a month or more, but it was quite certain that she'd eventually return to full health and to all her strength.

Volodyovski, who hardly took a step away from her bedside in all of this time, seemed to fall in love with her all over again, and—if this were possible for a man who loved her almost to the point of adoration—to care for her even more. Sometimes, as he sat beside her and watched that drawn little face into which her old joy of life was beginning to return, and those merry eyes which filled each day with more of her loving and lighthearted spirit, he felt like laughing and weeping all at the same time, and like shouting out: "She's getting better, my Baska! She is getting well!"

And then he covered her hands with kisses, and kissed those poor small feet which had pushed so bravely through the snows to Hreptyov, and he knew that his love and admiration for her had now soared to a wholly new realm of affection. He also felt an immense gratitude to God.

"I'm not a rich man," he said one day in front of Pan Zagloba and all his officers, "but even if I were to work my fingers to the bone, I'll manage to put up a little church somewhere, even if it's only a wooden one. That way each time I hear the bells I'll remember God's mercy and I'll be grateful all over again."

"God grant that we first get through the Turkish war," Pan Zagloba offered.

But the little knight only smiled a little and twitched his whiskers with a thoughtful nod.

"The Almighty knows what would please Him best," he said. "If it's to be the church, then he'll bring me through unharmed. But if He'd rather that I spilled my blood for Him, then I won't skimp on it, you can be sure of that."

★   ★   ★

Along with her health, Basia was quick to recover her good humor. Two weeks later she had her door left ajar in the evening, and when the officers gathered in the hall as usual, she called out to them in her silvery voice: "Good evening gentlemen! I'm not going to die any more, so there!"

"Praise be the God on high!" the officers answered in a single chorus.

"*Slava Bohu, detyno mylenkaya!*" Pan Motovidlo called out all alone. He looked at Basia with a particularly fatherly affection and he always spoke in Ruthenian when he was especially moved. "Glory to God, sweet child!"

"Isn't it incredible what happened?" Basia went on, invisible behind her door. "Who'd have thought it possible? But all's well that ends well, don't you think?"

"God watches over the innocent!" they all chorused again.

"Ha! And Pan Zagloba used to laugh at me that I've more liking for a saber than for a spinning wheel. Good enough! But a lot of good I'd have done with a spindle or a sewing needle! Still, I expect you'll agree that I did well out there?"

"An angel wouldn't have done it better!"

Pan Zagloba worried that Basia would be tired by this exchange and brought it to an end by closing the door. But she didn't thank him for it. On the contrary, wanting to keep chatting—and, above all, to hear herself praised for her courage and determination—she hissed at him angrily like a cat. Now that the danger was long past, she was extremely proud of how she'd treated Azia, and demanded an inordinate amount of praise and attention.

"I did do well, didn't I!" she'd say over and over to the little knight. "Don't you think I did?"

And he, obedient to her will, praised her and kissed her hands and eyes, until Pan Zagloba pretended to be disgusted with it all.

"She'll get as spoiled as rotten apple," he'd mutter gruffly to hide his own adoration of the little warrior. "There will be no living with her after this."

★ ★ ★

The great joy that gripped everyone in Hreptyov, was darkened only by the thought of how much damage Azia's treason did to the Commonwealth, and by the terrible fate of old Pan Novovyeyski, Zosia and her mother, and Evka. What happened in Rashkov was already known in detail not only in Hreptyov but in Kamyenetz as well, and Basia almost fell ill again with worry. Pan Myslishevski, who still hoped to convert the turncoat *Lipki* to the service of the Commonwealth, was the first to tell the story in Hreptyov. Pan Bogush arrived a few days after him, and then came reports directly from Mohilev and Yampol.

There Azia failed to surprise the little garrisons. Pan Gorjhenski proved a better soldier than he was an orator and didn't let himself be taken unawares. He intercepted Azia's message to the *Lipki* left in Mohilev, attacked them himself with his handful of Mazurian infantry, and either killed them all or took them prisoners. Moreover, he sent a timely warning to the garrison in Yampol, so that this border town also escaped a massacre and destruction, and the regular troops which had been chasing shadows in the Steppe, returned to their posts soon after.

Rashkov alone fell victim to Azia's treason, and Pan Volodyovski received a long report from Pan Bialoglovski who had been sent there to replace young Adam Novovyeyski.

'It's a good thing I came here,' Bialoglovski wrote, *'because Novovyeyski isn't in a fit condition for any military function. He looks more like a skeleton these days than a human being and I fear we'll lose a splendid cavalier because his pain and grief have quite broken him. And why wonder? His father was butchered like an ox, his sister's was given to Adurovitch to use at his pleasure, and his little fiancee is now*

*the slave of Azia himself. There's no help for them now, even if there
was some way to buy them back to freedom.*

'We know this from one of Azia's Lipki who twisted his back in the
river crossing,' the letter went on, 'and whom our men caught and
questioned on the coals. Azia, Krytchinski and Adurovitch have gone
south, heading for Adrianople. Novovyeyski is mad to go after them,
saying he has to get his revenge on Azia even if he has to tear him right
out of the Sultan's camp. He was always ready to jump into the hottest
fire so it's no surprise, especially now when it's a matter of his little
Zosia, over whose fate we are all in tears because she was a sweet and
gentle child who won all our hearts.*

'I do what I can to calm Novovyeyski, telling him that Azia will
come to us on his own, because the war is now a certainty and it's just
as sure that the Tartars will come first as they always do.*

'I've word from Moldavia,' Bialoglovski wrote, 'and even from
some Turkish traders, that the Sultan's army is already assembling
below the Balkans. All the Hordes are coming, and so are the Spahis,
which is what they call their picked cavalry, and the Sultan with the
janissaries is due any day. My dear friend, all of the East is marching
against us and we have no more than a handful of troops! Our only
hope is to hold them at Kamyenetz which, I pray to God, has been well
prepared. It's Spring already in Adrianople, and it will be here soon as
well, because the rains are already with us and new grass is starting to
show. I'm falling back on Yampol because Rashkov is just a pile of ashes
with neither food nor shelter. Besides, the way I see it, they'll be calling
us all in from these border outposts before very long.'*

★ ★ ★

The little knight had heard from another source, and possibly
a better one, that the war was now inevitable, because he kept
in touch with the Turkish governor of Khotim, his blood-
brother and opposite number in Moldavia just across the Dniester. He had even forwarded the Turk's warning to the Hetman
a short time before. However Bialoglovski's letter made a powerful impression since it came from the Commonwealth's farthest listening post and confirmed all he'd heard before. But it
wasn't the certainty of war that worried him just then. He was
terribly concerned about Basia's safety.

"The Hetman's orders pulling us out of here will come any
day," he shared his anxiety with Pan Zagloba. "And in the

meantime here's Baska, unable to travel, and in such foul weather too!"

"Let there be ten sets of orders!" Pan Zagloba huffed. "Baska comes first! We'll sit here till she's back to health. The war isn't going to start right away, not until the rains stop and the floods recede. After all, they'll be hauling heavy guns and a siege train to Kamyenetz and they need solid ground for that."

"And you're always ready to act on your own," the little colonel snorted with impatience. "Orders aren't something you can ignore for the sake of your own private business."

"Ha! If you're fonder of your orders than of Basia, then by all means load her on a cart and go! I know, I know... You're ready to help her with a pitchfork if she can't climb into a wagon on her own, and all for the sake of your precious orders! May the Devil take you all with your discipline and orders! In the old days a man did what he could, and he left alone what he couldn't do. You're full of love and concern for Baska when it comes to talking, but let somebody shout *'Let's go get the Turk'* and you'll spit all that caring and compassion out of your mouth like a cherry pit, and you'll drag that poor little thing beside your horse on a rope!"

"I'm not concerned about Basia?" the little knight shouted in amazement. "You should worry about God's anger when you say such things!"

★ ★ ★

But Basia's safety was far too important for them both to bicker about it. Pan Zagloba huffed and puffed for a while longer, really angry that his beloved little warrior wasn't getting the first consideration, but one look at Volodyovski's worried face stirred him to some compassion of his own.

"Michal," he began. "Take what I say the way I mean it. I love her. She's like a daughter to me. My worry comes from a father's heart. You know me. We've done some great things together but have I ever risked my head without a good reason? Would I still be here, waiting like a horseshoe under the Turkish hammer, if it weren't for her? Wouldn't I be better off taking my ease in some quiet backwater, far from any war, to which my age entitles me anyway, and to which nobody in his right mind could object? And who was it that tied you and Baska together in the first place? If it wasn't me, then order me to gulp down a bucket of water without flavoring it with something stronger."

"My life wouldn't be enough to pay you with for that," the little knight replied. "I've thought for some time that once the war begins you'll take Baska to the Skshetuskis in the Lukov country. It's hard to imagine that the *tchambuls* will get that far into the Commonwealth."

"I'll do it for you," the fat knight assured him hastily, "even though I'd really like to take another crack at those thieving Turks. There's nothing worse on earth than that filthy nation that won't touch pork and doesn't drink wine!"

"There's just one thing that I'm afraid of," the little knight confided.

"Such as what?"

"That Baska will put up a fight to go to Kamyenetz to be there beside me. I shake like a leaf, I tell you, when I think about it. And she'll put up a fight, you know she will, as there's a God in Heaven!"

"So you'll forbid it. Haven't we had enough harm done around here just because you let her have her way in everything, and that you agreed to that Rashkov expedition even though I cried out against it from the start?"

"Now there's a lie!" Volodyovski snorted in derision. "You wouldn't give any advice at all."

"When I refuse to give advice," the old knight sniffed loftily, "it's even worse than if I argued for a week against it."

"Baska should've learned her lesson, but you know how she is! If she sees a sword hanging over my head she'll insist on being there too!"

"So you'll forbid it, I repeat. For God's sake! What a henpecked husband you turned out to be!"

"Henpecked or not, I'll confess one thing," the little knight sighed. "When she pushes those tiny fists into her eyes and begins to weep, or even if she only pretends that she's weeping, all my resolution melts like butter in a frying pan. There's no help for it. She must've put some kind of spell on me. Oh, I'll send her off, alright, because her safety is a lot dearer to me than my life, and you know that too. But when I think that I'll have to upset her like I will, then I swear I'd rather choke to death."

"Michal!" the old knight cried. "Put God in your heart and don't let yourself be led by the nose!"

"Huh! Some advice! And who was it who said just a while ago that I had neither mercy nor compassion for Baska?"

"What was that?" Pan Zagloba cocked a palm beside his ear, pretending not to hear.

"You're known for your perspicacity, my friend. Your mind is a wonder. But here you are, just as stumped for a good idea and scratching your head like the worst of us."

"That's because I'm pondering the best arguments to use."

"And what if she puts her fists in her eyes straight away?"

"Ay, ay! And she'll do that, as there's a God in heaven!" Pan Zagloba cried, clearly as worried about it as Volodyovski.

So they racked their brains, knowing full well that Basia could impose her will on them in almost anything she wanted.

Her illness, in which she'd come so close to death, frightened them both to such an extent that they truly let her have her way in everything. They loved her so much that the need of doing something that would cause her any kind of grief made them shake with terror.

Neither of them doubted for a moment that, in the end, she'd comply dutifully with their cruel verdict. No wife of that era could or would oppose a husband's will for long, and Basia was a good and caring wife along with all those other qualities that made her loved by everyone around her. But when it came to seeing those little fists clenched tight and clamped against her eyes, even Pan Zagloba would much rather charge a regiment of janissaries singlehanded.

Chapter Fifty-six

IN THE MEANTIME, something happened that very afternoon
which, they were both sure, would solve the problem of convincing Basia that she should not accompany Pan Michal to Kamyenetz.

This unexpected help came in the form of very welcome
guests when, close to evening, and without any advance warning
whatsoever, Sir Hassling and Lady Ketling appeared in Hreptyov. The joy and amazement at this surprise reunion were
beyond description. The visitors were also overjoyed to hear
that Basia felt much better. Krysia ran at once into Basia's room
and the squeals and cries that came out of there immediately
announced Basia's own great joy.

Ketling and Volodyovski clung to each other a long time,
holding each other at arm's length only long enough to take a
good look at a friend that neither of them had seen for half a
dozen years, and then embracing each other joyfully all over
again.

"As God's my witness!" the little knight said at last. "A
Hetman's baton wouldn't please me more than seeing you again.
But what are you doing in these parts?"

"The Hetman has appointed me commander of artillery in
Kamyenetz," Ketling told him, "so my wife and I are now living
there. The first thing we heard was the story of your troubles
here so we set out for Hreptyov straight away. God be thanked
that everything turned out so well for you and Basia after all that
happened. To tell you the truth, we rode here in a great anxiety,

532

not knowing if we were coming to share your mourning or your joy."

"The joy! The joy!" Pan Zagloba broke in, interrupting. "Now there's another reason for a celebration!"

"But how did that whole thing come about?"Ketling pressed.

The little knight and Pan Zagloba raced each other to tell the whole story, and Ketling only raised his eyes and arms to the ceiling, full of admiration for Basia's courage and spirit. Then it was Ketling's turn to tell his friends how he and his wife had prospered since their last time together.

"After our wedding we settled close to the Courland border," he reported. "And we're so happy there that Paradise couldn't be any better. Marrying Krysia, I knew very well that I was taking on a celestial being, a creature not of this earth so to speak, and now I'm more sure of it than ever."

Pan Zagloba and Volodyovski immediately remembered the old Ketling they knew, the one who always expressed himself in lofty and poetic terms, and for whom women tended to become objects of distant adoration.

"Tell me, though," Pan Zagloba asked. "Did some earthy event happen to befall that celestial creature? The kind that kicks its legs about and sucks on its thumb?"

"God gave us a son!" Ketling said. "And now again, as you might have noticed..."

"I noticed," Pan Zagloba broke in again and bent a stern eye on the little knight who started moving his mustache nervously up and down at once. "We've nothing like that to report around here."

"Baska asks you all to join us if you would," Krysia said just then, appearing for a moment in the doorway to the inner room.

★ ★ ★

Krysia's return to the main hall put a quick end to further revelations, and they followed her to Basia's room where their joyful greetings resumed once again. Ketling kissed Basia's hands, Volodyovski kissed the hand of Krysia, and all of them peered at each other with great curiosity, like all people do who haven't seen each other a long time.

Ketling had altered least of all. His hair was cut short now in the Polish fashion, which made him look much younger. Krysia, however, was changed almost beyond recognition. She was no longer as lithe and lissome as before. Her complexion had become more pale, which made the soft down above her upper lip more pronounced and darker.

All that seemed to be left of the breathtaking girl who had so entranced Pan Volodyovski were her magnificent dark eyes, their long, curving lashes, and a warm and sunny gentleness in her face. But those delicate features which had once been so subtle in their line and shading had lost their purity and shed their enchantment. Her body had thickened. This could have been just a passing thing, Pan Michal supposed, due to her condition, but when he compared her with his Basia, he couldn't get over his own amazing luck.

'For God's sake!' he asked himself. 'How could I've fallen for her when they were both together? Where did I lose my eyes?'

Basia, in contrast, seemed beyond the ordinary criteria of beauty to the delighted Ketling, and she was indeed dazzling with her tawny hair tumbling across her forehead and with her pale complexion which had lost its customary, healthy flush during her long illness, and which seemed as delicate and translucent as the petals of a fresh white rose. Now her small face was aglow with joy and her little nostrils quivered with excitement. She looked so young just then that she seemed hardly older than a child, and at first sight she appeared ten years younger than Ketling's own Krysia.

But her childlike beauty had only one effect on the poetic and sentimental Ketling. He looked at his own wife with even greater caring and affection, because he always felt somewhat guilty where she was concerned.

★   ★   ★

The two women had already told each other everything that could be related in such a short time, so now the whole gathering settled around Basia's bed and started recalling their old times together. But this conversation didn't work too well. Those old times contained some matters that none of them wanted to talk about or even to remember. There were the liberties that Pan Volodyovski had taken with Krysia. There was his indifference to his adored Basia, and there were various broken promises and acts of desperation. The time they had all spent together in Ketling's little manor had a great deal of charm for everyone, and all of them remembered it with pleasure, but talking about it was another matter.

Finally Ketling reached for another subject.

"I haven't told you yet," he said, "that we stopped off at the Skshetuskis on our way south from the Courland border. What wonderful friends they are! They wouldn't hear of our leaving for a full two weeks and gave us such a welcome that Heaven itself couldn't be any better."

"For God's sake!" Pan Zagloba cried. "And how are the Skshetuskis? Did you find Yan at home as well?"

"We did because he'd just come home on leave, along with three of his older sons who are already serving in the Hetman's regular contingent."

"I haven't seen Skshetuski since the time of our wedding," sighed the little knight. "He and his sons were here in the Wild Lands with their regiment later on, but we didn't get a chance to see each other."

"They all miss you terribly, by the way," Ketling told Zagloba.

"And I miss them!" the old noble sniffed. "But here's how it is. I sit here and I miss them over there, but if I go there I'll be lost without this kitten here... That's the way it goes in life, I expect. You get a cold wind blowing in one ear or the other and there's no help for it... And it's worst for a lonely old man who doesn't have a child or a corner of his own, because if I had something of my own to love I wouldn't have to love what belongs to others."

"Your own children wouldn't be able to love you more than Michal and I," Basia said.

Pleased and moved, the old knight quickly shelved his thoughts of loneliness, fell into an excellent good humor, huffed a few more times to voice his satisfaction, and announced: "I was a fool that time in Ketling's house when I played the match-maker for the four of you and never gave a thought to myself! There was still time then..."

And here he turned to the two young women.

"Admit it!" he ordered. "You were both desperately in love with me and each of you would've far rather married me than Michal or Ketling!"

"That goes without saying!" Basia cried.

"Helen Skshetuska would also have rather picked me in her time," the old knight observed. "Ha! It's too late now! Ah, but that's a fine, steady, settled woman, that Helen of mine, made to my quiet tastes, not some harum-scarum whipper-snapper who runs around scaring people and knocking the teeth out of some Tartar's head. And how is she doing? Healthy? Well?"

"She's well," Ketling answered. "Only she's a bit troubled at the moment because her two middle sons just ran away from school and joined the army. Skshetuski himself is quite pleased about it, I mean that the youngsters have so much spirit in them, but a mother is always a mother!"

"Do they have a lot of children, then?" Basia asked and sighed.

"They've twelve boys," Ketling said. "And now they've started on the fair sex."

"Ha! There's a special blessing on that house," Pan Zagloba nodded. "I raised that whole brood at my own breast, so to speak, like a pelican who feeds her young with her own flesh. But I've got to twist the ears off that middle pair. If they had to run off to the army, the least they should've done is run here to Michal... Hmm, which ones could they be? Must be Mihalko and Yasiek. There's such a swarm of them over there that their own father can't keep their names straight. Nor will you see a crow for a mile around the house because those rascals shot them all out of the trees years ago. I tell you, you wouldn't find another woman like Helen if you were to search for one with a lighted candle! Each time I told her, *'sweetheart, the lads are growing up, I need another pup to pester and torment me,'* she'd snort at me to behave myself, but nine months later there'd be another little fellow kicking at the air! You could make bets on that! Imagine this, it came to such a pass that if there's a woman in the district who can't quite manage to effect her own maternal state, she'll borrow a piece of clothing from Helen to wear, and it works every time!"

Everyone was quite amazed by this revelation and all of them sat in silence for a while, and the little knight murmured suddenly: "Baska! Did you hear that?"

"Michal, will you be quiet?" she replied.

★   ★   ★

But Michal didn't want to keep quiet just then because a new idea popped up in his head, especially since it suddenly appeared possible to combine two important matters, the one that dealt with his own long delayed family and Basia's safety too, so he began to speak in a deliberately off-hand and careless manner, as if he was merely musing to himself, and as if it were the most normal and expected thing in all the world.

"By God's grace!" he said. "It'd be worthwhile to pay the Skshetuskis a visit! He won't be there, I know that, because he'll be back with the Hetman before very long, but she has a good brain in her head and she never tempts God's patience and forbearance, so she'll be at home."

And here he turned to Krysia.

"Spring's on its way and the weather will be fine for traveling. It's too soon for Basia just now to make any kind of journey, but later on, when she's fit to travel, I wouldn't put up much of an objection. It's a friend's duty to look in on an old war comrade. Pan Zagloba could escort the two of you, and come Fall, when things quieten down around here, I'd make my way up there myself and join you..."

"That's a great idea!" Pan Zagloba cried. "I have to go anyway because I've fed them quite enough of my ingratitude. Ha! They must think I've forgotten they are still alive! That's quite enough to shame me for ever!"

"What would you say to that, milady?" Volodyovski asked, peering anxiously into Krysia's eyes.

"I'd be pleased to go," she answered with her usual gentleness and quietness. "But I'm afraid I can't."

"And why's that?"

"Because I'll stay in Kamyenetz with my husband and I won't leave him there alone no matter what happens."

"Dear God, what am I hearing?" Volodyovski shouted, seeing his best laid plans crumbling so unexpectedly around him. "You'll be in a fortress which is bound to be besieged! And by an enemy who shows no consideration for anyone: man, woman or child. I wouldn't say much if it was a war with some civilized opponent, but this is pure barbarism we'll be facing there. Do you have any idea, milady, what happens in a city that's taken by assault? Do you have any notion of captivity among the Turks and Tartars? 'Struth! I can't believe my ears!"

"However," Krysia said, calm and firm as always. "That's how it has to be."

"Ketling!" the little knight appealed in despair. "Don't you have any say in this matter? Put God in your heart, man! Don't let yourself be controlled like this!"

"We talked about it all a long time," Ketling said. "And that's what we decided."

"Our son is also in Kamyenetz," Krysia said, "under the care of a kinswoman of mine. And is it so inevitable that Kamyenetz must fall?"

And here she raised her sunny smile towards the ceiling and the skies beyond it.

"God is more powerful than the Turk," she said. "He won't break our trust. And since I promised my husband that I wouldn't leave him until death, my place is with him."

The little knight was thrown into complete confusion because that was the last thing he expected to hear out of Krysia. But Basia, who'd caught on from the start where Michal was heading, shot him a sly little grin and mimicked his own earlier question.

"Michal! Did you hear that?"

"Baska!" he shouted, totally defeated. "Will you please keep quiet?"

His last hope lay with Pan Zagloba, and he threw him a glance of utter desperation, but the old knight had no help to offer.

"Somebody ought to give some thought to supper," he said and stood up. "Man does not live by the word alone."

And he beat a hasty retreat of his own.

Pan Michal soon seized a chance to run after him, caught up with him outside and stepped in his path.

"Well, and what now?" Pan Zagloba asked.

"What now?" Volodyovski echoed.

"Damn that Ketling woman anyway! For God's sake! How is the Commonwealth not to fall when women rule the roost?"

"But can't you think of something?"

"How can I think of something that might help you when you're scared to death of your own wife? Tell the blacksmith to nail some horseshoes to your heels, that's what you can do! And how about a nice ring in your nose?"

Chapter Fifty-seven

THE KETLINGS STAYED in Hreptyov for about three weeks. Basia insisted on getting up as soon as they left, anxious to get back fully into the life around her, but it was soon clear that she still wasn't well enough for that. Life was pouring back into her faster than her worn, weakened body could accept with ease, and the Greek physician ordered her to stay in bed until she was completely strong again.

In the meantime, Spring came to the wilderness. A vast, warm wind ascended from the Wild Lands and the Black Sea. It ripped and shredded the thick shroud of clouds as if they were old clothes rotting with old age, then seized those scattered grey wisps, bundled them together, and chased them through the sky like a sheepdog that drives his flock across an open pasture. The clouds fled before it, drenching the land below with thick streams of water, in which the individual droplets were often bigger than a berry. The melted remnants of snow-drifts and ice created lakes in the even plains; ribbons of water trickled off the frozen overhanging roots along the canyon walls; the ravines filled with fresh running streams; and all of it rushed loudly, raucously, and with great commotion south into the Dniester, much as a crowd of children runs towards their mother.

Bright sunlight of especial clarity gleamed and dimmed among these scurrying clouds, flashing the presence of a renewed sun that had a fresh, scrubbed look, as if it had bathed in all that water everywhere below it.

Then pale green shoots of new grass began to stretch out of the sodden soil, and the frail tips of tree and shrub branches

thickened under an abundance of buds. The sun burned ever
hotter. The sky filled with birds, flights of cranes and herons,
wild geese and storks flying home from their Winter exile; and
then the wind brought skimming clouds of swallows. Frogs
boomed out their croaking chorus out of the warmed pond
waters. All the small, grey fraternity of starlings and sparrows
twittered from dawn to dusk, and one vast joyful sound burst in
the forests, the plains and the canyons, as if all nature cried out
in vast exaltation: "Spring! U-u-ha! Spring!"

But what that year's Spring was bringing to those unhappy
lands was not joy but mourning, and not new life but death. A
few days after the Ketlings went back to Kamyenetz, the little
knight received a last, desperate message from Pan Myslishevski
who was still trying to hold the peace together at the Sultan's
court, but who had lost all hope and was coming home.

*'The plains above Adrianople are swelling with armies. The Sultan
sent a great amount of gold to the Crimea. The Khan and fifty thousand
of the Horde is riding to join Doroshenko. The Tartar avalanche, when
it falls upon us, will come along the Black Trail and the Kutchmanski
Track. The Turks will march straight up out of the Balkans. May God
have mercy on the Commonwealth!'*

Volodyovski immediately forwarded this message to the Hetman but made no special efforts to evacuate and abandon Hreptyov. He wouldn't have done that in any event without the
Hetman's orders, but years of experience in fighting the Tartars
all across the Wild Lands taught him that the *tchambuls* never set
out as quickly as all that. The flooding in the Steppe was still too
wide and deep, the rivers rushed too swiftly across the swollen
fords, the grass wasn't tall and rich enough for fodder, and
Doroshenko's Cossacks were still in Winter quarters.

The Turks, he thought, wouldn't show themselves much
before the Summer, because even though they'd been assembling at Adrianople for some months, such an enormous siege
and wagon train, such vast crowds of warriors, camp servants and
drovers, and such a mass of baggage, horses, camels and other
beasts of burden, could move only at a snail's pace. Their cavalry
armies could be expected earlier, perhaps in late April or the first
days of May, but even they wouldn't come in one solid, overwhelming mass. Just as single raindrops spatter the ground before
a massive rainstorm, so the main force of the Sultan's horsemen

which—when assembled—could be counted in tens of thousands and filled the horizons, was always preceded by swarms of small *tchambuls* and smaller *vatahas*.

But these were nothing for Volodyovski to worry about. If even picked *tchambuls* of Dobrudjan Tartars could seldom stand up to the regular cavalry of the Commonwealth, such bands of scouts and foragers were no special danger. They had the habit of scattering like dust before the wind at the first hint that regular troops were coming out against them.

★　★　★

In any event, Pan Volodyovski thought, there was time enough; and if it should run a little short, he wouldn't be averse to brushing against some *tchambuls* in a manner they'd find both memorable and painful. He was a soldier born and bred, a soldier by vocation and a lifelong practice, so that war brought him a kind of inner peace and woke a hunger for the enemy's destruction.

Pan Zagloba's thinking was considerably different. His long life made him quite at home in a variety of dangers, but he was much less matter-of-fact about them, or calm at their prospect. He could show great courage in a desperate moment, especially when he had no other choice, building his valor and his reputation piece by piece through many violent encounters, most of which happened quite against his will. He had done great things and won great fame and glory, but the first murmurs of a war always had a nervous and unsettling effect upon him. He had, however, an immense faith in Volodyovski's military skills and profound admiration for his campaign experience, and when the little knight explained his viewpoint to him, even he began to feel much better about the situation.

"When Christian nations fight each other," he held forth to anyone who'd listen, "then our Lord Jesus mourns, and all the saints start scratching their heads, because that's the way it is in Heaven as it is on Earth: when there's a worried master, there are worried servants. But whoever hammers on the Turk, brings joy to the heavens; in fact there's nothing that brings greater pleasure to the holy martyrs. I heard this from a certain high personage in the Church, that the saints get the belly-ache at the sight of those pagan sons of bitches, which spoils their appetite for heavenly foods and drink and interferes with their eternal bliss."

"I'm sure that's the way it is," the little knight agreed. "It's just that the might of the Turks is beyond all counting, while we have merely a handful of soldiers."

"But they can't conquer the whole Commonwealth, can they? Didn't *Carolus Gustavus* bring a whole mess of perfumed plunderers to pollute our air, and weren't there wars against the Russians and the Cossacks and Hungarians and the Prussians going on at the same time? And where are they all today? We not only drove them out of our own country but carried our swords and fire into their backyards."

"That's true enough. I wouldn't fear this war if it was just a matter of my life or death, especially since I've got to do something important to pay our Lord and the Holy Mother for taking care of Baska. Let God just send me a chance! But I worry about these territories which might pass into pagan hands along with Kamyenetz, even if it's only for a time. Think of all those profaned churches and all those Christian people living in op-pression."

"Just don't ask me to shed any tears for the Cossacks! Damn the dogs! They raised their sacrilegious hands against their own mother, so now let them have what they wanted. The main thing is for Kamyenetz to hold out. What do you think, Michal? Will it hold?"

"I don't think Pan Pototzki, the General of Podolia, equipped it well enough, trusting in the natural strength of the town and castle. The burghers also didn't do their part, thinking the place impregnable. But Ketling says that the foot regiments of Bishop Tshebitzki have come in recently and that they're well disci-plined and armed. We should do well enough and I expect we will. Why not? We beat off overwhelming odds at Zbarajh not so long ago from behind a miserable little earthwall and a couple of fish ponds, and Kamyenetz is an eagles' nest in comparison with that..."

"Ha! An eagle's nest, but who knows if there'll be an eagle in it, such as Vishnovyetzki? We could find some empty-headed crow hopping about in there. How well do you know His Lordship of Podolia?"

"He's a great lord and a good soldier but a little on the careless side."

"Yes, yes, I know him too. I've pointed it out to him often enough. The Pototzki family wanted me to take him abroad for his education so he could learn some courtly manners at my side. But I said: *'I won't go. He's so scatterbrained and careless about his property he doesn't have a pair of bootstraps left on any boot, and he'll walk about in mine to make a good showing in all those royal chambers, and shoe leather's expensive.'* And later on, at the court of Marie-Louise, he dressed like a Frenchman but his stockings were always falling down and he strutted about with his bare calves showing. No, no, he won't measure up to Vishnovyetzki!"

"The Kamyenetz merchants and shopkeepers are also whining about the siege because it's bad for business. They'd just as soon belong to the Turks as long as they can keep on making money."

"Dogs!" said Pan Zagloba.

And both he and the little knight slumped into a grim anxiety, thinking about the fate and future of Kamyenetz. They also worried terribly about Basia who'd have to share the destiny of all the other women in the city if the town and castle had to be surrendered.

★ ★ ★

But after a while Pan Zagloba slapped himself on the forehead as if to drive away all his troubling thoughts.

"For God's sake!" he said. "Why are we chewing our finger-nails about this? Why should we go to that flea-bitten rock-pile and lock ourselves in there? Wouldn't you rather stay with the Hetman's army and fight in the field? And if you did that, Baska would hardly enlist in the cavalry, would she? She'd have to go somewhere safe, and not to Kamyenetz either but to some faraway place, like maybe to the Skshetuskis. Michal! God looks into my heart and sees how much I want to fight that heathen vermin, but taking her to the Skshetuskis is the least I can do for Baska and you."

"Thank you with all my heart, my dear old friend," Volody-ovski said. "It stands to reason that if I weren't in Kamyenetz she wouldn't put up any fuss about going there. But what else can I do once the Hetman sends me the orders I expect from him?"

"What can you do when you get your orders? I wish the Devil

snatched and chewed up all the orders that were ever written!
What can be done, you ask? Ah! Ah! I'm getting an idea. You
have to... anticipate the order!"

"What do you mean?"

"Write at once to Pan Sobieski, like maybe you're just passing
on some news, and then drop a hint that when the war begins
you'd like to be with him, out of the great love that you have
for him, and serve in the field. By God's wounds! That's a prime
idea! First, because it makes no sense to lock up such a Steppe
hawk as you behind some wall, instead of using him where he'd
be used the best, and in the second place, that kind of letter will
make the Hetman even fonder of you than he already is and he'll
want you with him. He's not exactly overrun by loyal soldiers,
is he... And there's another thing! If Kamyenetz holds out, all
the glory will go to the General of Podolia, but whatever great
things you do in the field under Pan Sobieski will go to the
Hetman. Don't worry, the Hetman won't let you go to the
General! He'd give up anybody else before he'd part with you!
Even I wouldn't be able to get you from him if I needed you,
though there's nothing he'd ever deny me...! Write that letter!
Nudge him! Refresh his memory about you! Ha! My wits are
worth a lot more than chicken feed, that's certain! Michal, let's
have a drink to celebrate this happy flash of genius! Sit down and
start writing!"

Overjoyed at this possible solution, Volodyovski threw his
arms around Pan Zagloba.

"What's more," he added, "I won't be shortchanging anybody—neither God, nor our country, nor the Hetman—because
I'll really be able to do a lot more in the field than behind the
walls. Thank you, my friend! Thanks with all my heart! I also
think that the Hetman will want to have me near, especially after
getting such a letter. But, to give a little something also to
Kamyenetz, d'you know what I'll do? I'll raise and equip an
infantry company and send it over there. And I'll write to the
Hetman about that as well."

"Better and better! But where will you get the men?"

"I've got about forty cut-throats in the cellars here. They'll
do for a start. Baska, who always pesters me to spare a life
whenever I have some footpad hanged, urged many times that I

turn all these bandits into proper soldiers. I never have, because I wanted the executions to serve as a warning to other marauders. But now that there's a war hanging over our necks everything's allowed. Right now they're more like beasts then men, and they've smelled their share of blood and gunpowder, but we can hammer them into decent shape with discipline and training. I'll also post announcements that whoever comes to enlist out of all the canyons and lairs in the forests will have his crimes forgiven and get a fresh start. We ought to get a hundred men without any trouble. Baska will also be pleased as Punch about it... It's a great, heavy load, my friend, that you've lifted off my heart!"

★　★　★

That same day the little knight dispatched a fresh courier to the Hetman, and announced to the cut-throats chained in the Hreptyov cellars that they could have their lives and freedom in exchange for service in the infantry. They leaped at the chance and swore to recruit others of their kind. Basia was delighted. Tailors were brought in from Kamyenetz and Ushitza to make the uniforms. The former bandits drilled all day in the Hreptyov *maydan*, and Pan Volodyovski was pleased that he'd be fighting the enemy in the open field, that he wouldn't expose his wife to any kind of danger, and that he'd help both Kamyenetz and his country all at the same time.

This work went on for several weeks when Pan Michal's courier returned on one evening with a letter from Hetman Sobieski.

'*My dear and well beloved Volodyovski,*' the Hetman had written. '*I and the country both owe you a great debt for the information you are getting to me. The war is certain. I've other reports that the Turkish armies massing around Adrianople threaten us with very heavy odds. Counting the Horde, they're three hundred thousand strong already, and more come each day. The Tartars will be on the move almost any hour, but nothing matters more to the Sultan than Kamyenetz, because that's the key to the back door of Europe. What's more, those traitor Lipki know every track and trail throughout that whole region, and they'll teach the Turks everything about Kamyenetz that they have to know. I hope God throws that viper son of Tuhay-bey into your hands, or those of Novovyeyski whose agony I share, so that he*

*may pay for his terrible crimes against that fine young soldier and the
entire Commonwealth as well.*

'*As for your serving with me in the field,*' the Hetman continued,
'*nothing would please me better, but it just can't be. The General of
Podolia wasn't always well-disposed towards me after the King's
election, and he did his best to undermine my credibility in Warsaw,
but I want to send him my very best soldier because Kamyenetz is more
important to me than both my eyes and ears. There'll be a lot of men
there who've had a lick or two of war, but they're like people who once
sat down to a memorable meal and then talk about it for the rest of their
lives. What you won't find there are men for whom war is their daily
bread, or if you do find a few, they won't have the stature and position
to influence events.*

'*That's why I want you there,*' Pan Sobieski wrote. '*Ketling's a
good soldier but he's not as well known as you. You, on the contrary,
will be the center of everyone's attention, and the way I see it, they'll
listen to what you have to say even if somebody else is the nominal
commander.*

'*It's dangerous service,*' the Hetman concluded. '*Death will come
thick as hail, as likely as not, but we're used to standing out in the
downpour while everybody else runs for shelter to keep their coat-tails
dry. Fame and a grateful memory is all that any of us can ever expect,
but the main thing is always service to our country, and I don't need to
goad you or harangue you into that.*'

When this letter was read out that night to the officers, who
assembled in the main house to hear the Hetman's order, it
saddened everyone. All of them would have rather fought in the
open field than in a besieged fortress, and Volodyovski let his
head hang low.

"What are you thinking, Michal?" Pan Zagloba queried.

The little knight raised a calm, unworried face to the subdued
old knight, and his voice was as quiet and steady as if none of his
hopes had been disappointed.

"What's to think about?" he asked in turn. "We're going to
Kamyenetz."

He looked and sounded as if he had never thought about it
one way or another, only his little whiskers moved rapidly up
and down.

"Hey, good comrades!" he said after a while. "We'll go to
Kamyenetz. But we won't give it up as long as we're alive!"

"As long as we're alive!" the others repeated.

"Death comes only once, one way or the other, so we might as well make it count for something!" Pan Mushalski said.

Pan Zagloba said nothing for a long time, peering with some anxiety from one face to another and knowing that everyone was waiting to hear what he thought about it. Once more, as so often in his turbulent and extraordinary life, he had to make a choice between great dangers and the safety of his skin, and between his own comfortable and secure well-being and standing by his friends.

Then he sighed.

He took a deep breath.

"Ah, to the Devil with it all," he said finally. "I am going with you!"

Part VIII

Chapter Fifty-eight

WHEN THE STEPPE DRIED, and the lush new grass rose above the Wild Lands, fifty thousand Astrakhan and Crimean Tartars set out to help Doroshenko and his rebel Cossacks.

The Khan himself rode with them along with all his kinsmen, lesser khans, beys and more important murjahs; and all of them wore rich kaftans of honor sent as gifts by the *Padishah*, or *'Ruler of all the Rulers'* as the Sultan of the Turks was known; and they marched upon the Commonwealth not for the loot and captives that were their usual quarry, but to wreak death on all Christianity, to give no quarter, and to exterminate that cursed *Lehistan* in a Holy War.

A second and much greater storm gathered at Adrianople, with only the rock of Kamyenetz crouching in its path on the Polish border. No other barrier stood between that human flood and the defenseless Commonwealth that lay as prostrate as an open plain, or like a sick man too weak to defend himself or even able to stagger to his feet.

After years of Swedish, Prussian, Russian, Cossack and Hungarian wars—all of them won eventually but at a staggering cost in men and resources—the Commonwealth lay exhausted. Weakened by the innumerable *confederations* or mutinies in a sullen army, drained to the last by the rebellions of the cursed George Lubomirski who disrupted every effort to strengthen the country, she was a vast arena for misrule and anarchic chaos which almost any enemy could enter.

Her prospects, like her vistas, were ruined trade and cities that were barely stirring to life again. Empty treasuries and slaughtered populations. And then—as if this were not enough for calamity—the seeping wounds created by eruptions of unrest, domestic chaos, quarrels among the powerful, a population of indifferent gentry who were blind to anything but their own concerns, the threat of civil war, and a helplessly inept King frightened of his mother, who wanted to be loved by each and every party.

The great Sobieski appealed in vain for the means to turn the coming avalanche. No one wanted to face reality. No measures for defense were taken; the treasury had no money and the Hetman had no troops. Fewer than ten thousand men were to face a military power that could challenge all the Christian Kings and peoples of the world.

★ ★ ★

But in the Eastern world, where all that happened did so by the will of the Padishah, and the nations were like one sword gripped by a single fist, just the reverse was true. With the moment that the Banner of the Prophet was unfurled, and the horsetail standards were affixed to the Sarai tower, and the *mullahs* began to preach a Holy War, half of Asia Minor and Arabia, all of Turkish Europe, and all lands and provinces of North Africa from Syria to Morocco, erupted like a flood.

The Sultan himself pitched his pavilions in the Spring in the plains of Thrace and started to assemble a host that numbed the watching world. One hundred thousand Spahis and janissaries surrounded his holy person. All the armies of all the satrapies and possessions began to pull towards him as if drawn by invisible steel strings, and Southeastern Europe spilled out all her warriors.

There came the scarlet cohorts of the Bosnian beys, as deadly as lightning; clans of wild warriors who swarmed out of their Albanian mountains, clutching the long knives with which they fought on foot; legions of Serbs who had embraced Islam and now served the Sultan; the people of the Lower Danube and the lands below it, Rumelia, Macedonia, Silistria and all the nations that inhabited the Balkans north of the Thracian mountains.

Each pasha, or provincial viceroy, led an entire army that could overwhelm the defenseless Commonwealth on its own.

Valachians and Moldavians. All the Dobrudjan and Belgorodian Tartars. Several thousand *Lipki* and *Tcheremisy*, led by the terrible Azia Tuhaybeyovitch, who were to be the pathfinders along familiar trails into their own country.

Then came the Asian levies. The pashas of Siva, Basra, Kufa, Aleppo, Damascus and Baghdad not only brought their regular standing armies but also the armed cohorts of their subject peoples. There came the levies raised among the wild mountaineers who lived in the cedar-covered mountains of Asia Minor, the dusky-skinned inhabitants of Syria and Mesopotamia, the Mamelouks of the Nile, the mounted archers who ranged between the Red Sea and the Persian Gulf, and all the warrior peoples who lived along the Tigris and Euphrates Rivers.

Nor were the Arabs wanting in reply to the call of the Caliph; their white burnous headwear dotted the Rumelian plain like a sheet of snow. Bedouin wanderers of the deserts crouched at the campfires beside city troops from all the towns between Mecca and Medina. Nor did tributary Egypt fail to hear the call. All those uncounted thousands who used to swarm through the streets of Cairo, or sit at sunset to watch the shadows of the pyramids, and all who wandered through the ruins of Thebes or lived in those murky regions which feed Father Nile, now stood in arms in the Adrianople plains, and prostrated themselves in prayer for a triumphant Islam and for the final end of that hated nation which shielded the world for centuries from the Sons of the Prophet.

There were armed warriors by the tens of thousands. Hundreds of thousands of horses neighed in the pastures beside vast herds of buffalo, sheep and camels. It seemed as if God's command drove those multitudes out of Asia and pointed them towards those northern lands where the sun is pale and the snow quilts the plains in Winter. So they came, obedient to God's will, along with all their herds, in swarms beyond counting: dark-skinned and white and burned as black as coal by their distant suns.

How many different languages crossed in that clement air. How many different armaments and costumes gleamed in the April sun. One nation stared curiously at another, their customs strange and never seen before, their weaponry and their ways of fighting unknown to the rest. It was only their faith that united these migrating peoples, and it was only when the *muezzin* sent out the call to prayer that these many-languaged legions faced towards the east and cried out to Allah with a single tongue.

The Sultan's household servants outnumbered all the forces of the Commonwealth, while even greater masses of merchants and traders trailed behind the armies. A fleet of ships carried their wagons north by river along with the military wagon train and baggage. It took two pashas, each entitled to have a triple horsetail standard carried over him and each leading an entire army, to supply food and fodder to these human masses, and the forage was always abundant. The powder train was like a mobile city. Two hundred cannon rolled behind this army, ten of them of such size, range and caliber that no European monarch possessed anything to match them.

★   ★   ★

In camp, the Asian beys occupied the right flank and the European satraps took the left. Their tents spread over such vast distances that the city of Adrianople seemed like a little market town beside them. The Sultan's camp alone was a separate city that gleamed with purples, silken ropes, velvets and gold thread. It swarmed with armed guardsmen, black eunuchs from Ethiopia in blue and yellow kaftans, huge Kurdish porters, beautiful young boys from the Uzbekh tribes dressed in silken shawls, and a glittering array of grooms, table servants, lamp bearers, messengers and other retainers whose many-colored robes turned the dry southern plains into a flowering Steppe.

In the flat, beaten space around the Sultan's court, which brought to mind the joys and opulence of the Paradise promised to the faithful, stood the pavilions of the Grand Vezir, the Imams of the Faith, and of young Kara Mustapha, the Bey of Anatolia, who was looked upon with awe and admiration even by the Sultan as the future *sun of war* and the sword of Islam.

None of these magnificent pavilions matched the splendor of the Sultan's compound but each could have served as a Summer residence for any European monarch. Before them, as before the tents of the Padishah, stood gleaming ranks of infantry, armed with scimitars and spears, who wore such huge turbans that they seemed like giants. Their canvas shelters spilled as far as the tents of the Sultan's household. Beyond them sprawled the camp of the terrible janissaries, armed with spears and muskets, who were the core of the Turkish military power. Neither the German Emperor nor the King of France could boast of such infantry, neither in quantity nor skill. In all the wars against the Commonwealth, few of the Sultan's peoples could face an equal force of Polish-Lithuanian regulars and crushed them only with overwhelming numbers, but the janissaries stood firm even against the elite *husaria* whose irresistible charges broke any other enemies and scattered them like chaff. They were the terror of Christendom, and the Sultan himself took care to keep on the good side of these praetorians, whose commanding Agha was one of the chief dignitaries of the Divan.

Beyond the janissaries stood the camps of the mounted Spahis, then the regular armies of the various pashas, and then all the territorial and provincial levies. All of this vast assembly had waited for several months outside Istanbul until all the contingents of the Ottoman Empire came to swell their numbers, and the Spring sun sucked the moisture from the soil and let the march to *Lehistan* begin.

And the sun shined brightly, as if obedient to the Sultan's will. Only a few warm showers bathed those canvas cities in April and May. The rest of the time the sky seemed like a clear canopy hung by the hand of God above the Sultan's armies. The brilliant sunlight gleamed on the snowy canvas, on the enormous turbans, on cloaks and kaftans as brightly colored as the rainbow, on the steel of helmets, spears, javelins and scimitars, and on the gold crescent tops of banners and standards, drowning the camps and tents and men and herds in one vast sea of brightness. At nightfall, when the crescent moon rose above these thousands who marched behind its symbol, and hung in a cloudless sky like a prophecy of conquest, it seemed to dwindle in the glare of the countless campfires. But when the Arab runners from Aleppo and Damascus lit the green, red, blue and yellow lamps around the tents of the Padishah and the Grand Vezir, it was as if the sky had fallen on the bright-lit plain and filled it with stars.

An exemplary discipline and order ruled among those cohorts. The pashas bent like reeds before the Sultan's will and the armies bowed before the pashas. There was never a lack of food and fodder for the men and horses. Everything came on time and in amounts that exceeded the provisioning quotas. Hours of drill and training and nourishment and prayer passed in perfect order. The moment that the *muezzins* cried their call to prayer from wooden minarets scattered among the camps, the entire army faced east, spread out its prayer rugs, and fell to its knees as one man. The sight of that controlled power filled their own hearts with faith, inflamed their spirits with an eagerness for war, and sent their minds soaring to the stars with the certainty of triumph.

★   ★   ★

The Sultan entered the camp at the end of April but he didn't begin the march until six weeks later, waiting for the roads ahead to harden and dry. Meanwhile he drilled his armies, ruled, received ambassadors, and sat in judgment under a purple baldachin.

His principal wife, Casseca, a woman as beautiful as a dream, accompanied him on the expedition. A gilded cart carried her under a purple canopy made of airy fabrics, other wagons followed, along with burdened strings of white Syrian camels also dressed in purple.

Houris and *bayaderes* sang to her to please her on the journey. Whenever she wearied, the dulcet tones of soft flutes and strings sounded the moment that she closed her eyes and lulled her to sleep. Ostrich and peacock fans waved over her in the heat of the day, and priceless eastern perfumes burned in censers before her tents when she stopped to rest. Traveling with her were all the treasures, wealth and wonders that the East and the Sultan's power could provide, and all of it—the whole procession of dancers, singers, black eunuchs and musicians, fan-bearers, angelic serving lads, white camels and Arabian horses—gleamed and glittered with silks, satins, velvets, cloth-of-gold, and the rainbow fire of diamonds, rubies, emeralds and sapphires.

All the peoples of the Empire threw themselves down on their faces as she passed, not daring to look upon that being that only the Padishah had the right to see, and it seemed to them that this caravan was some unearthly vision, or a mystical reality transferred for the moment to the Earth from the realms of visions and illusions.

★   ★   ★

But the sun burned hotter every day and, at last, came the dry days of Summer, and in the cool of a certain evening the war flag of the Turks rose to a pole outside the Sultan's tents, and a cannon boomed the signal that the march on *Lehistan* has begun. The Holy Drum thundered in the *maydan*, and all the other drums and fifes boomed and shrilled in unison in the evening air, the dervishes whirled and howled, and the human river lurched into the night so that it might avoid the heat of the day.

The army didn't march until several hours later. First went the wagon train and those pashas who chose the camp sites and assembled the fodder and provisions. Then went the legions of artisans and laborers who were to pitch the tents and set up the encampments, and then the lowing herds of beef and baggage cattle. Each night's march was to take six hours, and it was to be so tightly organized and planned that the fighting cohorts would find their tents and dinners ready at each halt.

When it was finally time for the army's march-out, the Sultan rode onto a hilltop so that he might take pleasure in the sight of his strength and power. Riding with him were the Vezir, the chief imams, and young Kara Mustapha along with a guard battalion of Silistrian Turks.

The night was warm and clear. The moon was full and bright. The Sultan could have seen each and every one of his advancing columns if it weren't for the fact that no human eye could sweep and contain those masses that stretched across the miles. But he was pleased in any event. His heart filled with gratitude and gladness that he was master of such immense armed hosts, and he raised his eyes in thanks to Allah as he fingered the sandalwood beads of his Moslem rosary.

Then, when the head of the siege train began to vanish in the darkened distance, he interrupted his prayer for a moment and turned to Kara Mustapha beside him.

"I forget," he said. "Who leads our advance?"

"Light of Paradise," the young general addressed him. "Leading the vanguard are the *Lipki* and the *Tcheremisy*, and leading them is your dog, Azia, son of Tuhay-bey."

Chapter Fifty-nine

AFTER A LONG ENCAMPMENT in the southern plains, Azia Tuhay-beyovitch and his *Lipki* soldiers did indeed lead the march of all the Turkish armies towards the borders of the Commonwealth.

Basia's brave resistance thwarted his great plans, wounded his pride as well as his body, and damaged his reputation in his own harsh eyes. But now the star of his good fortunes appeared to be rising.

He had fully recovered all his faculties and strength. True, his handsome face was ruined. One of his eyes was gone altogether, the bridge of his nose was mashed into his cheekbones, and his fierce, hawklike features had turned into the gruesome mask of a one-eyed monster. But it was this sense of horror that he inspired in people that gave him an especially honored and respected place among the wild Dobrudjans and this soon spread to all the other Tartars.

His arrival in the Tartar camp was almost triumphant and his exploits grew with each admiring tale into something almost mystical in weight and proportion. His legend soon had him bringing all the *Lipki* and the *Tcheremisy* of the Commonwealth into the service of the Padishah. He was said to have struck the Poles with such stealth and cunning that it overshadowed even his great father, that he burned all the Dniester towns, slaughtered their garrisons, and got away with great amounts of loot. Those young warriors who had never raided in *Lehistan* before, those who had come from the farthest reaches of the Sultan's realms, and those whose pulses quickened nervously at the thought of those devastating charges for which these infidels

558

were famous, saw him as a young, bloodied war chief who had already faced those dreaded horsemen, who felt no fear of them, and who defeated them and gave the war a lucky beginning. The sight of this young *baghadir* filled them with faith in their own good luck; and his name as the son of Tuhay-bey, whose legend lived throughout the East, turned more eyes upon him every day.

"The *Lahiv* raised the cub,"the warriors told each other about him. "But he's the son of a lion. He tore them with his teeth and came back to the Sultan's service."

The Vezir himself expressed a wish to see him, while Kara Mustapha, the young general who loved savage warriors and lived for fame and glory, was fascinated by him. Both of them questioned him about the Commonwealth, the Hetman, the army and Kamyenetz and liked what they heard; the war he painted for them would be an easy one with the *Lahiv* destroyed, the Sultan triumphant, and both of them getting the prized title of *Ghazi*, which meant *conqueror*. After that he often had the chance to throw himself facedown before the Vezir and to sit near the entrance to Kara Mustapha's tents. Both gave him rich gifts of weapons, camels and horses. The Grand Vezir presented him with a silver kaftan and this raised him immeasurably in the eyes of all his *Lipki* soldiers. The silver kaftan was a sign of favor and raised the wearer to the rank of *murjah*. Krytchinski, Adurovitch and all the other renegade commanders placed themselves unconditionally under his command, honoring his descent, his qualities as a warrior, and as a man who received a kaftan.

His star, he thought, shined brightly overhead. He had become an important *murjah*, one who led two thousand cavalry who were infinitely better fighting men than ordinary Tartars. The war could raise him high. He could find in it all the honors, dignities, fame and power he wanted.

★　★　★

And yet bitterness gnawed at him. His pride seethed within him. The Turks treated Tartars with indifference, if not with contempt, as if they were no more than a pack of hunting dogs trotting at their heels. He may have had some standing among them, but the Turks looked generally at the Tartars as inferior people. They needed them, and sometimes even feared them, but in the rigid hierarchy of rank that started with the janissaries and the Spahis, the Tartars were looked upon as tribal horsemen of a lower order.

Azia saw this as soon as he rode into the Turkish camp and he had his *Lipki* pitch their tents away from the horse-hair *yurts* of all the other Tartars, as if they were a superior branch of the Turkish service. All that this did for him, however, was to enrage the Dobrudjan and Belgorodian *murjahs*, while failing to convince the Turkish officers that his *Lipki* were any better than the common *tchambuls*.

Furthermore, raised as he was in a Christian country among knights and gentry, and treated courteously even by the Hetman, he couldn't get used to the servile customs of the East. He had been only a junior officer in the Commonwealth and his Tartar Horse didn't have the standing or importance of the regiments in which only well-born gentry were serving in the ranks, but he didn't have to humble himself before his superiors the way he had to do it among the Turks, even though here he was a favored *murjah* and chief of all the *Lipki*.

He had to go down on his face, like a slave, before the Grand Vezir when that dignitary deigned to send for him. Kara Mustapha called himself his friend, but Azia had to beat salaams before him on his hands and knees. He had to prostrate himself before the pashas, the imams, and the chief Agha of the janissaries, and his savage soul seethed with rage at this humiliation. He never lost sight of whose son he was, his pride boiled within him, and because his ambitions for himself soared in the clouds high among the eagles, he felt himself dishonored by this ritual abasement.

What seared him the most, however, were his memories of Basia. Ah, he could live with the thought that she—a mere woman—had bested him in a struggle, knocked him off his horse and got away from him. He could swallow the shame and the disgrace, hard as it came to him; bad luck, he knew with truly Eastern fatalism, could strike even the luckiest warrior, and it could come from almost any hand. But this was a woman he wanted at all cost and hungered for beyond all reason! He'd give his soul, he knew, if he could have her here in his tent to look at, touch, kiss, whip, possess, whatever came to mind! If he could choose between the gold and ivory throne of the Padishah, ruler of half the world, and the possession of that single woman—his to embrace at will, her heart beating against his, her warm breath on his face, his lips fixed hungrily on hers—he'd take her any day, even if he were offered a Caliphate in exchange!

He wanted her because he loved her. He wanted her because he hated her. He wanted her all the more because she belonged heart and soul to another man, and because she was clean, faithful, undefiled and beyond his reach. When he recalled those kisses he had burned into her closed eyes after that fight against Azbah-bey's marauders, or that last moment before Rashkov when he felt her breast pressed against his chest, he thought he'd go mad with unfulfilled desire.

He didn't know what had happened to her, whether she managed to get back to Hreptyov or died on the way. The thought that she was dead eased his rage a little but then it would give place to an immeasurable grief. There were moments in his tent when he thought it would have been better not to try to carry her off by force, not to burn Rashkov, not to cast his lot with the Turks and Tartars, but to stay in Hreptyov as a simple soldier in the Tartar Light Horse, if that was the only way that he could be near her.

Hatred and disappointment gnawed at him, because instead of that unattainable woman he craved more than life, all he had in his tent was poor Zosia Boska.

★ ★ ★

Zosia's life had now become one of servitude, terror and utter degradation because Azia showed her no mercy whatsoever. He exercised a willful and unbridled cruelty on her for his hatred of her, and he hated her because she wasn't Basia. She had the sweetness and the charm of a country flower, and she had youth and beauty, and he sated himself on that beauty whenever he wanted. But then he'd lash out at her or kick her with his boots, or flail her white body with a rawhide whip at the slightest pretext.

Life in Hell could be no worse for her because she had no hope of any other existence in all the years ahead; and the most tragic part of it was that this life had only just begun; that it had come into flower only recently in Rashkov, blooming like Spring with love for young Novovyeyski. She loved that brave, chivalrous and yet simple and unaffected soldier with all the newly-wakened passion of her heart and soul, and here she was now, the slave and plaything of that one-eyed monster, trembling before him like a spiritless, whipped dog, crawling towards him on her hands and knees, watching his face and hands in terror to see if he was about to seize a bull whip, and hold her breath and hold back her tears.

She had no illusions about ever being able to evoke any mercy in him, nor could she hope for any other kind. She knew that even if some miracle tore her out of those inhuman hands, there was no coming back to what she had been. She was no longer that other Zosia, as fresh and new as the first snow of Winter, as clean and pure as a crystal spring, and able to give love for love with an honest heart. All that was gone for ever and swallowed up in darkness as if it had never existed at all. And because there was no sense or reason to that abysmal degradation in which she found herself, because she had done nothing to deserve it, she couldn't understand why she was being so terribly and mercilessly punished. She'd always been a quiet, decent girl with no more blemish than a newborn lamb, as gentle as a dove, as trusting as a child, and full of a childlike simplicity and love. Why then was she the victim of such a terrible injustice? Why did God's anger lie upon her with such a crushing weight?

This mental anguish, as much as the physical agonies of her slavery, added to her suffering and despair beyond any measure.

Days, weeks and months passed for her with a terrifying sameness. It was Winter when Azia dragged her to these Turkish plains and the march upon the Commonwealth didn't begin until the middle of June. Each moment of that intervening time meant only shame, submission, and back-breaking labor.

If Azia could have loved her—or if, at least, he was capable of kindness—her captivity might have been endurable in some way. But he was unmoved by her childlike sweetness and her unspoiled beauty. He hated her because she wasn't who and what he wanted. He looked at her as no more than a common captive, less valuable to him than his riding horses, and so she worked like a slave from before dawn until long after nightfall. She took his horses and camels to the river at dusk and in the morning. She carried water for his baths and wood for his fire. She spread the hides on which he slept at night and she cooked his food.

Custom and the fear of the janissaries kept all the other women in the Turkish camps confined to their tents, but the *Lipki* bivouac stood outside the general encampment, and the oriental custom of secluding and segregating women was still foreign to them. The few women they kept in their camp didn't even cover their faces with the obligatory *yashmak*. They were forbidden from crossing the *Lipki* picket lines, where—as they all knew anyway—they would be seized and carried off at once, but they could go in safety wherever they had to within the encampment and do all the camp work that was required of them.

* * *

Despite this dreadful burden, Zosia found some relief in those trips for loads of firewood, and to water the camels and the horses, because she could cry. Nothing inflamed Azia more than the sight of her tears and she hid them from him as best as she could. But out in the *maydan* and away from his tent she could weep all she wished.

One day, as she walked under a load of firewood, she came across her mother whom Azia had given to Halim. They threw themselves into each other's arms and had to be pried apart and torn away by force. Azia flogged Zosia for it afterwards, whipping her about her head and face as well as her body, but it was a precious moment for all that.

On another day, while she was at the river laundering Azia's body-wraps and foot-cloths, she caught sight of Evka carrying pails of water. Evka groaned under the heavy yoke. Her body had already thickened, she was carrying her master's unborn child, and she was dull and sluggish in her shuffling movements. Her features coarsened in captivity. But even though half her face was covered with a *yashmak*, it reminded Zosia so powerfully of Adam that a savage pain stabbed through her like a knife and the world spun dizzily around her. Fear made them mute, however, and stopped them from speaking to each other.

That awful, ever-present fear overwhelmed all her other

feelings and gradually took over her entire being. Hope, wishes, memory were all gone, consumed by the dread of her anticipation. Her only goal in life was to avoid the whip. In her place, Basia would have knifed Azia to death after the first day, without a thought about the consequences, but the fearful, timorous little Zosia was still half a child and she had none of Basia's courage and determination.

At last she reached such a state of terror and abasement that she thought it a privilege and an act of grace when Azia, stabbed by a sudden lust, suspended his disfigured face over hers and reached for her body.

Sitting like a trembling animal on the floor of his tent, she kept her eyes fixed on her master's face to guess his mood before he exploded in anger over her. She watched every movement of his hands and tried to anticipate his wishes, and when as often happened she made the wrong guess, and the long yellow canines glittered under the Tartar's mustache in just the way that old Tuhay-bey's used to do when he was enraged, she crawled at his feet, half dead as she was with terror, pressing her pale lips to his boots and clutching convulsively at his knees, and crying out like a tormented child:

"Don't beat me Azia! I won't do it again! Forgive me! Don't beat me!"

He almost never bothered to forgive. He invented refined cruelties for her not only because she wasn't Basia but also because she had once been the promised bride of Adam Novovyeyski. Azia didn't really understand the meaning of fear. But there was such a terrible accounting to be made between him and Adam, that he felt queasy at the thought of that huge, raging soldier with vengeance burned into his heart as if he were branded. They would most likely meet each other in the war, Adam would see to that. Azia didn't want to think about that inevitable accounting, even though he was both powerful and fearless, but he couldn't help it. And because one look at Zosia reminded him immediately of Adam, he wreaked his own vengeance on her in advance, and spent his fury on her, as if that whistling rawhide could silence his own alarm.

★   ★   ★

At last the Sultan ordered the march to begin. He had ar-

ranged with the Grand Vezir and Kara Mustapha that the Dobrudjan and Belgorodian Tartars were to lead the way, with
Azia's *Lipki* ranging far ahead as the pathfinders and advance
guard, but in the beginning, or at least as far as the lower
Balkans, all of them went together. They marched in easy,
comfortable stages in the cool of the night, with only six hours
on the road from one halt to the next. Barrels of pitch burned
beside their trails and marked their line of march, while the
Damascus runners lighted the Sultan's way with their multicolored lanterns. They flowed like a sea across the plains, filled the
valleys like a swarm of locusts, and spilled across the mountains.
Behind the warriors rolled the wagon trains, with the harems
within them and the herds beyond them.

But then something happened. The gold and purple conveyance that carried the beautiful Casseca sunk and became en-
meshed in the soft soil of the marshlands that lay along the
southern edge of the Balkan plain and ten teams of water-buffalo
couldn't pull it out of the mire.

"An evil omen, Lord!" the Grand Mufti told the Sultan. "A
bad sign for you and all of your army."

"An evil omen!" howled the half-mad dervishes and holy men,
and the Sultan responded to their panic with a superstitious fear
of his own. He decided to have the whole army stripped of all
its women, and that included his own beautiful Casseca and all
her attendants.

His decree was read out in all the encampments that very day
and every pasha, agha, murjah, bey and warrior hurried to obey
it. Those of the common soldiers who had nowhere to send their
slave girls, and who loved them too much to give them up for
another's pleasure, simply cut their throats. Others were bought
in thousands by the traders from the Caravanserai and later sold
in the markets of Istanbul and in all the closer towns of the
Middle East and Asia.

The great sale lasted three full days. Azia put Zosia on the
auction block without hesitation and sold her for a good price
to an old Istanbul dealer in sweetmeats who bought her for his
son. He was a kindly man, responsive to Zosia's tears and
pleading, so he also bought her mother from Halim. He got the
older woman at a bargain price and the two of them set out for
Istanbul the next day with a convoy of other girls and women.

In Istanbul, Zosia's fate improved. Her new owner fell in love
with her and, after a few months, raised her to the status of a
wife. Her mother was never parted from her again.

Many captives sometimes returned to their homes even after
years of living among the Turks, and sometimes these were
women; although once taken, few of them were ever seen again.
There was even someone for a time who searched for Zosia
through Armenian go-betweens, through merchants and traders,
and even through men in the service to the various Commonwealth ambassadors, but he failed to find her. Then this search
ended, as suddenly as if cut off with a knife, and Zosia never
again saw her homeland or the faces of those she had loved
there.

She lived in the harem for the rest of her life.

Chapter Sixty

A GREAT DEAL of activity gripped the army posts all along the Dniester even before the Turks set out from Adrianople. Messengers from the Hetman, and couriers bearing orders for all the detachments stationed on the border, galloped into Hreptyov which lay closest to Kamyenetz, and the little knight either carried out these orders by himself or sent them on by trusted messengers of his own.

The result of these dispatches was that the garrison of Hreptyov shrunk considerably. Pan Motovidlo took his companies all the way to Uman, to reinforce the Cossack Ataman Hanenko, who struggled as best he could with just a handful of Cossacks loyal to the Commonwealth, against the rebel swarms of Doroshenko and the Crimean Horde which the Khan had brought to help him in his war.

Pan Mushalski, the incomparable archer, Pan Snitko, Pan Nenashinyetz and Pan Hromyka led the nobles' regiment and the Linkhauz dragoons to Batoh, the scene of a former humiliation of the Commonwealth, where Pan Lukojhetzki kept his eye on Doroshenko's other busy flank. Pan Bogush was ordered into Mohilev where he was to stay until he saw the invading *tchambuls* with his naked eye. The Hetman's orders also searched urgently for Pan Rushtchitz, the former Rashkov *stannitza* commander who had no peer other than Volodyovski in the hit and run warfare of the open Steppe, but that famed borderer vanished as completely as if the earth had swallowed him up. He had taken a few dozen men into the Steppe and no one knew where he was to be found. He surfaced later, appearing like a vengeful spirit along the edges of the enemy encampments, to snatch patrols and sentries and to disrupt their provisioning and communications. But at this time he had disappeared.

★ ★ ★

Volodyovski's orders stayed unchanged. He was to go to Kamyenetz because that's where the Hetman needed him the most. The Hetman wanted him there because he knew that the sight of the famous little soldier would raise the spirits of both the garrison and the inhabitants, harden their resolve, and fill their hearts with hope.

Pan Sobieski had no doubt that Kamyenetz would soon be under a terrible Turkish siege, that it would be stormed and that it would fall. But he wanted the clifftop city to hold out as long as it could, awaken the rest of the country to its dreadful danger, and buy the time for the Commonwealth to gather some sort of forces for its own defense.

He knew that he was sending the country's foremost soldier to a certain death but he felt neither pity nor regret. The Grand Hetman always said that death and soldiering went hand in hand together, and that war put a final seal on that unwritten contract. He was quite ready to give his own life in battle and thought that this was a soldier's ordinary duty. And if that death could also render great service to the country, then the sacrifice was its own reward and a sign of favor. He also knew that the little knight held the same opinion.

Finally, this was no time for him to think about saving one individual soldier or another, not when total destruction was about to fall on all the churches, towns and territories in the east, and on the unprepared Commonwealth itself; nor when all of Islam rose up against Europe with a power not seen since the days of Genghis Khan, to overwhelm and trample all Christianity. Safe and shielded by the Commonwealth, as it had been for centuries, this Christian Europe didn't think it necessary to help in its own defense, because this Commonwealth had always managed it alone.

It might have managed it this time as well, the Hetman was sure, if it weren't for the anarchy of its institutions. As it was, he didn't even have the troops he needed for patrols, far less to fight a war. A mere few dozen men sent in one direction, opened up a gap through which an enemy avalanche could pour in some other area. The Sultan's generals posted more men as sentries around their encampments than he had under his command. The onslaught was coming from two separate directions, out of the southern valleys of the Danube, north across the Dniester, and from the seething Ukrainian cauldron beyond the Dnieper River in the east. Since Doroshenko and his Tartar allies were closer at this time, and since they already started to pour into the country with their swords and fires, the few regular companies he had went in that direction. Only the town and castle of Kamyenetz were left to guard the approaches from the south, and the Hetman didn't even have the men to scout the country near it and beyond it.

★ ★ ★

It was in this desperate moment that the Grand Hetman found the time to write these few words to Pan Volodyovski:

'I thought of sending you out to Rashkov, right under the noses of the enemy, but it occurred to me that you might get cut off, and not be able to get back to Kamyenetz where you're sorely needed, which could easily happen once the Horde crosses from Moldavia through the Seven Fords. Just yesterday, however, I thought of Novovyeyski. He's an experienced soldier who never thinks twice about danger when duty is at stake, and because a man who loses everything is ready for anything I think he'll do well in that assignment. Send him whatever light cavalry you can, and let him go as far towards the enemy as he's able. Let him be seen everywhere, and let him spread the word about our great new armies, and once the enemy has caught sight of him, then let him stay in sight but not allow himself to be surprised and taken. We know how they'll come and the roads they'll take, but if he spots anything unusual he is to let you know at once, and you'll send word immediately to me and to Kamyenetz. Let Novovyeyski go as soon as possible, and you be ready to go to Kamyenetz yourself any day. But stay where you are for now and wait until you have sure news from Moldavia and from young Novovyeyski.'

Since Novovyeyski happened to be in Mohilev at this time, and since he was supposed to come to Hreptyov anyway, the little knight merely sent him word to speed up his arrival because there was a job of work waiting for him by the Hetman's orders, and three days later young Adam was there.

★   ★   ★

No one who knew this huge, fearless, laughing and confident young man could recognize him in the bowed, yellowed apparition that arrived in Hreptyov, and everyone's first thought was that Pan Bogush had been right to call him both a skeleton and a living corpse. His gaunt, hollowed frame made him look even taller than before, but this was no longer that lighthearted giant who threw himself on the enemy with bursts of laughter like a neighing horse. He stared about with dull, blinking eyes, as if he were unable to recognize even his best friends; and everything had to be said twice to him because he didn't seem to understand anything the first time he heard it.

It was clear to all, as Pan Zagloba observed quietly the moment he saw him, that *'acid was now flowing through his veins instead of blood,'* and that he willed himself into that dull, vacant-eyed detachment so that he wouldn't think about things that would drive him mad.

True, there wasn't a single human being in those parts of the country, nor one family in the *Kresy* borderlands, nor one officer in the army, who hadn't lost someone dear to them at the hands of one barbaric invader or another. But Novovyeyski had been simply buried by an avalanche of horrors. In one day he lost his father, his sister, and the girl he loved with all the passion of his elemental soul. It would have been better for that sister and that beloved, sweet girl to die under the knife like the murdered father than to live as they were surely living. Their fate was such that the worst torments of medieval torture would be nothing for him in comparison with the agony of thinking about it. He knew that he would lose his mind if he couldn't silence those screaming visions in his brain, and he tried to bury them under a leaden, unresponsive dullness, but he couldn't do it.

That impenetrable, stony numbness he wore like a mask was a facade that fooled nobody who knew him. There was no shred of fatalistic resignation or acceptance anywhere within him. One glance was enough to show that something frightful and malevolent crouched under that stillness, and that if this suppressed volcano of rage, pain and bitterness should ever break out and explode, then this grim, skeletal giant would perpetrate horrors beyond description, like all the unleashed forces of unbridled nature. This was so clear to all that even his closest friends approached him with caution and avoided any mention of what happened in Rashkov.

★ ★ ★

But the sight of Basia apparently stirred up all his buried pain, because his eyes filled with blood, the veins on his neck thickened into ropes, and he began to groan like a dying bison when he kissed her hands. And when Basia burst into tears and hugged his head to her breast like a consoling mother, he threw himself at her feet and it took a long time to get him up again.

Told what the Hetman had in mind for him, he blinked suddenly awake like a dying man coming back to life. His attention sharpened, and then the lurid glare of a frightful joy flashed across his face.

"I'll do it," he said coldly. "And I will do more."

"And when you meet that cursed spawn of the Devil," Pan Zagloba threw in without thinking, "give him a hot welcome!"

Novovyeyski didn't seem to understand at first. He merely stared at the old knight as if trying to knot these words together into a coherent whole, and then the light of madness glittered in his eyes. He rose from his bench, took a slow step forward, and then lurched towards Pan Zagloba as if he were about to hurl himself upon him.

"Do you believe, sir," he began, "that I never did that man any harm, and that I've always tried to be decent to him?"

"Oh I do, I do!" Pan Zagloba answered hastily and took a swift, protective step behind the little knight. "I'd go with you myself only the rheumatism is chewing on my legs."

"Novovyeyski!" the little knight said sharply. "When do you want to start out?"

"Tonight."

"You're sure you'll be ready?"

"I am ready now."

"I'll give you a hundred dragoons. That'll leave me with another hundred and the infantry. Come with me to the barracks!"

They went out together to give the necessary orders, but just beyond the threshold they found Zydor Lusnia waiting at attention. The news about the expedition had already spread throughout the *maydan*, and the sergeant-major came to ask his colonel, in the name of all his dragoons as well as in his own, to be allowed to go with Novovyeyski.

"What's this?" Volodyovski never expected a request for a transfer from his favorite soldier. "You want to leave me?"

"We swore an oath against that motherless son, commandant," the old sergeant said. "So maybe we'll get our hands on him!"

"Oh yes," the little knight nodded, remembering. "Pan Zagloba told me about that oath of yours."

But Lusnia was now speaking to Novovyeyski. "Commandant," he began.

"What do you want?"

"If we get him, sir... If we get him... I'd like to be the man that takes care of him."

Such a savage, unforgiving hatred glowed in the face of the old Mazurian that Novovyeyski bowed at once to the little colonel and asked to have that man on his expedition. Volodyovski saw no reason to refuse and that same night a hundred troopers clattered out of Hreptyov behind Novovyeyski.

★   ★   ★

They took the old trail for Mohilev and Yampol. In Yampol they found the former Rashkov garrison where the Hetman's orders detached another two hundred men to add to Novovyeyski's. Pan Bialoglovski was to take the rest to Mohilev to reinforce Pan Bogush.

Meanwhile Novovyeyski led his command to Rashkov. The countryside around them was now a total wilderness, empty and abandoned. The little town itself was just a pile of ashes which the winds had already blown far into the Steppe, while the few inhabitants who escaped the slaughter had made themselves scarce before the expected storm. These were the early days of May, the new grass was lush and the Steppe had dried and the Dobrudjan Horde could appear in these territories at almost any moment, so it was dangerous to stay there too long. In point of fact, the Hordes were still camping with the Turks in the Rumelian plain, but nobody knew that in the caves and canyons where the survivors clustered, so each man and woman who managed to emerge alive from the massacre of Rashkov wasted no time in getting away wherever they thought best.

All the way through their march south along the Dniester, Zydor Lusnia plotted the various ambushes and forays through which—in his opinion—Pan Novovyeyski could harass the enemy and bring his men back with their skins intact. Nor did he keep these gems of military wisdom to himself.

"You young numbskulls," he told his listening troopers, "don't know a thing about how this is done. But I'm an old war horse and I know. We'll go to Rashkov. There we'll go to ground in the caves and wait. When the Horde comes to the river crossing, they'll send a few small sweeps across, like they always do, while the *tchambul* will pull up and wait until the coast is clear. Then we'll slip out behind those scouting parties, cut them off from the rest, and drive them all the way to Kamyenetz if we have to."

"So maybe we won't get that son of a bitch we want?" one of the troopers asked.

"Shut your damn fool mouth!" Lusnia snarled. "Why shouldn't we get him?"

"Well, how do we know he'll come over with that early bunch?"

"And who do you think will be the first across if it's not the *Lipki?*"

★ ★ ★

It seemed at first as if the sergeant-major's supposition was correct. Novovyeyski gave his men a day's rest once they got to Rashkov, and they were all quite sure that the next thing they'd do would be to ride out to the huge caves and caverns that dotted the limestone cliffs throughout that whole region, and that they'd lie low in there, keeping out of sight, until the first Tartar scouts came across the river.

But the next morning Novovyeyski put the regiment on the road again and led it south of Rashkov.

"Where the hell's he taking us?" the old sergeant muttered. "All the way to the Yahorlik, or what?"

In the meantime they came close to the Dniester River and, some minutes later, they halted at a crossing known as the Bloody Ford. Novovyeyski rode right into the water and started straight across without a word.

"What's this now?" The soldiers stared at each other in surprise. "Are we going all the way to Turkey?"

But this wasn't the sheep-clipping, argumentative landed gentry of the General Levy who were always ready for protests and discussions of each and every order. These were simple soldiers, used to the iron discipline of the border service, so the first rank rode into the river right behind their commandant, and all the others followed. None of them gave another thought to this unexpected turn. Some of them were a bit surprised to be invading the Ottoman Empire with just three hundred men but they went nonetheless.

But even their surprise didn't last too long. The roiled water began to slap and slosh against the flanks of their horses and they got too concerned about keeping their feed bags dry for any further thought about where they were going. It was only when they were all standing on the other bank that they stared at each other wide-eyed and open-mouthed.

"As God's my witness," one or another of them whispered to the man beside him. "We're in Moldavia now!"

And one or another glanced back towards the Dniester which glowed behind them in the setting sun like a ceremonial sash streaked with gold and crimson. The cliffs and caves beyond the river were also gleaming with that scarlet brightness. They rose like a forbidding wall between this handful of men and their receding country. 'For some of us,' Lusnia thought, 'this could be the last time we see it.'

It flashed through old sergeant-major's brain that his commandant had finally lost his mind, and that his company was now following a madman, but it was a commandant's job to lead and a soldier's to follow.

Meanwhile the wet horses now began to snort and shake their manes, which all the men took for a lucky omen.

"*Zdrov! Zdrov!*" they called out, wishing good health and fortune to themselves and their snorting horses.

"Forward!" Novovyeyski ordered.

The ranks moved at a trot towards the setting sun, riding steadily closer to those tens of thousands of enemies that swarmed ahead of them, to those human seas that washed restlessly across the Adrianople plains, and to that vast assembly of peoples and nations.

Chapter Sixty-one

NOVOVYEYSKI'S CROSSING of the Dniester, and his march with only three hundred men against those countless thousands, may have looked like an act of madness to those who didn't know much about Steppe warfare. In reality it was only a bold military raid, following well tried campaign procedures, which had a good chance of success.

To begin with, it wasn't all that rare for the borderers of those days to face odds of a hundred to one when fighting the Tartars in their own special manner. They would allow the great *tchambuls* to catch a glimpse of them, tempt them into a chase and then make a running fight of it, striking out of ambush in which they inflicted bloody punishment. It was a way taught by the wolves which sometimes lured a village dog pack into a baying chase only to turn on it when the time was right and tear the throat out of the nearest mongrel. The running animal was always just as much the hunter as he was the quarry. He ran, hid, went to ground, circled his pursuers, leaped out on them when they least suspected, savaged them, darted off and disappeared again. This was the famous *'Proceder'* or *Rule of Tartar Warfare*—in part a specialized form of military tactics, and in part a game that called for great courage, skill, cunning and imagination—in which the best Steppe soldiers competed with each other in ruses, ambushes and deceptions.

Pan Volodyovski was the acknowledged Polish master of this game, followed closely by Pan Rushtchitz; and with both Pan Pivo and Pan Motovidlo as the most famous among the Ruthe-

nian officers of the Commonwealth; but Novovyeyski was also
one of those who were often mentioned. He was a Steppe
borderer since childhood, living by the Rule since he was a boy,
so it wasn't likely that he'd let the Horde engulf him once it
caught sight of him somewhere in Bessarabia.

His expedition had an even better chance once he crossed the
Dniester, because beyond it lay a thinly populated, barren wilderness, full of broken ground, where it was easy to hide a large
detachment. Once in a while some small settlement hugged the
bank of a river but inhabitants were rare. Brown hills and
yellowing escarpments lined the river courses in the northern
reaches, just as they did among the rocky walls and cliffs along
the Dniester, but the rest of northern Bessarabia was an arid
Steppe, faded prairie, and thickly tangled woods in which herds
of wild pigs, deer and water-buffalo made their endless migra-
tory journeys. Because the Sultan craved a taste of his own vast
military power, and wished to judge his strength before the
campaign with his own eyes, all the Belgorodian Hordes which
occupied the lands below the Lower Dniester, and the Dobrudjans who lived even farther south of Bessarabia, rode by his order
to the great muster around Adrianople rather than waiting for
the Sultan's armies to come to their countries. So did the
Turkish governors of Moldavia and all the other satraps of the
upper Balkans. Wide open to begin with, the land emptied even
more with this exodus, so that a raiding column could ride for
weeks without being seen.

Moreover, no one needed to tell Pan Novovyeyski that the
tchambuls exercised every caution once they crossed the border
of the Commonwealth, sniffing the air like dogs at every river
crossing, and eying everything around them as suspiciously as
wolves. But here, still in the Sultan's empire, they'd come in a
wide, far-flung mass, anticipating no threat whatsoever. The
Tartars would expect death to strike them in their own backyards before they thought of meeting Commonwealth troops so
far in Bessarabia. And why shouldn't they? Who'd expect this
Commonwealth which couldn't even defend its own borders to
send any columns to their grazing grounds?

So Novovyeyski felt confident that his expedition would
surprise, alarm and confuse the enemy—thus being even more

useful than the Hetman hoped—and that it could bring disaster to Azia and his *Lipki*. It was easy for the young lieutenant to guess that the *Lipki* and the *Tcheremisy* would spearhead the onslaught, being so terribly familiar with the Commonwealth, and it was in this certainty that he placed all his remaining hopes. Having lost everything that could ever matter to his kind of man, his shattered soul lived only for revenge. He wanted nothing more in life than to fall like a thunderbolt on the unsuspecting *Lipki*, get his hands on Azia—perhaps even tear his sister and Zosia out of their terrible captivities—and then wreak his vengeance and die in the war.

With such plans and hopes coursing through his mind, Novovyeyski shook himself out of his stony trance and came alive again. New trails, the wide Steppe winds blowing in his face, and the hazards of the expedition, restored the haggard giant; a sharp light glowed once more in his extinguished eyes and his old strength came back.

The borderer woke within him.

The sufferer subsided.

Before, there was no room in him for anything but recollection of his own agony and torment; now he had to think, plan, steal a march on the enemy, and tear him to pieces.

* * *

Once across the Dniester, they slanted southwest towards the River Pruth, often going to ground in daylight and lying low in the thickets or in some hollowed gorge. Even today this country is sparsely settled; in that time it was almost wholly empty. Only occasionally did they come across cleared land or a stubbled corn field with some desolate little settlement huddled nearby.

Stealing south as secretly as wolves, they gave wide berth to any larger hamlet, but rode in boldly among the smaller clusters of huts and shelters, some even numbering a dozen cabins and ramshackle dwellings, knowing that no one there would even think of running to warn the Tartars. Lusnia took care that this didn't happen anyway, keeping a tight grip on whatever wretches fell into their hands, but even he gave up any extra measures after a few days; he soon caught on that these few rare settlers that they came upon, all of them subjects of the Sultan, feared the approach of their master's armies no less than the border settlers of the Commonwealth. Nor did they have any idea whose troops had come so unexpectedly among them, taking the column for yet another tributary detachment that rode south like the rest by the Sultan's order.

No one put up any opposition when Novovyeyski's men helped themselves to supplies of corn cakes, cherry raisins and dried buffalo meat. Every settler had his sheep, water buffalo and horses hidden near the rivers. Once in a while they came across wandering, half-wild herds of buffalo, each guarded by a dozen or more nomadic herdsmen, who stayed in any one place only as long as the fodder lasted, and then moved on and pitched their tents elsewhere. There were often old Tartars among them, so Novovyeyski approached their camps with all the care he'd take if they were a *tchambul*. He made sure that none of them—the Tartars in particular—got away alive to pass the word of his coming to some local *murjah*, but first he questioned them about all the tracks, paths and cross-country trails that were known only to such men as they who spent their whole lives drifting through the prairies. Then he took whatever livestock he needed and went on.

The farther south they rode, the more numerous such wandering herds became. The southern herdsmen were almost always Tartars, banded together in far greater numbers around their sheep and cattle than in the northern prairies. In fifteen days of hard but careful riding, Novovyeyski surrounded and crushed three armed companies of herders, each numbering up to sixty or seventy half-wild Tartar *tchabantchuki*. The dragoons always stripped them of their greasy sheepskin hats, capes and coats, scorched the lice and vermin out of these crude garments over an open fire, and wore them for disguises, so that in two weeks all of them looked from a distance like a Tartar *tchambul*. Only their matched weapons and trained cavalry horses could give them away on closer inspection. They stuffed their dragoon helmets and uniform *kolety* into their saddle bags, and only their light blue eyes and pale Mazurian mustaches betrayed who they were; but glimpsed in the Steppe or up along a ridge line they fooled the most experienced eyes, especially since they drove their own beef cattle and sheep herd before them.

★ ★ ★

When they came to the Pruth River, they turned due south along the left bank, trying to anticipate the route that the Sultan's army would follow when it came. The Kutchmanski Track, the traditional route of Tartar invasions, promised to be a hungry route for an advancing army, so it was a good guess that the Sultan's cohorts would take the Valachian Trail into Bessarabia, and then either turn northeast and force the Dniester above Kamyenetz, or march straight up the length of the Bessarabian plain and debauch into the Commonwealth somewhere near Ushitza. Either way, they'd follow the Pruth as far as they could because they'd need the river for their supply galleys.

Novovyeyski was so sure of this that he gave up speed for the sake of caution, scouting far ahead and moving his column in short, watchful marches. Time was of no importance now, since he and the *tchambuls* were on a collision course, and he didn't want to come upon them without any warning.

At last, in the fork of the tributary Sarat and Tekitch Rivers, he went to ground to rest his men and horses in a thicketed, well hidden place, and to wait for the spearhead of the Tartar vanguard.

He chose carefully and well. The place was a natural hideout. The whole fork of the river crouched under a stand of leafy crab apple and wild cherry trees, and so did the outer banks of both the rivers. The thickets ran as far as the eye could see, hiding the ground under a mass of tangled tree crowns, undergrowth and bushes, or forming dense groves with many clear, natural bivouac sites between them. The blooms had already given way to thick leaf at this time of the year, but early Spring must have turned this entire region into a sea of white and yellow flowers. Nothing human lived there, or showed any sign of having spent more than a night or two in that wilderness oasis. But the thickets were full of animals—deer, does, wild hares and a swarm of birdlife—and here and there along the cool freshwater springs that ran into the rivers, the soldiers came upon the tracks of a bear. Two days after they slipped into that natural refuge, a bear did attack two of the sheep they drove as their marching rations, and Lusnia promised himself the pleasures of a bear hunt. But Novovyeyski forbad the use of muskets so Lusnia and his beaters went after the sheep-killing bear with axes and spears.

A few days later the soldiers found traces of some old camp fires near one of the springs, but these looked as if they were made long ago, perhaps the year before. It was safe to suppose that the *tchabantchuki* camped here now and then along with their flocks, or perhaps Tartars came to the cherry groves to cut hardwood clubs and handles for their horsehead axes. But not even the most careful search of the entire area showed any traces of a live inhabitant.

This, Novovyeyski decided, was the place to wait. A month might go by before the Turkish army showed on the horizon, but the young borderer was certain that this was the way they'd come. "We'll go to camp here," he ordered, and Lusnia set the men to building comfortable lean-to shelters out of woven branches, and screening their fires. Pickets watched night and day from the outer edges of the trees, and small patrols—often led by the young commandant himself—ranged silent and unseen far into the country, searching for the first sign of the Turks' approach.

They knew what to look for and the weather couldn't have been better for the job at hand. The countryside was dry, but neither parched nor arid. There was good grass and swift running water. The days were hot, but it was easy to find a shaded spot on the cool thicket floor, and the nights were clear, soft and filled with moonlight, while the massed shrubbery shook to the singing of the nightingales.

It was on such nights as these, however, that Adam Novovyeyski suffered more than ever. Unable to sleep, he drifted into memory, reliving in his mind all of the brief happiness he'd enjoyed in Rashkov, as well as every detail of his present calamity and torment.

One thought alone kept him clinging to life, such as it had become, and helped to hold back the crimson clouds of madness. Vengeance. Retribution. Sated, he might find some form of peace or perhaps even another reason for staying alive. And in the meantime each day brought closer the moment of that confrontation in which he'd either extract that dreadful payment or die in the attempt.

The weeks passed slowly in this quiet camp as they watched and waited and scouted the country, learning the run of every trail, river, stream, canyon and ravine, trapping and cutting down a few more bands of herdsmen and driving off another herd or two. But for all their careful scouting and patrols, there was something far older and primeval about this interlude. Novovyeyski and his border soldiers had become a single animal, as dangerous as it was implacable and cunning, that crouched beside a known trail and waited for its prey.

And finally the awaited moment came.

Chapter Sixty-two

BIRDS WERE AS ALWAYS the heralds of invasion, soaring in the skies and winging along the ground. Wild turkeys, bustards, partridges, blue-legged plover and quail darted towards the thickets through the grasses, while crows and ravens swarmed darkly overhead, along with the wild geese and marsh fowl startled into flight on the banks of the lower Danube and off the Dobrudjan wetlands in the south.

"They're coming!" the word flew one morning from one man to the next, and the dragoons looked narrowly up at the sky and then at each other. "They're coming!"

No sign of trepidation showed in those fierce, mustached faces that suddenly looked grimly eager and as tensed as predators when they've scented prey. A lifetime in the Steppe lived by the only rule that assured survival, which was the famed *Proceder* of Tartar warfare that governed every moment awake or asleep, sharpened all their senses.

Their eyes gleamed as they grinned fiercely at each other. They had the honed instincts of hunting dogs and wolfhounds that catch the scent of quarry and stiffen in anticipation. But when they snapped into swift, silent motion they didn't waste a moment.

The campfires were swamped at once with buckets of water.

The thin ribbons of carefully dampened smoke were too pale in the bright dawn sky to betray the men hidden in the thickets and the sharp morning breeze soon dispersed them in the lightening air.

The horses were saddled and the whole column stood ready

to ride without a need for orders. All that remained was to calculate the exact time and distance to where the enemy would halt for the night, so that they might sweep down upon the Tartars like a thunderbolt and strike them when they were least able to resist: scattered, on foot and with their horses tethered, and pitching their tents.

Novovyeyski knew very well that the Sultan's armies wouldn't be coming in a tight, battle-ready mass here in their own territories where any kind of danger was utterly unlikely. He also knew that the Turkish vanguard always rode a day's march ahead of the main body, and he surmised correctly that the *Lipki* would be the tip of the Tartar spearhead. He wondered if he ought to move invisibly towards them along the hidden routes and trails he discovered in his weeks of scouting, or if he should ambush them from his leafy fastness. He chose the latter because the thickets would keep his men hidden until the last moment, and give him a chance to strike out of the blue any time he wanted. One more day and night passed while the fleeing birds were joined by whole packs of scampering animals that ran before that vast human avalanche behind them, and the next morning the enemy came in sight.

South of the cherry thickets ran a long, ridged plain that dipped from sight below the horizon, and now a dark, swiftly moving mass appeared upon it and flowed rapidly towards the left arm of the river fork ahead. The dragoons watched out of their concealment while the mass drew nearer, now and then vanishing behind the hunched round tops of the rolling high ground, and then reappearing and spilling out in the open flatlands.

Lusnia, who was gifted with a truly extraordinary eyesight, peered tensely at these nearing masses for some time, and then trotted up to Pan Novovyeyski.

"Commandant," he said. "There's hardly more than a troop out there. It's mostly horses driven out to pasture."

A few minutes later Novovyeyski could see this with his own two eyes and a terrible, hungry joy spread across his face. "That means they'll make camp a mile from these thickets?" he murmured.

"Yes sir," Lusnia nodded. "Mile to a mile and a half, like they always do. Looks like they're marching nights, so's to keep out

of the heat, and rest in the daytime. And the horses get sent out
to pasture until nightfall."

"How many men d'you see around those horses?"

Lusnia slipped quietly to the edge of the thicket and stayed
there for a while. Then he appeared again beside Pan Novovyeyski.

"There's about fifteen hundred horses and twenty five men to
guard them,"he reported. "They're in their own country so they
think they've nothing to fear. They don't even have any sentries
posted."

"What are they? Could you tell?"

"They're still quite a ways off but they're *Lipki*, sir! They
won't get away from us now!"

"That's right!" said Novovyeyski.

He could be certain that not one of those nearing horsemen
would get away from him. This was an easy exercise for such a
borderer as he and for the kind of men he commanded here.

Meanwhile the pasturing detachment drove the *Lipki* horses
closer by the minute to the cherry thickets. Lusnia edged forward once more and his face was alight with cruelty and a savage
joy when he slipped back again.

"Lipki, sir," he murmured once again. "There's no doubt
about it!"

★   ★   ★

Hearing this, Novovyeyski cried shrilly like a hawk and the
disguised dragoons turned and slipped at once into the deepest
part of the cherry thickets. There the command split into two
detachments. One company rode into a long ravine to circle the
horseherd and the *Lipki* and to stay concealed until it could
debauch into the plain behind them, while the other formed a
single crescent rank and waited.

All of this happened in such utter silence that the most
sensitive and experienced ear couldn't have picked up a whisper
of movement among the trees. Not a spur jingled, not a single
saber rattled against a stirrup. Not one horse neighed. The
matted grass which floored this natural orchard deadened the fall
of hoofbeats. Even the horses seemed to understand that success
depended upon stealth and silence, since they had done this sort
of thing many times before. Only the shrill, dwindling cry of a

hawk echoed for some time longer from the ravine and out of the thickets.

The horseherd and the *Lipki* drovers came to a halt within an arrow's flight of the leafy ambush and spilled across the pasture in small groups and clusters. Novovyeyski himself now crouched at the edge of the undergrowth and watched every move made by the horseherders. The sky was clear, the day had reached midmorning, but the sun stood already high and a sweltering heat blazed down upon the earth. The pasturing horses started to roll in the dusty soil and to drift closer to the shrubs and bushes. The drovers trotted up to the edge of the thicket, jumped to the ground and let their horses feed freely on loose rein, while they themselves pushed into the grove in search of cool shelter.

Soon a campfire blazed brightly near a thick clump of bushes where the herders stretched out to rest and eat. When the dry twigs and branches burned down into glowing charcoal, the herdsmen threw half a carcass of a slaughtered colt across the coals and ashes, and settled down nearby, away from the heat. Some of them sprawled on the matted grass, others squatted on their heels in the Turkish fashion, and one of them started warbling a thin, tuneless monody on a set of pipes made of a hollowed marrow bone. The still depths of the thicket loomed in total silence everywhere around them, and only a hawk shrilled there briefly now and then.

The stench of burned meat signaled at last that the roast was ready, and two of them dragged the scorched carcass into the shade of a thorn bush. There they hunched around it like a flock of vultures, tore into it with their knives, and gnawed the half raw lumps of meat with animal ferocity while the blood caked their clawing fingers and dripped down their chins. They washed down this barbaric feast with fermented mares' milk that they gulped out of goatskin gourds. Their bellies swollen, and their bodies sated, they slumped back into sluggish lethargy. A few of them talked listlessly for a little longer and then they sunk into a heavy stupor.

★ ★ ★

Then it was noon. The sun seemed to spew molten fire from the quivering sky and the heat grew thicker by the minute.

Flickering patches of sunlight flashed on and off in the matted scrub on the thicket floor, seeping through the tree crowns overhead. There was no sound of any kind in that soporific stillness. Even the hawk was silent.

A few *Lipki* got slowly to their feet and straggled off to the edge of the copse to check on the horses. The others sprawled like corpses on a battlefield, sated with raw meat and wearied by the swelter, and soon began to snore. But their stuffed bellies must have given them some ominous dreams because one or another of them groaned now and then, or stirred restlessly, or muttered *"Allah... Bishmillah..."* while his eyelids flickered open to escape the nightmare.

But suddenly a thick, strangled sound came from the edge of the grove, as if a man was being throttled before he could howl a warning to the others, and the horseherders jerked out of sleep as if doused with water. Either their hearing was so sharply honed that they picked up the soft, gurgling gasps through the fog of sleep, or some animal instinct warned them of their danger, or perhaps Death itself breathed its icy exhalation on their sweated bodies, but all of them were immediately awake.

"What's that?" they babbled at each other. "Where's that lot that went to look at the herd?"

And then a voice said in Polish out of the darkness of the grove: "They're not coming back!"

One hundred and fifty men burst out of the coppice all around the herdsmen and fell on them with such savage fury that their howl of terror choked in their own throats. A scant handful managed to clutch a knife before they were slaughtered. The tight circle of their assailants swarmed over them and covered them completely. The thorn bush shook in the press of bodies that piled on each other in a chaotic jumble, out of which came the hiss of saber blades, gasping breaths, sometimes a moan or the whistling groan of a dying man, and then all sounds ceased.

"How many are alive?" asked a voice among the attackers.

"Five, commandant."

"Check the dead. Make sure they're not faking. Slit their throats to make sure. And get the live ones to the fire."

*   *   *

The order was carried out at once. The dead were nailed to

the ground with their own knives. The prisoners were roped together, their feet stripped bare and bound with rawhide to stout, wooden staves that the dragoons quickly cut and trimmed out of the cherry branches, and thrown around the camp fire which Lusnia stirred so that the glowing coals lay piled on top of the ashes.

The prisoners watched Lusnia and these preparation with empty, hopeless eyes. There were three former Hreptyov *Lipki* among them and they knew the old sergeant-major very well. He also recognized them.

"Well, comrades," he said. "It's time for you to sing for your supper, and if you don't sing out loud and clear, you'll walk into the next world on roasted feet. I won't skimp on the coals for old friends like you."

With this he tossed some dry branches on the coals so that they flamed at once. Novovyeyski came up just then and the interrogation started. The prisoners' confessions more or less confirmed what he had supposed to begin with.

The *Lipki* and the *Tcheremisy* were, indeed, riding as the spearhead of all the Sultan's armies, a day's march ahead of the other Tartars. Azia led them. They rode at night, to avoid the swelter, and sent their horses to pasture in the daytime. They took no precautions because nobody expected an attack even near the Dniester, and far less down here on the Pruth, right next to the home grounds of the Hordes. They were relaxed, unsuspecting, and riding at their ease along with their remount herds and camels that carried the tents of the chiefs and senior commanders. Azia's tent was easy to spot among the others because it had a horsetail standard affixed to its top, and the various *Lipki* companies grounded their banners in front of it during the day-long halts. The *Lipki* division was camped about a mile south, two thousand strong according to its roster, but part of it had been left with the Belgorodian Horde which rode another mile behind.

Novovyeyski questioned his prisoners closely about the best routes to the *Lipki* camp, about the layout of the tents and their disposition in the *maydan*, and then about what mattered to him the most.

"Does he have any women in his tents?" he asked.

The *Lipki* were now trembling for their lives. Those of them

who had served in Hreptyov knew that Novovyeyski was the
brother of one of those women, and the fiance of the other, so
they could guess the rage that would seize him when he discovered the whole truth. This rage would explode on them before
anybody else, so they hung their heads, peered fearfully at each
other, and slumped into a gloomy silence.

"Let's warm their feet a little, commandant!" Lusnia growled.
"Then they'll talk alright!"

"Do it!" Novovyeyski said.

"Have mercy!" cried Eliashevitch, an old Tartar trooper from
the Hreptyov squadron. "I'll tell you all I saw with my own eyes,
or heard from the others...!"

Lusnia shot a quick glance at his commandant, in case he
wanted the man tortured anyway, but Novovyeyski merely
waived his hand.

"Start talking!" he snapped at the Tartar.

"We're not to blame, lord!" Eliashevitch answered. "We were
just doing what we were told to do! The *murjah* gave the orders.
He gave Your Honor's sister to Pan Adurovitch who kept her in
his tent. I saw her carrying water back there in Rumelia, and I
helped her carry it a few times myself, because she was heavy
with child already...."

"I'm burning," Novovyeyski hissed.

"And the other young lady was in our *murjah's* tent. We didn't
see that much of her like we did your sister, but we heard her
screaming many times, because though the *murjah* kept her for
his pleasure, he'd flog her with a bullwhip and kick her every
day...."

Novovyeyski's lips were now the color of ashes and he began
to shake throughout like a man in the grip of fever. The old
Tartar barely caught his next whispered question.

"Where are they now?"

"Sold. In Istanbul."

"To whom?"

"I don't know, lord. I wouldn't think the *murjah* knows
himself. There was this order from the Padishah to get rid of the
women. Everybody sold theirs in the bazaar, so the *murjah* did
too."

* * *

The interrogation was over and silence settled once more around the camp fire, broken only by the rustling of the underbrush and the hiss of a hot southern wind that seeped through the bushes. The wind quickened swiftly and the thicket rustled louder, filling the air with a murmur like a gathering tide. The air was suddenly parched and heavy with storm warnings. Dark clouds, edged with an eerie, coppery light, boiled up from below the horizon.

Novovyeyski left the fireside. He staggered off like a blind, mindless man, with no idea of where he was going. At last he threw himself facedown into the turf, clawed at the soil with his fingernails, bit his own fists, and then began to groan hoarsely like a dying man. Spasms seized and shook his enormous body, and hours passed before he finally shuddered into a silent stillness. The dragoons eyed him worriedly from a distance, but even Lusnia didn't dare to come close to him.

But thinking that the commandant wouldn't be displeased if the Lipki were dispatched to another world, the grisly old sergeant simply stuffed their mouths with soil to muffle their cries, and slaughtered them like oxen.

He kept only Eliashevitch alive, thinking that he'd be useful as a guide. He finished off the last of the dying *Lipki*, dragged their cadavers away from the fire and lined them up in a row under the trees, and went to take a closer look at his young commander.

"Even if he's gone mad," he growled under his mustache, "we'll get that other fellow anyway."

★ ★ ★

It was then well past noon, the sun marched steadily across the burning void, and the day dipped towards the west. But those early clouds glimpsed earlier along the horizon had now spilled across the entire sky, grown heavier and blacker, without losing that coppery glow along their outer edges. Gigantic coils rolled and twisted darkly overhead, and rumbled like millstones grinding against each other; they coiled and wound around each other, boiling and erupting like a vast ravine full of agitated serpents, and pushed each other in dense, swirling masses down towards the ground.

The wind whistled in among the trees, striking the branches

like the wing of a bird of prey. It bowed the trees to the ground, whipped clouds of dry leaves high into the air and scattered them with fury, and died abruptly in moments of sudden stillness as if it had sunk into the soil. In those hushed, breathless pauses, as threatening as they seemed unnatural, the blackness overhead filled with foreboding growls and hisses and mysterious rattling, as if cohorts of thunderbolts were gathering for a battle, goading each other into rage and fury with deep, booming snarls, before they burst and hurled themselves at the trembling soil beneath them.

"Storm! There's a storm coming!" the dragoons whispered to each other.

And the maelstrom drew nearer. The day darkened further. Thunder boomed and rumbled in the east behind them and began to roll heavily across the sky from the lower Dniester. It paused at the Pruth, as if to draw a hot, chaotic breath, and then pealed out again, burst among the rolling hillocks of the wilderness, and started tumbling across the horizon.

The first thick drops of a cloudburst splashed in the parched Steppe grasses.

It was then that Novovyeyski suddenly appeared before the dragoons.

"Mount up!" he bellowed in a voice as violent as thunder.

In moments, no longer than it took to say a hasty prayer, he rode out of the thickets at the head of one hundred and fifty men.

Out in the prairie, his troop joined up with the other half of their column which had been watching for any *Lipki* herders who might have got away. The dragoons swiftly surrounded the pasturing horses, uttered the shrill, savage howl common to all the Tartar *tchabantchuki*, and headed south, driving the herd before them.

The sergeant-major held Eliashevitch close on the end of a rope, and shouted in his ear so that he could be heard above the crash of thunder: "Show the way, dogsblood, and no tricks! Or it's a knife in the throat for you!"

★   ★   ★

Meanwhile the clouds had sagged so low that they were now practically dragging along the ground. A wave of heat struck suddenly, like a fist, and a savage windstorm howled into the plain. A blinding light tore through the thick black curtain with a clap of thunder, lightning flashed; a thunderbolt struck with an unearthly roar, and then a second and a third. There was an overpowering reek of sulfur and darkness fell again.

Terror seized the horseherd. Goaded by the fierce yells of the dragoons behind them, the horses hurled themselves into a wild stampede, running with flared nostrils and windswept manes and barely touching the ground with their flying hooves. Lightning and thunder lashed the plain in an unceasing drumroll of fiery explosions, the wind shrieked around them, and they—the men along with the running horses—flew in that furious riot of the elements as if they were part of the hurricane themselves, swept in a headlong rush without mind or feeling, hurtling like demons through that towering darkness amid the thundering roars that seemed to crack the earth beneath their hooves, driven by the storm and their thirst for vengeance, less like men in that howling wilderness than an aerial cavalcade of warlocks and malignant spirits.

Space shrunk before them. They didn't need a guide because the panicked herd plunged straight for the encampment of the *Lipki* which neared them at each bound. But the storm burst around them in all its savage fury even before they reached it. The sky and the earth seemed to reel with madness. White sheets of light leaped and flared like a permanent illumination around the horizon, showing the tents crouched in the Steppe ahead. The whole world seemed to shake and quiver under the pounding of the thunderbolts, and it was surely just a matter of moments before the dense black tangle of the clouds would rip itself free of the sky and crash down to earth.

And then the floodgates burst open overhead and streams of rain began to drown the Steppe. The downpour seemed to swallow the entire world, blinding them to everything that lay more than a step or two ahead, and thick clouds of steam boiled up from the parched soil beneath them.

A moment more and they'd be in the camp.

But the maddened horseherd burst apart and swept around the campground, leaving a clear space for the men behind them; and then three hundred voices uttered one terrifying battlecry, three hundred sabers glittered amid the lightnings, and the dragoons fell upon the tents.

The *Lipki*, half-blinded as they were by the glare of lightning, caught sight of the approaching herd just before the cloudburst, but they had no idea what deadly drovers were whipping it along. Surprised and alarmed that the herd was running straight for the encampment, they spilled out of their shelters and started shouting and waiving their arms to turn the stampede. Azia himself flung back the flaps of his pavilion and stepped into the rain with anger glaring on his gruesome face.

But in just that moment the herd split and swerved, and he caught sight of some sinister apparitions—many times the number of the drovers he'd sent out—among the sheets of rain and the fog of steam.

And then a single roar boomed out in three hundred voices: "Kill! No quarter! Kill!"

There was no time for anything, not even for terror. No time to wonder what happened and what was happening now. The human whirlwind swept into the encampment, more maddened than the elements, fiercer than the storm.

Before Azia could take one step back towards his tent, some unearthly force seemed to reach down to him and sweep him up in a terrible embrace. He felt himself carried through the air in the grip of some monstrous claw which strained his bones and crushed his ribs and robbed him of breath. Darkness enveloped him. But just before he sunk into that vertiginous pool of blackness, just before the last gleam of consciousness ebbed out of his eyes, he glimpsed a face that loomed before him as if through a mist, and he knew that he'd much rather look into the face of Satan.

★   ★   ★

What happened next was less a battle than a massacre. The storm, the darkness, the suddenness of the attack and the unknown number of the attackers, and the scattered horseherd, stripped the panicked *Lipki* of their will to fight. Mad with shock and terror, they hardly bothered to defend themselves. None of them knew where to run, or where to look for refuge. Many of them had run out of their tents unarmed, some had barely leaped out of sleep, and now—stunned, uncomprehending and struck blind with fear—they crowded together in a formless mob, knocking each other down in their frightful panic and trampling everyone who fell. Pushed inward by the press of horses, cut down by sabers and crushed underhoof, the *Lipki* must have thought that the sky had fallen down upon them and that the earth had cracked wide-open under their boots.

A windstorm doesn't smash, uproot and devastate a stand of young trees as terribly as the dragoons sabered and trampled them. Blood ran in streams along with the downpour. The boom of thunder, the whip and crack of lightning, and the hiss and roar of the rain in the riven darkness, played in terrible counterpoint to the sounds of the slaughter. The dragoon horses had gone mad with terror of their own and hurled themselves blindly into that churning mass, splitting the dense mob, crushing it, and trampling it into the sodden soil.

At last the beaten mass burst apart and broke into the open. But the battered *Lipki* had lost the sense of place and direction to such an extent that they flung themselves into a panicked run all around the battlefield, spilling to right and left rather than straight ahead into the windswept darkness. Colliding with each other like two opposing waves, they fought with each other until the dragoon sabers whistled down upon them.

And finally they were smashed and scattered altogether, pursued and sabered without mercy or any thought of quarter, until the bugles sounded recall in the captured camp and the dragoons abandoned the chase.

No attack that any of them could recall had ever been more of a surprise to an enemy, nor was there ever a more terrible disaster. Three hundred men had smashed and scattered close to two thousand elite cavalry, immeasurably superior to ordinary Tartars. Most of them lay prone among the pools of rainwater and blood. The rest fled blindly and on foot into the sheltering darkness, not knowing if they weren't running into another ambush, and so demoralized as to be quite useless.

But the darkness and the storm that saved them had also been the prime cause of their destruction. Riding back into the captured camp, the victors knew that the wrath of God had fought beside them against traitors.

★   ★   ★

Night fell before Novovyeyski led his dragoons back towards the frontiers of the Commonwealth. Trotting between him and Sergeant-major Lusnia was a remount horse with Azia Tuhay-beyovitch, the chief of all the *Lipki*, trussed upon its back. He was unconscious. All his ribs were crushed. But he was still alive.

They, in the meantime, glanced at him constantly with care and concern, as if they carried a precious treasure they were afraid to lose.

The storm was passing. Stray clouds still galloped through the skies. But stars began to show in the clear gaps between them, and to glitter in the pools scattered across the Steppe.

In the far distance, somewhere along the borders of the Commonwealth, echoed the grim residue of thunder.

Chapter Sixty-three

THE REMNANTS of Azia's shattered *Lipki* stumbled into the encampment of the Belgorodians, babbling in terror about their
incomprehensible defeat, and couriers carried the news from there
to the Sultan's camp, where it created amazement, consternation
and alarm.

Pan Novovyeyski didn't have to *'run hard before the wolves,'* as
the saying went, because no one even thought of launching a
pursuit, and not just at the first word of the disaster but for the
next two days as well. The Sultan was so astonished that he
simply didn't know what to do. The only thing he did at first
was to dispatch some *tchambuls* of the Belgorodian and Dobrudjan Hordes to comb the countryside for any other enemy forces
that might be threatening him. These went unwillingly, worried
about their own skins.

Meanwhile the news, fueled by rumor and anxious speculation, flew like the wind through the Sultan's armies. Those
warriors who lived in the far reaches of Asia or Northern Africa,
and who never made war on *Lehistan* before, were shocked and
dismayed. Legend and folk tale made fire-breathing dragons out
of the terrifying cavalry of these infidels, and here they were, not
content to wait for them inside their own country, but coming
out to seek them in theirs. Even the Grand Vezir and Kara
Mustapha were puzzled. How, they asked, can this Commonwealth whose helplessness was common knowledge in the eastern world, go on the attack? Every Turk in the camp was
scratching his head about that, worried and unsure, because their
whole expedition became suddenly a dangerous and uncertain

venture, a far cry from that easy triumph they thought it would be.

Anger lay thickly in the Sultan's face when he summoned his generals and pashas to a council of war and this dangerous displeasure chilled the Grand Vezir and Kara Mustapha.

"You lied to me," the Padishah accused them. "The *Lahiv* can't be as weak as you said if they come looking for us. You told me that Sobieski wouldn't defend Kamyenetz. But here he is, and so probably is his entire army..."

The Vezir and the brilliant young Anatolian general tried to explain that this was only some foolhardy local band of cut-throats and marauders, but a few muskets and dragoon uniforms stuffed in saddle bags found on the battlefield, made it hard for them to believe their own words. All of the Padishah's inner circle were shrewd, thoughtful men, skilled in the arts of survival and advancement, and all of them bore in mind Sobieski's lightning thrusts into the Ukraine, when he won a whole string of stunning victories despite the most appalling odds. It didn't seem out of character for this fearless *Lion of the North* to forestall and surprise his enemies in this war as he did in others.

"He has no soldiers," the Grand Vezir said to the Anatolian general when they stepped out of the Padishah's pavilions. "But in his heart lives a lion that doesn't know fear. If he is here, and if he has at least ten thousand others with him, then we shall walk in blood all the way to Khotim."

"I'd like to match my skills with his some day," said Kara Mustapha, future *Sword of Islam*, whose destiny was to lead the faithful against the walls of Vienna.

"May Allah shield you from calamity when you do!" the Grand Vezir said.

In time, however, the Dobrudjan and Belgorodian *tchambuls* convinced themselves that there were no large armies anywhere around. Indeed, they found no one. They did, however, find the tracks of a small detachment, numbering about three hundred mounted men, who were riding rapidly for the Dniester. Keeping in mind what happened to the *Lipki*, the Tartars didn't follow.

The attack on the *Lipki* became something that no one could explain or understand. But order and calmness soon returned to the Grand Encampment, and the armies of the Padishah moved forward once more like a fearsome flood.

★ ★ ★

Meanwhile Novovyeyski rode back, unpursued, towards Rashkov with his living booty. He made a rapid march but his experienced borderers could tell within two days that there were no enemies pressing on their heels, so they didn't push their horses as much as they could.

Their prisoner rode between Novovyeyski and Sergeant-major Lusnia, roped to the back of a Tartar pony, and he gave the implacable old Mazurian many anxious moments. Two of his ribs were crushed; the wounds he'd suffered from Basia broke open in his struggle with Novovyeyski, and in the long, fast ride head-down across a horse; and the implacable Lusnia nursed him like a child, wanting to keep him alive until they came to Rashkov.

The young Tartar knew what awaited him and did his best to die. He refused to eat. But Lusnia pried his teeth open with a knife and forced him to drink vodka and Moldavian wine thickly laced with dry powdered hardtack. Whenever they halted, Lusnia splashed water over Azia's wounds, driving the flies out of his bleeding nose and eye socket, where they clustered thickly during the long, dusty hours on the trail. Otherwise, the terrible sergeant feared, gangrene might save the young *Lipki* turncoat from a frightful vengeance.

Novovyeyski said nothing to him all the way. Just once, when Azia offered at the start of the journey to return Zosia and Evka as the price of his freedom, the lieutenant called him a lying dog.

"You sold them both to an Istanbul trader who'll peddle them in the Sarai bazaar," he said with such apparent coldness that it chilled the blood in Azia's veins.

Dragged up at once, Eliashevitch, confirmed this and more in front of all the others.

"It is so, lord," he said. "You sold her and you don't even know who you sold her to. And Adurovitch did the same with the sister of this *baghadir*, even though she was pregnant by him..."

★ ★ ★

It seemed to Azia that Novovyeyski would crush him to death

in his monstrous arms when these words were heard, so later, when he determined to die before his judgment, he did all he could to goad the young giant into murdering him out of hand in a fit of uncontrollable fury, and so spare him the agonies he expected. And because Novovyeyski kept step by step beside him, not wanting to let him out of his sight even for a moment, he started boasting about all the horrors that he perpetrated. He told in shameless detail how he sawed his knife back and forth across the throat of old Pan Novovyeyski, how he indulged himself in Zosia's innocence and raked her white body with his rawhide whip, and how he trampled on her and kicked her with his boots. Sweat streamed thickly down Novovyeyski's gaunt, grey face as he heard and listened; his hands trembled, locked with white knuckles upon his reins, and his whole body leaped and quivered as if in convulsions; but he had neither the strength nor the desire to get away from the sound of that taunting voice. He listened with such profound attention as if he were eager to hear this catalog of horrors, but he kept as tight a grip on himself as he did on his horse, and didn't kill the Tartar.

However, while inflicting torment upon his enemy, Azia was also tormenting himself. Talking about his own tyranny reminded him of how low he'd fallen. Just a few days earlier two thousand men jumped at his every order and he indulged his every whim and pleasure; he was a *murjah* favored by the powerful young Kara Mustapha who was sure to be a Padishah someday. And now he was heading for a horrific death, thrown like a sack across a horse's back, in pain, dripping blood, and eaten alive by flies. The only ease that came to him in this terrible new transformation was when he fainted out of pain and physical exhaustion, and this became so frequent that Lusnia started worrying if he'd get him to the Dniester alive.

But they rode night and day, stopping only long enough to keep their horses going, and Rashkov was nearer by the hour. His harsh, Tartar spirit clung stubbornly to his battered body. Day by day he slid into a deeper fever and into ragged bouts of unconsciousness or sleep where he drifted in a jumble of dreams and hallucinations. He was in Hreptyov with Volodyovski. They were about to set out for a great war. No, he was taking Basia to Rashkov, that's what this was about. No, he'd seized her, she was his, he had her in his tent. Sometimes he saw great massacres and battles, with himself as the Hetman of all the Tartars of the Commonwealth, issuing orders from under a horsetail standard.

Each time, however, consciousness returned all too soon. He'd open his eyes and see the face of Novovyeyski turned grimly towards him. He would see Lusnia. He'd glimpse the helmets of the dragoons who had thrown away their sheepskin disguises, and he'd know himself to be a part of such a terrifying reality that it seemed like a frightful vision sprung out of a nightmare.

Each of his horse's movements sent a shard of pain driving through his body; his seeping wounds burned hotter by the moment; he'd faint only to be revived and drift into fevered visions that led to yet another nightmare, from which he would invariably awake once again. There were moments when he found it impossible to believe that the ruined wretch he had become could be a son of the great Tuhay-bey, and that his life—which was so full of amazing and mysterious matters, and which seemed to point to such a brilliant destiny—could come so swiftly to such an awful end. At times it would occur to him that, as a son of Islam, he'd step from the agonies of his death into the delights of an eternal paradise promised to the faithful. But because he had once been a Christian and spent all but his infancy among Christian people he was afraid of Christ. He, the confused young Tartar was quite sure, would have no mercy for him, and He was clearly stronger than the Prophet, because if the Prophet were the mightier he'd never let Azia fall into Novovyeyski's hands.

But maybe the Prophet would show him some mercy, Azia hoped and prayed. Enough to send for his soul before they tortured him to death.

★ ★ ★

Meanwhile the hours passed and Rashkov was now near. They rode into a rocky landscape that heralded the Dniester. Near evening, Azia fell into a fevered, shallow sleep in which the real and the unreal drifted into one. He thought that they'd arrived and that they were stopping. The word "Rashkov! Rashkov!" echoed in his ears. Then he thought he heard axes cutting down a tree.

He felt the sudden chill of water thrown into his face, and

then the sharp bite of millet liquor poured into his throat. He
was fully conscious. The sky was full of stars and a dozen torches
flamed in the night around him.

Someone said: "Is he conscious?"

"He is. He sees... he understands..." And looking straight
ahead, up towards the stars, he saw the face of Lusnia peering
down at him. "Your time's come, fellow," Lusnia was saying to
him in a calm, matter-of-fact voice.

Azia lay on his back. He was breathing freely. His arms were
pulled up and stretched past his head, so that his chest could
draw deeper draughts of air than when he was trussed across the
back of a horse. He couldn't move his hands, however, because
they were tied to a thick oak sapling that ran past his shoulders.
They were, he noted, wrapped in pitch-soaked straw. He knew
what this meant. But, in that same moment, he noticed other
preparations that told him his agonies would be frightful and last
a long time.

He'd been stripped naked from the waist down.

When he raised his head slightly to look past his pale, parted
knees, he saw that they were raised and that the white point of
a rough-hewn, freshly-sharpened stake protruded between
them. The thick end of that stake lay wedged against a tree
stump.

From each of his ankles ran a rope that ended in a set of traces
and a harnessed horse. The torchlight showed Azia only the
backs of the horses and the dim outlines of men standing at their
bridles.

One glance told the story. The young Tartar knew beyond the
shadow of a doubt each detail of what was about to happen.
Then, looking straight into the sky, he fixed his eyes on the stars
and the crescent moon.

'They'll be impaling me,' he thought.

He clamped his teeth together so hard that a spasm gripped
and convulsed his jaws. Sweat burst out at once on his fevered
forehead but his face chilled, cold as death, as the blood drained
out of it in horror. Then it seemed to him as if his body had
leaped free of the soil and that it was flying into some bottomless
abyss, where neither place, nor time, nor anything that happened, had the slightest meaning. But then the sergeant's knife

was prying his clenched teeth apart, and more raw liquor was poured down his throat.

Azia choked, spitting out the harsh, burning liquid, but he had to drink a lot of it as well. He fell into a strange state, neither drunk nor sober. Indeed, his awareness had never been sharper nor his perceptions clearer. He saw everything around him. He understood it all. But he was seized by a sudden, inexplicable excitement, and by a sort of strange impatience that it was all taking so long and nothing had yet started.

★ ★ ★

He heard heavy footfalls and saw Novovyeyski looking down at him. All the nerves in his body seemed to leap in a single spasm. He had no fear of Lusnia, he had too much contempt for him to be afraid of him; but he couldn't despise Novovyeyski who'd never given him a reason for contempt. But every glimpse of Novovyeyski's face filled Azia with superstitious terror, loathing and disgust, which—for some reason Azia couldn't understand—was aimed at himself.

He thought: *'I'm at his mercy and I'm afraid of him.'* And the hair on his head grew as stiff as wire at this flash of feeling.

"For what you've done, you'll die in agony," Novovyeyski said.

Azia made no reply. His breath quickened into a sudden gasping.

Novovyeyski stepped aside. There was a brief silence, broken all too soon.

"And you've tried to hurt our lady," Lusnia grunted hoarsely. "But the lady's back home with her husband now, and you're here with us! Your time's come!"

For Azia, his torture started with these words. Nothing could pain him more, he thought, than this bitter knowledge in his final moments: that all he'd done never had a meaning; that all his cruelties were wasted; and that even his treason didn't make a difference to anyone but himself.

He'd gained nothing!

He might as well have left things as they were! The least he'd have if Basia had died on her way to Hreptyov was the consoling thought that she'd belong to nobody if she didn't belong to him. But even this comfort was taken from him at this of all moments, when he could see the point of a sharpened stake gleaming between his knees!

Ah, it was all for nothing! So many plots and treasons, so much blood, such a terrible punishment so near... for nothing! Lusnia had no idea how bitterly his final taunt had added to Azia's dying torments. If he had known, he'd have repeated it all the way across Bessarabia.

But it was too late now for realizations and regrets. Lusnia stooped down, grasped Azia by the hips so that he'd be able to move them back and forth, in much the way that a seamstress moves the eye of a needle she is about to thread, and barked an order at the men who held the waiting horses.

"Move out! Slowly and together!"

★   ★   ★

The horses started forward. The ropes tightened and pulled on Azia's legs. His body slid along the ground for barely a moment before it struck the crudely sharpened point of the young, felled tree. The point plunged into him, and slid ever deeper, and then something indescribable began to happen to his tormented body, something that violated every law of nature and all human feeling. His bones cracked and parted. Flesh ripped apart, his body split in two. A pain of such inexpressible intensity, and of such tearing agony that it almost stepped into the realm of some monstrous joy, burst throughout his entire being. And the stake thrust deeper. Tuhaybeyovitch clenched his jaws but the cawing, crow-like screech burst through his bared teeth anyway, and the long, grating howl that followed was like the scream of an impaled raven.

"Slowly!" the sergeant growled.

Azia's screams came faster.

"Ah, cawing, are you?" the sergeant asked quietly, then snapped at his men: "Together now! Hold it straight! Easy now! That's it!"

They quickly unharnessed the horses and unchained the traces. The stake was raised. The thick untrimmed end was dropped into a pit dug before the torture, and then the rest of the pit was filled up with soil. Azia looked down upon all this from his dreadful height. He was fully conscious. This form of execution, which came to the Commonwealth from Valachia a long time before, was all the more dreadful because an impaled victim sometimes lived as long as three days. Azia's head was dangling on his neck. His lips smacked thickly together, as if chewing something. Most of what he could feel just then was dizziness and a blank, weary lassitude. His solitary eye fixed on an infinite white mist which seemed somehow frightful, full of pain and horror. But he could see the faces of the sergeant and the dragoons hanging in that mist. He knew that he was impaled, on a stake, and that his body sagged ever deeper upon that grizzly point, dragged down by inches by its own dead weight.

Darkness sometimes fell upon that dreadful milky fog and then he blinked rapidly with his one good eye, wanting to pierce this blindness and to see everything all at once before he died. His dimmed sight wandered with particular insistence among the flaming torches because it seemed to him that each flame had acquired a halo of rainbows.

But his torture wasn't over yet. He saw the sergeant coming over to the stake, a wood-drill in his hand. He heard him tell the dragoons to lift him up and to hold him steady, and two muscular troopers hoisted him to their shoulders. Still blinking, still not quite able to pierce the drifting darkness, Azia began to stare at him as if wondering who it was, and who'd have the temerity to ascend to his own lofty level from which he could look down upon all around him.

"The lady knocked out one of your eyes," he heard the sergeant saying. "And I took me an oath I'd drill out the other."

With this he plunged the point of the drill into Azia's eye, turned it once or twice, and when the eyelid and the delicate flesh around the eye had wound around the spirals, he jerked it all out.

Twin streams of blood burst out of the two empty sockets, and flowed like two streams of dark tears down the Tartar's face.

Under that blood, that face was now drained of any color and it became ever more pale and grey. The dragoons began to douse their torches without a word, as if ashamed to cast a light on such a dreadful act, and then only the pale, silver of the crescent moon painted Azia's body.

His head was now hanging down upon his chest, and only his upraised arms, swathed in pitch-soaked straw and bound to a stave behind him, lifted towards the sky in silent supplication, as if this son of the East was crying out to the Turkish crescent for vengeance on his torturers.

"Mount up!" cried Novovyeyski.

Just before he mounted, the sergeant set fire to the Tartar's hands, using the last of the pine torches to do so, and then the column set out towards Yampol. All that remained among the ruins of Rashkov, casting a grim red light into the empty darkness, was the impaled Azia, son of Tuhay-bey. He had become a torch that glowed a long time.

Chapter Sixty-four

THREE WEEKS LATER Pan Novovyeyski brought his men to Hreptyov. It took him that long to get there from Rashkov because he crossed the Dniester several times more along the way, raiding the *tchambuls* and the men posted in the riverside forts by the local Turkish governors. Later on, when the Sultan's armies arrived in Moldavia, they heard widespread tales about Polish troops raiding everywhere, which fueled the speculation about a great army that would surely come out to bar their way, and challenge the Padishah in the field rather than wait for him in Kamyenetz.

This both surprised and displeased the Sultan. He'd been assured by everyone around him that the Commonwealth was helpless, his to sweep up in passing any time he wished, like dust in the field. But all this energetic activity implied the reverse. Wondering about it, the Padishah sent out all the Hordes from the Danubian basin, the Valachians and his remaining *Lipki* to check and occupy all the lands before him, while he followed cautiously and slowly. Despite the sea of warriors he commanded, he was most uneasy about an open battle with the regular contingents of the Commonwealth.

Volodyovski was away from Hreptyov when Novovyeyski got there because he'd gone to join Pan Motovidlo and the troops that fought against Doroshenko and the Crimean Horde. New fame came to him there, adding a fresh luster to all his other achievements.

Basia, meanwhile, made ready to leave Hreptyov because the

nearness of the approaching storm made it too dangerous to stay there any longer.

She was leaving the little wooden fortress where she experienced so many moving moments and dangerous adventures, but where she'd also spent the happiest year of her life. To live so close to the man she loved, among such famous soldiers and so many hearts that glowed fondly towards her, wasn't something that happened to every other woman. And now she was leaving, going to Kamyenetz by her own request, changing these warm, wooden walls for the uncertainties and danger of a town under siege.

She was *'a golden heart,'* as Pan Zagloba used to call her fondly, but it was also a heart with a lot of steel, so she didn't let regret get the better of her and took charge of all the preparations, supervising both the soldiers and the wagon train. Pan Zagloba, whose wisdom soared above all others in every adventure, added the fruits of his experience to this military bustle; while Pan Mushalski, the unequaled archer who was also a tested and accomplished soldier, gave her the practical assistance.

All of them were happy to see Novovyeyski although one glance at his face was enough to show that he didn't manage to get Evka and the gentle Zosia out of the hands of their Muslim captors. Basia wept for them both as if they were dead, because that was the only way to think of them from that moment on. Sold to unknown buyers, and then auctioned off in Istanbul, they could be anywhere in Asia Minor, on the Turkish islands of the Mediterranean, Ionian and Aegean seas, or in North Africa and Egypt, shut away in harems and lost to the world. Asking about them to trace their whereabouts in these circumstances, finding them, and then buying them from whoever owned them, had no chance of success.

So Basia wept for them and for Novovyeyski, and Pan Zagloba wept right along beside her, with Pan Mushalski sniffing and snuffling beside him, and only Novovyeyski's eyes remained dull and dry. He had, quite simply, no more tears to shed. But when he told them how he'd marched far south into the Danube basin, how he penetrated all the way down the Pruth to the Tekitch, right next to Dobrudja, how he attacked and shattered the *Lipki* right under the noses of the Hordes and the Padishah himself, and then how he caught the venomous

Azia Tuhaybeyovitch, both the older knights started to pound their sabers with their fists and shout in excitement.

"Get him over here! He should die right here in Hreptyov!"

"He's dead already," Novovyeyski said. "Not here but in Rashkov, which is simple justice. And one of your sergeants thought up such an end for him, that his death couldn't have come too soon."

★ ★ ★

Here he told the others how Azia had died, and they listened to him with horror but with little mercy.

"That God pursues the evildoer is a well known fact," Pan Zagloba observed eventually. "But it's a wonder that the Devil does such a poor job defending his servants."

Basia sighed, remembering how much she owed to God's protection, raised her eyes gratefully to the ceiling. "That's because he lacks the power to match himself with God," she said with conviction.

"Right on target, my lady!" Pan Mushalski cried. "You couldn't have hit it better! Because if ever the Devil gets the upper hand, which God forbid should happen, then it'll be all up with justice in the world, and the Commonwealth will wither away bit by bit and go down altogether."

"Which is why I don't give two hoots about the Turks," Pan Zagloba fired off at once. "First because they're all the sons of Belial, and next because the Devil himself doesn't know who their mothers were!"

★ ★ ★

That seemed like a good way to end that conversation, so they sat quietly for a while, looking with pity at Pan Novovyeyski. The young giant sat hunched on his wooden bench, his hamlike fists clenched around his knees, and stared with glassy eyes at the floor before him.

"Tell me, though," Pan Mushalski turned to him as gently as he could. "Are you feeling a little easier about everything now that he is dead? A good vengeance is a measureless consolation."

"Yes, tell us," Basia urged with all her generosity and compassion. "Is it easier for you? Can you be happier now?"

The grim young giant sat in deep silence for a while longer, as if wrestling with his own conclusions. But when he spoke, his

voice came as softly as a puzzled whisper, as if he was astonished
to hear his own words.

"Imagine, my lady and gentlemen, if you would," he seemed
locked in a struggle with his own confusion, "as God is my
witness... that's what I thought myself, that I'd find a little ease
once I killed that man... I saw him die. I watched him on the
stake. I watched when they were drilling out his eye. I kept
telling myself that this was good, that this made me feel better.
But it's not true! It's not true...!"

Here the racked Novovyeyski seized his head between his
two great fists and groaned through clenched teeth.

"He was better off on the stake," he muttered, "better with
the drill twisting in his eye and better with his hands on fire,
than I am right now with all that lives inside me, and tears at me,
and thinks and remembers... Only death can put an end to that
torment. Only death. That will be my only real consolation."

And here Basia showed how right all these soldiers were to
love her, honor her and respect her courage. She rose like a
soldier, placed her gentle hand on the sufferer's bowed head, and
said quietly but firmly:

"May God allow you to find it in Kamyenetz because what
you say is true. Death ends every torment."

"Yes!" the bowed young man said, fervent suddenly with
longing, and nodded with closed eyes. "Yes. May God repay
your kind thoughts, my lady..."

And that same evening they left for Kamyenetz.

Once through the gate, Basia turned to look for a long time
behind her, as if to fill her memory with those thatched roofs
that gleamed like gold at sunset, that earthwall on the little
mound and that wooden palisade that glowed so redly in the
warm rays of an evening sun, and then at last she sighed in
farewell and made the sign of the cross over them while they
sunk out of sight in the advancing darkness.

"May we come back to you someday, dear Hreptyov, Michal
and I!" she murmured. "May nothing worse happen to us while
we are away...!"

Two small tears rolled down that rosy face. A strange regret
gripped everyone around her and they rode on in silence.

★   ★   ★

Night fell soon after.

They made their way slowly to Kamyenetz because the wagon train couldn't be hurried beyond a snail's pace. It crept surrounded by herds of horses, oxen and heavy-laden camels, with the camp servants acting as the drovers. Some of the artisans and soldiers got married while in Hreptyov so that the wagons also carried women.

There were no soldiers in this exodus other than those led by Novovyeyski, and the two hundred Hungarian Infantry raised and equipped at his own expense by the little knight, whom Basia took into her special keeping. None of the men were, of course, real Hungarians; they were just drilled, uniformed and armed in the Hungarian manner with muskets and sabers, playing the role of *foot cavalry* on the battlefield. Their corporals and sergeants were veteran dragoons and the rank and file were former cattle thieves, bandits and marauders from the *vatahas* that the little colonel stamped out in his region, and condemned to death. They snatched at the offer of their lives in exchange for brave and loyal service in the infantry. Nor were they all reprieved felons, cut off the end of a hangman's noose in Hreptyov; at least half of them were volunteers who abandoned their lairs in the caves and forests, preferring service with "the Little Falcon" to the dread of his sword hanging over their necks.

As soldiers, they still left much to be desired. They needed discipline and training of the kind that only years in the infantry can give. But they were fierce fighters, used to hard times and bloodshed. Basia was especially fond of them as her Michal's own accomplishment, and they were soon devoted to their beautiful patroness and lady. Now they marched around her carriage with sabers slapping against their boots and muskets across their shoulders, proud to be her escort, and ready to fight like wolves if some *tchambul* ran across their path.

But the road ahead was still clear. Pan Volodyovski loved his wife too much to expose her to any kind of danger, and he was too farsighted to allow any more delays in the evacuation of his outpost station, so the rest of the journey passed without alarms. They started from Hreptyov in late afternoon, rode all night and well into the morning, and saw the craggy cliffs of Kamyenetz the next afternoon.

★ ★ ★

The sight of those tall crags, with the battlements and towers of the town and castle perched thickly above them, filled them all with confidence and hope. It seemed impossible for any hand other than that of God to topple that eagles' nest, built as it was on those rocky peaks, and held safe by the loops of the river that flowed through the gorges at its foot. The Summer day was beautiful beyond belief and miraculously clear. The domes and steeples of temples and churches gleamed like gigantic candles in the golden sun. Peace, happiness and quiet drifted above this bright-lit, open country.

"Take a look, Baska!" Pan Zagloba said. "The heathens gnawed at these walls many times before and they always cracked their teeth doing it. Ha! How many times have I seen them bolting out of here, holding their snouts because their teeth were hurting! It'll be just the same this time, if God lets it happen!"

"Of course He will!" cried the glowing Basia.

"Come to think of it, one of their Sultans had been here already. Osman. It was in 1621, I remember it like it was yesterday. The dog came at us right from over there, from Khotim across the Smotritza. His eyes bulged out, his mouth flapped open, and he looked and looked and didn't like anything he saw. *'Who made this place?'* he asked the Vezir. *'God did,'* the Vezir said. *'Then let God storm it because I'm not crazy,'* Osman said, and he turned right around and went where he came from."

"And a lot faster than he came!" threw in Pan Mushalski.

"That's right!" Pan Zagloba said. "Because we prodded their backsides with our lances, after which the knighthood carried me in their arms to Pan Lubomirski."

"You mean to say, sir, that you fought at Khotim?" asked the peerless archer, and it was hard to say whether he was amazed or amused. "Is there anywhere in history that you haven't been and anything that you didn't accomplish?"

Somewhat piqued, the old knight tossed the archer an unfriendly glance.

"Not only was I there," he replied, "but I took a wound which I can bare for your inspection anytime you wish. Only we'd better step into the bushes because it's in a rather private place and I wouldn't want to excite the ladies."

The peerless archer knew when he was the target of a joke. But because he didn't feel qualified to cross wits with the incomparable Zagloba, he swallowed his answer. Instead he changed the subject.

"What you both say is the truth," he said. "When a man's far away and hears people saying *'Kamyenetz isn't ready for a siege! Kamyenetz will fall!'* it's enough to scare anybody. But when he sees the place then, as God's my witness, hope fills him up again!"

"And Michal will also be there!" Basia cried.

"And Pan Sobieski may send a relief column!"

"God be praised!" Pan Mushalski nodded. "We're not so badly off, after all! No, not by a long shot! Ha! It's been a lot worse than this and we got through alright!"

"But even if it's the worst it's ever been," Pan Zagloba had the final word as always. "The main thing is to keep the faith and to stay resolute and determined. They didn't gulp us down before and they won't do it now! Just as long as we've our hearts and our spirit!"

★ ★ ★

The hopeful light which filled them at these words led to a moment of grateful thought and silence, but this quiet passage was soon broken for them when Pan Novovyeyski rode up to the side of Basia's open carriage.

His face, usually so grey with suffering and so crushed with hopelessness and despair, was now suffused with a strange, enigmatic smile, and his distant eyes were fixed in a glassy stare on the sun-drenched walls and towers of Kamyenetz. Basia and the two knights were surprised to see this sudden transformation, and wondered how the sight of the fortress could lift the burdens that weighed down his soul, and how it could do it so unexpectedly and swiftly.

"God's name be praised!" he greeted them loudly. "There was a lot of worry, but now joy is ready and waiting!"

And here he turned to Basia.

"They, the both of them," he said, "are with Tomashevitch, the alderman for the Polish merchants in Kamyenetz, and it's a good thing they went there, because that cut-throat won't get to them in a fortress as powerful as that!"

"Who are you talking about, sir?" Basia asked in a frightened voice.

"Zoska and Evka."

"God save you, lad!" the old knight cried out. "Don't let the Devil get you!"

"Besides," Novovyeyski babbled on. "What people say about my father, I mean how Azia cut his throat, that's also a lie!"

"His wits are addled," Pan Mushalski whispered.

"You'll permit, my lady, if I ride out ahead?" Novovyeyski babbled out again. "It's been so long since I've seen them that it's hard to wait! Oy, but the heart is empty with loving at a distance! So empty!"

His huge head started wagging from side to side like an ungainly burden, and then he nudged his horse forward with his heels and trotted ahead. Pan Mushalski beckoned to a few dragoons and rode after him, to make sure that the poor madman wouldn't hurt himself.

Basia hid her fresh young face in both her hands and tears flowed slowly through her shielding fingers, while Pan Zagloba heaved a heavy sigh.

"He was pure gold, that man," he said. "The best of his kind. But no one can carry more grief than he's able. Besides, the soul needs better nourishment than vengeance."

Part IX

Chapter Sixty-five

KAMYENETZ STIRRED AND HUMMED like a roiled beehive with preparations for defense against the coming siege. The town's various national and ethnic mercantile communities—such as the Poles, the Ruthenians, the Armenians, the Jews and the Gypsies—toiled on the walls of the old castle and on the city gates, each under its own aldermen and council; with special efforts being made on the Ruthenian Gate; and with Tomashevitch, the hard-fisted leader of the Polish townsmen, enjoying the most authority among them due to his courage, hardiness, and skills as a gunner.

For the time being the cannon lay quiet and still on the walls and gates which each of these communities would defend under its own leaders, and the Polish artisans, the Ruthenian tradesmen, the Armenian merchants and the Jewish craftsmen competed with each other with shovels and barrows, each wanting to have the strongest walls and the best defenses. The officers of the various regiments had the overall direction, the sergeants and the troopers did the heavy labor, and even the resident and visiting gentry worked gamely with their hands, forgetting that 'God gave them fists so they might grasp a saber' and left all other work to people of a lower order. Pan Humyetzki, the Seneschal of Podolia, led the way and shined by example, trundling a wheel-barrow full of rocks and boulders, indifferent to his age, his honors, his rank and his position.

A fever of work gripped the town and castle. Priests and friars—like the Dominicans, the Jesuits, the Carmelites and the

615

brothers of St. Francis—moved among these crowds, blessing the work of others. Women brought food and drink to their laboring men. The beautiful, sloe-eyed wives and daughters of rich Armenian merchants, and the even more beautiful Jewish girls and women from the outlaying townships of Zhvanyetz, Zhinkovyetz and Dunaygorod, drew the eyes of the soldiers in fond admiration.

But the attention of the crowds focused on Basia's entry into the town. There were undoubtedly many women in Kamyenetz whose rank and position far exceeded hers, but there wasn't one whose husband walked in greater fame and glory. Lady Volodyovska herself had become something of a legend. Folklore gave her a spine of steel, the fist of a soldier, and a heart full of dash, fearlessness and fire. She was, after all, a woman who wasn't afraid of life among fierce, primitive people in a wilderness *stannitza*, who went to war right beside her husband, and one who not only tore herself out of the clutches of a Tartar when he seized her and tried to carry her off to Asia, but who struck him down like a thunderbolt as well. Her fame, however, painted an erroneous picture for those who didn't know her; she was imagined as a giantess who could rip armor with her bare hands and snap horseshoes with her fingers. They gaped wide-eyed when they saw her small, pink face tilted curiously towards them from her open carriage, and looked into her brightly smiling eyes which were as mild and gentle as a child's.

"Is that her ladyship herself?" they asked, bemused, in the crowds around them. "Or is it her daughter?"

"It's she herself," replied those who knew.

A sense of wonder swept the burghers, their curious wives, the priests, the begging friars, and the watching soldiers. No lesser admiration met the Hreptyov garrison, made invincible by their own hardwon legend: the dragoons among whom rode the smiling, blank-eyed Novovyeyski, and the fierce-faced cut-throats who'd been transformed into Volodyovski's Hungarian Infantry. There were five hundred men riding or marching into the town with Basia, every one of them a hardened, well-tried warrior by profession, as unworried in the heat of battle as peddlers in the bustle of a country fair, so that a fresh wave of confidence surged at once into the shopkeepers and merchants.

"That's more than just an ordinary reinforcement," they cried in the crowds. "They'll look the Turk in the eye without qualm or worry!"

Some of the burghers and few of the soldiers thought that Pan Volodyovski himself rode somewhere in the column, so they began to shout and cheer his name.

"Long life to Pan Volodyovski!"

"Let him live and prosper, our defender! The most famous knight!"

"Vivat Volodyovski! *Vivat!*"

Basia heard and listened and her heart swelled with pride, because few things could please a woman more in those times than her husband's glory, especially when she heard it honored among people who live in a great town.

'There are so many great knights here,' she thought. *'But nobody shouts for them, only for my Michal.'*

And she felt like adding her own silvery voice to that ringing chorus and shout out: *'Vivat* Volodyovski!' But Pan Zagloba begged her to sit still and act like a lady.

"You're a distinguished person here," he admonished. "So will you behave? Sit still. Stop squirming. Don't shout anything! If people take you for a personage then be a personage, and bow to both sides of the carriage like royalty when they enter their own capital."

He himself bowed regally left and right, either raising his cap or wagging his hand to the cheering masses, but when a fresh burst of *vivats* exploded in his honor he forgot his own admonitions about dignity.

"My lords and ladies!" he boomed out at the crowd. "Who could take it in Zbarajh can take it in Kamyenetz!"

★　★　★

Pan Volodyovski left instructions for the cavalcade to stop at the newly-founded convent of St. Dominic. He had his own small townhouse in Kamyenetz, but he picked that secluded convent for his Basia's refuge because it lay at some distance from the inner walls and beyond the reach of besieging cannon. Since he was one of the convent's benefactors, he expected her to be well received.

Nor was he wrong in that. Podolia was Pototzki and Lantzk-

618 Fire in the Steppe

oronski country, although those magnates held vast possessions everywhere else in the Commonwealth as well, so the prioress, Mother Victoria, was a daughter of Pan Stefan Pototzki, the *Voyevode* of Bratzlav. But she received Basia with open arms, like mother and daughter. Straight from these warm embraces, Basia ran into the waiting arms of her aunt, Pani Makovyetzka, whom she hadn't seen since her wedding day. Both of them wept with joy, and so did her uncle, Pan Makovyetzki, whose favorite ward she had been before she was married.

They'd barely dried their sentimental tears when Krysia came running, so the fond greetings started all over again, and then Basia was surrounded by the convent sisters and other gentlewomen, eager to question her about everything at once. Some, like Lady Bogush, wanted news of their absent husbands who were still on outpost duty, patrolling the Dniester. Others wanted Basia's views about the Turks and the avalanche that was about to fall upon them all. Yet others wanted her opinion about whether Kamyenetz would hold out. She was thrilled to see that they all took her for a military expert who might reassure them, and she didn't skimp on confidence and enthusiasm.

"There's no question about holding out against the Turks!" she told them. "Of course we will do it! Michal will be here any day, today or tomorrow, and when he takes charge of the defense you won't have a worry in the world! And the fortress is a hard nut to crack as well, as I might well tell you, since thanks to God's mercy I know a bit about it."

★ ★ ★

Basia's confidence reassured the women who were especially heartened by the promise of the little knight's arrival. He was, indeed, so honored and respected throughout the whole country that eager visitors were soon streaming to the convent. Evening had fallen but the various local officers kept coming to pay their respects to Basia, and the first thing they asked after the bows of greeting, was how soon the famous little borderer would come to Kamyenetz and if he really meant to lock himself within the walls.

Basia was too tired to receive them all but she found time for Ketling and two or three others. The rest didn't even get past the convent gate that day. Her ladyship was tired by her journey, they were told, but in truth she was busy with Pan Novovyeyski. The deranged young man had lost consciousness and fallen off his horse at the convent gates and now lay senseless in a borrowed cell.

She sent at once for a medic, the same knowledgeable Greek who looked after her in Hreptyov, and who foresaw a dangerous inflammation of the brain, an irreversible imbalance of the humors, and didn't hold out much hope for the stricken victim. Basia sat with the old knight and Pan Mushalski long into the night, thinking about the sad fate of the young lieutenant.

"The medic told me," Pan Zagloba said, "that if he stays alive, then proper bleedings might restore the humors and his wits won't stay scrambled like they are. Then maybe he'd take his suffering with a lighter heart."

"No," Basia said. "There is no way for anything to console him now."

"A man would be better off sometimes if he had no memory at all," observed Pan Mushalski. "But even the *animalia* aren't free of that."

But the old knight took umbrage.

"If you had no memory you wouldn't be able to go to confession," he roared at the startled archer. "And that would make you no better than a Lutheran and fit to roast in Hell! Didn't Father Kaminski cautioned you enough about your blaspheming? Ah, but you can preach as many sermons as you like to a wolf, and he'll still steal goats!"

"Me a wolf?" the archer asked mildly. "Call Azia a wolf!"

"And didn't I do just that?" demanded Pan Zagloba. "Who was the first to say: *'that's a wolf!'*"

"Novovyeyski told me before we left Hreptyov," Basia said and sighed, "that he hears them crying out to him night and day, both Evka and Zosia, begging him to save them. And how is anybody to do that? It had to end in sickness because no one can live through such torments without going mad. He could make his peace with their deaths perhaps, but not their degradation."

"And now he just lies there, dead to the world like a piece of timber," Pan Mushalski nodded. "And that's a rare pity because he was a first-rate fighting man."

A servant lad interrupted them to report a fresh excitement in the town, and that new crowds were gathering to see Pan

Mikolai Pototzki, the Ordinate-General of Podolia, who had just entered the town with a substantial household and a few dozen infantry.

"The chief command here will be his, by virtue of his office," Pan Zagloba said and wagged his finger sadly. "It's decent of his lordship to come here in person rather than do his commanding from a safer distance, but I still wish he'd stayed away. Ha! He was as much a thorn in the Hetman's side as the rest of them! He didn't want to believe in any danger or hear a word about any war! And now, who knows, he might pay for it with his head!"

"Maybe some of the other Pototzki lords will follow him here," suggested Pan Mushalski.

"One thing is clear now," Pan Zagloba answered, and scrawled a hasty cross across his chest and belly. "The Turks must be near! In the name of the Father, the Son and the Holy Ghost! May his lordship turn into a second Yeremi Vishnovyetzki and Kamyenetz into a second Zbarajh."

"That's how it'll be or we'll die for it," some voice stated quietly from the threshold.

"Michal!" Basia cried, leaped up and threw herself into his arms.

★   ★   ★

The news Volodyovski brought fresh from the battle fields would be presented to the commanding council the next day, but Basia heard it first in the secluded cell she used as her chamber. Luck rode beside him as always, and he crushed a few of the smaller *tchambuls* while riding rings around Doroshenko's rebels and the Crimean Tartars. He also brought with him a few dozen prisoners who could tell how strong the Khan and his Cossack allies were.

Other Polish borderers hadn't fared so well. A strong force led by Pan Lujhetzki, the Chamberlain of Podlasye, was shattered in a murderous battle against Doroshenko; Pan Motovidlo, who was out scouting the Valachian trails, was overwhelmed by Krytchinski with help from the Belgorodian Horde and what was left of the *Lipki* Tartars. The little knight also stopped in Hreptyov to look once more at the place of his greatest happiness.

"I was there right after you left," he said. "In fact I could still feel your warmth about the place, and I could've caught up with you in an hour. But I crossed the Dniester at Ushitza to sniff along the southern trails for a day or two. Some of the leading *tchambuls* are already on our side of the river and they might catch a lot of people unawares. The others ride as a screen for the Turks' main army and will be here before very long. There'll be a siege, my love, there's no help for that, but we won't let them get us. Our people will fight all the harder because they'll be defending their own livelihoods as well as their country."

He was clearly moved. His little whiskers twitched up and down for a silent moment. But then he took his wife in his arms, started to kiss her cheeks, and they said nothing more to each other for the rest of the night.

★ ★ ★

The next morning Pan Volodyovski shared his news with the council of war called at the residence of Bishop Lantzkoronski, whose other members were several civil and military dignitaries of Podolia and a number of serving officers. Beside the bishop were Pan Mikolai Pototzki, whose rank as Ordinate-General of Podolia made him the chief military officer of the territorial gentry; Pan Hieronimus Lantzkoronski, the bishop's brother who was the *Podkomorzy* or Chamberlain of Podolia; Pan Revuski, the *Scriptor* or secretary of the Podolian diet, who had commanded the Mohilev garrison from Warsaw but who was a good fighting soldier for all that; the brave old Seneschal Humyetzki who wasn't afraid to soil his hands with work; Pan Makovyetzki, the *Stolnik* or magistrate of Latitchev and Basia's former guardian; Ketling and a few other ranking officers as well. The one thing, however, that upset Pan Volodyovski from the start was the Ordinate-General's opposition to a single, unified command. Instead, his lordship surrendered his duties to the council.

"Danger needs quick decisions, not discussions!" Volodyovski warned. "There must be a single head and a single will to meet the unexpected! There were three Commonwealth generalissimos at Zbarajh, appointed by the King and chosen by the senate, who could have commanded there by the right of their commission and authority, but they handed all their powers to Prince

Yeremi Vishnovyetzki because they judged, and rightly, that it's best to have one source of orders in moments of danger."

He might have saved his breath, however, for what good this did him. Nor did it help when the studious Ketling cited the example of the ancient Romans who, as he put it, were the greatest soldiers of their age, but who invested one man with all the powers of the senate in times of dire danger, giving the word *Dictator* to all the civilized languages on earth.

This eloquent appeal also fell on indifferent ears because Bishop Lantzkoronski didn't care for Ketling, having convinced himself that the young Scotsman had to be a heretic at heart. He replied loftily that Poles didn't need foreign newcomers to teach them about history.

"We have our own minds," he said. "Neither do we need to imitate the Romans since we don't have to take second place to them in much; and perhaps, at times, we even surpass them in eloquence and military prowess.

"And," he went on, "just as there's a brighter flame from a bundle of kindling wood than from a single twig, so many heads are better than one."

With this he praised the decorous modesty of Pan Mikolai Pototzki—although there were some who thought it might be fear of responsibility—and urged negotiations. But that word sent every soldier leaping from his chair as if scorched by fire.

Pan Volodyovski, Ketling, Makovyetzki, Humyetzki, Revuski and Major Kvasibrodski, started to grind their teeth in rage and to slap their sabers. "Now we know what's really in your minds!" they shouted to the civil dignitaries. "We didn't come here to chit-chat with the Turks but to fight them! Your clerical skirts protect you, excellency, or you wouldn't dare to speak to us like that!"

Major Kvasibrodski even shouted: "Back to your pulpit, sir! You don't belong in a military council!"

It looked for a moment as if a tumult was about to break out in the council room.

"I'd be the first to lay my head for the churches and for my flock!" the bishop thundered in a great voice, rising to his feet. "And if I mention negotiations it's only to gain time! Not to surrender the fortress, may God witness that, but to let the

Hetman bring some help to us. Pan Sobieski's name is terrifying to the Turks. Let them just hear that he is on his way, even if he's not really strong enough to face them, and the pagan will soon turn his back on Kamyenetz."

★ ★ ★

This powerful speech silenced everyone. Some of the officers were even pleased with it, since it didn't touch upon surrendering.

Then Volodyovski spoke up suddenly.

"If it's a matter of buying time," he said, "there's a better way. Before laying siege to Kamyenetz, the enemy must take Zhvanyetz, the property of his lordship, Pan Lantzkoronski who is here with us, because there is no way he'd leave a garrisoned castle at his back. With his lordship's permission, I'll lock myself in Zhvanyetz and buy us just as much time as his grace, the bishop, would through his diplomatic maneuvers. I'll take loyal men and Zhvanyetz will hold as long as I'm alive."

"Impossible!" the shout came from every throat at once. "You're needed here! The burghers will lose heart if they hear you're gone, and even the soldiers won't fight so well without you! Who has the most experience among us? Who else served in Zbarajh? And when it comes to making a night attack against the enemy, who would lead it better? No, no, first you'll die in Zhvanyetz and then we'll fall for sure!"

"All I need is an order," said Volodyovski.

"Just send some smart, resolute young man to help me in Zhvanyetz," said Pan Lantzkoronski, "and I'll go myself."

"Let Novovyeyski go there!" several voices cried.

"Novovyeyski can't go anywhere because his wits are scrambled," said Volodyovski. "He's on his back and blind to the world around him."

"In the meantime," broke in the bishop, "let's decide who is to stand where, and who's to defend which gates."

All eyes turned at once on Pan Mikolai Pototzki but he demurred again, still being either modest or doubtful about their chances. Or possibly he was anxious to cover himself against future charges in case the fortress fell.

"Before I give the orders," he said, "I'd like to hear the views of experienced soldiers. And since Pan Volodyovski stands above the rest of us in military matters, let him speak first."

★ ★ ★

Volodyovski urged that the hardest stand be made in the old stone castle that loomed above the town, and in the outlaying batteries that protruded from the city walls, against which the main enemy attacks were sure to come. The Turks, as everyone agreed, couldn't storm the gates and the earthwalls thrown around Kamyenetz while the castle guns were showering them with fire. The defenders had sixteen hundred infantry in the town and castle, which they divided between seven bastions in such a way that all approaches to the town were covered.

Pan Myslishevski took charge of the right or eastern ramparts of the castle. Pan Humyetzki, famous for his stand at Tzudnov, took the western flank. Pan Volodyovski faced the greatest danger, barring the way that led directly from Khotim, with a detachment of Hungarian Infantry entrenched lower down the slopes before him. Major Kvasibrodski held the walls that overlooked the fields and the road from Zhinkovyetz, while Pan Vonsovitch and Captain Bukar covered the southern slopes and the remaining side. None of them were time-serving volunteers, all were lifelong, trained professionals, who sweated less under artillery bombardments than most gentry did in the swelter of a Summer day. Moreover, serving since youth in the skimpy forces of the Commonwealth, they were quite used to great odds against them and took them as normal. The handsome Ketling, who knew more than anyone about guns and cannon, would direct all of their artillery, while the little knight would be the castle commandant, directing them all. Pan Pototzki also gave him a free hand with forays against the enemy if need and opportunity arose.

Told at last where each would stand and fight, the officers raised a ringing cheer, and Pan Pototzki felt a warm flush of confidence and a surge of spirit. *'I didn't think we'd manage to defend ourselves,'* he thought. *'Nor did I have much hope when I came to this place, responding only to the voice of conscience. But who can tell what happens with soldiers like these? They could hold off the enemy, the glory will fall on me, and I'll be hailed as the second Yeremi*

Vishnovyetzki. And if that happens, then I'll be damned if the star that guided me here wasn't a lucky one!'

And just as he'd doubted earlier the possibility of holding Kamyenetz, so now he started doubting that it could be taken. Full of determination, he settled down to planning how to defend the town's various ramparts, and the gates, and the walls around it.

What they decided that night was that in the town itself Pan Makovyetzki was to man the Russian or Ruthenian Gate with a handful of gentry, some of the Polish artisans and townsfolk, and several dozen Armenians and Jews, the last of which proved to be excellent cannoneers. Pan Grodetzki would hold the Lutzk Gate, with Pan Zuk and Pan Matchinski in charge of his cannon. The guard before the Town Hall in the city square was entrusted to Pan Lukas Dyevanovski, while Pan Hotchimirski took charge of the Gypsy fighters on the wall beyond. Assigned to guard the stretch from the castle bridge to the Sinitzki mansion was Pan Casimir Humyetzki, brother of the seneschal, with Pan Stanishevski quartered just beyond him. Pan Dubravski took over the command of the Butchers' Tower. Pan Martin Bogush, now back from his outpost in Mohilev, would hold the Polish Gate; Pan Jezhy Skarzhinski would guard the Iron Tower; and Pan Yatzkovski would man the smaller of the city ramparts and watch the gap towards the mud flats known as the White Marsh. The main city rampart was given to Alderman Tomashevitch and his Polish townsmen, and orders were sent out to start work on a third rampart from which, once the siege began, a certain Jewish gunner wreaked quite considerable havoc on the Turks.

With these dispositions made, the council adjourned for dinner at the house of Pan Mikolai Pototzki who went out of his way to honor Volodyovski. He treated him to one of the highest places at the table, choice wines, a meal of several courses, and flattering attentions. He foresaw that future generations would know Pan Volodyovski not only as the Little Knight, but as the Hector of Kamyenetz as well.

For his part, Volodyovski said that he'd do his best. "And there's a vow in that connection I'd like to make tomorrow in the cathedral,"—he turned to the bishop—"that I hope your grace won't forbid."

Bishop Lantzkoronski was pleased to consent, thinking that something good and uplifting could come out of it.

★ ★ ★

Early next day, a solemn high Mass was sung in the cathedral, and heard with thoughtful gravity by the assembled knights, gentry, soldiers and the commons.

Pan Volodyovski and Ketling lay prostrated before the main altar. Krysia and Basia knelt at the altar rail behind them, with tears streaming down their pale faces, because they knew that these vows could expose their husbands to unusual danger. After the last notes of the Mass dwindled among the arches, the bishop turned to the congregation with the holy sacrament in a golden monstrance.

The little knight rose then, knelt on the altar steps, and began to speak in a moved but steady voice.

"In gratitude for the many special blessings," he began, "and the particular protection given to me and mine by Almighty God and his one true Son, I make this solemn oath, that just as He and his Son helped me in a time of fear and despair, so I will defend the Holy Cross to my dying breath. And since command of the Old Castle is placed in my hands, I swear that as long as I can move an arm or bend a knee, I won't allow the heathen enemy to set foot within it, nor will I leave the walls, nor will I ever raise a white flag above them, even if I have to bury myself in their rubble... So help me God and the Holy Cross! Amen."

A breathless, ceremonial silence hung through the cathedral. And then Ketling spoke.

"I swear," he said, "in gratitude for the many kindnesses that this country has bestowed on me, to defend the castle to my last drop of blood, and to die under its ruins if I must, before an enemy might set foot in it. And since I take this oath out of true gratitude and affection, so may it be received by the Lord my God. Amen!"

The bishop brought the monstrance to the lips of each man in turn—first to Pan Volodyovski and then Ketling—and each sealed his vow by kissing the sacrament within it, and a great commotion swept through the knights and soldiers at this sight.

"We all swear to this!" cried many voices. "We'll fall and die across each other's corpses before we surrender! This fortress will not be taken! We swear! We swear! Amen! Amen! Amen!"

Sabers and rapiers grated out of their scabbards, their bared steel shining in the morning light that fell upon the grim, solemn faces and eyes alight with fire. A storm of enthusiasm swept through the gentry, the soldiers and the people. Suddenly all the bells rang out and went on ringing, the organ boomed, the bishop intoned the *'Sub Tuum praesidium'* and a hundred voices echoed his responses.

And so they prayed for that fortress which had become the outpost of the Christian world and the key to the Commonwealth.

★ ★ ★

After the Mass, Ketling and Volodyovski left the church with their arms linked like brothers. People cried out their blessings and their farewells to them, because no one doubted that they would die before they'd give up the castle. But it was not the shadow of death that seemed to hover over them as they walked together; victory and glory were shining in their eyes, and they were probably the only men within those cheering crowds who realized how final and how terrible their solemn vow could be if the city fell.

Two other hearts must have sensed by instinct that destruction now hung above their heads because neither Basia nor Krysia could find any peace for themselves, or stop their tears from flowing. And when Volodyovski found himself at last alone with his wife, alone with her sobbing and her bitter weeping, she clung to him and wailed like a forlorn child.

"Remember, *Mihalku,*" she sobbed. "That if... God forbid...something should happen to you... Then I'll... I'll... I don't know what'll happen to me...!"

Her slight, childlike body quivered in his arms and the little knight was profoundly moved. His little yellow mustache thrust in and out rapidly for some time.

"Well," he said at last. "Well, Baska... I had to. There was no other way..."

"I'd rather be dead!" she cried out.

The little knight's whiskers twitched and moved even faster than before as he tried to soothe and comfort this woman whom he loved more than anything. "Quiet now," he urged as he would a despairing child. "Quiet now, Baska. Quiet..."

And then he said:

"Do you remember what I said when God returned you to me back there in our Hreptyov? I said I would show my gratitude with everything I could afford. *'Lord God,'* I said. *'After the war, if I come back alive, I'll raise a chapel to your honor and glory. But I must do something notable in the war as well, so that you'll know that I'm truly grateful.'*

"What's one castle for such a blessing as I've had from Him?" he asked simply. "It's time for the payment! Would it be right for the Savior to say to himself: *'Promises are easy. But how about putting something on the line?'* May every stone in that castle come tumbling on my head before I break my word, given to anyone, not to mention a solemn oath given to God himself! It had to be, Baska... It really has to be. And Baska, let's keep trusting God...!"

Chapter Sixty-six

THAT SAME DAY Pan Volodyovski rode out with the cavalry to support young Pan Vasilkovski who'd darted out towards the settlement of Hrinchuk, because word came that Tartars had swept down on it unexpectedly, taking the people captive and driving off the cattle, but not sending the place up in flames so that the smoke wouldn't betray their presence.

Pan Vasilkovski made short work of them, recovered all their captives, and even took some prisoners of his own whom Pan Volodyovski brought back with him to Zhvanyetz. He had Pan Makovyetzki put them to the question, setting down all their replies in writing, so that they might be sent by courier to the Hetman and the King. The captured Tartars readily confessed that they were sent across the Dniester by the Turkish commandants in Moldavia, who'd even given them a Valachian cohort under Captain Stingan as a reinforcement. They could not say, however, even under torture, how far away the Sultan himself might be with his advancing army; riding in loose bands so far ahead of the main body of the Turks, they maintained no contact.

All of them, however, agreed on three things: that the Ottoman emperor had brought together his entire power, that he was marching upon the Commonwealth, and it was likely that he'd reach Khotim almost any day.

None of this was news to the future defenders of Kamyenetz; they had expected nothing else for months. But because there was still no credence given to the war at the King's court in Warsaw, Pan Lantzkoronski meant to have these captives sent to

629

the capital along with their reports, while he himself went to garrison his Zhvanyetz.

The raiding column came back, pleased with the results of their first expedition in the war, and in the meantime, the secretary of Habareskul Pasha, Volodyovski's blood-brother among the Turks and the senior Moldavian commandant of Khotim, slipped in to see him shortly after nightfall. He brought no letter because the Turkish general was afraid to put his words on paper, but Habareskul sent a verbal warning to his *'beloved blood-brother who is dearer to me than the iris of my eyes,'* to keep a sharp watch, and to leave Kamyenetz under any pretext if the fortress didn't have enough troops to defend itself, because the Sultan and his entire army were expected in Khotim within two days.

Volodyovski sent back his warmest thanks, had Habareskul's messenger properly rewarded, and immediately informed all the other commanders in the town and castle of the approaching danger. The news had been expected almost by the hour but it made the greatest possible impression nonetheless. Work on the defenses went on with doubled fervor, and Pan Lantzkoronski set out at once for Zhvanyetz from where he'd be able to keep an eye on Khotim.

★ ★ ★

Some time passed in waiting but then, on July 2, one of the feasts of Mary and St. Urban, the Sultan came to Khotim. The regiments and cohorts filled the plains around it like an unbounded sea, and the sight of this last fortress that lay within the northern boundaries of the Padishah brought one vast cry of "Allah! Allah!" bursting from the throats of hundreds of thousands of exultant warriors. Across the Dniester lay the helpless Commonwealth which these immense multitudes were to flood in a final deluge, or devour like a sea of fire. Masses of warriors, unable to find quarters within the city walls, pitched their camps in those same fields where a Turkish host no smaller than their own, was shattered by a Polish Hetman fifty years earlier. But now it seemed as if the hour of vengeance had come for them at last, and no one among these savage cohorts, from the Sultan down to the meanest camp laborer and servant, could even suspect that these plains would run with Turkish blood again, or that the green, crescent banners of Islam would be turned back once more by Polish sabers, here in two more years and a dozen years later on at Vienna, as they had been so many times before.

Sure of their victory, their hearts filled with fire. Dense ranks of janissaries and Spahis shouted to be sent at once into *Lehistan*; and massed warriors from throughout the Balkans—and from Rumelia and Silistria, the islands of the Aegean and the mountains of Lebanon and Assyria, the arid wilderness of Arabia and the banks of the Tigris and the Euphrates—joined the throngs from the palm groves of the lower Nile and the sun-baked sands of Africa, in one vast, echoing demand to stand at last on the infidels' bank of that border river.

In the meantime the cry of the *muezzin* came from the Khotim minarets, calling for evening prayer, and that boiling human sea quietened down at once. Heads swathed in turbans, or dressed in the white burnous hoods and tasseled crimson fezzes of the Bedouin and Egyptian *Djamak*—as the Sultan's tributary levies were known in the empire—bowed to the ground beside the spiked damascene helmets of the Mamelouks and the janissaries. Their murmured prayers swept in a deep growl across the plains like the massed droning of a countless bee swarm, and flew towards the Dniester and the Commonwealth on the evening breeze.

Then drums, horns and squealing fifes and whistles signaled a time of respite. The armies had made an easy and comfortable journey, but they had marched all the way from Adrianople, and the Padishah wanted to give them a good rest. He bathed in a clear spring that flowed not far from the city and rode to the governor's mansion in Khotim, while the fields behind him glistened with the white of the regimental tents as if it were Winter, and as if fresh snow had sheeted all the surrounding country.

The weather couldn't have been better and the day was ending under a clear sky. After the final prayer of the night, the great encampment settled down to rest. A hundred thousand campfires glittered in the darkness, counted anxiously and in vain from the little castle of Zhvanyetz across the river. There were so many of them, and they covered such vast distances, that the soldiers sent on a reconnaissance that night reported that "all of Moldavia seemed to be on fire." In time, as the hours passed and the moon climbed brightly into the starry sky, all of these fires dimmed and flickered out, except for those at which the sentries crouched on through the night. The bivouacs grew silent, sleep settled on the Hosts of the Prophet, and only the neighing of the horseherds and the bellow of the water buffalo grazing in the pastures, broke into the stillness.

★   ★   ★

At sunrise the next day, the Sultan ordered the janissaries, the Tartars and the *Lipki* to cross the Dniester and occupy the little town and castle of Zhvanyetz. Pan Hieronimus Lantzkoronski didn't wait for them behind his walls. He charged them at the crossing with his bodyguard of forty Household Tartars, eighty Kievan nobles and his own horse regiment of Podolian gentry, and he struck so hard into the thick of their musket fire that he scattered this elite infantry and drove it back into the water.

But, in the meantime, the Tartars and the *Lipki* crossed the river downstream and broke into the township. Smoke and the sound of shouting alerted the gallant chamberlain that his town was in the hands of the enemy, and he ordered a retreat from the crossing to bring some help to his wretched people. The janissaries, being infantry, couldn't follow hard upon his heels, and he galloped hell for leather to the rescue.

He'd almost reached the town when his Household Tartars threw down their Polish banner and went over to the enemy. It was a dangerous moment. The *tchambul*, stiffened by the chamberlain's own *Lipki*, struck fiercely at Pan Lantzkoronski's riders in the belief that the treason of his Tartar bodyguard would throw them into panic and confusion. Luckily, the Kievans caught fire from their courageous leader and put up a fierce resistance of their own, while the chamberlain's regulars soon broke through the *tchambul* and drove it off the field.

Fallen men and horses littered the sun-dried plow land before the town when the *tchambul* fled. Most of the dead were *Lipki* who could put up a fiercer fight against regular cavalry than ordinary Tartars and took the greatest losses. More of them were sabered down in the streets when the fight erupted into the little town. Then, seeing janissaries advancing from the river, Pan

Lantzkoronski sent for help from Kamyenetz and withdrew behind his castle walls.

But the Padishah didn't intend to storm the little castle that first day. He judged correctly that he'd turn it into a heap of rubble the moment all his forces were across the river. All he wanted for now was to occupy the town and secure the crossing. Sure that the forces he dispatched were enough to carry out his wishes, he sent neither more janissaries nor Tartars. Those, in the meantime, who had already crossed, retook the town after Pan Lantzkoronski withdrew to the castle. They didn't send it up in smoke as was their usual custom, wanting to save it as future quarters for themselves or others, but they set about their housekeeping straight away with their knives and sabers. The janissaries hunted for young women, dragging them out of hiding for their murderous amusement, and slaughtered men and children with their battle axes, while the Tartars busied themselves with pillage.

★ ★ ★

But just then the lookouts in the keep of the little castle spotted some cavalry, riding from the direction of Kamyenetz, and Pan Lantzkoronski himself climbed into the tower with a few of his gentry soldiers. He looked long and hard into the distance, peering through a field telescope he thrust through a loophole.

"That's the Light Horse from the Hreptyov garrison," he said at last. "The same troops that Vasilkovski took with him on the raid to Hrinchuk. They probably sent him out this time as well."

He peered a little longer. "I see some irregulars as well. Gentry volunteers. That must be Humyetzki."

And then: "God be praised! Volodyovski himself is out there because I see dragoons. Gentlemen, let's charge out ourselves! With God's help we'll drive the enemy not just out of the town but back across the river."

He sprinted back down into the courtyard to muster his Kievans and his fighting gentry. In the meantime the Tartars in the town caught sight of the approaching horsemen, ran to mount and gather into their formations, filling the air with their warbling, ear-piercing war cries. Drums boomed and rattled in every street, war horns growled and shrilled, and the janissaries

massed in battle order with a speed that few infantry in the world
could equal.

The Tartar *tchambul* whirled out of the town as if a great wind
had swept them into the open plain and hurled itself at the light
cavalry, whom it outnumbered by more than three to one.
Indeed, not even counting the *Lipki* whom Pan Lantzkoronski
punished so severely, the Tartars were three times as strong as
the garrison of Zhvanyetz and the relieving cavalry combined,
so they threw themselves on Pan Vasilkovski's horsemen without a qualm of fear. But Vasilkovski was a wild, unbridled youth
who didn't care about the odds against him, and he charged the
Tartars as hungrily as they erupted against him. Blind and indifferent to any kind of danger, he launched his men into an all-out
charge right from the beginning, and now roared down on the
tchambul like a desert whirlwind.

The Tartars were thrown off stride. They never liked to fight
at close quarters and this reckless courage shook them even
further. In spite of the shouts of their *murjahs* who were galloping behind them, the shrill screech of their goading whistles and
the booming of the ceremonial drum that signaled *No Quarter* to
the unbelievers, they started pulling up their horses and turning
aside. Their thirst for battle dwindled by the moment. At last,
when they were barely a bowshot away from the charging
regiment, they split in two, released a cloud of arrows on their
enemies and broke to the flanks.

Pan Vasilkovski knew nothing about the janissaries who
formed for battle behind the buildings and closer to the river,
and he swerved at full gallop in pursuit of the fleeing *tchambul*,
or rather the half of it that was nearest to him. He caught up
with the Tartars only a moment later and started sabering those
who rode the slowest horses and couldn't get away as readily as
the others. The second half of the *tchambul* turned at once,
wanting to surround him, but Pan Humyetzki's volunteers
struck them from one side while Pan Lantzkoronski charged out
of his gates and hit them with his Kievans from the other.

Pressed on all sides, the *tchambul* split and scattered like a
fistful of sand thrown into the air, and the fight broke at once
into a swirl of swift, individual clashes, in groups and alone, with
one man running down another, and one band of horsemen
pursuing the next. The Tartars fell thickly in this running fight,

many of them at the hand of Pan Vasilkovski, who threw himself alone against whole clusters of the enemy, oblivious of danger, in just the way that a peregrine rips into a swarm of sparrows.

But Pan Volodyovski kept his dragoons out of this wild scramble and pursuit. He was an experienced, coldly calculating soldier who held his best-trained men for just the right moment, and he peered across the mass of fleeing and pursuing horsemen to see if there weren't any janissaries or Spahis beyond this lesser prey.

His men raged to charge but they were forced by discipline to wait for his order, and he held them back, ignoring the shattered *tchambul* that spilled everywhere around him, much like a watchful hunter who holds his snarling wolfhounds on tight, straining leashes, not letting them leap on just any quarry, but waiting until he sees the red eyes and the gleaming tusks of a rogue boar breaking from the thicket.

★ ★ ★

Pan Hieronimus Lantzkoronski galloped up to him just then with his Kievan horsemen. "My dear friend!" he cried. "The janissaries are making for the river. Let's squeeze them a little!"

"Forward!" Volodyovski barked an order and unsheathed his rapier.

Each dragoon took a firm grip on his reins the better to control his horse, the whole rank swayed forward, and then stepped out as smartly as if on parade. They started at a swift trot, then surged into a canter, but they kept their horses on tight reins from breaking out into an all-out gallop. And then, after they rounded the cluster of huts and dwellings that spilled east of the castle towards the river, they caught sight of the tall white hats of the infantry marching towards the Dniester, and knew that this wasn't going to be any tussle with some irregular *Djamak* like the Horde. Those thick ranks garbed in snowy capes and towering felt hats were the janissaries.

"Charge!" cried Volodyovski.

The horses leaped, each animal hurled forward like an arrow, with their bellies stretched low above the ground, and with their hooves flinging clods of hard, parched earth behind them.

Not knowing the strength of the forces that had come to the relief of Zhvanyetz, the janissaries were pulling back to the river crossing. One battalion, numbering some two hundred and three score men, was already on the riverbank and its leading ranks were stepping aboard the ferries. Another was coming up at a rapid quickstep but in perfect order when it caught sight of the charging cavalry. It halted and spun about at once to face the attack. A wall of muskets snapped down at every shoulder and a volley thundered out at the rushing horsemen. Moreover, thinking that their comrades on the riverbank would cover them with supporting fire, the janissaries gave a ringing cheer, drew their curved sabers and charged into the smoke.

It was an act of almost suicidal bravery. Only infantry as fierce and fearless as the janissaries would ever charge cavalry on foot and they paid heavily for their recklessness. Unable to halt their horses even if they wished to, the dragoons crashed into them, bowled them over like an avalanche, shattered their ranks at once, and spread instant terror and destruction among them.

The shock of the charge hurled their leading ranks to the ground but many of them leaped up again, uninjured, and ran for the river, where their first battalion sent musket volleys into the dragoons, shooting over the heads of their running comrades.

There was a moment of uncertainty among the janissaries on the riverbank, as if they wondered whether to go aboard the ferries or charge the cavalry, sword in hand, like the men who were now fighting and running in the field. What made up their minds for them finally was the sight of the fleeing bands that the cavalry bowled over and sabered with a savagery that compared only with their skill. At times, such a fleeing cluster would turn around, stand at bay, and fight like a hunted animal that sees no way out. But it was then that the men on the riverbank could see, as clearly as if it were etched into their palms, that no one would be able to withstand that matchless cavalry with cold steel.

They were the supreme masters of their dreadful trade. Their sabers hissed down on heads, necks and faces with such speed and practice that it was almost impossible for the naked eye to catch a glimpse of the whirling blades. They brought to mind the huskers on a rich, well-managed estate, who flail dried peas on a threshing floor, pounding the mound of desiccated pods with such celerity and fervor that the whole barn resounds with their blows, while the husked peas fly to all sides as if fired from sling-shots. The whole plain before the river filled with just such a sound of rapid saber strokes, and the hard-pressed bands of janissaries, flailed without mercy, burst in all directions.

★ ★ ★

Pan Vasilkovski threw himself about at the head of his light cavalry as if his life had lost all its value for him. But just as a skilled harvester goes steadily forward, scything the wheat rows steadily before him, while a stronger but less experienced farm-hand is soon soaked with sweat and runs out of breath, so Pan Volodyovski overshadowed the fierce younger man.

Just before the dragoons burst in among the janissaries, he swerved aside and took his post slightly to the rear so as to keep a watchful eye on the whole encounter. Standing nearby, he noted everything that happened, leaped time and again into the swirl of fighting men and horses, struck like a hawk, corrected some error or took care of some dangerous situation, let the battle roll away from him so he could observe the whole of the action, then watched and struck once more.

As always happens in a fight against infantry, the horsemen charged past a few of the fugitives, and several of these turned back towards the town, wanting to hide in the sunflower patches that clustered before the dwellings. Pan Volodyovski spotted them, went after them, caught up with a pair, sent two slight saber strokes among them and they fell at once, twitching and kicking on the ground while their blood seeped into the soil. Seeing this, another janissary fired a pistol at him but missed, and Volodyovski slashed him across the face, killing him at once. He went after the rest of the fleeing dozen without a moment's pause, picking them off faster than a village lad can pluck a clump of mushrooms, and killed all but two before they reached the sunflowers. Some Zhvanyetz men fished out the remaining pair whom the little knight ordered kept alive.

The exercise warmed him up.

The janissaries, as he saw at once, were now largely backed up against the river.

He turned and galloped straight into the fight, took his place in the forefront of the battle line, and set to work among his dragoons. Sometimes he sent his strokes straight ahead of him.

Sometimes he turned slightly to one flank or another, let his blade flick down in a shallow thrust and didn't even look to note the result, but each stroke sent a white-robed body hurtling to the ground. The howling janissaries started to crowd together and mill in panic before him, and he doubled the speed and force of his attack, and even though he seemed as calm and unruffled as the eye of a hurricane, no eye could catch the flash of his rapier or tell his thrusts from strokes, because his blade created only one burst of whirling light around him.

★ ★ ★

Pan Lantzkoronski, who had long heard about him as a master swordsman but who'd never watched him at his work before, now couldn't believe his eyes. He was so amazed that he stopped fighting and merely sat and stared, unable to grasp how one man—no matter how famous nor how much of a master—could achieve so much, so quickly, and with what seemed like so little effort. He sat his horse, shaking his head in disbelief, and saying over and over to himself: "They didn't say enough about him, as God is my witness!"

Others around him shouted: "Watch! Watch! Because you'll never see anything like this anywhere in the world!"

Meanwhile Pan Volodyovski went on with his work. The janissaries were now jammed together on the riverbank and crowding aboard the ferries. But because there were enough of these flat-bottomed barges to bring over an entire cohort, and less than half of it was now coming back, they got aboard quickly and with room to spare. The heavy sweeps swung out and began to move and the gap between the horsemen and the janissaries widened by the minute.

Muskets flashed on the ferry decks. The dragoons replied with musketoons and pistols. Smoke billowed in a thick cloud above the water and then spread into long feathery streamers overhead.

The barges and the janissaries drew further away. The dragoons who had won the field now raised a fierce cheer and shook their fists at the repelled invaders.

"Back to your kennels, dogs!" they shouted. "Heel, you mongrels! Heel!"

★ ★ ★

The musket balls were still splashing along the shore when

Pan Lantzkoronski threw his arms around the little knight. "I didn't believe my eyes!" he cried. "You performed miracles, my dear friend, worthy of record with a golden quill!"

"It's just a smidgen of talent and a lot of practice," Volodyovski shrugged. "There've been so many wars, after all."

And then he freed himself from the chamberlain's bear hug and pointed down the shore. "Ah, but look there, Your Worship, and you'll really see something!"

Pan Lantzkoronski turned and saw an officer stringing a bow on the edge of the river. It was Pan Mushalski. Up until now the famous archer had fought at close quarters along with everybody else, sabering the enemy just like all the others, but now that the janissaries drew out of range of musketoons and muskets, he reached for his bow. He stood on horseback on a point of land that thrust somewhat higher above the riverbank, tested the bowstring with his fingernail, and when it twanged with a satisfactory sound he fitted a long, feathered arrow to it, raised the bow and started to take aim.

It was a sight for a painting, Pan Lantzkoronski thought. The archer sat erect on his horse, with his left arm thrust out straight before him, and his fist clutched the bow stave as if in a vise. His right hand drew the bowstring slowly past his breastbone until the veins bulged in his forehead with the effort, and he took a long, careful aim. Beyond him, in the near distance, several dozen barges slid across the water, which was so high and clean due to the heavy melting of the Winter snows, that the barges and the janissaries reflected in it as if in a mirror. The shooting on the shore had died away by then, and everyone was either watching Pan Mushalski or staring out towards the spot where the murderous arrow would strike when released.

And then the bowstring gave a mournful twang and the feathered messenger of death winged into the air. No one could spot the arrow in its flight but everyone saw the thickset janissary standing at the sweep who suddenly flung his arms wide, spun around, and fell into the water. The crystal mirror shattered as he vanished in it.

"That one's for you, Didyuk!" Pan Mushalski said.

Then he reached into his quiver for another arrow. "In honor of the Hetman!" he said to his comrades.

They held their breaths. The air hissed again and another

janissary sunk to the bottom of the barge. All the sweeps and oars began to strike a hasty beat on all the ferry barges, pounding the water in a frenzied hurry, and the peerless archer turned with a smile to the little knight.

"In honor of your distinguished lady, sir!" he said.

He bent his bow for the third time, and once again released a bitter arrow, and it plunged once more into a man's body, burying itself half way to its feathers.

A shout of triumph rang out on the riverbank. A howl of rage answered from the barges. Pan Mushalski cased his bow and turned away from the riverbank, and all the others who'd won their fight that day followed his example, and then the troops reformed and rode back to the town.

Chapter Sixty-seven

THEY LOOKED WITH SATISFACTION at the result of their day's work as they rode back to Zhvanyetz. Not many Tartars had fallen in the plain because they never managed to form a battle line or to make any kind of stand; quickly scattered and driven off the field, they wasted no time in fording the river back to where they'd come from. But dead janissaries lay everywhere, stacked like baled hay. A few were still kicking and twitching in their death throes but all were already stripped and looted by the chamberlain's servants.

"Good infantry," Pan Volodyovski said, looking down at them. "They charge into the smoke like a herd of tuskers. But they're not half as well drilled as the Swedes."

"Even so, they snapped out a volley as smartly as a nut-cracker," Pan Lantzkoronski noted.

"That could've happened pretty much by chance because they do hardly any training whatsoever. These were the Sultan's guards, and they do go through some drill now and then, but there are also other janissaries who are a lot more slack."

"Hah! But we gave them a good *pro memoriam* anyway, didn't we! God be praised that we're starting off the war with such a fine and notable success!"

But the experienced Volodyovski disagreed. "There's nothing specially fine about it, sir, and it's not worth noting. It'll do to put some heart into people who don't know much about war and combat, and it'll stiffen the shopkeepers' backbones, but that's about all we can expect from it."

"You don't think, then, that the heathen will lose heart?"

"The heathen won't lose heart," said Volodyovski.

★ ★ ★

Talking over their day's work in this way they rode into the town where the local people handed over the two Turks who tried to hide in the sunflowers from Pan Volodyovski's saber and who'd been seized alive. One had a gunshot wound but the other escaped without a scratch. Nor had he lost any of his arrogance.

Once they'd come to the castle, the little knight had Pan Makovyetzki interrogate this prisoner thoroughly. Like most border soldiers, the little knight understood Turkish very well but he wasn't fluent in it, and Pan Makovyetzki's first two questions were whether the Sultan was in Khotim in person and how soon he intended to move against Kamyenetz.

The Turk snapped out his answers as if he didn't have anything to hide and didn't care who knew it since a Turkish victory was inevitable no matter what happened.

"The Padishah is there in his own person," he said and stared at the assembled officers as if they were hardly worth his notice.

"So when's he coming over?"

"The word in the camp is that Halil-basha and Murad-basha are crossing tomorrow. They're bringing the *mehentees* with them, and they'll start cutting the trenches right away. You're time's as good as up. You'll all be dead meat day after tomorrow."

Sure of the power of the Sultan's name, he jerked his head proudly in the air, cocked his fists on his hips and stared at the Polish leaders with contempt.

"You must be mad," he said, "to throw yourselves on the Great Lord's people right under his nose! What's wrong with your heads? D'you think you'll get away without a frightful punishment? D'you think this piddling little castle will protect you? What are you going to be in a few days other than his slaves, that's if you're not dog food in the Great Lord's kennels? What are you now if not barking dogs snarling at your master?"

Pan Makovyetzki said nothing, carefully noting all this on a sheet of parchment, but Pan Volodyovski knew how to handle the men of the East. He stepped up to janissary and cracked him smartly across the jaws without a word of warning. The Turk immediately lost all his arrogance, looked at the little knight with stunned admiration, and answered the rest of Pan Makovyetzki's questions with respect.

"We have to send these prisoners and their testimony to the King at once," Pan Volodyovski said when the captive Turk was led out of the room. "There's no time to waste! The people at the court in Warsaw still don't believe there's going to be any war at all!"

"What are these *mehentees* that Halil and Murad are bringing over tomorrow?" Pan Lantzkoronski asked.

"Sappers," said Pan Makovyetzki. "They'll put up the siege-works, burrow the approaches, and entrench the cannon."

"Hmm. And what do you gentlemen think about that prisoner's replies? Was he telling us the truth or was he just lying?"

"We can warm his heels for him, if you like," Volodyovski shrugged. "I've a sergeant among my dragoons who took care of Azia Tuhaybeyovitch and who's *exquisitissimus* at that kind of thing. But I think the prisoner tells it as straight as he can. They'll start crossing almost anytime and there is nothing we can do to stop them. Indeed, we'd be unable to hold them here if we were a hundred times stronger than we are. So the only thing left for us to do is pack up and head for Kamyenetz with this information."

"Hmm. Things went so well for me around this Zhvanyetz of mine that I'd just as soon make my stand right in this little castle," the chamberlain said and flashed a quick smile at Volodyovski. "All I'd need is to know that you, sir, will dart out of Kamyenetz now and then and give me a hand. After that, let things go as they may!"

"They've two hundred cannon," Volodyovski said. "And once they get their ten big guns across the river this castle won't last a day. I had a mind to fight from here myself but now that I've seen the place I know it'd be for nothing."

The others agreed. Pan Lantzkoronski clung stubbornly to his view for a while longer, largely to demonstrate his determination and for the sake of his reputation as a fighting man, but he had too much military experience to hold out much hope for his little Zhvanyetz. What finally made up his mind, however, was Pan Vasilkovski who galloped back from the field in a tearing hurry.

"Gentlemen!" he cried, rushing in among them. "You can
hardly even see the Dniester, there're so many rafts and barges
on it!"

"They're crossing, then?" all the others asked at once and
together.

"As I live and breathe! The Turks are coming over on the rafts
and the Tartars are crossing on horseback."

★ ★ ★

That put a quick end to Pan Lantzkoronski's hesitation. He
ordered the few old castle guns taken off the walls and sunk in
the fishponds and everything else of any use or value to the
enemy packed up and either buried or shipped to Kamyenetz.
Meanwhile Volodyovski leaped into his saddle and rode out with
his men to watch the river crossing from a distant height.

The two Turkish pashas, Halil and Murad, were indeed ferry-
ing their divisions across the Dniester. Rafts and barges stretched
along the river as far as the eye could see, and their sweeps and
oars struck the water with a rhythmic beat. The Spahis and the
janissaries came across in great numbers all at the same time
because a huge fleet of transport ferries had been gathered and
readied at Khotim many months before, and a vast array of
soldiers stood massed and waiting their turn on the shore beyond
them. Volodyovski thought it likely that they'd begin building
bridges straight away.

Meanwhile Pan Lantzkoronski came riding up with his own
men and soon afterwards he and the little knight set out for
Kamyenetz where Pan Pototzki met them in the town. All the
leading officers were gathered in his quarters, and great crowds
of anxious, curious and uneasy people, about equally divided
between men and women, stood before his house.

"The enemy is coming over and Zhvanyetz is taken," the little
knight reported.

"Our preparations are complete and we're waiting for them!"
Pan Pototzki answered.

The news soon found its way out to the crowds which began
to mutter like a swelling tide. "To the gates! To the gates!"
people began to shout all over the town. "The enemy's in
Zhvanyetz!"

The burghers and their wives ran to the bastions, thinking

that they'd be able to see the enemy from there, but the soldiers wouldn't let them into their positions.

"Go home!" they shouted. "You'll just get in the way! Mess up the defenses and your wives will soon be getting a real close look at the Turks!"

But it was hard to shake the burghers' confidence and to repress the general enthusiasm. No one in town seemed worried or afraid because the news of that day's success had already run like lightning through the city and—as usual—it was a mass of wild exaggerations. The soldiers themselves helped to inflate the victory out of all proportion, telling sky-high tales about the fight at Zhvanyetz.

"Pan Volodyovski smashed the janissaries!" the word flew from mouth to mouth. "The Sultan's guards, no less! He's too much for the pagans! He sliced up a Turkish pasha with his own hand! Ah, the Devil's not as terrible as they paint him...! They couldn't match our lads for all their vast numbers... Serves you right, you heathen dogs! Down with you all and your Sultan too!"

The merchants' wives and daughters showed up once more that night at the towers and bastions. But now they came bearing baskets of vodka, wine and mead and the soldiers were soon having a rollicking time. Pan Pototzki didn't interfere with this celebration, wanting to keep up the men's high spirits and morale, and because the city and the castle were both well supplied with powder and munitions of all kinds he even allowed the firing of salutes. If the enemy was near enough to hear them, he supposed, this might make him wonder.

★ ★ ★

Meanwhile Pan Volodyovski, wanting to slip undetected through the crowded streets, had waited until twilight in the quarters of the General of Podolia. Then, accompanied only by his body servant and anxious to be with his wife as soon as he could, he set out for the convent where Basia was staying. But all his stealth failed him that evening. He was soon recognized and eager crowds swarmed around his horse, calling out and cheering, and blocking the way.

"Behold the man!" cried the women, holding up their children so that they might see the famous little soldier. "Look at him and remember!"

As it happened, he was as much an object of amazement to the gaping burghers as he was of awe and admiration. People who didn't know anything about soldiering and war couldn't get over how small he was, perched on his horse like a grey, bright-eyed sparrow on a massive statue. The shopkeepers racked their brains how such a tiny man, with such a mild, merry and inoffensive face, could be the most terrifying soldier of the Commonwealth, one whom nobody could match with saber in hand. He, in the meantime, made his way as best as he could through the admiring crowds, smiling and moving his little yellow mustache now and then, and as much embarrassed as pleased by all this adulation.

Once in the convent, he threw himself into Basia's welcoming arms. She already knew everything he had done that day because Pan Hieronimus Lantzkoronski called on her only a few minutes earlier and gave her an eyewitness account of the little soldier's every thrust and sword stroke. Right at the start of his account she called in the prioress and all the other ladies who were staying there, delighting in their admiring cries at Pan Lantzkoronski's story, and swelling up with pride. Volodyovski arrived just when the ladies took their leave.

Tired as he was, Volodyovski sat down to his supper. Basia plopped down beside him, filling his plate and cup with her own hands, and he ate and drank eagerly because he'd hardly had a bite in his mouth all day. In between mouthfuls he'd drop some snippet of the day's events and Basia stared at him with shining eyes, tossing her curls in impatience to hear more, and pressing him with questions.

"Aha! And then what? And then what?"

"There are some hefty fighters among the Turks," the little knight went on, "and fierce as the Devil. But you'll seldom find a real swordsman among them."

"So even I'd be able to try my hand with them?"

"You could but you won't because I won't take you out with me and that's that!"

"Just once! Please? One Turk would be enough! You know, my love, that I'm not even worried when you go out to fight

beyond the walls. I know that no one will be able to touch you
with a sword."

"They can shoot me, can't they?"

"Quiet, for God's sake! God will turn the bullets to where
they'll do no harm. But you won't let them cut you down, and
that's the main thing."

"One or two won't cut me down, that's true."

"Nor three! Nor four!"

"Nor four thousand," Pan Zagloba mimicked and turned to
Pan Michal. "If you just knew what a show she put on here
when the chamberlain was telling his story. I thought I'd burst
my breeches, may God be my witness! She was snorting around
like a young goat, her nose in the air, and she kept peering at all
the other females to see if they were sufficiently impressed. I got
afraid in the end she'd start turning cartwheels, which would've
been a most peculiar sight."

The little knight stretched his arms and shoulders, having
finished supper, and drew his wife closer to himself. "My quarters are ready at the castle," he told her. "But it's so hard to break
away from you... Baska, maybe I'll spend the night here? What
do you think?"

"As you like, Mihalku!" she said and dropped her glance.

"Ha!" Pan Zagloba grunted. "They must take me for a with-
ered mushroom around here rather than a man since the Mother
Superior lets me stay in this nunnery among all these women...
But she'll have reason to weep for that oversight, I'll just see to
that! Maybe you noted how Pani Hotchimirska was winking at
me? Eh...? She's a widow... Hmm! And that's all I'm going to
say about it!"

"By the Lord," said the little knight. "I think I will stay."

"Just make sure you get enough rest," Basia murmured.

"And why shouldn't he?" Pan Zagloba asked.

"Because we'll be talking and talking and talking!"

But Pan Zagloba started searching for his cap so that he might
also get to bed that night, then found it and jammed it on his
head.

"No you won't be talking and talking and talking!" he said.

And he left.

Chapter Sixty-eight

AT FIRST LIGHT THE NEXT MORNING, the little knight rode out towards the settlement of Knahin where he attacked some Spahis and captured Buluk-basha who was a famous warrior among the Turks. The whole day passed for him in hard work in the field, he sat through most of the night that followed in council with Pan Pototzki, and it was only when the roosters started to announce yet another dawn that he could finally get a little rest. But he'd no sooner fallen into a deep and satisfying sleep when the roar of cannon brought him wide awake.

His servant Pyentka, a Zmudyan groom who had been with him for so long that he was practically a friend, burst into the room along with the sound of the bombardment.

"Master!" he cried. "The enemy's right outside the town!"

The little knight leaped out of bed at once. "And what guns are those?"

"Ours, sir! Making the heathen run for a bit of cover. There's a big column out there rounding up the cattle in the pasture fields."

"What are they, then? Janissaries or cavalry?"

"Cavalry, Your Honor. And black as pitch, every one of them! Our men are showing the holy cross to them, 'cause they could be Devils!"

"Devils or not, we have to go and meet them," the little knight replied. "Go to her ladyship and tell her I am in the field. She can go up to the castle is she wants to get a good look at the fighting but only if she comes with Pan Zagloba. I count on his good sense more than anything!"

Pyentka took off at a run, heading for Basia's quarters, while half an hour later Pan Volodyovski galloped into the fields beyond the walls at the head of his dragoons and some volunteer gentry who hoped to show off their mettle in a mounted skirmish.

The enemy horsemen—about two thousand Spahis and Egyptian Mamelouks of the Sultan's guard—were in plain sight below, easy to see from the Old Castle walls. The Mamelouks were especially brilliant in their gleaming armor made of overlapping, silvered scales and burnished chain-mail, in their white desert cloaks ballooning behind them, in their tall, bright-hued turbans embroidered with gold thread, and with their richly jeweled and ornamented weapons. Only the wealthiest, bravest and most high-minded lords of the Nile served in this picked corps of horsemen who were the most magnificent-looking cavalry of their time. They were armed with javelins set in bamboo shafts and exaggeratedly crooked scimitars and daggers. Riding on horses as swift as the wind, they swept across the plain like a rainbow cloud, yelping their high-pitched battle cries and twirling their murderous lances in their fingers, and the observers on the castle walls couldn't get their fill of them.

Pan Volodyovski led his own horsemen towards them at an easy trot but it was hard for both sides to close with the other; the castle cannon forced the Turks to keep a safe distance, while their numbers made it impossible for the little knight to charge them and to settle with them beyond the reach of the guns. For a short time both sides contented themselves with milling about the field, riding back and forth beyond the reach of pistols, musketoons and arrows while shaking their weapons at each other and uttering sharp cries, but empty threats soon bored the fiery desert horsemen. First singly, then in groups, the Mamelouks started breaking away from the brilliant, multicolored mass and to gallop closer, calling on the Poles to come out and meet them hand to hand. They were soon swirling across the field like flowers in the wind and Pan Volodyovski glanced back at his own men.

"Gentlemen!" he cried. "They're inviting us! Who's for a skirmish, then?"

★ ★ ★

The hot-blooded Vasilkovski was the first to spur towards the Turks, with Pan Mushalski, the incomparable archer, close behind—eager to show off his skill with the saber as well as the bow—and more than a dozen other cavaliers and dragoons. The gentry rode for glory and the love of the fight. The dragoons had their eyes on rich booty, especially the priceless Arab horses, and Sergeant Lusnia spotted the best and the richest-looking from afar as he rode at the head of his men and gnawed the ends of his pale whiskers.

The day was bright and clear. Everyone in the field was easy to see. The cannon on the walls died down one by one until all were silent, because the gunners feared hitting their own men among the skirmishers and because they too wanted to watch the fighting rather than aim their guns at darting single riders. They, in the meantime advanced towards each other at a walk, no longer in a hurry now that the game was about to begin, and then at a trot. They came in loose groups rather than in any kind of line, each picking his opponent as he rode. They halted within bowshot range to curse and revile each other, all the better to stir themselves into a battle fury.

"You won't get fat on us, you heathen dogs!" called the Polish riders. "Come and taste our steel! Nor will you get much help from your worthless prophet!"

The others shouted back in Arabic and Turkish, and many of the Polish skirmishers knew both these languages well, having spent hard years of captivity among them just like Pan Mushalski, and they understood every jibe and insult. The Moslem horsemen were especially blasphemous about the Virgin Mary, and the hair rose in rage on the heads of the knights, each of whom thought himself the servant of the Holy Mother, and who charged out to avenge the profanation of Her name.

Who struck first? And who robbed another of his precious life? Pan Mushalski's arrow struck a young *bey* who wore a purple turban, burying itself half way up its shaft under his left eye, and the Mamelouk tilted his handsome face to the rear and slid from his saddle. The archer had just enough time to case his bow, reach his victim before he toppled to the ground, and pierce him with his saber. Then he seized the dead youth's superb ornamental weapons and drove his horse back towards

Kamyenetz, while shouting in Arabic over his shoulder: "I wish this was the Sultan's own son! He'd rot here before you sent your last charge against us!"

Horrified, the Turks and the Egyptians sent two *beys* charging against Pan Mushalski, but Lusnia crossed their paths at a sudden angle and sabered one of them to death almost as fast as it takes to blink an eye. First he whisked the scimitar out of Turk's hand, and when the man leaned forward to retrieve it, he cut him so terribly across the back of the neck that he almost lopped his head off his shoulders. The second *bey* broke away and turned his horse for flight, but Pan Mushalski drew out his bow again, sent another arrow winging after him, and buried it up to the feathers between his shoulder blades.

The third to best his opponent was Pan Plotzki who struck a Turk so powerfully in the head with the sharp end of his battle hammer that the blade cut right through the helmet and chain-mail headpiece, pierced the silver and velvet of the lining, and drove so deep into the victim's skull that Pan Plotzki couldn't free it for some time.

Others fought with varying degrees of luck and success but victory went mostly to the skilled swordsmen of the Polish gentry. Two dragoons, however, fell in quick succession before the powerful Hamdji-bey, who then split Prince Ovsyany's face with one great blow of his crooked scimitar and stretched him on the ground. The Ruthenian prince bled out his life into his homeland's soil, and Hamdji turned on Pan Sheluta whose horse had stepped into the hidden tunnel of a marmoset and couldn't free itself to run or maneuver. Sure that his last hour had come, Pan Sheluta leaped out of his saddle and tried to meet the charging *bey* on foot, but Hamdji ran him down with his horse, bowled him over with his animal's chest, and sliced through his shoulder with the sharp tip of the scimitar as he fell. The knight's arm hung limp and useless at one stroke and the terrible *bey* galloped off in search of new opponents.

Many, however, lacked the heart to meet him. He seemed superhuman. The wind rushed through his white silk cloak and let it float high above his shoulders, lifting it like the wings of a giant bird of prey; the gilded scales of his body armor threw a malignant light on his blue-black features; his eyes glared wildly, shining with strange fires; and the curved scimitar gleamed over his head exactly like the silver crescent of a rising moon on a clear night.

The famous archer had sent two arrows already after him, but each rang harmlessly against the gilded steel scales of his armor and spun into the grass, so that Pan Mushalski began to wonder what he ought to do. Should he try one more arrow into the neck of the Egyptian's horse, or should he charge the *bey* with his saber in hand? But Hamdji-bey spotted him first as he sat weighing the alternatives and sent his coal-black stallion charging into him.

They met in midfield.

Pan Mushalski wanted to show off his great physical strength and to take Hamdji-bey alive, so he struck the scimitar high into the air with an upward blow, grasped the *bey* by the throat with one fist and by the sharp, high point of his helmet with the other, and drew him powerfully towards him. But the girth of his saddle snapped under him just then, he twisted off his horse together with his saddle, and Hamdji smashed the hilt of his scimitar down upon his head and stunned him as he toppled to the ground.

A shout of joy burst from the watching Mamelouks and Spahis who had begun to worry about Hamdji-bey. A cry of grief broke out from the Poles. Then both sides leaped at each other in a pell-mell rush, charging in thick clusters, one to seize the fallen archer and carry him away, and the other to retrieve and protect his body.

★   ★   ★

The little knight had taken no part in the skirmishing so far because his colonel's rank didn't permit him to indulge his pleasures like a private soldier. But when he caught sight of Pan Mushalski's fall and saw the damage wreaked by Hamdji-bey's successes in the field, he decided to avenge the archer and put fresh heart into his own men at the same time. Spurred by this thought, he spurred his horse as well and darted across the field as swiftly as a hawk that slants across the sky towards a scattering of wild doves above a fresh-sowed field. Basia, who stood on the battlements of the Old Castle high above him, caught sight of him through a field telescope, and turned at once to Pan Zagloba who stood near by.

"Michal is coming out!" she cried out. "Michal is coming out!"

"Then you're about to discover something new about him!" Pan Zagloba answered. "Watch where he strikes first! Watch carefully! And don't worry about him!"

The telescope was trembling in Basia's hands. She wasn't all that worried about her husband since there was no more shooting in the field, either with bows or firearms, but she was swept by enthusiasm, made avid by curiosity, and also somewhat nervous and uneasy. It was as if her heart and soul had burst from her body and now flew after her husband on the battlefield. Her breath came swiftly. Her breast rose and fell. A bright red flush set fire to her cheeks. At one point she leaned so far forward through the gunport in the castle wall that Pan Zagloba caught her by the waist so that she wouldn't topple into the moat below, and then she cried out: "There are two of them coming against Michal!"

"So there'll be two fewer," Pan Zagloba answered.

★ ★ ★

Two tall, broad-backed Spahis did indeed ride out against the little knight just then. His dress suggested that he was somebody important and his small stature promised an easy victory. Fools! They were hurrying to their deaths because the little knight didn't even slow his horse as he passed between them. He merely gave each of them a swift saber stroke, as light and careless as a mother's tap given in passing to a pair of unruly children, and they immediately plunged to earth and started clawing at it and quivering upon it like two wildcats shot off a tree-limb at the same time.

The little knight flew on towards other riders who milled on the field and started a carnage among them. The image that came then to the observers' minds was of an altar boy who puts out the candles after Mass, snuffing the flames with a metal cup set on a long pole while the lights died instantly one by one and plunged the altar into murky shadows. So he extinguished the splendid Turkish and Egyptian horsemen, turning his saber lightly to the left and right as he passed among them, and sent them into the eternal darkness. The Moslem riders recognized him soon enough for the master that he was and tried to avoid him. Their courage ebbed out of them and their spirits fell. Now and again one or another of them reined back so as not to cross his path, and he darted like a horsefly after those who ran and stung them to death.

The castle gunners started to shout with joy, following his progress with excited eyes. Some ran to Basia, carried away by their own enthusiasm, and kissed the trailing edges of her skirt. Others jeered at the Turks below.

"Baska! Control yourself!" Pan Zagloba shouted every other moment, holding onto the Colonel's Lady as if she were about to fly out of his grasp and soar through the air; she, in turn, wanted to laugh and cry and shout and clap her hands and look all at the same time, and to run after her husband into the plain before her.

He, in the meantime, went on with his harvest among the Turkish Spahis and Egyptian *beys* until the cries of *"Hamdi! Hamdi!"* echoed across the battlefield as the Moslem warriors called on their champion to come at last and put an end to that terrible little horseman who seemed to be the personification of death itself.

*   *   *

Hamdi had taken note of the little knight some time before that but he was in no hurry to try his hand against him. Fear brushed against him as he watched the grim little man's achievements. He didn't want to stake his reputation and his young life against such a terrible antagonist, so he pretended not to notice him and kept to the other end of the battlefield, circling like a wolf among less deadly victims. He had just snatched the life out of Pan Yalbrik and Pan Kos when the desperate cries of *"Hamdi! Hamdi!"* echoed in his ears. He knew then that he couldn't hold back any longer, that he had to try, and that he'd either win immortal glory for himself or pay with his head. He uttered such a piercing shriek that all the cliffs around him sounded with an echo, and sent his swift horse hurtling like the wind against the little soldier.

Volodyovski saw him from afar and also nudged his chestnut Valachian runner with his heels and galloped towards him. All other fighting ceased as both sides watched and waited. Up on the castle walls, Basia grew slightly pale. She'd watched all the earlier triumphs of the deadly Hamdi. She had a boundless faith in her husband's matchless swordsmanship but now she couldn't help a swift lick of fear.

But Pan Zagloba couldn't be more indifferent.

"I'd rather be that heathen's heir than himself," he announced and shrugged.

Pyentka, the slow phlegmatic Zmudyan that he was, showed even less concern. He was so sure about his master that he broke into a short Zmudyan ditty as he watched the galloping Egyptian.

> *"Dumb dog, what's your hurry?*
> *Dumb dog, you better worry.*
> *That's a wolf acomin' from the wood*
> *Bark all you want but you'll do no good."*

Meanwhile the combatants came together in midfield between the two long ranks of opposing warriors and everyone held his breath as if their hearts stood still. But suddenly lightning seemed to flash above the dueling horsemen, the glittering scimitar flew out of Hamdi's hand and curved high into the air like an arrow hurled out of a bow, and the black *bey* bowed his head towards his saddle horn and closed both his eyes.

Pan Volodyovski, however, didn't want to kill him. He merely caught him by the neck, pressed the point of his saber into Hamdi's armpit, and drove his horse beside his own towards his own men. Hamdi did not resist. He seemed quite stunned by what had happened to him. His arms hung limp beside him. Indeed, he hurried his own horse along with his heels, feeling the point of Volodyovski's saber against his flesh above the edge of his scaled armor, and tears of shame traveled down his face. Volodyovski handed him over to the savage Lusnia and turned again towards the battlefield.

But now the horns and flutes sounded the calls for assembly and retreat in the Turkish cohorts and the Spahis and the Mamelouks galloped away towards their own lines. They rode off with shame and worry twisting in their hearts, and with the frightening memory of a deadly horseman.

"It was Sheitan himself," they told each other as they rode away. "It was the Devil, no less. Had to be. He who comes near him dies."

The Polish skirmishers stayed in the plain for a while longer to show that they had won the field. Then they gave three great cheers and drew back under the cover of their guns which Pan Pototzki ordered to resume their firing. But the Turks were also in full retreat just then. Their white cloaks, glittering chain-mail and many-colored turbans shined and gleamed for a while longer in the ebbing sunlight and then they vanished altogether in the bluing distance. Only the sabered bodies of dead Poles and Turks remained in the field. Camp servants came out of the castle to collect and bury the fallen Polish riders and to loot the Turks. Soon afterwards came the carrion birds to attend to the burial of the Moslem dead. But their funeral supper didn't last too long because the armies of the Prophet returned in force later in the evening.

Chapter Sixty-nine

THE GRAND VEZIR HIMSELF arrived at Kamyenetz the next day, coming at the head of a large corps of Spahis, janissaries and Asian tributary levies. Judging by their numbers, the besieged believed that he'd storm the walls, but all he wanted was to see their fortifications. His siege engineers took a long look at the defenders' fortress and their city earthworks. This time it was Pan Myslishevski who went out against the Vezir with some infantry and a horse detachment, some skirmishing followed, the defenders got the better of it but didn't do as well as the day before.

At last the Vezir ordered the janissaries to try an assault on the fortifications. The roar of cannon shook the walls in both the castles and throughout the town. The janissaries marched up to the sector held by Pan Podtchaski, uttered a fierce yell and fired a volley, but Pan Podtchaski's men replied with well-aimed fire from above. And then, because they thought that cavalry might come out and charge them in the flank, the janissaries turned about, withdrew without further effort, and took the Zhvanyetz road back to their main forces.

Later that evening a Czech postilion escaped from the Turks and fled to the city. He was a household servant of the Janissary Agha who had the soles of his feet whipped in punishment. He brought the news that the Turks were already entrenched in Zhvanyetz and in the broad fields all the way to the settlement of Dluzka.

"What's the consensus among the Turks?" the besieged commanders questioned eagerly. "Do they think they'll take Kamyenetz or not?"

657

The fugitive replied that their morale was good and all the omens favorable. A pillar of smoke rose suddenly from the earth a few days ago in front of the Sultan's pavilion. Thin and narrow at the bottom, it spread as it rose into a wide funnel, soaring towards the heavens like a plume; and this, the *mullahs* explained, meant that the glory of the Padishah would reach to the skies and that he'd be that mighty Turkish ruler who finally crushed Kamyenetz.

This, as the Czech reported, sent the spirits soaring throughout the Sultan's armies. They, he went on, were very much afraid that Hetman Sobieski might come to break the siege; the memory of the regular Commonwealth contingents, met sword in hand in the in the open field, was painful among the Turks for a generation, and they'd much rather clash with Venetians, Hungarians or any other peoples. But since they knew that the Commonwealth had no ready forces, they were confident that they would take Kamyenetz, although at some cost.

"Kara Mustapha wanted to take the walls by storm," he reported, "but the Vezir wants a regular siege with earthworks, sapping, mines and artillery bombardments to bury the town." The Sultan's view, he said, swung to the side of the Vezir after the first few encounters in the field and now the defenders could expect a protracted siege.

Hearing him, the assembled officers grew somber. Pan Pototzki, Bishop Lantzkoronski, the chamberlain and Pan Volodyovski became glum and pensive. All of them counted on the Turks to storm the walls with overwhelming forces, and they expected to inflict heavy losses on the charging enemy. Experience told them that assaulting fortified positions always caused immeasurably greater casualties among the assailants than for the defenders, that each repulsed attack helped to sap the besiegers' spirits, and that every repelled assault put a fresh heart into the besieged. They thought that just as the knights who had defended Zbarajh in the Cossack Wars came to love battle, sallies, danger and the flames of their own resistance, so also would the citizens of Kamyenetz, especially if each attempt against them ended in a crushing disaster for the Turks. A regular siege, however, was a different story. Here all depended on engineers and gunners, the digging of approaches, the laying of mines, and the construction of batteries for the siege guns, all of which could weary the defenders, undermine their spirit, and make them more willing to negotiate. Sorties out of the fortress would also prove more difficult here than in Zbarajh. The walls could not be safely stripped of soldiers, while a sally beyond the walls by armed camp servants and citizens' militias wouldn't fare well against janissaries.

Pondering all this, the senior officers grew worried, and a successful defense started to seem unlikely. But it wasn't the overwhelming power of the Turks that was their greatest danger, as most of them knew it; if and when it came, their defeat would be due largely to themselves.

Pan Pototzki, their supreme commander, wasn't a warlike man or an experienced military leader. Moreover, he lacked the necessary confidence in himself to have much faith in others, and he saw no more hope for the Commonwealth. The bishop counted mainly on negotiations. His brother, the chamberlain, had a hard and heavy hand but also a head to match it. Pan Volodyovski was a peerless soldier but he didn't have the inborn inner power and imagination of a Sobieski, a Tcharnyetzki or a Vishnovyetzki; he lacked that ineffable majestic quality of greatness that could affect events. Just as the man who carries the sun within him can warm and inspire everyone around him, so the man who is himself no more than a flame can only touch those near him. The little knight could spark the courage in others by the fire of his own example, but he couldn't flood everyone around him with his own great-hearted dedication any more than he could pass on his talent for the saber.

Nor was it likely that the Commonwealth would come to their aid. Relief was unlikely because Pan Sobieski didn't have either the men or money; he had the needed greatness but not the resources. The King was just as helpless and so was the Commonwealth herself.

★　★　★

Then finally on August 16 the Crimean Khan arrived before Kamyenetz with the Horde and Doroshenko's Cossacks. Their vast camps stretched across all the fields towards Orynin and beyond. That same day the Tartar Sufankazi-agha invited Pan Myslishevski for a talk where he advised surrender. If the defenders gave up without more delay, they could obtain such generous conditions that nothing like them could be found in the history of sieges, he assured the Poles. The bishop wanted to know more about this generosity but he was shouted down in council and the invaders' offer was refused.

Two days later the Turks themselves began to arrive with their Padishah among them.

They came like a sea, immeasurable in its vastness. True tidal waves of Spahis, janissaries and *Djamak* infantry spilled behind each other. Each pasha led the armies of his *Pashalik* on the continents of Asia, Africa and Europe. Behind them came the siege train and the *tabor*—a wagon train that spread across the plain like a moving city drawn by water buffalo and mules. A rainbow of a hundred colors glowed from these swarming co-horts, a hundred different kinds of armaments and armor glittered in the fields, and countless different costumes dazzled the observers. They marched in all day long from dawn to dusk, without a break in their flowing masses; they moved from place to place, deployed their formations, occupied all the fields and made their encampments; and when the watchers looked down from the castle towers, they could see nothing but a sea of tents between the horizons. It seemed to them that a great snow had fallen to sheet the whole region.

Gun and musket fire accompanied the deployment of the siege train because the janissaries who screened the emplace-ments kept up a constant stream of musketry against the walls, while the castle gunners replied with their cannon. Echoes thundered among the cliffs and smoke climbed thickly to cover up the sky. By nightfall, Kamyenetz lay in such a tight embrace that nothing other than a bird could have slipped out of it. The cannonade died down only when the first stars of the night glittered overhead.

During the next few days the constant fire from and against the walls inflicted heavy losses among the besiegers. White plumes of gunsmoke erupted from the walls each time a group of janissaries clustered within range, cannonballs whirled among them, and they scattered like a flock of sparrows peppered with a load of birdshot. Moreover, the Turks weren't apparently informed that there were long-range guns in both the castles and the town, and they pitched their tents too close to the defenses.

The defenders took the little knight's advice and let them do just that. But later, when the heat of the day drove the besiegers to shelter under canvass, the cannon thundered on the walls in an uninterrupted roar. Panic followed. The iron shot slashed through the canvass and splintered the tent-poles. Shards of rock and timber flew among the soldiers, and the janissaries fell back in confusion—shouting and running, and knocking over other tents as they tried to get out of the cannons' range—and spreading consternation throughout the encampments. Pan Volodyovski charged these jumbled masses with the cavalry and cut them to ribbons until powerful Turkish reinforcements galloped to the rescue.

However the Turks were also hard at work in digging approaches that snaked towards the walls, constructing the earthworks, and emplacing their batteries of long-range heavy cannon. But before they settled to a regular bombardment, the Sultan gave Kamyenetz one more chance to lay down its arms. A Turkish emissary rode up to the walls and showed the defenders a letter from the Padishah which he fixed to a bamboo lance.

'My armies,' wrote the Sultan, 'are like the leaves of a forest and the sands that lie beside the seas. Look at the skies at nightfall, count the stars, and then tell yourselves that such is the power of the Faithful. And since I am a just and merciful king over other kings, and a nephew of the One True God, then it is from God that I derive my power. Know then that I hate obdurate and disobedient men, bow before my will, and open your gates before me. But if you resist me and persist in your stubborn errors each and every one of you will die by the sword and no voice on earth will be raised against me.'

Much thought went into the composition of an answer. "Cut off a dog's tail and send him that!" Pan Zagloba counseled but the commanders decided on a more courteous and diplomatic message.

'We have no wish to anger Your Imperial Majesty,' they wrote back politely but firmly, 'but it is not our duty to bow before your will since it is not to you that we gave our oaths but to our own master. Our oaths bind us to defend the fortress and the churches to the death.'

*   *   *

The officers went back to the walls after this reply but Pan Pototzki and Bishop Lantzkoronski seized on a chance to write another letter asking the Sultan for a four-week armistice, and had Pan Yuritza take it to the Turks. The news, when it reached the bastions and the gates, caused an immediate uproar.

"Now you see their true colors!" one or another of the serving gentry shouted at the others. "Here we are, sweating at the guns and there they go, sending letters behind our backs and without our knowledge, even though we too belong to the council!"

Greatly upset and worried by this unexpected turn, the little knight and Pan Makovyetzki led all the officers back to the general's quarters after the evening stand-down.

"How is it then?" Pan Makovyetzki cried out at the commander. "Are you already thinking about giving up, since you've sent off another messenger? And why was this done behind our backs?"

"Really!" added the little knight. "It's not right! We sit in the council. No letters to the enemy should be sent without us. Nor will we allow any talk about surrender, and if there's someone in the leadership who has that in mind then let him step down!"

His little whiskers twitched fiercely up and down as he spoke because this was a highly disciplined and dedicated soldier and it went hard on him to challenge his superiors. But that, he thought, was what he had to do since he had sworn to defend the castle until death.

Thrown off stride, and perhaps a little shamed as well, Pan Pototzki tried a conciliatory smile. "I thought this was the general consensus," he suggested.

"There's no consensus!" several voices shouted. "This is where we'll die!"

"I'm glad to hear it," their General nodded gravely. "I too hold my faith dearer than my life. Fear had nothing to do with my decision and it never will. Stay here for supper, gentlemen, and we'll get all this ironed out much better..."

But they didn't want to stay.

"Our place is at the gates, not at dinner tables!" said the little knight.

★   ★   ★

Bishop Lantzkoronski arrived just then, discovered what the trouble was about, and turned at once to the little knight and Pan Makovyetzki.

"Good people!" he said. "Everyone here shares your faith and courage and no one had surrender in mind. I wrote to ask for a four-week armistice, explaining that this would give us time to send for reinforcements and instructions from our king, after which let things happen as God wills them to."

Pan Volodyovski didn't know if he should shout in anger or laugh like a fool. Such ignorance of war was simply beyond him. His whiskers twitched as fiercely as before but this time because he couldn't believe his ears. In all his years as a soldier he'd never heard of anyone asking an enemy for an armistice so that he might have time to send for help. He started casting puzzled glances at Pan Makovyetzki and the other officers and they peered back worriedly at him.

"Is this a joke?" someone asked, and other voices queried: "Is he being serious?"

Then everyone stood silent.

"Your Eminence!" Volodyovski said at last. "I've fought in wars against Tartars, Cossacks, Russians, Swedes, Prussians and Hungarians but I've never heard anything like this before. The Sultan didn't come here to be helpful to us, but for his own reasons and convenience. How is he to agree to an armistice when we tell him that we need this time to wait for a relieving army?"

"If he doesn't agree, we'll have what we have right now, no more and no less!" said the troubled bishop.

"He who begs for an armistice betrays his own fears and displays his weakness," replied Volodyovski. "He who counts on relief from beyond the walls shows that he doesn't trust his own powers of resistance. Now that heathen dog knows these things about us, and the damage this has done to us is incalculable."

Glum at last, and saddened by the truth, the bishop appealed for understanding.

"I could've kept far away from here," he murmured. "I had no need to come. But these are my churches and my people. And now that I stayed with my flock in a time of need I have to listen to such accusations."

The sentimental little knight was moved at once to pity. "God keep me from making any accusations," he said and went down on his knees before the bishop as he would to his own natural father. "But this is a council, so I say what my experience tells me."

"What should we do, then? Let it be *mea culpa* if it has to be, but what can we do to show them that we lack neither the strength nor the determination? How can we repair the damage?"

"How to repair the damage?" Pan Volodyovski echoed. He thought long and hard and finally lifted up his head with a merry smile. "There's a way!" he said. "Come with me, gentlemen!"

He left and all the officers followed. A quarter of an hour later all of Kamyenetz quivered to the sound of the cannon, while Pan Volodyovski sallied beyond the walls with some volunteers, attacked the janissaries who slept in the nearest earthworks, and slaughtered them in dozens before they broke and fled all the way to their wagon trains.

Then he made his way back to the quarters of the General where Bishop Lantzkoronski also waited for him.

"As you see, gentlemen," he said happily. "There was a simple way."

Chapter Seventy

THE REST OF THE NIGHT passed in sporadic gunfire, but at dawn the watch gave word that several Turks were standing on the slopes outside the castle gates, waiting for someone to come to talk to them. No matter if the council wished to have no more dealings with the Turks, it had to find out what these emissaries wanted, so Pan Makovyetzki and Pan Myslishevski were appointed to go out to them and find out. Pan Casimir Humyetzki joined them before they left.

There were three Turks: Muktar-bey, the Pasha Salomi, and an interpreter named Kozra. The meeting took place under the open sky beyond the castle gate. The Turks began to bow as soon as they caught sight of the Polish envoys, placing the tips of their fingers on their foreheads, mouths and hearts; the Poles in turn showed them every courtesy, while asking what they had come about.

"Dearly beloved!" Salomi replied in the fulsome phrases of his time and customs. "Our Lord and Master has suffered a grave injury at your hands, one over which all righteous men must weep, and also one for which the Eternal One will punish you, if you don't hurry to make amends. You sent us an envoy, a certain Yuritza, who went on his knees before our Grand Vezir and begged for a ceasefire, and when we stepped into the open from behind the cliffs and out of our trenches, trusting in your goodwill and your virtuous intentions, you opened fire on us. Furthermore, not content with cannon, you leaped upon the Faithful sword in hand and paved the road with our dead all the way to the pavilions of the Padishah. Which act, dearly beloved, cannot go unpunished unless you show great sorrow and regret by turning over to us both your castles and the town."

"Yuritza is a dog who did more than he was told to do," Pan Makovyetzki answered, "in as much as he even had his groom carry a white flag. He'll be tried for that. Our bishop had merely inquired if an armistice was possible and he wrote purely on his own without consent of the council. But since you also kept up your cannonade during this exchange—and I'm a witness to that, because splintered stonework struck me in the face—then you can't expect us not to shoot at you. If you now come with a new armistice proposal then all's well and good. If not, then tell your master, dearly beloved, that we'll keep on defending our castles and our town as long as we live, or—as is more likely—until you all perish in those rocks and trenches. That, dearly beloved, is all we have to say beyond wishing you long life and God's mercy, so that your days may be multiplied and you may reach the contentments of old age."

After that the Turks went back to the Vezir while the three Polish envoys hurried to the castle. "What did they want?" everyone wished to know. "How did you handle them? What did the Turks offer?"

"Nothing you'd want to think about, dear brothers," Pan Humyetzki said. "Put simply, those mongrels want the town keys by nightfall."

"They won't get fat on us, the heathen dogs!" many voices cried out the popular slogan. "We'll drive them off with their tails dragging!"

Then everyone went back to his post and the cannonade opened up at once. The Turks had already managed to emplace much of their siege artillery and their projectiles skimmed across the breastworks and fell on the town. The town and castle gunners sweated at their cannon through the remainder of the day and throughout the night but there were no replacements for those of them who fell at their guns. Nor were there enough men to handle the powder and shot. The roars of the bombardments didn't start abating until dawn.

★   ★   ★

No sooner had the grey light of day seeped into the sky, and no sooner did the dawn's pink circlet with its golden rim appear in the East, when bells, drums and trumpets sounded the alarm in both the cliff castles. The townsmen leaped out of sleep all across the city. Bleary-eyed people poured into the streets.

"They're getting ready for an assault!" people told each other, pointing at the fortress.

"And is Pan Volodyovski there?" others asked uneasily.

"Yes he is!"

The castles, in the meantime, rang with chapel bells and growled with drum rolls. In that morning twilight, in that first light of dawn, these somber sounds created an air of mystery, and in that instant the Turks sounded their morning *kindja*, a long, wailing fanfare played by all of their musicians, summoning the Faithful to their morning prayer. One band passed this music to another, replacing another so that the repetition sounded like an echo, and these endless echoes flew on and on through the vast Turkish camp. The Turkish swarm began to stir and spill out of its tents.

As the sun edged higher below the horizon so the besieging earthworks loomed taller in the halflight. Tiered bastions, smaller earth-forts, and the covered trenches that snaked towards the town, rose near the castle walls. And suddenly heavy cannon bellowed all along this line. The cliffs along the river replied with their echoes, and the air filled with such an overwhelming roar that it seemed as if all the thunderbolts stored in the heavens had burst overhead and were now falling down to earth along with the skies.

The castles and the town thundered in reply. It was soon clear that no assault was coming but the artillery duel would go on all day. The smoke soon blotted out the sun, covered the Turkish earthworks, and seemed to swallow the very Earth itself. Kamyenetz disappeared along with all the bastions, batteries and trenches that lay ranged against it, and all its spaces turned into a single cloud, grey and colossal like a prehistoric monster, that boomed and bellowed amid gleams of lightning.

But the Turkish cannon had the range on the defenders' guns, and their shot soon started to spread death and damage through the town. Several Polish guns were smashed or disabled. The crews of the swivel-guns died several at a time. A wooden wedge hurled into the air from under the wheels of an exploding carronade, struck a Franciscan friar who walked along the walls praying for the gunners and blessing their cannon; it tore off his nose and half his face. It also killed two gunlayers, both of them resolute and determined Jews, who fought heroically at their gun.

Pounded the hardest, however, was the City Rampart. Pan Humyetzki crouched there like a salamander lizard amid flame and fires; half his company was dead, and of the living nearly all were wounded. The sounds that shattered eardrums everywhere around him robbed him of speech and hearing, but he and the alderman of the Polish burghers stayed at their guns, pouring fire into the Turkish battery before them, and eventually knocked it out for as long as it took the Turks to drag out the smashed artillery and roll in new cannon.

Three days and nights passed like that and the terrible *colloquium* of the guns went on without a moment's pause. The Turkish cannoneers changed watch four times a day but there was no relief for the city gunners. They stood on the walls round the clock hour after hour; sleepless, with hardly anything to eat, they staggered with exhaustion. Many were wounded by flying shards of iron ripped out of their demolished gun carriages and splintering debris; half-choked on gunsmoke, they endured because they had no choice. How long could this go on? The soldiers held out, fighting grimly through the endless hours, but the burgher volunteer militia began to give out. Finally they had to be driven with staves and cudgels to their guns where they died in dozens.

Relief came only on the night of Thursday, the third day of that terrible bombardment, when the chief fury of the Turkish guns turned upon the castles. Huge mortars hurled firebombs and grenades high across their walls, swirling in thickest clusters into the Old Castle, but these feared projectiles inflicted only minor casualties *"since"* (as the chronicles of the times related) *"a man could spot them coming in the darkness and get away from them without a lot of trouble."* It wasn't until later, close to dawn, when the men's weariness undermined their nimbleness and caution, that they began to fall in greater numbers.

Kettling, the little knight, and Pan Myslishevski answered the Turkish fire from the newer castle, one that protruded on its rocky summit well before the city. Pan Pototzki looked in on them there now and then, stalking worriedly among the shot and shell but paying small attention to the danger. However when the firestorm didn't ebb by nightfall, and as the barrage increased along with the darkness, the General edged up to Pan Volodyovski.

"Colonel," he said. "We won't hold out here."

"We'll hold out as long as they're satisfied with bombarding us," the little knight answered. "But they'll blow us out of here with landmines. They're already tunneling."

"What? Tunneling? Are you sure?"

"Seventy guns are firing so it's hard to hear it. But even so there's a quiet moment now and then. As soon as one comes, Your Excellency, give a little listen and you'll hear the miners working on the rock below."

They didn't have long to wait for such a silent moment and an accident speeded it along. One of the Turks' monster guns, the so-called Destroyers, burst suddenly in its earthen layer and shattered apart; in the confusion, with curious gunners peering out of other bastions and messengers coming on the run to find out what happened, there was a sudden hiatus in the shooting and the night grew momentarily quiet. Pan Pototzki and Pan Volodyovski took the opportunity to edge out into the farthest angle of the nearest salient, and after a while their ears caught the thin, tinny tapping of pickaxes chipping at the rock-face under them.

"They're tunneling," Pan Pototzki nodded.

"Tunneling," echoed the little knight, his voice flat and dry.

Then both were silent. A great anxiety crept out on Pan Pototzki's face. He raised his hands and pressed them numbly to his temples, looking into distance.

"It's normal siege-work," said Volodyovski. "At Zbarajh they burrowed under us night and day."

The General looked up. "And what did Vishnovyetzki do about that?"

"We tightened our lines, moved to inner walls, and raised new ones behind them."

"And what's the best thing for us to do?"

"The best thing is to take the guns, and all else we can carry, and move out of here. The Old Castle stands on solid granite and they'll never drive their landmines into that. I always thought that the new castle would serve only like a sort of barbican, enough to blunt the first assaults of the enemy, but that the real defense would start in the old one."

There was another silence. The General stared worriedly at the ground. "And what if we have to fall back from there?" he asked in a stricken voice. "Where shall we go then?"

The little soldier drew himself up at that, a sudden twinge of feeling moved his mustache swiftly up and down, and he pointed his finger at the broken soil.

"That's where I'll go!" he said.

★   ★   ★

Just then the cannon opened up again. A whole swarm of firebombs hissed towards the castle like a flock of comets. But it was dark already by that time, and the grenades were easily spotted by their fiery tails. Pan Volodyovski took his leave of General Pototzki and walked along the walls. He peered into the gunpits, one after another. He stopped at every embrassure and each gun emplacement. He made suggestions, gave advice, and raised the gunners' spirits, and at last he came to Kettling's battery.

"So what's new here?" he said.

Kettling's smile seemed almost angelic. "The grenades light up this place as bright as daylight," he said and shook hands warmly with the little knight. "The Turks aren't skimping on their fireworks."

"They lost a big cannon. I expect you blew it up for them?"

"I expect I did."

"God, but I'm sleepy."

"So am I." The young Scotsman yawned. "But there's no time for it."

"And our wives must be getting anxious about us," the little knight muttered. "It's hard to sleep thinking about that."

"They are praying for us," Ketling said and raised his eyes towards the hurtling bombs.

"May God keep them well, both of them."

"There's none like them among all the women in the world," said Ketling and got ready to say more.

★   ★   ★

But he never finished what he wished to say because just then the little knight turned towards the interior of the castle and suddenly shouted: "Great God Almighty! What's this I see there?"

And then he leaped down the stone steps to the courtyard. Ketling turned, curious and surprised. A scant twenty paces distant, he saw Basia hurrying across the open space with Pyentka the Zmudyan, and with Pan Zagloba panting close behind her.

"Get under cover, for God's sake!" The little knight dragged them all at once into the shelter of the curtain wall. "What's the matter with you? For God's sake...!"

"Ha!" Pan Zagloba gasped out amid gulps of air. "Do something with her, will you? I beg her. I persuade. *'You'll doom yourself and me too!'* What's the use? I kneel. I plead. Nothing helps! Was I to let her come alone...? Ooof! Nothing did any good. Nothing! Nothing! *'I'll go and that's that,'* she says. So what could anybody do? You know what she's like!"

Basia looked truly frightened and her eyebrows quivered as if she were about to burst into tears. But it wasn't the terrible cacophony of the bombs that frightened her; she hardly noticed the iron shards and cracked stone that hissed all about her. Fear of her husband's anger, even though he'd die before he ever hurt her, pounded so violently in her mind that it quite drowned out the roar of the bombardment.

"I couldn't, *Mihalku!*"She gave way to a paroxysm of sobbing, clasping her hands before her like a child about to be punished. "I just couldn't sit there! I love you, I couldn't! Don't be mad at me *Mihalku*! I can't just sit waiting while you're here in danger! I just cant, I can't...!"

He was, indeed, angrier than she'd ever seen him. He had already shouted: "Baska! You undermine God's patience!" But suddenly his sentimental nature grasped him by the throat, his voice choked with feeling, and it was only when her small, bright head lay pressed against his chest that he could speak again.

"Ah what a friend you are to me," he murmured. "A friend for a lifetime...!"

And he put both his arms powerfully around her.

★ ★ ★

In the meantime, Pan Zagloba squeezed himself in haste into

a sheltered angle of the inner buttress and rattled breathlessly at Ketling.

"Yours wanted to come too," he babbled. "But we fooled her. Told her we weren't going.... I mean, in her condition? Your new baby's going to be a general of artillery, no question about it; use my brains for a tinker's cuss if I'm lying! Ha! The bombs pelt that city bridge like pears in a windstorm. I thought I'd shake apart. Not out of fear, you understand, out of anger! I fell the other day, you see, on some sharp stones, and tore the skin on my backside so badly that I won't sit comfortably for a week. The nuns have to apply ointments to me there, and God only knows what that does to their vows of chastity. Ooof! Ha! And in the meantime those heathen dogs are shooting all the harder! May lightning bombard them! Pan Pototzki wants me to take over the command, but I don't know... Hey, why don't you get these poor soldiers something good to drink? They won't hold out without it... Ha! Look at that grenade! By God, it's going to hit somewhere close by... Shield Baska! Protect Baska! God, it's going to be close!"

But it wasn't close. The mortar bomb sailed all the way to the Old Castle where it hit the roof of the Lutheran chapel. Because the roof and ceiling there were particularly strong, the church was now the munitions store, but the projectile pierced the ceiling and set off the powder. A powerful blast, much louder than the cannon, shook both the castles to their foundations. Cries of terror rose from the battlements and all the guns grew silent on both sides of the walls.

Ketling turned his back on Zagloba, Pan Volodyovski tore himself away from Basia, and both ran to the ramparts. Their orders rang out, even though both were out of breath and panting. But a sudden growling of janissary drums welled out of the Turkish earthworks and drowned out their commands.

"They'll be attacking now!" Zagloba hissed to Basia.

Hearing the explosion, the Turks must have thought that both the castles were blown into ruin, and their defenders were either dead and buried in the rubble or struck numb with terror, and they prepared to storm the walls. They had no way of knowing that it was only the chapel that was wrecked. The explosion did no other damage; not a single gun tumbled off its carriage in the newer castle. Their drums acquired a frenzied beat. Swarms of janissaries slid off their entrenchments and ran towards the walls. All the watch fires in the castle and in the nearby Turkish outer works had long since died out, but the night was clear, and a bright silver moonlight bathed the dense, bobbing mass of white janissary caps, surging at a run like a foaming wave. Several thousand janissaries and a few hundred of the irregular *Djamak* infantry poured up the slope, coming straight for the wall between two flanking bastions. Many of them would never see the minarets of Istanbul again, nor the bright waters of the Bosphorus, nor the lofty Cypress trees of Asia, but now they charged with fire in their eyes and a firm conviction of victory in their hearts.

Meanwhile Volodyovski flitted silently as a ghost all along the walls.

"Hold your fire!" he ordered at each gun post. "Wait for the command!"

★   ★   ★

The dragoons lay prone on the ramparts, their muskets thrust out before them, panting with impatience. A deep silence settled among the crouched Mazurians; only the rapid beat of the janissaries' boots rolled ever closer like a muffled thunder. The closer they came the more assured they were that they'd take both the castles at one blow. Many believed that the surviving soldiers had pulled back into the town and that the walls were without defenders.

At last they came to the moat, filled it in moments with thick bundles of reeds, bags of raw wool and bales of straw, and surged towards the wall.

No sound came from there.

But when the leading ranks stepped onto the sacks, bales and fascines with which they'd filled the moat, a pistol shot cracked in one of the outer angles of the wall while a shrill voice screamed out:

"Fire!"

A long belt of flame leaped at once like a stream of lightning from both the bastions and their connecting wall. Cannon roared. Muskets blazed. Handguns rattled out. A fierce yell burst out of the defenders and a savage howl came from the attackers. The image that came to mind was of a stricken bear, whose belly had been pierced by a javelin hurled by a powerful hunter, and who now twists, roars, lurches, throws himself about, clutches at himself and then springs erect only to twist again. In just that way the mass of janissaries and *Djamak* infantry coiled, snapped open and coiled upon itself again. No musket ball fired off the walls failed to find a target. Canisters full of stone and iron pellets fired from the cannon, sweeping across that heaving mass like a cyclone across a field of wheat, scythed whole ranks into the ground all at the same time. Those Turks who'd stormed the wall that linked the two protruding outer bastions, found themselves in a crossfire that swept from three sides. Panicked and driven half-mad with terror, they turned to flee, jammed against the ranks that had pushed behind them, and turned into a formless mob that heaved and thrashed about amid such heaps of corpses that they seemed like a range of dreadfully twitching hillocks. Ketling pounded that vast human logjam with two carronades, and when it finally broke out and lurched towards escape, he closed the only exit between the two bastions with a storm of iron and hot lead.

★   ★   ★

The assault was beaten off all along the line, so when the *Djamak* and the janissaries finally broke and fled—and they streamed back towards their trenches like wild, mindless cattle, bellowing with terror—the Turkish batteries began to hurl pitch pots and flaming torches into the plain before them, and to set off aerial rockets and illuminations. A white day-like glare replaced the night's darkness to light the way for the fleeing masses and hinder a pursuit.

Meanwhile Volodyovski caught sight of the mass trapped between the bastions, called his dragoons together, and slid down the angled wall towards it. The wretched crowd tried to break out to safety once again but Ketling buried the escape route in such a hail of iron that the whole exit was soon blocked with corpses, stacked on each other like another wall. "No prisoners!" Volodyovski ordered. Those Turks who were still alive had no choice but death and so they fought back with the ferocity of despair. Big, broad-backed men, armed with spears, halberds, *yataghans* and sabers, backed up against each other in clumps of three, four or five, and hacked savagely at anyone who neared them. All of their fear, terror and certainty of death erupted as a single rage. The furies of the battlefield seized them by the hair. Some charged the dragoons singlehanded and died hacked to pieces by a dozen sabers, and the dragoons met their rage with one of their own. Their weariness, sleeplessness and hunger came together in a wave of hatred. They threw themselves like wild beasts at this enemy who caused them their torments; and because they were much better swordsmen than the Turks they wreaked a terrible carnage in their ranks.

Wanting more light, so that his gunners could tell friends from enemies, Ketling ordered barrels of flaming pitch hoisted above the walls, and their glaring light cast a lurid glow on the uncontrollable Mazurians and the janissaries who fought with sabers, fists and bare hands, clutching at necks and beards. The terrifying Lusnia raged there like a maddened bull. Pan Volody-ovski fought on the other flank, exceeding all his previous feats because he knew that Basia watched him from the wall behind. It was as if a fierce vixen had burst into a nestful of fieldmice in a stand of corn, slaughtering mercilessly everything around her. The little knight flew and darted among the janissaries as if he'd suddenly become their spirit of destruction. His name was well known already in the Sultan's armies, as much from other battles as from the tales told about him by the Khotim Turks. Only death could come to anyone who met him, according to his legend, so now many of the janissaries who saw him coming at them didn't even bother to defend themselves, but died on his rapier with eyes closed and *"Kismet"* on their lips.

Then their resistance dwindled. The survivors threw themselves onto the wall of corpses that barred their escape and there they were cut down to a man.

★   ★   ★

The dragoons came back across the buried moat, shouting and singing, panting with exhaustion and splashed and smeared with blood. The Turks fired a few more shots out of their emplacements, a few Polish cannon answered for a while, and then there was silence. The great gun duel that had lasted for several days now came to an end.

"Thank God for that," said the little knight. "We'll get to rest, at least until the morning *kindja*. Nor can I think of anybody who deserves it more."

But they both knew, he and the experienced Ketling, that it would be a deceptive rest at best, because no sooner had the silence settled, and the night grew both darker and quieter, than the soft chipping sounds of the miners' picks came from the rock below.

"That's worse than bombardments," Ketling said, nodding towards the sound.

"Ah what wouldn't I give for a sortie now!" said the little knight. "But that can't be, not tonight. The men are done in. They've had no sleep or food for days, even though there were full rations handy, because there wasn't time. Besides, the Turks' mining parties always have a few thousand Spahis and the *Djamak* on guard against surprises. We'll have to blow up these outer works and pull back into the Old Castle. There's no other way."

"But not tonight," said Ketling. "Take a look. The men are out like a light everywhere around us. The dragoons didn't even wipe the blood off their sabers."

"Baska!" the little knight ordered suddenly. "Back to the town and to bed with you!"

"Very well, *Mihalku,*" Basia answered meekly. "I'll go if you want me to. But the cloisters are locked for the night back there and I'd rather stay here watching over you."

"It's a strange thing," said the little knight, "but I don't feel the least bit tired just now and sleep's the last thing that I have in mind."

"That's because you've stirred up all your blood playing with the janissaries," Pan Zagloba noted. "That always happened with me in my time. But as far as Baska is concerned, why should she drag herself to a locked gate tonight? Let her stay here with you until the morning *kindja.*"

Basia threw her arms joyfully around Pan Zagloba, and seeing how much it meant to her, the little knight gave way. "Then let's go inside," he said.

And they went.

★ ★ ★

But they soon discovered that all the castle chambers were

thick with mortar dust shaken loose by concussion during the bombardment. It was impossible to breathe there or stay for any length of time, so they came out again, and made their way back towards the walls, and found a shelter in the arch of an old walled-up gateway.

There he sat down and she nestled like a child against him. The August night was warm and filled with sweetness. The moon cast its silver light into that niche and brushed against their faces. Groups of sleeping soldiers lay in the courtyard below them, along with those others who fell during the bombardment and for whom there hadn't been any time for burial. The moon shined its light in passing into all those faces as if to see who was merely sleeping and whose rest was both final and eternal. Beyond them loomed the main inner structure of the castle which cast its dark shadow over half the courtyard. Men's voices rose out of the moving shadows on the other side where the camp servants stripped and plundered the slaughtered janissaries, along with those dragoons who wanted loot even more than they needed sleep. Their reddish lights and torches glittered in the plain like darting fireflies. Some called out softly to each other and one started singing a quiet lilting love song that didn't fit his present occupation.

> *"I need neither gold nor silver*
> *Nor this costly gear,*
> *I'd die gladly by the roadside*
> *'S long as you are near.*

After a while, however, all sounds and movement ceased beneath the wall. Silence came down on the sleeping castle. The only sounds were the drawn-out, intermittent calls of the huddled sentries and the faroff, muffled clink of the picks that chipped persistently at the face of the rock below. That silence, that silvered night and that quiet moonlight fell like a soothing balm on the little knight and Basia. A sense of longing and regret which neither of them could really understand lay just below their peacefulness and contentment.

"Mihalku?" Basia was first to raise her eyes and to see that her husband's were wide open and fixed upon distance. "You aren't sleeping, are you?"

"Odd to say, I don't even want to."

"Are you happy here?"

"And how. And how about you?"

Basia began to twist her bright, shining head. "Oh so happy! Oy! Oy! Did you hear what that other man was singing?" And here she repeated the last lines of the song: *"I'd die gladly by the roadside s'long as you are near."*

They sat in silence for a moment longer. "Baska!" the little knight broke into their musing. "Listen a minute, will you? Listen now..."

"What is it, Mihalku?"

"Well, to tell the truth, we're so happy together that it seems to me we'd each mourn the other way beyond all reason if one of us should fall."

Basia knew very well that the little knight had himself in mind when he spoke of falling. It came to her that he didn't believe he would come out of the siege alive, and that he wanted to prepare her for this final moment and let her mind get used to the idea. A terrible premonition seized her and chilled her to the bone.

"Mihalku!" she cried and pressed her hands together as if in a prayer. "Don't talk like that! Have mercy on me and on yourself!"

The little knight's voice trembled a little with emotion but he was calm and quiet. "Because the way it is, you see," he said in his quiet, simple and straighforward manner, "you're speaking against logic. Think, what is this life about? What's all this struggling for? Who can live on love and happiness when everything else around is as fragile as a dried out twig?"

But she was quivering with sobs and cried over and over: "I don't want that! I don't want that! I don't want to hear that!"

"You're wrong there, as God's dear to me," the little knight insisted. "Look now, up there beyond that moon is a land of eternal happiness. That's the kind to shoot for! Whoever gets into those high pastures can really draw a deep breath, take his ease at last like a lost, strayed sheep that's found its way home, and graze there in peace. When my time comes—and that, after all, is part and parcel of being a soldier—you ought to tell yourself at once: *'It's alright. It doesn't mean a thing. Michal's gone away for a time, that's all. True, it's a long way off, farther even than to Lithuania, but that's still alright because I'll be following him in my proper time.'* Baska, stop crying, I tell you. Whichever of us goes first will find good quarters for the other, and that's all there's to it."

He may have caught a glimpse of the future just then because his voice softened even further, he raised his eyes to the moon, and said: "What's all the fuss about existence anyway? Who'd want to care about the things of this world, the way those things are? Imagine that I'm already up there and there's this knocking on the heavenly gates. St. Peter opens up and what do I see? Who's there? My Baska! That's when you'll see me jump like never before! That's when I'll shout and cry out louder than you've ever heard! What joy it'll be. Dear God, give me the words to say it as it is! And there'll never be any tears up there. It'll all be joy and happiness and love, like a wedding party that never has to end. There'll be no Turks or Tartars or any other heathen, no guns, no mines under the walls. There'll just be peace and peacefulness and happiness that'll never end. The rest of it... all this *reality* we're so concerned about down here, it's nothing! Remember Baska: it doesn't mean a thing."

"Michal, Michal...!" Basia kept repeating.

And then there was another silence, interrupted only by the muffled clink of hammers and pickaxes battering and chipping the cliff-face below.

"Let's say a prayer together, Baska," Volodyovski said at last.

And so these two honest, decent, simple and loving souls began to pray together, and peace and acceptance flowed gradually into them as their prayers unfolded, and then sleep came to them and they slept in each other's arms until the first light of dawn. Then, even before the morning *kindja* sounded in the Turkish camps, Pan Volodyovski took Basia all the way to the bridge that connected the Old Castle with the town.

Parting from her at last he said: "Remember. It's nothing."

Chapter Seventy-one

THE THUNDER OF THE GUNS shook both the castles and the town right after the *kindja*. The Turks had already dug an assault ditch of some five hundred feet towards the defenses and in one place they started to dig under the New Castle itself, as the newer outer works were known. A ceaseless fire of janissary muskets, the so-called *yantcharki*, poured from this ditch upon the defenders. The besieged made parapets and breastworks for themselves out of leather sacks stuffed with bundled cotton, but since the Turkish batteries hurled a constant stream of solid shot and firebombs against them, men fell in large numbers around the Polish cannon. Six men of Volodyovski's convict infantry died from one mortar bomb at one of the guns. Other cannoneers dropped beside the others. By evening the officers concluded that they couldn't hold these walls much longer especially since the mines could go off under them almost any time. That night the captains assembled their companies and hauled all the cannon, ammunition and provisions out of the newer outer works to the Old Castle itself, even though the shooting went on uninterrupted. Since the older fortress stood high on solid rock it could resist much longer, and the mining operations against it would be much more difficult. Asked about that at the council, Pan Volodyovski said he was ready to defend it for a year if only no one undermined his efforts with negotiations. What he said soon spread throughout the town. It filled the townsfolk with encouragement and hope. Everyone knew that the little knight would keep his word even if he paid for it with his life.

They set powerful mines under both the bastions and the

connecting wall before they marched out of their old defenses. These went off close to noon with a massive roar, but they did little damage to the Turks who'd learned a painful lesson the day before and were in no hurry to occupy the deserted walls. Both the abandoned bastions, however, along with the fronting battlements and the best part of the New Castle itself, became at once a single heap of rubble. Strewn in huge piles below the castle gates, these barricades of broken bricks and timber made it harder for the Turks to storm the fresh defenses, but they also screened the janissary musketeers who burrowed inside them. What seemed more dangerous than the Turkish sharpshooters, however, was the fact that the wreckage hid the sappers who got to work at once on another tunnel. Skilled Italian and Hungarian engineers, in the pay of the Sultan, watched over these expert preparations, and the work went swiftly. The besieged couldn't disrupt this massive burrowing because they couldn't see the burrowers. Their cannon and muskets were as good as useless. Pan Volodyovski thought hard about another sortie but that would have to wait. The soldiers were simply too weary and exhausted. Huge purple swellings rose on the shoulder of every dragoon, stamped there by the repeated recoil of their muskets. Some of the soldiers were no longer able to lift their right arm. It became clear, moreover, that if the tunneling went on uninterrupted long enough, the main gate of the castle would be mined and blown into the air without any question. Pan Volodyovski ordered a tall earthwall raised behind that gate in anticipation of a breach and didn't worry any more about it.

"What do I care?" he said to Pan Pototzki. "If they blow up the gate we'll fight them off the earthwall. If they blow up the earthwall we'll hold them on a new one we'll raise in the meantime. And so it'll go until the last foot of ground behind us is used up."

But the General-Ordinary of Podolia had now lost all hope. "And what if that last foot is also gone?" he asked.

"Then we'll be gone too," the small knight said simply.

* * *

Meanwhile he ordered hand bombs tossed down on the burrowing enemy, causing heavy losses. Lieutenant Dembinski proved the most effective at this work, bowling over the tunneling Turks like nine-pins, until a short-fused bomb blew off his right arm. The brave Captain Schmidt died in the same way. Many others fell to cannon fire, many more died in the hail of musketry which rattled out from the janissaries hidden in the rubble. The Polish guns were largely silent during all this time, which worried the gentlemen of the council even more.

"They've stopped shooting," they said to each other, far out of range of the Turkish fire. "That means Volodyovski himself has lost faith in holding out."

None of the officers at the council wanted to be the first to say that further resistance was useless, and that all that could now be done was to get the best possible terms from the Turks before surrender, but the bishop had no military reputation to protect.

"In my opinion there's nothing else to do," he said. "We should sue for an immediate ceasefire and negotiate the terms for a capitulation."

But before making a final decision, the council sent Pan Vasilkovski to the castle to consult with the General of Podolia.

'In my opinion,' Pan Pototzki wrote back to the council, *'the castle won't hold out until evening. But the others here don't agree with me.'*

After that, even some of the military members of the council started to talk about surrendering.

"We did what we could," they assured each other. "We gave it our best, and no one here is worried about his own skin. But if we can't go on then we can't, and we have to ask for terms."

It wasn't long before word of this decision seeped through the town and brought about a huge gathering in front of the Town Hall. The crowds stood in uneasy silence, not especially opposed to negotiations but not favoring surrender. Some rich Armenians were pleased that the siege might end sooner and that normal business could start up again, but these were a few; the great majority of the Armenian merchants, long settled within the boundaries of the Commonwealth, favored resistance along with the Poles and the Ruthenians.

"If they were going to surrender they should've done it straight off," they muttered to each other. "That way the terms would be generous, now they won't. We'd do better to bury ourselves in the rubble and fight on."

★ ★ ★

The muttering began to grow loud and angry, so that the deliberating dignitaries started getting worried, but suddenly it turned into shouts of joy and cheers at the sight of Pan Volodyovski and Pan Humyetzki riding from the castle. Pan Pototzki had lost all hope of holding out, but he was anxious to be seen as a fair-minded man, one who was always willing to consider all sides of any question, and so he sent the two of them to the council anyway to give their own views on whether they could hold off the Turks.

Wild enthusiasm seized the crowds at the sight of them. Some of the people raised a yell as loud as if the Turks had already broken into the city, others' eyes filled with tears when they saw their admired defender. The little knight looked weary and worn down with hardships. His thin, hollowed face was dark with smoke and blackened with powder. Dark circles rimmed his reddened eyes but he looked about him cheerfully enough. Once he and Humyetzki managed to make their way through the cheering crowds and reached the council chamber, the assembled gentry greeted them like heroes.

"Dearest brothers!" the bishop cried out immediately. *"Nec Hercules contra plures,* as the saying goes. Not even Hercules could manage against overwhelming numbers. Pan Pototzki has already sent word to us that you must surrender."

"Pan Pototzki has lost his head!" said Pan Humyetzki sharply. He was an outspoken man, whose old Ruthenian family was very well connected, and he could say largely what he pleased. "The only good thing about that head of his is that he risks it in the castle like the rest of us. As for how long we can defend the castle, I'll let Pan Volodyovski do the talking, because he knows more about that than all of us together."

All eyes turned at once on the little knight whose little yellow mustache twitched powerfully up and down and whose voice echoed with anger and amazement.

"For God's sake!" he said. "Who said anything about surrender? Didn't we all swear to God that we'd fall before such a thing could happen?"

"We swore we'd do all we could," the bishop said quickly. "We've done all we could!"

"Let everyone keep whatever oath he gave!" Pan Volodyovski answered. "Ketling and I swore before God not to give up the castle, and we won't! Not while we're alive! Good God, gentlemen! If I'm obliged to keep my word given to a man, how could I break a promise made to the Almighty?"

"But what about the castle?" many voices asked. "We heard the gate is mined. How long will you be able to defend yourselves there?"

"Yes, the gate is mined, or if it isn't yet then it will be soon. But I've had an earth-fort built behind the gates and the cannon are already on it. Dearest brothers, have God in your hearts! Have mercy! Think what will happen to the churches once the heathen take possession of them. Think of the pagan rites practiced before Christ's altars! How can you talk so lightly about giving up? We are the gateway to the Commonwealth! Nothing else stands between our country and the Turk! How will you make peace with your conscience, every one of you, if you throw this gate open to such a terrible enemy? I sit in the castle and I don't worry about any mines, and you're here, safely in the town, and you're afraid of them? In God's name brothers, let's never give up! Let's hold as long as we're alive! Let's make a stand here that future generations will remember just as they remember the defense of Zbarajh!"

"The Turks will turn the castle into a heap of rubble," someone said.

"Let them! We can fight them out of rubble just as well as from behind a rampart!" But here the little knight started to lose his patience. "And as God's my witness, that's just what I'll do. I won't give up the castle and that's my last word. Do you hear me?"

"And you'll doom the town?" asked the bishop.

"I'd rather see it leveled than go to the Turks!" the little knight exploded. "I took an oath! I won't waste any more words on you here. I'm going back to my cannon. They, at least, are defending our country, not trading it away!"

* * *

With this he burst out of the room and Pan Humyetzki slammed the door behind them. They hurried away because they really felt better in those heaps of rubble, under the gunfire and among the corpses, then with weak, vacillating men whose frail faith could be shaken with so little effort. But Pan Makovyetzki ran out after them and caught up with them on the stairs before the door.

"Michal," he asked the little knight, "tell me the whole truth. Were you talking about resistance just to raise our spirits or can you really keep up a defense?"

"As God's my witness! As long as they don't surrender the city I can fight off the Turks for a year!"

"Then why aren't you shooting? People don't understand this, they take it for the worst possible sign, and that's why they're talking about giving up."

"We weren't shooting because we were busy throwing hand grenades to disrupt the tunneling and knock out the miners."

"But listen, Michal," Pan Makovyetzki worried. "D'you have enough guns in the castle to turn a few my way? God forbid the Turks should break through me at the Ruthenian Gate, I'll hold them while I can, but it's hard to do much with just a company of merchants."

"Don't give it a thought, dear brother," the little knight grinned whitely. "I've already laid fifteen guns to bear on that quarter. And don't worry about the castle either. We can defend ourselves without any trouble and if necessary we'll send you help at the gate as well."

Delighted to hear this, Pan Makovyetzki turned to let them go when the little knight stopped him for a moment longer. "Tell me," he said. "You go to those council meetings a lot more than I. Are they just testing us or do they really want to give Kamyenetz to the Sultan?"

Pan Makovyetzki looked down at the ground.

"Michal," he said. "Be honest with yourself. Isn't that what must happen in the end? We'll keep resisting for a while longer... a week or even a month perhaps... but the result will have to be the same."

Pan Volodyovski looked at his sister's husband with a bitter stare. "And you too, Brutus, stand against me then?" he cried and raised his fists in a surge of anger. "Ha! So be it then! Chew your shame without my help, if that's what you want, because I'm accustomed to a different diet!"

And they parted bitterly, with anger between them.

*   *   *

The mine under the main gate went off shortly after Volodyovski returned to the Old Castle. Bricks and masonry sailed into
the air. Smoke and dust blotted out the sky. A quick flash of fear
and alarm stunned the gunners on the wall for a little while. The
Turks swarmed into the breach at once, pouring in at a run like
a herd of cattle that drovers lash into their gaping stable. But
Ketling lashed them with canister and chain-shot fired from six
cannon mounted well ahead of time on the backup earthwall;
then he lashed out twice more and swept them from the courtyard. Volodyovski, Humyetzki and Myslishevski came running
with the dragoons and the infantry who threw themselves onto
the wall as thickly as flies on a carcass.

There then began a firefight with muskets and handguns. Lead
balls rattled down like rain on a tin roof, or like a shovelful of
grain that a broad-backed peasant hurls into the air. The Turks
were everywhere in the ruins of the abandoned New Castle, or
what had been the outer works of the main defenses; they
crouched singly, in twos and threes, in dozens and in scores in
every hole and declivity, behind every heap of masonry and each
pile of rubble, and they kept up an unending stream of musketry
against the defenders. Fresh regiments marched to reinforce
them from the direction of Khotim, crowded into the debris one
after another, and immediately began to add their own continuous barrage. The whole area of ruin, wreckage and destruction
that spread beyond the breach seemed alive with Turks; their
turbans massed as densely as cobble stones across every yard of
visible open space. Now and then this roiled swarm of turbans
erupted with a frightful howl and hurled itself pell-mell into the
breach, and stormed the defenses, and Ketling's cannon blew it
out again. The deep bass roar of the artillery overwhelmed the
crack and clatter of firelocks and muskets; the massed lead balls
spewed out of the cannon, shrilling through the air like a flock
of furies; a wall of lead fell upon that throng, crushed it and
turned it into heaps of torn flesh and stacks of lifeless bodies, and
filled up the breach with this fresh human rampart.

Four times the janissaries charged and each time Ketling
threw them back and swept them down the hillside like a
windstorm that scatters a mound of leaves.

He stood untroubled and unmoved in that maelstrom of fire and smoke, oblivious of the shards of iron and debris that whirled everywhere, with a quiet smile on his face among the bursting firebombs and grenades, and without a line of worry on his clear, high forehead. His eyes were fixed on the breached gates and the rubble around it. Sometimes he took the smoldering fuse from a gunner's hand and touched it to the touch-hole; at other times he shielded his eyes with his hand to see the effect of a cannon's discharge; and now and then he turned to the officers around him.

"They won't get through!" he'd say with a smile.

Never before did such a furious enemy assault meet with such a savagely determined resistance. Private soldiers competed with their officers; they seemed oblivious of the deaths among them, and yet death cut a bloody swath in their ranks as well. The brave Pan Humyetzki fell among the others. So did Pan Mokoshitzki, the commander of the Kievan gentry volunteers. The snowy-haired Pan Kalushovski clutched his chest at last and started to fall. He was an old friend of Volodyovski, an old soldier who could be as gentle as a lamb and as implacable as a lion, and the little knight caught him up at once.

"Give me you hand! Quick! Quick! Give me your hand!" the dying man murmured. Then, having clutched it briefly, he added: "Glory be to God."

And then his face became as white as his beard and mustache.

* * *

This happened just before the fourth assault. A janissary cohort broke in through the breach but then couldn't get away again through the wall of corpses piled up behind them. Volodyovski leaped down on them with his Hreptyov infantry and hammered them all into the ground with musket butts and timbers used by the gunners to shore up their cannon.

Hours passed and the firefight went on unabated. But word of the heroic stand flew into the town, excited the imaginations and fired warlike spirits. The Polish townsmen, and especially the young apprentices among them, started to call each other out into the streets, nudge and eye each other, and dare each other to take a hand in the fighting.

"Let's help them out at the castle!" they challenged each other.

"Let's go, lads! Let's get going! We won't let our brothers die without giving them a hand! Come on, lads, let's go!"

Such cries echoed in the town square and at all the gates, and soon a crowd of several hundred people, armed with whatever came to hand but with courage and determination glowing in their hearts, started out towards the bridge that led to the castle. The Turks raked it with an immediate hurricane of fire. It was soon paved with corpses. But the rest of the eager volunteers got through, climbed up on the earth-fort, and started working at once against the Turks.

They beat back that fourth assault with such devastating losses to the enemy that it seemed as if a moment of respite might come after all. But such hopes were vain. The flash and rattle of the janissaries' muskets didn't end till nightfall. Not until the evening *kindja* did the guns grow silent and the Turks pulled back from the rubble of the outer works. Then the remaining Polish officers slid down the wall to the Turkish side to inspect the damage.

The little knight ordered the breach closed up with whatever could be heaved and dragged into the gaping hole, and soon a thick barrier of logs, earth, bundled reeds and rubble started to rise within it. The foot soldiers, the serving gentry, the dragoons, privates, officers and nobles worked side by side without regard for rank. They expected that the Turkish guns would bellow out again at almost any moment, but this had been a day of great success for the besieged over the besiegers, so all their faces were untroubled and clear, hope glowed within them, and their spirits soared in anticipation of victories to come.

Chapter Seventy-two

AFTER THE WORK on the breech was done, Ketling and Volody-ovski linked arms like brothers and strolled along the walls. They circled the courtyard, leaned out through the battlements to look into the terraces of the outer works, and took pride in the damage they had done the Turks.

"They're piled on one another over there," the little knight pointed at the bodies among the ruins. "And the stacks at the breach are so tall you have to climb them with a ladder. Your cannon did that, Ketling."

"The best of it is that we've blocked that breach so thoroughly they'll have to tunnel under it all over again. They can't break in without it. They may have hordes of men to spare but they'll get tired of this kind of siege in a month or two."

"And in that time the Hetman will get here," said the little knight. "But no matter what happens we've an oath to keep."

Here the two knights looked into each other's eyes and Volodyovski asked in a quieter voice: "Did you do what I asked you to?"

"Everything is ready," Ketling murmured back. "But I don't think it'll come to that. We really can hold this place a long time, and there'll be many more days like this one."

"God give us one tomorrow."

"Amen," Ketling said.

Cannon fire interrupted them. Once again the mortar bombs flew towards the castle, dragging their fiery tails. A few of them burst high overhead like Summer lightning and went out at once. Ketling cast an expert eye on the battery they came from. "They're putting too much sulfur into the fuses,"he said.

"And now all the others are opening up,"said Volodyovski.

★ ★ ★

Just as a single dog might break the silence of a peaceful night, and others answer him one by one until the whole village echoes with their barking, so the one Turkish cannon seemed to wake every other gun, and a thundering, fiery wreath surrounded the city. This time the Turks hurled their bombardment at the town rather than the castle. The clink of sledge hammers and wedges, however, now came from three sides of the granite rock below. It seemed clear the Turks wanted to blow that clifftop eagles' nest skyhigh at all cost, no matter how that stone foundation frustrated their efforts.

Ketling and Volodyovski sent their grenadiers to the walls again, and had them throw hand bombs towards the sound of the picks and hammers, but darkness made it impossible to tell if this did any good even though streaks of flame whirled across the sky. It seemed to the men upon the walls as if huge flocks of fiery birds were hurtling through the dark firmament above them and settling on the town, and the attention of almost everyone turned in that direction. Some of the projectiles exploded in the air, but others arced downward, trailing fire behind them, and fell onto the roofs of the homes below. A lurid glow rose in the night sky above several areas of the town. The church of St. Catherine was soon in flames, St. Yuri's Orthodox church burned in the Ruthenian quarter, and fire broke out again in the Armenian cathedral which had been burning earlier in the day. The fires spread and widened by the minute and illuminated the entire city. The shouting came all the way to the battlements so that it soon seemed as if the conflagration had already burst throughout the town.

"This is bad,"said Ketling. "The burghers will lose heart."

"I don't care if everything burns to ashes!" the little knight shouted. "Just as long as this rock stands solid under us and we can keep on fighting!"

Meanwhile the shouting in the town swelled into a continuous cry of anger and fear. The flames in the Armenian quarter leaped from the cathedral to the warehouses built for that section of the population around their own town square. Rich stores of gold and silverware, costly leatherwork, and bales of Persian carpets, Indian silks and Venetian satins sunk into the flames. After a moment scarlet tongues of fire licked at the roofs of the surrounding houses.

Volodyovski noted the quick spread of the fire and glanced towards the convent of St. Dominic. "Ketling!"he said, suddenly alarmed. "Keep an eye on our grenadiers and do what you can to disrupt that tunneling. I'm going to run down to the town because I'm worried sick about the convent. Thank God they've left the castle alone so that I won't be needed here for a while."

★　★　★

There really wasn't much to do in the castle just then so the little knight mounted up and rode to the city. He was back two hours later along with Pan Mushalski, who'd quite recovered from that blow he'd taken in the fight with Hamdi-bey, and who now hurried to the castle with his bow and arrows. If the Turks launched any more assaults, he thought, his archery would be useful.

"Welcome!" Ketling greeted them. "I was getting anxious about you with all that bombardment in the town. What's the word from the convent, then?"

"Everything's fine,"said the little knight. "Not a single bomb fell anywhere near it. It's a quiet, safe place."

"God be praised for that! And how's Krysia doing? Not too worried, is she?"

"She couldn't be calmer. She and Basia are sitting together in one of the nuns' cells and Pan Zagloba's with them. Novovyeyski is also there. He's conscious again and he wanted me to bring him to the castle but he's still too weak to stand up without help. You go there now, my friend, for a couple of hours, and I'll take over your watch here."

Ketling threw his arms gratefully around Volodyovski because he was most anxious to visit with Krysia and ordered a horse saddled straight away. But he had time before the horse was ready to question the little knight a little more closely about the conditions in the town.

"The townsmen are fighting the fires with great courage," Volodyovski told him, "but the richer merchants among the

Armenians are desperate because their best goods are burning
up. They've sent a delegation to the bishop, begging him to
surrender the town straight away. I swore I wouldn't go again
to one of those councils but I had to hear this for myself so I
looked in there. Lost my temper, too. Belted one of those
pleaders in the snout because he was really pressing the bishop
to give up, and now His Eminence is looking down his nose at
me. Ah, it's bad there, brothers, really bad!"

"How bad?"

"It stinks of fear in that council room, you'd think a skunk
had got in among them. They're acting more and more like
cowards and turning against us because we're ready to keep on
resisting. We're the villains now, don't you see, not the heroes!
They're accusing us of endangering the city for nothing. I've
heard they also gave Makovyetzki a bad time for speaking up
against negotiations. The bishop himself told him: *'We're neither
denying our Faith nor abandoning our King, and what's the use of any
further fighting? You fear the profanation of the churches,'* said His
Eminence, *'the danger to the women, and innocent children dragged
into captivity? We'* (he said) *'can secure their fate with a good
agreement, and get free passage for ourselves as well!'* That's what the
bishop said and my lord the General only sighed and nodded and
kept muttering: *'I'd rather die than do it, but that's God's own
truth!'*"

"Let God's will be done!" Ketling said.

Volodyovski twisted his hands in anger and frustration. "If
only it *were* the truth!" he shouted bitterly. "But it isn't! We *can*
keep on fighting!"

In the meantime Ketling's horse was brought from the stables.
Ketling mounted quickly.

"Be careful on the bridge," Volodyovski warned him as he
pulled away. "The grenades come pretty thick out there!"

"I'll be back in an hour," Ketling said and trotted away.

★ ★ ★

Left alone with Mushalski, the little knight began to pace the
walls. The grenadiers worked in three separate places where the
sounds of the tunneling came from the darkness of the rock
below. Sergeant Lusnia was in charge of the bomb throwing on
the castle's left side.

"How's it going here?" asked Volodyovski.

"Bad, commandant!" the sergeant reported. "The sons of bitches are already inside the rock and it's only near the entrance hole that a piece of shrapnel gets one or another. We haven't done much good."

It was even worse elsewhere, especially since the sky clouded over, starlight and moonlight had both disappeared, and a thick rain began to fall, soaking the fuses which protruded from the hand grenades. The darkness also deepened to protect the miners.

Suddenly Volodyovski led Pan Mushalski aside.

"Listen," he said, urgently but quietly. "Why don't we go after those moles ourselves? We can stamp them out right inside their holes!"

"Seems to me like that's certain death," Pan Mushalski answered. "They've got whole janissary regiments watching over them. But why not? Let's try it!"

"They're well guarded, there's no doubt about that, but the night is dark and it'll be easy to throw them into panic or disorder. Just think, back in the town they're talking surrender. And why? *'They've put mines under you,'* they tell us. *'You can't resist that!'* But what if we sent word this night that there are no more mines? Wouldn't that shut their mouths? Is that worth risking our necks for or isn't it?"

Pan Mushalski gave that a little thought and then cried out: "It's worth it! Yes, by God, it's worth it!"

"One of those tunnels is only just begun," Volodyovski said. "We'll leave that alone. But they've cut their way deep into the rock down here, and out there on the left. You'll take fifty dragoons, I'll take the same number, and let's try to smoke them out of their holes before they know what happened. Well? How do you feel about that?"

"I feel good! And it's getting better! I'll take along a few spiking nails too. Maybe we'll come across some carronade."

"I doubt we'll get that close to their batteries," Volodyovski shrugged, "although they do have a few swivel guns quite near to the tunnels. But take your nails. We'll just wait for Ketling to get back. He'd know better than anyone how to help us if we run into any trouble."

★   ★   ★

Ketling returned exactly when he said he would, not a minute late, and half an hour later two dragoon detachments, each numbering fifty men, crept up to the breach, edged their way through the breach to the slopes outside, and vanished in the darkness.

Ketling let the grenading go on for some time longer, then stopped it and waited. His heartbeat quickened with anxiety. As an experienced soldier who served in many sieges, he knew how daring this venture truly was. The minutes dragged. They became an hour. It seemed to him that the two assault parties should have reached their goal by now. The action should have started. But when he pressed his ear to the rock below he heard only the steady, regular chipping of the hammers.

And suddenly there came the dry, popping sound of a pistol shot at the bottom of the cliff far beneath the wall. It was so soft, so muted in the rainy night, and so insignificant beside the booming roar of the Turkish mortars, that it might have passed unnoticed on the walls above it if a wild uproar hadn't broken out immediately after it.

'They've got there!' Ketling thought. 'But will they get back?'

And down below him the night filled with frenzied cries, feverish drumming, the shrill scream of signal flutes and whistles, and finally the hurried and frenetic thunder of janissary handguns. Mass volleys and single shots crashed and cracked out from every direction. It seemed that whole regiments came charging up to save the engineers but, as the little knight expected, the darkness and the suddenness of the attack confused the janissaries and created chaos; afraid of opening fire on their own kind, they milled about, shouting at the top of their voices, and shooting off their muskets at everything and nothing and mostly in the air.

The howling and the musketry grew more frantic with every passing minute. Just as greedy weasels break at night into a sleeping henhouse, and the silent structure suddenly explodes with sound in every direction, so the whole plain around the besieged castle filled with a blaring uproar. Fire bombs arced out of the Turkish siegeworks to throw some light into the sodden darkness. Ketling, who brought more than a dozen carronades to bear on the Turkish cohorts protecting the miners, replied with canister. Musket fire swept the Turkish trenches. Musketry rattled in reply off the Polish walls. Bells clanged out in alarm on the city churches; and yells of panic sounded in the streets as most of the townsmen thought that the Turks had finally burst into the castle. Up on the ramparts before the town, however, the city companies took this clamor for yet another sally by Volodyovski—one in which the besieged had attacked all the Turkish earthworks simultaneously—and beat to quarters in a general alarm.

The night seemed made to order for the dare-devil enterprise of the little knight and the famous archer. It turned dark as pitch. Gun muzzle blasts and grenade explosions ripped whitely through the murky gloom, to be followed by an even deeper darkness than before. At last the heavenly sluices sprung open overhead and spilled streams of rain. Thunder displaced the roars of the cannonade and rolled among the cliffs with terrifying echoes.

Ketling leaped off the wall and ran to the repaired breach with several dozen men. He didn't have to wait long before dark forms appeared in the greater darkness among the logs which filled the gap torn out of the gatehouse.

"Who goes there?" Ketling cried.

"Volodyovski!" came the instant answer, and the two knights threw themselves into each other's arms.

"So how was it?" questioned other officers who now came running to welcome the raiders. "How did it go out there?"

"Well, God be praised! The sappers are cut down to a man. All their equipment's smashed and scattered. Their work's all for nothing!"

"God be praised!"

"And where's Mushalski? Is he back with his people yet?"

"No, not yet. They're still out there."

"So how about going out to give them a hand? Well, gentlemen? Who's willing to try it?"

★ ★ ★

But in that moment the rubble that filled the breach darkened with newcomers; Mushalski's men came swarming back, in a hurry to get behind the walls, and in far fewer numbers than they started out with because the musketry had raked them heavily. But they came back exulting because they'd done just as well as Volodyovski's party. Some of the soldiers brought drills, pick-axes and sledge hammers as proof that they were inside the mine itself.

"And where's Pan Mushalski?" Volodyovski asked.

"Hey, that's right! Where's Pan Mushalski?" several others echoed.

The men who had gone out with the famous archer started to peer anxiously at each other.

"Pan Mushalski's dead," a badly wounded dragoon said in a weak voice. "I saw him fall. I fell right next to him. Only I got back up, he didn't..."

Deeply saddened by the death of the incomparable bowman, who was after all one of the most respected soldiers in the army, the other officers questioned the dragoon as to how it happened, but he could tell them nothing. Blood streamed out of him, he could no longer speak, and at last he toppled over like a falling tree.

The knights, meanwhile, mourned the lost Mushalski.

"His memory will live in the army," Pan Kvasibrodski said. "And whoever lives through this siege will heap praises on his name."

"We won't see an archer of his kind again," some other voice added.

"He was the strongest man in Hreptyov," said the little knight. "He could press a silver thaler with his thumb right into a plank if it was fresh cut. There's only one man I ever knew who was physically stronger, and that was Pan Podbipyenta, a Lithuanian who fell at Zbarajh. Novovyeyski, perhaps, could come close in arm-wrestling, but that's about all."

"Ah, it's a great loss!" others said. "A great loss to all of us. You don't get cavaliers like him born nowadays."

* ★ ★

Back at their posts again, the officers turned their thoughts to duty. Volodyovski sent off a messenger to the bishop and the General of Podolia with news that the tunnels had been wrecked and the sappers slaughtered, but this caused more consternation than delight. The general and the bishop may have tried to hide what they felt but neither could conceal his dismay. Both believed that these passing, temporary victories wouldn't save the city but only enrage the Turkish lion even more. As they saw it, such raids were useful only if they played a role in the negotiations, eased the transition between defiance of the Turks and capitulation, and helped the defenders to accept their inevitable surrender in due time. The bishop and the general kept the news a secret from the city leaders and decided to keep seeking terms.

Neither Ketling nor Pan Volodyovski imagined even for a moment that their good news would take such a turn. On the contrary, they were now quite sure that even the worst of the defeatists would take heart, and that a fresh flame of resistance would blaze in everyone. The Turks couldn't take the town without first capturing the castle, and if the castle not merely held them off but actually launched its own thunderbolts upon them, there was no need to talk to them at all. Provisions, powder and munitions were in plentiful supply; all the townspeople had to do was watch their gates and put out their fires.

This, as they both knew, was the happiest night for Ketling and the little knight since the siege began. They never felt so sure that they'd not only come out of it alive but that they'd also save their wives, those two dear creatures who meant so much to them.

"A few more assaults," the little knight said happily, "and, as God's my witness, the Turks will get discouraged, quit storming, and try to starve us into a surrender. And our stores are full. September's almost here. The rains and the cold are just a month away and the Turks aren't much for enduring weather. Let them get well chilled just once and they'll pull away."

"That's so," Ketling nodded. "A lot of them come from beyond the Nile and the first frost will be a shock to them. If the worst should happen, we can hold them at bay for two months even with assaults. Nor can it be that the Commonwealth won't send us some relief. They'll wake up in Warsaw. And even if the Hetman won't have the strength to attack the Sultan he can still wear him out with raids and maneuvers."

"Ketling!" Pan Michal cried. "It looks to me as if we've not yet come to our final destination, you and I. Our last hour hasn't struck."

"It's all in God's hands. But I also think that we won't have to die here."

"Unless one of us falls like Pan Mushalski. That's how it goes at times and there's no way to help it. Ah, I feel really badly about Pan Mushalski, although he died like a real cavalier."

"May God give us as good an end when it comes. But not just yet. I don't mind telling you, Michal, that I don't want to bring so much grief to Krysia... not now, of all times..."

"I feel the same way about Basia," the little knight confided. "Well... We've got our work cut out for us, my friend, but I feel that God's mercy is with us. I tell you, my soul's really jumping I'm so pleased with everything. We'll have to do something notable tomorrow, just as we did today!"

"The Turks have put up timber parapets and wicker screens on their nearer earthworks. I've thought of a way to burn them out, the same way that warships are set on fire in a sea fight. I've the rags for the fire canisters soaking in pitch right now. I've every hope of burning down all their outworks by mid-day."

"Ha!" said the little knight. "If that's so, I'll take out another sortie! The fire will cause enough confusion among them, and it'll never even dawn on them that we'd sally out in daylight! Ketling, my friend, tomorrow could be even better than today."

★   ★   ★

So they talked and chatted, their hearts full of feeling, and then they each went to their quarters because they were really tired and needed some rest. The little knight, however, managed to snatch no more than three hours of uninterrupted sleep when Sergeant Lusnia knocked upon his door.

"Commandant!" he said, coming in. "There's news!"

"What is it?" the watchful small soldier was immediately awake and springing to his feet.

"Pan Mushalski's here, sir!"

"For God's sake!" cried the little knight. "Are you sure?"

"Yes sir! He's here. I was watching at the breach and I heard somebody crying out in Polish *'Don't shoot! It's me!'* I took a look and there was Pan Mushalski coming back, dressed up like a janissary!"

"Glory be to God!" said the little knight and ran to greet the returning archer.

The light had greyed. Dawn wasn't far away. Pan Mushalski had already clambered through the breach and stood on this side of the wall, so much like a real janissary in his white camel-hair cloak and chainmail armor that it was impossible to tell the difference. He caught sight of Volodyovski, jumped to greet him, and the two of them embraced each other joyfully for a while.

"We've already mourned you for dead!" Volodyovski cried.

A crowd of other officers came running up just then with Ketling among them. All looked astonished and hardly able to believe their eyes. They practically drowned the returning archer under a flood of eager and excited questions. His resurrection was astonishing enough without the added mystery of his janissary costume.

He, in the meantime, took center stage among them and began to speak.

"I tripped over a dead Turk and hit my head on a spent cannon ball," he told them, "and even though I wore a cap reinforced with wire, that blow I took from Hamdi-bey still makes me prone to dizziness and I blacked out at once. So I came to, a little later, and there I was: asleep on a dead janissary like on a saddle blanket. My head hurt a bit but I couldn't even feel a bump on it. *'Good enough!'* said I. I took off my cap, the rain cooled my head, and my mind started working. Why not strip this Turk, I thought, and go visiting for a while among them? Don't I speak Turkish as well as I do Polish? And who could tell me from a real janissary just by my face alone? *'I'll go,'* I told myself. *'I'll look around. I'll hear what they're saying to each other.'* I got a bit worried now and then, remembering the kind of life that I lived among them, but I went.

"The night was dark. They hardly had any lights or fires anywhere and I walked about among them as I'd do right here among our own kind. Many of them were lying behind the lines in their covered bunkers and communications trenches, and I went there too. *'What are you creeping about for?'* they'd ask here and there. And I'd say: *'I don't feel like sleeping.'* Others sat huddled together, talking about the siege. They're really bitter about the way things are going for them. I heard with my own ears how they muttered against our Hreptyov commandant who is here among us."

Here Pan Mushalski bowed his lanky frame to Volodyovski.

"Since the curses of an enemy are the sweetest praise," he resumed, "I'll cite them *verbatim*. *'We'll never take that castle,'* they're saying to each other, *'as long as that small dog is defending it.'*

"Small dog," he bowed once more to Volodyovski, "is what those mongrels call Your Excellency, even though each of them had a dog for a father. But there's more. *'Neither lead nor steel can make a mark on him,'* they tell each other, *'and death breathes out of him like the plague.'*

"And at that point they all started muttering and complaining," the archer resumed. *"'We're the only ones who are doing any fighting,'* is what they're all saying. *'The Djamak dogs are scratching their bellies in the sun, the Tartars grab the pillage, and the Spahis twiddle their thumbs in the bazaar. The Padishah calls us his beloved lambs, but he can't love us very much if we've been led to this butchery. We'll do our best here,'* they say, *'but not for much longer. Then we'll go back to Khotim. And if they don't let us go when we feel like going we might just take a few important heads with us.'"*

"D'you hear this, gentlemen?" Volodyovski cried. "When the janissaries snarl even the Sultan listens! Let him just think that a mutiny is brewing and he'll soon take note and break off the siege!"

"And that's the truth of it!" Pan Mushalski added. "Mutinies are easy to come by among the janissaries, and they're already fed up with everything here. It seems to me they'll try another assault or two, and then they'll bare their teeth at the Janissary-Agha, at Kara Mustapha, and even at the Sultan himself!"

"So it'll be!" the officers cried out together.

"Let them try twenty more assaults!" others shouted. "We're ready for them all!"

And at once their hard fists slapped and rattled the sheaths of their sabers, their breaths thickened into an angry snarl, and they began to stare at the Turkish ramparts with hot, eager eyes.

"Another Zbarajh!" the little knight whispered to Ketling, lifted to heights of certainty and joy by this determination. "As God is my witness, we'll have another Zbarajh here!"

★   ★   ★

But Pan Mushalski wasn't finished yet.

"That's what I heard," he said. "It was a pity that I had to leave, I might've heard more, but I didn't want daylight to catch me there. So I went forward, back among the batteries that weren't firing then, to slip through in darkness. I took a good look and there weren't any sentries or pickets posted anywhere! Just little clusters of janissaries wandering about every which way, as they do in all their encampments. I looked again, and there was this great destroyer cannon with nobody near it. Pan Volodyovski knows that I took a handful of spiking nails with me. So I slipped one into the touch-hole. It wouldn't go in without a mallet, as they never do. But since God gave me a pretty fair fist—as some of you gentlemen might've noted now and then in Hreptyov—I pushed it down by hand. It caught and grated a bit going in, but it went in all the way to the nail head. I was really pleased!"

"For God's sake! You did that?" the questions and the exclamations poured on the grinning archer from all sides. "You spiked the great gun?"

"I did. And also another. It went so well the first time, I wanted to stay around a little longer. My hand hurts a bit but all the nails went in!"

"Gentlemen!" Volodyovski cried. "No one among us has accomplished more! No one has won such glory! *Vivat* Pan Mushalski!"

"Vivat! Vivat!" all the officers cheered in a single voice.

The soldiers joined in, and the cheering swelled to such a roar that even the Turks heard the celebration, and the spirits of the janissaries flagged even further in their dismal trenches. Meanwhile the pleased archer was bowing joyfully to his fellow officers, and showed them his great palm—broad as a shovel and heavy as a bear's paw—on which two round blue bruises were visible to all.

"It's all true, gentlemen!" he repeated, slightly out of breath. "Every word of it! And here's the evidence!"

"We can believe it!" everybody shouted. "Thank God you've come back to us safe and sound!"

"I got through those wooden palisades of theirs," the archer explained. "I'd have been glad to set fire to them but I didn't have anything to do it with."

"You know something, Michal?" Ketling cried out happily. "My flammables must be ready by now. Let me give a little thought to those palisades myself! Let them get the idea that we're starting first!"

"Start it, then!" cried Volodyovski.

He himself ran to the orderly room to send a new report down into the city.

'Pan Mushalski didn't die in the sortie,' he wrote hurriedly. *'He has returned, having spiked two big Turkish cannon. He was among the janissaries who are talking mutiny. We'll bombard and burn their timbered defenses in an hour, and if I can I'll lead another sortie.'*

His courier had barely reached the middle of the city bridge when the walls shook under the concussion of the bellowing cannon. This time the castle was the first to start the thunderous conversation. Flaming sheets of pitch-soaked tarpaulin and canvas hurtled like scarlet streamers through the sky, looking like angry banners unfurled in the pale light of the dawning day, and fell on the Turks' wooden palisades and siege screens. It didn't help the Turks that the wood was still damp with the night's rain. The fires soon bit into the timbering and the palisades smoldered into flame. After his rain of fire, Ketling followed with a barrage of grenades. Weary mobs of janissaries abandoned their ramparts. There was no morning *kindja* played by the Turks that day. The Grand Vezir himself rode into the siege lines at the head of a new corps of besiegers, but doubt must have crept into his heart as well, because the surrounding pashas heard him as he murmured: "They'd rather fight then rest! What kind of people are they in that castle?"

And throughout the masses of soldiers around him one phrase went the rounds in fearful repetition:

"The small dog is starting to bite! The small dog is biting!"

Chapter Seventy-three

AFTER THAT JOYFULLY SUCCESSFUL night, so thickly laden with omens of victory, came the momentous day of August 26 which would decide the outcome of that war.

The castle garrison expected some prodigious effort on the part of the Turks. With sunrise came fresh sounds of tunneling under the west wall, stronger and louder than ever before; it looked as if the Turks were drilling their biggest and most dangerous mine. Powerful cohorts stood guard over the laboring engineers. A human swarm stirred in the janissary batteries and redoubts; fresh cannon were hauled and emplaced in their embrassures. The fields that sloped distantly towards Dluzek bloomed with such numbers of many-colored banners that the defenders guessed at once that the Grand Vezir himself had come to direct the storming of the castle. Moreover, dense crowds of janissaries settled into the moats and ruins of the abandoned outer works, ready to charge the breach and scale the walls when the moment came.

The castle was the first to speak in that debate of cannon, hurling its iron arguments so successfully that panic broke out for a moment in the Turkish trenches. But the *Bimbashim*, or janissary company commanders, instantly restored discipline and order in their ranks, and all the Turkish siege guns bellowed in reply. Solid shot, grenades and grape-shot flew across the sky upon the defenders; rubble, bricks and plaster rained upon their heads; dust and smoke became a single blinding curtain, and the fire of the guns became one with the heat that poured down from the sun. Throats gasped for air, chests and lungs struggled for a breath, smoke-filled eyes saw nothing. The blast of the guns, the crash of exploding shrapnel-bombs, the crack and rumble of cannon balls skittering across the cobblestones in the castle yard, blended into the howls of the Turks and the shouts of the defenders to form a hellish music that boomed against the cliffsides in a hundred echoes.

The barrage threatened to bury the embattled castle in rubble and iron, swamp the town with a flood of fiery projectiles, and overwhelm all its gates and towers. But the castle fought back with a savage fury, hurled its thunderbolts into the gaping maws of the Turkish cannon, shook with concussion, smoked, gleamed with lightning flashes, roared, spat out streams of flame, spread death and destruction like an angered Zeus, and raged as if all thought and reason vanished from men's minds in that holocaust of fire, except determination to beat and stamp the Turks into a sullen silence and either win or sink beneath the soil.

In all that chaos, amid the shell and shot, and in the clouds of brick-dust, smoke and fire, the little knight leaped from one cannon to the next, from one wall to another and into every bastion, angle and emplacement, seeming less like a man than a burning flame himself. It was as if he knew how to multiply himself into twos and threes. He was everywhere. His shouts and cries spread encouragement and faith. He took the place of fallen gunners, restored sagging spirits, inflamed resistance and determination, and ran to the next endangered post to heal, calm and inspire yet other defenders. His enthusiasm swept over other soldiers. Seeing him, they could believe that this terrible Turkish firestorm was the last that they'd have to endure, and that both peace and glory would be theirs thereafter. Faith in their victory filled them to the brim. Their hearts and minds hardened with resistance and the rage of battle seized them by the hair. Fierce shouts and curses tore out of their throats. Such madness seized some of them that they clawed their way up and across the walls to come to grips with the janissaries hand-to-hand.

Twice on that morning dense janissary masses hurled themselves into the blocked breach under the cover of impenetrable smoke; twice repulsed, they stumbled back, shattered and confused, leaving behind a littered hillside that seemed paved with their slaughtered dead.

At noon, fresh waves of territorial levies and the *Djamak* infantry were brought to their assistance and thrown against the walls. But these less disciplined warrior masses refused to storm the castle, even though they were goaded with spears from the rear, and milled among the stacks of janissary corpses, howling with rage and fear.

Kara Mustapha, the young field marshal of all the Turkish forces, rode up in person to stiffen them with his own courage and example, but it was all for nothing. It was, as everyone could see, just a matter of time before a blind, fear-crazed panic seized these swarming cohorts. Another hour and they would break and run. Hardly able to believe their own casualties, the Turks eventually resigned themselves to temporary failure, withdrew their infantry and left the duel only to their cannon.

These worked without pause or rest. The iron thunderbolts swept through the sky hour after hour. Lightning followed lightning. The sun—a red, hazy orb shrouded in dust and gun-smoke—dipped coldly towards the afternoon.

★ ★ ★

By three o'clock in the afternoon, the gunfire rose to such intensity that the defenders couldn't hear the loudest words shouted right into their ears. The air in the castle became as hot as the exhalations of a smelting furnace. The water with which the gunners doused their cannon boiled instantly into clouds of steam that robbed them of whatever visibility was left by the dust and gunsmoke but the guns went on thundering none the less.

Two of the biggest Turkish siege guns were hit and smashed shortly after three. A nearby mortar blew up a few minutes later, hit by the castle round-shot. The gunners died like flies. Every moment made it clear to the Turks that this unconquered, hellish castle would get the better of them, that it would out-roar their thunder and have the last word in that terrible debate, and that this word would be victory.

The Turkish fire weakened then.

"The end is coming soon!" Volodyovski howled into Ketling's ear, wanting his friend to hear him through that frightful clamor.

"I think so too!" Ketling tried to answer. "Will they give up until tomorrow? Or longer?"

"Maybe longer. We're the winners today!"

"We'll have to give some thought to that new mine."

The Turkish fire weakened even further.

"Let's keep on shooting!" Volodyovski shouted and leaped among the cannoneers. "Fire, lads!" he cried. "Keep firing until their last gun is quiet! For the glory of God and the Holy Mother! For the life and glory of the Commonwealth! Fire!"

The soldiers sensed that this assault was about to end just like all the others. They answered with a single booming cheer and bent to their guns even more eagerly than before.

"We'll play your evening *kindja* for you, you scurvy sons of bitches! Here's your evening *kindja!*"

*   *   *

What happened then came so suddenly and so unexpectedly that no one knew what to make of it at first. All Turkish guns fell silent. No sound came from the janissary muskets in the wrecked New Castle. The Old Castle boomed and thundered for some time longer but at last the officers started peering oddly at each other and to ask: "What is this? What's happened?"

Ketling, also alarmed by the sudden silence, brought his own cannonade to an end.

"They must have a mine under us," one of the officers said loudly. "They'll set it off any minute now!"

Volodyovski pierced him with a steely glare. "The mine's not ready yet," he snapped. "And even if it was, it would blow up just the left flank of the castle! We'll fight in the rubble if we have to, do you hear me, Mister?"

A deep silence followed. Not a single shot rang out from the city walls or the Turkish ramparts. After the suffocating fire-storm that choked the air with thunder, there was a strange solemnity in that total silence, as if a dreaded prophecy was nearing fulfillment. Everyone stared intently at the silent earth-works, straining their eyes through the layered smoke, but it was like staring through a curtain.

Suddenly they heard something. The measured clicks and rattles of the miners' hammers came to their ears from below the left wall of the castle.

"I said they were still tunneling!" said Volodyovski. Then he turned to Lusnia. "Sergeant! Take twenty men and comb the New Castle for me. See what's going on there!"

Lusnia moved off at once, detailed twenty men, and vanished with them beyond the breach in the barricaded ruins of the gatehouse.

The silence returned, broken only by the rattling breath of mortally wounded men and the clenched, final gasps of men who were dying. The subterranean chipping went on as before.

It took a long time for Lusnia to return.

"Commandant!" he reported. "The New Castle's empty. There's not a pagan soul anywhere near it."

"Could they be breaking off the siege?" Volodyovski turned in surprise to Ketling. "I can't see a thing through that smoke!"

But the billowing sheets of smoke ebbed and faded everywhere around them, and eventually lifted altogether from above the town, and in that moment some shocked, cracked voice cried in astonishment and terror off the nearest tower:

"There are white flags on all the city gates! We're surrendering!"

Everyone—all the officers and soldiers in the castle—turned at once towards the town. Their eyes gaped wide in dumbstruck amazement. Their mouths hung open, silent and without a word. White flags, seen clearly through the drifting smoke, flapped weakly on two of the main gates of the city and, farther on, on the Bathory tower.

The little knight's face became just as white as those unexpected banners. "Ketling!" he whispered. "Do you see?"

"I see." Ketling was as pale as Volodyovski.

Nothing more needed to be said by these two loyal and devoted soldiers who had never stained their honor in any way, and who would never break their given word, and who had taken an oath before God to die before they gave up the castle.

They stared mutely into each other's eyes, and read in them their own final tragedy.

So it was now? Now? After such resistance? After such fighting that it brought to mind the heroism of Zbarajh? They were being told to break that solemn oath after throwing back such an assault and winning such a victory, ordered to break it, surrender the castle, and then go on living?

Grim, deadly thoughts crowded through their heads like
those grenades and bombs of just an hour earlier. A grief beyond
human measurement gripped them both at the thought of those
two, dear beings whom they would never see again, and whose
anticipated pain added to their torments.

They saw all the happiness and all those years of fruitfulness
and joy they would never know. They looked at each other with
hopeless, leaden eyes that swung in despair now and then towards the town as if to make sure that there was no mistake, no
possibility of error, and that their last hour on earth had indeed
rung out.

★   ★   ★

Meanwhile there came the sound of rapid hoofbeats from the
town and, a moment later, a youth who served as one of the
gentlemen-in-waiting for the General of Podolia, came galloping among them.

"Orders for the commandant!" he cried, reining his horse to a
sliding halt.

Volodyovski took the order, read it without a word, and
turned to the officers who waited in a graveyard silence.

"Gentlemen!" he said. "Our peace commissioners have already
crossed the river on their way to Dluzek to sign the terms of the
capitulation. They'll be coming back this way at any moment.
We're to take out all our men by nightfall and the white flag is
to be flown at once."

Nobody spoke. Only the quick, panting breaths and heavy
sighs broke into the silence.

"Well... then we'd better hang out that white flag," one
officer said at last. "I'll get the men in formation straight away..."

Orders rang out soon after in the castle courtyard and the
soldiers started to form and dress their ranks and shoulder their
muskets. The sharp, dry rattle of their grounded weapons and
the thick, rhythmic tread of their boots echoed dully off the
castle walls.

Ketling drew closer to Volodyovski.

"Is it time?" he asked.

"Wait for the commissioners. Let's hear the conditions. Besides, I'll go down there myself."

"No, I'll go! I know the cellars much better than you and I know where everything is stored."

"The commissioners are coming back!" a scattering of voices cried out suddenly, drawing their attention. "The commissioners are coming!"

A short time later the three unhappy men who had been sent to sign the terms of the surrender appeared in the castle. They walked in grim silence, heads hung low. The gold brocades of the kaftans with which the Sultan had rewarded them glittered on their shoulders. Volodyovski waited quietly for them, leaning on a cannon aimed towards the distant fields of Dluzek. The gun was still warm under his hand. Its iron jaws were still seeping smoke.

They nodded to him in greeting but in silence.

"What are the terms?" he asked.

"The town won't be looted. Whoever lives here can live as before, safe in life and property. Whoever wants to leave can go where he likes."

"And Kamyenetz? Podolia?"

The commissioners' heads bowed even lower. "To the Sultan... for ever..."

★   ★   ★

Then the commissioners walked away. They didn't go down to the city bridge because thick crowds had already spilled out of the town and blocked the way at the other end, but slipped out to the left, through the southern gate. They climbed into a boat at the foot of the castle slope which was to take them to one of the city gates lower down the Dniester. Janissaries began to appear in the low, flat gaps between the craggy cliffs that stretched along the river. A dense swarm of anxious and uncertain townsmen churned in the open square beyond the city end of the castle bridge. Some of the people wanted to run to the castle but they were turned back, by order of the little knight, by the detachments which were marching out.

With the last of his companies formed up for the march-out, the little knight beckoned to Pan Mushalski.

"Old friend," he said. "Do me one last favor. Go to my wife. Tell her from me,"—and here his voice choked briefly in his throat—"tell her... that it's nothing!"

The archer nodded. He turned and walked away. The troops began to march out towards the bridge behind him. Volodyovski climbed into his saddle and watched over their departure. The castle emptied slowly. The ruins and debris littering the court-yard everywhere around them blocked their passage and got in their way.

Ketling drew close to the little knight.

"I'm going down," he murmured through clenched teeth.

"Go. But take your time until the troops are all out of the castle... Go!"

Here the two knights turned towards each other and threw their arms around each other and held each other like brothers for a time. An unearthly light glowed in the eyes of both.

Then Ketling turned and vanished in the entrance to the castle cellars.

Volodyovski unstrapped and removed his helmet. He looked for a while longer at that heap of ruins, at that field of his own undying glory, at that rubble and at all those dead brave men scattered everywhere around him, at the broken masonry, at the battlements and cannon, and then he raised his eyes towards the sky and began to pray.

His last words were:

"Give her the strength, Lord God, to endure this moment. Give her the peace...!"

But Ketling must have been in too much of a hurry. He hadn't even waited for all of the garrison to pass the castle gate which suddenly heaved and shuddered all around them, hurling the bastions and the walls and towers into the fiery air. A huge roaring flame leaped up and seized it all—the men, the horses, the living and the dead, the rock and the soil—seized it and crushed it into a single sacrificial offering and threw it into the sky.

★   ★   ★

So died Volodyovski, the Hector of Kamyenetz as history has called him; and the First Soldier of the Commonwealth, as his contemporaries knew him in his time.

His funeral was such as no fallen general of his time had ever commanded.

He lay in two coffins. Wood and lead enclosed his little body.

The catafalque stood amid a sea of burning candles in the center of the collegiate basilica in Stanislavov, far from lost Podolia, where all the exiles had been brought under Turkish escort. The lids had been already hammered shut and the leave-taking was coming to an end.

It was the widow's wish that her husband's body be interred in Hreptyov, but since all of Podolia now lay in the hands of the enemy, he was to rest in a temporary grave here in Eastern Malopolska until such time as the Turks could be driven out again.

All the bells rang in all the cloisters. The church was packed from wall to wall with gentry and with soldiers who wanted one last look at the coffin of their fallen hero. It was the Hector of Kamyenetz who lay there, after all, they whispered to each other. The First Soldier of the Commonwealth... The Grand Hetman himself was to come to this funeral... But since he hadn't come before it started, and since the Tartar *tchambuls* were expected at almost any moment, they started the final rites without Pan Sobieski.

Old friends and soldiers whom Volodyovski led in battle ringed the funeral bier. Among them stood the archer, Pan Mushalski, and Pan Motovidlo, and Pan Snitko with Pan Hromyka and Pan Nenashinyetz, and the mad Adam Novovyeyski, and many other officers from the old *stannitza*. By a strange twist of fate all of them had come through the war unscathed; hardly anyone was missing among those who used to gather in the evenings around that Hreptyov fireside; and only he who was their leader and exemplar was absent from their ranks. Only that good and decent knight who had been such a deadly terror to the enemy but who was such a patient and forgiving friend—the matchless swordsman who was also as gentle as a dove—now lay high above them amid candle flames, bathed in immeasurable glory but also steeped in the silence and stillness of death.

Grim hearts and minds, tempered to steely hardness by years of war and slaughter, now cracked and crumbled at this painful sight. The yellow candlelight glittered in brimming eyes and gleamed on the tears that flowed down those fierce and troubled faces. Among them, in that circle formed by the grieving soldiers, Basia lay on the stone floor with her arms flung out in the

form of a penitential cross. Beside her lay the old, infirm, broken
and quivering Zagloba.

It was she who had brought this precious body here, walking
on foot beside the cart that carried it all the way from Kamyenetz, and now the time had come to give that body back to the
soil that bred it. She had walked blindly, mindlessly, as if no
longer belonging to life and among the living, and she repeated
that last phrase he sent her each step of the way, and now she
whispered it over and over like a litany at the foot of the
gleaming catafalque.

"It's Nothing," her cold lips mouthed numbly. *'It's Nothing,'*
she murmured within her without a sound, forming the words
only because they came from that lost, irreplaceable and beloved
man, and because they were his last message to her.

"It's Nothing," she said but this was only a sound without
meaning; it contained neither truth, nor hope, nor any consolation.

But no, it wasn't *'nothing.'*

It was grief. It was darkness. It was despair and a dulled,
numbed deadness thrust on all her senses; a promise of a life
stripped of any feeling, a tragedy beyond recall or simple understanding. It was a young existence snapped and broken and never
to be healed; it was awareness that she would never know
another moment of kindliness or mercy, and that there would
never be anything within her or around her except an empty
void that only God could fill with death in His own good time.

The bells clanged overhead. The funeral mass was ending
before the main altar. The priest's voice soared high as if ascend-
ing from the depths.

"Requiescat in pace!"

A feverish tremor seized Basia's crumpled body and shook her
like a doll, while a single thought leaped up in her mind and
filled her entire being.

'They'll take him from me now!'

But the ceremony still had some time to go. The gathered
knights had prepared many funeral orations which were to be
given while the coffin was lowered into the ground, and in the
meantime Father Kaminski mounted to the pulpit. It was the
same old priest who visited so frequently in Hreptyov and who
had given Basia her last rites while she was so ill.

People began to cough and clear their throats throughout the church, as always happens before a Sunday sermon, and then the congregation settled down, a hush fell upon them, and all eyes turned expectantly towards the raised pulpit which suddenly erupted with a threatening drumroll.

The drum boomed and rattled as if summoning troops to arms. The listeners gaped, astonished. The priest beat out an urgent, snarling rhythm as if to wake a sleeping city or alert an army. He paused. The silence was as absolute as that of the grave. Then he hurled another drumroll at the congregation, and then yet another, and finally threw the drumsticks on the ground before him.

"Colonel Volodyovski!" he cried in a great voice.

Basia's choked scream was his only answer. An icy clutch of terror gripped everyone in the church and brought a cold sweat to their straining faces. Only Pan Zagloba moved in that sudden stillness. He staggered painfully to his feet and, helped by Pan Mushalski, carried the unconscious woman into the fresh autumn air outside.

"For God's sake, colonel!" the priest cried on behind him as if appealing to the fallen soldier. "They're calling you to arms, sir! War is upon us, sir! The enemy has pierced the borders! And you don't jump to your feet at once as you always did? You don't grasp your saber? You don't leap upon your battle charger? What's happened to you, soldier? Have you turned your back so totally on all those ancient virtues that gave your life its meaning, that you leave us here alone and unprotected in our time of need? That you provide us with nothing but mourning and fear?"

Pain ripped through all those hardened chests around the bier. Tears ran down the bowed, scarred and weathered faces. A sudden tide of sobbing surged across the church and it flowed in waves, again and again, as the priest eulogized Volodyovski's virtues, his love of country and his heroic courage.

The priest's own words seized him and carried him away. His face was white with feeling. Sweat gleamed on his forehead. His voice broke and shook. Grief for the fallen knight, for the lost Kamyenetz and for the Commonwealth tormented by the followers of the Moslem crescent, lifted him into prophecy and visions, and so his prayer ran slowly to its end.

"Your churches, Lord, will now be pagan temples!" he cried. "They will chant the Koran in those places where we heard the Gospels! You've spurned us, Lord! You've turned your face against us and you've given us into the Turk's unclean hands. You are unfathomable, Lord, and so is your judgment, but who'll oppose that enemy now? What armies will come to drive him from our borders...?

"You!" cried the priest. "For whom nothing is hidden or unknown! You know that there is no one like our knighthood! What cavalry will charge as readily as ours? Why do You deprive your Church and your people of such irreplaceable defenders? Why do you break that living shield behind which all of Christianity may live in safety, worshiping Your name...?

"Kind Father!" he cried. "Don't abandon us! Show us Your great mercy! Send us a defender, a nemesis for the blasphemous Muhammad, let him come here, let him stand among us, let him uplift our hearts and fill them with fresh hope! Send him to us! Send him to us, Lord!"

A sudden murmur broke out at the rear of the church and the Grand Hetman, Jan Sobieski, marched into the nave. All eyes turned upon him. A strange anticipation ran like an icy tremor among all the people. He marched on to the sharp ringing of his spurs—magnificent, with the face and bearing of a Caesar, and so powerful in stature that he seemed colossal—until he came to the foot of the catafalque.

Deep ranks of armored knights marched in right behind him.

"*Salvator!*" the priest cried out, swept into prophecy by his exaltation. "Our savior!"

And Jan Sobieski knelt beside the bier and began to pray for the peace of Volodyovski's soul.

Translator's Afterword

That was the end of the man but not of the story. A year and a half after the fall of Kamyenetz, when the various squabbling factions had finally got together, the Commonwealth did rouse herself to her own defense and fell upon the Turks. Sienkiewicz writes a lengthy epilogue that recounts the years of Poland's later history, and paints a vivid picture of the Second Battle of Khotim (or *Chocim* in Polish) in which the Grand Hetman, Jan Sobieski, destroyed the armies of the Turkish viceroy, Hussein Pasha, and restored Kamyenetz and Podolia to the Commonwealth; he then went on to become that King Jan III of Poland who crushed the Turks in 1683 at the relief of Vienna, turning the seemingly irresistible tide of Turkish conquest under the leadership of Kara Mustapha, *the Sun of War and the Sword of Islam,* and inflicting such a stunning defeat upon the Turks that they would never again try to conquer Europe. Many of the men who played such vital roles in the lives of Basia and Volodyovski, both the historical figures and the border gentry created for the novel, are mentioned in this account and their exploits and final fates are noted. The interested reader is directed to the history books for that information while we attempt to tie the last loose threads of an epic novel.

Of those whose lives existed only in the pages of the Trilogy —and that is all that must concern the modern story-teller— Sienkiewicz tells us that Pan Yan Skshetuski, now a grey-haired colonel, led six of his own sons in battle at Khotim, two of them fighting in their first campaign, and that the sons proved worthy of the father.

Of those who used to gather around the fireside in Hreptyov, Pan Motovidlo and Pan Mushalski were killed in the battle—the last, by a strange stroke of fate, shot through the throat by a Turkish arrow as he was reaching into his own quiver after the Turks collapsed and their armies fled, and the first at the hands of his own blood-brothers, Hohol's rebel Cossacks, who clung to the Turks and Hussein to the end.

Pan Snitko, Pan Nenashinyetz and young Novovyeyski were also in that battle. After the *Lipki* of the renegade Krytchinski trapped and defeated Pan Motovidlo earlier in the war, Pan Novovyeyski tracked them all across Podolia, captured the vicious Adurovitch and had him skinned alive, but not even this terrible revenge brought him the peace he'd lost. He looked for death in every battle and found it at Khotim, shot after he had killed the Pasha Kyaya, known as the *Lion of God* among the Turks, who had all but managed to rally the shattered janissaries and turn the Turks' terrible defeat to victory. Together with Pan Motovidlo and the famous archer, the tragic young man was buried on the battlefield under a great stone cross on which their names were carved in gratitude by their grieving comrades. Such a cross does stand on the old battlefield of Khotim and those three names can still be read on it. The grave of Pan Volodyovski can still be found in Stanislavov, although that country town, just like the little settlement of Hreptyov, no longer stands within the boundaries of Poland.

Sienkiewicz tells us nothing of the later years of Basia and Krysia, nor does he leave us a picture of Pan Zagloba beyond the moment when the crushed old man staggered to his feet to carry the unconscious widow out of the Stanislavov church. Perhaps he did so because their grief had such a terrible finality, rare in our own times but common in the days of Pan Volodyovski, when the death of a husband virtually ended the life of his widow.

It would be good to think that this didn't happen, and that some measure of peace returned to Basia and Krysia in just the same way that the Commonwealth returned to power, glory and new life under Jan Sobieski. Krysia would have devoted her life to her sons, raising them to the same qualities of patriotism and honor for which their father died. Basia could have found within herself all those qualities of courage and endurance that have made Polish women the symbols of their nation across the generations, and she would have lived a full and useful life in service to her country.

As for Pan Zagloba, who embodied so many hidden virtues among so many faults, and who was surely the true example of that raucous, fractious, valiant, quarrelsome and intractable gentry that was both the glory and despair of their Commonwealth, we hope that he returned to the love and care of Pan Yan and Helen, that he helped them to raise the rest of their prophesied twelve sons and half a dozen daughters, and that he finally found his rest under their linden tree on a warm Spring day, with a quiet smile on his lips, contentment in his soul, and a tankard of mead clutched in his firm old hands.

So pass old orders, giving way to new, and every generation learns from those which have gone before.

—Wieslaw Stanislaw Kuniczak, 1992

BALTIC
SEA

GULF OF
RIGA

• Wolr
LIV
• Kies

PITTEN LAND
• Pitten
• Goldinga
Dyjament • Riga
Lenwarc

C O U R L A N D
• Mitawa
SEMI

• Birze

• Wornie • Szawle
• Poniewież

SAMOGITIA   • Rosienie   **ZMUDYA**
• Onikszt

Królewiec
N I E M E N   • Kiejdany   • Wilkopież

Lebark   Labiawa   Tilsit
Kowno   • Troki
• Wilno
(Vilnius)
• Oszmiana

Słupsk   • Pucka
Gdańsk

Brunsberga
Bartoszyce
Lidzbark   • Lec

Starogard
Malbork

Tuchola

DUCAL PRUSSIA

Walcz
Bydgoszcz • Chełmno
Olsztyn

Lida

NOTEC
Nakło   Toruń
Grudziądz

Grodno
Nowog

Ostroróg
Inowrocław
Kruszwica

DUCHY OF
MAZOVIA
Tykocin

Wołkowysk
Słonim   My

Międzyrzecz
Poznań
• Gniezno
• Płock
Pułtusk

B L A C K

• Grodzisk

Leszno
Łęczyca
Pjątek

N A R E W
PODLASIE

Warszawa
(Warsaw)

Węgrów   Biała   Brest
Litovsk
• Kobryń   Pińsk

Kalisz
Sieradz
Uniejów
Sochaczew
Łowicz
Rawa

Piotrków
Wieluń

Bodzentyn
Radom
Opatów

Radomsko
Częstochowa

Kielce

VISTULA
Łuków
• L

Chęciny
Kazimierz

Olsztyn
Jędrzejów

CHELMLAND   BUG

Sandomierz
Zamość

DETAIL OF ACTION IN
Fire in the Steppe

Siewierz
Olkusz
Baranów

Kraków

LITTLE POLAND

Bełż
• Sokal
Kamionka Strumiłowa

━━━━━━━━━
**Turkish Invasion Route
1672**

Zator
Wieliczka
Bochnia
Tarnów
Przaworsk
Jarosław

• Gliniany

Łańcut

•••••••••••
Basia's Journey to Raszkow

Kęty
Nowy Sącz
Stary Sącz
Krosno
Przemyśl
Sambor
Krasiczyn
Sadowa

Lwów (Lvov)

▨▨▨▨▨▨
Basia's Escape Route

Żywiec

Sanok
Drohobycz

RED RUTHENIA

DNIESTR

Stryj
Żydaczów
Halicz

Rohatyń

P

Buczacz
Czerwo

Obertyn
Gwoźdźiec
Kołomyja

KAMIENIEC
PODOLSKI   CHREPTIÓW

USZYCA

MOHYLÓW

JAMPOL

WAŁADYNKA

RASZKÓW